César,

Jules Vernes is an author that will amaze you with his imagination. I hope that you'll enjoy reading his books as much as I did.

Love,

Lila

EVERYMAN,
I WILL GO WITH THEE,
AND BE THY GUIDE,
IN THY MOST NEED
TO GO BY THY SIDE

JULES VERNE

JOURNEY TO THE CENTER OF THE EARTH

TWENTY THOUSAND LEAGUES UNDER THE SEA

ROUND THE WORLD IN EIGHTY DAYS

WITH AN INTRODUCTION
BY TIM FARRANT

EVERYMAN'S LIBRARY
Alfred A. Knopf New York London Toronto

351

THIS IS A BORZOI BOOK
PUBLISHED BY ALFRED A. KNOPF

First included in Everyman's Library, 1908 (*Twenty Thousand Leagues
Under the Sea*), 2013 (*Journey to the Center of the Earth, Round the World
in Eighty Days*)
Introduction Copyright © 2013 by Tim Farrant
Bibliography and Chronology Copyright © 2013 by Everyman's Library
Typography by Peter B. Willberg
Third printing (US)

Twenty Thousand Leagues Under the Sea and *Round the World in Eighty Days*
are translated by Henry Frith. *Journey to the Center of the Earth* is by an
anonymous translator. A note on the translations appears on page xliv.

All rights reserved. Published in the United States by Alfred A. Knopf,
a division of Penguin Random House LLC, New York, and in Canada
by Penguin Random House of Canada Limited, Toronto. Distributed by
Penguin Random House LLC, New York. Published in the United
Kingdom by Everyman's Library, 50 Albemarle Street, London
W1S 4BD and distributed by Penguin Random House UK, 20 Vauxhall
Bridge Road, London SW1V 2SA.

www.randomhouse.com/everymans
www.everymanslibrary.co.uk

ISBN: 978-0-307-96148-8 (US)
978-1-84159-351-7 (UK)

A CIP catalogue reference for this book is available from the
British Library

Library of Congress Cataloging-in-Publication Data
Verne, Jules, 1828–1905, author.
[Novels. Selections. English]
Three Novels: Journey to the Center of the Earth, Twenty Thousand
Leagues Under the Sea, Round the World in Eighty Days /
by Jules Verne; with an introduction by Tim Farrant.
p.   cm.—(Everyman's Library)
"This is a Borzoi book."
Includes bibliographical references.
ISBN 978-0-307-96148-8 (hardcover : alk. paper)
1. Verne, Jules, 1828–1905—Translations into English.   I. Title.
PQ2469.A2   2013   2013018818
843'.8—dc23   CIP

Book design by Barbara de Wilde and Carol Devine Carson
Typeset in the UK by AccComputing, Wincanton, Somerset
Printed and bound in Germany by GGP Media GmbH, Pössneck

JULES VERNE

CONTENTS

INTRODUCTION

We all 'know' Jules Verne – or at least, we think we do. Anyone who has ever thrilled to the exploits of a round-the-world yachtsman, or a jungle explorer, or an astronaut; anyone who has been transfixed by a mountaineer, by a deep-sea diver, by a Jacques Cousteau or a David Attenborough, in some sense 'knows' Verne, for without him it is difficult to imagine that we would be quite as alive to the excitement of exploration, adventure and discovery, that we would get quite the same fix from the new. The novels presented here, *Journey to the Centre of the Earth, Twenty Thousand Leagues under the Sea* and *Round the World in Eighty Days* are three key texts from the pivotal phase of his career: beginning with his first major success, *Five Weeks in a Balloon* (1863), and *The Adventures of Captain Hatteras* (1864), the first of the *Extraordinary Journeys*, the defining series of his work; and ending with the outstanding triumph of *Round the World in Eighty Days* and the consecration of the *Extraordinary Journeys* by the French Academy in 1872. In the meantime Verne had acquired the Legion of Honour, and a fishing-boat – the first of three ever more pretentious vessels on which he would write and sail to destinations as various as Gravesend and the Mediterranean. In 1867 the first English translation of his fiction had appeared – *From the Earth to the Moon*, in the *New York Weekly Magazine*. From 1873 he would go global, publishing a run of outstandingly popular novels – including *The Mysterious Island, Michel Strogoff, The Steam House, Robur the Conqueror, Propellor Island, An Antarctic Mystery* and *Master of the World* (the last before his death in 1905) – and multiple stage adaptations of his work. Verne is, according to UNESCO, still one of the world's most translated writers (behind Walt Disney Productions and Agatha Christie, but ahead of Shakespeare and Enid Blyton). The present renderings, first published in 1876 and 1879, can give some impression of how Verne's earliest English readers encountered him.

Two things found Verne's career: trade and travel. Born in 1828, of a lawyer father and a minor-noble mother, into a family

of ship-owners and merchants in the busy maritime city of
Nantes, Verne himself was sent to Paris to study law. But, like
many another young man of the period, and, spurred on by
another repentant lawyer, Alexandre Dumas, he turned to the
theatre in his twenties, writing a number of moderately successful – if insufficiently lucrative – plays, an operetta, and several
stories. In 1857 he would marry and begin a seven-year (if
unsuccessful) career as a stockbroker, and, between 1859 and
1861, make his first major journeys abroad (to England and
Scotland, then Norway and Denmark, followed by major trips
to Liverpool and the States in 1867, to Algiers in '78, to Scotland
again in '79, to Copenhagen in '81, to Rome in '84). But it was
his 1862 meeting with Pierre-Jules Hetzel which really transformed his fortunes. Hetzel, the Republican publisher of some
of the major writers of his age, among them Balzac, Hugo and
George Sand, would follow the first success of *Five Weeks in a
Balloon* with the myriad fictions of the *Extraordinary Journeys*
(fifty-four novels, in eighty-two volumes, plus some twenty-five
stories) over more than forty years. Of nineteenth-century literary enterprises, only Balzac's ninety-six-work *Human Comedy*
(another Hetzel publication) can rival it; Zola's twenty *Rougon-
Macquart* novels (1871–93) seem modest alongside.

Hetzel was central in determining what (and how) Verne
wrote; his left-leaning, improving, pedagogic influence is ubiqui-
tous. But it would be absurd to reduce Verne to Hetzel: there
are also other dialogues, of imagination and reality, mobility or
displacement and stasis, which probably had their origins in
Nantes. Verne, like another Breton (and relation by marriage),
Chateaubriand, grew up with the sea in his blood. Aged eleven,
he allegedly attempted to run away to sea to India, before being
caught and promising henceforth to travel only in his dreams.
The tension between the armchair and adventure, between
security and possibility, lies at the heart of Verne, as of his age
– an age of scientific, technical, industrial, colonial expansion,
but also questioning and reverie. The two threads are evident
from his first stories, written in the 1850s, *A Drama in the Air,
A Winter amid the Ice* and *Master Zacharias*. They nod to earlier
speculative adventure writing (such as de Bergerac's 1657
Journey to the Moon), but also to the contemporary vogue for

Hoffmann and Germanic fantasy. They typically feature an eccentric technical genius, like previous tales of frenzied artisans and artists – Hoffmann's *Master Martin the Cooper* and *The Trill*, Balzac's *Master Cornelius* (1831) – but also like Verne's imminent novels. France/Germany, imagination/reality: this dual inheritance is significant, revealing something fundamental both to Verne and to what would be called, somewhat inaptly, his science fiction: a whimsy appealing to something prospective, curious, enquiring, in Verne's (and many another contemporary reader's) mind, tempered by a supposedly Teutonic literalism, a countervailing strain of practicality, of artisan craft and technical potential, of excitement at what human ingenuity could achieve.

The twin threads of fancy and practicality are embodied in the two significant works he wrote aged twenty-five, *Five Weeks in a Balloon* and *Paris in the Twentieth Century*. *Five Weeks in a Balloon* bears the trademarks of what Timothy Unwin has more appropriately dubbed Verne's 'science-in-fiction'. It takes a known technical reality, balloon travel (then being demonstrated by Verne's friend, the great photographer Nadar), and makes it extraordinary, placing it in the realm of fantasy, in a journey preternaturally impossible, because headed west against insuperable winds. Yet because we begin with the familiar, we believe. Taking the familiar and pushing it is a recurrent ploy of Verne's – firing the gentlemen of the Gun Club from a cannon, led by Nadar anagrammatically present as Ardan in *From the Earth to the Moon* (1865); imagining a steam-driven elephant (*The Steam House*, 1880), or an electro-mechanically powered island (*Propellor Island*, 1895). Verne segues from the real to the unbelievable, to the strange but seemingly true. This is the opposite of the uncanny: the strange is made familiar, rather than the familiar, strange. *Paris in the Twentieth Century*, conversely, his next offering to Hetzel after *Five Weeks in a Balloon*, reads perhaps as the uncanny, Verne's imagining of a world we (but in many ways also Verne's contemporaries) would recognize, with mass-culture, long-distance communication, metros, electric lighting, fax, and cars: technologically advanced but also totalitarian, philistine, materialistic. Such candour would have sunk him; Hetzel, indeed, refused it, its vision being doubtless too dystopically off-message. Verne's *Twentieth Century* would not appear until 1994, by which time it was almost historical.

Five Weeks in a Balloon and *Paris in the Twentieth Century* thus represent two currents in Verne's production – optimism, technology, the forward-looking on the one hand, and on the other a recurrent undertow of apprehension about mankind's ability to handle its own inventions. But to these two currents must be added a third: a new, thing-based world of modernity and alienation, the realm, indeed, of what we now call science fiction, conceived, if not completely realized, in *Paris in the Twentieth Century*. Science fiction had been somewhat anticipated by the Goncourt brothers, themselves apostles of a fastidious realism, who had noted, in 1856, after reading Edgar Allan Poe,

a new literary world, the signs of the literature of the twentieth century. The scientific miraculous, the fable via A + B; a sickly, lucid literature. No more poetry: imagination by analysis, blow by blow [...] Something monomaniacal – Things with more role than people; love giving way to deductions and other sources of ideas, phrases, tales and interest; the basis of the novel transported from the heart to the head and from passion to the idea, from drama to its solution.

But when Verne writes on Poe in 1864, he observes something the Goncourts pass over: not technology, but the human elements in Poe's fictions. Where Ann Radcliffe uses the '*genre terrible*, always explained by natural causes', and Hoffmann a 'pure fantastic, which no physical reason can explain', Poe's characters are, in contrast, possible, Verne says, and

eminently human, though endowed with an overexcited, supra-nervous sensibility, exceptional individuals who are galvanized, so to speak, like people breathing air with extra oxygen, whose life were but an active combustion. Though not mad, Poe's characters are doomed to go mad by abusing their brain as others abuse strong liquour; they push the spirit of reflection and deduction to its limit; they are the most awe-inspiring analysts I know who, beginning from an insignificant fact, reach the absolute truth.

This appraisal contains the template of Verne's great novels, and of what might be called his human science: a fusing of myth and the real; a new, modern, awestruck apprehension of the man-made and the natural; a dream – yet sometimes nightmare – of the possibilities of mankind, technology and the sublime.

*

Our first such novel is *Journey to the Centre of the Earth* (1864). It begins with the enthusiastic return of the narrator's uncle, Professor Lidenbrock, to his home on a precisely indicated date, 24 May 1863, with an exciting new discovery. We do not find out what the discovery is until the second chapter, for the first is taken up with an account of Lidenbrock's eccentricity, and the firm establishment of this protagonist as a mad scientist, a stuttering, Hoffmannesque, imperious egomaniac. The first chapters lead us circuitously to the novel's core, the journey. That journey is triggered by Lidenbrock's purchase of a runic manuscript, which he gradually deciphers; an echo, perhaps, of Champollion's 1822 elucidation of the Rosetta stone, but also a recollection of the more distant fictional past of a sixteenth-century scholar and alchemist, Saknussemm (chapter III), who interpreted the manuscript and made the journey to the centre of the earth, entering via an Icelandic volcano. Saknussemm, decoded by Lidenbrock, places the reader on the familiar if unsettling ground of the Faustian pact characterized by Goethe's drama (translated by Nerval in 1827), but also of alchemy and the quest for the absolute explored in Balzac's eponymous novel of 1834, itself about a fictional sixteenth-century Flemish alchemist, Balthasar Claës. But Lidenbrock, unlike Claës, is ultimately successful, and both pedagogic and edifying: Lidenbrock's reading of the runes (chapter II) is but the first of many episodes in which the learned professor will lecture and educate his nephew, and the reader, about a succession of subjects, from cryptograms to geology, to zoology, and the history of the earth, freighting his explanations with footnotes (though also assuming a wide vocabulary), his seriousness redeemed only by the fact that he is German, stutters, and is thus supposedly a figure of fun. He is an early example of a role which would become fundamental to the formation of nineteenth-century French identity: the teacher.

It is that target of Second-Empire, and later Third-Republic, pedagogy, the citizen, who is at the heart of *Journey to the Centre of the Earth.* If Lidenbrock is mocked, at the outset, because of his egotistically subjective lectures (chapter I), such self-obsessed and disorganized idiosyncrasy is but the obverse of the infinitely more ordered education which Axel, and the reader, will receive. The whole odyssey, which actually never reaches the earth's centre, combines recurrently Poesque claustrophobia with a remarkable amount of subterranean actual and mental headroom, and develops from that point of subjectivity which is the reader – whether the *savant* represented in many of Verne's novels, and here by Professor Lidenbrock – or the real live recipients of the fiction, you and I. It is in the reader's imagination that the journey ultimately occurs. This geo-historical itinerary is as much a journey around books (indeed, chapter XXXVIII compares dinosaur fossils to a library devised for Lidenbrock's personal satisfaction) – not just Hoffmann and his French emulators in the jocular, indulgent picture of the German scientist cum artisan-artist, but also Poe, the major inspiration for the journey's confinements and inertia, in particular via the below-decks scenes from *The Narrative of Arthur Gordon Pym* (1838), to which Verne would produce a sequel, *An Antarctic Mystery*, in 1897.

It is digression, however, which constitutes the novel's fundamental essence. Its linear drives towards the centre, towards knowledge, are counterpointed by redeeming divagations, relieving what might otherwise be a relentless (and potentially tedious) stress on progress by an enlivening, at times almost vaudevillian humour and caprice. Many dangers, obstacles actual and potential, are faced and overcome: the storm on the *Valkyria* (chapter IX); the ascent of Mount Snäffell (chapter XV); the descent into the crater (chapter XVII); exhaustion of the explorers' water supplies (chapter XIX). This uncertain itinerary of advances and set-backs, breakthroughs, mistakes and dead-ends, mimics the very business of discovery and disappointment: science, as Lidenbrock remarks, is made of mistakes which are worth making (chapter XXXI); the journey is very far from being as straightforward as a notional descent along the earth's plain radius might lead us to expect. The expedition which begins with an unremarkable railway journey from Kiel, and heads via Copenhagen and Iceland to end in the Mediterranean, via a spectacularly life-threatening ejection from a volcano (chapter XLIV) is measured by misadventure.

Yet over-spanning all is the novel's generic fundamental, romance. Mentioned in the exposition but tangential for most of its length is Lidenbrock's god-daughter, Gräuben, whom the narrator loves and will eventually marry. For most of the time, she is scandalously absent (as women generally are in Verne): present only, like Lidenbrock's servant Martha, as the domestic and/or spouse she ultimately becomes. Just as the narrative takes us from the ordinary to the extraordinary, so it also leads us via incredible adventures back to the familiar, and marriage, at its end. The ploy by which the unbelievable is made plausible is the report of Lidenbrock's explorations in 'the leading journals' (chapter XLVI): the press, ostensibly the ultimate benchmark of veracity, provides, with the novel's opening date, the framing grains of truth. Yet the leitmotif of madness running throughout the novel is ultimately overturned: Lidenbrock's compass, which has led them astray, is revealed to have done so not because it has gone 'mad', but because it was re-magnetized in their final ejection from the earth. It is an elegant reversal: north is south, and south is north; the rational is insane, and, by implication, the fictional real. The scientist's 'madness' is finally validated by the rational; the extraordinary journey by its supposed corroboration in the press; in a vertiginous self-mirroring in the last chapter, the novel even circulates under its own title, within its own fictional world. Writing acts to validate the 'real', but also teases about its very nature, status and existence.

*

Our next novel, Verne's masterpiece, *Twenty Thousand Leagues under the Sea*, was published in 1869 and 1870. Since *Journey to the Centre of the Earth* he had published *From the Earth to the Moon* and *The Children of Captain Grant*, and was to produce *Round the Moon* before 1869 was out. Conceived as early as 1865, partly at George Sand's instigation, *Twenty Thousand Leagues* was Verne's most ambitious novel to date, its wide-ranging explorations coloured by his simultaneous labour on an illustrated geography of France and its colonies, also for Hetzel, between 1866 and 1868, as well as by his own transatlantic journey on Brunel's *Great Eastern* in 1867. *Twenty Thousand Leagues* persuades and engages by moving out from the familiar – from the supposedly real-life press and social validation which had ended *Journey to the Centre of the Earth*, and by developing as its central premise known technology – the submarine built by Fulton in 1800 (and subsequently emulated by others), helping us gradually to suspend disbelief. Uncertainty about the unknown enemy's identity, whether a whale or man-made, sets up the tension that drives the entire narrative; when the submerged adversary is revealed as a submarine, focus falls less on nature than artifice, in the shape of exploring the impressive technology of this machine (called, like Fulton's, the *Nautilus*). From the moment it and its tracker, Captain Farragut, converge, the *Nautilus* becomes central, and Dr Aronnax, the narrator, the indispensable exegete of its captain's, Nemo's, craft and its arcana. Much that is discovered through the journey, natural and technological, geological, geographical, zoological, engineering and electrical, forms part of the stock-in-trade of the *Magasin d'éducation et de récréation*, the bi-monthly popularizing pedagogic journal established by Hetzel in 1864 – a kind of *National Geographic*, but aimed (like Verne's novels) at the whole family, in which *Twenty Thousand Leagues* first appeared. The novel combines frequent commentary on natural phenomena – geology, zoology, geography, on subjects from whales to mermaids and geysers to volcanoes – with breathtakingly poetic descriptions and thrilling crises.

But its real enigmas are twinfold. First is science: once Aronnax and his companions have been captured by the *Nautilus*, discovery of its nature and mode of functioning become central. His extraordinary seaborne library with its twelve thousand volumes like a gentleman's cabinet (chapter XI) is the place from which everything radiates. The library is a metaphor for the centrality of book learning, of encyclopaedic knowledge conquering the world, and a reflection of the didactic enterprise the novel itself enshrines. To the alternation of experiment and proof, question and answer, crisis and resolution of Verne's earlier (and subsequent) works, Verne adds real engineering questions: how, for example, the submarine could replenish its air, and not least an interest in electricity, the motive force of the *Nautilus*, as of (though Verne does not stress this) a future, now our own, age. The technical details are never given (for most readers they would doubtless be tedious, and no more than any contemporary could Verne give them). But electricity's very presence is intriguing. The *Nautilus* really is seriously forward-looking, more plausibly perhaps than any of Verne's other scientific imaginings.

The second and more fundamental enigma is human. The novel draws on numerous previous motifs, from Verne and others – expulsion via a volcano (part II, chapters V–VI), entrapment beneath an iceberg – episodes echoing moments in *Journey to the Centre of the Earth* and *Hatteras*, and, in the case of the iceberg and the maelstrom, Poe (*Pym* and *A Descent into the Maelström*). This is literature as experience, but experience at the limits: the battle with the octopus reflects Gilliatt's, in Hugo's *The Toilers of the Sea*; the crew's scavenging for food, *Robinson Crusoe* (which Verne emulates in *The Mysterious Island* and *Two Years' Holiday*); Verne's pirate Nemo recalls Scott's in *The Pirate* (1821) – Nemo's status as a lone enemy of society is Gothic in resonance, echoing Maturin's *Melmoth the Wanderer*, Balzac's Vautrin, or, in his quest for revenge, Dumas's Monte Cristo.

Yet what is peculiar and disconcerts here is the sinister and dystopic subversion of these models. Nemo is (unlike Vautrin, Monte Cristo, or Hugo's Valjean in *Les Misérables*) seemingly incapable of redemption, a doomed outsider exciting reprobation. Enigmatic, inscrutable, a human black hole, he receives all queries, and yet gives nothing away. He has his vessel, and, by extension, the world, under total control; even episodes which might give his hosts some liberty, and even the possibility of escape (the hunting expedition, for example, of part I chapters XV and XVI) take place under confined circumstances, with the hunters in cumbersome diving suits. The artificial has replaced nature, innovation the ordinary. Nemo has thought of everything, and that is precisely what is so alarming. There seems to be no space for the chance embodying possibility: Nemo's responses are so watertight that they leave no purchase for the uncertainty which gives opportunity for development (and regression), in human relations as elsewhere.

JULES VERNE

Nemo is, more than Verne's previous scientists, a sinister, autocratic monomaniac, presiding over the *Nautilus* as over a prison. His absolute management is emblematized by the black flag which he plants at the South Pole near the end (part II, chapter XIV): a pirate flag, but not quite. Absolute management does not signify absolute meaning: Nemo fights adversaries to the death, but not in a combat of good and evil. He embodies no moral superiority over his opponents. He is Aronnax's counterpart, but only insofar as Aronnax signifies meaning and Nemo the opposite, engaged in an endless, nameless, ostensibly motiveless vendetta, the embodiment of all tyranny past, present, and to come – a very modern form of Gothic. Unable to make meaning through relations, his failure is temporarily (but devastatingly) encapsulated by his weeping over the picture of his (doubtless now lost) wife and children. Nemo's victory, then, is, like his black flag, Pyrrhic, no victory at all. The technologized forces he employs imply progress yet also amorality, purposelessness and void; the water hissing into the tanks of the *Nautilus* could as easily sink as steer it; his triumph is ultimately hollow. The motto we meet early on, 'Mobilis in Mobile', surmounting a giant 'N' seems, when we finally see the flag, to figure but a great negation – Capitain Nemo, Captain Nobody, *non*. And the 'N' cannot but recall Napoleon III, whose tightly controlled yet oppressive regime Nemo's submarine appears to figure, in 1869 and 1870, on the very point of its downfall. Verne's text buries these meanings many leagues beneath its surface, on the shadow side of its creator's optimistic consciousness, yet awaiting the intrepid adventurer.

*

Round the World in Eighty Days (1872), Verne's next major novel after *Twenty Thousand Leagues*, is based on a similar proposition to its predecessor: an adventure against all odds, hatched in a gentleman's club like the Gun Club of *From the Earth to the Moon*, here the London Reform Club; an enigmatic, mysteriously rich, and solitary hero, who, for a bet, sets out on the title's seemingly impossible enterprise. Fogg, like Lidenbrock, like Nemo, is a know-all, and, perhaps even more than Nemo, seems to embody total control: an absolute, clockwork order more achievable in his more earthbound and domestic realm. Fogg is first of a protagonist trio, with his servant Passepartout ('Passe-partout' in our translation) and their unwanted minder Inspector Fix, who endure a riveting itinerary of combat against obstacles natural and man-made, desolating setbacks and triumphant advance, nail-biting cliff-hangers and near-death experiences alternating with passages of pedagogy, including the only actual lecture in these novels (on Mormon history, in chapter XXVII), and an eleventh-hour disquisition on how Fogg in fact manages to traverse the world in not eighty but seventy-nine days by travelling eastwards.

But there are also key differences from previous fictions. First, the narrator is anonymous, an unidentified centre of conscious-ness: this novel seems to anticipate a global version of *Le Tour de France par deux enfants*, the celebrated popular topographical volume aimed at the geographical education of children which first appeared five years later, in 1877 – or would anticipate it, were it not for Fogg's refusal to countenance any kind of tourism. Second, the descriptions, if succinct, are more atmo-spheric and suggestive of lived experience: the snow-dogged train journey in chapters XXVI–XXX, for example, is convinc-ing because of its combination of tedium, tension, and event, and perhaps because Verne's Rockies were in part inspired by Scotland. There is also greater engagement with the lands traversed, their peoples, instanced by the treatment of British India, characters such as the Hindu Mrs Aouda or the boorish American Colonel Proctor, or the account in chapter XXVI of railway development in the States – with the peoples, but also their politics. When Verne reminds us that British dominance in India was less complete than we might think, he gives the respectable face of a secret history which Verne (and France) perhaps does not dare admit: the novel's striking silence, in its American chapters, over France's loss of some half of the States she had controlled but fifty years before – a subject doubtless too delicate immediately after Prussia's 1871 annexation of Alsace-Lorraine. The novel's sole overtly political scene – the chapter XXV American hustings which virtually degenerates to a brawl – suggests a nightmare reflection of the highly unstable situation in France as the Third Republic was coming into being. More latently, two key religious episodes – Passe-partout's pursuit by priests when he blunders into a temple, and his rescue of the Indian widow, Mrs Aouda from suttee – embody a criticism of religion which is certainly the author's own, and which was to see its achievement with the separation of Church and State in 1905, the year in which Verne died.

As if to leaven this more substantial matter, the novel contains more plot complications and convincingly motivated plot reversals than before; more mishaps and moments where the polarity is switched by something other than chance. The ironically named comic sidekicks, Passepartout, and to a lesser extent Inspector Fix, seem to exist in order to derail things: Passepartout's temple blunder leads to his pursuit by priests, and the bringing of Fogg to trial; Fix, in contriving this impedi-ment, and in pursuing Fogg across the world, finally (if fleet-ingly) imprisoning him, believing him to be the thief who has stolen an enormous £55,000 from the Bank of England, causes Fogg to miss his deadline and lose his bet. It is only when Fogg realizes, thanks to Passepartout, that he has miscalculated, in fact reaching home a day early, that the situation is saved, making Fogg arrive on time. It is an amazing eleventh-hour, or last-minute, reversal, which gives the novel effectively two endings. The first, in chapter XXXIV, is a failure: Fogg arrives five minutes late; the second, two chapters later, is a success: Fogg comes in on (or just before) the dot. They imply a dual conclusion: first, that even the imperturbably linear, controlling Fogg is more fallible than he admits; second, that the ostensibly less perfect Passepartout, who is sometimes more of an obstacle than an assistant, is endowed with a kind of creativity, insight and kindness which Fogg manifestly lacks.

As a whole, the novel has more coherence through the over-determination of key episodes than its predecessors, making its characters more convincing, helping the reader to assess them more objectively. Passepartout's previous career in a circus is indicated early, because it will be necessary when he needs to turn a penny as a clown (chapter XXIII). And when Fogg's train is attacked by Indians, Passepartout's acrobatics enable him to crawl underneath and halt it, allowing him to save the day (chapter XXIX). Likewise Fogg is redeemed by his devotion in risking his life to save Passepartout from the Sioux, and by waiving his heartless intention of making him pay for the gas he has carelessly left burning throughout their absence. There are nonetheless some moments of contrivance: the Sioux attack opportunely releases Fogg from his impending duel with Proctor; Fogg is oddly absent from the narrative when it has to be decided whether to rush his train over Medicine Bow rapid, as if Verne could not bear facing this model of order with deciding an impossible risk; the astonishing climax of the journey, when, having missed his steamer, Fogg suborns the crew of a ship, imprisoning its captain, only then to purchase his vessel in order to burn its upperworks to fuel his return home. It is a climax which, like many of Verne's climaxes, impresses in direct proportion to its implausibility. And it would not be Verne without this vertiginous verging on the extraordinary, which, like some glimpsed abyss, makes us want to go on.

Yet, at the core of this brilliantly realized and impressively economical novel lies a love-narrative more central than in any of Verne's earlier works. Fogg's rescue of Mrs Aouda from what is explicitly presented as the barbaric practice of suttee will take her on his journey across the world, leading to attachment, affection, love and marriage. No relativism here: Fogg does not doubt that he is right to abduct her, despite the dangers he is thereby creating, just as the novel does not doubt that the attacking Sioux are savages. The novel is generally positive about progress and modernity: the world is smaller, Fogg asserts, because of the increased rapidity of communication – an idea familiar to us, if novel then. This is, indeed, a pre-eminently bourgeois, capitalist work, focused on time and calculation. On many occasions, Passepartout calculates their location, or what he has cost his master, at one point even comparing the sun to a gold coin. But so relentless is the stress on money that we begin to question its rectitude. Fogg throws cash at every problem, solving most of them in this way: bailing himself from Indian prison, paying to rescue Passepartout, purchasing the ship which will take him home. We never know the source of his wealth, and may, for much of the novel, like Fix, suspect him of being the thief. This world is a hard one – as hard as Fogg himself, unpitying with his servants, imperturbable when challenged by Proctor to a duel. In the final chapter, as his 'friends' are waiting to see whether he will return on time, Fogg is traded like a bond (as he had been when he set out), his stock swinging wildly as the market, and his friends, speculate on his position – geographical, moral, and financial. They appear entirely happy as long as they win their bet, showing no concern for his whereabouts or well-being. Above all, the female protagonist, Mrs Aouda, is important chiefly as the passive recipient of his salvation, and the foil to this materialism. The two endings – the first, when he is ruined, and she nonetheless declares her love for him, the second when she accepts him even though he is rich – say that love conquers all and that wealth does not matter. It is the first time that Verne has made romance, and a woman, so central, even if she is squeezed into a conformist mould; but then the end is hard to take seriously, given all that has gone before, and despite Verne's careful motivation of her affection (itself indebted to Hetzel, who would have liked more romance in Verne's novels. Verne himself was reticent about such matters). More memorable is the novel's rollercoaster of experience, not least Fogg's on the stock exchange; and the widespread excitement which brings about Fogg's financial fall and rise, greeting his return and helping to convince us of its reality. So convincing was this fiction that its first readers bet on whether Fogg would arrive on time as the novel was being serialized in the newspaper *Le Temps*. But the novel might also remind us of the crowd's amoral power to sweep us up, for good or evil, for better or for worse – the power which Verne exploited in his triumphantly successful enterprise, whose ambiguities and intriguing heroes can still enthral us today.

Tim Farrant

SELECT BIBLIOGRAPHY

Works in French are published in Paris, those in English in London, unless otherwise indicated.

1. EDITIONS

FIRST EDITIONS AND DOCUMENTATION

Verne's *Voyages extraordinaires* were generally first serialized in newspapers or magazines, usually Hetzel's *Magasin d'éducation et de récréation*, before book publication (again by Hetzel) in an economical, unillustrated in-18, and a lavishly illustrated bound octavo brought out in the last quarter aimed at the Christmas gift market. Our novels first appeared as follows:

Voyage au centre de la terre: Hetzel, in-18, 25 November 1864 (no previous serialization); octavo, 13 May 1871, with two new chapters (37–38), and illustrations by Édouard Riou.

Vingt mille lieues sous les mers. Tour du monde sous-marin: Le Magasin d'éducation et de récréation, 20 March 1869 – 20 June 1870. Book publication: in-18, 28 October 1869 (vol. I), 13 June 1870 (vol. II); octavo, 16 November 1871, illustrated by Alphonse de Neuville and Édouard Riou.

Le Tour du monde en quatre-vingts jours: Le Temps, 6 November – 22 December 1872; in-18, 30 January 1873; octavo, 25 September 1873, illustrated by Alphonse de Neuville and Léon Benett.

Vivid illustration was integral to their appeal: material on this and many other aspects of Verne, including a bibliography, is at jv.gilead.org.il/. A comprehensive collection of these editions is held by the *Centre de documentation Jules Verne* in Amiens http://www.jules-verne.net; a major vendor is the Librairie aux deux éléphants: www.aux2elephants.fr/.

MODERN EDITIONS AND TRANSLATIONS

(i) *French:*

Voyages extraordinaires, ed. J.-L. Steinmetz (Gallimard-Pléiade, 2012, 2 vols) contains only four of the journeys, yet includes *Vingt mille lieues sous les mers*, with authoritative scholarly apparatus and bibliography. Verne's original texts and illustrations are encountered more economically in the Librairie générale française Livre de poche series, offering some twenty of the *Voyages extraordinaires,* beyond our three novels, in mock nineteenth-century-style bindings, but only three with

critical introductions; Garnier Flammarion and Folio offer only five
and two novels respectively, but all with scholarly apparatus.

(ii) *English:*
W. Butcher's Oxford World's Classics translations vastly improve on
the foibles of earlier versions, with insightful introductions and biblio-
graphies; they have recently been supplemented by *Journey to the Centre
of the Earth*, tr. F. Wynne, ed. P. Cogman, intr. J. Smiley (London,
Penguin, 2009), and a worthy addition to *Around the World in Eighty
Days*, tr. M. Glencross (London, Penguin, 2004), which is interestingly
introduced by a major contemporary practitioner of science fiction,
Brian Aldiss.

2. SECONDARY LITERATURE

(i) *Biographies:*
W. Butcher, foreword A. C. Clarke, *Jules Verne: The Definitive Biography*
(2nd edn, Acadian, 2008): vivid, scholarly, iconoclastic; justifies its
title. O. Dumas, *Voyage à travers Jules Verne* (2nd edn, Montreal, Stanké,
2000): readable, semi-thematized intellectual biography; J.-J. Verne,
Jules Verne (Paris, Hachette, 1973; Eng. tr. R. Greeves, Macdonald
and Jane's, 1976): authoritative biography by Verne's grandson. M.
Soriano, *Jules Verne (Le Cas Verne)* (Juillard, 1978): psycho-literary
exploration of conflicts and contradictions in Verne's life and work.
J.-P. Dekiss, *Jules Verne L'Enchanteur* (Éditions du Félin, 1999): extensive,
expository, contextualized.

(ii) *Introductory guides and overviews:*
J.-P. Dekiss, *Jules Verne: Le Rêve du progrès* (Paris, Découvertes Gallimard,
1991): attractive, compact, lavishly illustrated overview; D. Compère,
Jules Verne. Parcours d'une oeuvre (Amiens, Encrage, 1996): brief, clear
introduction. C. Legrand, *Dictionnaire des Voyages extraordinaires* (Amiens,
Encrage, 1997) and F. Angelier, *Dictionnaire Jules Verne* (Garnier Flammarion, 2006): invaluable vade-mecums. *The Jules Verne Encyclopedia*,
ed. B. Taves and S. Michaluk (Lanham, MA, and Folkestone, Scare-
crow, 1996): interesting essays, aimed primarily at American readers.

(iii) *Critical studies:*
W. Butcher, *Verne's Journey to the Centre of the Self. Space and Time in the
Voyages* extraordinaires (Macmillan, 1980): rigorous, vigorously
argued defence of Verne as a literary writer. A. B. Evans, *Jules Verne
Rediscovered: Didacticism and the Scientific Novel* (N.Y., Westport, CT,
Greenwood, 1988): no-nonsense exploration of ideological intentions,
contexts and techniques. A. Martin, *The Mask of the Prophet: the
Extraordinary Fictions of Jules Verne* (Cambridge, 1990): bold yet attentive

SELECT BIBLIOGRAPHY

examination of ideological and other tensions. E. Smyth (ed.), *Jules Verne. Narratives of Modernity* (Liverpool, Liverpool U.P., 2000): stimulating essays on divers topics. T. Unwin, *Jules Verne: Journeys in Writing* (Liverpool, Liverpool U.P., 2005): deft, intelligent, accessible exploration of Verne as an experimental writer.

In French: M. Moré, *Le Très Curieux Jules Verne* (Gallimard, 1959, repr. 2005): psycho-analytical explication of the author. S. Vierne, *Jules Verne et le roman initiatique* (Sirac, 1973): compendious investigation of the mythic appeal of Verne's works, supplemented more accessibly, with discussions of and extracts from our novels, in *Jules Verne* (Balland, 1986), and poetically in *Jules Verne: mythe et modernité* (P.U.F., 1989).

(iv) *Scholarly journals:*

The *Bulletin de la Société Jules Verne* (1935–39, 1967–): www.societejulesverne.org/bulletins/bulletins.cgi), the *Revue Jules Verne* (Amiens, Centre International Jules Verne, 1996–: www.jules-verne.net/revue-jules-verne.html) and *Verniana. Jules Verne Studies* (2008–: www.verniana.org) contain innumerable useful articles.

CHRONOLOGY

DATE	AUTHOR'S LIFE	LITERARY CONTEXT
1827	Marriage of Verne's parents in Nantes.	Cooper: *The Red Rover, The Prairie.* Goethe: *Faust* (pt I), tr. Nerval. Hugo: preface to *Cromwell.* Manzoni: *The Betrothed.*
1828	Verne born in Nantes, 8 February.	Scott: *The Fair Maid of Perth.*
1829	Birth of Verne's brother Paul; the Vernes move to Quai Jean-Bart, overlooking the Loire.	Balzac: *Les Chouans.* Dumas: *Henri III et sa cour.* Hugo: *Les Orientales.* Mérimée: 'Mateo Falcone', 'La Vision de Charles XI'.
1830	Verne's first memories are of hearing gunfire in Nantes during the July Revolution.	Cooper: *The Water-Witch.* Hugo: *Hernani.* Stendhal: *Le Rouge et le noir.*
1831		Balzac: *La Peau de chagrin.* Hugo: *Notre-Dame de Paris.* Sue: *Plik et Plok: scènes maritimes.*
1832		Sainte-Beuve: *Critiques et portraits littéraires.* Sand: *Indiana.* Death of Scott and Goethe.
1833		Balzac: *Eugénie Grandet.* Michelet: *L'Histoire de France* (17 vols to 1867). Sand: *Lélia.*
1834	Attends boarding-school with Paul (to 1836). Summers are spent at the country house of his great-uncle Prudent, a retired slave-trader with a colourful buccaneer past.	Balzac: *La Recherche de l'Absolu.* Sand: *Jacques.* Bulwer-Lytton: *The Last Days of Pompeii.*
1835		Balzac: *Le Père Goriot.* Gautier: *Mademoiselle de Maupin.* Vigny: *Chatterton.* Poe: 'The Unparalleled Adventure of One Hans Pfaall'. Tocqueville: *De la Démocratie en Amérique* (vol.I 1835, vol. II 1840).

Battle of Navarino, last sea battle fought entirely by sailing ships.

Conquest of Algiers. July Revolution: abdication of Charles X, accession of Louis-Philippe, new constitutional Charter.

Anti-clerical riots, insurrection of Lyons silk-workers. Faraday invents dynamo. Cholera epidemic (to 1832).

Attempted revolts by Royalists (Vendée, April) and Republicans (Paris, June); Napoleon's son, the duc de Reichstadt, dies.

Guizot Law establishing public education. Daguerre and Niépce pioneer photographic techniques. Brutus de Villeroi demonstrates submarine at Noirmoutier.

Repression of growing trade union movement in France. Revolt in Lyons. Paris unrest suppressed (rue Transnonain massacre).

Fieschi attempts to assassinate Louis-Philippe.

JULES VERNE

DATE	AUTHOR'S LIFE	LITERARY CONTEXT
1836	Transfers to the École Saint-Stanislas, a junior boys' seminary (to 1840).	Dumas: *Kean*. Lamartine: *Jocelyn*. Loudon: *The Mummy: A Tale of the Twenty-Second Century*. Balzac's *La Vieille Fille* launches newspaper serialization of fiction in *La Presse*.
1837	Birth of Verne's sister Anna. Henceforth the Vernes spend summers at Chantenay on the Loire. The boys teach themselves to sail; Jules steeps himself in adventures: *The Swiss Family Robinson, Robinson Crusoe* and Fenimore Cooper.	Balzac: *Illusions perdues* (1837–43). Sand: *Mauprat*.
1838		Cooper: *Homeward Bound*. Poe: *The Narrative of Arthur Gordon Pym*. Dickens: *Oliver Twist*. Gautier: *La Comédie de la mort*. Hugo: *Ruy Blas*.
1839	Birth of Verne's sister Mathilde. Verne allegedly attempts escape to India.	Poe: *Tales of the Grotesque and Arabesque*. Stendhal: *La Chartreuse de Parme*.
1840	Vernes move to 6 rue J.-J. Rousseau in Nantes. Jules and Paul attend the Petit séminaire de Saint-Donatien (to 1842). Begins to write.	Cooper: *The Pathfinder*. Mérimée: 'Colomba'. Proudhon: *Qu'est-ce que la propriété?* Sainte-Beuve: *Port-Royal* (6 vols to 1859).
1841		Cooper: *The Deerslayer*. Lammenais: *Le Livre du peuple*. Musset: *Le Souvenir*.
1842	Birth of Verne's sister Marie.	Bertrand: *Gaspard de la nuit*. Bulwer-Lytton: *Zanoni*. Sand: *Consuelo*. Sue: *Les Mystères de Paris*.
1843	Studies at the Collège Royal de Nantes (to 1846).	Dickens: *Martin Chuzzlewit* (to 1844). Hugo: *Les Burgraves*.
1844	Experiments with plays and short prose. In love with cousin Caroline.	Dumas: *Les Trois Mousquetaires*; *Le Comte de Monte-Cristo*. Sue: *Le Juif errant*.
1845		Mérimée: 'Carmen'.

CHRONOLOGY

First attempted *coup d'état* by Louis Napoleon. Government of Molé; death of Charles X. First long-distance (England–Germany) balloon flight. Colt patents the revolver.

First railway from Paris, to Saint-Germain. Accession of Queen Victoria. Morse demonstrates electric telegraph.

Death of Talleyrand. Daguerre perfects daguerrotypes. Wheatstone patents the stereoscope. Invention of Morse Code. Brunel's *Great Western* begins first regular transatlantic steamship service.

Fall of Molé. Revolt of Abd el Kader. Goodyear discovers vulcanization.

Inauguration of Bastille Column. Napoleon's ashes returned to Paris. Louis Napoleon attempts second *coup d'état*. Government of Thiers, ministry of Guizot.

Franco-British *rapprochement*.

Duc d'Orléans (Louis-Philippe's son) killed in a carriage accident. Railway mania (1842–6).

Flora Tristan promotes international workers' union. Henson designs aerial steam carriage.

Potato famine (to 1846).

DATE	AUTHOR'S LIFE	LITERARY CONTEXT
1846	Passes *baccalauréat*.	Balzac: *La Cousine Bette*. Baudelaire: *Salon de 1846*. Sand: *La Mare au diable*. Dickens: *Dombey and Son* (to 1848).
1847	Goes to Paris to study law; Paul joins the merchant navy. Unrequited love for Herminie Arnault-Grossetière. Begins novel, *Un Prêtre en 1839*, which remains unfinished.	Cooper: *The Crater*. Balzac: *Le Cousin Pons*. Lamartine: *Histoire des Girondins*. Michelet: *Histoire de la révolution française* (7 vols to 1853). Thackeray: *Vanity Fair*.
1848	Reads Molière, Hugo, Musset, Shakespeare, German Romantics. Friendship with composer Aristide Hignard; begins writing librettos for operettas. Passive support for February revolution; writes play about Guy Fawkes.	Dumas *fils*: *La Dame aux camélias*. Sand: *La Petite Fadette*. Thackeray: *Pendennis*. Marx and Engels: *Communist Manifesto*.
1849	Frequents literary salons, meets Dumas *père* and *fils*.	Chateaubriand: *Mémoires d'outre-tombe*. Dickens: *David Copperfield* (to 1850). Sue: *Les Mystères du peuple*.
1850	Mentored by Dumas *père*; one-act comedy *Les Pailles rompues* staged at Dumas's Théâtre-Historique. Graduates as a lawyer.	Ferry: *Le Coureur des bois*. Hawthorne: *The Scarlet Letter*. Turgenev: *A Month in the Country*.
1851	Friendship with explorer Jacques Arago. First stories (*Les Premiers Navires de la marine mexicaine* and *Un Voyage en ballon*); first attack of facial paralysis, treated with electricity.	Melville: *Moby-Dick*. Nerval: *Voyage en Orient*. Sainte-Beuve: *Causeries du lundi* (15 vols to 1862).
1852	Appointed secretary of Théâtre-Lyrique (formerly Historique); involvement in Paris theatre life. Refuses father's legal practice; Verne *père* withdraws support. Publishes three more stories and a play.	Hugo: *Napoléon le petit*. Thackeray: *The History of Henry Esmond*.
1853	Operetta *Le Colin-Maillard* (co-authored with Michel Carré) performed at Théâtre-Lyrique.	C. Brontë: *Villette*. Hugo: *Les Châtiments*.

CHRONOLOGY

HISTORICAL EVENTS

Louis Napoleon escapes from prison. Morse demonstrates electric telegraph.

Economic crisis in France. Anti-government banqueting campaign.

February Revolution, abdication of Louis-Philippe. Provisional government proclaims universal suffrage; slavery abolished. Constituent Assembly (April), Constitution of Second Republic (November), Louis Napoleon elected president.

Legislative Assembly (May); failed Paris uprising (June). Invention of safety pin (US).

Loi Falloux extending clerical control of education. Left-wing wins in by-elections, franchise restricted. Bauer builds first German submarine.

Legislative Assembly rejects constitutional reform. Louis Napoleon's *coup d'état* (2 December). Plebiscite. London Great Exhibition. Singer builds first commercial sewing machine.

Plebiscite and proclamation of empire (November–December). Crédit Foncier and Crédit Mobilier founded. Opening of Paris *Bon Marché* department store. Giffard makes first powered dirigible airship flight. Otis instals first lift. Foucault invents gyroscope.

Marriage of Emperor Napoleon III to Eugénie de Montijo. Hausmann begins reconstruction of Paris. Cayley demonstrates manned glider. First heavier-than-air aircraft.

DATE	AUTHOR'S LIFE	LITERARY CONTEXT
1854	'Maître Zacharius' published in *Le Musée des familles*.	Defontenay: *Star, ou Psi Cassiopea.* Dumas *père*: *Les Mohicans de Paris* (to 1858). Nerval: *Les Chimères.*
1855	Second attack of facial paralysis. *Les Compagnons de la Marjolaine*, co-authored with Carré and Hignard, performed at Théâtre Lyrique.	Dickens: *Little Dorrit* (to 1857). Dumas *fils*: *Le Demi-monde.*
1856	Meets a young widow with two daughters, Honorine de Viane Morel.	Hugo: *Les Contemplations.* Tocqueville: *L'Ancien Régime et la Révolution.* Turgenev: *Rudin.*
1857	Marries Honorine on 10 January. Begins work as stockbroker; publishes first book, on the 1857 *Salon* of art-works.	Baudelaire: *Les Fleurs du mal.* Champfleury: *Le Réalisme.* Flaubert: *Madame Bovary.*
1858		Mazzini: *The Duties of Man.*
1859	Travels to England and Scotland; writes *Voyage en Angleterre et en Écosse*, unpublished during his lifetime.	Darwin's *Origin of Species* (first French translation 1862). Dickens: *A Tale of Two Cities.* Eliot: *Adam Bede.* Hugo: *La Légende des siècles.*
1860		Collins: *The Woman in White.* Eliot: *The Mill on the Floss.* Erckmann-Chatrian: *Contes fantastiques.* Hawthorne: *The Marble Faun.* Turgenev: *On the Eve.*
1861	Visits Germany, Sweden, Denmark and Norway. Birth of only child, Michel.	Dickens: *Great Expectations.* Eliot: *Silas Marner.* Goncourt brothers: *Soeur Philomène.*
1862	Meets Pierre-Jules Hetzel, republican publisher of Balzac, Hugo and Sand. Hetzel accepts *Cinq semaines en ballon*, his first work from Verne.	Flammarion: *La Pluralité des mondes habités.* Flaubert: *Salammbô.* Hugo: *Les Misérables.* Turgenev: *Fathers and Sons.*
1863	*Cinq semaines en ballon* published, with good reviews but moderate sales. Verne offers, but Hetzel refuses, *Paris au XXe siècle*.	Huxley: *Evidence as to Man's Place in Nature* (first French translation 1868). Renan: *Vie de Jésus.* Sainte-Beuve: *Nouveaux lundis* (13 vols to 1870).

CHRONOLOGY

France enters Crimean War. Tyndall demonstrates principles of optical fibre.

Paris Universal Exhibition attracts more than five million visitors. Fall of Sebastopol. Bauer builds 52-ft submarine for Russia.

Peace of Paris ends Crimean War.

Garibaldi founds Italian National Association. Development of Pullman railway sleeping car.

Nadar takes first aerial photographs. Lenoir builds early internal combustion engine. First vision at Lourdes.
Construction of Suez Canal begins. War of Italian Unification; battles of Magenta and Solferino. De Villeroi build 32-ft submarine in Philadelphia.

France acquires Nice and Savoy. Anglo-French free-trade treaty and occupation of Peking. Expedition to Syria. First Italian parliament meets in Turin.

Beginning of American Civil War. Victor-Emmanuel first king of Italy. First bicycles manufactured in France. Yale patents cylinder lock.

France annexes Cochin-China. Bismarck becomes Prussian chancellor. Gatling gun patented. De Villeroi builds *Alligator* submarine for US Navy.

Legislative elections. Burn and Bourgeois launch 140-ft *Le Plongeur* submarine. Nadar builds a huge balloon called *Le Géant*, inspiring Verne's *Five Weeks in a Balloon*.

JULES VERNE

DATE	AUTHOR'S LIFE	LITERARY CONTEXT
1864	'Edgard Poë [*sic*] et ses oeuvres', *Le Musée des familles*. Signs one-book contract with Hetzel. Serialization of *Aventures du capitaine Hatteras* in Hetzel's *Magasin d'éducation et de récréation* (March to February 1865). *Voyage au centre de la terre* published (25 November); commercial success. Moves to Auteuil, gives up stockbroking.	Dickens: *Our Mutual Friend* (to 1865). Tolstoy: *War and Peace* (to 1869). Goncourt brothers: *Germinie Lacerteux*.
1865	New contract with Hetzel, specifying three volumes annually. *De la terre à la lune, Les Enfants du capitaine Grant*, and a story, 'Les Forceurs de blocus'.	Berlioz: *Mémoires*. Carroll: *Alice's Adventures in Wonderland*. Hugo: *Les Chansons des rues et des bois*. Zola: *La Confession de Claude*.
1866	Moves to Le Crotoy, a fishing port at the mouth of the Somme (but retains a flat in Paris). Buys a 25-ft fishing vessel and converts it to a yacht, the *Saint-Michel I*. Begins extended sailing trips, writing many works aboard this boat and its successors.	Dostoevsky: *Crime and Punishment*. Hugo: *Les Travailleurs de la mer*.
1867	*Géographie de la France et de ses colonies* (to 1868). Travels with Paul to Liverpool and thence to America on Brunel's *Great Eastern*, visits New York and Niagara Falls.	Dumas *fils*: *Les Idées de Madame Aubray*. Marx: *Das Kapital*. Verlaine: *Poèmes saturniens*. Zola: *Thérèse Raquin*.
1868	Sails up the Thames to London. Publication of illustrated versions of *De la terre à la lune* and *Les Enfants du capitaine Grant*.	
1869	*Vingt mille lieues sous les mers* serialized in *Le Temps* to great acclaim (to 1870). *Autour de la lune* in *Le Journal des débats*. Verne settles in Amiens.	Baudelaire: *Petits poèmes en prose*. Collins: *The Moonstone*. Flaubert: *L'Éducation sentimentale*. Hale: 'The Brick Moon'. Hugo: *L'Homme qui rit*.
1870	*Découverte de la terre* (first volume of *Histoire générale des grands voyages*). *Une ville flottante*. Verne made Chevalier of the Légion d'honneur. Serves as a National Guard coastguard at Le Crotoy.	

CHRONOLOGY

Schleswig-Holstein War. Maximilian proclaimed emperor in Mexico. Papal Syllabus of Errors. First Workers' International opens in London. Pasteur discovers link between bacteria and disease. Foundation of International Red Cross.

Slavery abolished in US. Lincoln assassinated. Duruy modernizes French education. Mouchout builds first solar energy device.

Austro-Prussian War. Nobel invents dynamite. Brunel's *Great Eastern* lays first durable telegraph cable across the Atlantic. Whitehead invents torpedo. Ku Klux Klan founded in US.

Napoleon III announces constitutional changes. Paris Universal Exhibition. Lister develops antiseptic surgery. Roper builds first steam motorcycle in US. Michaux makes velocipedes.

French press laws relaxed. Discovery of helium.

Government of Ollivier. Suez Canal opens.

Franco-Prussian War; surrender and capture of Napoleon III at Sedan. Siege of Paris. Pénaud experiments with rubber-powered model helicopters.

JULES VERNE

DATE	AUTHOR'S LIFE	LITERARY CONTEXT
1871	Financial difficulties, briefly returns to stockbroking. New Hetzel contract reduces Verne to two volumes per year. Father dies. *Vingt mille lieues* published in octavo, illustrated by Neuville and Riou.	Bulwer-Lytton: *The Coming Race.* Dostoevsky: *The Possessed.* Eliot: *Middlemarch.* Zola: *La Fortune des Rougon.*
1872	*Le Tour du monde en quatre-vingts jours* serialized in *Le Temps. Voyages extraordinaires* awarded Grand prix de l'Académie française. Verne elected to the Académie d'Amiens.	Butler: *Erewhon.* Carroll: *Through the Looking-Glass.* Daudet: *Tartarin de Tarascon.* Hugo: *L'Année terrible.* Nietzsche: *The Birth of Tragedy.* Zola: *La Curée.*
1873	Book publication of *Le Tour du monde en quatre-vingts jours. Le Docteur Ox* and *L'Île mystérieuse.* Verne's first flight in a balloon.	Bulwer-Lytton: *The Parisians.* Dostoevsky: *The Idiot.* Rimbaud: *Une saison en enfer.* Tolstoy: *Anna Karenina.*
1874	Successful and spectacular stage adaptation, with Adolphe d'Ennery, of *Le Tour du monde en quatre-vingts jours.* Verne interns son Michel in Dr Blanche's asylum.	Flaubert: *La Tentation de Saint-Antoine.* Hugo: *Quatre-vingt-treize.* Verlaine: *Romances sans paroles.*
1875	Verne sued, unsuccessfully, for plagiarism in *Voyage au centre de la terre*; unwittingly inspires Offenbach's *Le Voyage dans la lune.*	Trollope: *The Way We Live Now.*
1876	*Michel Strogoff.* Wife Honorine falls ill, Michel sent to reformatory. Verne launches the *Saint-Michel II*, sails coasts of northern France and southern England.	Mallarmé: *L'Après-midi d'un faune.* Twain: *Tom Sawyer.*
1877	*Hector Servadac. Voyages et aventures à travers le monde solaire.* Hosts lavish themed ball on *De la terre à la lune*; Honorine, sick, cannot attend. Buys *Saint-Michel III*, a 100-ft ten-man steam-and-sail yacht.	Turgenev: *Virgin Soil.* Zola: *L'Assommoir.*
1878	Serialization of *Un Capitaine de quinze ans.* Sails to Portugal, Morocco and Algeria.	

CHRONOLOGY

HISTORICAL EVENTS

Paris, bombarded, surrenders (January). Assembly elected; government of
Thiers (February), Paris Commune (March–May). William I of Prussia
declared emperor of a united Germany. Starley invents Penny Farthing
bicycle. Adams patents chewing gum (US).

Thiers resigns, Mac-Mahon president. Last German troops leave France.
Napoleon III, in exile in England, dies at his home in Chislehurst.
Bollée builds 12-passenger steam car.

First Impressionist exhibition in Paris.

Garnier's Opéra de Paris opens.

Alexander Graham Bell patents telephone.

Republicans form government under Dufavre. Edison invents phonograph.
Muybridge creates the first moving pictures.

Afghan War. J. P. Holland creates a prototype submarine for the Fenians.

JULES VERNE

DATE	AUTHOR'S LIFE	LITERARY CONTEXT
1879	*Les Tribulations d'un Chinois en Chine.* Honorine recovers. Sails to Scotland. Michel expelled from home.	James: *Daisy Miller.*
1880	*La Maison à vapeur. Michel Strogoff,* stage adaptation with d'Ennery. Michel elopes with actress Thérèse Tâton.	Dostoevsky: *The Brothers Karamazov.* Maupassant: *Boule de suif.*
1881	*La Jangada.* Cruise to Holland, Germany and Denmark.	France: *Le Crime de Sylvestre Bonnard.* James: *The Portrait of a Lady.*
1882	*Le Rayon vert* and *L'École des Robinsons.* Rents larger house in Amiens.	
1883	*Kéraban-le-têtu* published in newspaper and book form, fails on stage.	Villiers de l'Isle-Adam: *Contes cruels.* Henty: *Under Drake's Flag.* Maupassant: *Une Vie.* Stevenson: *Treasure Island.*
1884	Michel marries Thérèse, then elopes with Jeanne Reboul, a minor. Verne and Honorine tour Mediterranean; audience with Pope Leo XIII.	Huysmans: *À Rebours.* Maupassant: *Miss Harriet.* Verlaine: *Les Poètes maudits.*
1885	*Mathias Sandorf.* Sells *Saint-Michel III.* Second themed fancy dress ball in Amiens, on *Le Tour du Monde.* Michel divorces, marries Jeanne, who bears two children within a year.	Jefferies: *After London.* Maupassant: *Bel-Ami.* Zola: *Germinal.*
1886	*Robur-le-conquérant.* Verne's nephew Gaston attempts to kill but maims him, causing permanent limp. Hetzel dies.	Villiers de l'Isle-Adam: *L'Eve future.* Stevenson: *Dr Jekyll and Mr Hyde; Kidnapped.* Haggard: *King Solomon's Mines.*
1887	*Nord contre sud.* Mother dies. Verne and Michel reconciled. Lecture tour in Belgium and Holland.	Haggard: *She.* Mallarmé: *Poésies.* Zola: *La Terre.*
1888	*Deux ans de vacances.* Enters politics as a Republican and is elected town councillor of Amiens, serving until 1903. Michel Verne begins collaborating on father's work.	Bellamy: *Looking Backward: 2000–1887.* Kipling: *Plain Tales from the Hills.*
1889	*Sens dessus dessous* and 'In the Year 2889', written by Michel but signed Verne.	Bourget: *Le Disciple.* Flammarion: *Urania.* Stevenson: *The Master of Ballantrae.*

C H R O N O L O G Y

Zulu War. Edison patents electric light bulb.

Ewing, Gray and Milne develop seismograph.

Tsar Alexander II assassinated.

Germany, Austria-Hungary and Italy sign Triple Alliance against France.

Berlin Conference partitioning Africa.

Foundation of Indian National Congress. Pasteur inoculates child against rabies. Benz builds first practical internal combustion car. Starley produces first 'safety bicycle'. First petrol-engined motorcycle.

Hertz demonstrates radio waves. US Navy announces $2 million prize for a workable torpedo-firing submarine.

Dunlop patents pneumatic tyre. Eastman invents Kodak camera and rolled photographic film. Tesla builds first AC motor and transformer. Edison develops motion picture camera. Berliner pioneers discs for recording sound.

Universal Exhibition; Eiffel Tower opens. Daimler and Wilhelm Maybach build workable internal combustion vehicle. Benz demonstrates his Model 3.

JULES VERNE

DATE	AUTHOR'S LIFE	LITERARY CONTEXT
1889 *cont.*		Twain: *A Connecticut Yankee in King Arthur's Court.*
1890	*César Cascabel.* Suffers from stomach problems.	Frazer: *The Golden Bough* (to 1922). Hamsun: *Hunger.* Morris: *News from Nowhere.*
1891	*Adventures de la famille Raton.*	Gissing: *New Grub Street.* Hardy: *Tess of the D'Urbervilles.* Wilde: *The Picture of Dorian Gray.*
1892	*Le Château des Carpathes.* Elected President of the Académie d'Amiens and Officer of the Légion d'honneur. Pays Michel's debts.	Doyle: *The Adventures of Sherlock Holmes.* Feydeau: *Champignol malgré lui.*
1893	*P'tit-Bonhomme, Claudius Bombarnac.*	Flammarion: *La Fin du monde.*
1894	Finishes *Le Superbe Orénoque* and *L'Île à hélice.* Suffers from dizziness and tinnitus, develops cataract in left eye.	Barrès: *Du sang, de la volupté et de la mort.* Hope: *The Prisoner of Zenda.* Kipling: *The Jungle Book.* Du Maurier: *Trilby.*
1895	*L'Île à hélice.*	Crane: *The Red Badge of Courage.* Wells: *The Time Machine.*
1896	*Face au drapeau.* Health deteriorates.	Wells: *The Island of Dr Moreau; The Invisible Man.* Hardy: *Jude the Obscure.*
1897	Death of Verne's brother Paul. *Le Sphinx des glaces.*	Lasswitz: *Two Planets.* Rostand: *Cyrano de Bergerac.* Stoker: *Dracula.*
1898	*Le Superbe Orénoque.* Verne, an *antidreyfusard*, joins *Ligue de la patrie française.*	James: *The Turn of the Screw.* Wells: *The War of the Worlds.* Zola: *J'Accuse.*
1899	*Le Testament d'un excentrique.*	Wells: *When the Sleeper Wakes.* Wilde: *The Importance of Being Earnest.*
1900	*Seconde patrie*, Verne's sequel to *The Swiss Family Robinson.* Develops bilateral cataracts.	Baum: *The Wonderful Wizard of Oz.* Colette: *Claudine* novels (to 1904). Conrad: *Lord Jim.* Freud: *The Interpretation of Dreams.*
1901	*Le Village aérien.* Undergoes cataract operation.	Griffith: *A Honeymoon in Space.* Kipling: *Kim.* Wells: *The First Men in the Moon.* Zola: *Travail.*

xl

CHRONOLOGY

Bismarck resigns chancellorship. Brazilian aviator Alberto Santos-Dumont circles Eiffel Tower in airship.

Lilienthal makes first manned aircraft (glider) flight. J. W. Reno introduces escalator.

Colonial uprisings in French Africa. Dewar invents vacuum flask.

President Carnot assassinated. Beginning of Dreyfus affair.

Lumière brothers screen first public film. Lilienthal flies first biplane gliders.

First film by Georges Méliès. Ford builds his first car. Langley's steam-powered plane. Lilienthal dies in glider accident.

Thomson discovers electron. In US 'Holland VI' is the first successful naval submarine. Parsons develops steam turbine for high-speed liners and warships. First lightweight steam cars go on sale.
Curies discover radium.

Boer War (to 1902). Dreyfus exonerated. Marconi establishes first wireless communication between France and England.

First Zeppelin flight. Planck formulates quantum theory. Aspirin patented by Bayer.

Death of Queen Victoria. Gillette invents double-edged safety razor. First successful radio receiver.

JULES VERNE

DATE	AUTHOR'S LIFE	LITERARY CONTEXT
1902	*Les Frères Kip*. Works on *Maître du monde*.	Conrad: *Heart of Darkness*. Doyle: *The Hound of the Baskervilles*. Gide: *L'Immoraliste*. Herzl: *Altneuland*.
1903	*Bourses de voyage*.	Conrad: *Typhoon*. London: *The Call of the Wild*. Rolland: *Jean-Christophe* (to 1912) Wells: *The Land Ironclads*.
1904	*Maître du monde*.	Barrie: *Peter Pan*. Chesterton: *The Napoleon of Notting Hill*.
1905	Suffers a severe stroke. Dies March 24 in Amiens. *L'Invasion de la mer* and *Le Phare du bout du monde*. Further volumes will appear posthumously, most reworked by Verne's son Michel.	Kipling: 'With the Night Mail'. Wells: *Kipps*; *A Modern Utopia*.

CHRONOLOGY

NOTE ON TRANSLATIONS

The anonymous translation of *Voyage au centre de la terre* was first published in London by Routledge in 1876, under the title *A Journey to the Centre of the Earth*, from which the redundant indefinite article has been removed.

The translation of *Vingt mille lieues sous les mers* by Henry Frith was first published in London by Routledge in 1876. It is reprinted here with its original (if inaccurate) title of *Twenty Thousand Leagues under the Sea*, with 'sea' in the singular – perhaps a homage to 'those in peril on the sea' in William Whiting's well-known hymn 'Eternal Father, strong to save'.

The translation of *Le Tour du monde en quatre-vingts jours* by Henry Frith was first published by Routledge in London and New York in 1879 under the title *Round the World in Eighty Days*, which is retained for reasons of authenticity here.

All three translations have been out of print for very many decades. The present republications offer an invaluable opportunity to encounter Verne in the versions his first English readers knew, giving unique access to his voice as heard in the idiom of his time. Their occasional archaisms, approximations and omissions lend spice to their overwhelming faithfulness, and make a telling contrast with perhaps more accurate if blander modern renderings. They will be of particular interest to students and historians of nineteenth-century literature, translation, and mentality, to those concerned with the archaeology of the text and the story of international cultural exchange, and to anyone in quest of a pleasurable and authentic record of Verne's work as it initially appeared.

JOURNEY TO
THE CENTER OF
THE EARTH

CHAPTER I

IT WAS ON Sunday, the 24th of May, 1863, that my uncle, Professor Lidenbrock, came rushing suddenly back to his little house in the old part of Hamburg, No. 19, Königstrasse.

Our good Martha could not but think she was very much behind-hand with the dinner, for the pot was scarcely beginning to simmer, and I said to myself:

"Now, then, we'll have a fine outcry if my uncle is hungry, for he is the most impatient of mortals."

"Mr. Lidenbrock, already!" cried the poor woman, in dismay, half opening the dining-room door.

"Yes, Martha; but of course dinner can't be ready yet, for it is not two o'clock. It has only just struck the half-hour by St. Michael's."

"What brings Mr. Lidenbrock home, then?"

"He'll probably tell us that himself."

"Here he comes. I'll be off, Mr. Axel; you must make him listen to reason."

And forthwith she effected a safe retreat to her culinary laboratory.

I was left alone but, not feeling equal to the task of making the most irascible of professors listen to reason, was about to escape to my own little room upstairs, when the street-door creaked on its hinges, and the wooden stairs cracked beneath a hurried tread, and the master of the house came in and bolted across the dining-room, straight into his study. But, rapid as his flight was, he managed to fling his nutcracker-headed stick into a corner, and his wide-brimmed rough hat on the table, and to shout out to his nephew:

"Axel, follow me."

Before I had time to stir he called out again, in the most impatient tone imaginable:

"What! Not here yet?"

In an instant I was on my feet and in the study of my dreadful master.

Otto Lidenbrock was not a bad man. I grant that, willingly. But, unless he mightily changes, he will live and die a terrible original.

He was a professor in the Johannæum, and gave the course of lectures on mineralogy, during which he regularly put himself into a passion once or twice. Not that he troubled himself much about the assiduity of his pupils, or the amount of attention they paid to his lessons, or their corresponding success. These points gave him no concern. He taught *subjectively*, to use a German philosophical expression, for himself, and not for others. He was a selfish *savant* – a well of science, and nothing could be drawn up from it without the grinding noise of the pulleys: in a word, he was a miser.

There are professors of this stamp in Germany.

My uncle, unfortunately, did not enjoy great facility of pronunciation, unless he was with intimate friends; at least, not when he spoke in public, and this is a deplorable defect in an orator. In his demonstrations at the Johannæum the professor would often stop short, struggling with some obstinate word that refused to slip over his lips – one of those words which resist, swell out, and finally come forth in the anything but scientific shape of an oath. This put him in a great rage.

Now, in mineralogy, there are many names difficult to pronounce – half Greek, half Latin, barbarous appellations which would blister the lips of a poet. I have no wish to speak ill of the science. Far from it. But when one has to do with rhomboidal crystallizations, retinasphaltic resins, galena favosite, molybdates of lead, tungstates of manganese, and titanites of zircon, the most nimble tongue may be allowed to stumble.

The townsfolk were aware of this pardonable infirmity of my uncle's, and they took advantage of it, and were on the watch for the dangerous passages; and when he put himself in a fury laughed at him, which was not in good taste, even for Germans. His lectures were always very numerously attended, but how many of those who were most regular auditors came for anything else but to make game of the professor's grand fits of passion I shouldn't like to say. Whatever my uncle might be, and I can hardly say too much, he was a true *savant*.

Though he sometimes broke his specimens by his rough handling, he had both the genius of a geologist and the eye of a mineralogist. With his hammer and steel pointer and magnetic needle, his blow-pipe and his flask of nitric acid, he was a master indeed. By the fracture, the hardness, the fusibility, the ring, the smell, of any mineral whatever, he classed it without hesitation among the six hundred species science numbers to-day.

The name of Lidenbrock was consequently mentioned with honour in gymnasiums and national associations. Humphry Davy, Humboldt, and Captains Franklin and Sabine, paid him a visit when they passed through Hamburg. Becqueul, Ebolmann, Brewster, Dumas, Milne-Edwards, Sainte Clarice Deville, took pleasure in consulting him on the most stirring questions of chemistry, a science which was indebted to him for discoveries of considerable importance; and in 1853 a treatise on Transcendent Crystallography, by Professor Otto Lidenbrock, was published at Leipsic, a large folio, with plates, which did not pay its cost, however.

Moreover, my uncle was curator of the Museum of Mineralogy, belonging to M. Struve, the Russian ambassador, a valuable collection, of European celebrity.

Such, then, was the personage who summoned me so impatiently.

Fancy to yourself a tall, spare man, with an iron constitution, and a juvenile fairness of complexion, which took off a full ten years of his fifty. His large eyes rolled about incessantly behind his great goggles; his long thin nose resembled a knife-blade; malicious people declared it was magnetized, and attracted steel filings – a pure calumny; it attracted nothing but snuff, but, to speak truth, a superabundance of that. When I have added that my uncle made mathematical strides of three feet at every step, and marched along with his fists firmly clenched – a sign of an impetuous temperament – you will know enough of him not to be over-anxious for his company.

He lived in his little house in Königstrasse, a dwelling built partly of brick and partly of stone, with a crenated gable-end, which looked on to one of those winding canals which intersect each other in the centre of the oldest part of Hamburg, which happily escaped the great fire in 1842.

The old house leaned forward slightly, and bulged out towards the passers-by. The roof inclined to one side, in the position a German student belonging to the *Tugendbund* wears his cap.

The perpendicular of the house was not quite exact, but, on the whole, the house stood well enough, thanks to an old elm, firmly embedded in the façade, which pushed its flower buds across the window-panes in spring.

My uncle was pretty rich for a German professor. The house was his own, and all its belongings. These belongings were his godchild Gräuben, a Virland girl, seventeen years old, his servant Martha, and myself. In my double quality of nephew and orphan, I became his assistant in his experiments.

I must confess I have a great appetite for geological science. The blood of a mineralogist flows in my veins, and I never grow weary in the society of my beloved stones.

On the whole, it was possible to live happily in this little house in Königstrasse, notwithstanding the impatience of the owner; for though he had a rough fashion of showing it, he loved me for all that. But, the fact was, he was a man who could not wait, and was in a greater hurry than nature.

When he used to plant mignonette and convolvuluses in his terracotta pots in the spring, every morning he went regularly and pulled their leaves, to hasten their growth.

With such an original, there was no alternative but to obey, so I darted into the study immediately.

CHAPTER II

THE STUDY WAS a complete museum, every specimen of the mineral kingdom was to be found there, all labelled in the most perfect order, in accordance with the three great divisions of minerals – the inflammable, the metallic, and the lithoid.

How well I knew this alphabet of mineralogical science. How many a time, instead of loitering about with boys of my own age, I amused myself by dusting these graphites, and anthracites, and pit coal, and touch-stones; and the bitumens, and the resins, and organic soils, which had to be kept from the least particle of dust; and the metals, from iron up to gold, the relative value of which disappeared before the absolute equality of scientific specimens; and all those stones, enough to build the little house in the Königstrasse over again, and an extra room besides, which I would have fitted up so nicely for myself.

But when I entered the study now, I scarcely thought of those wonders. My mind was entirely occupied with my uncle. He had buried himself in his big arm-chair, covered with Utrecht velvet, and held a book in his hands, gazing at it with the most profound admiration:

"What a book! What a book!" he exclaimed.

This reminded me that Professor Lidenbrock was also given to bibliomania in his leisure moments; but an old book would have had no value in his eyes unless it could not be found anywhere else, or, at all events, could not be read.

"What! don't you see it, then?" he went on. "It is a priceless treasure! I discovered it this morning while I was rummaging about in Hevelin's, the Jew's shop."

"Magnificent!" I replied with forced enthusiasm.

Really, what was the good of making such a fuss about an old quarto volume, the back and sides of which seemed bound in coarse calf – a yellowish old book, with a faded tassel dangling from it?

However, the professor's vocabulary of adjectives was not yet exhausted.

"Look!" he said, asking himself questions, and answering them in the same breath; "is it handsome enough? Yes; it is first-rate. And what binding! Does it open easily? Yes, it lies open at any page, no matter where. And does it close well? Yes; for binding and leaves seem in one completely. Not a single breakage in this back after 700 years of existence! Ah! this is binding that Bozerian, Closs, and Purgold might have been proud of!"

All the while he was speaking, my uncle kept opening and shutting the old book. I could not do less than ask him about the contents, though I did not feel the least interest in the subject.

"And what is the title of this wonderful volume?" I asked.

"The title of it?" he replied, with increased animation. "The title is 'Helms Kringla', by Snorre Turleson, the famous Icelandic author of the twelfth century. It is the chronicle of the Norwegian princes who reigned in Iceland."

"Indeed!" I said, doing my best to appear enthusiastic. "And it is translated into German, of course?"

"Translated!" cried the professor, in a sharp tone. "What should I do with a translation? Who cares for translations? It is the original work, in the Icelandic – that magnificent idiom at once grand and simple – which allows of the most varied grammatical combinations and most numerous modification of words."

"Like German," I said, making a lucky hit.

"Yes," replied my uncle, shrugging his shoulders; "without taking into account that the Icelandic language has the three numbers like the Greek, and declines proper names like the Latin."

"Does it?" said I, a little roused from my indifference. "And is the type good?"

"Type? Who is talking of type, you poor, ignorant Axel. So, you suppose this was printed! You ignoramus! It is a manuscript, and a Runic manuscript, too."

"Runic?"

"Yes. Are you going to ask me to explain that word, next?"

"Not if I know it," I replied, in a tone of wounded vanity.

But my uncle never heeded me, and went on with his instructions, telling me about things I did not care to know.

"The Runic characters were formerly used in Iceland, and, according to tradition, were invented by Odin himself. Look at them, and admire them, impious young man! – these types sprang from the imagination of a god."

The only reply I could think of was to prostrate myself, for this sort of answer must be as pleasing to gods as to men, since it has the advantage of never embarrassing them. But before I could do this the current of the conversation was changed in an instant by the sudden appearance of a dirty parchment, which slipped out of the old book and fell on the floor.

My uncle pounced on this treasure with avidity, as can easily be supposed. An ancient document, shut up in an old volume, perhaps from time immemorial, could not fail to be of priceless value in his eyes.

"What is this?" he exclaimed, carefully spreading out on his table a piece of parchment, five inches long and three wide, on which some incomprehensible characters were inscribed in long transverse lines.

I give the exact *fac-simile*, for great importance attaches to these fantastic marks, as they led Professor Lidenbrock and his nephew to undertake the strangest expedition of the nineteenth century.

The professor looked at the queer characters for some minutes, and then pushed up his spectacles and said:

"It is Runic! these marks are exactly like those in the manuscript of Snorre Turleson. But what can they mean?"

As Runic appeared to me an invention of learned men to mystify the poor world, I was not sorry to see that my uncle could not decipher it. At least I judged so from the convulsive working of his fingers.

"Yet it is the ancient Icelandic!" he muttered to himself.

And Professor Lidenbrock could not but know this, for he was considered a veritable polyglot. Not that he could speak fluently the 2,000 languages and 4,000 dialects used on the surface of the globe, but he was familiar with a good part of them.

A difficulty like this, then, was sure to rouse all the impetuosity of his nature, and I was just expecting a violent scene, when two o'clock struck and Martha opened the study door and said:

"Soup is on the table."

"Pitch the soup to the devil and the cook too, and those who eat it."

Martha fled and I scampered after her, and hardy knowing how, found myself in my accustomed seat in the dining-room.

I waited a few minutes. The professor did not come.

This was the first time to my knowledge that he had ever neglected the grave business of dinner. And what a dinner, too! Parsley soup, a ham omelette, and sorrel *à la muscade*, a loin of veal, and a *compôte* of plums; and for dessert, *crevettes au sucre*, and all washed down with sparkling Moselle wine.

All this was what my uncle was going to lose for the sake of an old paper. Really, as a devoted nephew, I felt obliged to do his share of eating as well as my own, and I did it conscientiously.

"I never saw the like of this!" exclaimed our good Martha, "Mr. Lidenbrock not to come to dinner! It is incredible! This bodes something serious," went on the old servant, shaking her head.

In my opinion it boded nothing except a frightful outbreak when my uncle found his dinner devoured.

I was just finishing my last *crevette* when a loud thundering summons tore me away from my voluptuous enjoyment. I made one bound into the study.

CHAPTER III

"IT IS EVIDENTLY RUNIC," said the professor, knitting his brows, "but there is a secret in it, and I will discover it, or else—"

A violent gesture completed his sentence.

"Sit down there," he added, pointing to the table with his fist, "and write."

I was ready in an instant.

"Now, then, I am going to dictate to you each letter of our alphabet which corresponds to one of these Icelandic characters. We shall see what that will give us. But by St. Michael take care you make no mistake."

The dictation commenced. I did my best. Every letter was called out one after another, and formed the following incomprehensible succession of words:

m. rnlls	esreuel	seecJde
sgtssmf	unteief	niedrke
kt,samn	atrateS	Saodrrn
emtnaeI	nuaect	rrilSa
Atvaar	.nscrc	ieaabs
ccdrmi	eeutul	frantu
dt,iac	oseibo	KediiI

When I had finished it my uncle snatched the paper from me and examined it attentively a long time.

"What can it mean?" he repeated mechanically.

On my honour I could not tell him. Besides, he did not ask me, he was speaking to himself.

"It is what we call a cryptogram, where the meaning is concealed by confusing the letters designedly, and to make an intelligible sentence they must be arranged in proper order. To think that here perhaps lies the explanation or indication of some great discovery!"

For my own part, I thought it was absolute nonsense, but I was wise enough to keep my opinion to myself.

The professor took up the book and the parchment again, and compared them.

"The two writings are not done by the same hand," he said. "The cryptogram is of later date than the book. On the very face of it there is an irrefragable proof of it. The first letter is a double *m*, which would be sought in vain in Turleson's book, for it was only added to the Icelandic alphabet in the fourteenth century. Consequently, there are at least 200 years between the manuscript and the document."

This certainly seemed logical enough.

"I therefore come to the conclusion," continued my uncle, "that these mysterious characters were inscribed by some one who came into possession of the book. But who on earth was it? Could he have put his name, I wonder, in any part of the manuscript?"

And my uncle pushed up his spectacles, and taking a powerful magnifying-glass, began to examine carefully the first pages of the book. On the back of the first leaf he discovered a spot, which looked like a blot of ink. But, on closer inspection, sundry letters, half obliterated, could be distinguished. My uncle saw instantly that this was the chief point of interest, and fastened on it furiously, poring over it through his big magnifying-glass, till at last he made out these marks, Runic characters, which he read off immediately.

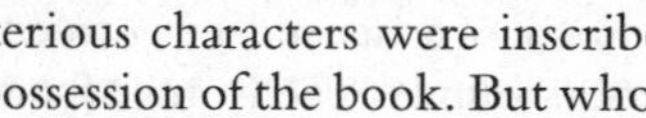

"Arne Saknussemm!" he cried, in a triumphant tone. "Why, that is a name, and an Icelandic name, too; that of a celebrated alchemist, a *savant* who lived in the sixteenth century."

I looked at my uncle with a feeling of admiration.

"These alchemists," he went on, "Avicenna, Bacon, Lully, Paracelsus, were the true, the only *savants* of their times. They made discoveries which may well astonish us. Why should not this Saknussemm have hidden under this incomprehensible cryptogram the secret of some surprising invention? It must be so. It is."

The professor's imagination was enkindled at this hypothesis.

"No doubt," I ventured to reply; "but what interest could the *savant* have in concealing a wonderful discovery?"

"Why? Why? Ah, don't I know? Didn't Galileo act so about Saturn? Besides, we shall soon see. I will get the secret of this document; I will neither eat nor sleep till I find it out."

"Oh!" thought I.

"No more shall you, Axel!"

"Plague it!" said I to myself. "It's a good job I have had a dinner for two to-day!"

"The first thing to be done," said my uncle, "is to find the language of the cipher."

I pricked up my ears at this. My uncle continued his soliloquy.

"Nothing is easier. In this document there are 132 letters, in which there are 79 consonants and 53 vowels. Now this is just about the proportion found in the words of southern languages, while the northern idioms are far richer in consonants. Consequently this must be in a southern language."

His conclusions were very just.

"But what language is it?"

It was this I waited for him to tell me, for I knew he was a profound analyst.

"This Saknussemm," he went on, "was a learned man, and since he did not write in his mother tongue, he would be sure to employ the language in common use among the cultivated minds of the sixteenth century; I mean the Latin. If I am mistaken, I could try the Spanish, the French, the Italian, the Greek, the Hebrew. But the learned in the sixteenth century generally wrote in Latin. I may rightly, then, say, *à priori* – this is in Latin."

I started, for my recollections of Latinity revolted against the pretension of this assemblage of uncouth words to belong to the soft tongue of Virgil.

"Yes, Latin," repeated my uncle; "but tangled Latin."

"So be it," thought I. "And if you disentangle it, my uncle, you'll be clever."

"Let us examine it thoroughly," he said, taking up the sheet again on which I had been writing. "Here are 132 letters in evident disorder. In some words there are nothing but consonants, as in the first, *mrnlls*; others where the vowels, on the contrary, abound – the fifth, for example, *unteief*, or the last but one, *oseibo*. Now this arrangement has, clearly, not been designed. It is the mathematical result of the unknown law which ruled the succession of these letters. It seems to me certain that the primitive phrase has been written regularly, and then turned upside down, according to some law I must find out. Any one who had the key of the cipher could read it fluently. But where is the key? Have you got it, Axel?"

I made no reply, and for a good reason. My gaze was fixed on a portrait hanging on the wall opposite me, the portrait of Gräuben, my uncle's ward, who was just now at Altona, on a visit to her relations, and her absence made me very unhappy, for – I may as well confess it now – the pretty Virlandaise and the professor's nephew loved each other with true German patience and placidity. We were betrothed, though unknown to my uncle, who was too much of a geologist to understand such sentiments. Gräuben was a charming young girl, a blonde, with blue eyes, rather inclined to be grave and solemn, but loving me none the less for that. For my part, I worshipped her, if there is such a word in the Teutonic language. The image of my little Virlandaise transported me in an instant from the world of realities to a world of fancies and memories.

I could see my faithful companion in labours and pastimes. Every day she helped me to put my uncle's precious collection of stones in order and put on the labels. Indeed Miss Gräuben was quite a mineralogist. She would have put more than one *savant* to the blush. She loved to dive into the deepest questions of science. What delightful hours we had spent in studying together, and how often I had envied the unconscious stones handled by her charming hands!

And when our tasks were over, how we used to go out and wander along the shady walks by the Alster, and then repair to the old black, tarred mill, which looks so picturesque at the far end of the lake, chatting all the way and holding each other's hands! I used to tell her droll stories which made her laugh heartily, and beguiled the time till we reached the banks of the Elbe, and after saying "Good night" to the swans, which swim about among the tall white irises, we returned to the quay of the steamboat.

I had just got to this point when my day-dream was rudely interrupted by a violent rap on the table from my uncle's knuckles, which recalled me to reality.

"Look here!" he said, "it seems to me that if one wished to mix up and confuse any sentence, the first thing he would think of would be to write the words vertically instead of horizontally, in groups of five or six."

"Indeed!" thought I.

"We must see what that makes. Write some sentence on this bit of paper, but, instead of putting the letters one after the other, put them in vertical columns, grouping them in numbers of five or six."

I understood what he meant, and immediately wrote from top to bottom.

*J	m	n	e	G	e
e	e	,	t	r	n
t'	b	m	i	ä	!
a	i	a	t	u	
i	e	p	e	b	

"Very good!" said the professor, without reading it. "Now arrange these words in horizontal lines."

I obeyed, and this sentence was the result:

JmneGe   ee,trn   t'bmiä!   aiatu   iepeb

"Perfectly so," said my uncle, seizing the paper from my hands. "This has the look of the old document already. Vowels and consonants are grouped in the same disorder. There are even capitals in the same way in the middle of words, and also commas, exactly as in the parchment of Saknussemm."

I could not but think these remarks very ingenious.

"Now, then," said my uncle, addressing me, "I don't know what sentence you have written, but all I need to do to enable me to read it is to take the first letter of each word in succession, and then the second, and then the third, and so on."

* I love thee well, my little Gräuben.

And to his great amazement, and certainly still more to mine, my uncle read:

Je t'aime bien, ma petite Gräuben!

"Eh, what?" said the professor.

Positively, like a love-sick fool, I had written this tell-tale sentence, without knowing it.

"Ah! you love Gräuben," resumed the professor, in a thoroughly magisterial tone.

"Yes – No——" I stammered out.

"Ah! you love Gräuben," he repeated, mechanically. "Well, well, let us try my method with the document in question."

My uncle was completely absorbed again in his subject of contemplation, and had already forgotten my imprudent words. I say imprudent, for a *savant*'s head cannot understand *affaires du cœur*, but fortunately the great business of the document carried him away completely.

Professor Lidenbrock's eyes flashed like lightning through his spectacles, and his fingers trembled as he took up the old parchment again to make his important experiment. He was greatly excited. At last he coughed violently, and in a grave tone read out the following letters, naming successively the first of each word, and then the second, and so on as he had done in my unfortunate sentence.

mmessunkaSenrA.icefdoK.segnittamurtn
ecertserrette,rotaivsadua,ednecsedsadne
lacartniiiluJsiratracSarbmutabiledmek
meretarcsilucoIsleffenSnI

I must confess I felt excited as I ended the series. The letters themselves, named one by one, sounded perfectly meaningless, but I fully expected to hear my uncle come out in a pompous style with some magnificent piece of Latinity.

But who could have thought it! instead of this a tremendous thump of his fist sent the table spinning, jerked out the ink, and made my pen fly out of my hands.

"That's not it," he thundered out. "It does not make sense."

Next minute he was off like a shot, rushing down the stairs with the speed of an avalanche, and away out into the street as fast as his legs could carry him.

CHAPTER IV

"HE IS GONE!" cried Martha, running up to see what the noise was about, for the door closed with such a bang that it shook the house from top to bottom.

"Yes," I replied, "clean gone."

"And without his dinner?"

"He won't have any!"

"Nor supper either?" said the old domestic.

"Nor supper either," I said.

"What!" exclaimed Martha, clasping her hands.

"No, my good Martha, he will neither eat any more himself, nor allow any one else in the house to eat."

"Goodness me! Then there is nothing for us but starvation?"

I did not dare to say that with such an autocrat as my uncle this was our inevitable fate.

The old servant was evidently alarmed, however, and went back to her kitchen sighing.

Now that I was alone, the thought came into my head, that I would go and tell Gräuben the whole affair. But how could I get away? The professor might be back any moment. And suppose he called me, and wanted to recommence his logogryphical labours, which old Œdipus himself would not have undertaken? And if I am not forthcoming, what would be the consequence?

The wisest plan was to stay, and I had plenty to do, for a mineralogist in Besançon had just forwarded us a collection of silicious nodules, which had to be classified. I set to work, picking out, labelling, and arranging in their glass-case all these hollow stones, full of small glittering crystals.

But this occupation did not engross me entirely. Strangely enough, I could not get the old document out of my mind. My brain was disturbed, and an uneasy feeling began to steal over me. I had the presentiment of some approaching catastrophe.

In the course of an hour, all the stones were in their right places, and I ensconced myself in the large velvet easy-chair, swinging myself, and throwing back my head. I lighted my "hookah", the carved bowl of which represented a Naiad reclining carelessly. I amused myself with watching the progress of carbonization which was gradually turning my Naiad into a thorough negress, and kept listening for footsteps on the stair. But there was not a sound. Where could my uncle be? I fancied him striding along the road to Altona, among the beautiful trees, gesticulating, and making cuts at the wall with his stick; thrashing the grass vigorously, nipping off the tops of the thistles, and disturbing the tranquillity of the solitary storks.

Would he come back triumphant or dejected? Would he master the secret, or give it up? As I was thus questioning myself, I mechanically took up the paper on which I had written the incomprehensible series of letters, and I said:

"What can this mean?"

I tried to group the letters so as to form words. It was impossible. Let me arrange them as I might, putting two or three, or five, or six together, I could make no intelligible sense. True, the 14th, 15th, and 16th would make the English word *ice*, and the 83rd, 84th, and 85th would make *sir*, and also, in the middle of the document, I noticed the Latin words, *rota, mutabile, ira, nec, atra.*

"Hang it!" I said to myself, "these last words certainly do go to prove my uncle is right about the language in which the document is written." And in the 4th line again, I noticed the word *luco*, which means the *sacred wood*. On the other hand, I read in the 3rd line the word *tabiled*, a thoroughly Hebrew expression, and on the last, the vocables *mer, arc, mère*, which are pure French.

It was enough to craze one. Four different idioms in this meaningless sentence. What connection could there be between the words *ice, sir, colère, cruel, sacred wood, chair, grant, mère, arc*, or *mer*? The first and the last might easily be brought together since there was nothing astonishing in finding a *sea of ice* mentioned in a document written in Iceland. But as for understanding the remainder of the cryptogram, that was quite another thing.

I fought and fought with this insurmountable difficulty, gazing fixedly at the document till my brain grew giddy, and the letters seemed whirling round my head.

A sort of hallucination came over me. I felt stifled, as if from want of air, and involuntarily began to fan myself with the sheet of paper. The back and front of it alternately met my eye, and as it waved rapidly to and fro I fancied I could see on the back some perfectly legible Latin words, amongst others *craterem* and *terrestre*.

Light broke in on my mind instantly. I caught a glimpse of the clue. I had found the key to the cipher. To understand this document it was not even necessary to read it through the back of the page. No, just as it was, exactly as he had dictated it to me, it could be spelt out easily. The professor was right in his arrangement of the letters, and right about the language of the document. A mere nothing would enable him to read the whole sentence fluently, and this mere nothing chance had just revealed to me.

It may be imagined how excited I was. My eyes began to swim and I could scarcely see. I had spread out the paper on the table, and one glance would make me possessor of the secret.

At last I managed to calm myself somewhat. I made myself walk twice round the room to quiet my nerves, and then dropped again into the capacious arm-chair.

"Now, then, we'll read it," I exclaimed, taking a long breath.

I leaned over the table, and, placing my finger on each letter in succession, read the whole sentence aloud.

But what stupefaction, what terror seized me! I sat motionless, as if paralysed. What! Had any one really ever done what I had just read? Had any mortal man been bold enough to make the search?

"But no, no!" I cried, leaping up from my chair; "my uncle shall not know it. He would not be satisfied with the mere knowledge of the fact. He would undertake the journey for himself. Nothing could hinder him. Such a daring geologist as he is would start off in spite of everything, come what might! And he would drag me with him, and we should never return. Never! Never!"

I cannot describe my state of agitation.

"No, no, that shall never be," I said, passionately, "and since I can prevent my tyrant from getting such a notion into his head, I will. If he were to begin twisting and turning the document about he might chance to discover the key. We'll destroy it."

There was still a spark of fire in the grate. I snatched up both the sheet of paper and the parchment of Saknussemm, and, with a feverish hand, was just going to fling them on the hot embers, and make an entire end of the dangerous secret, when the study door opened and my uncle appeared.

CHAPTER V

I HAD ONLY just time to replace the unfortunate document on the table. Professor Lidenbrock seemed absorbed in his own meditations. His ruling thought allowed him not a moment's respite. He had evidently been poring over the subject and analysing it, and bringing all the resources of his imagination to bear upon it during his walk, and he had come back to try some new combination.

In fact, he was no sooner in than he seated himself in his arm-chair, and taking up his pen, began a fresh formula, which resembled some algebraic calculation.

My eyes followed his trembling hand; not one of his movements escaped me. What unhoped-for result was he suddenly about to produce? I trembled, and yet needlessly, for since the right combination and the only one had been already found, all further search must of necessity be useless.

For three long hours my uncle continued his labours without speaking or even lifting his hand, blotting out and doing again, erasing and making a fresh beginning a thousand times.

I knew quite well that if he succeeded in arranging the letters in all the relative positions they could occupy the right sentence would come out. But I also knew that twenty letters only can form two quintillions, 432 quatrillions, 902 trillions, 8 billions, 1,175 millions, 640,000 combinations. Now there were 132 letters in the sentence, and these 132 letters would make a number of different sentences, composed of 133 ciphers at least, a number almost impossible to enumerate or adequately conceive.

I therefore reassured myself on the score of this heroic method of solving the problem.

However, the time passed away and night drew on. The noisy street had become still, but my uncle, still stooping down over his task, saw nothing, not even his good old Martha, when she ventured to open the door partially and say:

"Will you take any supper, sir?"

He never heard her, and the worthy old servant had to go away without getting an answer. For myself, I held up as long as I could, but at last weariness overpowered me completely, and

I fell sound asleep on the end of the sofa, while my uncle still continued his calculations and erasures.

When I woke next morning the indefatigable worker was still at his task. His red eyes and wan face, and wild disordered hair, through which he was constantly drawing his feverish fingers, and the crimson spots on his cheeks, all told the story of a terrible struggle with the impossible.

Really he moved my pity. I could not but feel for him, much as I might justly blame him. The poor man was so completely engrossed with one idea that he forgot to put himself in a passion. All the vital powers were concentrated on one single point, and I began to fear the long strain on them, without any escape by their usual safety-valve, would positively end in some internal explosion.

I could have relaxed this tension by a single gesture or word, and yet I did not.

Still, I was acting from a kind motive. For my uncle's sake I remained silent.

"No, no," I said to myself, "I won't say a word. He would want to go then, I know he would. He would risk his life to do what no other geologist has done. I'll say nothing about it, I will keep this secret chance has revealed to me. It would be the professor's death. Let him guess it if he can. I'll not have to reproach myself, at any rate, with having disclosed it."

My resolution taken, I crossed my arms and waited. But I was not prepared for a circumstance which occurred some hours later.

When Martha went to go out as usual to market, she found the door locked. The great key was gone. Who had taken it? My uncle must, of course, when he returned from his hasty walk the night before.

But had he taken it purposely, or through inadvertence? Did he really want to subject us to the horrors of starvation? This seemed to me going too far. Were Martha and I to be victimized for what did not concern us in the least? No doubt of it, for I remembered a precedent which might well frighten us. Some years before, when my uncle was engaged on his great mineralogical classification, he ate nothing whatever for forty-eight hours, and made his entire household feed on this scientific diet. I well remember the sharp twinges in my internal regions I got through it, for such diet was not very satisfying for a boy like me, naturally inclined to be rather voracious. It certainly appeared we would have to dispense with breakfast, as we had with supper the preceding night. However, I determined to be heroic and stand out in spite of hunger. Martha was quite distressed, and looked very grave over it. What troubled me most was that I could not get out of the house. That was a great grievance, as may easily be supposed.

My uncle still laboured on. His imagination was wandering in the ideal world of combinations. He lived above the earth, and really above earthly wants.

Towards noon the pangs of hunger made themselves seriously felt. Martha, innocently enough, had eaten up all that was left in the larder the night before. There was nothing whatever in the house. I still stood out, though; I made it a point of honour.

Two o'clock struck. The thing was becoming ridiculous, and even intolerable. I began to see matters in a different light, and thought I had been exaggerating the importance of the document; that my uncle would not believe in it, that he would consider it a mere hoax, and that even if the worse came to the worst, and he wished to attempt the adventurous journey, he could be prevented by main force; and finally, I thought he may, perhaps, discover the secret for himself, and I shall only get my fasting for my pains.

These appeared excellent reasons to me now, though the night before I had rejected them indignantly. I even thought I had been acting absurdly in waiting so long, and determined to give the solution of the mystery without further delay.

I was just waiting for a suitable opportunity, not wishing to be too abrupt, when the professor got up, and taking his hat, was about to go out.

What! Was I going to let him leave the house, and shut us all in again? Never.

"Uncle!" I said.

He did not seem to hear me.

"Uncle Lidenbrock!" I repeated in a louder tone.

"Eh? What?" he said, like a man suddenly roused from sleep.

"Well! Have you got the key?"

"What key? The key of the door!"

"No," I replied; "the key of the document."

The professor looked at me above his spectacles, and no doubt noticed something unusual in my face, for he seized my arm sharply, and, without saying a word, gazed at me inquiringly.

Never was question put more plainly.

I nodded my head.

He shook his in a pitying sort of manner, as if he thought he had to do with a fool.

I made a still more affirmative gesture. His eyes sparkled, and his grip became threatening.

This mute conversation of ours would have interested the most indifferent spectator, and really I hardly dared to speak now, for I was afraid he would stifle me with embraces in his joy. But he became so pressing, that I was forced to reply.

"Yes," I said, "this key has by chance—"

"What are you saying?" he cried, with indescribable agitation.

"Here! Take this," I replied, handing him the piece of paper on which I had written what he dictated. "Read."

"But there is no sense in that!" he said, crushing up the paper.

"No, not if you begin at the beginning, but if you begin at the end—"

Before I had time to finish the sentence, the professor gave a cry, or rather I should say a perfect roar. A revelation had come to him. He looked transfigured.

"Ah! ingenious Saknussemm!" he exclaimed. "Your phrase was written backwards then!"

And, snatching up the sheet, he read in tones full of emotion, the entire document, beginning at the last letter. It was as follows:

In Sneffels Yoculis craterem Rem delibat umbra Scartaris Julii intra calendas descende, audas viator, et terrestre centrum attinges. Kod feci. Arne Saknussemm.

Bad Latin, which may be translated thus:

Descend the crater of the Jokul of Snäfell, that the shadow of Scartaris softly touches before the Kalends of July, bold traveller, and thou wilt reach the centre of the earth. Which I have done. Arne Saknussemm.

My uncle gave a leap as he read this, as if suddenly touched by a Leyden jar. He was magnificent in his joy, and daring, and conviction. He went up and down the room, clasped his hands over his head, moved about the chairs, piled up the books. It seems almost incredible, but he began to toss about his precious specimens of stones; he gave a thump with his fist here and a tap there. At last he grew calmer, and sank down in his arm-chair as if exhausted.

"What time is it?" he asked, after a brief silence.

"Three o'clock," I replied.

"Stop! I have had no dinner! I'm starving. Let us go and have it at once, and then afterwards—"

"Afterwards?"

"Pack my trunk."

"Eh? What?" I cried.

"And your own, too," added the merciless professor, as he passed into the dining-room.

CHAPTER VI

THESE WORDS MADE me shudder, but I restrained myself, and resolved to put a good face on it. Only scientific arguments would be of any avail with Professor Lidenbrock. But such arguments there were, and good ones, against the possibility of such a journey. To go to the centre of the earth! What folly! However, I reserved my dialectics for a fitting moment and concerned myself about dinner.

It would be useless to repeat my uncle's imprecations when he found a bare table. All was explained and our worthy domestic was forthwith liberated. She hurried immediately to the market, and made such successful purchases that, in about an hour, my hunger was appeased and I was able to realize my situation fully.

During the meal my uncle was almost merry. He then indulged in a few jokes – very harmless ones certainly. After dessert he beckoned me into his study.

I obeyed. He seated himself at one end of the table and I took the other.

"Axel!" he said, in a rather gentle tone, "you are a very ingenious fellow. You have done me a noble service just when, weary of the struggle, I was about to give up the combination. What wrong tracks should I have got into then? Who can say? I shall never forget this, my boy, and you shall have a share in the glory we are about to gain."

"Come," thought I, "he's in a good humour; now's the time to discuss the glory."

"Above all," continued my uncle, "I enjoin upon you the most absolute secrecy. You understand me. There are *savants* who are envious of me, and many would undertake this journey who will never know of it till we return."

"Do you think there are so many bold enough to venture?"

"Certainly. Who would hesitate to win such fame? If this document were known, a whole army of geologists would rush after Arne Saknussemm."

"That is just what I doubt, uncle, for there is no proof of the authenticity of the document."

"What! Didn't we discover it in the book?"

"Yes, and I grant that Saknussemm wrote those lines; but does it follow that he really accomplished the journey, and may not this old parchment be all a hoax?"

This last word was rather hazardous, and I almost regretted I had said it. The professor knitted his brows, and I was afraid I had seriously damaged my cause. Fortunately no remark was made. A faint smile, indeed, was discernible on my stern inter-locutor's lips, as he replied:

"That is what we shall see for ourselves."

"Ah!" said I, "but perhaps you will allow me to exhaust my stock of objections to the document?"

"Speak your mind freely, my boy. I allow you perfect liberty of opinion. You are no longer my nephew, but my colleague. Go on, then."

"Well, I should like to know at the outset what this Jokul, and Snäfell, and Scartaris are. I have never heard of them before."

"I have no difficulty in telling you that. I happened, just a short time ago, to get a map from my friend Augustus Peterman, of Leipsic, and it could not have come more opportunely. Fetch the third Atlas, in the second row of the large library, list G, plate 4."

I got up, and, thanks to these precise directions, found the atlas wanted. My uncle opened it and said:

"Here is one of the best maps of Iceland – Handersen's, and I daresay it will solve all our difficulties."

I leaned over it, and the professor said:

"Look at this island, composed of volcanoes, and notice that they all bear the name of Jokul. This word means *Glacierus*, Icelandic; and in the high latitude of Iceland most of the eruptions break out through sheets of ice. The name Jokul applies, therefore, to all the eruptive mountains in the island."

"Well, and what is this Snäfell?" I replied.

I hoped he would not be able to answer this query, but I was mistaken; my uncle began again:

"Follow me along the western side of Iceland. Do you see Reikiavik, the capital? Yes. Well, go up the innumerable fiords on the shore, and stop a little below the 65° of latitude. What do you see there?"

"A sort of peninsula, like a long bare bone, ending in an enormous knee-pan."

"A very good comparison, my boy. Now do you see nothing on this knee-pan?"

"Yes, a mountain, which seems to have risen out of the sea."

"Well, that is Snäfell."

"Snäfell?"

"Its very self. It is a mountain 5,000 feet high, one of the most remarkable in the island, and assuredly the most celebrated in the whole world, if its crater leads to the centre of the globe."

"But that is impossible!" I exclaimed, shrugging my shoulders.

"Impossible?" repeated the professor sternly; "and pray why?"

"Because the crater is evidently blocked up by lava, burning rocks, and because——"

"And what if the crater is extinct?"

"Extinct?"

"Yes. The number of active volcanoes on the surface of the globe is only about 300, but extinct volcanoes are to be found in far larger numbers. Now, among these last is Snäfell, and the only eruption on record took place in 1219. From that date the rumblings began to die away gradually, till now it is no longer ranked among the active volcanoes."

To positive declarations like these I had absolutely no reply to make. I had, therefore, to pass on to the other obscurity in the document.

"What does this word *Scartaris* mean? and what have the Kalends of July to do with it?" I asked.

My uncle took a few minutes to think, and I began to hope. But only for an instant, as he soon went on again, and said:

"What you call obscurity is to me light. This proves the ingenious pains Saknussemm has taken to make his discovery clear. Snäfell is composed of several craters, it was therefore necessary to indicate which one led to the centre of the globe. How has the Icelandic *savant* done it? He has remarked that 'as the Kalends of July approached', that is to say, about the end of June, 'one of the mountain peaks, the *Scartaris*, projects its shadow over the opening of the crater in question'; and this fact he states in the document. Could any one imagine a more exact indication, and the summit of Snäfell once reached, could there be the least doubt which road to take."

Positively, my uncle had an answer for everything. I soon saw all attack against the words of the parchment would be useless. I therefore ceased to discuss the subject, and went on to the scientific objections to the journey.

"Well then," I said, "I am obliged to confess, the sentence is plain enough, and leaves no doubt on the mind. I even grant that the document appears perfectly authentic. This *savant* has been to the bottom of Snäfell; he has seen the shadow of Scartaris fall softly over the edges of the crater, towards the Kalends of July; he has even heard legendary tales, that this crater leads to the centre of the earth; but to believe that he has reached it himself, that he ever made the journey, or came back if he did, no! a hundred times no! I say to that."

"And your reason?" said my uncle, in a peculiarly bantering tone.

"My reason is, that all the theories of science prove the impracticability of such an enterprise."

"All the theories say so?" replied the professor good-humouredly. "Ah! those tiresome theories! How they hamper us, those poor theories!"

I saw he was making fun of me, but I went on notwithstanding.

"Yes," I said. "It is well known that heat increases about $1°$ in 70 feet below the earth's surface. Now, at this rate, the temperature at the centre must be over $20,0000°$, since the radius of the earth is about 4,000 miles. Everything in the interior must consequently be in an inflamed gaseous state; for metals, gold or platinum, and even the hardest rocks, could not resist such a heat. I am justified, therefore, in asking if it would be possible to get there?"

"So it is the heat, then, Axel, that stumbles you?"

"Undoubtedly. If we even only reached the depth of the earth's crust, we should find the temperature was above 1,300°."

"And you are afraid of passing into a state of fusion?"

"I leave you to settle that question," I said crossly.

"This is what I settle," replied Professor Lidenbrock, mounting the high horse; "that neither you, nor anyone else, knows anything certain that is going on in the centre of the earth, seeing that we scarcely know the 12,000th part of its radius, that science is eminently perfectible, and that each theory has constantly to give way to a fresh one. Was it not believed, till Fourier's time, that the temperature of the planetary spaces was constantly decreasing, and is it not known now that the greatest cold does not exceed 40° or 50° below zero? Why should it not be so with the internal heat? Why should there not be a certain limit beyond which it cannot increase?"

I could not reply to this, since my uncle now placed the question in the regions of hypothesis, and he went on to say:

"And now let me tell you that many learned men, Poisson amongst others, have proved that if the temperature of the centre of the earth was 20,000°, the incandescent gases, arising from the molten materials, would acquire such elasticity that the crust would burst like a steam boiler."

"That is only Poisson's opinion, uncle, that's all!"

"Certainly; but other distinguished geologists agree with him in thinking that the interior of the globe is neither formed of gas nor water, nor of the heaviest minerals known, for in that case the earth's gravity would be twice less."

"Oh, figures can be made to prove anything!"

"And facts, too, my boy. Is it not unquestionable that the number of volcanoes has considerably decreased since the early days of the world; and if great central heat existed, would it be likely to get less powerful?"

"If you enter the field of suppositions, uncle, I have nothing more to say on the subject."

"And I have to say that my opinion is supported by that of very competent judges. Do you remember a visit Sir Humphry Davy, the celebrated chemist, paid me in 1825?"

"Not the least, since I only came into the world nineteen years afterwards."

"Well, Humphry Davy came to see me, in passing through Hamburg, and, among other topics, we had a long discussion on the hypothesis that the centre of the earth was in a liquid state. We both agree that this liquidity was impossible, for a reason to which science can find no reply."

"And what is it?" I asked in surprise.

"It is this — that the liquid mass would be subject, like the ocean, to the moon's attractions, and that, consequently, twice a day there would be tides which would heave up the earth's crust, and cause periodical earthquakes."

"But still it is evident that the face of the globe has undergone combustion at some period, and it is allowable to suppose that the exterior crust cooled first, and the heat took refuge in the centre."

"It is erroneous," replied my uncle. "The earth has been heated by the combustion of its surface, not otherwise. This surface was composed of a great quantity of metals, such as potassium and sodium, which have the property of igniting by mere contact with air and water. These metals take fire when the atmospheric vapours fall on the ground in the form of rain, and as the water gradually penetrates the cracks in the earth's crust, they cause fresh fires, which burst out in explosions and eruptions. This is why volcanoes were so frequent in the early ages."

"That certainly is a clever hypothesis!" I could not help exclaiming.

"And Humphry Davy made me see it by a very simple experiment. He made a metallic ball of those metals, chiefly which I have just mentioned, which perfectly represented the globe. On this he squirted a sort of fine dust, and the surface began to puff up and get oxydized, and assume the shape of a little mountain. A crater opened in the top, and an eruption took place, which communicated such intense heat to the whole ball that it could not be held in the hand."

Positively I began to be shaken by the professor's arguments, heightened as their effect was by his usual fire and enthusiasm.

"You see, Axel," he added, "geologists have raised diverse hypotheses about the earth's centre, but nothing has been less proved than the existence of great heat. According to me it does not exist, it cannot exist, but we will go and see, and, like Arne Saknussemm, find out for ourselves who is right."

"Yes, that we will!" I exclaimed, carried away by his enthusiasm. "We shall see, that's to say, if we can see at all there."

"And why not? May we not reckon on some electric light, and even on the atmosphere, for the pressure, as it approached the centre, would render it luminous."

"Yes, it is possible after all."

"It is certain," replied my uncle triumphantly. "But silence, remember; silence about the whole business. Let no one take it into his head before us to try and discover the centre of the earth."

CHAPTER VII

SO ENDED THIS memorable conversation. It had put me in a perfect fever. I was quite giddy when I left my uncle's study, and there was not air enough in the streets of Hamburg to revive me. I went along the shore of the Elbe, beside the little stream which conveys passengers to the Hamburg railway station.

Was I convinced by what I had been hearing, or was it merely the professor's power that had conquered me? Must I treat this project seriously? Had I been listening to the mad speculations of a fool, or the scientific deductions of a great genius? And in it all, where did the truth end and error begin?

A thousand contradictory hypotheses floated before my mind, and there was nothing I could lay hold of.

However, I recollected I had felt convinced, though my enthusiasm began to cool down, but I would have liked to start immediately, before I had time for reflection. Yes, I could have strapped my portmanteau and set off that moment.

But, I must confess that, within an hour, this unnatural excitement left me. My nervous tension relaxed, and I was able to ascend from the depths of the earth to the surface once more.

"It is absurd!" I exclaimed. "It is not common sense. It is not a rational proposal to make to a sensible lad. Nothing of the sort exists. I have not slept well, and I have had a bad dream."

Meantime I had followed the shores of the Elbe, and got past the town. After I came out of the harbour, I took the road to

Altona, in obedience to a presentiment which after events justified, for I soon descried my little Gräuben tripping along on her
way home to Hamburg.

"Gräuben!" I shouted in the distance.

The girl stopped, rather put about, I should imagine, at hearing her name called out on the public road. A few steps, and I was
beside her.

"Axel!" she said, in surprise. "Ah! you came to meet me;
I know you did, sir."

But when she looked at me she could not but notice how upset
and worried I looked.

"What is the matter?" she said, holding out her hand.

"The matter, Gräuben?"

A few brief sentences told her the whole affair. She was silent
for a minute. Did her heart throb like mine? I didn't know, but
the hand I held in my own did not tremble in the least. We had
gone a hundred steps without speaking, and then she said:

"Axel!"

"Dear Gräuben," I replied.

"This will be a great journey."

I gave a jump.

"Yes, Axel, a journey worthy of the nephew of a *savant*. It is
right for a man to distinguish himself by some great enterprise."

"What! Gräuben! Wouldn't you dissuade me from attempting
such an undertaking?"

"No, dear Axel. I would gladly accompany you and your
uncle, but a poor girl like me would only be an encumbrance."

"Is that the truth?"

"Perfect truth."

Ah, those women and young girls – female hearts – always
incomprehensible. You are either the most timid or the bravest
of beings. Reason has nothing to do with you. The idea of this
child encouraging me in this expedition, and being willing to go
herself, too; even urging me to it, though she loved me!

I was somewhat nettled, and why should I not own it –
ashamed as well.

"Gräuben," I replied, "we'll see if you will say so to-morrow."

"To-morrow, dear Axel, I shall say the same as to-day."

We walked on together, hand in hand, in profound silence.
I felt quite worn out by the exciting scenes of the day.

"After all," thought I to myself, "the Kalends of July are a long way off yet, and many things may happen before that which may cure my uncle's craze for an underground journey."

It was late in the evening when we reached the house in Königstrasse. I expected to find everything quiet and my uncle gone to bed, as usual, and Martha in the dining-room with her dusting-brush, making all straight for the night.

But I had not allowed for my uncle's impatience. I found him shouting and running about among a troop of porters, who were unloading sundry goods in the passage. The old servant was at her wits' end.

"Come along, Axel, pray!" he called out, as soon as I came in sight. "Unfortunate fellow! Here is your portmanteau not packed, and my papers not arranged, and the key of my travelling-bag not to be found, and my gaiters not come!"

I stood dumbfounded. Voice failed me. My lips could scarcely articulate the words:

"We are going, then?"

"Yes, unlucky boy, wandering about instead of being here!"

"We are really going?" I repeated feebly.

"Yes; the day after to-morrow, at dawn."

I could not bear to hear more, and flew to my own little room.

There could be no doubt about it. My uncle had been employing his afternoon in getting some of the articles and utensils necessary for the journey. The passage was full of rope-ladders, slip-nooses, torches, gourds, cramp-irons, pickaxes, alpenstocks, mattocks, enough articles to load ten men at least.

I spent a terrible night. Next morning, I heard myself called quite early. I determined not to open the door, but who could resist the soft voice which said:

"Axel, dear Axel!"

I came out of my room thinking to myself that Gräuben would change her mind when she saw my pale, haggard face and eyes, red with want of sleep.

But as she met me, she said:

"Ah! you are better to-day, dear Axel, I see. Your night's rest has quieted you."

"Quieted me!"

I rushed to my mirror, and looked at myself. Well, I must confess I did not look so bad as I supposed. It was incredible.

"Axel," said Gräuben, "I have been having a long talk with my guardian. He is a bold *savant*, a man of great courage, and you must not forget his blood runs in your veins. He has told me all his plans and hopes, and why and how he expects to gain his object. He will succeed, I have no fear of it. Ah! Axel, it is a grand thing to devote one's self to science. What glory awaits Mr. Lidenbrock, and will be reflected on his companion! When you come back, Axel, you will be a man, an equal, free to speak, free to act, free to—"

The girl blushed, and did not finish the sentence. Her words animated me, but I still refused to believe that we were really going away. I dragged Gräuben off with me to the professor's study.

"Uncle!" I said, "is it quite settled that we are to go?"

"What! Have you any doubt about it?"

"No," I said, afraid of vexing him. "Only I want to know what's to hurry us so?"

"Why, time, to be sure – time which is fast flying, and can never be overtaken."

"But this is only the 26th of May, and between this and the end of June—"

"And do you suppose, you ignoramus, that we can get to Iceland so easily? If you had not gone off like a fool, I would have taken you with me to the Copenhagen office at Liffender's & Co., where you would have learnt that there is only one service between Copenhagen and Reikiavik, and that is on the 22nd of every month."

"Very well?"

"Very well; why if we wait till the 22nd of June, we shall arrive too late to see the shadow of Scartaris touch the crater of Snäfell. We must, therefore, get to Copenhagen as quickly as we can, and find out some means of transport. Go and pack your portmanteau."

There was not a word to say, and I went upstairs again to my room. Gräuben followed me. She undertook to arrange and stow away in a little portmanteau everything I needed for the journey. She was as cool and collected as if I had been going on a mere pleasure-trip to Lubeck, or Heligoland. Her little hands went quickly to work without the least haste or fluster. She talked calmly, and gave me most sensible reasons in favour of our expedition. She enchanted me, and I felt furious at leaving her. Sometimes I was going to break out in a passion, but she took no notice, and went on methodically with her tranquil occupation.

At length the last strap was buckled. I went down to the ground-floor.

All this day philosophical instruments, arms, electrical machines were being brought to the house. Martha did not know what to make of it.

"Is the master mad?" she said.

I made an affirmative gesture.

"And he is going to take you with him?"

I repeated the affirmative gesture.

"Where to?" she asked.

I pointed with my finger towards the heart of the earth.

"Into the cellars?" cried the old domestic.

"No," I said, at last; "lower down than that."

Evening came. I didn't know how the time went now.

"To-morrow morning," said my uncle, "we start at six precisely."

At 10 p.m. I fell on my bed like a lump of inert matter.

During the night my fears returned in full force.

I dreamt of abysses. I was delirious. I felt myself in the iron grip of the professor, being dragged away and engulfed. I was falling down terrific precipices, always getting lower and lower, with the ever-increasing velocity of bodies falling in space, and yet I never reached the bottom. It was one interminable descent.

At five o'clock I awoke, exhausted with fatigue and emotion. I repaired to the dining-room, and found my uncle already at table, devouring all that came in his way. I almost shuddered when I looked at him. But Gräuben was there, and I said nothing. I could not. At half-past five I heard the rattling of a vehicle coming down the street. It was a big coach to take us to the railway station at Altona. It was soon packed with my uncle's luggage.

"And where is your portmanteau?" he said to me.

"It is ready," I replied, turning faint.

"Make haste and fetch it down then, or you will make us lose the train."

To struggle against my fate seemed impossible. I went up to

my room, rolled my portmanteau down the stairs, and followed it immediately.

My uncle was just putting the reins of government solemnly into Gräuben's hands. My pretty Virlandaise retained her habitual composure and embraced her guardian passionately, but she could not keep back a tear, which dropped on my face when her sweet lips touched my cheek.

"Gräuben!" I cried.

"Go, dear Axel, go!" she said. "You are leaving your betrothed, but you will find your wife when you come back."

I clasped her once more in my arms and then took my place in the coach. Martha and the young girl stood at the door waving us a last adieu, and next minute we were dashing along at a gallop towards Altona.

CHAPTER VIII

AT ALTONA, WHICH, in fact, was only a suburb of Hamburg, commenced the line of rail to Kiel, by which we were to get to the shores of the Belt.

In less than twenty minutes we entered the territory of Holstein, and at half-past six the coach stopped before the railway station. The numerous packages of my uncle were unloaded, weighed, labelled, and deposited in the luggage van, and at seven we took our seats opposite each other in the same compartment. A shriek from the whistle and we were off.

Was I resigned? Not yet. However, the fresh morning air and the constant variety of scene, as the train bore us swiftly on, diverted my mind somewhat from its preoccupation.

As to the professor, the engine was evidently much too slow for his impatience, and his thoughts were far ahead of it. We were alone in the carriage, but neither of us spoke. My uncle was turning out his pockets and his travelling-bag, and investigating everything with the most minute attention. I soon saw that he had secured whatever was necessary for the execution of his projects.

Among others there was one sheet of paper, bearing the heading of the Danish Consulate, with the signature of M. Christiensen, the consul at Hamburg, and a friend of the professor. This would give us every facility for obtaining introductions at Copenhagen for the governor of Iceland.

I also perceived the famous document carefully stowed away in the most secret pocket of his portfolio. I anathematized it in my deepest heart, and turned away to look out again at the window. The country through which we were passing was a vast succession of uninteresting, monotonous, muddy plains, though tolerably fertile; a country very favourable for making railroads, as it would allow of the straight lines so prized by railway companies.

But this monotony had not time to grow wearisome, for in three hours from the time we started, the train stopped at Kiel, a few steps from the sea.

Our luggage was registered for Copenhagen, so we did not need to trouble ourselves about it. However, the professor looked anxiously after his property, as it was being carried on board the steamer, till it disappeared into the hold.

My uncle, in his haste, had calculated so well that we found a whole day would be lost here, as the steamer, the *Ellenore*, did not sail till night.

Nine hours' fever was the result, during which the irascible traveller stormed and swore at the managers of the railways and steamers, and the Government which allowed such abuses. I had to join in with him when he attacked the captain on the subject, insisting on the furnaces being lighted, and the vessel put in motion immediately. The captain merely sent him about his business.

But at Kiel, as everywhere else, a day must come to an end. By dint of walking along the verdant shores of the bay, in the heart of which the little town is situated, and roaming through the thick woods, which give it the appearance of a nest among the branches, and admiring the villas, and racing about and fuming, the time passed, and ten o'clock struck.

Clouds of smoke puffed out from the *Ellenore*, and the bridge shook with the vibration of the boiler when we came on board and took possession of our berths in the one solitary cabin of the steamer.

At a quarter past ten the cable was let go, and the steamer began to thread her way rapidly through the gloomy waters of the Great Belt.

The night was dark. There was a fine breeze and a strong sea.

Here and there, on the coast, lights glimmered. Farther on – I don't know where – a lighthouse shone brilliantly over the waves, and this is all I recollect about this first stage of our journey.

At 7 a.m. we disembarked at Korsör, a little town on the eastern side of Zealand. Here we jumped into a fresh railway, which carried us over a country quite as flat as the plains of Holstein.

We had a three-hours' journey still before reaching the capital of Denmark. My uncle had not closed an eye. In his patience I do believe he was pushing the carriage along with his feet.

At last he caught sight of the sea in the distance.

"The Sound!" he cried.

On our left there was a huge building resembling a hospital.

"It is a mad-house," said one of our travelling companions.

"Well, now," I thought to myself, "that is an establishment we certainly ought to end our days in; and large as it is, it would still be too small to contain all the madness of Professor Lidenbrock."

At ten in the morning we set foot in Copenhagen. The luggage was put on a conveyance, and we drove to the "Phœnix Hotel", in Breda Gate. This occupied about half an hour, for the station was outside the town. There my uncle, after a brief toilette, dragged me out with him. The porter of the hotel spoke German and English, but the professor being a perfect polyglot, interrogated him in good Danish, and it was in good Danish that the man directed him to the Museum of Northern Antiquities.

The curator of the curious establishment, where a new history of the country might be compiled out of the old stone weapons, and bowls, and jewels, was Professor Thomson, a *savant*, and a friend of the consul in Hamburg.

My uncle had a warm letter of recommendation to him. As a rule, one *savant* is not very cordial to another, but here was an exception. M. Thomson, being an obliging man, gave Professor Lidenbrock a hearty welcome, and his nephew also. It is hardly necessary to say that we kept our secret from the worthy curator. We were simply visiting Iceland as disinterested amateurs.

M. Thomson placed himself entirely at our disposal, and ran about the quays for us, trying to find a vessel that was going there.

I fervently hoped his search would be unsuccessful. But it was nothing of the sort. A small Danish schooner, the *Valkyria*, was to sail on the 2nd of June for Reikiavik. The captain, M. Bjorne, was on board. His intending passenger almost crushed his hand by the hearty grip he gave it in his joy. The worthy man was a little astonished, for going to Iceland was an every-day occurrence to him. My uncle thought it sublime, and the brave captain took advantage of his enthusiasm to ask him double fare. But we did not look at matters too closely.

"Be on board on Sunday, at 7 a.m.," said M. Bjorne, pocketing the dollars coolly, as the bargain was concluded.

We then returned to the "Phœnix", after giving our best thanks to M. Thomson for his trouble.

"This is capital! Most capital!" repeated my uncle. "What a fortunate chance to have found a ship ready to sail. Now we'll have breakfast, and then go and look at the town."

We went first to Kongens-Nye-Torw, an irregular square, where two harmless cannons were posted. Close by, at No. 5, there was a French "restauration", kept by a cook named Vincent. Here we breakfasted very well for the modest sum of four marks each.*

Then I wandered about the town with absolutely childish delight. My uncle walked along, but he saw nothing – neither the magnificent palace of the king, nor the pretty bridge built in the sixteenth century, which stretches across the canal in the front of the Museum, nor that immense cenotaph of Thorwaldsen adorned with horrible mural paintings outside, and containing in the interior the works of the sculptor, nor the Castle of Rosenberg, in a tolerably fine park, a miniature structure, looking like a *bon-bon* box; nor the Exchange, a handsome *renaissance* edifice, nor its tower, composed of the twisted tails of four dragons in bronze, nor the great windmills on the ramparts, the vast sails of which swelled out before the breeze like the canvas of a ship in a breeze.

What charming walks my pretty Gräuben and I would have had along the harbour where the two-deckers and the frigates sleep peacefully, below the red roof of the shed, and along the verdant banks of the strait, through the leafy shades of which the citadel peeps out, and its black line of cannon stretches along among the branches of the elders and willows.

* About 2s. 6d.

But, alas! she was far away, and might I ever hope to see her again?

However, though my uncle noticed none of these enchanting views, he was much struck by the sight of a certain steeple in the island of Amack, which forms the south-west quarter of Copenhagen.

I was ordered to bend my steps towards it, and hailed a little steamer which ferried passengers over the canal. In a few minutes we landed on the quay of the dockyard.

After having traversed several narrow streets, where the galley-slaves, in their yellow and grey short trousers, were toiling under the baton of the sergeants, we came in front of the Vor-Frelsers Kirk. There was nothing remarkable in this church. But this was why the steeple had attracted the attention of the professor. It was of considerable height, and rising from the top of the tower there was a staircase outside which wound round the spire to the very top.

"Let us go up it," said my uncle.

"But it will make us giddy."

"All the more reason for going. We must accustom ourselves to it."

"But—"

"Come, I tell you; do not lose time."

I was forced to obey. The man who kept the church lived on the other side of the street and I got the key from him and we commenced the ascent.

My uncle went first with a nimble foot. I followed him in some alarm, for I was desperately inclined to turn giddy. I had neither the steadiness nor the nerves of an eagle.

As long as we were inside the spiral I got on well enough, but after 150 steps I felt the wind in my face, and we reached the platform of the steeple where the outside stair commenced. It was protected by a frail balustrade, and the steps growing narrower and narrower seemed to climb up into space.

"I shall never do it!" I exclaimed.

"Would you be a coward? Go on!" replied the inexorable professor.

I was compelled to obey, clinging with all my might. The strong wind made me giddy, I felt the steeple oscillate at every gust. My legs gave way and I had to climb up soon on my knees and then on my stomach. I shut my eyes; I felt sick.

At last I reached the ball, my uncle dragging me by the collar.

"Look down," he said, "and look well. We must take *abyss lessons.*"

I opened my eyes. I saw the houses, looking flat and as if crushed by a fall, in the midst of thick smoke. Above my head scattered clouds were passing, and by an optical inversion they seemed to me motionless, while the steeple, and ball, and myself were whirling down with fantastic swiftness. In the distance, on one side lay the green plains, and on the other the sparkling sea. The Sound spread out before Elsinore, and sundry white sails, like the wings of sea birds, and in the mist, to the east, appeared the faint outlines of the Swedish coast. All the universe was swimming round before my eyes.

But for all that I was obliged to rise and stand up and gaze. My first lesson in *vertigo* lasted an hour, and when at last I was allowed to descend and my feet touched the solid pavement of the street, I was lame.

"We will begin again, to-morrow," said my master.

And so we did. For five days in succession this dizzy exercise was repeated, and in spite of myself I made sensible progress in the art of "high contemplation".

CHAPTER IX

THE DAY OF departure arrived. Our obliging friend, M. Thomson, brought us hearty letters of introduction to Baron Trampe, the governor of Iceland; to M. Pictursson, the suffragan of the Bishop; and M. Finsen, Mayor of Reikiavik, for which my uncle thanked him by the heartiest shake of the hand.

On the 2nd, at 6 a.m., our precious luggage was carried on board the *Valkyria*, and we were conducted to our narrow cabins by the captain.

"Have we a fair wind?" asked my uncle.

"Excellent!" replied Captain Bjorne; "a sou'-wester. We shall go out of the Sound in full sail."

A few minutes later the schooner got under weigh, and with

her mizzen, brigantine, and top-gallant sails spread, was running before the breeze through the Strait. An hour afterwards the capital of Denmark seemed to sink beneath the distant waves, and the *Valkyria* was coasting along by Elsinore. In my excited nervous state I expected to see the ghost of Hamlet wandering on the legendary terrace.

"Sublime madman!" I said to myself. "You would approve our proceedings, undoubtedly. Maybe you would follow us to the centre of the globe, to seek there a solution of your eternal doubt!"

But nothing appeared on those ancient walls. The castle, more-over, is much younger than the heroic Prince of Denmark. It is used now as a sumptuous lodge for the toll-keeper of the Sound, through which 15,000 vessels of all nations pass every year.

The Castle of Kronsberg soon vanished in the mist, as also the town of Helsingborg, on the Swedish coast, and the schooner began to catch the breezes of the Cattegat.

The *Valkyria* was a good sailer, but one cannot reckon on a sailing vessel. She was loaded with coal for Reikiavik, and house-hold utensils, earthenware, woollen clothing, and a cargo of wheat. Five men, all Danes, composed the crew.

"How long will the voyage take?" my uncle asked the captain.

"About ten days," was the reply, "if we don't get a taste of a 'nor'-wester' as we pass the Faroes."

"But, as a rule, are you liable to be much delayed?"

"No, M. Lidenbrock. Make your mind easy, we'll get there soon enough."

Towards evening the schooner doubled the Skagen, the north-ern point of Denmark, and during the night we passed through the Skager Rack, coasted along the extremity of Norway, by Cape Lindness, and out into the North Sea.

Two days afterwards we sighted the coast of Scotland off Peterhead, and the *Valkyria* began to steer straight towards the Faroe Islands, passing between the Orkneys and Shetlands.

The waves of the Atlantic were soon dashing against our schooner, and she had to tack to avoid the north wind, and had considerable difficulty in getting to the Faroes. On the 8th the captain sighted Myganness, the most easterly of the islands, and from that time steered a straight course for Portland Bay, situated on the southern coast of Iceland.

Nothing particular occurred during the passage. I stood the sea pretty well, but my uncle, to his great vexation and still greater shame, was ill the whole time.

He was unable consequently to have any conversation with the captain about Snäfell and the means of communication with it or modes of transport. All these questions he was obliged to postpone till his arrival, and passed his time lying down in his cabin, the sides of which cracked and shivered with the pitching of the vessel. It must be owned he rather deserved his fate.

On the 11th we sighted Cape Portland. The weather happening to be clear just then allowed us a glimpse of Myrdals-Jokul, which rises above it. The cape is simply a low, broad hill, with very steep sides, standing alone on the shore.

The *Valkyria* kept a good way out from the coast in a westerly direction, sailing through numerous shoals of whales and sharks. Presently an immense rock was seen, pierced with holes, through which the foaming waves dashed furiously. The Westman islets seemed to rise out of the ocean like rocks strewed on the liquid plain. After this the schooner made a wide sweep to round Cape Reikianess, which forms the western angle of Iceland.

The stormy sea prevented my uncle from coming on deck to admire the broken, jagged shores, constantly beat upon by gales from the south-west.

Forty-eight hours later, just as we got out of a storm which obliged the schooner to take in every inch of canvas, we sighted, in the east, the beacon light of Cape Skagen, whose dangerous rocks extend a great distance below the waves. An Iceland pilot came on board, and three hours afterwards the *Valkyria* moored before Reikiavik in the Faxa Bay.

The professor emerged from his cabin at last, a little pale and exhausted, but as enthusiastic as ever, his eyes beaming with satisfaction.

The inhabitants of the town stood in a group on the quay, peculiarly interested in the arrival of a vessel which had brought everyone's commissions.

My uncle was all haste to leave his floating prison, or we might say hospital. But before leaving the deck of the schooner he dragged me away to the bow, and, pointing with his finger to the mouth of the bay, showed me a high mountain with two peaks, a double cone covered with eternal snows.

"Snäfell! Snäfell!" he exclaimed.

Thus reminding me by a gesture to keep silence, he took his seat in the boat which was waiting for us. I followed, and our feet soon touched the shores of Iceland.

Next minute a fine-looking man appeared in the uniform of a general. However, he was simply a magistrate, the governor of Iceland – Baron Trampe himself. The professor speedily discovered his rank, and presented him with his letters of introduction from Copenhagen. Then followed a brief conversation in Danish, which I did not understand a word of, and for a good reason. But the outcome of it all was that Baron Trampe placed himself entirely at the disposal of Professor Lidenbrock.

From the mayor, M. Finsen, no less military in costume than the governor, and equally pacific in temper and calling, my uncle received a most kindly welcome.

The bishop's suffragan, M. Pictursson, was making an episcopal visitation in the north, so we had to give up meantime the pleasure of being introduced to him. But there was one most fascinating man we met with, whose society became very precious to me; this was M. Fridrikson, professor of natural science in the school at Reikiavik. This modest *savant* only spoke Icelandic and Latin. It was in the soft tongue of Horace that he came to offer his services, and I felt at home with him at once. In fact he was the only person with whom I could exchange a word during my stay in Iceland.

Out of the three rooms which his house contained, this excellent man placed two at our disposal, and soon we were installed in them bag and baggage, the quantity of which rather astonished the good folks of Reikiavik.

"Come now, Axel," said my uncle, "we are getting on famously. The worst part of the business is over."

"How do you make that out?" I exclaimed.

"Why, all we have to do now is to make the descent."

"Oh, if you look at it in that way you are right; but we have got to get up as well as to get down, I fancy."

"Oh, that does not trouble me at all. Come, there is no time to lose. I am going to the library. Perhaps there is some manuscript of Saknussemm's to be found there; and I should like very much to consult it."

"And while you are there I will look over the town. Won't you do that much too?"

"Oh, that has but little interest for me. The most curious part of Iceland is not what is on the surface, but what is below."

I went out and wandered at hap-hazard. It would have been difficult to lose one's way in Reikiavik, seeing there are but two streets, so I was not obliged to ask my way by making signs, which exposes one to many mistakes.

The town lies between two hills, on a somewhat low and marshy soil. An immense layer of lava covers it on one side and slopes gently down to the sea. The wide bay of Faxa stretches out on the opposite side and is bounded by the enormous Snäfell glacier, and in this bay the *Valkyria* was the only vessel then at anchor. Generally the English and French fishery-keepers are moored in the offing, but just now they were wanted on the eastern coast of the island.

The longer of the two streets lies parallel with the shore. It is here that the merchants and traders live in wooden huts, made of red planks laid horizontally; the other street, more to the west, runs down to a little lake, between the houses of the bishop and others not connected with trade.

I had soon made my way through these dull, melancholy-looking streets, here and there catching a glimpse of a bit of faded turf, like an old threadbare carpet, or occasionally of a garden, the scanty produce of which, consisting of a few potatoes, cabbages, and lettuces, might have easily figured on a Lilliputian table. A few sickly gillyflowers were also trying to lift up their heads in the sunlight.

About the centre of the non-commercial street I found the public cemetery, enclosed by a mud-wall, and apparently with plenty of room in it. A few steps farther brought me to the governor's house, a hut compared with the town hall of Hamburg, though a palace beside the huts of the Icelanders.

A church rose between the little lake and the town, built in the Protestant style and with calcined stones which the volcanoes brought up from the earth at their own expense. When strong gales blew from the south-west it was evident that the red tiles of the roofs would be scattered in all directions, to the great danger of the faithful worshippers.

On a neighbouring eminence I perceived the national school
where, as I was subsequently informed by our host, Hebrew,
English, French, and Danish are taught; four languages of which,
I am ashamed to say, I didn't know a single word. I should have
stood at the bottom of the class in the little college numbering
forty scholars, and been unworthy to sleep with them in one of
those double closets where more delicate boys must have died of
suffocation on the very first night.

In three hours I had gone over both the town and its environs.
Its general aspect was singularly gloomy. No trees, no vegetation
worth speaking of; everything bare volcanic rocks. The Icelandic
huts are made of earth and turf, and the walls slope within. They
resemble roofs laid on the ground; but these same roofs are
meadows comparatively fertile. Thanks to the internal heat,
tolerably good grass grows on them, which is carefully cut down
in the hay season, for, if left, the domestic animals would come
and graze on these green dwellings.

During my ramble I met but few of the inhabitants. In coming
back, though, along the commercial street, I saw the greater part
of the population engaged in drying, salting, and loading cod-
fish – the principal article of exportation. The men looked
robust, but heavy, a species of Germans, with fair hair and pensive
eyes, feeling themselves a little outside the pale of humanity;
poor exiles relegated to this land of ice, who should properly
have been Esquimaux, since they were condemned by nature to
live on the edge of the Arctic circle. I tried in vain to catch a smile
on their features. Sometimes they laughed by a sort of involuntary contraction of the muscles, but they never smiled.

Their costumes consisted in a coarse jacket of black woollen
stuff known as *vadmel* in Scandinavian countries, a wide-
brimmed hat, trousers bordered with red, and a piece of leather
wound round the feet for shoes.

The women had sad resigned faces, agreeable enough, but
without expression, and were dressed in a gown and petticoat of
dark *vadmel*. The girls wore their hair in plaits round their heads,
and a little brown knitted cap over it; and the married women
donned a coloured handkerchief with a white peak of linen on
the top.

When I returned to M. Fridrikson, after a good long walk,
I found my uncle already in the company of his host.

CHAPTER X

DINNER WAS READY, and eagerly devoured by Professor Liden-brock, whose compulsory abstinence on board had converted his stomach into a deep gulf. About the meal itself, which was more Danish than Icelandic, there was nothing remarkable, but our host, who was more Icelandic than Danish, reminded me of the hospitable heroes of ancient times. It was evident that he considered the house ours rather than his so long as we were his guests.

The conversation was carried on in the idiom of the country, though my uncle put in a little German now and then, and M. Fridrikson a little Latin for my especial benefit. It turned on scientific questions, as befitted *savants*, but Professor Lidenbrock displayed great reserve, and at every sentence warned me by a look to be careful not to breathe a word about our plans.

Almost the first question asked by M. Fridrikson was how my uncle had got on at the library.

"The library!" exclaimed my uncle. "Why, it only consists of a few odd volumes on a lot of empty shelves."

"What!" said M. Fridrikson, "we have 8,000 volumes, many of them very valuable and rare, and in addition to works in the old Scandinavian tongue, we have all the novelties every year that Copenhagen can furnish us."

"And where are these 8,000 volumes? For my part—"

"Ah, M. Lidenbrock, they are all over the country. In our ancient island of ice there is a taste for study. Not a farmer nor a fisherman could be found who cannot read, and who does not read. We are of opinion that instead of letting books grow mouldy behind an iron grating, far from the vulgar gaze, it is better to let them wear out by being read. These volumes, there-fore, circulate freely from hand to hand, and are turned over and read and re-read, and often only come back to their shelves after a year or two of absence."

"And, meantime," replied my uncle, a little snappishly, "strangers—"

"What would you have? Strangers have their own libraries at home, and our first business is to educate our countrymen. I say again the love of study is in the Icelandic blood. That is how, in 1816, we started a literary society which is now flourishing. Learned foreigners are proud to be members of it. It publishes books compiled for the instruction of our fellow-countrymen, and is a valuable boon to the island. If you will consent to be one of our corresponding members, M. Lidenbrock, you will confer on us the greatest pleasure."

My uncle belonged already to a hundred scientific societies, but he consented – with so much grace that M. Fridrikson was quite touched by it.

"And now," he said, "if you will please to tell me what were the books you hoped to find, I may, perhaps, be able to give you some information about them."

I looked at my uncle. He had now to reply, for this was a question that immediately affected his project. However, after a minute's reflection, he said:

"M. Fridrikson, I wanted to know whether there are any writings of Arne Saknussemm among the ancient works."

"Arne Saknussemm!" replied the Reikiavik professor. "You mean a *savant* of the sixteenth century, who was at once a great naturalist, a great alchemist, and a great traveller?"

"Precisely."

"One of the glories of Icelandic science and literature."

"Exactly so."

"An illustrious man everywhere."

"That's the very man."

"His daring equalled his genius."

"Ah! I see you know him thoroughly."

My uncle's eyes beamed at this eulogy of his hero, and he listened eagerly to every word.

"Well!" he said at last; "and what about his works?"

"Ah! his works; haven't one of them!"

"What? Not in Iceland!"

"They are neither to be found in Iceland nor anywhere else."

"And why?"

"Because Arne Saknussemm was persecuted for heresy, and in 1573 his books were burnt at Copenhagen by the hands of the common executioner."

"Very good! that's capital," exclaimed my uncle to the great scandal of the professor of natural science.

"Yes," continued my uncle, "all hangs together, all is clear now, and I can understand how it was that Saknussemm, when he found himself placed on the *Index Expurgatorius*, and obliged to conceal the discoveries of his genius, had to bury his secret in an incomprehensible cryptogram."

"What secret?" asked M. Fridrikson, sharply.

"A secret that – which—" stammered out my uncle.

"Is it some secret document that you have come into possession of?"

"No, no; a mere supposition that I was making."

"Oh! that was it," said M. Fridrikson, and kindly dropped the subject when he saw the embarrassment of his guest. "I hope," he added, "that you will not leave the island without having seen some of its mineralogical wealth."

"Certainly not; but I fear I am a little too late. The island has been already visited by learned men, I believe."

"Yes, M. Lidenbrock. The labours of MM. Olafsen and Povelson, undertaken by order of the king, the researches of Troil, the scientific mission of MM. Gaimard and Robert, in the French corvette *La Recherche*,* and lastly the observations made by *savants* on the frigate *La Reine Hortense*, have largely contributed to our knowledge of Iceland. But believe me, there is plenty to do yet."

"Do you think so?" said my uncle, carelessly, trying to look unconcerned.

"I do. How many mountains and glaciers and volcanoes there are about which little or nothing is known. Stop! – without going a step farther – look at that mountain on the horizon! That is Snäfell."

"Ah, indeed!" replied my uncle. "That is Snäfell?"

"Yes; one of the most curious volcanoes, and its crater has been seldom visited."

"Is it extinct?"

"Yes, for the last 500 years."

"Well, then," said my uncle, crossing his legs frantically, to keep himself from giving a great jump, "I should like to commence my geological explorations at this Seffel, or Fessel, did you call it?"

---

* The *Recherche* was sent out in 1835 by Admial Duperré to find the traces of a lost expedition, that of M. de Blossville in the *Heloise*, which was never heard of.

"Snäfell!" replied the worthy M. Fridrikson.

This part of the conversation was in Latin. I understood every word of it, and could scarcely keep grave to see my uncle trying to hide his satisfaction. He was brimful and bubbling over with delight, but wanted to put on an innocent, simple look. All he managed, however, was a sort of diabolical grin.

"Yes," he said, "what you tell me has decided me. We will attempt the ascent of Snäfells, and perhaps even study its crater."

"I greatly regret," replied M. Fridrikson, "that my occupations prevent me from accompanying you. It would have been most pleasant and profitable to me."

"Oh no, no," returned my uncle, quickly; "we should not like to disturb anybody, M. Fridrikson. I thank you most heartily. Your company would have been very useful to us, but the duties of your profession, of course—"

It pleases me to think that in the innocent guilelessness of his Icelandic nature, our host did not see through my uncle's clumsy manœuvres.

"I quite approve your plan, M. Lidenbrock, of beginning with Snäfell," he said. "You will reap a rich harvest there of curious observations. But now tell me," he continued, "how you think of getting there."

"By sea. The quickest way will be to go across the bay."

"No doubt; but it is impossible to do it."

"Why?"

"Because we have not a boat in Reikiavik."

"Hang it!"

"You'll have to go by land – keeping along the shore. It is a longer way, but more interesting."

"Very good then, I must find a guide."

"I just happen to know of one that will suit you, I think."

"A reliable, intelligent man?"

"Yes; and who lives on the peninsula. He is an eider-down hunter, a very clever fellow, that will please you. He speaks Danish perfectly."

"And when can I see him?"

"To-morrow, if you like."

"Why not to-day?"

"Because he won't be here till to-morrow."

"Well, it must be to-morrow, then," said my uncle with a sigh.

This important conversation ended a few minutes later with hearty acknowledgements from the German professor to the Icelandic professor for his great kindness. My uncle had gleaned much valuable information during dinner. He had learnt the history of Saknussemm, the reason of his mysterious document, and, moreover, that his host could not accompany him in his expedition, and that next day a guide would be waiting his orders.

CHAPTER XI

IN THE EVENING I took a short walk along the shore, and came back early. I retired to rest, and was soon sleeping soundly in my big bed, made of rough planks of wood.

When I awoke I heard my uncle talking at a great rate in the next room. I got up immediately, and hastened to join him.

He was talking in Danish to a very tall man, of strong, well-built frame. This strapping fellow was evidently endowed with unusual strength. He had a very large head, and an innocent, simple-looking face. His pale blue eyes, dreamy as they were, seemed to me full of intelligence. Long hair, which would have been called red even in England, hung down over his athletic shoulders. His movements were full of suppleness, but he scarcely stirred his arms, and seemed to be a man who either disdained, or was unacquainted with the language of gestures. Everything about him revealed a temperament of the most perfect calmness, not indolent, but placid. You felt that he was not one to ask favours, and that he worked when it suited him; and that his philosophy would never be disturbed or surprised by whatever might happen.

I could tell all this by the way the Icelander listened to the torrent of words poured out by his interlocutor. He stood with folded arms, motionless, in face of the multiplied gestures made by my uncle. His head turned from left to right if he wished to give a negative reply, and gently bowed for an affirmative one, but so gently that his long hair scarcely moved. It was economy of motion carried to extremes.

Certainly I should never have guessed the man was a hunter. He would never frighten the game away, it was true, but how could he so much as get near it?

All was explained when M. Fridrikson informed us he was only an eider-duck hunter, a bird whose down is the principal wealth of the island. The down is called "eider-down", and no great amount of movement is required to get it.

Early in the summer the female, a pretty species of duck, builds her nest among the rocks of the fiords which fringe the entire coast. This nest she lines with the downy feathers off her own breast. Immediately the hunter, or rather the trader, comes, and takes the nest away and the poor bird recommences her task only to be robbed again. This is repeated till her breast is stripped bare, when the male steps in and feathers it in his turn. This time she is allowed to lay her eggs in peace, as the coarse hard plumage of her mate has no commercial value; so the nest is completed, the eggs laid, the young ones hatched, and the birds left undisturbed till the following year, when the harvest begins again.

Now as the eider does not choose precipitous crags for her nest, but rather low-lying horizontal rocks which stretch out into the sea, the Iceland hunter might pursue his calling without disturbing himself much. He was a farmer who neither needed to sow nor to cut down his harvest. All he had to do was to gather it in. This grave, phlegmatic, silent personage was named Hans Bjilke. He came on the recommendation of M. Fridrikson. This was our future guide. His manner strangely contrasted with that of my uncle.

However, they soon came to a mutual understanding. Neither of them cared about terms; the one was ready to take whatever was offered, the other ready to give whatever was asked. Never was bargain more easily settled.

The result of the agreement was that Hans engaged to take us to the village of Stapi, lying on the southern side of the peninsula of Snäfell, at the very foot of the volcano. The distance by land was about twenty-two miles, a two days' journey, my uncle reckoned.

But when he found that in a Danish mile there are 24,000 feet he was obliged to alter his calculations, and taking into account the indifferent roads, allow seven or eight days.

Four horses were to be placed at our disposal, two to carry him and me, and two for our luggage; Hans, according to his habit, would go on foot. He knew this part of the coast perfectly, and promised to take us by the shortest route.

His engagement with my uncle was not to end with our arrival at Stapi. He was to remain in his service during the whole time of his scientific expeditions, for the sum of three rix-dollars a week.* It was also expressly agreed, and indeed was a *sine qua non* of the engagement, that this sum should be paid down every Saturday evening.

The departure was fixed for the 16th of June. My uncle wished to pay "earnest money" on the conclusion of the bargain, but the man refused by pronouncing the single word:

"*Efter.*"

"*After,*" explained the professor, for my edification.

"A first-rate fellow," said my uncle, as Hans withdrew, "but he has no idea of the marvellous part he has to play in the future."

"He will go with us then into—"

"Yes, Axel, into the centre of the earth."

We had forty-eight hours still left before starting, but to my great regret they were obliged to be spent in preparations. We had to set all our wits to work to pack each article to the greatest advantage – instruments on one side, arms on the other: tools in this parcel, provisions in that; four sets in all.

The instruments comprised:

1. An Eigel's centigrade thermometer, graduated up to 150°, which seemed to me either too much or too little. Too much if the surrounding heat would rise to that, for we should be baked; too little if it was to be used for measuring the temperature of springs or any matter in a state of fusion.

2. A manometer for indicating higher atmospheric pressure than that at the level of the sea. An ordinary barometer would not have been enough, as the atmospheric pressure would increase in proportion to our descent below the surface of the earth.

3. A chronometer by Boisonas, jun., of Geneva, accurately regulated by the meridian of Hamburg.

4. Two compasses, for taking inclinations and declinations.

5. A night glass.

* About 12s.

6. Two of Ruhmkorff's apparatus, which, by means of an electric current, give a very portable safe light.*

The arms consisted of two of Purdey-Moore's rifles and two of Colt's revolvers. What did we need arms for? It was not likely we should encounter savages or wild beasts, I thought. But my uncle seemed to consider his arsenal as necessary as his instruments, and took special care to lay in a stock of gun-cotton, which damp cannot affect, and the explosive force of which is superior to that of ordinary gunpowder.

The tools comprised two pickaxes, two spades, a silk rope-ladder, three iron-tipped sticks, a hatchet, a hammer, a dozen wedges and iron hold-fasts, and long knotted ropes. A pretty sized package that made, for the ladder measured 300 feet.

Then there were provisions. But these did not take up much room, though it was comforting to know we had enough essence of beef and dry biscuits to last us six months. The only liquid we took was gin, and absolutely not a drop of water. But we had gourds, and my uncle reckoned on finding springs where we might refill them. Whatever objections to this I made, on the ground of their quality and temperature, or even their absence, was unsuccessful.

To complete the exact list of all we took with us, I must mention a portable medicine chest, containing blunt scissors, splints for broken limbs, a piece of unbleached linen tape, bandages and compressers, lint, a cupping glass, all terrible-looking things; and in addition to these a series of phials, containing dextrine,

---

* Ruhmkorff's apparatus consists of a Bunsen pile set in activity by means of bichromate of potash, which has no smell. An induction coil communicates the electricity produced by the pile to a lantern of peculiar shape. In this lantern there is a spiral tube where a vacuum has been made, and in which nothing remains but a residuum of carbonic-acid gas, or of azote. When the apparatus is put in motion this gas becomes luminous, producing a steady white light. The pile and the coil are placed in a leathern bag, which the traveller carries across his shoulder. The lantern placed outside gives sufficient light in deep darkness, and allows the adventurer, without fear of any explosion, to go through the most inflammable gases, and is not extinguished even in the deepest waters. M. Ruhmkorff is a *savant* and clever physician. His great discovery is this induction coil, by which electricity can be produced at high pressure. He obtained in 1864 the quinquennial prize of 50,000 francs, offered by the French Government for the most ingenious application of electricity.

spirits of wine and liquid acetate of lead, ether, vinegar, and ammonia – all drugs suggesting painful possibilities. Lastly, all the necessary articles for Ruhmkorff's apparatus.

My uncle did not forget to take a supply of tobacco, powder for hunting, tinder, and a leathern belt, which he wore round his waist, and in which he carried a sufficient sum of money in gold, silver, and paper. Good boots, made waterproof by a solution of india-rubber and naphtha; six pairs in all were stowed away among the tools.

"With such an outfit and equipment as ours, there is no reason why we should not go far," said my uncle.

The 14th was entirely taken up with settling all our different articles. In the evening we dined at Baron Trampe's with the mayor of Reikiavik and Dr. Hyaltalin, the principal physician in the country. M. Fridrikson was not among the guests. I afterwards heard that he and the governor had differed in opinion on some question of administration, and were no longer on speaking terms. I had no opportunity, therefore, of understanding a word of the conversation during this semi-official dinner. I only noticed that my uncle was talking all the time.

Next day, the 15th, our preparations were completed. Our host afforded my uncle the liveliest pleasure by presenting him with a map of Iceland, far more perfect than that of Handersen. It was the map of Olaf Nikolas Olsen reduced to $\frac{1}{480000}$ of the real size of the island, and published by the Iceland Literary Society. This was a precious document to a mineralogist.

The last evening was spent in close conversation with M. Fridrikson, for whom I felt a sympathetic attraction, and this was followed by a troubled sleepless night, as far, at least, as I was concerned.

At 5 a.m. the neighing of the four horses, as they stood pawing below the window, made me rise hastily and go down. I found Hans just finishing the loading of the horses, almost without stirring, one would say, but he did his work with uncommon cleverness. My uncle was making a great noise rather than helping, and the guide appeared to take no notice of his orders.

By 6 a.m. all was ready. We shook hands with M. Fridrikson, and my uncle thanked him most heartily for his great hospitality. As for myself, I launched out a cordial farewell in the best Latin I could find; then we jumped into our saddles, and M. Fridrikson repeated with his last adieux that line of Virgil which seemed to have been made for uncertain travellers on the road, like us:

Et quacumque viam dederit fortuna sequamur.

CHAPTER XII

THE SKY WAS gloomy when we started, but settled, so we had neither rain nor heat to fear. It was the very weather for tourists.

The pleasure of roaming over an unknown country on horseback easily reconciled me to this *début* of our enterprise. Indeed I felt quite in the mood of an excursionist rejoicing in his freedom, and, full of desires and expectations, I began to take my share in the business.

"Besides," I said to myself, "what risk is there? We are to travel through one of the most curious countries in the world, and to climb a most remarkable mountain, and, even at the worst, descend to the bottom of an extinct crater, for it is quite evident that is all that Saknussemm did. As to there being any passage out of it, right into the heart of the earth, that's a pure imagination, a sheer impossibility; so I shall make up my mind to get all the enjoyment I can out of this business, and not bother about the rest."

By the time I had reached this conclusion, we had quite got out of Reikiavik.

Hans was walking ahead at a rapid, even, continuous pace. The two baggage horses followed him without being led. My uncle and I brought up the rear, and really we did not cut a bad figure on our small but stout steeds.

Iceland is one of the largest islands in Europe. It is 14,000 miles in extent, and has only a population of 60,000. Geographers have divided it into four quarters, and we had crossed in a nearly diagonal direction the one called "Sudveste Fjordûnge" (the country of the south-west quarter).

After leaving Reikiavik, Hans kept straight along the coast. We went through scanty pastures, which tried their best to look green, and never succeeded in being anything but yellow. The rugged peaks of the trachyte rocks were faintly outlined on the misty eastern horizon. At times a few patches of snow, concentrating the scattered rays of light, glittered brilliantly on the tops of the distant mountains; certain peaks, bolder than the rest, pierced through the grey clouds, and reappeared above the moving matter like rocks out of the sea.

Often these chains of barren rocks made a sharp turn towards the sea, encroaching on the pasturage, but there was always room enough to pass. Our horses, moreover, instinctively chose the best footing, without once slackening speed. My uncle never even had the satisfaction of urging on his steed by voice or whip. He could not even get impatient with it. I could not help smiling, though, at seeing such a tall man on such a little horse. His long legs barely cleared the ground, and he looked like a Centaur with six legs.

"Good beast! good beast!" he said. "You will see, Axel, that a more intelligent animal does not exist than the Icelandic horse. Nothing stops him – neither snows, tempests, impassible roads, nor glaciers. He is brave, steady, and sure-footed. He never makes a false step – never shies. If we have to cross a river or fiord – and we shall be sure to meet with them – you will see him, without the least hesitation, plunge into the water as if he were some amphibious animal, and gain the opposite bank. But we must not be rough with him; leave him his liberty, and we shall get on at the rate of nearly thirty miles a day."

"I have no doubt *we* shall, but how about the guide?"

"Oh, I have no concern on that score. Men of his stamp get over the ground without perceiving it. He moves himself too little to get fatigued, and, besides, he shall have my horse at a pinch. I shall soon get the cramp if I have no exercise. I must study my legs as well as my arms."

We were getting on famously. The country was almost a desert already. Here and there a solitary farmhouse, called a *boër* in Icelandic, or a dwelling constructed of earth and wood and pieces of lava, stood up like a poor beggar by the roadside. These dilapidated-looking huts seemed as if asking alms from passers-by, and for two pins we would have given them a trifle. In this country there are neither roads nor paths, and, slow as vegetation is, travellers come so few and far between that their footsteps are soon overgrown.

And yet this part of the province, lying so near the capital, was reckoned among the inhabited and cultivated portions of

Iceland. What would it be then in districts more deserted than this desert? We had gone half a mile without seeing as much as a farmer at the door of his hut, or a rude shepherd tending a flock less wild than himself. Nothing had come in sight but a few cows and sheep wandering about as they pleased. What, then, must those convulsed regions be, overturned by eruptions, themselves the offspring of volcanic explosions and subterranean commotions?

We were doomed to know that in good time. But on consulting Olsen's map I saw they would be avoided by keeping along the winding coast. In fact, the great plutonic action is specially concentrated in the interior of the island. Then the piled-up rocks, in horizontal layers, called *trapp* in Scandinavian, trachytes, basalt, tuff, and all the volcanic conglomerates, streams of lava and porphyry in a state of fusion, invest the country with supernatural horrors. I little imagined, however, the spectacle which awaited us on the peninsula of Snäfell, where these fiery materials make a very chaos.

Two hours after leaving Reikiavik we arrived at the burgh of Gufunus, called *aoalkirkja*, or principal church. There was nothing remarkable about it, in fact there was nothing in it but a few houses, scarcely enough to make a German hamlet.

Hans stopped here half an hour. He shared our frugal breakfast, and said "yes" or "no" to all my uncle's questions, except when he asked where we were to pass the night, and to this he replied:

"Gardär."

I consulted the map to see where Gardär was, and found a little town of that name on the banks of the Hvalfjörd, four miles from Reikiavik. I showed it to my uncle.

"Only four miles!" he said. "Four miles out of twenty-two! That's a pretty walk, certainly."

He began some remark to the guide about it, but Hans took no notice, and resumed his place ahead, so we had to set off again.

Three hours later, still treading the faded grass, we had to go round the Kollafiord, a shorter and easier route than across the inlet. We soon entered a "pingstan", or parish named Ejilburg, the clock of which would have struck twelve, if the Icelandic churches had been rich enough to possess clocks; but they are like the parishioners, they have no clocks, and manage to do without them.

The horses were baited here, and then we struck into a narrow path between a chain of hills and the sea, which brought us to our next stage, the "aoalkirkja" of Brantär, and a mile further on to Sarnböre "Annexia", a chapel-of-ease on the south shore of the Hvalfjörd.

It was then 4 p.m. We had gone four miles, equal to twenty-four English miles in this part.

The fiord was at least half-a-mile in breadth. The waves were dashing noisily over the sharp rocks. The inlet had rocky walls on either side, or rather steep precipices, and crowned with peaks 2,000 feet high, remarkable for their brown strata, separated by beds of reddish tuff. However intelligent our horses might be, I did not augur anything good from attempting to cross a regular arm of the sea on the back of a quadruped.

"If they are really as intelligent as they are said to be," I thought to myself, "they won't try to pass it. Anyway, I'll be intelligent for them."

But my uncle would not wait. He spurred right on to the shore. His horse snuffed the wind, and stopped short. My uncle, who had an instinct too, urged him forwards, and again the animal refused, and shook his head. Then came oaths and smart lashes with the whip, but the beast only kicked and tried to fling his rider. At last the little horse bent his knees, and managed to slip out from under the professor's legs, leaving him standing upright on two boulders, like the Colossus of Rhodes.

"The confounded brute!" exclaimed the horseman, suddenly transformed into a pedestrian, and as much ashamed as a cavalry officer would be if degraded to a foot soldier.

"*Färja!*" said the guide, touching his shoulder.

"What? A boat?"

"*Der!*" replied Hans, pointing to a boat.

"Yes," I exclaimed, "I see a boat yonder."

"Why didn't you say so before, then? Well, let us get to it."

"*Tidvatten!*" said the guide.

"What does he say?"

"The tide," replied my uncle, translating the Danish word.

"No doubt he means we must wait for the tide."

"*Förbida,*" said my uncle.

"*Ja,*" replied Hans.

My uncle stamped his foot and the horses went on to the boat.

I quite understood the necessity of waiting for a particular state of the tide to undertake the crossing of the fiord, viz., when the sea is at the flood; for then the flux and reflux are not sensibly felt, and there was no risk of the boat being dragged to the bottom, or out into the broad ocean.

The favourable moment did not arrive till six in the evening, then my uncle, myself, the guide, two ferrymen, and the four horses, took our places on a somewhat frail raft. Accustomed as I was to the steamers on the Elbe, the boatman's oars seemed to me a very miserable species of propeller. It took us more than an hour to get over, but the passage was made without any accident.

Half an hour afterwards, we reached the "aoalkirkja of Gardär".

CHAPTER XIII

IT SHOULD HAVE been quite dark, for it was night, but under the 65th parallel the nocturnal light of the polar regions was not astonishing. During the months of June and July the sun never sets.

The temperature, however, had got much lower. I was cold, and worse still, very hungry. Welcome indeed was the *böer*, which hospitably opened its door to receive us.

It was only a peasant's hut, but, in point of hospitality, equal to a king's palace. The master of it came to meet us with outstretched hand, and without further ceremony, beckoned us to follow him!

Literally to follow him, for to accompany him would have been impossible. A long narrow dark passage led into the dwelling, which was built of roughly squared planks. All the rooms opened into this passage. These were four in number; the kitchen, the weaving shop, the *badstofa* or sleeping room for the family, and best of all, a visitor's room. My uncle, whose height had not been considered in building the house, of course knocked his head three or four times against the projecting beams of the ceiling.

We were conducted to our room, a large room with an earth floor well beaten down, lighted by a window, the panes of which were formed of sheep's bladder, none too transparent. The bed consisted of dry fodder thrown into two wooden frames, painted red and ornamented with sentences in Icelandic. I did not expect such comfort, the only drawback was the unpleasant smell of dried fish, hung beef, and sour milk, which pervaded the house. When we had doffed our travelling attire, we heard the voice of our host inviting us into the kitchen, the only place where there was a fire, even in the coldest weather.

My uncle lost no time in obeying the friendly summons, and I followed.

The fire-place of the kitchen was in the ancient fashion – the hearth in the centre of the room, and a hole in the roof above it, to let out the smoke. The kitchen also served for the dining-room.

On our entrance, the host, as if he had not yet seen us, greeted us with the word *sallvertu*, which means *be happy*, and kissed us on the cheek.

Then his wife pronounced the same words, followed by the same ceremonial, and afterwards, they both laid their right hand on their heart, and bowed profoundly.

I hasten to say that this Icelandic woman was the mother of nineteen children, big and little, buzzing about the room in the midst of the dense smoke which filled it. Every instant some little fair head, and rather melancholy face, would peep out of the clouds constantly curling up from the hearth. One would have said they were a band of angels, though their faces would have been the better for soap and water.

My uncle and I were very kind to this brood of youngsters, so before long we had three or four of the little monkeys on our shoulders, as many on our knees, and the rest among our legs. Those who could speak, repeated "*sallvertu*" in every imaginable tone, and those who could not, shrieked their loudest to make up for it.

This concert was interrupted by a summons to the repast. Our hunter just at this moment came back after seeing that the horses were provided with food, that is to say, he had, by way of economy, turned them out on the fields to find for themselves what moss they could on the rocks, and a few innutritious seaweeds, and they would return of their own accord in the morning to resume their labours.

"*Sallvertu!*" said Hans.

Then quietly, automatically, and impartially, he kissed the host and hostess, and the nineteen children.

This performance over, we sat down to table, twenty-four in number, and consequently, we were literally one on the top of another. The most favoured of us had at least two of the small fry on our knees.

But the appearance of the soup soon made silence in the little world, and the taciturnity which was natural, even among the *gamins* of Iceland, resumed its sway. The host assisted us to soup made of lichen, and not at all unpleasant. And this was followed by a huge piece of dried fish swimming in butter that had been kept twenty years, and was of course perfectly rancid – a qualification which made it greatly preferable to fresh butter, according to the gastronomical ideas of Iceland. With this we had *skyr*, a sort of clotted milk, and biscuits and the juice of juniper berries. Our beverage was whey mixed with water, called *blanda* in this country. I really am no judge of the merits of this singular diet, for I was enormously hungry, and at dessert I ate to the very last mouthful a plate of thick buckwheat porridge.

The moment the meal was over, the children disappeared and the grown-up folks gathered round the hearth, where not only peat was burning, but whins, cow-dung, and fish-bones. After this "pinch of heat" the different groups retired to their respective rooms. According to custom, our hostess offered to pull off our stockings and trousers, but after a most polite refusal on our part, she left us, and I was at last able to bury myself in my bed of moss.

At five next morning we bade the Icelandic peasant farewell, after persuading him with difficulty to take a fair remuneration, and Hans gave the signal to start.

About a hundred steps from Gardär the soil began to change its aspect. The ground became boggy and less favourable to our progress. On the right the chain of mountains extended indefinitely, like an immense system of natural fortifications, the counterscarp of which we were following. Often we came to streams, which we had to ford carefully, to prevent our baggage from getting wet, if possible.

The solitude deepened as we advanced. But now and again the shadow of a human being seemed to flee away in the distance as we approached. If a sudden turn brought us unexpectedly near one of these spectres I fell back in disgust at the sight of a swollen head and shining scalp destitute of hair, and loathsome sores visible through the tattered rags that covered them.

The poor wretch would not approach us nor hold out his misshapen hand, but dart away as fast as his legs could carry him, though Hans would always manage to greet him with the usual salutation, *Sallvertu.*

"*Spetelsk,*" he said.

"A leper," repeated my uncle.

The mere word had a repulsive effect. This dreadful disease of leprosy is pretty common in Iceland. It is not contagious but hereditary, and consequently marriage is forbidden the poor creatures.

Such apparitions as these were not calculated to enliven the landscape, which became more gloomy at every step. The last tufts of grass had disappeared. Not a tree was to be seen, unless a few dwarf birches, no higher than brushwood; not an animal, except a few horses, some which their owner could not feed, and had turned out to live as best they could.

Sometimes we could descry a hawk poising herself in the grey clouds and then flying away to the south. Such a dreary region made me melancholy, and my thoughts began to revert to my native country.

Before long we had to cross several small unimportant fiords and then a wide gulf. The tide being high just then, we got over without delay and reached the hamlet of Alftanas, about one mile beyond.

In the evening, after having forded two rivers, rich in trout and pike, the Alfa and the Heta, we were obliged to pass the night in a deserted building, worthy of being haunted by all the hobgoblins in Scandinavia. Jack Frost had certainly chosen it for his own abode, and he played us pranks all night.

Nothing unusual occurred next day. There was still the same boggy soil, the same uniformity and dreary outlook. By the evening we had gone half our journey, and we spent the night at the "annexia" of Krosolbt.

On the 19th of June, for about a mile, we walked over a stream of hardened lava. This ground is called *hraun* in the country. The furrowed surface of the lava presented the appearance of cables –

sometimes stretched long, sometimes coiled up. An immense torrent of the same hardened material ran down the neighbouring mountains, which were extinct volcanoes; but the ruins round attested their former power. Here and there jets of steam were still visible, issuing from hot springs beneath the surface.

We had no time to observe these phenomena; we had to go on steadily. Soon the boggy soil appeared afresh, intersected by little lakes. We were now pursuing a westerly direction. In fact we had gone round the great bay of Faxa, and the white peaks of Snäfell stood up against the clouds less than five miles off.

The horses held out well, undeterred by the difficulties of the soil. For my own part, I began to be very tired. My uncle was firm and upright as on the first day. I could not but admire him, even in comparison with the hunter, who looked on our journey as a mere promenade.

On the Saturday, June 20th, at 6 p.m., we reached Büdir, a village on the sea-shore. Here the guide claimed his promised wage and my uncle paid him. It was Hans' family, that is his uncle and cousins, who had offered us hospitality. We were kindly received by them, and without abusing the hospitality of those good people, I would willingly have stayed there a little to recruit myself after our fatigues. But my uncle, who had no need to recruit himself, would not hear of it, and next morning we had to remount our steeds.

The soil was plainly affected by the vicinity of the mountain, the granite foundations of which appeared above the ground, like the roots of an oak. We went round the immense base of the volcano, the professor devouring it all the time with his eyes, gesticulating, and apparently defying the giant, and saying, "There stands the giant I am going to conquer." At last, after four hours' walking, the horses stopped of their own will before the priest's house in Stapi.

CHAPTER XIV

STAPI IS A VILLAGE composed of about thirty huts, built of lava and lying in the sunlight reflected by the volcano. It extends along a small fiord, inclosed in a basaltic wall, which has the strangest effect.

Basalt, as is well known, is a brown rock of igneous origin. It affects regular forms, the disposition of which is often surprising. Here, nature proceeds geometrically, working after the manner of men with square and compass and plummet. Though everywhere else her art is seen in large masses thrown down in disorder, in unfinished cones, in perfect pyramids with the most fantastic succession of lines, here, as if to form an example of regularity and in advance of the very earliest architects, she has created a severe order which has never been surpassed by the splendours of Babylon and the marvels of Greece.

I had heard of the Giants' Causeway in Ireland, and Fingal's Cave in the Hebrides, but I had never before seen a basaltic formation.

This phenomenon I was to witness at Stapi in all its beauty.

The wall of the fiord, like all the coast of the peninsula, is composed of a succession of vertical columns thirty feet high. These straight shafts of perfect proportions supported an architrave, made of horizontal columns, the overhanging portion of which formed a semi-arch over the sea. At certain intervals under this natural shelter there were vaulted openings of admirable design, through which the waves came dashing and foaming. Fragments of basalt, torn away by the fury of the ocean, lay along the ground like the ruins of an ancient temple, ruins which never grew old, over which ages had passed without leaving an imprint behind them.

This was the last stage of our terrestrial journey. Hans had proved himself an intelligent guide, and it was a comfort to think he was not going to leave us here.

On arriving at the door of the rector's house, just a low cabin like his neighbour's, neither grander nor more comfortable, I saw a man engaged in shoeing a horse, hammer in hand, and a leather apron round him.

"*Sallvertu*," said the hunter.

"*God-dag*," replied the blacksmith in pure Danish.

"*Kyrkoherde*," said Hans, turning to my uncle.

"The rector!" said my uncle. "Axel, it appears this good man is the rector."

Meantime our guide was explaining about us to the *Kyrkoherde*, who left off his work, and gave a sort of cry, no doubt in common use among horses and jockeys. A tall vixenish-looking shrew instantly made her appearance. If she did not measure six feet high she certainly was not much less.

I was afraid she would offer me the Icelandic kiss, but I need not have alarmed myself, for her manner was too ungracious for any such politeness.

The visitors' room to which she conducted us seemed to be the worst in the house, being close-smelling, dirty, and narrow. However, we were obliged to put up with it. The rector was clearly not given to ancient hospitality. Before the day was over, I saw we had to do with a blacksmith, a fisherman, a hunter, a carpenter, and not at all with a minister of Christ. True, we came on a week day. Perhaps he was a better man on Sundays.

I don't want to say anything bad of these poor priests, who, after all, are miserably off. The sum they receive from the Danish Government is ridiculously small, and all they have besides is a fourth part of the tithe, which does not amount to more than sixty marks (about £4). Consequently, they are obliged to work for a living. But fishing, and hunting, and shoeing horses gives a man at last the tone and habits and manners of fishermen and hunters and farriers and such-like people. I found at night that even sobriety could not be reckoned among his virtues.

My uncle quickly understood his man. Instead of a good and honourable man of learning, this was a coarse, lumpish peasant. He therefore resolved to commence his great expedition with the least possible delay, and to get out of this inhospitable parsonage. In utter disregard of his fatigue, he determined to go and spend a few days in the mountain.

The very next morning our preparations began. Hans hired three Icelanders to take the place of the horses and carry our luggage, but it was distinctly understood that as soon as they had deposited it in the crater they were to turn and go back, and leave us to do the best we could.

My uncle took this opportunity of apprising Hans of his intention to explore the volcano to its furthest limits.

Hans simply nodded. To go there or anywhere else, into the bowels of the earth, or on the surface, was all alike to him. For myself, hitherto I had been amused by the incidents of the journey, and been somewhat forgetful of the future, but now my terrors returned in full force. But what was to be done?

If I wished to resist Professor Lidenbrock, it was at Hamburg I should have done it, and not at Snäfell.

One thought especially tormented me – one which might appal stouter nerves than mine.

I said to myself, "We are going to ascend Snäfell. That's well enough. We are going to visit the crater. Well enough too. Others have done that, and they came up alive. But that is not all. If there should actually be a passage into the bowels of the earth, and that unlucky Saknussemm spoke truth, we shall go and lose ourselves in the subterranean windings of the volcano. But what is there to prove that Snäfell is extinct? Who will guarantee that an eruption is not preparing to break out? Because the monster has been sleeping since 1229, does it follow that he will never wake up again? And if he does wake up what will become of us?" This was worth thinking about, and I did think about it. I could not sleep without dreaming of eruptions, and I must say I did not feel inclined to play the part of scoria.

At last I could not bear myself any longer and resolved to submit the case to my uncle with as much tact as possible and under the form of an impossible hypothesis.

I went in quest of him, and told him my fears, and then drew back to let his first outburst of passion pass over.

But all he said was:

"I have been thinking of it."

What could he mean? Was he really going to listen to the voice of reason? Could he be going to suspend his project? It was too good to be true.

After a few minutes' silence, which I did not venture to interrupt, he repeated again:

"I was thinking of it. Ever since we arrived here at Stapi my mind has been occupied with the grave question you have just submitted to me, for it would not do for us to be imprudent."

"No, indeed," I said emphatically.

"For 600 years Snäfell has been silent, but he may speak. Still, eruptions are always preceded by well-known phenomena. I have been therefore interrogating the inhabitants of this district on the subject. I have examined the ground and I am in a position to say there will be no eruption."

I was amazed at this declaration, and could make no reply.

"Do you doubt what I tell you?" resumed my uncle. "Well, come with me!"

I obeyed mechanically. The professor took a direct course away from the sun by going through an opening in the basaltic wall. Soon we were in the open country, if the word can apply to an immense heap of volcanic matter. The whole region seemed to have been overwhelmed with a flood of enormous fragments of trap, basalt, granite, and all the pyroxene rocks.

Here and there I could see puffs of white vapour rising in the air. These are called by the Icelanders "reykir", and issue from the thermal springs, which, by their violence, indicate the volcanic activity of the soil. This seemed to justify my fears. But I fell from the clouds when my uncle went on to say:

"You see all this smoke, Axel. Well, they prove that we have nothing to fear from the fury of the volcano."

"What an idea!" I exclaimed.

"Remember this," continued the professor; "at the approach of an eruption these vapours redouble their activity, but disappear entirely while the phenomenon lasts, for the electric fluids being relieved from pressure, escape by the crater instead of finding their way out through the cracks in the ground. Since, then, these vapours are now in the usual state, and there is no increase of energy, and also that the wind and rain have not given way to a heavy dead calm, you may be sure no eruption is at hand."

"But—"

"Enough. When science has spoken, it is for us to hold our peace."

I went back to the parsonage, very crestfallen. My uncle had vanquished me by scientific arguments. One hope, however, still remained; and this was that, on our reaching the bottom of the crater, we should find no passage, in spite of all the Saknussemms in the world.

I passed the night in all the miseries of nightmare. I was in the midst of a volcano, in the depths of the earth; I felt myself hurled into the planetary spaces, in the form of ejected rock.

The next day, the 22nd of June, Hans was ready, waiting us, with his companions bearing the provisions, tools, and instruments. Two stout sticks, tipped with iron, and two rifles and two shot-belts were reserved for my uncle and myself. Hans, like a wise man, had added to our baggage a leathern bottle filled with water, which, with our gourds, would be a sufficient supply for a week.

It was 9 a.m. The rector and his tall shrew stood at the door of the parsonage, doubtless to bid us farewell. But their adieux took the shape of a tremendous bill! They charged us for everything, even to the air we breathed, and that was polluted enough, I can vouch for it. This worthy couple fleeced us like any Swiss hotel-keeper, and made us pay a good price for their make-believe hospitality.

My uncle settled the account, however, without any higgling. A man who is just about to start for the centre of the earth does not care about a few rix-dollars.

This matter arranged, Hans gave the signal for starting, and a few minutes afterwards we left Stapi.

CHAPTER XV

SNÄFELL IS 5,000 feet high. Its double cone terminates in a trachytic belt, which stands out from the mountain system of the island. From our starting-point we could not see its two peaks outlined against the grey clouds. I could only see an enormous cap of snow coming down low over the giant's forehead.

We walked in file, preceded by the hunter, who was climbing by such narrow paths, that two could not go abreast. All conversation was therefore nearly impossible.

Beyond the basaltic wall of the fiord at Stapi the ground was herbaceous, fibrous peat, the remains of the ancient vegetation of the bogs on the peninsula. The quantity of this unworked combustible was enough to warm all the people in Iceland for a century. This vast turf-pit measured in certain ravines seventy feet deep, and presented successive layers of carbonized detritus separated by sheets of tufaceous pumice.

As a true nephew of Professor Lidenbrock, and notwithstanding my mental preoccupation, I was interested in observing the mineralogical curiosities displayed in this vast cabinet of natural history, and, at the same time, was going over in my mind the whole geological history of Iceland.

This most curious island has evidently risen from the depths of the sea at a comparatively recent epoch. Perhaps it may be even still rising by an insensible motion. If that be so, its origin can only be attributed to the action of subterranean fires, and, in this case, Humphry Davy's theory and Saknussemm's document, and my uncle's speculations, too, all vanish in smoke. This hypothesis made me carefully examine the nature of the soil. I could soon account for the successive phenomena which attended its formation.

Iceland being wholly destitute of alluvial soil, is entirely composed of volcanic tufa, that is, a conglomeration of stones and rocks of a porous texture. Prior to the existence of volcanoes it was composed of trappean rock, slowly upheaved from the sea by the central forces. The interior fires had not yet burst forth.

But at a subsequent period a large fissure appeared running in a diagonal direction from south-west to north-east, by which all the trachyte gradually forced its way out. This phenomenon was not attended with any violence, but the issue was enormous, and the fused matter thrown up from the bowels of the earth spread slowly in vast sheets or rounded protuberances. To this epoch the felspars, syenites, and porphyries belong.

But thanks to this outflow, the thickness of the island increased considerably, and in consequence its powers of resistance. It can be imagined what quantities of electric fluids had accumulated within its bosom when no channel of escape presented itself after the trachytic crust had cooled and hardened. There came then a time when the mechanical force of these gases became such that they upheaved the heavy crust, and made for themselves tall chimneys. The upheaval of the crust first formed the volcanoes, and then a crater suddenly opened at the summit.

To the eruptive phenomena succeeded the volcanic. By the newly-created openings the basaltic ejections first escaped, of which the plain we were just crossing presented the most wonderful specimens. We were walking over grey rocks, which had cooled into hexagonal prisms. In the distance a great number of truncated cones were visible, each of which had formerly been a mouth of fire.

After the basaltic eruption, the volcano, which increased in force by the extinction of other craters, made a passage for lavas and for tufa, viz., ashes and scoria, long streams of which I could see on the mountain sides, hanging down like flowing hair.

Such was the succession of phenomena which produced Iceland, all proceeding from the internal fire, and to suppose that the mass within was not still in a state of fusion was folly. And, surely, to pretend to try and reach the centre of the globe was the very climax of folly.

I reassured myself, therefore, about the issue of this enterprise, even while we were on our way to the assault of Snäfell.

The route became more and more difficult – the ground was rising. The loose masses of rock trembled, and the utmost care was needed to prevent dangerous falls.

Hans walked on as quietly as if he were on level ground. At times he would disappear behind great blocks, and for a moment we lost sight of him, then a sharp whistle told us the direction in which to follow him. Often, too, he stopped, picked up some fragments of rock, and arranged them in a recognizable manner, making landmarks in this way all along the road, to show us the route back – a good precaution on his part, though future events rendered it useless.

Three hours of fatiguing walking had only brought us to the base of the mountain. There Hans made a signal to stop, and a hasty breakfast was shared among us. My uncle took two mouthfuls at a time, to despatch it the quicker. But this halt was not only for breakfast, but for rest, and Hans did not make a start till one hour had elapsed. The three Icelanders, as taciturn as their comrade, never uttered a syllable, and munched away with solemn gravity.

Now the steep ascent of Snäfell commenced. His snowy summit, by an optical illusion, common enough in the mountains, seemed very near, and yet what long hours it took to reach it. Above all, what toil! The stones not being cemented by any earth, nor adhering together by any roots of herbage, rolled away under our feet, and rushed down the plain with the speed of an avalanche.

In certain places the sides of the mountain formed an angle of 36° at least with the horizon. It was impossible to climb them; and these stony cliffs had to be rounded, which was no easy matter. We had to assist each other with our sticks.

I must say that my uncle kept as close to me as possible. He never let me out of his sight, and many a time his arm was my powerful support. He himself certainly had some inner sense of equilibrium, for he never stumbled. The Icelanders, in spite of their loads, climbed with the agility of mountaineers. To look at the height of Snäfell it seemed impossible to reach the summit. But after an hour's fatigue and athletic exercise, a sort of staircase suddenly appeared in the midst of the vast carpet of snow lying on the croup of the volcano, and this greatly simplified our ascent. It was formed of one of those torrents of stones ejected by the eruption, and which the Icelanders called *stinâ*. If this torrent had not been arrested in its fall by the formation of the mountain sides, it would have dashed down into the sea, and new islands would have been the result.

As it was, it did us good service. The steepness increased, but these stone steps helped us to climb up easily, and indeed so rapidly, that when I stopped for a moment behind the rest, I perceived them already so diminished in size by distance that their appearance was microscopic.

At seven in the evening we had gone up the 2,000 steps of the stair, and risen above an extinct cone of the mountain, a sort of bed on which the actual cone of the crater rested.

The sea stretched below us 3,200 feet. We had passed the limit of perpetual snow, which, on account of the humidity of the climate, is rather lower in Iceland. It was bitterly cold. The wind blew violently. I was exhausted. The professor saw that my legs refused to carry me, and, in spite of his impatience, he determined to stop. He made a sign to the hunter to that effect, but Hans shook his head, and said:

"*Ofvanför*."

"We must go higher it seems," said my uncle, and asked the reason.

"*Mistour*," replied the guide.

"*Ja, mistour*," repeated one of the Icelanders, in a terrified tone.

"What does the man mean?" I asked, uneasily.

"Look!" replied my uncle.

I gazed down below. An immerse column of pulverized pumice, sand, and dust was rising, whirling round like a waterspout. The wind was driving it on to the side of Snäfell, to which we were clinging. The thick curtain across the sun projected a great shadow on the mountain. Should this waterspout-like column bend over it would inevitably catch us in its whirl. This phenomenon, not uncommon when the wind blows from the glaciers, is called in Icelandic *mistour*.

"*Hastigt, hastigt!*" cried our guide. Though I was unacquainted with Danish, I understood we were to follow Hans as quickly as possible. He began to go round the cone of the crater, but diagonally, to make the task easier. Before long the huge column fell on the mountain, which trembled at the shock. The loose stones caught up in its circling eddies flew off in a shower as during an eruption. Fortunately, we had gained the opposite side and were in safety. But without this precaution on the part of our guide, our mangled bodies, reduced to dust, would have been carried away far into the distance, and considered as the product of some unknown meteor.

Hans did not think it prudent though to pass the night on the sides of the cone. We had to continue our zigzag ascent. The 1,500 feet remaining took us nearly five hours to climb; the circuitous windings, the diagonal and counter-marches, measured three leagues I am sure. I was "dead beat", sinking with cold and hunger. The somewhat rarefied atmosphere scarcely allowed my lungs full play; but at length, at 11 p.m., in the dead of the night, the summit of Snäfell was reached, and before seeking shelter in the crater, I had time to see the midnight sun at his lowest point gilding the sleeping island at my feet with his pale rays.

CHAPTER XVI

THE SUPPER WAS quickly despatched, and the little company housed themselves as best they could. The couch was hard, the shelter rather insufficient, and the situation trying, for we were 5,000 feet above the level of the sea. But in spite of everything my slumbers this night were particularly peaceful. It was the best sleep I had had for a long time. I did not even dream.

Next morning, we awoke half frozen by the keen air. The sun was shining gloriously, when I rose from my granite bed, and went out to enjoy the magnificent panorama that awaited my gaze.

I was on the summit of one of the twin peaks of Snäfell, the southernmost. I commanded a view of almost the whole island. By an optical effect common to all great elevations, the shores looked raised and the centre depressed. I could have said that one of Helbesmer's relievo maps lay before me. I saw deep valleys intersecting each other in all directions, precipices seemed mere walls, lakes changed into ponds, and rivers into little streams. On my right there were glaciers without number, and innumerable peaks, over some of which there was a plume-like cloud of white smoke. The undulating lines of these endless mountains, on which the snow lay like foam, reminded me of a stormy sea. If I turned to the west, there lay old Ocean in all his majesty, like a continuation of these foamy summits. I could scarcely tell where the earth ended and the waters began.

I was revelling in the magical delight which is awakened in the mind by all great elevations, and this time without giddiness, for at last I had become accustomed to "sublime contemplations". My dazzled eyes were bathed in a flood of radiant sunshine. I forgot who I was, and where I was, to live the life of elves and sylphs, imaginary beings of the Scandinavian mythology. I gave myself to the luxury of the heights, without a thought of the depths into which I must shortly plunge.

But I was recalled to reality by the appearance of the professor and Hans, who rejoined us on the summit.

My uncle turned westward and pointed out to me a light vapour, a sort of mist, an appearance of land just above the waves, and said:

"That's Greenland."

"Greenland?" I cried.

"Yes; we are only thirty-five leagues from it, and when thaws come the white bears find their way to Iceland on the ice-floes from the north. But that's no matter. We are on the top of Snäfell, and here are two peaks, the one to the south, the other to the north. Hans will tell us what the Icelanders call the one we are on at this moment."

The question was put, and Hans replied:

"Scartaris."

My uncle glanced at me triumphantly, and said:

"To the crater, then!"

The crater of Snäfell resembled an inverted cone, the orifice of which was perhaps half a league in diameter. Its depth I estimated was about 2,000 feet. Imagine such a reservoir full of thunders and flame. The bottom of the shaft could not measure more than 500 feet in circumference, so that the gentle slope permitted us to get down easily. I involuntarily thought of an enormous wide-mouthed mortar, and the comparison made me shudder.

"To go down into a mortar," I thought, "when it is perhaps loaded, and may go off at any moment, is to act like fools!"

But I could not draw back. Hans, with an air of perfect indifference, took his place at the head of the party. I followed without saying a word.

In order to facilitate the descent, Hans pursued a winding track down. He was obliged to go through eruptive rocks, some of which, shaken out of their beds, rushed bounding down the abyss. Their fall awoke echoes of wonderful clearness.

Certain parts of the cone form glaciers. Hans would then walk with extreme precaution, sounding the ground at every step with his iron-tipped stick, to discover any *crevasses*. At doubtful parts we were fastened together by a long rope, so that any one who missed his footing would be supported by his companions. This arrangement was prudent, but it did not exclude all danger.

However, notwithstanding all the difficulties of the descent, down steeps unknown to the guide, the journey was accomplished without any accident, except the loss of a coil of rope, which fell from the hand of one of the Icelanders, and took the quickest road to the bottom of the gulf.

At mid-day we reached it. I looked up and saw the upper orifice of the cone framing a bit of sky, much reduced in size, but almost perfectly round. Just on the edge appeared the sunny peak of Scartaris, which lost itself in immensity.

At the bottom of the crater were three chimneys, out of which, in its eruptions, the central fire of Snäfell had belched out smoke and lava. Each of these chimneys had a diameter of about 100 feet. They gaped at us with wide-open mouths. I had not the courage to look at them. But Professor Lidenbrock had made a rapid survey of all three. He was quite panting, rushing from one to another gesticulating, and talking incoherently. Hans and his companions, seated on blocks of lava, looked wonderingly at this procedure, and evidently thought him mad.

All at once my uncle gave a cry. I thought he had lost his footing, and was falling into one of the holes. But no, there he was with outstretched arms, and legs wide apart, standing in front of a granite rock, laid in the centre of the crater like an enormous pedestal ready to receive a statue of Pluto. He was in the posture of a man who is stupefied, but whose stupefaction will soon give place to the wildest delights.

"Axel, Axel!" he cried; "come, come!" I ran to him. Neither Hans nor his companions moved.

"Look!" said the professor.

And sharing at least his stupefaction, if not his joy, I read on the western face of the block, in Runic characters half eaten away by time, this thrice-accursed name:

ᛏᛑᚿᛐ ᛋᛏᛒᚿᛐᛋᛋᛏᛪ

"Arne Saknussemm!" cried my uncle. "Do you still doubt?"

I made no reply, but went back to my seat in consternation. This evidence crushed me. How long I sat lost in my own reflections, I cannot say. All I know is that when I looked up again only Hans and my uncle were in the crater. The Icelanders had taken their leave and were now on their way down the side of Snäfell back to Stapi.

Hans was sleeping quietly at the foot of a rock in a stream of lava, where he had improvized a bed for himself. My uncle was pacing about like a wild beast in a trapper's pit. I had neither the wish nor the power to rise, and, following the guide's example, I fell into a troubled sleep, fancying I could hear the noises and feel the tremblings of the mountain.

Thus passed the first night in the bottom of the crater.

Next day a grey, gloomy, heavy sky overshadowed the mouth of the cone. I did not know it so much by the obscurity of the gulf as by my uncle's rage over it.

I understood the reason, and a ray of hope dawned on me. This was why:

Of the three routes open to us, only one had been followed by Saknussemm; and, according to the learned Icelander, it was to be recognized by the particular fact mentioned in the crypto-gram, that the shadow of Scartaris would come and fall softly over the edge of it during the last days of June. That sharp peak might, in fact, be considered as the gnomon, or pin, of an immense sundial, whose shadow on a given day would point out the road to the earth's centre.

Now, no sun, no shadow, and consequently no indication. It was the 25th of June now, and, should the sky remain overcast four days longer, our observations would have to be deferred till another year.

I cannot attempt to depict the wrath of Professor Lidenbrock. The day passed and no shadow appeared. Hans never stirred, though he must have asked himself what we were waiting for, if, indeed, he could ask himself anything at all. My uncle never once addressed me, but kept his eyes fixed on the gloomy sky.

On the 26th there was still nothing. Rain mingled with snow kept falling all day long. Hans made a hut of pieces of lava. I rather enjoyed watching the thousands of cascades that came rushing down the sides of the cone, the deafening noise increasing at every stone they came against.

My uncle was beside himself with passion.And certainly it was enough to irritate a far more patient man than he. It was like foundering within sight of the harbour.

But Heaven never sends great sorrow without great joy, and there was satisfaction in store for Professor Lidenbrock to compensate for his agonizing suspense.

The next day was again overcast, but on Sunday, the 28th of June, the last day but two of the month, with the change of moon came the change of weather. The sun poured a flood of rays into the crater. Every hillock, each rock and stone, every projection had its share in this affluence of light, and threw its shadow forthwith on the ground. Amongst the others was the shadow of Scartaris, which lay like a sharp peak, and it began to move round insensibly with the radiant orb. My uncle moved with it. At noon, when it was at its least, it fell softly on the edge of the middle chimney.

"It is there! it is there!" exclaimed the professor, adding in Danish:

"Now let's away to the centre of the globe!"

I looked at Hans.

"*Forüt!*" was his quiet reply.

"Forward!" returned my uncle.

It was nineteen minutes past one.

CHAPTER XVII

THE REAL JOURNEY now commenced. Hitherto our fatigues had been more than our difficulties, but now the latter would multiply at every step. I had not yet even looked down the bottomless well, in which I was about to be engulfed. The moment had come. I must now take my part in the enterprise, or refuse the risk. But I was ashamed to draw back before the hunter, and Hans accepted the adventure so coolly, with such indifference, and such a perfect disregard of danger, that I blushed at the idea of being less brave than he. Had we been alone I should have renewed my arguments, but in the presence of the guide I kept silent. Memory recalled for an instant my pretty Virlandaise, and I approached the central chimney.

I have already said that it measured 100 feet in diameter and 300 feet in circumference. Holding on by a jutting rock I looked down into it. My hair stood on end. The feeling of vacuity took possession of my being. I felt my centre of gravity becoming displaced, and my head began to reel as if I were intoxicated. There is nothing stranger than this abyss attraction. I was about to fall in when a powerful hand held me back. It was that of Hans. Evidently I had not taken enough *abyss* lessons at the Frelsers-Kirk in Copenhagen.

But short as my survey had been of this well I had a good idea of its conformation. Its walls, which were nearly perpendicular, were thick with sharp projections, which would greatly facilitate descent. But if the staircase was there, the rail was wanting. A rope fastened to the edge of the orifice would have been sufficient support, but how could we unfasten it when we reached the lower extremity?

My uncle employed a very simple method to obviate this great difficulty. He undid a coil of rope, about the thickness of a finger and 400 feet long. He let half of it slip down first, then he rolled it round a block of lava, which jutted out, and threw down the other half. Each of us could then descend by holding both lines of rope in his hand, which could not get loose. When he had gone 200 feet nothing could be easier than to haul the rope in by pulling one end. Then the exercise would begin again and go on *ad infinitum*.

"Now," said my uncle, after these preparations were completed, "let's see about the luggage. We will divide it into three parts, and each of us will strap one on his back. Of course I mean only fragile articles."

The daring man evidently did not include us in the category.

"Hans," he said, "will take charge of the tools and a portion of the provisions. You, Axel, will take another third of the provisions and the arms, and I will take the rest of the provisions and the delicate instruments."

"But who is to take the clothes?" said I, "and that heap of ropes and ladders?"

"They will take care of themselves."

"How?"

"You'll see."

My uncle liked to employ grand means. He ordered Hans to make a bundle of all the non-fragile articles, which was then firmly roped and thrown right down into the abyss. I could hear the loud roaring noise it made in whizzing through the air, and my uncle stooped down and watched its progress till it was out of sight. Then my uncle said:

"That's all right. Now it is our turn."

I ask any sane man if it was possible to hear these words without a shudder.

The professor forthwith fastened the package of instruments on his back, and Hans took the tools, and I the arms. The descent commenced in the following order: – Hans first, then my uncle, then myself. It was made in complete silence, only broken by the fall of fragments of rock into the abyss.

I let myself drop, as it were, frantically clutching the double cord in one hand, and propping myself with my stick with the other. One idea possessed me. I was afraid the support would give way. The cord seemed to me so frail to bear the weight of three persons. I hung upon it as little as possible, performing wonderful feats of equilibrium upon the projections of lava which my feet sought to catch hold of like a hand.

Whenever one of these slipping steps shook beneath Hans' foot, he said in his quiet voice:

"*Gif akt!*"

"Attention!" repeated my uncle.

In about half an hour we found ourselves on the slab of a rock that was firmly embedded in the wall of the chimney.

Hans pulled the rope by one end and the other rose in the air. After passing the upper rock it fell down again, and a shower of stones and lava came rattling after it like rain, or dangerous hail rather.

Leaning down over the edge of our narrow plateau, I noticed that the bottom of the hole was still invisible.

Then the rope manœuvre began again, and half an hour afterwards we had gone another 200 feet.

I don't know whether the maddest geologist would have attempted to study, during his descent, the nature of the rocks through which he passed. For my own part, I didn't trouble myself about it. I didn't care whether they were pliocene, miocene, eocene, cretaceous, jurassic, triassic, permian, carboniferous, devonian, silurian, or primitive. But, no doubt the professor was taking observations or making notes, for he said to me:

"The farther I go the more confident I feel. The disposition of these volcanic formations strongly supports the theory of Humphry Davy. We are now among the primitive rocks, on which the chemical operation took place produced by the contact of metals with air and water. I reject absolutely the theory of a central heat. However, we shall soon see."

Always the same conclusion. I was not inclined to amuse myself by arguing, and he took my silence for agreement.

The descent began afresh, but at the end of three hours, I could not yet catch a glimpse of the bottom. When I looked up, I perceived the orifice narrowing sensibly. The sides seemed to approach each other, and it was gradually getting dark.

Still we went on; down, down. I fancied the loosened stones fell quicker to the bottom, and with more noise.

I had taken care to keep an exact account of our manœuvres with the ropes, so that I knew exactly the depth attained and the time elapsed.

Each descent occupied half an hour, and we had made fourteen. I calculated then that we had been seven hours, and three hours and a half extra for rest and meals, as we had allowed us a quarter of an hour between each manœuvre. Altogether ten hours and a half. We had started at one. It must therefore now be eleven.

As to the depth – fourteen times 200 feet gave a depth of 2,800 feet.

At this moment, I heard the voice of Hans, calling:

"Halt!"

I stopped instantly, just in time to keep my feet from knocking my uncle's head.

"We are there!" he cried.

"Where?" said I, slipping down beside him.

"At the bottom of the perpendicular shaft."

"Then there is no outlet?"

"Yes, there is a passage, I think, to the right. I only caught a glimpse of it, but we shall see to-morrow. We'll sup now, and then go to sleep."

The darkness was not yet complete. We opened the bag of provisions and took some food, and then we all three settled ourselves for the night, as comfortably as we could on the stones and fragments of lava.

As I lay on my back, I chanced to open my eyes and perceived a bright spot at the extremity of the tube, 3,000 feet long, transformed now into a gigantic telescope.

It was a star, but deprived of all scintillation by the distance. By my reckoning, it was β Ursa Minor.

Then I fell fast asleep.

CHAPTER XVIII

AT EIGHT NEXT morning, a ray of daylight came to awaken us. The myriad facets on the lava walls received it and threw it back in a shower of sparks.

This light was strong enough to enable us to discern surrounding objects.

"Well now, Axel, what do you say to it?" cried my uncle, rubbing his hands. "Did you ever pass a quieter night in the old house in Königstrasse? No noise of carts, or street cries, no boatman's vociferations."

"Certainly, we are quiet enough, but the very calm has something terrifying about it."

"Now, now!" cried my uncle, "if you are frightened already, how will you get on by-and-by. We haven't gone one inch yet into the bowels of the earth."

"What do you mean?"

"I mean that we have only reached the level of the island. This long vertical tube which opens in the crater of Snäfell ends almost at the level of the sea."

"Are you sure of that?"

"Quite sure. Consult the barometer."

I found the mercury, which had risen gradually in the instrument, in proportion as we descended, had stopped at twenty-nine inches.

"You see," continued the professor, "we have only yet the pressure of the atmosphere, and I am impatient for the manometer to replace the barometer."

The barometer, in fact, would become useless, from the moment the weight of the air should exceed the pressure at the level of the sea.

"But," said I, "isn't there reason to fear that this always-increasing pressure will be very painful?"

"No. We shall descend slowly, and our lungs will get accustomed to the denser air. Aeronauts end by having too little air, as they rise constantly higher, and we shall have too much perhaps. But I prefer that. Don't let us lose an instant. Where is the bundle we rolled down before us?"

This reminded me that we had looked for it the night before and could not find it.

My uncle asked Hans about it, who, after gazing round with the keen eye of a hunter, replied:

"*Der huppe.*"

"Up there."

Sure enough there was the bundle hanging on a rocky projection 100 feet above our head. The agile Icelander climbed up after it like a cat, and in a few minutes the bundle was in our possession again.

"Now," said my uncle, "let us breakfast, and eat like men who are likely to have a long day's walk before them."

The biscuit and extract of beef were washed down with a drink of water mixed with a little gin.

After breakfast my uncle drew a notebook out of his pocket for observations. Then he took up his different instruments and wrote down the following result:

"*Monday, June 29th.*

"Chronometer, 8h. 17m. a.m.

"Barometer, 29' 7 in.

"Thermometer, 6°.

"Direction, E.S.E."

This last observation applied to the dim passage, and was indicated by the compass.

"Now, Axel!" exclaimed the professor, enthusiastically, "we are actually going to push our way into the heart of the earth. This is the exact time when our journey commences."

So saying my uncle took up the apparatus of Ruhmkorff suspended from his neck, with one hand, and with the other placed it in communication with the electric coil in the lantern, and immediately a light was produced, bright enough to illumine the dark passage.

Hans carried the other apparatus, which was also set in action. This ingenious application of electricity would enable us to go on for a long time, creating an artificial day, safe even in the midst of the most inflammable gases.

"Forward!" said my uncle.

Each one resumed his load; Hans undertook to push the bundle of ropes and clothing before him along the ground, and I came behind him into the gallery.

Just as I was about to enter the gloomy passage, I looked up through the distant aperture and saw once more the sky of Iceland, which I should never gaze upon again.

At the time of the last eruption, in 1229, the lava had forced this passage for itself, and the sides of it were covered with a thick shiny coating of it, which reflected and intensified the electric light. The great difficulty of the route was to avoid slipping too rapidly down an incline of forty-five degrees. Happily, certain erosions and protuberances served for steps, which we descended, letting our luggage slip before us from the end of a long rope.

But what were steps under our feet became stalactites in every other part. The lava, which was porous in certain places, was covered with small rounded blisters – crystals of opaque quartz adorned with clear drops of glass, and suspended from the roof like chandeliers, which seemed to light up as we passed. It looked as if the genii of the abyss were illuminating their palace for the reception of their terrestrial visitants.

"It is magnificent!" I exclaimed, involuntarily. "What a sight, uncle! Don't you admire all those shades of lava, from reddish brown to bright yellow? And those crystals looking like luminous globes?"

"Ah, you like that, Axel!" replied my uncle. "You call that splendid, my boy; you will see many of those, I hope. Let us walk on."

He would have been more correct if he had said slide, for we let ourselves slip, without effort, down the steep inclines. It was the *facilis descensus Averni* of Virgil. The compass, which I consulted frequently, indicated the south-east with undeviating regularity. This stream of lava neither turned aside to the east nor west. It had the inflexibility of the straight line.

However, there was no sensible increase of heat. This supported the theories of Davy, and more than once I was astonished when I consulted the thermometer. Two hours after it only marked 10°, that is to say, an increase of 4°. This authorized me to suppose that our descent was more horizontal than vertical. The depth reached might have been easily ascertained, as the professor measured with exactitude the angles of deviation and inclination on the road, but he kept his observations to himself.

About 8 p.m. he gave the signal to stop; Hans sat down immediately. The lamps were hung up to a jutting piece of lava. We were in a sort of cavern, but the air was not deficient. Quite the contrary. Certain puffs of it even reached us. What had produced them? To what atmospheric disturbance must we attribute their origin? I did not care just now to pursue the subject, however. I was too hungry and tired to argue the question. A seven hours' descent involves considerable expenditure of strength. I was exhausted, and rejoiced to hear the word, "Halt!" Hans spread provisions for us upon a block of lava, and we all ate heartily. One thing, however, made me uneasy. Our supply of water was half consumed. My uncle reckoned on replenishing it from subterranean springs, but hitherto not even one had appeared. I could not help drawing his attention to this fact.

"And are you surprised at seeing no springs?" he replied.

"Most certainly, and what's more, I am very uneasy; we only have water enough for five days."

"Don't worry yourself, Axel. I'll answer for it we shall find water, and more than we want."

"And when?"

"When we get out of this lava that envelops us. How can you think springs could burst through such walls as these!"

"But perhaps this passage runs to a great depth. It seems to me that we have not made great progress vertically."

"What makes you think that?"

"Because the heat would be much greater if we had penetrated very far through the crust."

"According to your system," replied my uncle. "What is the thermometer?"

"Scarcely 15°, which shows only an increase of 9° since we started."

"Well, and what is your conclusion?"

"This is my conclusion. According to the most exact observations the increase of heat in the interior of the globe is 1° in 100 feet. But certain localities may modify this figure. For instance, at Yakoust, in Siberia, the increase is 1° in 36 feet. This difference evidently depends on the conducting power of rocks. I may add, too, that in the neighbourhood of an extinct volcano and through gneiss it has been observed that the elevation of the temperature was only 1° in 125 feet. Let us adopt this last hypothesis and calculate."

"Do so, my boy."

"Nothing is easier," I said, writing down the figures in my notebook. "Nine times 125 feet make 1,125 feet of depth."

"That's it exactly. Well, then?"

"Well, according to my observations, we are 10,000 feet below the level of the sea."

"Is it possible!"

"Yes; or figures are no longer figures."

The professor's calculations were exact. We had already exceeded by 6,000 feet the greatest depth ever reached by man, such as the mines of Kitz-Bahl in the Tyrol, and those of Wuttembourg in Bohemia.

The temperature, which ought to have been 81°, was scarcely 15°.

This was certainly well worth thinking over.

CHAPTER XIX

NEXT DAY, TUESDAY, June the 30th, at 6 a.m., the descent was resumed.

We still followed the gallery of lava, a real natural staircase, sloping as gently as those inclined planes which are found in place of stairs even yet in some old houses. We went on till 12.17, the exact time when we overtook Hans, who had just stopped short.

"Ah!" cried my uncle, "then we have come to the end of the gallery!"

I looked round me. We were in cross roads. Two paths lay before us, both dark and narrow. Which should we take? Here was a difficulty.

However, my uncle would not allow himself to show any hesitation before me or the guide. He pointed to the eastern tunnel, and soon we were all three treading it.

Besides, we might have stood hesitating for ever, for there was nothing to determine the choice. We were absolutely forced to trust to chance.

The slope of this fresh gallery was scarcely perceptible, and its sections very unequal. Sometimes a succession of arches would be disclosed, like the nave of a gothic cathedral. The architect of the middle ages might have studied here all the forms of church architecture which start from the ogive. A mile farther and we had to stoop our heads beneath elliptic arches in the Roman style, and massive pillars in the wall bent beneath the abutments of the arches. In other places this arrangement gave place to low substructures, like beavers' huts, and we had to crawl along narrow tube-like passages.

The heat was always bearable. But involuntary thoughts came over me of its intensity when the lava, ejected by Snäfell, rushed along by the route which was now so quiet. I imagined the torrents of fire dashing against the angles of the gallery, and the accumulation of heated vapours in this narrow channel.

"It is to be hoped," thought I, "that the old volcano may not take it into his head to play his old pranks again!"

These reflections I did not communicate to my uncle Lidenbrock. He would not have understood them. His one thought was to get forward. He walked, he slid, he even tumbled over with a resolution that, after all, was worth admiring.

At 6 p.m., after a not very fatiguing walk, we had made two leagues south, but were scarcely a quarter of a mile deeper. My uncle gave the signal to rest. We ate without talking much, and went to sleep without thinking much.

Our preparations for night were very simple. A railway rug, in which we each rolled ourselves, composed our bedding. There was neither cold to fear nor nocturnal intruders. Travellers in the heart of Africa, among the Saharas, in the old world, or in the bosoms of forests in the new, are obliged to take turns at watching each other during the hours of sleep, but here there was absolute solitude and complete security; neither savages nor wild beasts were to be feared.

We woke up next morning fresh and bright. The route was resumed. We followed the passage of lava as on the preceding day. It was impossible to tell the nature of the rocks. The tunnel, instead of going down, seemed gradually becoming absolutely horizontal. I thought even it seemed rising to the surface. This upward inclination became more evident about 10 a.m., and consequently so fatiguing that I was obliged to slacken pace.

"Come on, Axel, what's keeping you?" said the professor, impatiently.

"I must stop; I can't keep up with you," I replied.

"What! after only three hours' walking on such an easy road!"

"Easy, it may be, but most certainly very tiring."

"What! when it is all down-hill?"

"All up-hill, if you please."

"Up-hill!" exclaimed my uncle, shrugging his shoulders.

"Undoubtedly. For the last half-hour the slope has changed, and if we continue this way we shall certainly get back to Iceland in time."

The professor shook his head like a man determined not to be convinced. I tried to resume the conversation, but he would not answer me, and gave the signal to go on. I saw quite well that his silence was mere temper.

However, I shouldered my load bravely and went quickly after Hans, who was following my uncle. I was always afraid of letting them out of sight, for the idea of losing myself in the depths of this labyrinth made me shudder.

Besides, though the upward route was more fatiguing, I had the comfort of thinking it was bringing us always nearer to the surface of the earth again. Each step confirmed me in this, and I rejoiced in the idea of seeing my little Gräuben once more.

At noon I noticed a change in the appearance of the walls of the tunnel. I was first aware of it by the reflection of the electric light becoming fainter, when I discovered that solid rock had displaced the lava coating. This rock was composed of sloping layers, often disposed vertically. We were among strata of the transition or Silurian period.*

"It is plain enough!" I exclaimed. "There are the sedimentary deposits of the waters, these shales, limestones, and grits. We are leaving the granitic rock behind us. It is just as if Hamburg people should take the train to Hanover to go to Lubeck!"

I had better have kept my observations to myself. But my geological temperament got the better of my prudence and my uncle heard my exclamation.

"What's all that about?" he asked.

"Look!" I replied, pointing to the varied succession of grits and limestones, and the first indications of the slaty cleavage.

"Well?"

"We have reached the period when the first plants and first animals appeared."

"Ah! so that's what you think?"

"Look for yourself and examine carefully."

And I made him turn his lamp so as to throw the light on the wall. I expected some outburst, but he did not make the slightest remark and walked on.

Had he understood me or not? Or was it that the *amour-propre* of uncle and *savant* was too great to allow himself to admit that he had chosen the wrong tunnel? Or had he determined to explore it to the very end? It was so evident that we had left the lava route, and that this road would never take us to the heart of Snäfell.

However, I began to wonder whether, after all, I was not attaching too much importance to this change of strata. Perhaps

---

* So called, because rocks of this period are extensively found in England in districts once peopled by the Silures, a Celtic race.

I myself might be mistaken. Were we really going through the layers of rock above the granite base?

"If I am right," I said to myself, "I ought to find some remains of primitive vegetation. I will look round and see."

I had not gone a hundred steps before incontestable proof met my eyes. And necessarily, for at the Silurian period the seas contained upwards of 1,500 species of vegetables and animals. My feet, accustomed to treading on the hard lava, suddenly came in contact with the dust, the *débris* of plants and shells. On the walls were distinct impressions of fucoids and lycopodiaceæ. Professor Lidenbrock could not be deceived. I fancy he first shut his eyes, and walked straight on.

It was obstinacy in the extreme, and at last I could not stand it longer. I picked up a shell in a complete state of preservation, which had belonged to an animal nearly resembling a woodlouse; and I turned to my uncle and said:

"Look!"

"Well," he replied calmly, "it is the shell of a crustacean of the trilobite species, now extinct. That's all."

"But does it not bring you to the conclusion that—"

"To the same conclusion as yours? Yes. Perfectly so. We have left the granite rock and the lava passage. It is possible I have made a mistake, but I shall not be sure of it till we have reached the very end of this gallery."

"You are quite right, uncle; and I should approve your intention, if we were not threatened with a danger which becomes each moment more imminent."

"And what is it?"

"The want of water."

"Well, we must put ourselves on rations, Axel."

CHAPTER XX

AND THIS, INDEED, we were forced to do. Our provisions would not last three days longer. I saw that when supper-time came; and, unhappily, we had little hope of meeting with a spring in the transition system.

All next day we continued our course through an interminable succession of arcades. We walked on without saying a word. The taciturnity of Hans seemed to have infected us.

The path was not rising now, at least not sensibly. Sometimes even it appeared to slope. But this tendency, besides being very slight, could not reassure the professor, for the nature of the layers remained unmodified, and the transition period became more distinct.

The electric light made the schists and limestone and old red sandstone sparkle magnificently. We might have thought ourselves examining some excavations in Devonshire, a county which gives its name to this series. Specimens of magnificent marbles clothed the walls, some of a grey agate, fantastically streaked with white; others of rich crimson or yellow, with red patches. Then came specimens of speckled marbles in dark colours, relieved by the light shades of the limestone.

The greater part of these marbles bore the imprint of primitive animals. Since the day before, creation had made evident progress. Instead of the rudimentary trilobites, I noticed the *débris* of a more perfect order: amongst others of fishes, the Ganoids and the Sauropterygia, in which palæontologists have sought to discover the earliest forms of reptiles. The Devonian seas were peopled with a large number of animals of this species, and they deposited them by thousands in the rocks of the new formation.

It became evident that we were ascending the scale of animal creation of which man is at the top. But Professor Lidenbrock seemed not to notice it.

He was expecting one of two things, either that a vertical well would open below his feet, and allow him to resume his descent, or that some obstacle would prevent him from continuing this route. But evening came, and neither hope was realized.

On Friday, after a night during which I began to feel the torments of thirst, our little company again plunged into the windings of the gallery.

After ten hours' walking, I noticed that the reflection of our lamps on the walls had strangely become fainter. The marble, the schist, the limestone, and the sandstone of the walls gave way to a dark dull lining. Just then we came to a very narrow part, and I leaned my left hand against the wall. When I removed it, I saw it was quite black. I looked closer. We were in a coal mine!

"A coal mine!" I exclaimed.

"A mine without miners!"

"Indeed, who knows that?"

"I know it," said the professor curtly; "and I am certain that this gallery through coalpits has not been bored by the hand of man. But whether it is Nature's work or not, is nothing to me. It is supper-time. Let us sup."

Hans prepared the meal. I scarcely ate anything, and drank the few drops of water that fell to my share. Our guide's gourd, and that only half full, was all that remained to quench the thirst of three men.

After the repast, my companions lay down on their rugs, and found the remedy for all their fatigues in sleep. But I could not close my eyes, and counted the hours till morning.

On Saturday, at 6 a.m., we set off again. Twenty minutes later, we arrived at a vast excavation. I owned then that human hands could never have dug out such a pit; the vaults would have been shored up, and certainly they must have been supported by some miracle of equilibrium.

The cavern we were in was 100 feet wide, and 150 feet high. It was evidently a hole, made in the coal formation by some violent subterranean commotion.

The whole history of the coal period was written on these gloomy walls, and a geologist could have easily made out the different phases. The beds of coal were separated by strata of sandstone or compact clay, and appeared crushed by the upper layer.

In that age of the world which preceded the secondary period, immense types of vegetation clothed the earth, owing to the double action of a tropical heat and continued moisture. An atmosphere of vapours enveloped the earth completely, depriving it still of the sun's rays.

Thence arises the conclusion that the high temperatures were not caused by this new fire. Perhaps even the orb of day was not yet prepared for his glorious mission. Climates did not yet exist, and a torrid heat overspread the entire surface of the globe, alike at the equator and the poles. From whence did it come? From its interior.

In spite of the theories of Professor Lidenbrock, a fierce fire brooded then within the spheroid; its action was felt to the last layers of the earth's crust. The plants, deprived of the beneficent influences of the sun, yielded neither flowers nor perfumes; but the roots drew a vigorous life from the burning soil of those primeval days.

There were but few trees, nothing but herbaceous plants, immense grasses, ferns, lycopods, sigillaria, asterophyllites, rare orders now, but then numbering thousands of different species.

Now it is from this very period of exuberant vegetation that the coal formation dates. The crust of the globe, still in an elastic state, obeyed the movements of the liquid mass it covered. Hence arose numerous fissures and depressions. The plants, dragged down by the waters in great numbers, formed gradually considerable heaps below.

Natural chemical action then ensued. The vegetable masses beneath the waters first changed into peat, then, owing to the influence of the gases, and the heat of fermentation, they underwent complete mineralization. Thus were formed those immense coal fields, which excessive consumption must exhaust, however, in less than three centuries, if the industrial world does not see to it.

These reflections occupied my mind while I was gazing at the wealth of combustibles stored up in this portion of the earth. They will doubtless never be discovered. The working of such deep mines would involve too great sacrifices. Besides, what would be the use when coal deposits are lying, one might say, on the surface of the globe in a great many countries! None but I saw these untouched mines, so they would remain till the last day of the world.

Meantime we were walking on, and I alone of the little company forgot the length of the way in geological contemplations. The temperature remained as it was during our passage through the lava and schists. Only my sense of smell was affected by the exceedingly strong odour of protocarburet of hydrogen. I recognized immediately the presence in this gallery of a large quantity of that dangerous fluid known among miners as fire-damp, the explosion of which has often caused such frightful catastrophes.

Happily we were illumined by Ruhmkorff's apparatus. If we had unfortunately been so imprudent as to have ventured to explore the gallery with torches in our hands, a terrible explosion would have made an end of the journey and the travellers.

This excursion in the mine continued till evening. My uncle could scarcely contain his impatience at this horizontal route. The darkness, quite deep twenty steps distant, prevented the length of the gallery from being reckoned, and I began to think it was positively interminable, when at six o'clock a wall appeared suddenly in front of us. There was no opening right or left, above or below. We had reached the end of a blind alley.

"Well, so much the better!" exclaimed my uncle. "I know at least what I'm about now. We are not on Saknussemm's route, and must just turn and go back to where the road forks."

"Yes," said I, "if our strength holds out."

"And why shouldn't it?"

"Because to-morrow, every drop of water will be gone."

"And of courage too, it seems," said the professor, looking sternly at me. I did not dare to reply.

CHAPTER XXI

THE DEPARTURE WAS fixed for an early hour next morning. No time was to be lost, for it would take us five days to reach the cross roads.

I need not dwell on the sufferings of our return. My uncle bore them like a man who is angry with himself for yielding to weakness: Hans, with the resignation of his placid nature; and I, to speak the truth, complaining and despairing the whole time. I could not bear up against this stroke of ill-fortune.

As I had foreseen, the water came to an end the very first day of our journey back. Our only store of liquid now was gin, but this horrible drink burnt the throat, and I could not even endure the sight of it. I felt the temperature stifling. Fatigue paralysed me. More than once I fell motionless. Then we had to come to a halt and my uncle or the Icelander did their best to revive me. But I saw already that the former was struggling painfully against the extreme fatigue and the tortures of thirst.

At last, on Tuesday, the 7th of July, dragging ourselves along on our knees and hands, we arrived half dead at the junction of the two passages. There I lay like an inert lump, stretched full length on the lava floor. It was 10 a.m.

Hans and my uncle, clinging to the wall, tried to nibble a few bits of biscuit. Long moans escaped my swollen lips. I fell into a profound stupor.

After a little, my uncle came to me, and, lifting me in his arms, said in a tone of genuine pity:

"Poor child!"

His words touched me, for I was not accustomed to tenderness from the austere professor. I seized his trembling hands in mine. He let me do it and looked at me. Tears stood in his eyes.

I saw him lift the gourd slung at his side, and, to my great bewilderment, he put it to my lips, and said:

"Drink!"

Had I heard him right? Was my uncle mad? I looked at him stupidly. I could not understand him.

"Drink!" he repeated.

And lifting up his gourd, he drained the contents into my mouth.

Oh! infinite boon! A gulp of water moistened my burning mouth, one only, but it sufficed to call back my ebbing life.

I thanked my uncle with clasped hands.

"Yes," he said, "a mouthful of water! The last, do you hear, the last? I kept it on purpose for you. Twenty times, aye, a hundred times, I have had to fight with my fearful longing to drink it; but no, Axel, I kept it for you."

"Oh, uncle!" I murmured, and big tears started to my eyes.

"Yes, poor child, I knew, when you reached these cross roads, you would drop down half dead, and I kept my last few drops of water to revive you."

"Thanks, thanks!" I cried.

Slightly as my thirst was quenched, I had somewhat recovered my strength. The muscles of my throat, which had become contracted, now relaxed, and the inflammation of my lips subsided. I could speak.

"Well, come," said I, "there is only one course open to us now; our water is done, and we must go right back."

While I was speaking, my uncle avoided looking at me, and hung down his head, unwilling to meet my eyes.

"We must go back," I cried, "and find our way to Snäfell. May God give us strength to climb to the summit of the crater."

"Go back!" said my uncle, speaking to himself, it seemed, more than to me.

"Yes, go back, and without losing an instant."

A pretty long silence ensued.

Then, in an odd tone, the professor went on to say:

"Well then, Axel, those few drops of water have not restored your strength and courage?"

"Courage!"

"I see you are as down-hearted as ever, and still speak despairingly."

What sort of man was this I had to do with, and what projects was his bold spirit still entertaining?

"What! you are unwilling?—"

"Shall I give up this expedition at the very moment when everything promises success? Never!"

"Then we must make up our minds to perish!"

"No, Axel, no! Start off! Let Hans go with you. Leave me alone!"

"Leave you behind?"

"Yes, I tell you; leave me here. I have commenced the journey, and I will complete it or never return. Go, Axel, go!"

My uncle was violently excited. His voice, which had softened for an instant, sounded harsh and threatening. He was struggling with gloomy energy against impossibilities. I was unwilling to leave him at the bottom of this abyss, and yet the instinct of self-preservation urged me to fly from it.

The guide watched this scene with his accustomed indifference. He understood what was going on, however. Our gestures showed him that each was trying to drag the other a different road; but Hans evidenced no interest in the question, though his own life was involved in it. He was ready to go if the signal to start was given, and ready to stay in obedience to the slightest wish of his master.

What would I not have given that minute to have been able to make him understand me! My words and groans and accent would have moved his cold nature. I would have pointed out dangers which he never seemed to suspect. I would have made him fully alive to them, and together we might, perhaps, have succeeded in convincing the obstinate professor. Nay, if all other means failed, we might have compelled him to regain the summit of Snäfell.

I went up to Hans and laid my hand on his. He did not stir.

I pointed to the way out of the crater. He still remained motionless. My gasping breath showed my sufferings. The Icelander
gently shook his head, and quietly pointing to my uncle, said:

"Master!"

"The master!" I cried. "Madman! He is not the master of your
life. We must fly, we must drag him along. Do you understand?"

I had grasped Hans by the arm, and was trying to make him
get up. I struggled with him, but my uncle interposed and said:

"Be calm, Axel, you will get nothing out of that impassible
servant. Listen, therefore, to what I propose."

I crossed my arms and looked my uncle firm in the face.

"The want of water," said he, "is the only obstacle in our path.
In this tunnel to the east, composed of lavas, schists, and coal, we
have not found a single drop of liquid. It is possible we may be
more fortunate if we explore the one to the west."

I shook my head with profound incredulity.

"Hear me to the end," said the professor, in a constrained
voice. "While you were lying motionless, I went to examine the
conformation of the passage. It leads straight into the heart of
the globe, and in a few hours we shall reach the granite foundation. There we must meet with springs in abundance. The nature
of the rock favours this, and instinct agrees with logic in support of my conviction. Now, this is what I propose to you. When
Columbus asked his ships' crews for three days longer to let him
discover new countries, the men, sick and dismayed as they were,
allowed the justice of his demand, and he discovered the New
World. I am the Columbus of these subterranean regions, and
I ask you to give me one day more. If I have not found water
before the time expires, I swear to you we will return to the
surface of the earth."

In spite of my irritation, I was moved by my uncle's words and
by the violent restraint he was putting on himself.

"Very well," I said. "It shall be as you wish, and may God
reward your superhuman energy. You have only a few hours to
try your fortune, so let us start at once."

CHAPTER XXII

THE DESCENT COMMENCED this time by the new gallery. Hans walked first as usual. We had not gone a hundred steps, when the professor, throwing the light of his lantern on the wall, exclaimed:

"Here are the primitive rocks. We are in the right track. Forward! forward!"

When the earth's surface gradually cooled in the first stages of its formation, the diminution of its bulk produced disruptions, rents, contractions, and chasms. The passage itself was a fissure of this kind, through which the eruptive granite had forced a passage at some time. Its myriad windings formed an inextricable labyrinth through the primordial rock.

The deeper we went, the more clearly defined became the successive layers of the primitive period. Geological science considers this primitive rock as the basis of the mineral crust, and she recognizes in it three distinct layers – the schist, the gneiss, and the mica-schist, resting on the immovable rock called granite.

Never before were mineralogists in such wondrously favourable circumstances for studying their science. What the boring machine, an insensible inert instrument, could not bring to the surface, we could examine with our eyes, and touch with our hands.

Through the beds of schist, coloured with beautiful shades of green, metallic threads of copper and manganese, mixed with traces of platinum and gold, were twisted and intertwined. I could not but think what riches are hid in the depths of the earth, which covetous humanity will never appropriate. These treasures have been buried so deep by the convulsions of primeval times, that neither mattock nor pickaxe will ever disinter them.

To the schists succeeded the gneiss, of a stratiform structure, and remarkable for the regularity and parallelism of its laminæ. Then the mica-schists disposed in great flakes, which are revealed to the eye by the sparkles of the white mica.

The light of our lanterns, caught by the little facets of the rocky mass, flashed up by brilliant jets at every angle, and I could have fancied myself travelling through a hollow diamond, in which the rays crossed and mingled and shot out in a thousand brilliant coruscations.

About six o'clock this illumination began to lose its splendour and almost ceased. The walls assumed a crystallized but sombre appearance, the mica became more closely mingled with the feldspath and quartz, to form the rock *par excellence*, the hardest of all stones, that bears, without being crushed by it, the weight of the four systems. We were shut up in a prison of granite.

It was 8 p.m., and no sign yet of water. My sufferings were terrible. My uncle still pushed forward. He would not stop, and kept listening for the murmur of some spring. But there was not a sound.

However, I could not hold out long, for my legs refused to carry me. I struggled against my tortures as long as I could, for I did not want to make him stop. This would be to him the death-knell of all his hopes, for the day was fast drawing to an end, and it was his last.

At length my strength failed completely. I screamed out, "I'm dying! Come to me." And then I fell flat on the ground. My uncle turned back, folded his arms, and looked at me attentively. Then I heard him mutter in a hollow tone:

"This finishes it." A frightful gesture of rage met my glance, and I closed my eyes.

When I opened them again, I saw my two companions lying motionless, wrapped in their rugs. Were they asleep? For my part, I could not get a moment's sleep. I was in too much suffering, aggravated, too, by the thought that there was no remedy for it. My uncle's words echoed in my ears, for in such a feeble state the idea of regaining the surface of the globe was out of the question.

A league and a half of terrestrial crust lay above us. The whole weight of it seemed to lie upon my shoulders. I felt crushed, and exhausted myself in frantic efforts to turn round on my granite couch.

Some hours elapsed. Deep silence reigned – the silence of a tomb. Nothing could reach us through these walls, the thinnest of which was five miles thick.

However, in the midst of my stupor, I thought I heard a noise. It was dark in the tunnel, but looking closely, I fancied I could see the Icelander disappearing, lamp in hand.

Why was he going? Was Hans really forsaking us? My uncle was asleep. I tried to call out, but my voice could not make itself heard through my parched lips. The gloom had deepened into blackness, and the faint echo of the sound had died away.

"Hans has abandoned us!" I cried. "Hans, Hans!"

But these words were spoken within me. They never left my lips. However, after the first moment of fear, I was ashamed of suspecting a man who had given us no ground of suspicion. His departure could not be a flight. Instead of going up the passage he was going down farther in it. A bad intention would have dragged him upwards, not downwards. This reasoning calmed me a little, and I came back to another train of ideas. Hans was so tranquil that only some grave motive could have induced him to give up his rest. Had he gone on a voyage of discovery? Had he heard some distant murmur break on the silent night, though I had not?

CHAPTER XXIII

FOR A WHOLE hour I was imagining in my delirious brain all the reasons which might have actuated the quiet Icelander. A perfect tangle of absurd ideas got into my head. I thought I was going mad.

But at last, a noise of footsteps was heard in the depths of the abyss. Hans was coming up again. The faint light began to glimmer on the walls, and then shone fully at the opening of the passage. Hans appeared.

He went up to my uncle, put his hand on his shoulder, and gently awoke him. My uncle sat up and asked what was the matter.

"*Vatten*," replied the hunter.

Violent pain certainly seems to make one become a polyglot, for though I did not know a single word of Danish, I instinctively understood what the guide meant.

"Water! water!" I cried, and clapped my hands, and gesticulated as if I were crazy.

"Water!" repeated my uncle. "*Hvar?*" he asked, addressing the Icelander.

"*Nedat!*" replied Hans.

"*Where? Down below?*" I understood every word. I seized the hunter's hands and grasped them in mine, but he looked at me with perfect calmness.

We were soon ready, and set out along a passage that made a slope of two feet in the fathom.

In about an hour we had gone 1,000 fathoms, and made a descent of 2,000 feet.

That very moment I heard an unusual sound of something running within the granite wall, a sort of dull roar, like distant thunder. I had been beginning to give way again to despair when we had walked half an hour, and still no spring had come in sight, but my uncle apprised me that Hans was not mistaken in his announcement, for that noise I heard now was the roaring of a torrent.

"A torrent?" I exclaimed.

"There is not a doubt of it. A subterranean river is flowing round us."

We hastened our steps, spurred on by hope. The sound of the murmuring water refreshed me already. It increased sensibly. The torrent which was running above us at first was now taking its course along the left wall, roaring and leaping. I passed my hands frequently over the rock, hoping to find some traces of moisture. But in vain.

Another half-hour passed, and another half-league.

It was evident that the hunter could not have gone farther than this while he was away. Guided by an instinct, peculiar to mountaineers, he felt this torrent through the rock, but certainly he had not seen the precious liquid at all, nor drank of it.

It soon became evident too, that if we went farther, we should be going away from the stream, for the rush was growing fainter.

We turned back. Hans stopped at the precise spot where the torrent seemed nearest.

I sat down beside the wall, the waters dashing within two feet of me with extreme violence, but still the granite wall between.

Instead of thinking over the likeliest means of getting over this barrier, I yielded once more to despair.

Hans looked at me, and I fancied I caught a smile on his lips.

He rose, and took the lamp. I followed him. He went to the wall, and I saw him lay his ear against the dry stone, slowly moving his place, and always listening intently. He was plainly trying to find out the exact part where the current made most noise. This point he discovered in the side wall to the left, about three feet from the ground.

How excited I felt! I could not venture to guess what he was going to do. But I soon understood and applauded, and loaded him with caresses when he lifted his pickaxe to attack the solid rock.

"Saved!" I shouted.

"Yes!" cried my uncle, in rapture. "Hans is right! Ah! the brave fellow! We should never have hit upon that!"

I quite believe it. Such an expedient, simple enough as it was, would never have entered our heads. Nothing seemed more dangerous than to give a blow with a pickaxe in this part of the earth's frame. Suppose some dislodgement should occur which would crush us? And what if this torrent should burst through the opening and engulf us! There was nothing chimerical in these dangers, but they could not hinder us. Our thirst was so intense, that we would have risked being crushed or drowned, and dug in the very bed of the ocean to relieve it.

Hans did the work, for neither my uncle nor myself could have done it. Our impatient hands would have made the rock fly off in fragments under our hasty blows. The guide, on the contrary, was calm and collected, and gradually wore away the rock by little but continuous strokes, till he had dug an opening about six inches wide. I could hear the torrent getting louder, and I seemed already to feel the beneficent water touch my lips.

Soon the pick had buried itself two feet in the granite. The operation had already lasted an hour. I waited with impatience, and my uncle wished to employ stronger measures, though I did all I could to dissuade him. He had already seized his pickaxe, when suddenly there came a hissing noise, and then a jet of water spouted out violently, and dashed against the opposite wall.

Hans, who was almost upset by the force of the shock, gave a cry of pain, the cause of which I soon understood, and cried out in my turn when I found, on plunging my hands into the water, that it was boiling.

"Water at 200°!" I exclaimed.

"Well, it will cool," replied my uncle.

The passage was filled with steam, and a stream formed, which began to run away and lose itself in the subterranean windings. Soon we were able to indulge in our first draught.

Oh, how delicious! What a priceless luxury this was. It mattered not what the water was or whence it had come. It was water, and though still warm, it brought back the ebbing life. I drank without stopping, without even tasting.

But after my first moment's delectation I exclaimed, "Why it is mineral water! It tastes of iron!"

"Capital for the stomach," said my uncle, "and highly mineralized! This journey is as good as going to Spa or Töplitz!"

"Oh, isn't it good?"

"I should think so, water obtained two leagues below the ground. There is an inky taste about it, but it is not disagreeable. No, it is really a famous tonic Hans has procured us, so I propose this health-giving stream shall receive his name."

"By all means," said I. And the river was called "Hansbach" forthwith.

Hans was not the least proud of the honour. After he had refreshed himself moderately, he sat down in a corner with his accustomed placidity.

"Now," said I, "we must not let this water run away."

"Why not?" replied my uncle. "I suspect the spring is un-failing."

"Never mind, let us fill our gourds and the leather bottle, and then try and stop up the hole."

My advice was followed. Hans made a bung of granite and tow, and did his best to drive it in. But it was not so easily done. We scalded our hands over the business, and our efforts were fruitless after all. The pressure was too great.

"It is evident," I said, "that the source of this river is at a great height, to judge by the force of the jet."

"There is no doubt of it," replied my uncle. "If this column of water is 32,000 feet high, it has the weight of 1,000 atmos-pheres. But an idea has just struck me."

"What is it?"

"Why should we be so bent on bunging up this hole?"

"Why, because—"

Here I stopped, for it was not easy to find a reason.

"When our gourds are empty again, how do we know for certain that we shall be able to fill them?"

"That's true."

"Well, then, let the water run. It will flow down naturally, and be both our guide and refreshment on the route."

"That's a capital idea," I exclaimed, "and with this river for our companion, there is no reason now why our projects should not succeed."

"Ah! you are coming round to my way of thinking, my boy," said the professor, smiling.

"I am doing better than coming, I have come."

"Not quite yet. We must have a few hours' rest."

I actually forgot it was night. But the chronometer reminded me of the fact, and before long. After we had recruited our strength with food, we lay down, and were soon all three sleeping soundly.

CHAPTER XXIV

NEXT DAY WE had already forgotten our past sufferings. I was amazed at first when I awoke, not to feel thirsty, and asked myself what could be the reason. The stream running at my feet gave me sufficient answer.

We breakfasted and drank of this excellent chalybeate water. I felt quite merry, and decided to go on. Why should not a man so thoroughly confident as my uncle succeed, when he had a zealous guide like Hans, and a determined nephew like me? Such were the grand ideas that came into my head. If any one had proposed my going back to Snäfell I should have refused indignantly.

But, fortunately, we had only to continue our descent.

"Come, let us start!" I shouted, awakening the old echoes of the globe by my enthusiastic tones.

We set out again on Thursday at 8 a.m. The granite passage, with its varied windings and unexpected bends, seemed almost like a labyrinthine maze; but, on the whole, the direction was uniformly S.E. My uncle consulted his compass constantly, that he might know exactly how much ground we had gone over.

The gallery extended almost horizontally, not sloping more than two inches in a fathom at most. The stream ran murmuring softly at our feet. I compared it to some kindly genius, who was guiding us underground, and I caressed with my hand the warm Naiad whose songs accompanied our steps. My gay mood involuntarily took a mythological turn.

As for my uncle, he kept fuming at the path for being so horizontal. He loved vertical lines, and it put him out of patience to be always going by an hypotenuse to the centre, instead of sliding along the radius, to use his own expression. But we had no choice, and so long as we were going towards the centre, however indirectly, we had no right to complain. Moreover, from time to time we came to steep slopes, down which the Naiad ran rushing and roaring, and we went with her.

On the whole, that day and the next we went over a great distance horizontally, though comparatively little vertically.

On Friday, July 10th, we reckoned we were thirty leagues to the south-east of Reikiavik, and two and a half leagues deep.

We were in front of a yawning abyss, and frightful enough it looked, though my uncle clapped his hands when he reckoned its depth.

"Famous!" he exclaimed. "This will take us a long way, and without any trouble, for the projections all the way down make a regular staircase."

The ropes were arranged, to avoid any risk of accident, and we commenced the descent. I dare not call it perilous, for I was already accustomed to that kind of exercise.

This abyss was a narrow chasm in the rock, called a "fault", in scientific language. It had been evidently caused by the unequal cooling of the earth's surface. If it had ever served as a passage for the eruptive matter ejected by Snäfell, I could not understand how there was no trace left of it whatever. We were going down a sort of spiral staircase, which one might have thought had been constructed by the hand of man.

We halted every quarter of an hour, to take needful rest, and to stretch our legs. Then we sat down on some projection, with our legs hanging down, eating and talking, and refreshing ourselves with a draught from the stream.

The Hansbach, of course, made a cascade down this fault, to the loss of its volume necessarily, but enough remained to quench our thirst, and we knew it must resume its quiet course when it reached more level ground.

In its present foaming, angry state, it made me think of my uncle in some of his passions, while its calm continuous flow hitherto reminded me of the tranquil Icelander.

On the 6th and 7th of July we were constantly following the

windings of the stairs, and had attained a further depth of two leagues. We were altogether nearly five leagues below the level of the sea. But on the 8th, at noon, the "fault", though still going S.E., began to get less vertical, only making an incline of 45°.

The road now became easier, though intensely monotonous. It could hardly be otherwise, for there was no scenery to enliven it.

On Wednesday, the 15th, we were seven leagues below the earth, and fifty from Snäfell. Though somewhat fatigued, we were in perfect health, and our medicine chest remained untouched.

My uncle noted down, every hour, the indications of the compass, the chronometer, manometer, and the thermometer, those which he has published in the scientific account of his journey. By this means he could always ascertain our exact position. When he apprised me that we had gone fifty leagues horizontally, I could not forbear an exclamation.

"What's the matter?" asked my uncle.

"Nothing; I was only making a reflection."

"What is it, my boy?"

"Just this: that if your calculations are correct, we are no longer below Iceland."

"Do you think so?"

"We can make sure at once."

I took my measurements, with the compasses, on my map, and found I was quite right.

"We have passed Cape Portland," I said, "and fifty leagues S.E. bring us to the open sea."

"Below mid-ocean!" cried my uncle, rubbing his hands.

"Then the ocean is really above our heads?"

"Of course, Axel. That's not so wonderful. Are there not coal mines at Newcastle extending far along under the sea?"

The professor saw nothing extraordinary in the fact, but my mind was quite excited with the idea of walking below the depths of the ocean. And yet what difference did it make whether the plains and mountains of Iceland were over our heads, or the waves of the Atlantic. It was all one, since the solid granite overarched us. I soon got used to the thought, for the passage, whether straight or winding, fantastic alike in its slopes and in its turns, but always running S.E., was rapidly leading us towards the heart of the globe.

Four days later, on Saturday, July 18th, in the evening, we reached a sort of grotto, of considerable size. Here my uncle came to a halt and paid Hans his weekly wage, and it was agreed that the morrow should be a day of rest.

CHAPTER XXV

I AWOKE CONSEQUENTLY on Sunday morning without the usual impression on my mind, that I must be up and off immediately. And though we were in the deepest depths, it was not disagreeable. We were quite fit for this existence of troglodytes. I scarcely thought of sun, or stars, or moon, or trees, or houses, or towns, or any of those terrestrial superfluities which are necessaries to sublunary beings. We were fossils now, and thought such useless marvels absurd.

The grotto was an immense hill. The faithful stream ran over the granite floor. At this distance from its source, the water was hardly lukewarm, and could be drank comfortably.

After breakfast, the professor determined to devote an hour or two to the arrangement of his daily notes.

"First," he said, "I am going to make calculations, that I may ascertain our situation exactly. I wish to be able on my return to draw a map of our journey, a sort of vertical section of the globe, giving a profile of our expedition."

"That would be a curiosity, uncle; but would your observations be sufficiently exact?"

"Yes. I have carefully noted the angles and inclines. I am certain there has been no mistake. Let us see first where we are. Take the compass, and observe its direction."

I looked at the instrument, and after watching it carefully, I replied:

"S.E. by E."

"Very good," said the professor, marking it down, and making some hasty calculations. "Well then, my conclusion is, that we have made eighty-five leagues from our starting-point."

"Then we are walking under the Atlantic now?"

"Just so."

"And perhaps, at this moment, a tempest is raging above our heads; and ships are being wrecked amid the wild hurricanes?"

"Likely enough."

"And whales are lashing the walls of our prison with their tails?"

"Don't be frightened, Axel, they can't shake them. But to return to our calculations; we are in the S.E., eighty-five leagues from the base of Snäfell, and according to my preceding notes, I reckon we have reached a depth of sixteen leagues."

"Sixteen leagues!" I exclaimed.

"Undoubtedly."

"But that is the extreme limit of the earth's crust, according to science."

"I don't say it is not."

"And if there is any law of increase in temperature, the heat here ought to be 1,500°."

"Ought to be, my boy."

"And all this granite would be in a state of fusion, as it could not possibly remain in a solid state."

"You see, however, that it is nothing of the sort, and that facts, as usual, give the lie to theories."

"I am obliged to own it, but still I am very much astonished at it."

"How does the thermometer stand?"

"$27\frac{6}{10}$."

"Then philosophers are out in their reckoning by $1,474\frac{4}{10}$. Then the proportional increase of temperature is a mistake, and Humphry Davy was right, and so was I to listen to him. What do you say to it now?"

"Nothing."

I could have found plenty to say if I chose. I could not admit Humphry Davy's theory in the least, and still believed in the central heat, though I did not feel the effect of it. I would really rather have admitted that this chimney of an extinct volcano, being covered with non-conducting lava, did not allow the heat to pass through it.

But, without stopping to seek for new arguments, I confined myself to the consideration of our actual situation.

"Uncle," I said, "I have no doubt all your calculations are right, but they bring me to a rigorous conclusion."

"And what is it, my boy? Speak your mind."

"At the point where we are, under the latitude of Iceland, the radius of the earth is scarcely 1,583 leagues."

"It is $1,583\frac{1}{3}$."

"Put down 1,600 leagues in round figures. Out of a journey of 1,600 leagues, we have gone twelve."

"That's just it."

"And at the cost of eighty-five degrees diagonally?"

"Perfectly so."

"In about twenty days?"

"In twenty days."

"Now sixteen leagues are $\frac{1}{100}$ of the earth's radius. If we go on at this rate, we should take 2,000 days, or nearly five and a half years to descend."

The professor made no reply.

"Without reckoning that if a depth of sixteen leagues is obtained by going eighty horizontally, that would make 8,000 leagues S.E.; and it would be a long time before we reached the centre, if we did not chance first to emerge at some point of the circumference."

"Hang your calculations!" cried my uncle, passionately; "and hang your hypothesis, too! On what ground do they rest? Who told you, pray, that this passage did not lead direct to the centre? Besides, I have a precedent. What I am doing, another has already done; and where he has succeeded I can succeed too."

"I hope so; but at least I may be allowed—"

"To hold your tongue, Axel, if you wish to argue in that senseless fashion."

I saw plainly the terrible professor was about to leap out of my uncle's skin, and I thought I had better be silent.

"Now," he said, "consult the manometer. What does it indicate?"

"Considerable pressure?"

"Well, then, you see in descending gradually we get accustomed to the density of the atmosphere, and are not the least affected by it."

"Not in the least, except a little pain in the ears."

"That is nothing, and you can get rid of it at once by breathing very quickly for a minute."

"Quite so," said I, determined not to contradict him again. "There is a positive pleasure even in feeling one's self getting into a denser atmosphere. Have you noticed the wonderful clearness of sound here?"

"Yes, indeed. A deaf man would soon get his hearing again."

"But this density will of course increase?"

"Yes, according to a somewhat indefinite law. It is true that the intensity of the weight will diminish in proportion as we descend. You know that it is on the surface that its action is most felt, and at the centre of the globe objects have no longer any weight?"

"I know that; but tell me, in the end will not the air acquire the density of water?"

"Undoubtedly, under the pressure of 710 atmospheres."

"And lower still?"

"Lower still of course the density will increase still more."

"How shall we descend, then?"

"Well, we must put stones in our pockets."

"I declare, uncle, you have an answer for everything."

I did not dare to go any farther into the field of hypothesis, for I should have been sure to have stumbled against some possibility, which would have made the professor start out again.

But it was quite evident that the air, under a pressure of possibly a thousand atmospheres, would pass at last into a solid state; and in that case, even supposing that our bodies might have held out, we should be forced to stop in spite of all the reasonings in the world.

But it was no use advancing this argument. My uncle would have met me with that everlasting Saknussemm, a precedent of not the slightest value, for even quoting the truth of the learned Icelander's narrative, this simple answer might be made to it: "In the sixteenth century neither barometers nor manometers were invented, consequently how could Saknussemm know that he had reached the centre of the earth?"

But I kept this objection to myself and waited the course of events.

The rest of the day passed in talking and making calculations. I always sided with Professor Lidenbrock, and envied the perfect indifference of Hans, who went blindly wherever destiny led him, without troubling himself about cause and effect.

CHAPTER XXVI

I MUST OWN that up till now things had not gone so very badly with us, and I should have been graceless to complain. If the average of difficulties did not increase, we must accomplish our purpose in the end. And what glory we should win! I began positively to reason like Lidenbrock himself. Seriously I did. I wonder if it was owing to my strange surroundings at present. May be it was.

For some days we came to a succession of steep inclines. Some of them almost frightfully perpendicular, which brought us a long way towards the interior. On some days we advanced a league and a half to two leagues. But these were perilous descents, in which we were greatly helped by the adroitness of Hans, and his marvellous *sangfroid*. Thanks to him we got over many a bad place that we could never have scrambled through by ourselves.

His absolute silence, however, increased every day. I even think it grew upon us also. External objects have an actual influence on the brain. Any one shut up within four walls loses the faculty at last of associating words and ideas. Look at prisoners in solitary cells. How they become imbeciles, if not insane, by the disuse of their thinking faculties!

During the fortnight which followed our last conversation, nothing occurred worth mentioning. I can only recall to mind one event of any importance, and that I can never forget. I have reason to remember every particular of it, even the smallest detail.

On the 7th of August our successive descents had brought us to a depth of thirty leagues, that is to say, we had over our heads thirty leagues of rocks, ocean, continents, and cities. We must have been then 200 leagues from Iceland.

That day the tunnel was but very slightly slanting. I was ahead of the others. My uncle was carrying one of Ruhmkorff's apparatus, and I had the other examining the beds of granite.

All at once, on turning round, I found myself alone.

"All right!" I thought. "I have been going too fast, or Hans and uncle may have stopped for a minute on the road. Come, I must get back to them. Fortunately, the path is not steep."

I retraced my steps, and, after walking for a quarter of an hour, looked round me. Nobody was in sight. I called out. No answer. My voice was drowned in the midst of the hollow echoes awakened by the sound.

I began to be uneasy, and a shudder crept over me.

"Be calm," I said to myself, aloud. "I am sure of finding them again. There are not two roads. I was walking in front, so I must just keep going back."

I went back for half an hour longer, and then I listened to hear if any one called me, for in so dense an atmosphere I should hear a long way off. There was not a sound. A strange silence reigned throughout the gallery.

I stopped. I could not believe in my isolation. I had lost my way; I was not lost; I should get right again presently.

"There is only the one passage," I kept saying to myself, "and as they are in it, I must come up to them soon. I have only to keep ascending. Unless, not seeing me, and forgetting I was in front, they had gone back to look for me. But even then, by hurrying, I shall overtake them, that's evident."

I repeated these last words like a man who is not very certain, and moreover it took me a long time to put my ideas together at all in the shape of a conclusive argument, simple enough as they were.

Then a doubt crossed my mind. Was I really ahead of my companions when I got parted from them? Certainly I was. Hans was following me, and my uncle came after him. He had even stopped for a minute to fasten his packages on his shoulder. I remembered this circumstance distinctly. It was at this very moment I must have gone on too far.

"Besides," thought I, "it is impossible I could have gone far wrong, for I have a guide to lead me through this labyrinth; one that will never fail me – my faithful stream. I have only to follow it back and I cannot help finding my companions."

This conclusion reanimated me, and I resolved to set out immediately, without losing an instant.

How I blessed the foresight of my uncle now, in not allowing the hunter to stop up the hole in the granite. This beneficent spring, after having refreshed us on the road, was now to be my guide through the winding mazes of the earth's crust.

Before starting I thought I should be the better of sundry

ablutions. I dipped my face into the Hansbach; but judge of my stupefaction! I touched dry, rough granite! The stream no longer ran at my feet.

CHAPTER XXVII

I CANNOT DESCRIBE my despair. No human tongue could tell what I felt. I was buried alive, with the prospect before me of dying of cold and hunger.

I passed my burning hands mechanically over the ground. How dry the rock seemed!

But could I have forsaken the course of the stream? For here it certainly was not. Now I understood the cause of this strange silence, when I listened for the last time expecting to hear a call from my companions. I had not, till this moment, noticed the absence of the stream. It is evident that just as I took the first wrong step the gallery must have forked, and I had followed the new opening, while the Hansbach, obeying the caprice of another incline, had gone away with my companions towards unknown depths. How could I get back? There was not a track. My feet left no imprint on the granite. I racked my brain to discover the solution of this problem. One single word expressed all the misery of my situation – Lost!

Yes, lost at, what seemed to me, an immeasurable depth. These thirty leagues of the earth's crust were weighing down my shoulders terribly. I felt crushed.

I tried to bring my thoughts back to the upper world. But I scarcely succeeded. Hamburg, the house in Königstrasse, my poor Gräuben – all the living world, beneath which I was lost, passed rapidly before my terrified memory. I saw, as if in some hallucination, all the incidents of the journey – the voyage, Iceland, M. Fridrikson, Snäfell! I said to myself that to have the faintest shadow of hope in my position would be madness, and that I had far better despair.

What human power, indeed, could bring me back again to the surface of the globe, or tear down these enormous arches supporting each other above my head? Who could set me in the right track once more, and take me to rejoin my companions?

"Oh, uncle!" I cried in accents of despair.

This was the only word of reproach that came to my lips, for I knew how much the poor man would suffer while he was vainly searching for me.

When I saw myself thus wholly cut off from human succour, incapable of attempting anything for my deliverance, I thought of heavenly succour. Memories of my childhood, of my mother, whom I had only known in the sweet days of my infancy, came back to me. I began to pray, little as I deserved that God should know me when I had forgotten Him so long; and I prayed fervently.

This cry for help to heaven made me calm, and I was able to bring all my mind to the survey of my actual position.

I had provisions enough for three days, and my gourd was full. However, I could not stay where I was any longer, but what course should I take? Should I ascend or descend?

Ascend, evidently – always keep ascending. I must then inevitably come to the part where the gallery had forked, and, could I but regain the stream, I could at any rate get back to the crater of Snäfell.

How hadn't I thought of this sooner? There was clearly some chance of deliverance here. My very first business was to find the Hansbach again.

I rose up, and leaning on my iron-tipped staff, began to climb the gallery. The incline was pretty steep, but I walked on hopefully and unconcerned, like a man who has not the choice of roads before him.

For half an hour I met with no obstacles. I tried to recognize the way by the form of the tunnel, and by the projections of certain rocks, and the disposition of the fractures. But no particular appearance recurred to me, and I soon saw that this gallery would not bring me to the point of demarcation. It was a blind alley. I struck against an impenetrable wall and fell on the rock.

What terror and despair took hold of me then I have no power to depict. I was completely prostrated! My last hope was shattered against the granite wall!

Lost in a labyrinth amidst a perfect maze of windings, it was useless to attempt an impossible flight. The most terrible of all deaths stared me in the face! And, strangely enough, the thought crossed me that if some day my fossilized body should see the light, what grave scientific questions would be raised by its discovery thirty leagues below the earth's surface.

I tried to speak aloud, but hoarse accents alone issued from my parched lips. I was gasping for breath.

In the midst of my anguish, a new terror seized me. My lamp had gone wrong when I fell. I could not rectify it, and its light was paling and would soon go out.

I saw the luminous current always diminishing in the coil of the apparatus. A procession of moving shadows appeared on the gloomy walls. I did not dare to close my eyes, dreading to lose the least atom of this fainting light. Every instant it threatened to go out and enwrap me in the blackness of night.

At last there was only a faint glimmer in the lamp. I watched it with trembling eagerness, concentrating all my gaze on it as on the last ray of light that my eyes would ever see before total darkness should fall on me.

What a terrible cry escaped me! On the earth, even in the darkest night, the light never wholly abandons his rule. It is diffused and subtle, but little as may remain, the retina of the eye is sensible of it. Here there was nothing. Absolute darkness made me blind in the literal acceptation of the word.

Then I lost my senses. I got up with outspread arms, endeavouring to feel my way, but the attempt was most painful. I ran along wildly through inextricable labyrinths, always going down deeper into the heart of the earth, like a denizen of the subterranean regions; calling, shouting, howling, striking myself against projecting rocks, falling down and getting up again, feeling the blood trickling from me, and trying to drink it as it dropped from my face, and always expecting to come to some wall to dash my head against.

Whither did the said course lead me? That I am ignorant of to this day.

After several hours, no doubt, when all my powers were exhausted, I fell against the wall like a lifeless mass, and lost all consciousness of existence.

CHAPTER XXVIII

WHEN I REVIVED my face was wet – wet with tears. How long this state of insensibility had lasted I cannot say, I had no longer any means of reckoning time. Never was solitude like mine, never was abandonment so absolute.

After my fall I lost a quantity of blood – I felt myself deluged with it.

Oh! how sorry I was that death had still to come! That it was not over already. I refused to think, I banished every suggestion, and, overcome by grief, I rolled myself towards the opposite wall.

I could feel myself ready to swoon again, and I thought with satisfaction that with it would come the final unconsciousness, when a violent noise struck my ear. It was like a long rolling peal of thunder, and I heard the waves of sound lose themselves, and die away in the distant depths of the abyss.

Whence came the noise? Doubtless from some physical source in the bosom of the terrestrial mass. The explosion of some gas, or the fall of some of the vast beds of the earth's crust.

I listened again. I wanted to know if that noise would be repeated. A quarter of an hour passed. Silence reigned in the gallery. Nothing was audible but the beating of my heart.

Suddenly my ear, which happened to touch the wall, was startled by a sound like distant, undistinguishable, inarticulate words. I trembled.

"Is it a hallucination?" thought I.

But no! On listening more attentively, I could plainly hear a murmur of voices, but I was too weak to make out what was said; but that some one was speaking, I was certain.

I feared for a moment that it might be the sound of my own words brought back by an echo. Perhaps I might unconsciously have cried out. I closed my lips tightly, and again applied my ear to the wall.

Yes! yes! voices undoubtedly!

I dragged myself to some distance along the wall, and then heard the sounds more distinctly. I could catch an indistinct murmur of distorted and unmeaning words. They sounded as if some one was humming them in a low voice. Once or twice I caught the word "forlorad" repeated with an accent of sorrow.

What did it mean? Who was speaking? Clearly either my uncle or Hans. But if I could hear them, surely they might hear me!

"Here!" I called with all my strength. "Here!"

I listened, and watched in the darkness for an answer, a cry, a sigh. Not a sound. A crowd of ideas ran through my brain. I fancied my enfeebled voice could not reach my companions.

"For it is certainly they," said I. "What other mortals would there be here, ninety miles underground?"

I listened again. In trying backwards and forwards along the wall I found a point where the voices appeared to attain their maximum of sound. The word "forlorad" again reached my ear, and the thunder-sound which had at first arrested my attention.

"No!" I exclaimed; "it is not through this rock that I hear the voices. The wall is of granite, and the loudest sound would not penetrate it. The sound comes by way of the gallery itself. There must be a very peculiar acoustic effect!"

I listened once more. Yes! this time I heard my own name distinctly echoed through the gloom!

It was my uncle who uttered it! He was doubtless talking to the guide, and the word "forlorad" was a Danish word.

Then I understood it all. To make them hear me, all I had to do was to speak with my mouth close to the wall, which would serve to conduct my voice, as the wire conducts the electric fluid.

But I had no time to lose. If my companions happened to change their position, even by a few paces, the acoustic phenomenon would have been destroyed. I went close to the wall, and I said, slowly and distinctly:

"Uncle Lidenbrock!"

And I waited with painful anxiety. Sound does not travel quickly here. The density of the atmosphere increases its intensity but not its velocity. A few seconds, which seemed ages, passed, and at last I heard these words:

"Axel! Axel! is that you?"

*   *   *

"Yes! yes!" I answered.

*   *   *

"My child, where are you?"

*   *   *

"Lost in the most intense darkness."

*   *   *

"Where is your lamp?"

*   *   *

"Out!"

*   *   *

"And the brook?"

*   *   *

"Disappeared."

*   *   *

"Axel, my poor lad: take courage!"

*   *   *

"Wait a little; I am exhausted. I have not got strength to answer. But talk to me!"

"Have courage," said my uncle. "Don't try to speak, just listen to me. We searched up and down the gallery, looking for you. We failed to find you. I wept for you, my child! Then we came down again, firing as we came, always supposing you still on the channel of the Hansbach. Now that our voices meet it is by a purely acoustic phenomenon, and we cannot touch hands. But do not despair, Axel! To hear one another is something!"

*   *   *

During this time I had been thinking. A ray of hope, slight indeed, raised my spirits. First of all it was necessary to know one thing. I put my lips to the wall and said:

"Uncle?"

*   *   *

"My child!" he replied, after the lapse of several seconds.

*   *   *

"We must first ascertain what distance separates us."

*   *   *

"That is easy."

*   *   *

"You have your chronometer."

*   *   *

"Yes."

*   *   *

"Well, take it! Call my name, and note the exact moment. I will repeat it the instant I hear it, and you will again note the precise moment."

*   *   *

"Yes! and half the interval between the question and the answer will be the time required for my voice to reach you."

* * *

"Just so, uncle!"

* * *

"Are you ready?"

* * *

"Yes!"

* * *

"Well, listen now; I am going to call out your name!"

* * *

I put my ear to the wall, and as soon as the word "Axel!" reached me I instantly answered "Axel," and then waited.

* * *

"Forty seconds!" said my uncle. "Therefore the sound took twenty seconds to ascend. Now, at the rate of 1,020 feet per second, that makes 20,400 feet, or nearly four miles."

* * *

"Nearly four miles," I murmured.

* * *

"Well, that is a practicable distance, Axel!"

* * *

"But must I go up or down?"

* * *

"Down, and for this reason – we have come upon a vast hollow space, into which several galleries open. The one you have got into must lead here, for I feel certain that all these earth fractures radiate from the immense cavern in which we stand. Rouse yourself and go on. Walk, crawl, slide down steep inclines, if necessary, and you will find our strong arms waiting to support you at the end. Forward, my child, forward!"

* * *

These words filled me with new life.

"Good-bye, uncle," I cried; "I go. When I leave this spot we can speak to each other no more, so adieu!"

* * *

"Till we meet again, Axel!"

* * *

I heard nothing more.

This singular colloquy, uttered in the bowels of the earth,

exchanged at a distance of nearly four miles, ended with words of hope. I thanked God for having led me through the labyrinth of darkness to the only point at which the voices of my companions could reach me.

This astonishing acoustic effect was easily accounted for by physical laws alone; it was produced by the form of the gallery and the conducting power of the rock. There are many instances of imperceptible sounds being conveyed to a distance. I have experienced the phenomenon myself more than once, among others in the gallery of St. Paul's Cathedral in London, and notably in those curious caves in Sicily, and in the labyrinths near Syracuse, of which the most wonderful is known as Dionysius' Ear.

These recollections occur to me, and it seemed obvious that, as my uncle's voice reached me, there could be no solid barrier between us. If I travelled the road by which the sound came, I need not despair to reach him unless my strength failed me.

I rose – I dragged myself rather than walked. The slope was very great, and I let myself slide. After a little the rapidity of my descent was alarmingly increased, and threatened to turn into a falling motion. I had no strength to stop myself.

Suddenly my feet lost their hold. I felt myself rolling, and now and then striking the rough projections of what seemed to be a well, a sort of vertical gallery. My head struck a sharp point of rock, and I lost consciousness.

CHAPTER XXIX

WHEN I CAME to myself I was in semi-darkness, lying on thick rugs. My uncle was watching me, hoping for a sign of life in my face. At my first sigh he took my hand; when I opened my eyes he uttered a joyful cry.

"He lives! he lives!" he exclaimed.

"Yes," I answered, with a feeble effort.

"My child!" said my uncle, pressing me to his heart, "thank heaven you are saved!"

I was deeply touched by the tone in which these words were spoken, and more deeply still by the attentions which accompanied them.

But it required such dangers to excite the professor to such demonstrations.

Then Hans arrived. He saw my hand in that of my uncle. I may say at least that his eyes expressed great satisfaction.

"God-dag," said he.

"Good day, Hans," I whispered. "Good day. And now, uncle, tell me where we are."

"To-morrow, Axel, to-morrow; to-day you are too weak. I have bound up your head with bandages, which must not be disturbed; therefore, try to sleep now, and to-morrow you shall hear all I have to tell."

"Well," said I, "at least tell me what hour – what day is it?"

"Eleven o'clock in the evening, and to-day is Sunday, August 9th; and I will answer no more questions till the 10th of this month."

I was really very weak, and my eyes closed involuntarily. I was in want of a night's rest, so I went to sleep, with the knowledge that I had been four long days in my state of isolation.

Next day, when I awoke, I looked round me. My bed, composed of all the travelling rugs, was situated in a lovely grotto, adorned with magnificent stalactites, and the ground was covered with fine sand. Twilight reigned. No torch nor lamp was lighted, and yet gleams of light seemed to penetrate by a narrow opening in the grotto. I could hear, too, a gentle undefined murmur, like the moan of the waves breaking on the sands, and now and again the whisper of a breeze.

I wondered whether I was really awake, or if I was dreaming still; or if my brain, injured in my fall, was suggesting imaginary sounds. Still, neither my ears nor my eyes could be so far mistaken.

"It is really a gleam of daylight," thought I, "that peeps in at that crevice in the rock! And I am sure that what I hear is the murmur of the waves. There is the whistling of the wind. Can I be deceived? Or are we once more on the surface of the earth? Has my uncle abandoned his expedition, or has he brought it to a satisfactory close?" I was asking myself these questions, to which I could find no answer, when my uncle came in.

"Good morning, Axel," said he, joyously. "I would wager a good deal that you are better."

"Yes, indeed!" said I, sitting up under my blankets.

"That is right. You slept quietly. Hans and I sat beside you in turns, and we have seen you get better step by step."

"In fact, uncle, I feel quite a man again; and you will say so when you see the breakfast I shall make if you give me the chance."

"Certainly, my boy; you shall eat. The fever has left you. Hans has rubbed your wounds with some Icelandic nostrum, of which he knows the secret; and they have cicatrized with wonderful rapidity. Our hunter is very proud, I can tell you."

As he spoke, my uncle prepared some nourishment, which I ate greedily, in spite of his advice, while at the same time I overwhelmed him with questions, which he did his best to answer.

I then learnt that my providential fall had brought me to the end of an almost perpendicular gallery. As I arrived in the midst of an avalanche of stones, the smallest of which would have been sufficient to crush me, it was to be judged that part of the mass had fallen with me.

This fearful mode of locomotion had landed me in the arms of my uncle, where I fell bleeding and inanimate.

"I am truly astonished," said he, "that you were not killed a thousand times over. But, for God's sake, never let us part, for the chances are that we should never meet again."

"Let us never part again!" Then the voyage was not over? I opened my eyes with astonishment, which provoked the question:

"What ails you, Axel?"

"A question that I want to ask. You say I am safe and sound?"

"Beyond a doubt."

"All my limbs uninjured?"

"Certainly."

"And my head?"

"With the exception of some contusions, your head is safe on your shoulders."

"Well, I am afraid my brain is affected."

"Your brain?"

"Yes; we are not on the surface of the earth again?"

"No, indeed!"

"Well – then I am crazy; for I see the light of day, I hear the wind blowing, and the sea breaking."

"Oh! is that all?"

"Well, but explain to me—"

"I will explain nothing, for it is inexplicable; but you will see for yourself, and you will understand that geological knowledge is far from final."

"Let us go out, then," said I, rising suddenly.

"No, Axel, no; the open air might be injurious to you."

"The open air?"

"Yes; the wind is rather strong, and I forbid you to expose yourself."

"But I assure you I am perfectly well."

"A little patience, my boy! If you had a relapse it would be a serious matter for us all, and we cannot afford to lose time, for it may be a long distance across."

"Across?"

"Yes; take another day's rest, and we will embark to-morrow."

"Embark?"

The word made me jump!

What – embark? Had we a river, a lake, a sea at our disposal? Was there a ship anchored in some subterranean port?

My curiosity was strongly excited. My uncle tried in vain to quiet me, and when he at length saw that to deny me would do me more harm than to yield, he gave up the point.

I dressed quickly, and as a precaution wrapped one of the rugs round me and went out of the grotto.

CHAPTER XXX

AT FIRST I could discern nothing. My unaccustomed eyes closed against the light. When I was able to open them I was stunned rather than astonished.

"The sea!" I exclaimed.

"Yes," said my uncle. "The sea of Lidenbrock; and it pleases me to think that no navigator is likely to contest the honour of having discovered it, or deny my right to call it by my name!"

A great sheet of water, the commencement of a lake or ocean, stretched farther than the eye could reach. The shore, sloping gradually, presented to the waves a beach of fine golden sand, strewn with the small shells in which the first created things had lived. The waves broke there with the echoing murmur peculiar to vast hollow spaces. A light spray was blown by the breeze, which sprinkled a few drops on my face. On this gently shelving shore, about 300 yards from the fringe of foam, curved gradually the last undulations of the steep of the rocky counter-scarp, which rose with a widening sweep to an immeasurable height. Some of these had their edges torn into capes and promontories by the beating of the surf, and, farther still, the eye could follow their outlines sharply defined on the cloudy background of the horizon.

It was a real ocean, with the varying contour of terrestrial shores, but lonely and fearfully wild in aspect.

That I could see to a distance along this sea was owing to a "special" light, which irradiated the smallest details. It was not the light of the sun, with his glorious glittering darts, nor the pale, uncertain radiance of the star of night, which is only a cold reflection. No! The illuminating power of this light, its quivering diffusion, its clear, sharp whiteness, the low degree of its temperature, its more than moonlight brightness, all proclaimed its electric origin. It was like a continuous aurora borealis which filled this cavern, so vast in extent as to contain an ocean.

The arch, or sky, suspended over my head seemed composed of great clouds, moving bodies of vapour, which some day would certainly fall, by condensation, in torrents of rain. I should have thought that under such a heavy atmospheric pressure water could not evaporate, and yet, from some physical reason which I was unacquainted with, large clouds were spread above us. But it was then "fine weather". The electric masses produced a wonderful play of light on the very high clouds. Well-defined shadows were thrown on their lower folds, and often between two disjoined layers a gleam of singular brightness was thrown on us. In short, it was not the sun, for there was no heat. The effect was mournful – intensely melancholy. Instead of a sky, bright with stars, I felt that above these clouds was the granite vault crushing me with its weight; and this space, immense though it was, was not large enough for the orbit of the humblest satellite.

I then recalled the theory of an English captain who likened the earth to a vast hollow sphere, in whose interior air maintained its luminosity by reason of its compression; and that two stars,

Pluto and Proserpine, described within this sphere their mysterious orbits. Perhaps he was right, after all. We were really imprisoned in a vast hollow, of whose breadth we could form no
estimate, as the shore widened as far as we could see; nor of its
length, as the eye was soon stopped by an irregular horizon line.
Its height must be eight or nine miles. Where this vault meets
the granite buttresses the eye cannot decide, but a cloud was
suspended in the air, whose height must have been at least 2,000
fathoms, a greater height than is attained by terrestrial vapours,
owing, no doubt, to the greater density of the air.

The word "cavern" does not convey any impression of this
vast space. But the language of human speech is inadequate to
picture what may exist in the subterranean abysses.

Nor could I conjecture what geological cause could have produced this great excavation. Could the cooling process have
induced it? I knew, from the narratives of travellers, of the existence of celebrated caves, but none of them had such dimensions
as this.

If the Guacharo Cave in Colombia, which Von Humboldt
visited, was not exactly ascertained to be 2,500 feet deep, it was
measured with sufficient precision to warrant the assumption
that it was not much beyond that depth. The immense Mammoth Cave in Kentucky boasts of giant proportions, for its arch
rises 500 feet above an unfathomable lake, which has been
followed for thirty miles without coming to the opposite shore.
But what were these compared with the one I was contemplating, with its sky of clouds, its electric irradiation, and its vast
ocean.

I thought silently over all these wonders. I had no words to
express my sensations. I felt as if I had been transported to a
distant planet, Uranus or Saturn, and was gazing on phenomena
of which my Earth-nature had no cognizance. To express such
novel impressions, I wanted new words, and my imagination was
unable to supply them. I looked, I thought, I wondered with
amazement, not unmixed with fear.

The unexpectedness of the spectacle had brought back the hue
of health to my face; astonishment was called to my aid, and
cured me by a new system of therapeutics; and, in addition, the
dense air was a source of invigoration, by furnishing an abundant
supply of oxygen to my lungs.

It will be easy to understand that, after forty-seven days spent in a narrow gallery, there was infinite enjoyment in breathing this moist salt-laden atmosphere.

I had indeed no reason to regret having quitted my dark grotto. My uncle, already accustomed to these wonders, betrayed no surprise.

"Are you able to take a little walk?" he asked.

"Yes, certainly," said I; "and I should like nothing better."

"Well, take my arm, Axel, and let us follow the bend of the shore."

I eagerly consented, and we began to coast along this new sea. On the left, the abrupt rocks, piled one on the other, formed a Titanic group of imposing grandeur; down the sides poured countless waterfalls, which flowed away in clear gurgling streams. Light wreaths of vapour, curling here and there among the rocks, indicated the place of hot springs, and brooks ran down the declivities with a delicious murmur, and lost themselves in the common basin.

Among these rivulets I perceived our faithful travelling companion, the Hansbach, which here merged quietly into the sea, as if it had been doing nothing else since the world began.

"We shall miss it, now," said I, with a sigh.

"Bah!" said the professor, "what matters whether we have that or another?"

I thought him ungrateful. But at this moment my eye was attracted to an unexpected sight. Five hundred paces off, round a high promontory, rose a lofty forest, thick and close. It consisted of trees of medium height, shaped like parasols, with clear geometrical outlines; the wind did not seem to have clipped their leaves, and in the midst of gusts they remained motionless, like a forest of petrified cedars.

I quickened my steps. I could find no name for these singular growths. Did they belong to any of our already known 200,000 species, and were they to have a special place in the flora of lacustrine vegetation? No; when we arrived under their shade, my surprise was not greater than my admiration.

I found myself gazing on terrestrial products, cut on a gigantic pattern. My uncle named them instantly.

"It is nothing but a forest of mushrooms," said he.

He was right. Fancy the development of these cherished plants in a warm damp atmosphere. I knew that the "Lycoperdon giganteum" attains, according to Bulliard, a circumference of nine feet; but these were white mushrooms, thirty or forty feet high, with a head in proportion. They were in millions. The light could not pierce their dense shades, and complete darkness reigned beneath these domes, which lay side by side, like the domed roofs of an African city.

But I was anxious to go farther in. A deathly chill was reflected from these fleshy arches. For half an hour we wandered among the dusky shades, and I felt it quite a relief when we regained the sea-shore.

But the vegetation of this subterranean region did not stop at mushrooms. Farther on rose groups of other trees with dis-coloured foliage. They were easy to recognize – the humble arbutus of the upper earth, but of gigantic proportions; lycopods, 100 feet high; monster sigillarias, tree-ferns as tall as the northern pines; lepidodendrons, with cylindrical forked stems, terminating in long leaves and bristling with rough hairs.

"Astounding, magnificent, splendid!" cried my uncle. "Here is the whole flora of the second epoch – the transition epoch – the humble plants of our gardens which grew as trees in the early ages of the world! Look, Axel, and admire! No botanist in the world ever was at such a show."

"You are right, uncle. Providence seems to have preserved in this great hot-house the antediluvian plants, which scientific men have so successfully reconstructed."

"It is, as you express it, Axel, a vast hot-house; but you might with equal justice call it a menagerie."

"A menagerie?"

"Yes, indeed! Look at the dust beneath our feet – the bones scattered on the ground."

"Bones!" I exclaimed. "Bones of the antediluvian animals?"

I eagerly examined this primeval dust, formed of an indestructible mineral (phosphate of lime), and had no hesitation in naming these immense bones, which only resembled dried-up tree-trunks.

"There," said I, "is the lower jaw of the mastodon; here, the molars of the dinotherium; there is a *femur*, which can only have belonged to a megatherium. Yes, truly, it is a menagerie, for the bones cannot have been brought here by a convulsion of nature.

The animals to which they belonged must have lived on the shore of this subterranean sea, under the shade of the arborescent plants. Look! there are even whole skeletons. And yet—"

"Yet what?" said my uncle.

"I cannot understand the existence of animals in this granite cavern."

"Why not?"

"Because there was no animal life on the earth, except during the secondary period, when the sedimentary formation was produced by the alluvial forces, and replaced the igneous rocks of the primitive epoch."

"Well, Axel! there is a very simple answer to your objection, and that is, that this is a sedimentary formation."

"What, at such a depth below the surface of the earth?"

"Beyond a doubt! and the fact can be geologically explained. At a certain period the earth's crust was elastic, subject to alternate upward and downward movements, by reason of the law of attraction. It is probable that depressions were produced, and that portions of the sedimentary strata were engulfed in abysses opened suddenly."

"That may be so. But if antediluvian animals have lived in these subterranean regions, who can say that some of these monsters are not still wandering in the midst of these gloomy forests, or behind these inaccessible rocks?"

At the bare idea I involuntarily scanned the various points of the horizon, but no living being appeared on the desert shores.

I was a little tired. I went and sat down on the point of a promontory at whose feet the waves dashed with a hoarse noise. Thence I could see the whole of the bay formed by a bend in the coast. At the bottom a little harbour nestled between the pyramidal rocks. Its calm waters were sheltered from the wind. A brig and two or three schooners could have lain at anchor easily. I almost expected to see some ship come out in full sail and put to sea before the southerly wind.

But this illusion was soon dissipated. We were but too surely the only living creatures in this lower world. In a sudden hush of the wind, a stillness more intense than that of the desert fell upon these barren rocks, and hung over the ocean. I tried to see through the distant mists, to pierce the curtain that veiled the mysterious horizon. What questions crowded to my lips? Where did this sea end? Whither did it lead? Should we ever behold the other shore?

My uncle, at any rate, had no misgiving. As for me, I hoped and feared at the same moment.

After an hour passed in gazing on the wondrous panorama, we took the beach road once more to regain the grotto.

CHAPTER XXXI

I AWOKE NEXT day quite recovered. I thought a bath would be of service to me, and I went and took a dip in the waters of the Mediterranean Sea. Of all seas, surely this best deserved the name.

I came back to breakfast with a sharpened appetite. Hans was busy cooking our meal, and having fire and water at his disposal this time, he was able to vary our bill of fare. He supplied us with several cups of coffee, and that delicious beverage never seemed to me so palatable.

"Now," said my uncle, "it is nearly high water, and we must not lose the opportunity of observing the phenomenon."

"What, the tide?" exclaimed I.

"Undoubtedly."

"Do you think the influence of sun and moon is felt in this region?"

"Why not? Every particle of a solid body is governed by the force of attraction. This mass of water cannot escape the universal law, and, therefore, notwithstanding the atmospheric pressure on its surface, you will see it rise just like the Atlantic."

At this moment we reached the sandy shore, and the waves were gradually gaining ground.

"The tide is certainly coming in," said I.

"Yes, Axel, and you may see by these foam streaks that it rises at least ten feet."

"It is wonderful!"

"Not at all; it is in the natural order of things."

"You may say as you will, uncle. I cannot but think it extraordinary; in fact, I can hardly believe my senses. Who would have imagined that beneath the earth's crust there is a real ocean, with its ebb and flow, its breezes and its storms!"

"Why not? Is there any physical reason against it?"

"I know of none, if you abandon the central fire theory."

"Then, so far, Davy's theory is supported?"

"So it would seem; and if that is so, there may be seas and countries in the interior of the globe?"

"Yes, but uninhabited."

"Why so? Why may not these waters contain fish of some unknown species?"

"At any rate, we have met with none, so far."

"Well, we can make some line, and see if the fish-hook will be as successful here as in our sublunary waters."

"We will try, Axel; for we must do our utmost to find out all the secrets of these unexplored regions."

"But where are we, uncle? For I have not yet asked you that question. Your instruments will have told you our whereabouts."

"Our position is, horizontally, 1,050 miles from Iceland."

"So far?"

"I am certain within 500 fathoms."

"And the compass still pointing north-east?"

"Yes, with a western declination of 19° 40', just as on the surface. As to the inclination, there is a curious fact, which I have observed very carefully: the needle, instead of dipping towards the pole, as it does in the northern hemisphere, has an upward direction."

"Then we may conclude that the magnetic pole is a point contained between the surface of the globe and the depth we have reached?"

"Exactly; and I think it very likely that, if we arrived in the polar regions towards that 70th degree, where Sir James Ross discovered the magnetic pole, we should see the needle take a vertical position; therefore, this mysterious point is at no great depth."

"That is a fact which science has never guessed."

"Science, my boy, is made up of mistakes; but of mistakes which lead to the discovery of truth."

"And how far down are we?"

"About 100 miles."

"Well then," said I, after consulting the map, "the mountainous part of Scotland is above us, where the lofty Grampians raise their snowy summits."

"Yes," said the professor, smiling. "There is some weight to carry; but the arch is strong; the great architect of the Universe has used good materials, and no human builder could have given it such a span! What are the great arches of bridges and cathedrals beside this great nave, whose radius is nine miles, and under which there is space for an ocean and its storms?"

"Oh! I am not afraid of the roof falling over my head. But now, uncle, what are your plans? Do you not intend returning to the surface?"

"Returning! What a notion! On the contrary, we will go on, as we have had such luck so far!"

"Still, I do not see how we are to get below this watery plain."

"I do not intend to plunge into it head first; but as oceans are, properly speaking, nothing more than lakes, as they are surrounded by land, no doubt this interior sea is bounded by granitic masses."

"That is probable enough."

"Well then, on the opposite shore I am sure of finding new outlets."

"How long do you guess this ocean to be?"

"From 100 to 120 miles."

"Hem!" said I to myself, thinking that a very wild calculation.

"So you see we have no time to spare; we must put to sea to-morrow."

I involuntarily looked round for the wherewithal.

"Ah!" said I, "we are to embark to-morrow. On what vessel shall we take passage?"

"Not on a vessel, my lad, but on a strong safe raft."

"A raft!" said I, "but we can no more build a raft than a ship, and I don't see—'

"You don't see, Axel, but if you listened, you could hear. Those sounds of hammering might tell you that Hans is already at the work."

"Do you mean that he is making a raft?"

"I do."

"What? Has he felled trees with his axe?"

"Oh! the trees were all ready to his hand. Come and look at him at work."

After a quarter of an hour's walking, and on the farther side of the promontory which enclosed the little port, I could see Hans at work. A few more steps, and I was at his side. To my great surprise, a raft already half-completed lay on the sand! It was made of logs of a peculiar-looking wood, and a vast number of planks, knees, ties, strewed the ground. There was material for a fleet.

"Uncle," said I, "what kind of wood is that?"

"It is pine, fir, birch, all the northern conifers, mineralized by the action of sea-water."

"Is it possible?"

"It is called 'surtur-brand', or fossil wood."

"But, then, like lignite, it must be as hard as stone, and cannot float?"

"Occasionally, that is so. There are woods which become true anthracites; but others, like this, are only partially fossilized. But, look for yourself," said my uncle, throwing into the water one of these precious fragments.

The log first disappeared, then rose to the surface of the waves and followed their undulations.

"Are you satisfied?" said my uncle.

"I am convinced that it is incredible."

The next evening, thanks to the skill of our guide, the raft was ready. It was ten feet long by five feet wide; the logs of surtur-brand, bound each to each with strong rope, offered a solid floor, and once launched, this impromptu vessel floated quietly on the waters of the "Sea of Lidenbrock".

CHAPTER XXXII

ON THE MORNING of August 13 we were early astir. We were to commence our new kind of locomotion – a rapid and easy one.

A mast, made of two logs mortised together; a yard formed by a third, a sail made of one of our rugs, was all our rigging. We had plenty of ropes, and the whole affair was strongly put together.

At six o'clock the professor gave the signal to embark. Our provisions, baggage, instruments, firearms, and a good stock of fresh water collected among the rocks, were arranged on board.

Hans had set up a rudder, so as to be able to guide his vessel. He took the helm. I cast off the rope that moored us to the shore. The sail was set, and we rapidly left the land.

As we quitted the little harbour, my uncle, who made a great point of his geographical nomenclature, wished to fix on a name for it, suggesting mine, among others.

"Uncle," said I, "I beg to propose the name of Gräuben. Port Gräuben would look very well on a map."

"Well, Port Gräuben be it."

And thus it was that the name of my beloved Virlandaise came to be connected with our daring adventure.

A light breeze blew from the north-east. We made rapid way, with the wind aft. The density of the atmospheric strata gave great force, and the wind acted on the sail like an immense ventilator.

An hour enabled my uncle to estimate our speed.

"If this rate continues," said he, "we shall do about ninety miles in twenty-four hours, and shall soon gain the other shore."

I made no reply, but went and stationed myself in the fore-part of the raft. Already the northern shore was sinking below the horizon. The projecting arms of the land opened wide to let us go. A vast extent of ocean was spread before my gaze. Great clouds moved rapidly over its surface, casting grey shadows, which seemed to weigh down the melancholy waste of waters. The silvery rays of the electric light, reflected here and there by the spray, dotted our wake with luminous points. Soon we lost sight of land, and of every point of observation, and but for our track of foam, I could have believed that we were motionless.

Towards noon immense algæ were seen floating on the waves. I was aware of the powerful vitality of their growth, which enables them to exist at a depth of over 12,000 feet, at the bottom of the sea, and to fructify under a pressure of 400 atmospheres; I also knew that they sometimes form beds compact enough to impede the motion of a ship; but I think there can be no algæ so gigantic as those of the "Sea of Lidenbrock".

Our raft passed along by *fuci* 3,000 or 4,000 feet long, great serpentine bands twisting away far out of sight; I tried to follow their endless ribbons and never came to an end, and hour after hour increased my astonishment if not my patience.

What power of nature produces such growths, and what must have been the aspect of the earth in the first ages of its formation, when under the combined action of heat and moisture the vegetable kingdom alone developed on its surface!

Evening came, and, as I remarked the day before, the luminous state of the air seemed to suffer no diminution. It was a constant phenomenon on whose stability we could reckon.

After supper I lay down at the foot of the mast, and soon lost myself in sleep mingled with idle reveries.

Hans, motionless at the helm, had only to leave the raft to itself – the wind being astern we hardly needed steering.

Since leaving Port Gräuben, Professor Lidenbrock had appointed me to keep the "journal on board"; to note every observation; to record all interesting phenomena; the direction of the wind; the speed attained; the distance accomplished; in a word, all the incidents of this novel voyage.

I shall confine myself, therefore, to reproducing these daily notes, written, so to speak, from the dictation of events, so as to give a perfectly exact account of our voyage across this ocean.

Friday, August 14. – Steady breeze from the N.W. The raft goes fast, and in a straight line. We have left the coast ninety miles behind us in the direction of the wind. Nothing on the horizon. The intensity of the light is unvarying. Weather fine, that is, the clouds are high, not dense, and bathed in a white atmosphere like molten silver. Thermometer 58°.

At mid-day, Hans fastened a fish-hook to the end of a rope; he baited it with a morsel of meat and threw it into the sea. After two hours he had taken nothing. Then these waters are uninhabited? No! There is a bite. Hans draws in his line, and behold a fish which resisted violently.

"A sturgeon!" I exclaimed. "A small sturgeon!"

The professor looks, and does not agree with me. This fish has a round, flat head, the back of its body covered with bony plates, teeth wanting, pectoral fins large, no tail. The creature belongs to the order where naturalists have placed the sturgeon, but it differs from the sturgeon in very essential points.

My uncle, after a short examination, pronounced that this animal belongs to a family which has been extinct for centuries, and of which the Devonian beds alone show fossil remains.

"How," said I, "can we have taken a living specimen of an inhabitant of primeval seas?"

"Yes," said the professor, "and you see these fossil fishes have no identity with present species. To have obtained a living specimen is a glad era for a naturalist."

"But to what family does it belong?"

"It is a ganoid, one of the Cephalaspidæ, species Pterichthys, I am sure! But this individual offers a peculiarity common to the fish of all subterranean waters – it is blind! It not only does not see, but the organ of sight is wanting."

I looked closely and saw that this was really the case, but perhaps an exceptional one.

The line is baited again and thrown into the sea. This sea must be well stocked with fish, for in two hours we took a great number of Pterichthys, as well as some others belonging to another extinct family, the Dipteridæ – of what species, however, my uncle was unable to pronounce. All were deficient in organs of vision.

This unexpected take of fish was a welcome addition to our stock of provisions.

Thus much seems certain, that this sea is inhabited only by fossil species, of which the fish and the reptiles are more perfect as their date is more remote. Perhaps we shall meet some of the saurians which science has re-created from a fragment of bone or cartilage!

I take the glass and scan the sea. It is a desert. Perhaps we are still too near the shore. I turn to the air. Why do we see none of the birds reconstructed by the immortal Cuvier, flapping their great wings in this dense atmosphere: these fish would supply them with stores of food. I gaze into space, but the air is as lonely as the waters.

My fancy ran riot among the marvellous hypotheses of palæontology. I dream with my eyes open. I fancy this sea covered with chelonia, those antediluvian turtles that resembled floating islands. I peopled its gloomy strand with the giant mammifers of ancient times, the leptotherium, found in Brazilian caves, the mericotherium, from the icy region of Siberia. And, farther on, the pachydermatous lophiodon (the gigantic tapir) hides itself behind the rocks, ready to tear the prey from the anoplotherium, a strange animal akin to the rhinoceros, the horse, the hippopotamus, and the camel, as if in the hurry of creation one animal had been made up of several. The giant mastodon writhed his trunk and ground his tusks on the rocky shore, while the megatherium, propped on his mighty paws, turns up the earth, and roars till the granite echoes to the sound.

The whole fossil world lives again in my imagination. I go back in fancy to the biblical epoch of creation, long before the advent of man, when the imperfect earth was not fitted to sustain him. Then still farther back, to the time when no life existed. The mammifers disappeared, then the birds, then the reptiles of the secondary epoch, and then the fishes, crustaceans, molluscæ, articulata. The zoophytes of the transition period returned to oblivion. All life was concentrated in me, my heart alone beat in a depopulated world. Seasons were no more; climates were unknown; the heat of the earth increased till it neutralized that of our radiant star. Vegetation was gigantic. I passed under the shade of tree-ferns, trampling with uncertain step iridescent clay and particoloured sand: I leaned against the trunks of immense conifers; I lay down in the shade of sphenophylles, asterophylles, and lycopods 100 feet high.

Ages seemed to pass like days! I followed step by step the trans-formation of the earth. Plants disappeared; granite rocks lost their hardness: the fluid replaced the solid under the influence of growing heat; water flowed over the earth's surface; it boiled, it volatilized; gradually the globe became a gaseous mass, white hot, as large and as luminous as the sun.

In the centre of the nebulous mass, 14,000 times larger than the earth it was one day to form, I felt myself carried into plan-etary space. My body became ethereal in its turn and mingled like an imponderable atom with the vast body of vapour which described its flaming orbit in infinite space!

What a dream! Where is it carrying me? My feverish hand tries to note a few of the wild details. I was unconscious of all around – professor, guide, raft – everything. My mind was under a hallucination.

"What ails you?" said my uncle.

My staring eyes were fixed on him without seeing.

"Take care, Axel, you will fall into the sea!"

At this moment I felt Hans' strong grip on my arm. But for him, the delirium of my dream would have made me jump overboard.

"Has he lost his senses?" cried the professor.

"What is it?" said I at last, regaining consciousness.

"Are you ill?"

"No; I had a moment of hallucination, but it is over now. Is all going well?"

"Yes; a good breeze and a calm sea; and if my calculation is correct we shall not be long before we touch land."

As he spoke I rose and carefully scrutinized the horizon, but, as before, the line of sea is lost in the clouds.

CHAPTER XXXIII

Saturday, August 15. – The sea preserves its dreary monotony! No land in sight. The horizon looks very distant.

My head is heavy from the excitement of my dream. My uncle had no dream, but he is out of humour. He sweeps the horizon with his glass, and crosses his arms with an air of vexation.

I remark in Professor Lidenbrock a tendency to become, as of old, a man impatient of the past, and I record the fact in my journal. My danger and my sufferings barely sufficed to draw from him a spark of humanity; but since my recovery his nature has got the upper hand again. And yet what has he to complain of? Our voyage has been most favourable, and the raft sails with wondrous rapidity.

"You seem uneasy, uncle?" said I, seeing him constantly using his glass.

"Uneasy? Oh no!"

"Impatient, then?"

"One might be impatient with less reason."

"And yet our speed?"

"What is the speed to me? The speed is well enough, but the sea is too vast."

I remembered that the professor, before our departure, estimated the length of this subterranean sea at about 100 miles. We had sailed three times that distance, and the southern shore was not yet in view.

"We are not descending," said the professor. "All this is lost time, and in fact I did not come so far to make one of a boating party on a pond."

"But," said I, "if we have followed the route pointed out by Saknussemm—"

"That is the very question. Have we followed his route? Did he meet with this ocean? Did he cross it? Did the stream we followed mislead us utterly?"

"At any rate, we have no reason to regret having come so far. The scene is grand. . . ."

"The question is not of scenery. I have an object in view, and I wish to attain it. Don't talk to me of scenery."

I took the hint, and left the professor to bite his lips in silence. At six o'clock Hans claimed his wages, and his three rix-dollars were counted out to him.

Sunday, August 16. – Nothing new. Weather continues the same. Wind tends slightly to freshen. When I awake, my first thought is to observe the intensity of the light. I always fear the electric phenomenon may decrease, and die away. But there is no diminution. The shadow of the raft is sharply defined on the waves.

This sea seems boundless. It must be as large as the Mediterranean, or even the Atlantic. Why not?

My uncle has repeatedly taken soundings. He fastened one of our heaviest pickaxes to a long rope, and let out 200 fathoms. No bottom! We had great difficulty in hauling in the line. When the axe came up, Hans called my attention to some strongly-defined marks on its surface. It had the appearance of having been strongly compressed between two hard surfaces. I looked at the hunter.

"*Täuder!*" said he.

I did not understand. I turned to my uncle, but he was absorbed. I did not care to disturb him. I came back to my Icelander, who opened and closed his mouth, and I at last understood him.

"Teeth!" said I, with amazement, and looking more closely at the iron bar.

Yes! it was certainly teeth that made that impression. What prodigious power of jaw! Are some of those extinct monsters lying at the bottom of this deep ocean – monsters more voracious than the shark, more formidable than the whale? My eyes were fascinated to that half-gnawed bar. Is my dream of last night to be realized?

These thoughts agitated my mind all day, and my imagination only calmed down after a sleep of several hours' duration.

Monday, August 17. – I am trying to recollect the peculiar instincts of the antediluvian animals of the secondary period which, following the mollusca, the crustaceans, and the fish, preceded the appearance of the mammifers on the globe. These monsters were the monarchs of the Jurassic seas*. Nature furnishes them with the most complete organization. What giant forms! What enormous power! The saurians of our day, alligators or crocodiles, the largest and most formidable, are only feeble miniatures of their primeval ancestors!

I shudder at the phantoms I have evoked. No human eye has seen their living forms. They appeared on earth countless ages before man, but their fossil skeletons found in the calcareous clays known as *Lias* have allowed us to reconstruct them anatomically, and to become acquainted with their colossal figures.

I have seen, in the Hamburg Museum, the skeleton of one of these saurians, that measured thirty feet in length. Am I destined to behold face to face these representatives of an antediluvian family? No, it is impossible. And yet the mark of mighty teeth is stamped on that iron bar, and their impress shows that the teeth are conical like those of the crocodile.

I gazed nervously at the sea. I feared to see one of these inhabitants of submarine caves.

I suppose Professor Lidenbrock was struck with the same idea, though not by the same fears, for when he had examined the pickaxe, he threw a glance round on the ocean.

"What possessed him to take soundings," thought I; "he has disturbed some animal in its retreat, and if we are not attacked—"

I looked over our firearms to satisfy myself that they were in good order. My uncle observed me, and nodded approbation.

Already long swells on the surface of the sea indicated disturbances in the depths. The danger is at hand! We must be watchful!

Tuesday, August 18. – Evening came, or rather there came the moment when sleep weighed down our eyelids, for there is no night on this ocean, and the unvarying light fatigues our eyes, as if we were voyaging on the Arctic Seas. Hans was at the helm. During his watch I went to sleep.

Two hours after, I was awakened by a fearful shock. The raft was lifted off the water with indescribable force, and thrown on the waves again forty yards off.

"What is the matter?" cried my uncle. "Have we struck?"

---

* Seas of the secondary period, which formed the strata of which the Jura Mountains are composed.

Hans pointed to a dusky mass about 400 yards off, which rose and fell alternately. I looked, and then exclaimed:

"It is a colossal porpoise!"

"Yes," said my uncle, "and there is a sea-lizard of uncommon size."

"And beyond that a monstrous crocodile! See the great jaws and the rows of teeth! Ah! he is gone."

"A whale! a whale!" exclaimed the professor. "I see his enormous fins! And see the jets of air and water he expels from his blowholes."

I saw two liquid columns rising to a considerable height in the air. We stood, amazed, helpless, terrified in the presence of these monsters of the sea. They were of supernatural size, and the smallest of them could have crushed our raft with a snap of his teeth. Hans wanted to turn up into the wind to escape this dangerous neighbourhood; but on that side, new enemies, no less formidable, came into view; a turtle, forty feet long, a serpent, thirty feet, who moved his enormous head with a darting motion above the waves.

Flight was impossible. The reptiles were drawing nearer, they circled round the raft with a rapidity unequalled by an express train, they described concentric circles round us. I took my carbine. But what effect would a ball have on the scale-armour of these creatures?

We were dumb with fear. They came nearer! The crocodile on one side, the serpent on the other. The rest disappeared. I was about to fire. Hans stopped me by a sign. The monsters passed within 100 yards of the raft, fell on one another, and in their fury they overlooked us. The battle was fought 200 yards away from us. We could distinctly see the struggles of these monsters. But as I watched, it appeared to me that other creatures came and took part in the contest – the porpoise, the whale, the lizard, the turtle. I had momentary glimpses of them all. I pointed them out to Hans. He shook his head.

"*Tva!*" said he.

"What! two? He says there are only two."

"He is right," said my uncle, whose glass had never left his eyes.

"You are jesting, uncle."

"No! the one has the muzzle of a porpoise, the head of a lizard, the teeth of a crocodile, and that deceived us. It is the most formidable of all the antediluvian reptiles – the ichthyosaurus!"

"And the other?"

"The other is his great antagonist, a serpent hidden in the carapace of a turtle, whom we know as the plesiosaurus."

Hans was right. Two monsters only made all this commotion in the sea, and I really beheld two reptiles of the primitive age. I saw the bloodshot eye of the ichthyosaurus, as big as a man's head. Nature has provided him with an optic apparatus of great power, and capable of resisting the pressure of the water at the depth he inhabits. He has been justly named the whale of the saurians, for he has the shape and the speed. His jaw is enormous, and naturalists tell us he has no less than 182 teeth.

The plesiosaurus is a serpent with a cylindrical trunk, short tail, and claws arranged like oars; his body is entirely covered by the carapace, and his neck, as flexible as that of the swan, stretches to a height of thirty feet above the waves.

These animals fought with incredible fury, they raised mountainous waves, which flowed back towards the raft; hissing sounds of great force were heard. The two brutes had closed with each other. I could not distinguish one from the other. We had still to fear the fury of the victor.

An hour, two hours passed: the battle still raged with unabated vehemence. The combatants sometimes veered towards us, and sometimes away from us. We remained motionless, ready to fire.

Suddenly the two monsters disappeared, creating a maëlstrom in the waters. Some minutes elapsed. Were they fighting it out down below?

All at once an enormous head darted up – the head of the plesiosaurus. The great creature is mortally wounded. I could see nothing of his gigantic carapace, only his long neck, which rose and fell, curved and lashed the waters like a mighty whip, and writhed like a divided worm. The water was dashed to a considerable distance. It blinded us. But soon the struggles of the enormous body drew to an end; his motions diminished, his contortions became fewer, and his long serpent neck lay an inert mass on the calm waves.

As to the ichthyosaurus, we asked ourselves whether he had reached his submarine cavern, or whether he would again show himself on the surface.

CHAPTER XXXIV

Wednesday, August 19. – Fortunately the wind, which is blowing pretty fresh, has enabled us to make a rapid flight from the scene of the conflict. Hans is still at the helm. My uncle, who had been aroused from his absorbing reflections by the incidents of the struggle, relapsed into his impatient watching of the sea.

The voyage is as monotonous as ever, but I should not care to have the dreariness varied at the price of yesterday's dangers.

Thursday, August 20. – Breeze N.N.E. unsteady. Temperature hot. We are going about nine miles and a half per hour.

Towards mid-day we heard a very distant sound. I note the fact here without being able to account for it. It is like a continuous roar.

"There must be in the distance," said the professor, "some rock or island on which the sea breaks."

Hans crawled up the mast but could see no breakers. The ocean is undisturbed as far as the eye can reach.

Three hours pass, the noise assumes the sound of a far-off fall of water. I remark this to my uncle, who shakes his head, but I am convinced I am right. Are we running towards some cataract which will precipitate us into an abyss? Such a descent may suit the professor, as it approaches the vertical, but as for me –

Whatever it is, there must be a few miles off a phenomenon of a noisy kind, for now we can hear a violent roaring sound. Does it come from sky or sea?

I look towards the vapour suspended in the atmosphere and try to estimate its depth. The sky is tranquil. The clouds, which have risen to the roof of the vault, seem motionless, and are lost in intensity of light. Not there can I find the cause of the phenomenon.

Then I turn to the horizon, now clear and free from mist. Its aspect is quite normal. But if this noise comes from a fall or a cataract, or if the waters of this sea fall into a lower basin, if these roarings are produced by a falling mass of water, the current ought to increase, and its rate of acceleration may give us the measure of our danger. I try the experiment. There is no current; a bottle thrown into the water remains unaffected by aught but the wind.

About four o'clock Hans rises, takes a grip of the mast, and goes to the top. Thence his eyes wander over the circle of the ocean; at a certain point they stop. No surprise is visible on his face, but his eye is riveted.

"He sees something," said my uncle.

"I think so."

Hans came down. Then he extended his arm to the south and said:

"*Der nere.*"

"Down there?" said my uncle.

And seizing his glass he gazed attentively for a minute; which seemed to me an age.

"Yes, yes!" cried he.

"What do you see?"

"An enormous jet of water rising above the waves."

"Another marine animal?"

"Perhaps."

"Well, then, let us keep her head more to the west, for we have had experience enough of the danger of meeting the antediluvian monsters."

"No," said my uncle; "let her go."

I turned towards Hans – he kept the tiller with inflexible steadiness. But I cannot conceal from myself that if, at this distance, which must be thirty-six miles at the very least, we can discern the column of water he ejects, the creature must be of preternatural size. To fly would only be to obey the dictates of vulgar prudence. But we did not come here to be prudent.

So on we went. The nearer we approached, the higher the jet of water became.

What monster could imbibe and expel without cessation such a mass of water?

At eight o'clock in the evening we were not six miles from him. His enormous body, a dark mountainous mass, lay along the sea like an island. Am I under an illusion? Has fear got the better of me? His length seems to be over 2,000 yards. What great cetacean can it be, never predicated by Cuvier or Blumenbach. It is motionless, perhaps asleep; the sea cannot lift it, for the waves break on its flanks. The jet of water rising 500 feet high, falls again in rain with a deafening noise. And we are running madly on towards this mighty mass, which 100 whales would not suffice to feed for a day.

Terror seized me. I would go no farther. I resolved to cut the halyard, if necessary. I attacked my uncle, who made no answer.

All at once Hans rose, and pointing with his finger to the spot where the danger lay:

"*Holm!*" said he.

"An island!" cried my uncle.

"An island," I repeated, shrugging my shoulders.

"To be sure it is," said the professor, bursting into a laugh.

"But the column of water?"

"*Geyser,*" said Hans.

"Undoubtedly a 'geyser', like those in Iceland."

At first I was annoyed at having mistaken an island for a marine monster. But I cannot help myself, and must own my error. It is nothing but a natural phenomenon.

As we drew near, the dimensions of the liquid shaft became really grand. The island bears a wonderful resemblance to an immense cetacean, whose head rises sixty feet out of the water. The "geyser", which in Icelandic signifies "fury", rises majestically at its extremity. Muffled sounds of explosion occurred every moment, and the enormous jet rose with greater force, convulsed its canopy of vapour, and leaped up to the lower clouds. It was a solitary geyser. Neither fumerolles nor hot springs surround it. All the volcanic force is centred in itself. The rays of the electric light mingled with this dazzling fountain, investing every drop with the hues of the rainbow.

"Let us go round the island," said the professor.

But we had to be very careful to avoid the falling waters, which would have sunk the raft in a moment. Hans managed, with great skill, to bring us to the other end of the island. I jumped on the rock. My uncle followed me quickly, but the hunter stayed at his post like a man superior to such excitements.

We trod a granite soil mixed with silicious tufa. The ground vibrated beneath our feet, like the sides of a boiler full of superheated steam. The heat is intense. We came in sight of a small central basin, whence rises the geyser. I immersed our thermometer in the water, which runs away bubbling as it goes, and it marked 233°.

So that this water must come from a burning centre – contrary to the theory of Professor Lidenbrock. I could not refrain from giving utterance to this remark.

"Well," said he, "what does that prove against my doctrine?"

"Oh, nothing!" said I, perceiving that he was past reasoning with.

Nevertheless, I cannot deny that up to this time we have been singularly fortunate, and that for some reason unknown to me, we have made this voyage under peculiar conditions of temperature. But I look upon it as certain that we must, one time or other, arrive at the region where the central heat attains the greatest point, and leaves far behind all the gradations of our thermometers.

"We shall see." So the professor says. He has given his nephew's name to this volcanic isle, and now orders us to re-embark.

I stayed a few minutes longer to watch the geyser. I remark that its jets are irregular – sometimes the force is diminished, sometimes increased. And I attribute these variations to the fluctuating pressure of the vapours accumulated in the reservoir.

At last we start, making a circuit by the steep rocks at the southern end. Hans has taken advantage of our halt to repair the raft.

But before leaving I took some observation to ascertain the distance we had come, and I note them in my journal. We have made over 800 miles since leaving Port Gräuben, and we reckon that we are under England, 1,800 miles from Iceland.

CHAPTER XXXV

Friday, August 21. – Next day the magnificent geyser was out of sight. The wind freshened, and carried us rapidly away from Axel Island. The roaring sound died away gradually.

The weather, if I may use the expression, will soon change. The atmosphere is dense with vapours charged with the electricity generated by saline evaporation; the clouds are slowly falling, and are of a uniform olive tint. The electric rays can scarcely penetrate them; they look like a dark curtain let down before the stage on which the drama of the Tempest is to be played.

I have the kind of premonitory sensation that animals have

previous to a shock of earthquake. The "cumuli"* heaped up towards the south have a threatening look – they have the pitiless expression that I have so often noticed before a storm. The air is oppressive, and the sea calm.

In the distance the clouds resemble great bales of cotton piled up in picturesque disorder; gradually they swell, and lose in number what they gain in magnitude; they become so heavy that they lie close to the horizon, but the upper current seemed to melt them into a dark formless bank of cloud full of evil boding; now and then a ball of vapour, still illumined, will roll for a moment on the grey background, and then lose itself in the opaque mass.

The atmosphere is saturated with electric fluid, and my body also. My hair stands up as if an electric machine were at hand. I feel as if I should give a violent shock to my companions if they touched me.

At ten o'clock this morning the signs of a storm became more decisive – the wind seemed as if it paused to take breath. The cloud looked like a great bag in which the tempests were collected together. I tried not to believe in the stormy promise of the sky, but I could not help saying:

"Bad weather is brewing there!"

The professor did not answer. He is in an insufferably bad humour at seeing the sea extending farther and farther as we go. He shrugged his shoulders at my words.

"We shall have a storm," said I, pointing to the horizon. "Those clouds bear down on the sea as if they would crush it."

General silence. The wind has now died away. Nature has a death-like appearance, and seems not to draw a breath. From the mast, where I already see a faint halo like St. Elmo's fire, the sail is hanging in heavy folds. The raft lies motionless on the deep waveless sea. But if we are not stirring, why keep our sail up, and thus run the risk of destruction at the first blast of the storm?

"Let us take in the sail and lower the mast," said I. "It would only be prudence."

"No! by all the powers!" said my uncle; "a hundred times no! Let me only behold the rocks of the shore, and I care not if the raft is shivered into a thousand pieces."

* Clouds of a rounded form.

He had scarcely said the words, when the southern horizon underwent a change. The accumulated vapours descended in rain, and the air, rushing in to fill their place, produced a hurricane. It came from every quarter of the cavern. The darkness increased. I could do no more than make a few imperfect notes.

Suddenly the raft rises – makes a bound – my uncle is thrown down. He takes firm hold of a cable, and watches with delight the spectacle of the elements at war!

Hans does not stir. His long hair, beaten by the wind and driven across his stolid face, gives him a weird look, for at the end of every hair is a luminous tuft. He looks like an antediluvian man, a contemporary of the ichthyosaurus and the megatherium. The mast still survives. The sail swells out like a bubble on the verge of bursting. The raft spins along with a speed I cannot attempt to estimate; the water rushing past seems to fly faster still; it describes sharp, clear, arrowy lines.

"The sail! the sail!" I exclaim, making signs to lower it.

"No," said my uncle.

"*Nej*," said Hans, gently shaking his head.

The rain is like a roaring cataract between us and the horizon to which we are madly rushing. But before it reaches us, the cloud curtain tears apart and reveals the boiling sea; and now the electricity, disengaged by the chemical action in the upper cloud strata, comes into play. Loud claps of thunder; dazzling coruscations; networks of vivid lightnings; ceaseless detonations; masses of incandescent vapour; hailstones, like a fiery shower, rattling among our tools and firearms. The heaving waves look like craters full of interior fire, every crevice darting a little tongue of flame.

My eyes are dazzled by the intensity of the light, my ears deafened by the crash of the thunder. I have to hold firmly by the mast, which is bending like a reed before the tornado.

* * *

[Here my notes of the voyage become very fragmentary. I can only find a few fugitive remarks, which appear to have been written almost mechanically. But in their brevity, and even in their obscurity, they bear the impress of the excitement of the time, and portray my feelings better than I could do from memory.]

* * *

CHAPTER XXXVI

WHITHER ARE WE going? We are carried along with inconceivable rapidity.

The night has been appalling, and the storm gives no sign of abating. We live in an atmosphere of deafening sound – a ceaseless thunder. Our ears are bleeding. We cannot hear each other speak.

The lightning is incessant. I see flashes which describe a kind of backward zigzag, and, after a rapid course, seemed to return upward as if they would rive the granite vault above us. If that vault should be rent, what would become of us! Sometimes the lightning is forked, and sometimes takes the form of fiery globes which explode like so many bomb-shells, but whose report is lost amid the roar of the elements. The human ear can no longer measure the increment of sound. If all the powder magazines in the world were to blow up, I believe we should fail to perceive the shock. The surface of the clouds is constantly emitting scintillations of electric light. Their molecules seem continually to disengage electricity. The air seems parched, and countless jets of water are thrown up into the atmosphere and fall again in foam. Again I ask myself, "Whither are we tending?"

. . . My uncle lies stretched at full length on the raft.

The heat increases. On consulting the thermometer I find it marks. . . . [the figures are effaced].

Monday, August 24. – The storm has not ceased. It seems strange that after any modification in this dense atmosphere there does not come some definitive change.

We are broken down with fatigue. Hans is much as usual. The raft keeps driving to the south-east. We have already made more than 600 miles since leaving Axel Island.

At mid-day, the hurricane acquired tenfold force. We were obliged to make fast every article of cargo, and also to lash ourselves to the raft. The sea was washing over us.

For three whole days we had been unable to exchange a syllable. Even a word shouted in the ear was inaudible. My uncle leaned over to me, and said something. I fancied it was "We are lost!" I am not certain. It occurred to me to write the words, "Let us take in our sail." He nodded assent.

He had scarcely raised his head again, when a fiery disc appeared on the edge of the raft. The mast and the sail were swept away together, and I saw them flying at an immense distance above, looking like a pterodactyl, the primeval bird of whom geologists tell us.

We were petrified with fear. The great ball, half fiery white, half azure blue, the size of a ten-inch shell, moved slowly, spinning with great velocity. It was now here, now there – up on the timbers of the raft, over on the bag of provisions; then it glanced lightly down, made a bound, grazed the case of gunpowder. Horror! we shall be blown to atoms! No! the dazzling disc retreated, approached Hans, who stared calmly at it; then my uncle, who crouched on his knees to avoid it; then myself, pale and shuddering at the glare and the glow; it gyrated close to my foot, which I was powerless to withdraw.

An odour of nitrous gas filled the air. It attacked the throat and lungs; we were all but suffocated.

What can it be that hinders me from moving my foot? It feels as if riveted to the raft! I have it! The contact of this electric body has magnetized all the iron on board. Our tools, our firearms were stirred, clicking as they touched each other; the nails of my boots had forcibly adhered to a plate of iron sunk in the timber. I cannot stir my foot!

At length, by a violent effort, I succeeded in tearing it away, just as the ball was preparing to strike me in its next gyration, if—

Oh, what intensity of light! The ball bursts! We are covered with jets of flame. Then all was dark. I had just time to discern my uncle stretched on the raft, Hans motionless at the tiller, and "spitting fire" under the influence of the electricity which pervaded his body.

Again I exclaim, "Where are we going?"

Tuesday, August 25. – I have just recovered from a prolonged swoon; the lightnings are let loose in the atmosphere like a brood of serpents.

Are we still at sea? Yes, driving on with incredible swiftness. We have passed under England, under the British Channel, under France, perhaps under all Europe!

* * *

A new sound greets our ears. Surely the roar of breakers! But in that case

CHAPTER XXXVII

HERE ENDS WHAT I call "my journal on board," which fortunately has been saved from the wreck. I take up my narrative as before.

What happened after the raft struck on the rocks I can scarcely tell. I felt that I was thrown among the breakers, and if I escaped death, if my body was not mangled by the pointed rocks, it was the strong arm of Hans that plucked me from the waters.

The courageous Icelander carried me beyond the reach of the waves, and laid me on a burning, sandy shore, where I found myself side by side with my uncle.

Then he returned to the rocks, where the angry sea was dashing, in order to try and save some waifs from the wreck. I could not speak. I was worn out with excitement and fatigue; it was more than an hour before I recovered my faculties.

Even at this time a deluge of rain was falling, but with that accumulated force that betokens the end of the storm. Some rocks piled on others afforded us a shelter from the torrent. Hans prepared some food which I could not touch, and then, exhausted by our three nights' watch, we fell into a troubled sleep.

Next day the weather was glorious. Sky and sea united in soft repose. All trace of the tempest was dissipated. Such was the joyful news with which the professor greeted me on awaking. His gaiety jarred on my nerves.

"Well, my lad," said he, "I hope you slept well."

He spoke as if we were at home in the Königstrasse, and that I had just come down to breakfast on my wedding morning with poor Gräuben. Alas! if the storm has only impelled the raft to the eastward we should have passed under Germany – under my beloved town of Hamburg – perhaps under the very street where dwells all that is dearest to me in the world. Then there would only have been 120 miles between us – but 120 vertical miles through a granite wall, and in reality we had more than 3,000 miles to travel!

All these melancholy thoughts flashed through my mind before I replied to my uncle's question.

"Well," said he. "I asked you how you slept?"

"Very well," said I. "I am knocked up; but that is nothing."

"Nothing at all; merely a little fatigue."

"You seem in great spirits this morning, uncle," said I.

"Delighted, my lad! Delighted! We have arrived!"

"At the end of our expedition?"

"No, but at the end of the weary sea. We shall now resume our land journey; and, this time, we shall penetrate into the bowels of the earth."

"But, uncle, may I ask you a question?"

"You may, Axel."

"How are we to get back?"

"Get back! Is your mind on getting back before we have even arrived at our journey's end?"

"No; I merely wanted to know how it is to be accomplished."

"The simplest thing in the world. Once arrived at the centre of the spheroid, we shall discover a new route whereby to regain the surface; or else we shall return in a commonplace manner by the same road by which we came. It will not be closed behind us, that is one comfort."

"In that case the raft must be made tight."

"Of course."

"But have we provision for all this travelling?"

"We have. Hans is a right clever fellow, and I am sure he has saved the greatest part of our cargo. However, come and let us see."

We left the windy grotto. I had a hope, which was almost a fear. It seemed to me impossible that anything on board the raft could have survived that terrible landing. I was wrong. When I reached the beach, Hans was in the midst of a mass of objects arranged in order. My uncle pressed his hand with the liveliest gratitude. This man, whose superhuman devotion is probably without a parallel, had toiled while we slept, and had saved all that was most precious to us, at the risk of his own life.

Not that we had not serious losses. Our firearms, for example; but those we could do without. The powder was uninjured, having missed explosion during the storm.

"Well," exclaimed the professor, "as the guns are gone, we cannot be expected to go hunting; that is something."

"That is all very well," said I, "but what of our instruments?"

"Here is the manometer, the most useful of all, and for which I would have given all the rest. Having that, I can calculate our depth, and ascertain when we are at the centre. Without it we should run the risk of coming out at the antipodes."

His joking manner appeared to me ferocious.

"And the compass?" said I.

"Here it is on the rock, quite unharmed, and the chronometer and thermometer. Oh, the hunter is an invaluable fellow!"

This could not be gainsayed. Not one of our instruments was missing. As to tools and implements, I saw scattered on the sand, ladders, ropes, pickaxes, mattocks, &c.

There only remained the victualling question.

"And the provisions?" said I.

"Ay! let me see the provisions," said my uncle.

The cases which contained them were lying in a row on the strand in a perfect state of preservation. The sea had spared them for the most part; and taking everything together – biscuit, salt meat, geneva, and dried fish – we had sufficient for four months.

"Four months!" cried the professor. "Why, we have enough to go and come back; and with what is left I will give a grand dinner to my colleagues at the Johannæum."

I ought to have been used to my uncle's eccentricities by this time, but still they never ceased to surprise me.

"Now," said he, "we can replenish our water stores from the granite basins which the storm has filled with rain; so we are in no danger of suffering from thirst. As to the raft, I should recommend Hans to make the best job he can of it, although I do not at all expect to want it again."

"Why not?" said I.

"A fancy of mine, my boy. I do not think we shall come out where we came in."

I looked at the professor with great misgiving. I wondered if he had gone crazed, but he spoke quite collectedly.

"Let us go to breakfast," said he.

I followed him to a high promontory after he had given directions to the hunter.

There, dried meat, biscuit, and tea made up an excellent meal, one of the best I ever made in my life. Fasting, the fresh air, and rest following strong excitement, all combined to give me an appetite.

During breakfast I questioned my uncle as to the means of ascertaining where we were at this moment.

"That," said I, "seems to me very difficult to calculate."

"Well, yes; to calculate exactly," he answered; "in fact it would be impossible, because during the three days' storm, I could take no note of the rate or direction of our course; but still, by reckoning, we can estimate our position approximately."

"Our last observation was taken at the Geyser Island—"

"At Axel Island, my lad. Do not decline the honour of giving your name to the first island discovered in the centre of the earth."

"Be it so. At Axel Island we had crossed 810 miles of sea, and we were more than 1,800 miles from Iceland."

"Just so; therefore, starting from that point, let us reckon four days of storm, during which our speed was certainly not less than 240 miles in the twenty-four hours."

"I think that is about it. So that will be 900 miles to add."

"Yes, the 'Sea of Lidenbrock' must be 1,800 miles across! Do you know, Axel, it will rival the Mediterranean."

"Yes, especially if we have only crossed the breadth."

"Which is quite possible."

"Another curious thing," said I, "if our calculations are correct, the Mediterranean must be just over our heads."

"Really!"

"Yes, for we are 2,700 miles from Reikiavik!"

"That is a good step from here, my lad; but whether we are under the Mediterranean rather than under Turkey or under the Atlantic, we cannot decide unless we are sure that we have not deviated from our course."

"Well, it is easy to ascertain by looking at the compass. Let us go and see."

The professor made for the rock on which Hans had arranged the instruments. He was lively, sprightly, rubbed his hands, threw himself into attitudes as he went! He was young again. I followed him, anxious to know if my calculation was correct.

Arrived at the rock, my uncle took up the compass, laid it horizontally, and watched the needle, which, after a few oscillations, settled itself into its place. My uncle gazed; he rubbed his eyes, and looked again. Then he turned to me with a bewildered air.

"What ails you, uncle?" said I.

He motioned me to look at the instrument. I uttered an

exclamation of astonishment. The needle indicated north, where we had believed the south to be. It turned to the shore instead of to the open sea.

I shook the compass. I examined it; it was in good order. No matter which way I turned it, it persisted in making this unexpected declaration.

We could only conclude that during the tempest we had failed to note the change of wind which had brought back the raft to the shore, which my uncle hoped he had left behind him.

CHAPTER XXXVIII

NO WORDS COULD depict the succession of emotions which agitated the professor – bewilderment, incredulity, rage. I never saw a man so discomfited at first or so enraged afterwards. After all the fatigues of the journey, all the risks we had run, all must be done over again! We had gone back instead of forward.

My uncle soon recovered himself.

"What a trick fate has played me! The very elements are against me. The air, the fire, the water conspire to bar my passage. Well! they shall know what my will can accomplish! I will not yield: I will not go back a step, and we shall see whether man or nature will win."

Standing upright on the rock, betraying his irritation by his menacing attitude, Otto Lidenbrock reminded me of Ajax defying the gods. I thought it time to interpose and put a check on his mad enthusiasm.

"Listen to me, uncle," said I, in a steadfast voice. "There is a limit to human ambition; it is useless to struggle after the impossible; we are badly equipped for a sea-voyage; 1,500 miles cannot be done on a raft of unsound timbers, with a rag of blanket for a sail and a stick for a mast, and in the face of all the winds of heaven let loose. We have no means of steering, we are the plaything of the storm, and it is the height of madness to attempt the voyage a second time!"

I set forth all this without interruption for about ten minutes, but this was owing solely to the inattention of the professor, who did not hear one word of my arguments.

"To the raft!" cried he.

That was his answer. In vain I entreated him to desist. In vain I stormed, in vain I spent my strength in warring against a will harder than granite. Hans had just completed his repairs of the raft. It was as if this whimsical being had divined my uncle's plans. With some pieces of surtur-brand, he had strengthened the vessel. A sail was already spread, and was flapping in the breeze.

The professor gave a few directions to the guide, who immediately put our belongings on board, and made everything ready for a start. The air was pretty clear, and the north-west wind held.

What could I do? How could I alone make head against these two? Impossible, even if Hans had sided with me. But the Icelander seemed to have put away all individual will, and taken a vow of abnegation. I could do nothing with a servant so enslaved to his master. There was nothing for it but to go on. Accordingly, I proceeded to take my usual place on the raft, when my uncle put out his hand to stop me.

"We shall not start till to-morrow," said he.

I made a gesture of resignation to everything that might be in store for me.

"I must omit nothing," said he. "Since fate has thrown me on this part of the coast, I will not leave it without a full examination."

This remark will be intelligible when it is understood that we had returned to the north coast, but not to the part from which we had started. Port Gräuben must be more to the west. So that, after all, there was nothing unreasonable in the professor's desire to explore carefully this new region.

"Let us go then and reconnoitre," said I.

And leaving Hans to his occupations, we set out. The space between the beach and the foot of the sea-rampart was very extensive. We walked for a good half-hour before reaching the rocky wall. Our feet crushed innumerable shells of every form and size, the former homes of extinct species. I also observed countless numbers of carapaces whose diameter often exceeded fifteen feet. They had belonged to those giant glyptodons of the pliocene period, of which the tortoise of our day is but a miniature copy.

The ground was also strewn with an immense quantity of rocky *débris*, a sort of pebbles rounded by the action of water and arranged in successive ridgy lines. I judged from this that the sea had at some time occupied this space. On the scattered rocks, now out of their reach, the billows had left evident traces of their passage.

This might account in some degree for the existence of an ocean 120 miles below the surface of the earth. But, according to my theory, this liquid mass must little by little lose itself in the bowels of the earth, and it is evidently replenished from the waters of the ocean which find their way through some fissure. Just now, however, the fissure must be closed, otherwise this cavern, or rather this immense reservoir, would be filled in a very short time. Or perhaps this body of water struggling against sub-terranean fires may be partly vaporized, which would account for the clouds suspended overhead, and for the electric disturb-ances which convulse the interior of the globe.

This seemed to me an adequate theory of the phenomena we ourselves had witnessed, for however vast the wonders of nature, they are always referable to physical causes.

We were walking on a kind of sedimentary stratum, formed by water, like all the strata of that period, so widely distributed over the earth. The professor pored attentively into every chink in the rock. He was convinced that some opening must exist, and it was vital to him to ascertain its depth.

We had followed the coast of the "Sea of Lidenbrock" for a mile, when suddenly the surface exhibited a change. It seemed to have been turned upside down – torn up by the convulsive heaving of the underlying strata. In many places the extent of the disturbance was attested by deep chasms and corresponding elevations.

We made but slow progress over these fragments of granite, mingled here and there with silex, quartz, and alluvial deposits, when we came in sight of a vast plain covered with bones. It was like an immense cemetery, where the generations of twenty centuries mingled their dust. Piles of remains rose behind each other in the distance, undulating like a sea towards the horizon, where they were lost in a soft haze. Here, on an extent of prob-ably 3,000 square miles, was concentrated the whole history of animal life – a history scarcely traceable in the too recent soil of the inhabited world.

An insatiable curiosity urged us on. Our feet crushed the

remains of pre-historic animals and fossils, whose rare and interesting relics are eagerly competed for by the museums of great cities. The lives of a thousand Cuviers would not suffice to reconstruct the skeletons that lie in this magnificent assemblage of organic remains.

I was speechless with amazement. My uncle threw up his arms towards the impenetrable vault that stood for a sky. His mouth wildly open – his eyes gleaming under his spectacles; his head moving up and down, right and left – his whole demeanour indicated how intense was his astonishment. He found himself in a priceless collection of leptotherium, mericotherium, lophodion, anoplotherium, megatherium, mastodon, protopithecus, pterodactyles – all the antediluvian monsters gathered together for his private gratification. Just fancy an enthusiastic bibliomaniac transported in an instant into that Alexandrian library which Omar burnt, and which some miracle had reproduced from its ashes. Such was my uncle Lidenbrock at this moment.

But there came a new phase of astonishment, when hurrying across this organic dust, he seized a skull, and, in a voice full of emotion, he cried:

"Axel, Axel! – a human head!"

"A human head, uncle!" said I, equally surprised.

"Yes, my lad. Ah! Milne-Edwards. Ah! Quatrefages, why are you not here with me to behold it?"

CHAPTER XXXIX

TO UNDERSTAND WHY my uncle invoked these illustrious *savants*, it should be understood that a fact of great importance in palæontology had been announced some time before we left.

On March 28, 1863, some workmen, under the direction of M. Boucher de Perthes, excavating in the quarries of Moulin-Quignon, near Abbeville, in the department of the Somme, in France, found a human jaw-bone fourteen feet below the surface. It was the first fossil of that kind ever brought to light. Near it were found stone axes and cut flints, clothed by time with a uniform coating of green.

This discovery made a great noise, not only in France, but in England and Germany. Many learned men of the French

Institute, among others, Messrs. Milne-Edwards and Quatre-fages, took up the matter warmly, proved the incontestable authenticity of the bone in question, and became the ardent partisans of the "maxillary process".

The learned men of the United Kingdom who accepted the fact as authentic, such as Messrs. Falconer, Busk, Carpenter, &c., were supported by the German *savants*, and foremost among these – the warmest enthusiast – was my uncle Lidenbrock.

The authenticity of a human fossil of the fourth epoch was thus incontestably established and admitted.

Their theory, it is true, had an implacable opponent in Monsieur Elie de Beaumont. This high authority held that the formation at Moulin-Quignon did not belong to the "diluvium", but to a less remote stratum, and, so far in accordance with Cuvier, he denied that the human race was contemporary with the animals of the fourth epoch. My uncle Lidenbrock and the great majority of geologists had maintained the opposite by discussion and controversy, and Monsieur Elie de Beaumont was left almost alone on the other side of the argument.

All these details were familiar to us, but we were not aware of the progress which the question had made since our departure. Other jaw-bones, identical in species, though belonging to other types and nations, had been found in the light soils of certain caves in France, Switzerland, and Belgium, as well as weapons, utensils, tools, bones of children, youths, men, and aged persons. The existence of man during the fourth epoch was daily confirmed.

And this was not all. New remains, exhumed from the tertiary pliocene, had enabled still bolder spirits to assign an antiquity even more remote to the human species. These remains, it is true, were not actually human, but relics of man's industry, tibias and thigh-bones of animals regularly striated – carved, so to speak – and which told clearly of human work.

Thus, at a bound, our species gained many steps on the ladder of time; he took precedence of the mastodon; he became contemporary with the "elephas meridionalis"; he dated 100,000 years back, for that is the figure assigned by the best geologists to the tertiary pliocene.

Such was the state of palæontological science, and the extent of our knowledge of it will account for our attitude as we gazed at this vast ossuary of the "Sea of Lidenbrock", and also for the bewilderment of joy with which – twenty paces farther – my uncle found himself face to face with an individual man of the fourth epoch.

It was a perfectly recognizable human body. Perhaps some peculiarity in the soil, as in St. Michael's cemetery at Bordeaux, had thus preserved it. Who can tell? But this corpse, the skin tightened and dried like parchment, the limbs still soft to all appearance, the teeth perfect, the hair abundant, the finger- and toe-nails of a hideous length, stood before us as in life.

I was dumb before this apparition of another age. My uncle, generally so loquacious, so full of energetic talk, was silent too. We had lifted the corpse and set it upright. He looked at us from his hollow orbits. We handled his body, which sounded at our touch.

After some minutes of silence, the uncle was superseded by the professor! Otto Lidenbrock, carried away by his ardent tempera-ment, forgot the circumstances of our voyage, the place we were in, the great cavern that held us. No doubt he fancied himself in the Johannæum, standing before his pupils, for he took the lecturer's tone, and addressing an imaginary audience, said:

"Gentlemen, I have the honour to introduce to you a man of the fourth epoch. Great *savants* have denied his existence; others equally great have maintained it. The Saint Thomas of palæon-tology, were he here, would touch him with the finger and believe! I know how necessary it is for science to be on her guard against discoveries of this kind. I am aware of the contriv-ances of Barnum, and others of the same class, to impose on the world a fossil man. I know about the knee cap of Ajax, the pretended body of Orestes, discovered by the Spartans, and the body of Asterius, nine cubits long, of which Pausanias tells. I have read the reports on the skeleton of Trapani, found in the fourteenth century, which it was sought to identify as Polyphemus, and the history of the giant disinterred near Palermo, in the sixteenth century. You also, gentlemen, are acquainted with the analysis made near Lucerne, in 1577, of those gigantic bones which the celebrated physician Felix Plater declared were those of a giant, nineteen feet high! I have read eagerly the treatises of Cassanio, and all the memoirs, pamphlets, essays and counter-essays published *à propos* of the skeleton of the Cimbrian king Teutobochus, the invader of Gaul, exhumed in a gravel-pit in Dauphiné in 1613. In the eighteenth century I would have contested with Pierre Campet the existence of the pre-adamites of Scheuchzer! I have in my hands the monograph called Gigan—"

Here was my uncle's natural infirmity; he could not in public pronounce difficult words without stumbling.

"The monograph called Gigan—," he repeated.

He got no farther.

"Giganto—"

No, the unfortunate word would stick there. How they would have laughed at the Johannæum!

"Gigantosteology!" At last he brought it out between two imprecations.

Then, more fluently than ever he went on:

"Yes, gentlemen, all that is familiar to me! I am aware that Cuvier and Blumenbach see in these bones simply the remains of the mammoth and other animals of the fourth epoch! But here, to doubt would be an insult to science! The body is there! You can see it, touch it! It is no skeleton, it is a perfect form, preserved for the purposes of anthropology!"

I had no desire to contravene the assertion.

"If I could wash it in a solution of sulphuric acid, I could free it from these earthy particles and glistening shells that encrust it. But the precious solvent is wanting. But, as he is, let him tell us his story."

Here the professor took the fossil corpse, and handled it with the dexterity of a showman.

"You see," said he, "it is not six feet long, far from giant pro-portions. As to the race it belongs to, there can be no doubt it is Caucasian, the white race; the race to which we ourselves belong. The cranium of this fossil is ovoid; without projecting cheek-bones, or protruding jaw. It presents no indication of prognathism, which modifies the facial angle.* If we measure this angle we find it almost 90°. But I will go farther with my deduc-tions; I will venture to assert that this specimen of the human

---

* The facial angle is formed by two lines, one (more or less vertical), which touches the forehead and the incisors, the other horizontal, passing from the auditory opening to the lower bone of the nasal sinus. The projection of the jaw, which modifies the facial angle, is called in scientific language – prognathism.

race is of the family of Japheth, which extends from India to the boundary of Eastern Europe. Do not smile, gentlemen!"

Nobody was smiling, but the professor was used to seeing faces relax during his learned dissertations.

"Yes," he continued, with renewed energy, "we have here a fossil man, a contemporary of the monsters who fill this vast amphitheatre. As to how he came here, how the layers of *débris* in which he was embedded came into this vast cavern, I cannot offer a speculation. No one can doubt that, during the quaternary epoch, there was considerable disturbance of the earth's crust. The gradual cooling of the globe produces gaps, chasms, faults, into which portions of the upper strata must fall. I assert nothing, but this much is certain. Here is the man surrounded by his handiwork, these axes, these wrought flints, which mark the Stone Age; and unless he came here as a tourist like myself, a pioneer of science, I cannot entertain a doubt of his origin."

The professor was silent, and I uttered my "unanimous applause". My uncle was perfectly right, and wiser people than his nephew would have found it difficult to controvert his statements.

Another point is, that this was not the only corpse in the great bed of bones. We met with others at every few steps in the dust, and my uncle had a choice of wonderful specimens wherewith to convince unbelievers. In truth it was an amazing sight to behold generations of men and animals in one mass of confusion in this great cemetery. But here came an important question to which we had no solution. Were these beings already dust when, by some throe of nature, they were brought down to the shores of the "sea of Lidenbrock", or had they lived here, in this subterranean world, with this false sky, in birth and death like the inhabitants of the earth? Up to the present time we had only seen sea-monsters and fish alive! Were we yet to meet some man of the abyss wandering on this lonely shore?

CHAPTER XL

FOR ANOTHER HALF-HOUR we wandered over these deposits of bones. We pressed on, impelled by intense curiosity. What other wonders would this cavern reveal? what new treasures for science? My eyes were on the watch for surprises, and my mind prepared for any degree of astonishment.

The sea-shore had long been shut out by the hills formed by the ossuary. The imprudent professor, little dreaming of losing his way, drew me on to a distance. We went on silently bathed in waves of electric light. By a phenomenon I cannot explain, the light seemed uniformly dispersed, not radiating from any centre, nor casting any shade. It was as if we were in the summer noon of the equatorial region, under the vertical rays of the sun. All vapour had disappeared. The rocks, the distant mountains, confused outlines of distant forests, presented a singular aspect under the equally diffused light. We were like the fantastic creation of Hoffman, the man who lost his shadow.

After walking about a mile we found ourselves on the skirts of an immense forest, but not of a fungoid growth like those we had seen in the neighbourhood of Port Gräuben.

It was the vegetation of the tertiary epoch in all its magnificence – great palms of a species now extinct, superb palmacites, yews, cypresses. Thujas represented the conifers, and were interlaced with an impenetrable network of lianas. The ground was thickly carpeted with mosses and hepaticas. Some small streams trickled through the groves, scarce worthy of the name, as they gave no shade. At the sides of the streams grew tree-ferns, like those of our hot-houses. But colour was wanting to trees and shrubs alike, debarred from the vivifying light of the sun. Everything was of a uniform brown, or faded tint. The leaves had no greenness, and the flowers themselves, so numerous at that epoch, now colourless and scentless, looked as if made of paper, and discoloured by the action of the air.

My uncle ventured into this gigantic labyrinth. I followed, not without apprehension. As nature had spread a vegetable banquet, why should we not meet with some of the terrible mammifers? In some openings, left by decayed and fallen trees, I saw leguminous plants, and acers and rubias and a thousand other shrubs dear to the ruminants of all ages. Then, blended in one group, I beheld the trees of dissimilar climates – the oak growing beside the palm, the eucalyptus of Australia elbowing the Norwegian pine, the birch of the North mingling its branches with the kauri of New Zealand. It would puzzle the most scientific botanist of the upper earth.

Suddenly I came to a stop. I held back my uncle. The diffused light made the smallest objects visible in the depths of the forest. I thought I saw – No! my eyes did not deceive me. I did see immense forms moving under the trees! They were the giant animals, a herd of mastodons, not fossil but living, of the kind whose remains were discovered in 1801 in the swamps of the Ohio River. I distinctly saw great elephants, whose trunks were coiling among the branches like a legion of serpents. I could hear the noise of their ivory tusks as they struck the bark of the trees. The branches cracked, and the leaves, torn off in masses, disappeared down the mighty throats of these monsters.

The dream, in which I seemed to see revived that pre-historic world – the third and fourth epochs – that dream was realized!

My uncle looked.

"Come!" said he, seizing my arm. "Come on; we will go on."

"No!" said I. "No! We are unarmed. What could we do in the midst of a herd of giant quadrupeds? Come, uncle, come! No human creature could brave the fury of those monsters."

"No human creature!" said my uncle, in a subdued voice. "You are wrong, Axel! Look down there! I think I see a human form! A being like ourselves! A man!"

I shrugged my shoulders while I looked, and resolved not to believe it unless belief was inevitable. But, in spite of myself, I was convinced. About a quarter of a mile off, leaning against the branch of an enormous kauri pine, a human being – a Proteus of these subterranean regions – a new son of Neptune, was herding that vast troop of mastodons.

"*Immanis pecoris custos, immanior ipse!*"

Yes, *immanior ipse!* It was no longer the fossil being whose corpse we had picked up on the ossuary, it was a living giant capable of commanding these monsters. His stature was over twelve feet. His head, as large as that of a buffalo, was lost in the mass of his tangled hair. It was a mane like that of the primeval elephant. He brandished an enormous limb of a tree, a fit crook for such a shepherd.

We stood motionless, petrified. But we ran the risk of being seen. We must fly.

"Come, come!" cried I, dragging my uncle, who for the first time in his life, allowed himself to be led.

A quarter of an hour after we were out of sight of this formidable enemy.

Now that I think of it all quietly; now that my mind is calm again, and that months have elapsed since that wonderful, supernatural apparition, what am I to think? What am I to believe? It seems impossible. Our senses must have played us false. Our eyes did not see what they showed to us! No human creature lives in that subterranean world. No generation of men inhabits those lower caverns of the globe without an idea of the inhabitants above, and without communication with them. It is madness – the height of madness.

I would rather admit the existence of some animal whose structure approximates to ours: some ape of a remote geological period, some protopithecus; some mesopithecus, like that which Lartet discovered in the bone-deposit of Sansau. But this one which we saw exceeded in size all the species known in modern palæontology. No matter! One can imagine an ape, however improbable. But a whole generation of living men, shut up in the bowels of the earth! Never can I believe it.

However, we left the light and luminous forest dumb with astonishment, overcome by a stupefaction which bordered on insensibility. We ran mechanically. It was a mad flight – an irresistible impulse, such as pervades some kinds of nightmare. Instinctively we returned to the "Sea of Lidenbrock", and I do not know into what vagaries my reason might have been betrayed, but that I was forcibly recalled to practical matters.

Although I was certain that we were treading virgin ground, I frequently noticed groups of rock that recalled to me those of Port Gräuben. This was further confirmation of the indication of the compass, and of our involuntary return to the north of the "Sea of Lidenbrock". It was sometimes very confusing. Hundreds of rills and cascades fell from the crags. I seemed to recognize the stratum of Surtar-brandur, our faithful Hansbach, and the grotto where I first regained my senses. Then again, at a little distance, lay the rocky sea-wall; the appearance of a streamlet, the striking outline of a rock, threw me into a state of indecision as to our whereabouts.

I imparted my doubts to my uncle. He, too, was in a maze. In a panorama so vast and so monotonous there was nothing the mind could fix on as a landmark. "At any rate," said I, "we have not landed at our point of embarkation. The storm has led us lower down, and if we follow the shore we shall come to Port Gräuben."

"If that is so," said my uncle, "we need explore no further. The best thing we can do is to get back to the raft. But are you sure you are correct, Axel?"

"It is difficult to say positively, uncle; all the rocks are alike. And yet I fancy I recognize the promontory at whose foot Hans put our raft together. We ought to be near the little port; unless, indeed, this is it," added I, scrutinizing the small creek.

"No, Axel. If that were so, we should find our own tracks; and I see nothing of the kind."

"But I see!" said I, darting towards something that shone on the sand.

"What is it?"

"Look!" said I.

And I showed my uncle the dagger stained with rust which I had picked up.

"Steady, now," said he. "Did you bring this weapon with you?"

"I! No, indeed. But you—"

"Not to my knowledge," replied the professor. "I never had such a thing in my possession."

"How strange!"

"Well, no! After all, it is simple enough, Axel. The Icelanders often have poniards of this kind. Hans must have dropped this one. No doubt it is his."

I shook my head. Hans never had anything of the kind.

"Is it the weapon," cried I, "of some antediluvian warrior – of a living man, a contemporary of the giant herdsman? But no! it does not belong to the Stone Age, nor to the Age of Bronze either. This blade is steel—"

My uncle stopped me short in this new digression, and in his coldest tone he said:

"Calm yourself, Axel, and collect your wits. This poniard is a weapon of the sixteenth century, a true 'dagger', such as noblemen used to carry in their belt to give the *coup-de-grâce*. It belongs neither to you, nor me, nor the hunter, nor even to the human beings who may live in the bowels of the earth."

"Would you venture to say—"

"See! That notch never came from cutting throats; the blade is covered with rust that dates not from a day, nor a year, nor an age."

The professor grew warm, as usual, when he gave the reins to his imagination.

"Axel," said he, "we are on the road to the great discovery! This blade has lain on the sand one, two, perhaps three hundred years, and that notch was made by the rocks of this subterranean sea."

"But," said I, "it did not come here by itself; it did not give itself this twist. Some one has been here before us."

"Yes! a man."

"And this man has graven his name with this dagger! He wanted to mark once more the road to the central point. Let us search everywhere!"

Intensely interested, we kept close along the high wall, prying into the narrowest crevices that looked like the entrance to a gallery. At last we came to a place where the shore narrowed. The sea almost washed the foot of the cliff, leaving a passage not more than six feet wide. Between two projecting points of rock we saw the entrance to a dark tunnel.

There, on a block of granite, stood the mysterious letters, half effaced, the initials of the bold traveller –

$$\blacksquare \cdot \mathbf{4} \cdot \mathbf{h} \cdot$$

"A.S.!" cried my uncle, "Arne Saknussemm! Always Arne Saknussemm!"

CHAPTER XLI

SINCE THE COMMENCEMENT of our travels I had passed through so many phases of wonder and surprise that I thought nothing could startle me any more, or excite a feeling of astonishment; but when I beheld these two letters, cut three hundred years ago, I stood there in a state of bewilderment akin to idiocy. Not only was the signature of the great alchemist before my eyes, but his stylet was in my hands. It would be an unbeliever indeed who could doubt the existence of the traveller and the reality of his travels.

While these thoughts were racking my brain, the professor went off into dithyrambics on Arne Saknussemm. "Wonderful genius!" cried he. "You neglected nothing that could open to other mortals the channels through the earth's crust; and your fellow-men can follow your traces, after three centuries, in the depths of these dark caves. You have done everything to enable others to behold these marvels. Your name, engraved from stage to stage, is an unfailing guide to any one bold enough to tread in your footsteps; and I believe your autograph will be found at the centre of our planet. Well, I too will write my name on this last page of granite. But henceforth this Cape, discovered by you near this sea, shall be called Cape Saknussemm."

That is the substance of what I heard, and my own enthusiasm was rising with his words. A fire seemed to burn in my breast. I forgot everything, the dangers of the voyage and the perils of the return. What another had done I would dare, and nothing appeared to me impossible.

"Forward! forward!" I exclaimed.

As I spoke I sprang forward toward the dark gallery, when the professor, usually so prone to hasty action, restrained me, and advised coolness and patience.

"First let us go back to Hans," said he, "and bring the raft round to this point."

I obeyed with a bad grace, and hastened to the beach.

"Uncle," said I, "do you know that circumstances have been very much in our favour up to now?"

"Do you think so, Axel?"

"I do. Why everything, even the storm, combined to set us in the right track. Blessings on the hurricane! It landed us on the very coast from which fine weather would have carried us far away. Just fancy if our prow (a raft with a prow!) had touched the southern shore of the Lidenbrock Sea, what would have become of us. The name of Saknussemm would never have greeted our eyes, we should be wandering on a shore without an outlet."

"Yes, Axel, there is really some providential guidance which brought us, going to the south, back to the north, and to Cape Saknussemm. I may say it is more than astonishing, and there is something in it that baffles my sagacity to explain."

"What does it matter?" said I. "We do not need to account for facts, only to make the most of them."

"Certainly, my boy, but—"

"But we are going northward again. We shall pass under the northernmost countries in Europe – Sweden, Russia, Siberia, who knows? – instead of penetrating under the deserts of Africa or the waves of the ocean; and what more do I want to know?"

"Yes, Axel, you are right, and it is all for the best, as we shall leave this horizontal sea, which can lead nowhere. We shall go down, down, always down! Do you know that before we reach the centre we have only 4,500 miles to travel?"

"Bah!" said I, "that is not worth mentioning. Let us start at once!"

We talked on in this mad tone till we returned to the hunter. Everything was ready for an immediate start. Every package was on board. We took our stations on the raft, and, the sail being hoisted, Hans steered for Cape Saknussemm, following the coast-line.

The wind was not very favourable to a craft that could not sail very close. In some places we had to resort to poles to assist our progress: often low submerged rocks compelled us to go far out of our course. At last, after about three hours of navigation, that is, about six o'clock in the evening, we reached a point that offered a good landing-place.

I leaped on shore, followed by my uncle and the Icelander. The short passage had not calmed my spirits. On the contrary, I proposed "burning our ship" to cut off all temptation to retreat. My uncle would not hear of it. I thought him very lukewarm.

"At any rate, let us lose no time in starting," said I.

"Yes," said my uncle; "but, as a preliminary, we must examine this new gallery, to ascertain whether we must prepare our ladders.'

My uncle got ready his Ruhmkorff apparatus, the raft, fastened to the shore, was left alone, the mouth of the gallery was not twenty paces off, and our little party bent their steps thither, myself leading the way.

The almost circular opening was about five feet in diameter; this dark tunnel was hollowed out of the living rock and carefully cleared by the eruptive matter to which it had once formed the outlet, so that we could enter without difficulty.

We followed an almost horizontal direction, when, after about six paces, our progress was cut short by an enormous block of stone.

I uttered an exclamation which was not a blessing when I found myself stopped by an insurmountable obstacle.

In vain we searched to the right and to the left, above and below, there was no passage, no outlet. I was bitterly disappointed; I would not allow the reality of the obstacle. I bent down, looked under the block. Not a chink! Above, the same granite barrier. Hans passed the lamp along every part of the wall, but found no solution of the difficulty. We had no alternative but to abandon all hope of passing.

I had seated myself on the ground. My uncle strode up and down the passage.

"What did Saknussemm do?" I exclaimed.

"Yes!" said my uncle. "Was he baffled by this stone barrier?"

"No! no!" said I, with warmth. "This rocky fragment must have suddenly closed this passage, set in motion by some shock, or by one of those magnetic phenomena which disturb the crust of the earth. Many years have gone by since the return of Saknussemm and the fall of that block. There can be no doubt that this gallery was once a channel for lava, and that the eruptive matters had a free circulation. Look, there are recent fissures furrowing the granite roof. It is composed of an assemblage of blocks, enormous stones that are arranged as if a giant had toiled to form it; but some sudden shock has displaced the mass, and, as if the keystone of the arch had been dislodged, the falling stones have obstructed all passage. It is a fortuitous obstacle which Saknussemm did not encounter, and if we do not remove it we are unworthy to reach the centre of the earth!"

That was my speech! The soul of the professor had passed into me. The spirit of a discoverer pervaded me. I forgot the past, I disdained the future! Nothing existed for me on the face of our planet, in whose bosom I was plunged, neither town nor country, neither Hamburg nor Königstrasse, nor my poor Gräuben, who must think me lost for ever in the bowels of the earth!

"Well," said my uncle, "with the mattock and the pickaxe let us cut our way! Let us break down this wall."

"It is too hard for the pick!" cried I.

"Well, then, the mattock!"

"Too tedious!"

"But—"

"Well, powder! Let us mine, and blow up the barrier."

"Powder! of course!" said my uncle. "Hans, set to work at once!"

The Icelander returned to the raft, and came back with a pick-axe, wherewith to dig a trench for the powder. It was no easy task. We had to make a hole large enough to contain fifty pounds of gun-cotton, whose expansive power is four times greater than that of gunpowder.

I was in a state of feverish excitement. While Hans was at work I helped my uncle to prepare a slow-match, made of damp powder in a tube of cloth.

"We shall pass it!" said I.

"We shall!" said my uncle.

At midnight we had finished. The charge of gun-cotton was put in, and the slow-match was brought along the gallery to the outside. A spark only was wanting to set this powerful agent in operation.

"To-morrow!" said the professor.

There was no help for it. I had to resign myself to wait six long hours.

CHAPTER XLII

THE NEXT DAY, Thursday, August 27, was a notable date in this subterranean voyage. When I think of it my heart still beats with terror. From that moment our reason, our judgement, our ingenuity went for nothing, we were to be the playthings of the elements.

At six o'clock we were afoot. The moment was at hand when we were to force a passage through the granite crust by means of powder.

I begged to be allowed the honour of setting light to the match. That done I was to rejoin my companions on the raft, which had not been unloaded: then we intended to sheer off a little, lest the explosion should not confine its effects to the interior of the rocky mass.

We reckoned that the match would take about ten minutes before reaching the chamber where the powder was; I should therefore have time to regain the raft.

I prepared to fulfil my part, not without trepidation.

After a hurried meal, my uncle and the hunter went on board, while I stayed on the beach. I was equipped with a lighted lantern with which to fire the train.

"Go now, my lad," said my uncle, "and come back immediately to us."

"Never fear," said I, "I am not likely to loiter on the way."

And I turned my steps to the entrance of the gallery; I opened my lantern, took up the end of the match, the professor held his chronometer in his hand.

"Ready!" cried he.

"Ready!"

"Well, fire! my boy."

I quickly put the match into the flame, which crackled at the contact, and running as quickly as I could, I regained the beach.

"Jump on board," said my uncle, "and let us push off!"

Hans, with a powerful stroke, impelled us from the land; the raft was about twenty fathoms from the shore.

It was an exciting moment. The professor watched the hand of the chronometer.

"Five minutes more!" said he. "Four! three!"

My pulse beat twice in a second.

"Two! One—Crumble ye hills of granite!"

What happened? I do not think I heard the explosion. But the form of the rocks seemed to change before my eyes; they opened like a curtain. An unfathomable abyss seemed to open on the shore. The sea seemed to become dizzy, and only formed one great wave, on whose back the raft rose perpendicularly.

We were all three thrown down. In less than a second the light was swallowed up in utter darkness. Presently I felt our support give way from beneath the raft. First I thought we were falling vertically, but I was mistaken. I thought of speaking to my uncle, but the hoarse roar of the waters would have prevented his hearing me.

In spite of the darkness, the shock, the emotion, I was able to understand what had happened.

Beyond the block which we had blown up, there was an abyss.

The explosion had produced a kind of earthquake in this fissured rock, and now the gulf was laid open, and the sea, changed into a torrent, was carrying us away in its course.

I gave myself up for lost. An hour, two hours, who knows how much longer passed thus. We pressed closely together, holding hands so as not to be thrown from the raft. We felt shocks of great violence when the raft touched the wall, but this was rarely, from which I drew the inference that the gallery had widened. Beyond a doubt this was the passage of Saknussemm; but instead of travelling along it by ourselves, we had, by our imprudence, brought a sea along with us.

It will be understood that these ideas passed vaguely and darkly through my mind. It was difficult to think at all in this giddy journey, which was so like a fall. Judging by the wind that lashed our faces, our pace must have far exceeded that of the most rapid train. To light a torch under these conditions would have been impossible, and our last electric apparatus was broken at the moment of the explosion.

My surprise was great, therefore, at seeing a bright light shine out suddenly beside me. The stolid face of Hans was illuminated. The undaunted hunter had succeeded in lighting the lantern, and although its flame flickered almost to extinction, it threw some gleams into the appalling darkness.

The gallery was wide, as I had judged. The faint light did not allow us to perceive both walls at a time. The steepness of the waterfall which carried us off was greater than the great cataracts of America. The surface was like a shower of arrows, launched with the utmost force. No comparison can convey my impression. Sometimes, caught by an eddy, the raft would veer to the right or left in its whirling course. When it neared the wall of the gallery I threw the light of the lantern on the rock, and could form an estimate of our speed by the fact that little points of rock seemed to form continuous lines, so that we appeared to be enclosed in a network of moving threads. I judged our speed to be ninety miles an hour.

My uncle and I looked at each other with haggard faces as we clung to the butt of the mast, which was broken short off at the moment of the catastrophe. We turned our backs to the current of air, so as not to be choked by the rapidity of a motion which no human power could slacken.

But still the hours passed. The situation was unchanged, except for a complication.

In trying to get our cargo in order, I found that the greatest part of our stores must have disappeared at the moment of the explosion, when the sea had been so violently agitated. I wanted to know exactly what we had to rely on, and, lantern in hand, I began my investigation. Of our instruments nothing was left but the compass and the chronometer. The ladders and ropes were represented by an end of cable round the remnant of the mast. Not a pickaxe, nor a mattock, not a hammer, and, irreparable loss! we had provisions only for a day.

I searched the interstices of the raft, the crevices formed by the beams and the floor-joints. Nothing! Our store consisted of a morsel of dried meat and some biscuits. I stared about me with a stupefied air. I was loath to believe it. And yet, what did it matter? If the provisions would have sufficed for months, how were we to escape from the abyss or from the irresistible torrent that was hurrying us down? Why fear the torments of hunger, when so many forms of death were presenting themselves? Could we even count on time enough to die of inanition?

And yet, by an extraordinary freak of imagination, I overlooked the immediate peril, and was overwhelmed with the future, which looked to me so terrible. Besides, it seemed just possible that we might escape the fury of the torrent, and regain the surface of the globe. How, I know not. Where, I cared not. What matter? A chance is a chance, even if it is only one to a thousand; while death by hunger left us no ray of hope, ever so faint.

I thought of telling my uncle, and showing him the destitution to which we were reduced, and to show exactly how long we had to live. But I summoned courage to be silent. I thought it best to leave him his self-possession.

At this moment the light of the lantern gradually sank, and then went out. The wick was burnt out. The darkness became absolute. No hope remained of illuminating it. We had a torch left, but it could not be kept alight. So, like a child, I shut my eyes to keep the darkness out.

A considerable time elapsed, and then our speed was increased twofold. I knew it by the current of air as it struck my face. The slope of the water became greater and greater. I think we no longer slid, we fell. It was to my sensations an almost vertical descent. The hands of my uncle and of Hans holding fast to my arms held me firmly down.

Suddenly, after a period whose duration was quite inappreciable, I felt a kind of shock, the raft had struck nothing solid, but its course was suddenly arrested. A waterspout, an immense liquid column, was falling. I was suffocated – I was drowning!

But this sudden flood did not last long. In a few seconds I was inhaling long breaths of pure air. My uncle and Hans squeezed my arms almost to breaking, and the raft still bore us all three.

CHAPTER XLIII

I SUPPOSE IT was now about ten o'clock at night. The first of my senses that began to act was that of hearing. Strange as the expression may appear, I heard first the silence produced in the gallery, after the roaring which for hours had filled my ears. At last I heard my uncle say, in a voice that sounded like a far-off murmur:

"We are ascending!"

"What do you say?" I cried.

"We are ascending, I say!"

I put out my hand, I touched the wall; my hand was bathed in blood. We were ascending with extreme rapidity.

"Now for the torch!" exclaimed the professor.

Hans, not without difficulty, succeeded in lighting it, and the flame was able to burn even with the ascending motion, and to throw light enough to illuminate the scene.

"Just as I thought," said the professor. "We are in a narrow well, not twenty-four feet in diameter; the water, arrived at the bottom of the gulf, regains its level, and we are ascending with it."

"Whither?"

"I do not know, but we must hold ourselves in readiness for any emergency. We are ascending at the rate of twelve feet per second – say 720 per minute, or nine and a half miles per hour. At that rate we shall make some way."

"Yes, if nothing stops us, and if the well has an outlet; but if it is closed, the air will be more and more compressed, and we shall end by being crushed."

"Axel," said the professor very calmly, "our situation is all but desperate; but there are chances of salvation, and those I contemplate. We may perish at any moment, but at any moment we may be saved. Therefore let us be on the alert to take advantage of any circumstance."

"What is there that we can do?"

"Recruit our strength by eating."

At these words I glanced sadly at my uncle. At last I should have to reveal my secret.

"Eat?" said I.

"Yes, without a delay."

The professor added some words in Danish. Hans shook his head.

"What!" said my uncle; "our provisions are lost?"

"Yes, there is all that remains – a piece of dried meat for the three of us."

My uncle looked vacantly at me.

"Well," said I, "do you still think we may be saved?"

My question received no answer.

An hour passed. I was suffering the pangs of hunger. My companions suffered also; but none of us would touch the miserable remnant of food. We continued to ascend with extreme rapidity. Sometimes the air cut off our respiration, as happens to aeronauts rising too swiftly. But as they experience cold as they rise, we experienced, on the contrary, an ever-increasing heat, and at this moment it must certainly have reached 70°.

What does this change indicate? Up till now the facts had confirmed the theories of Davy and of Lidenbrock; till now the peculiar conditions of refractory rocks, electricity, and magnetism had modified the general laws of nature, and given us a moderate temperature, for the central-fire theory still seemed to me the only true or explicable one. Were we hastening towards a medium where these phenomena were developed strictly in accordance with that theory, and in which the heat reduced the rocks to a state of fusion? This fear took hold of me, and I said to the professor:

"If we are neither drowned nor crushed, and if hunger does not put an end to us, we have still the chance of being burnt alive."

He merely shrugged his shoulders, and relapsed into meditation.

An hour passed, and no change save in the temperature, which kept increasing. At last my uncle broke the silence.

"Come," said he, "we must make up our minds."

"Make up our minds?" said I.

"Yes; we must recruit our strength. If we husband our little store in order to have a few more hours of life, we shall make ourselves weaker at the last."

"Yes, at the last! That will be very soon."

"Well, well! suppose a chance of safety presented itself, and that a sudden effort was necessary, how shall we have strength for it if we weaken ourselves by fasting?"

"Uncle," said I, "when that bit of meat is gone, what have we?"

"Nothing, Axel, nothing. But what good does it do you to devour it with your eyes? You reason like a being without will or energy!"

"Do you not despair?" cried I, exasperated at his coolness.

"No," replied he firmly.

"What! you still believe we have a chance?"

"Yes, a thousand times, yes! While the heart beats and the flesh palpitates, a creature endowed with will should never give place to despair."

What a speech. The man that could utter it under such circumstances was of no ordinary mould.

"Well," said I, "what is your plan?"

"To eat what remains, to the last crumb, and regain our lost strength. It may be our last meal, it is true, but at least we shall be strengthened to meet our fate."

"Well," said I, "let us fall to."

My uncle took the piece of meat and the few biscuits that had escaped the wreck; he divided them into three equal portions, and distributed them. That gave about a pound of food to each. The professor ate heartily, with a sort of feverish appetite; I ate my portion with loathing rather than relish, in spite of my hunger; Hans took his moderately, tranquilly, masticating little mouthfuls, eating with the indifference of a man whom no thought for the future disturbed. He had discovered a gourd half full of geneva; he offered it to us, and the vivifying liquor re-animated me a little.

"*Fortrefflig!*" said Hans, drinking in his turn.

"Excellent!" rejoined my uncle.

Hope revived in me a little. But our last meal was ended. It was now five o'clock in the morning.

Man is so constituted that his health is a purely negative result; once the desire for food is satisfied, he scarcely conceives the horrors of starvation; to understand them he must be suffering them. So in our case, a few mouthfuls of biscuit and meat triumphed over all our past troubles.

Still, after our repast, each one gave himself up to his own thoughts. What were the reflections of Hans, this man of the extreme West, possessed with the fatalism of the orientals? As for me, my thoughts were nothing but memories, and they carried me to the surface of the globe, which I ought never to have left. The home in the Königstrasse, my poor Gräuben, our good Martha, passed before me like dreams, and in the melancholy rumblings that echoed in the rock I fancied I could hear the hum of cities.

My uncle, always busy, was occupied, torch in hand, examining the nature of the formation; he was trying to ascertain our position by observing how the strata were grouped. Such a calculation could only be a very rough one; but a *savant* is always a *savant*, as long as he keeps his self-possession, and Professor Lidenbrock had that faculty in no common degree.

I heard him mutter geological terms; I understood them, and in spite of myself I was interested.

"Eruptive granite," said he. "We are still in the primitive period. But we ascend still! Who knows?"

He still hoped. He felt along the wall, and in a few minutes later he exclaimed:

"There is the gneiss! There are the mica-schists; soon we shall come to the transition rocks, and then—"

What did he mean? Could he measure the thickness of the crust suspended over head? What means had he of calculating? The manometer was gone, and nothing could supply its place.

The temperature rose rapidly, and I felt bathed in a burning atmosphere. The heat was comparable to nothing but the blast from a foundry furnace where melting is going on.

"Are we approaching a burning mass?" cried I, at a moment when the heat seemed to acquire double intensity.

"No," said my uncle; "it is impossible."

"And yet," said I, touching the wall, "this rock is burning hot."

As I spoke, my hand touched the water, and I quickly withdrew it.

"The water is burning hot, too."

This time the professor only replied by an angry gesture. From that moment I became the victim of terror I could not shake off. I apprehended a speedy catastrophe, such as the wildest imagination could not have conceived. First it was a vague idea which soon changed to certainty in my mind. I repulsed it, it returned with unabated strength. I could not put it into words. But some involuntary observations confirmed my conviction. By the uncertain light of the torch I remarked some fitful movement of the beds of granite; something was going to happen in which electricity would play a part; then this excessive heat, this boiling water. . . . I looked at the compass. It was stationary nowhere.

CHAPTER XLIV

YES; IT WENT round and round. The needle turned from pole to pole with abrupt movements, pointed to all the points of the compass, and turned as if touched by vertigo.

I was aware that, according to the most generally received theories, the mineral crust of the earth is never in a state of absolute repose. The changes brought about by internal decomposition, the agitation produced by great currents of fluid, the action of magnetism, tend to shake it incessantly, even when the beings scattered on its surface are not aware of any disturbance. This phenomenon, therefore, would not have filled me with terror taken alone.

But other facts, details quite *sui generis*, left me no room to doubt. The sounds of detonations became very frequent. I could only liken them to the sound of a multitude of carriages driven rapidly over a paved street. It was one continuous thunder.

Then the revolving compass, disturbed by electric shocks, confirmed my opinion.

The mineral crust threatened to break, the granite masses to close in again, the fissure to close up, and then, poor mortals! we should perish in the close embrace.

"Uncle! uncle!" said I, "we are lost!"

"What new terror has seized you?" said he, with amazing calmness. "What ails you?"

"What ails me? Look at those heaving walls, the dislocation that is gradually taking place in the mass, this torrid heat, this boiling water – every sign of an earthquake!"

My uncle only shook his head gently.

"An earthquake?" said he.

"Yes."

"My boy, I think you are mistaken."

"What! do you not perceive the signs?"

"Of an earthquake? No! I expect something better than that."

"What do you mean?"

"An eruption, Axel!"

"An eruption!" said I. "Then we are in the outlet of an active volcano?"

"So I think," said the professor, smiling, "and perhaps that is the best thing that could befall us."

The best thing! Was my uncle mad? What could he mean? Why this unnatural smiling calmness?

"What?" said I. "We are caught in an eruption; fate has thrown us into the track of the burning lava, the rocks of fire, the boiling torrents, all the eruptive materials. We shall be shot up into the air with rocky fragments, amid a rain of cinders and scoria, in a whirlwind of flame, and that is the best thing that can befall us!"

"Yes," said the professor, looking at me over his spectacles, "it is our only chance of reaching the surface again."

I passed all my ideas rapidly in review. My uncle was perfectly right, and I never saw him more confident or more satisfied than at this moment, as he waited and counted the chances of an eruption.

Still we were rising; the night passed in the same ascending movement; the surrounding noises increased; I was all but stifled; I thought my last hour had surely come, and still, imagination is such a strange faculty, I gave myself up to a childish curiosity. But I was the slave of my fancies, not their master.

It was evident that we were being forced upwards by an eruptive pressure; under the raft was boiling water, and under these waters a lava-mass, a collection of rocks which, on leaving the crater, would be scattered in every direction. We were in the chimney of a volcano. Not a doubt of it.

But this time, instead of Snäfell, an extinct volcano, it was a volcano in full operation. And I began to speculate what mountain it might be and on what part of the world we might be vomited forth.

Undoubtedly we were in the north. Before its derangement, the compass had never varied in that respect. Ever since Cape Saknussemm we had been carried directly northward for hundreds of miles. Had we returned under Iceland? Were we to make our exit by Hecla or one of the seven other craters of the island? Within a radius of 500 miles to the westward I recalled only the imperfectly known volcanoes of the north-west coast of America. Eastward, the only one existing under the 84th parallel of latitude was the Esk, in Jan Mayen Island, not far from Spitzbergen! There was no scarcity of craters spacious enough to belch forth an army! But what I wanted to know was, which one would serve our turn.

Towards morning the ascending motion was accelerated. The heat increased instead of diminishing as we approached the surface, but this was a local phenomenon, and due to volcanic influences. The quality of our locomotion was quite certain in my mind. We were undoubtedly propelled by an enormous force − a force of many thousand atmospheres produced by the vapours accumulated in the centre of the earth. But to what perils this force exposed us!

Presently reddish reflections penetrated the vertical gallery, which began to widen. I perceived, to right and left, deep passages like vast tunnels, whence arose thick vapours; tongues of flame coruscated as they licked the walls.

"Look, look, uncle!" cried I.

"Well," said he, "those are sulphurous flames, quite natural in an eruption."

"But if they close in upon us?"

"But they will not close in upon us."

"Suppose they stifle us?"

"They will not stifle us. The gallery is widening, and, if necessary, we can leave the raft and take refuge in some hollow of the rock."

"And the water still rising?"

"Axel, there is no more water – only a volcanic, pasty fluid, which is carrying us up on its surface to the crater mouth."

It was true: the liquid column had given place to eruptive matters, still dense, though boiling. The temperature became insufferable, and a thermometer exposed to this atmosphere would have marked more than 118°. I was bathed in perspiration. But for the rapidity of our upward movement we should have been suffocated.

However, the professor did not put into practice his proposition to abandon the raft, and he was right. Those ill-joined beams gave us a solid foothold, which we could not have found elsewhere.

About eight o'clock in the morning a novel incident occurred. The ascending movement ceased in an instant. The raft was absolutely motionless.

"What is it?" asked I, shaken by the sudden stoppage, as by a shock.

"A halt," replied my uncle.

"Is the eruption diminishing?"

"I hope not, indeed."

I rose. I tried to look about me. Perhaps the raft had caught on a point of rock, and offered a momentary resistance to the eruptive mass, in which case we must disengage it without delay.

Nothing of the kind. The column of cinders, scoria, and stony *débris* had itself ceased to rise.

"Has the eruption stopped?" cried I.

"Ah!" muttered my uncle, between his closed teeth, "you fear so, my boy; be consoled, this calm will not last long. Five minutes have already elapsed, and very soon we shall resume our ascent to the mouth of the crater."

As he spoke he continued to watch his chronometer, and he was destined to be right in his prognostication. Soon the raft began to move again in a rapid but irregular manner, which lasted about two minutes, and then stopped again.

"Good!" remarked my uncle. "In ten minutes we shall start again."

"Ten minutes?"

"Yes, this is an intermittent volcano. It lets us take breath also."

Nothing truer. At the appointed minute we started afresh with extreme rapidity. We had to cling to the raft, to avoid being thrown off. Then the pressure stopped again.

I have since reflected on this singular phenomenon, without finding any satisfactory solution. But I think it is clear that we were not in the main shaft of the volcano, but in an accessory passage, where the counter-shocks are felt.

How often this movement was repeated I cannot say, I only know that at each succeeding start the force was greater, and at last like the force of a projectile. During the intervals of rest we were stifled. I thought for a moment of the delight of finding one's self in a hyperborean region, at a temperature of thirty below zero. My overwrought imagination wandered on snowy plains in the Arctic regions, and I longed for the moment when I should roll myself on the frozen ground of the Pole. Gradually my senses, weakened by repeated shocks, gave way. But for the protecting arm of Hans I should more than once have had my head crushed against the granite wall.

I have no accurate recollection of what took place in the hours that followed. I have a confused idea of continuous detonation, of general convulsion, of a gyratory movement of the raft. It rocked on the lava sea in the midst of a rain of ashes. The roaring flames enveloped it. A hurricane like the blast of a furnace fed the subterranean fires. The last thing I recall is the face of Hans, lit up by the flames; and I felt like one of those poor wretches bound to the mouth of a cannon at the moment when the gun is fired and their dismembered atoms are shot into space.

CHAPTER XLV

WHEN I CAME to myself again, and opened my eyes, I felt my waist pressed by the powerful hand of our guide. With the other hand he supported my uncle. I was not seriously injured, but worn out by exhaustion. I was lying on the slope of a mountain, two steps from an abyss, into which the least movement would have precipitated me. Hans had saved me from death, while I rolled on the sides of the crater.

"Where are we?" said my uncle, who seemed rather put out at having returned to the surface.

The hunter shrugged his shoulders in token of ignorance.

"In Iceland?" said I.

"*Nej!*"

"What! no!" cried the professor.

"Hans is mistaken," said I, raising myself.

After the innumerable surprises of our voyage, yet another was in store for us. I expected to see a cone covered with eternal snows, in the midst of the barren wastes of the northern regions, lighted by the pale light of a polar sun, up in the higher latitudes, and now, contrary to these previsions, my uncle, the Icelander, and myself, were stretched on a mountain side, dried and burnt up by the heat of the sun, which was even now scorching us.

I could not believe my senses; but the roasting process my body was undergoing did not admit of a doubt. We had come out of the crater half naked, and the glorious orb from whom we had received nothing for two months, now lavished upon us his light and heat, and threw around us a flood of radiance.

When my eyes grew accustomed to the splendour, I endeavoured to correct the error of my imagination. I expected at least to be at Spitzbergen, and I felt it hard to give up the idea.

The professor was the first to speak:

"After all, it is not like Iceland."

"But Jan Mayen, perhaps?" said I.

"Not even that, my lad. This is no northern volcano, with its granite sides and cap of snow."

"Still—"

"Look, Axel, look!"

Above our heads, 500 feet at least, was a crater, by which escaped, at intervals of a quarter of an hour, with a loud report, a tall column of flame, mixed with pumice-stones, ashes, and lava. I could feel the convulsive movement of the mountain, which panted like a whale, casting up fire and hot air from its enormous blowholes. Lower down and on a very steep slope lay sheets of eruptive matter, covering a declivity 700 or 800 feet in extent, which gave the volcano a height of not quite 1,800 feet. Its base was lost in a basket-like mass of foliage, among which were distinguishable olives, figs, and vines, loaded with rosy grapes.

Not very like the Arctic regions, certainly.

Glancing across this belt of green, the eye was charmed with a lovely lake or sea, which made of this enchanted spot an island not many miles in extent. Eastward were a few houses, and then a little harbour, on whose blue waves there rode some vessels of peculiar form. Beyond these, groups of islands rose from the liquid plain, so numerous as to resemble a vast ant-hill. Looking towards the west, distant shores sloped to the horizon; on some there stood out the lovely outlines of blue mountains; on another more distant still, there towered a gigantic cone, on whose summit hovered a canopy of smoke. In the north an immense expanse of water sparkled in the sunlight, dotted here and there with tops of masts or the curves of a swelling sail.

The beauty of the scene was multiplied a hundred-fold by our entire unpreparedness for anything of the kind.

"Where are we? where are we?" I kept muttering to myself.

Hans closed his eyes, and was indifferent; my uncle gazed vacantly before him.

At last he remarked:

"Whatever mountain this is, it is rather warm quarters; the eruption is going on, and it would be a pity to have escaped a volcano to be crushed by a boulder. Let us go down, and then we shall find out all about it. Besides, I am dying of hunger and thirst."

Certainly, the professor was not of a reflective turn of mind. For my part, I was insensible to hunger or fatigue, and would have remained there for hours longer, but of course I had to follow my companions.

We encountered some very precipitous slopes in our descent from the volcano. We lost our footing among the ashes, and barely escaped the rivers of lava which ran along like fiery serpents. All the time we were coming down, I talked rapidly – my imagination was too much excited to let me be silent:

"We must be in Asia," cried I, "on the shores of India, or the Malay Islands, or Oceanica! We have crossed half the globe to come out at the antipodes of Europe."

"But how about the compass?" said my uncle.

"Yes, indeed! according to that we have gone uniformly northward."

"Then the compass lied!"

"Oh, uncle! Lied!"

"Yes, unless this is the North Pole!"

"Well, not the Pole; but—"

I had no solution to offer. I could think of nothing.

And now we were near the lovely vegetation, hunger assailed me, and thirst too. Fortunately, after two hours' walking, we came to a lovely plantation covered with olives, pomegranates, and vines, which looked as if they belonged to everybody. And indeed, in our state of destitution, we were not disposed to be too particular. How delightful we thought that fruit, and how eagerly we devoured the great bunches of rosy grapes. Not far among the shady trees we found a spring of water in the grass, and we bathed face and hands with the greatest enjoyment.

While thus revelling in the delights of rest, a child appeared between two clumps of olives.

"Ah!" exclaimed I, "behold an inhabitant of this happy land!"

It was a poor child, miserably clothed, scared-looking, and evidently frightened at our appearance; and in fact, half naked as we were, and unshaved, we must have looked rather queer, and unless the country was a nest of robbers, we were very likely to strike terror into the inhabitants.

Just as the little urchin was running off, Hans went and brought him back in spite of his kicks and cries.

My uncle began by comforting him, and asked him in German:

"My little friend, what is the name of this country?"

No answer.

"Very good," said my uncle; "we are not in Germany," and he repeated his question in English.

No answer. I was puzzled.

"Let us try Italian," said my uncle, and he asked, "*Dove noi siamo?*"

"Yes, where are we?" I repeated impatiently.

No answer.

"What! you won't speak," said my uncle, who was getting angry. He pulled the child's ears and asked:

"What do you call this island?"

"Stromboli," said the little herd-boy, and fled through the olives till he reached the plain.

We did not need him. Stromboli! How I was startled at this unexpected name. We were in the midst of the Mediterranean, in the Æolian archipelago of mythological memory – the ancient Strongyle, where Æolus held the wind and storms in fetters. And the blue mountains curving towards the east were the mountains of Calabria! And the volcano that rose on the southern horizon was Etna, the fierce Etna itself.

"Stromboli! Stromboli!" I repeated.

My uncle accompanied my gestures and words as if we were a chorus.

What a wondrous voyage! In by one volcano, out by another, and this other situated more than 3,000 miles from Snäfell; and from that arid Iceland, at the extreme end of the world. The chances of the expedition had brought us to the heart of the loveliest countries in existence. We had left the region of eternal snows for those of infinite verdure; and exchanged the grey fogs of the frozen zone for the azure blue of a Sicilian sky!

After an exquisite banquet of fruit and spring water, we set out again for the port of Stromboli. We did not think it prudent to divulge the manner of our arrival in the island; the superstitious minds of the Italians would certainly have looked on us as demons vomited forth from the infernal regions, so we made up our minds to pass as shipwrecked mariners. The glory was less, but the safety greater.

As we journeyed I heard my uncle mutter:

"But the compass – it always marked the north. How can we explain it?"

"Don't explain it!" said I, with a contemptuous air, "that is the easiest plan."

"What an idea! A professor at the Johannæum who could not find the reason of a cosmical phenomenon! It would be a scandal."

And as he spoke, my uncle, half naked as he was, girt with his leathern belt, and spectacles on nose, was once more the Professor of mineralogy.

An hour after leaving the olive wood we arrived at Port San Vicenzo, where Hans claimed the pay for his thirteenth week of service, which was paid to him with hearty good-will.

At this moment, if he did not participate in our emotion, he gave way to an expansion very unusual to him.

With the tips of his fingers he lightly pressed our hands and broke into a smile.

CHAPTER XLVI

HERE ENDS A story to which no credence will be given even by those who are astonished at nothing. But I am fore-armed against human incredulity.

We were received by the fishermen of Stromboli with the attention due to shipwrecked travellers.

They clothed and fed us. On the 31st of August, after a delay of forty-eight hours, we set sail in a speronar for the port of Messina, where a few days of rest made us forget our fatigues.

On Friday, September the 4th, we embarked on board the *Volturne*, one of the mail-packets of the *Messageries Impériales* of France, and, three days later, landed at Marseilles, having only one drawback to our satisfaction, namely, our mysterious compass. This inexplicable phenomenon worried me greatly. On September the 9th, late in the evening, we arrived in Hamburg.

I will not attempt to describe the amazement of Martha or the joy of Gräuben.

"Now that you are a hero," said my beloved, "you will not want to leave me again, Axel!"

I looked at her. She smiled through tears. The return of Professor Lidenbrock, I need not say, made a sensation in Hamburg. Owing to Martha's imprudent talk everybody had heard of his journey to the centre of the earth. Nobody believed it, and now that he had come back they believed it less than ever.

Still the appearance of Hans, and some reports received from Iceland, were not without effect on public opinion.

And thus my uncle became a great man, and I became the nephew of a great man, which is something. Hamburg gave a *fête* in our honour. A public meeting was held in the Johannæum, and my uncle related the history of the expedition, only omitting the facts about the compass.

The same day he deposited in the archives of the city the document of Saknussemm, and recorded his regret that circumstances stronger than his will had prevented him from following to the centre of the earth the footsteps of the Icelandic traveller. He was modest as to his achievement, and thereby increased his reputation.

So much honour of course raised up enemies, and as his theories, based on certainties, were opposed to scientific systems, on the question of central fire, he was engaged by tongue and pen in controversy with the *savants* of every country.

For my part, I cannot admit the theory of cooling. In spite of all I have seen I still cling to the doctrine of central fire; but I do not deny that certain circumstances, only dimly defined as yet, may co-operate with natural phenomena to modify this law.

While these questions were fermenting in the public mind my uncle had a great trial. Hans had left Hamburg, in spite of his entreaties. The man to whom we owed everything would not allow us to pay our debt. He was the victim of home-sickness.

"*Farväl*," said he one day, and with that little word of adieu he set out for Iceland, where he arrived safely.

We were deeply attached to our brave eider-duck hunter. Even in absence he will never be forgotten by the men whose lives he saved, and I certainly will see him again before I die.

In conclusion, I ought to add that this "Journey to the Centre of the Earth" made a great noise in the world. It was printed and translated into all languages; the leading journals extracted the principal episodes, which excited comment, discussion, and attack, sustained with great animation in the believing and unbelieving camps. My uncle had the rare felicity of being famous during his life, and Barnum, himself, proposed to exhibit him in the United States on very handsome terms.

Still, amid all this glory, there was an annoyance, I may say a torment; it was the one inexplicable fact – the compass. To a man of science, such a phenomenon unexplained is a mental torment. But my uncle was destined to be made entirely happy.

One day, in arranging a collection of minerals in his study, the well-known compass caught my eye, and I took a glance at it. It had lain there for six months, unconscious of the mischief it had done.

Suddenly, what was my surprise. I exclaimed—

The professor hastened to me.

"What is it?" said he.

"That compass!"

"Its needle is pointing south, not north!"

"What do you say?"

"Its pole is changed!"

My uncle looked, compared it, and then made a jump that shook the house.

What a light now broke upon us!

"Well then," said he, when he regained his speech, "after our arrival at Cape Saknussemm the needle of this confounded compass marked south for north."

"Clearly."

"Then our mistake is explained. What could have produced the change of polarity?"

"I think that is easy to explain," said I. "During the storm on the sea of Lidenbrock that fire-ball that magnetized all the iron in the raft, disorganized our compass!"

"Ha, ha!" laughed the professor, "then it was a prank of electricity?"

From that day my uncle was the happiest of sages, and I the happiest of men; for my lovely Virlandaise, abdicating her position of pupil, was installed in the Königstrasse house in double quality of niece and wife. I need not add that her uncle was the illustrious professor Otto Lidenbrock, corresponding member of all the scientific societies, geographical, and mineralogical, in the five quarters of the globe.

TWENTY THOUSAND LEAGUES UNDER THE SEA

CONTENTS

PART I

CHAPTER I
A MOVING ROCK

THE YEAR 1866 was marked by a very strange event, an inexplicable and unexplained phenomenon, which must still be in the recollection of our readers. Without mentioning rumours which agitated the population of the sea-ports, and extended to the interior of various countries, the maritime population were more particularly exercised in their minds. Merchants, ship-owners, ship-captains, skippers, and masters, both European and American, officers of the Marines of both countries, and, subsequently, the Governments of various States of these continents, were deeply engrossed respecting this phenomenon.

As a matter of fact, for some time many vessels had encountered "an enormous thing", long, spindle-shaped, phosphorescent at times – very much larger and swifter than a whale.

The facts relating to this apparition, as recorded in various "logs", agreed sufficiently respecting the formation of the object – or being – in question, the unheard-of celerity of its movements, its wonderful power of motion, the peculiar life with which it seemed endowed. If it were of the whale species, it exceeded in bulk all that science had hitherto classified. Neither Cuvier, nor Lacépède, nor Dumeril, nor M. de Quatrefages, had admitted the existence of such a monster.

But to strike a medium of the observations made at intervals, rejecting the timid estimates which pronounced this object to be 200 feet long, and putting away the exaggerated opinions which gave it a breadth of one mile and a length of three, we may state, nevertheless, that this extraordinary being exceeded anything hitherto discovered by ichthyologists – supposing it ever existed.

Now if it existed, the fact could not be denied, and with the instinct for the marvellous, indulged in by the average brain of humanity, one can understand the effect produced upon the world by this supernatural apparition. It was quite impossible to treat it as a mere fable.

In fact, upon the 20th July, 1866, the steamer *Governor*

Higginson, of the Calcutta and Burnach Steam Navigation Company, had encountered this moving mass five miles to the east of Australia. Captain Baker was at first under the impression that he had met with an unknown rock, and was preparing to take the bearings of it, when two columns of water, impelled by this extraordinary object, were spurted 150 feet into the air. So, unless this rock were subject to the intermittent expansions of a geyser, the *Governor Higginson* had in good earnest encountered some aquatic mammifer hitherto unknown, which spurted through its blow-holes two columns of water mixed with air and steam.

A similar occurrence was observed on the 23rd July in the same year, in the Pacific Ocean, by the *Christopher Columbus* of the West India and Pacific Steam Navigation Company. On this occasion the wonderful cetacean must have moved from place to place with extreme velocity, since the *Governor Higginson* and the *Christopher Columbus* had observed it at two places separate more than seven hundred nautical leagues.

Fifteen days later, two thousand leagues from the above latitude, the *Helvetia*, of the National Steamship Company, and the *Shannon*, of the Royal Mail, sailing between Europe and America, noticed the monster respectively 42° 15′ N. lat., and 60° 35′ W. long., of the meridian of Greenwich. In this simultaneous observation the minimum length of the mammifer was estimated at 350 feet, for the *Shannon* and *Helvetia* were smaller than it, inasmuch as they measured 300 feet only from stem to stern. Now the very largest whales – those which inhabit the neighbourhood of the Aleutian Islands, Kulammak and Umgillick – have never exceeded 180 feet, even if they reached that length.

These reports arrived in quick succession. Further observations made on board the Transatlantic "liner" *Pereire*; a collision between the *Etna* of the Inman Line and the monster; an official report sent in by the officers of the French frigate *La Normandie*; a very serious report obtained by the Secretary of State from Commodore Fitz-James of the *Lord Clyde*, stirred up public curiosity. In a country possessing some sense of humour the subject would have been treated as a joke, but in such grave and practical nations as England, America, and Germany, people were very much exercised in their minds.

In the large towns this monster became quite the rage; they

sung about it in the cafés, they derided it in the newspapers, and joked upon it in the theatres. The *canards* had now every opportunity to lay eggs of every colour. One might have noticed in the papers drawings and descriptions of all the terrible and imaginary beings, from the white whale – the fearful Moby Dick of the Arctic regions – to the immense Kraken, whose tentacles were sufficient to grasp a ship of 500 tons and drag it to the depths of the ocean. They reproduced even the statements of ancient writers, the opinions of Aristotle and Pliny, who admitted the existence of these monsters; the Norwegian narratives of the Bishop Pontopidan, the tales of Paul Heggede, and, finally, the reports of Mr. Harrington, whose good faith no one could impugn, when he declared he had seen, when on board the *Castillan* in 1857, that enormous serpent, which up to that time had only infested the waters of the ancient *Constitutional*.

Then there arose the interminable discussions between the credulous and the incredulous amongst scientific societies and publications. This "monster question" inflamed their minds. Journalists who professed themselves scientific in contradistinction to those who professed to be intellectual, "slung ink" to a great extent during this memorable campaign; some even shed a few drops of blood, for the sea-serpent gave rise to some very offensive personalities.

For six months this paper-war continued with varying success. To the leading articles of the Geographical Institute of Brazil, of the Royal Academy of Sciences at Berlin, of the British Association, of the Smithsonian Institute at Washington, to the discussions in the "Indian Archipelago", in the "Cosmos" of the Abbé Moigno, in the "Mittheilungen" of Petermann, in the scientific notices of French and other journals, the comic papers replied with unflagging energy, their lively writers parodying a speech of Linnæus, quoted by the opponents of the monster, maintained in effect that Nature did not do foolish things, and abjured their contemporaries not to give Nature the lie by admitting the existence of krakens, sea-serpents, "Moby Dick", and other inventions of drunken sailors. At length, in a very celebrated satirical journal, the editor attacked the monster, gave him a last blow, and conquered, amid universal laughter. Wit had vanquished science.

During the first months of the year 1867 the question

remained in abeyance, and did not appear likely to crop up again, when suddenly some new facts were brought to the knowledge of the public. These did not take the shape of a scientific problem which had to be solved, but of an actual danger to be avoided. Thus the question assumed a totally different aspect. The monster was still an islet, a rock, a reef, but a moving rock, indeterminable and unassailable.

On the 5th March, 1867, the *Moravian*, of the Montreal Ocean Company, in 27° 30' N. lat. 17° 52' W. long., during the night struck, on the starboard quarter, a rock, which no chart had ever laid down. Impelled by steam and wind, the vessel was progressing at the rate of thirteen knots. Had the *Moravian* not been very stoutly built she would have sprung a leak and have gone to the bottom with her 237 passengers and crew.

The accident happened at about 5 a.m., at daybreak. The officers of the watch hurried to the stern of the ship. They scanned the ocean with minuteness. They perceived nothing except a strong eddy, which broke about two cables' length distant, as if the surface of the sea had been violently disturbed. The bearings of the spot were accurately taken, and the *Moravian* continued her voyage apparently uninjured. Had she struck upon a sunken rock or on some wreckage? They could not tell, but upon examination in dock it was discovered that a portion of the keel had been carried away.

This occurrence, although sufficiently serious in itself, would perhaps have been forgotten, like many others, if, three weeks afterwards, it had not occurred again under exactly similar conditions. Only, thanks to the nationality of the ship, the victim of this system of running foul of vessels, and to the reputation of the company to which the ship belonged, the event created a great sensation.

No one can be ignorant of the name of Cunard, the celebrated English shipowner. This gentleman founded in 1840 a postal service between Liverpool and Halifax, N.S., with three wooden vessels and engines of 400 horse-power, and 1,162 tons measurement. Eight years afterwards the fleet of the company had increased by four ships of 650 horse-power and 1,820 tons, and two years later two other steamers of greater size were built. In 1853 the Cunard Company, which had again secured the concession to carry the mails, added successively to its fleet the *Arabia*, *Persia*, *China*, *Scotia*, *Java*, *Russia*, all vessels of the first-class, and the largest (except the *Great Eastern*) that had ever crossed the ocean. Thus, in 1867, the company possessed twelve ships, eight paddle and four screw-steamers.

I give these details so that every one may appreciate the importance of this company in maritime affairs. No enterprise connected with transatlantic transport has been conducted with such ability, or crowned with so great success. For six-and-twenty years the Cunard "liners" had crossed the Atlantic, and had never missed a voyage, had experienced no serious delays, nor even lost a man, a letter, or a vessel. So passengers choose them still, notwithstanding the great competition, as can be perceived from an abstract from the official reports. Under these circumstances it is not surprising that some excitement should have been created when the news came of an accident that had happened to one of the best steamers.

On the 13th April, 1867, the sea was smooth, the wind light, and the *Scotia* was in 15° 12' W. long. 45° 7' N. lat. She was steaming over thirteen knots. Her draught of water was about six metres and a half, her displacement 6,680 cubic metres.

About four o'clock in the afternoon, while dinner was proceeding in the saloon, a shock, but not a very great one, was distinctly felt somewhere on the starboard quarter abaft the paddles.

The *Scotia* had not struck; it had been struck, and, moreover, by some sharp or pointed thing, which contused her. This "hulling" of the vessel was so gentle that no one on board would have felt anxious had not someone run upon the bridge and exclaimed, "We are sinking! we are sinking!"

Of course the passengers immediately took alarm, but Captain Anderson soon reassured them. Indeed, the danger could not be imminent, as the *Scotia* is divided into seven water-tight compartments, and can put up with a little leakage.

Captain Anderson descended at once into the hold. He perceived that the fifth compartment had sprung a leak, and the rate at which the water was pouring in proved that the injury was of considerable extent. Very fortunately the furnaces were not situated in this portion of the ship, else they would have been quickly extinguished.

Captain Anderson stopped the *Scotia*, and sent one of the

sailors to examine the injury. He soon discovered a large hole in
the hull. Such damage could not be trifled with, and the *Scotia*
was put at half-speed for the rest of the voyage. She was then 300
miles from Cape Clear, and, after a delay of three days, which
caused great anxiety in Liverpool, she arrived in port.

The surveyors then set about their examination of the *Scotia*,
which was dry-docked for the purpose. They could scarcely
believe their eyes. About six feet below the water-line there was
a regular rent, in the shape of an isosceles triangle. The fissure in
the iron plating was perfectly even, and could not have been
more neatly done with a punch. It must have been caused by
an instrument of no common hardness, and after it had been
launched against the ship with such prodigious force as to pierce
an enormous hole in the iron, it had been withdrawn by a retro-
grade movement almost inconceivable.

This was the last occurrence which had so excited public
curiosity. From that time all disasters at sea which could not be
accounted for were put to the credit of the monster. This fantastic
animal bore the responsibility of all shipwrecks – whose numbers
are, alas! considerable – for out of the 3,000 vessels whose loss is
annually recorded, the number supposed to be lost, because no
intelligence concerning them has been received, scarcely reaches
200. Now this was the monster which, justly or unjustly, was
accused of their destruction; and, thanks to him, the communication between the continents became more and more dangerous, and the public demanded that the ocean should be cleared
of this formidable cetacean.

CHAPTER II
FOR AND AGAINST

WHILE THE EVENTS above described were taking place, I was
returning from a scientific expedition into the wild territory of
Nebraska, U.S.A. In my position as assistant professor to the
Natural History Museum in Paris, the French Government
had nominated me to the expedition. After six months passed
in Nebraska, I arrived in New York about the end of March, in
charge of a valuable collection. I had arranged to sail for France
at the beginning of May. In the meantime I was occupying

myself in classifying my mineral, botanical, and zoological collections, when the accident happened to the *Scotia*.

I was perfectly well acquainted with the topic of the day: how
could it be otherwise? I had read again and again the European
and American journals without being any more enlightened.
This mystery puzzled me. In the impossibility to form an opinion,
I drifted from one extreme to the other. That there was something was an undoubted fact, and the unbelieving were invited
to put their fingers into the side of the *Scotia*. When I arrived in
New York the subject was being freely discussed. The hypotheses
of the floating island and the unassailable rock, upheld by some
minds, had been altogether abandoned. And indeed, unless this
rock possessed a machine in its interior, how could it move at
such a tremendous pace! The floating hull of some large wrecked
vessel was also set aside as untenable, and for the same reason.

There thus remained two possible solutions to the question,
which called into existence two distinct clans or cliques – those
who believed in a monster of enormous size, on the other hand
those who supported the idea of a submarine vessel of a wonderful motive-power.

Now this last hypothesis, allowable after all, could not be
supported in face of the inquiry directed against it. That any one
person had such a mechanical power at his disposal was scarcely
likely. Where and when had he manufactured it, and how had
he kept the construction a secret?

A Government only could have possession of such a destructive machine, and in these disastrous days, when everyone is
bending his energies to multiply the effect of offensive weapons,
it was possible that one State might, unknown to others, attempt
such a formidable engine. After *chassepôts*, torpedos – after
torpedos, submarine rams; then – a reaction. At least, I hope so!

But the suggestion of an engine of war was dissipated by the
declarations of the various Governments. As the question agitated was of public interest, since inter-oceanic communication
was being interrupted, the statement of the Governments could
not be called in question. Moreover, how could the construction
of such a machine have escaped notice? To guard such a secret
under the circumstances would be a very difficult task for an
individual, and certainly impossible for a State, whose acts are
jealously watched by powerful rivals.

So, after inquiries had been instituted in England, France, Russia, Prussia, Spain, Italy, America, and even Turkey, the suggestion of a submarine monitor was definitely rejected.

The monster appeared by fits and starts, in spite of the incessant fire of jokes directed against it by the comic press, and in this direction imagination went to the most absurd lengths in fantastic ichthyology. On my arrival at New York many people had done me the honour to consult me upon the phenomenon in question. I had already published in France a work in two volumes quarto, entitled "The Mysteries of the Great Ocean Depths". This work, which was much relished by the scientific world, dubbed me a specialist in this somewhat obscure branch of natural history. My opinion was asked. So long as I could deny the reality of the occurrence I took refuge in absolute denial, but soon, driven to the wall, I was obliged to explain categorically; and "the Honourable Pierre Aronnax, Professor at the Museum in Paris", was formally called upon by the *New York Herald* to pronounce an opinion.

I complied with the request, because I was unable to remain silent. I discussed the question in all its bearings, politically and scientifically, and I give below an extract from a well-digested article which I published in the issue of the 30th April.

"Thus," said I, "after having examined one by one the various hypotheses, all other suppositions being rejected, we must necessarily admit the existence of a marine animal of great power.

"The profound depths of the ocean are entirely unknown to us. Soundings have never reached to the bottom. What goes on in these abysses? What beings inhabit or can inhabit the regions twelve or fifteen miles beneath the surface of the water? What is their organisation? One can scarcely even conjecture.

"Nevertheless, the solution of the problem which has been submitted to me assumes this shape—

"Either we are acquainted with all the varieties of beings which inhabit our planet, or we are not.

"If we do not know them all, if Nature has still secrets from us in ichthyology, nothing can be more rational than to admit the existence of fishes or cetacea of new species, or even new genera, of an essentially primary organization, which inhabit the beds of ocean inaccessible to the sounding line, and which some accident, a fancy or caprice, if they will it, impels, at long intervals, to the upper waters of the ocean.

"If, on the contrary, we *do* know all living species, we must, necessarily, seek for the animal in question amongst the marine animals already catalogued, and in this event, I am disposed to admit the existence of a gigantic narwhal.

"The common narwhal or sea-unicorn often attains a length of sixty feet. Five or ten times this extent would give to this cetacean a force proportionate to its size; increase its offensive power, and you obtain the animal you desire. It will have the proportions mentioned by the officers of the *Shannon*, the instrument needed for the perforation of the *Scotia*, and the force necessary to pierce the hull of a steamer. As a fact, the narwhal is armed with an ivory sword, or halberd – as some naturalists have termed it. It is a tooth of the hardness of steel. Some of these teeth have been discovered in the bodies of whales, which the narwhal can attack with success. They have also been extracted, and not without labour, from the hulls of ships, which they have pierced through and through, as a gimlet pierces a cask. The Museum of the Faculty of Medicine in Paris contains one of these weapons, two metres and a quarter in length, and forty-eight centimetres broad at the base.

"Well, then, suppose a weapon ten times as powerful, and the animal ten times as great as the ordinary narwhal, let it rush through the water at the rate of twenty miles an hour, multiply the mass by the velocity, and you will obtain a resultant capable of producing the shock required.

"So far as information can go, I am of opinion that this monster is a sea-unicorn of colossal dimensions, armed, not merely with a 'halberd', but with a veritable spur like an iron-clad or a 'ram', possessing, at the same time, a force and motive power in proportion.

"Thus I can explain this almost inexplicable phenomenon, unless there is really nothing at all – in spite of all that has been seen, written, and felt – which is still possible."

These last words were rather weak on my part, but I wished, up to a certain point, to shroud myself in my dignity as a professor, and not to give the Americans anything to ridicule, for they laugh well when they do laugh. I reserved a loophole for myself. In my heart I admitted the existence of the monster.

My article was warmly criticized, and this gave it popularity. It gained a number of adherents. The solution it advanced also gave free scope to the imagination. The human mind is pleased with great conceptions and supernatural beings. Now the sea is precisely the best vehicle for them, the sole medium where these giants, compared to which terrestrial animals, elephants or rhinoceros, are but dwarfs, can be produced and developed. These ocean depths contain the largest known species of mammalia, and perhaps contain molluscs of unheard-of size, crustacea frightful to behold, such as lobsters of 100 metres, and crabs weighing 200 tons! Why not? Formerly terrestrial animals of the geological epochs – the quadrupeds, apes, reptiles, and birds – were all formed upon gigantic models. The Creator cast them in a colossal mould, which time has by degrees reduced. Why cannot the sea, which never changes, while the earth is ever changing, still retain in its unknown depths these immense specimens of the animal life of former ages? Why cannot it hide within its bosom the last varieties of this Titanic species, whose years are centuries, and whose centuries thousands of years?

But I must not indulge in unbecoming speculations. A truce to these fancies, which time has shown me are terrible realities. I repeat the opinion then expressed of the nature of the phenomenon, and the public admits, without question, the existence of an enormous being which has nothing in common with the fabulous sea-serpents.

But if one party saw in this nothing but a scientific problem to be solved, the others, more positive, above all in England and America, were anxious to purge the ocean of this redoubtable monster, so as to secure safety in transatlantic communication. The commercial and trade journals took the matter up mainly with this view. The *Shipping and Mercantile Gazette, Lloyd's List, The Steamboat, The Maritime and Colonial Review,* all the papers devoted to the Insurance Companies, which threatened to raise their premiums, were unanimous on this point.

The opinion of the public being thus pronounced, the United States took the initiative.

Preparations were made at New York for an expedition destined to pursue this narwhal. A frigate of great speed – the *Abraham Lincoln* – was fitted out for sea at once. Commodore Farragut pushed forward the armament of the ship rapidly.

At this very time, as always happens, when they had determined to pursue the monster, the monster did not turn up. For two months nothing was heard about it. No vessel had fallen in with it. It seemed as if this unicorn had some knowledge of the toils being spread around it. Too much had been said about it, and by means of the Atlantic cable too. So argued the funny ones, who maintained that this "sly dog" had intercepted some telegram, which he had turned to his own advantage.

So there was the frigate supplied with material for a lengthened cruise, and formidable apparatus for the monster's capture, and no one knew whither she must sail. The general impatience was increased when, on the 2nd of July, it was announced that a steamer of the San Francisco and China line had seen the animal three weeks before in the South Pacific Ocean.

The excitement caused by this intelligence was intense. Commodore Farragut had not twenty-four hours' notice. His provisions were put on board. The bunkers were filled with coal. Not a man of the crew was missing. He had only to light the fires, get up steam, and put to sea. People would not have tolerated the delay of half a day. Besides, Commodore Farragut was only too anxious to set out.

Three hours before the departure of the *Abraham Lincoln*, I received a letter couched in the following terms: –

> "M. ARONNAX,
>   "Professor of the Museum of Paris,
>   "Fifth Avenue Hotel,
>   "New York.
>
> "SIR, –
>
> "If you wish to accompany the expedition on board the *Abraham Lincoln*, the United States' Government will be pleased that France should be represented by you, in this enterprise. Commodore Farragut will hold a cabin at your disposal.
>   "Yours very truly,
>   "J. B. HOBSON,
>   "Secretary to the Admiralty."

CHAPTER III
"JUST AS MONSIEUR PLEASES!"

THREE SECONDS BEFORE the arrival of Mr. Hobson's letter, I had no more notion of going in search of the unicorn than of attempting the North-West Passage. Three seconds after I had read the Secretary's letter, I quite believed that my true vocation, my only aim in life, was to hunt up this monster, and rid the world of him.

Meanwhile, I was about to undertake a trying journey, with all its fatigue and absence of repose. I had been wishing above everything to see my native land, my friends, my little house in the Jardin des Plantes, my cherished and valuable collections, once again. But now nothing would stop me. I forgot all this – friends, collections, and perils – and I accepted, without hesitation, the offer of the American Government.

Moreover, I thought every track leads to Europe, and the unicorn may be amiable enough to lead me to the coast of France. This worthy animal would doubtless permit himself to be taken in European waters, for my especial benefit, and I did not wish to bring back less than half a metre of his ivory halberd, for the Museum of Natural History.

But, meantime, it was necessary to search for this narwhal in the North Pacific Ocean; so to reach France, I should probably have to go by way of the antipodes!

"Conseil!" I cried peremptorily.

Conseil was my servant, a devoted fellow, who accompanied me in all my wanderings – a brave Fleming, whom I like very much, and who serves me well; phlegmatic by nature, regular on principle, zealous from habit, taking life very easy, very handy and apt in all things, and, his name notwithstanding, never giving advice, even when he was *not* asked for it.

In consequence of associating with *savants* in our little world in the Jardin des Plantes, Conseil had picked up some information. I possessed in him a specialist well up in the classification of natural history, who could run, so to speak, like an acrobat up the ladder of branches, groups, classes, sub-classes, orders, families, genus, sub-genus, species, and varieties. But there his scientific attainments stopped. To class was his *ultima thule*, but he knew nothing beyond that. Completely versed in the theory of classi-fication, but little in the practice, I do not believe he could distinguish a cachalot from a whale. Nevertheless, he was a brave and worthy fellow.

For the last ten years Conseil had followed me whithersoever science had drawn me. He never commented upon either the duration or the fatigue of a journey. He had no objection to start for any country, China or Congo it was all the same to him. He would go to one or the other and ask no questions. Moreover, he enjoyed excellent health, which set all illness at defiance; solid muscles, no nerves – not even the appearance of nerves – I mean moral nerves, of course. He was thirty years of age, and his age was to his master's as fifteen to twenty, so I need not add that I was forty years old. But Conseil had one fault. A strict formalist, he never addressed me except in the third person – enough to set your teeth on edge!

"Conseil," I repeated, as I began, with feverish hands, to make preparations for departure. Certainly, I was sure of this devoted fellow. In ordinary circumstances I never asked him whether it would suit him or not to accompany me in my travels; but this time it was upon an expedition which might be indefinitely pro-longed, and hazardous, in the pursuit of an animal capable of crunching a frigate like a nutshell. There was need of reflection in this, even for the most impassible man in the world. What would Conseil say?

"Conseil," I cried, for the third time.

Conseil appeared.

"Did Monsieur call?" he asked as he entered.

"Yes, my lad. Get my things and your own ready. We start in two hours."

"Just as Monsieur pleases," replied Conseil calmly.

"There is not an instant to lose. Pack up my trunk quickly."

"And Monsieur's collections?" asked Conseil.

"We will see about those later."

"What! the archiotherium, the hyracotherium, the oreodons, the cheropotamus, and the other specimens?"

"The hotel people will take care of them."

"And the babiroussa?"

"They will keep it during our absence. Besides, I will leave orders to forward our menagerie to France."

"We are not returning to Paris, then?" said Conseil.

"Well – yes – certainly," I replied evasively; "but we shall take a little round."

"Any *detour* that Monsieur pleases."

"Oh! that will not be of much consequence. By a less direct route, that's all. We shall sail in the *Abraham Lincoln*."

"As may be most convenient to Monsieur," replied Conseil quickly.

"You are aware, my friend, of the question about this monster – this narwhal. We are about to purge the sea of him. The author of a work in quarto, and in two volumes, upon the 'Mysteries of the Great Ocean Depths', cannot give up the idea of embarking with Commodore Farragut. A glorious enterprise, but dangerous. One cannot tell where they may go. These animals are very capricious; but we shall go all the same. We have a commander who has no fear."

"If Monsieur goes, I will go," replied Conseil.

"But mark well, for I have no wish to hide anything. This is one of the journeys from which one cannot always return."

"Just as Monsieur pleases."

A quarter of an hour afterwards our trunks were ready. Conseil had done everything, and I was sure nothing was forgotten, for this fellow could classify shirts and coats as well as birds and beasts.

The hotel "lift" deposited us in the great vestibule of the *entre-sol*. I descended to the hall, paid my bill, and gave directions to have my various collections of plants and animals forwarded to Paris. I opened a credit for the babiroussa, and, followed by Conseil, jumped into a carriage.

The fly, at twenty francs the course, descended Broadway as far as Union Square, proceeded along Fourth Avenue to its junction with Bowery Street, entered Katrin Street, and stopped at the thirty-fourth pier. There the Katrin ferry took us all over – men, horses, and carriage, to Brooklyn, the great suburb of New York, situated upon the left bank of the river; and in a few minutes we reached the quay, close to which the *Abraham Lincoln* was vomiting huge volumes of black smoke from her two funnels.

Our baggage was immediately put on board. I hurried after it, and asked to see the commodore. One of the sailors conducted me up to the poop, where I found myself in the presence of an officer of pleasant appearance, who offered me his hand.

"Monsieur Pierre Aronnax?" said he.

"The same," said I. "Have I the pleasure to address Commodore Farragut?"

"Yes, in person. You are welcome, sir, and your cabin is prepared."

I saluted him, and leaving the commodore to his duties, I descended to the cabin destined for my reception.

The *Abraham Lincoln* had been well selected and fitted out for its novel enterprise. She was a quick sailer, fitted with superheating apparatus, which permitted the expansion of the steam to seven atmospheres. With such a pressure, the *Abraham Lincoln* attained an average speed of eighteen miles and a quarter an hour, a very considerable speed, too, but not sufficient to cope with the gigantic cetacean.

The interior arrangements of the frigate were in keeping with her sea-going qualities. I was much pleased with my cabin, situated at the stern, opening to the ward-room.

"We shall be very comfortable here," said I to Conseil.

"Very much so, indeed, if Monsieur is not displeased to live like a hermit crab in a whelk-shell."

I left Conseil to arrange the cabin, and ascended to the deck to investigate the preparations for getting under weigh. At this moment Commodore Farragut gave orders to "let go", so, had I been a quarter of an hour later, I should have been left behind, and missed this extraordinary and improbable expedition, of which this truthful narrative may perhaps contain some incredible statements.

But Commodore Farragut did not wish to lose an hour in searching the seas in which the animal was reported to be found. He sent for the engineer.

"Is steam up?" he asked.

"Yes, sir," replied the engineer.

"Go ahead, then," said the commodore.

At this order, which was conveyed to the engine-room by a speaking tube, the engineers started the engines. The steam hissed into the cylinders, the long pistons set the connecting-rods of the shaft in motion. The blades of the screw beat the waves with increasing rapidity, and the *Abraham Lincoln* advanced majestically in the midst of a crowd of ferry boats and tenders, filled with spectators, which composed the procession.

The quays of New York and Brooklyn, bordering the East river, were crowded with the curious. Three cheers were given by half a million throats. Thousands of handkerchiefs were waved in salute to the frigate, until she reached the Hudson, at the point of the long peninsula on which stands the town of New York.

The frigate coasting the New Jersey side, on which so many pleasant villas are erected, passed the forts, which saluted. The *Abraham Lincoln* replied, dipping and hoisting the American flag three times, whose thirty-nine stars shone at the peak; then slackened speed, so as to make the buoyed channel which leads into the inner bay, formed by the point of Sandy Hook, where many thousands of spectators gave the frigate a parting cheer.

The procession of boats still followed the *Abraham Lincoln*, and did not quit her until they reached the light-ship at the entrance of the channel.

It was then three o'clock. The pilot got into his boat and was pulled on board his little schooner, which lay hove-to awaiting him. The frigate's fires were coaled up, the screw revolved quicker than before, the frigate passed the yellow low coast of Long Island, and at eight o'clock p.m., having lost sight of Fire Island, she proceeded at full speed across the Atlantic.

CHAPTER IV
NED LAND

COMMODORE FARRAGUT WAS a good sailor, and worthy of the frigate he commanded. His ship and he were one. He was the soul of it. On the question of cetaceans he entertained no doubt. He would not permit any discussion respecting it. He believed in it as some good women believe in Leviathan, by faith, not by reason. The monster was in existence, and he had sworn to rid the seas of him. He was a sort of Knight of Rhodes; a Dieudonné de Gozon, marching to encounter the serpent that was devastating his island. Either Farragut must kill the narwhal or the narwhal would kill Farragut. There was no compromising the matter.

The officers were of the same opinion as their commander. One could hear them speak, discuss, dispute, and calculate the various chances of an encounter, as they scanned the ocean expanse. More than one imposed a voluntary watch upon himself, and ascended to the fore-topmast cross-trees, which under other circumstances would have been voted an awful bore. So soon as the sun got hot, the masts were ascended by sailors, to whose feet the planks of the deck were too warm. Meanwhile, the *Abraham Lincoln* had not yet entered upon the suspected waters of the Pacific.

As for the ship's company, they asked for nothing better than a meeting with the unicorn, to harpoon him, hoist him on board, and to cut him up. They watched the sea with scrupulous attention. Moreover, Commodore Farragut had spoken of a certain sum of $2,000, reserved for whosoever he be, ship-boy or able seaman, master or officers, who should first signal the animal. So I leave you to imagine whether they used their eyes on board the *Abraham Lincoln*.

For my own part, I was not behind-hand with the others, and delegated to no one my part of the daily observations. The frigate might, with much reason, have been called *Argus*. Only amongst them all Conseil protested by his indifference on the question which absorbed us, and was somewhat a "damper" of the general enthusiasm on board.

I have already mentioned that Commodore Farragut had carefully provided proper apparatus to catch this enormous cetacean. A whaling ship could not have been better armed. We possessed all known weapons, from the simple hand-harpoon to the barbed arrows fired from a blunderbuss, and the explosive bullets of the duck gun. On the forecastle was trained the latest pattern of breech-loading cannon, of great thickness and accuracy, the model of which was in the Exhibition of 1867. This valuable weapon of American construction could carry with ease a conical shot, weighing four kilogrammes, to a distance of sixteen kilometres.

Thus no means of destruction were wanting on board the frigate. But there was better than this still. There was Ned Land, the king of harpooners.

Ned Land was a Canadian of almost incredible sleight of hand, and unrivalled in his perilous profession. Skill and coolness, bravery and tact, he possessed in a very high degree, and it must, indeed, be a very malignant whale, or a very astute cachalot, that could escape from his harpoon.

Ned Land was about forty. He was of large frame, and over six feet high, strongly built, grave, silent, sometimes passionate, and very angry when contradicted. He attracted attention by his appearance, and chiefly by the steadiness of his gaze, which gave a singular expressiveness to his countenance. I believe that Commodore Farragut had wisely engaged this man. He was worth the whole crew for steadiness of eye and hand. I can only compare him to a powerful telescope, which could be immediately used as a loaded cannon.

A Canadian is a Frenchman, and little communicative as Ned Land was, I think he conceived a certain liking for me. My nationality attracted him, no doubt. It was an opportunity for him to speak, and for me to listen to the old language of Rabelais, which is still in use in some parts of Canada. The family of the harpooner were originally from Quebec, and had already grown into a tribe of hardy fishermen when that town belonged to France.

By degrees Ned got to like a chat, and I was glad to hear the recitals of his adventures in the Arctic seas. He recounted his fishing exploits and his combats with much natural poetry of expression. His narratives assumed the epic form, and I could fancy I was listening to some Canadian Homer chanting an Iliad of the Arctic regions. I am now describing this hardy companion as I actually knew him. We have become quite old friends, united by the unalterable band of friendship, which is born of and cemented by the most terrible experiences in common. Ah, brave Ned, I only ask to live a hundred years so as to think the longer of you!

And now what was Ned Land's opinion respecting this marine monster? I should state that he scarcely credited the unicorn theory, and was the only one on board who did not share in the general conviction. He even avoided the subject, upon which I thought he ought to have entered some day.

One lovely evening, the 30th July, that is to say, three weeks after our departure, the frigate was about thirty miles to windward of Cape Blanco, on the coast of Patagonia. We had passed the tropic of Capricorn, and the straits of Magellan were scarcely 700 miles to the south. Before eight days had passed the *Abraham Lincoln* would be ploughing the waters of the Pacific.

Sitting on the poop, Ned Land and I were chatting of various things, watching that mysterious sea whose depths are still inaccessible to human research. I led the conversation up to the subject of the gigantic unicorn, and treated of the chances of success or failure of our expedition. Then perceiving that Ned permitted me to speak without replying, I put the direct question:

"How is it, Ned, that you cannot be convinced of the existence of this cetacean we are pursuing? Have you any particular reasons for being so incredulous?"

The harpooner looked at me for some seconds before he replied, then striking his forehead with a gesture habitual to him and closing his eyes, as if to collect his thoughts, he said at last, "Perhaps I have, M. Aronnax!"

"Why, Ned! a man like you, a 'whaler' by profession, and familiar as you are with all such marine animals – you, whose imagination can easily entertain the hypothesis of an enormous cetacean – you ought to be the very last person to harbour a doubt under such circumstances."

"It's just there where you make the mistake, sir," replied Ned. "That common people may believe in wonderful comets, or in the existence of antediluvian monsters inhabiting the centre of the earth, is not surprising; but neither the astronomer nor the geologist will admit such a theory. In the same way the whaler. I have hunted hundreds of cetaceans, harpooned quantities of them, killed them by dozens; but powerful and armed as they were, neither their tails nor their tusks were able to pierce or damage the hull of an iron steamer."

"But, Ned, there have been cases in which the tooth of the narwhal has pierced ships through."

"Wooden ships, perhaps," replied the Canadian. "All the same, I have never seen any. But, on the contrary, I deny that whales, cachalots, or narwhals can produce such an effect."

"Just listen to me, Ned."

"No, sir, no. Anything you like, except that. A gigantic polypus, for instance."

"Still less. The polypus is only a mollusc; and the name of it even indicates the consistency of its flesh. Is it 500 feet long ever? Why, the polypus does not belong to the branch of vertebrates, and is perfectly harmless towards such vessels as the *Scotia* and the *Abraham Lincoln*. We may, then, relegate to the land of fables all tales of the exploits of krakens and other monsters of like nature."

"Then, sir," said Ned, in a bantering tone, "you admit the existence of an enormous cetacean?"

"Yes, Ned; I repeat it with a conviction founded upon the logic of facts. I believe in the existence of a mammifer of a powerful organization, belonging to the vertebrate animals, like whales, cachalots, and dolphins, and furnished with a horny defence, whose power of penetration is very great."

"Hum," replied the harpooner, nodding his head with the air of a man unwilling to be convinced.

"Just consider, my worthy Canadian," I replied, "that if such an animal exist, if it inhabit the depths of the ocean, if it live some miles below the surface, it necessarily possesses an organism defying all comparison."

"And why should it have such a powerful organism?"

"Because it must possess a tremendous strength to enable it to live so far below the surface and resist the pressure of the water."

"Really?" inquired Ned, with a wink.

"Certainly; and figures can easily demonstrate it."

"Oh, figures!" cried Ned. "One can do anything with figures!"

"In business, Ned, but not in mathematics. Listen. Granting that the pressure of the atmosphere may be represented by the pressure of a column of water thirty-two feet high. In reality the column of water would be of less height, since it would be sea-water, whose density is superior to that of fresh water. Well, when you dive, Ned, so long as you have thirty-two feet of water above you your body is supporting a pressure equal to that of the atmosphere, that is to say a kilogramme for each square centimetre of surface. It follows that at 320 feet this pressure would be equal to 10 atmospheres, and to 100 atmospheres at 3,200 feet, and 1,000 atmospheres at 32,000 feet, which is about two and a half leagues. This is equivalent to saying that if you could reach this depth, each square centimetre of your body would bear a pressure of 1,000 kilogrammes. Now, my brave Ned, do you know how many square centimetres of surface there are in your body?"

"I cannot tell, M. Aronnax."

"About 17,000."

"So many as that?"

"And as, in fact, the atmospheric pressure is a little greater than one kilogramme to a square centimetre your 17,000 square centimetres are at this moment supporting a pressure of 17,568 kilogrammes (97,500 lbs.)."

"Without my being sensible of it?"

"Without your being sensible of it. And, if you are not crushed by this pressure, it is because the air enters the body with an equal force. So the inward and outward pressure are equal, and neutralize each other, and you can support it without inconvenience. But in the water it is a different thing."

"Yes, I understand," replied Ned, who was now very attentive, "because the water surrounds me, and does not enter the body."

"Precisely, Ned; so at thirty-two feet below the surface of the sea you would be subject to a pressure of 17,568 kilogrammes; at 320 feet ten times that pressure, that is to say, 175,680 kilogrammes; at 3,200 feet 100 times that pressure, viz., 1,756,800 kilogrammes; at 32,000 feet at least 1,000 times that pressure, viz., 17,568,000 kilogrammes. In other words, you would be flattened out as if you had been under a hydraulic press."

"The devil!" exclaimed Ned.

"So, my worthy harpooner, if vertebrates, many hundred metres long and large in proportion, live at such depths, and whose surface is represented by millions of centimetres, we must estimate the pressure to which they are subject by thousands of millions of kilogrammes. Calculate now what the strength of their bony structures and organism must be to enable them to resist such pressure."

"They must be like ironclad frigates," replied Ned.

"Just so, Ned; and now think of the damage such a mass could do, if, going at express speed, it encountered the hull of a ship."

"Well – yes – perhaps," replied the Canadian, staggered by these figures, but unwilling to yield to them.

"Well, are you convinced?"

"You have convinced me of one thing, sir, and that is that if such animals live at the bottom of the sea, they must necessarily be as strong as you state."

"But if they do not exist, how can you explain the accident to the *Scotia*?"

"Perhaps—" began Ned.

"Well, go on."

"Because it is not true," replied the Canadian, imitating unconsciously a celebrated reply of Arago.

But this reply only proved the harpooner's obstinacy – nothing more. I said no more upon that occasion. The accident to the *Scotia* was undeniable. The hole existed, and it had to be stopped up, and I do not think that the existence of any hole could be more conclusively demonstrated. Now as the hole did not get there of its own accord, and since it had not been produced by rocks or submarine engines, it must have been caused by some animal.

Now, according to my view, and for reasons already given, this animal belonged to the vertebrate branch, class mammalia, group pisciform, and to the order of cetacea. It was of the whale family (or of the cachalots or dolphins), its genus and species was a matter for later decision. To decide this it must be dissected; to dissect it, it must first be caught; to catch it we must have the harpooner – that was Ned Land's business; the harpooner must see it, which was the ship's affair; and to see it, it must first be in sight, which was a matter of chance!

CHAPTER V
"AT A VENTURE"

THE VOYAGE OF the *Abraham Lincoln* was not marked by any particular incident for some time. Nevertheless, a circumstance occurred which brought out the wonderful skill of Ned Land, and showed what confidence might be reposed in him.

On the 30th June the frigate communicated with some American whalers, and we learnt that they had seen nothing of the narwhal. But the captain of one vessel, the *Monroe*, hearing that Ned Land was on board the *Abraham Lincoln*, asked for his assistance in chasing a whale then in sight. The commodore, wishing to see Ned Land at work, gave him leave to go on board the *Monroe*. Chance favoured the Canadian, who, instead of one whale, harpooned two, "right and left", striking one to the heart, and taking possession of the other after a chase of some minutes. Certainly, if the monster should ever come into contact with Ned Land, it would be very bad for the monster.

The frigate ran along the south-east coast of America at a rapid rate. On the 3rd July we opened up the Straits of Magellan near Virgin Cape. But the commodore did not wish to enter upon this winding passage, so we directed our course round Cape Horn.

The crew thought him right. Was it at all likely that the narwhal would be encountered in the sinuous strait? A number of the sailors declared that the monster was too big to pass it.

Upon the afternoon of July 6th the *Abraham Lincoln* doubled the solitary island – that isolated rock at the extremity of the American continent named Horn by the Dutch sailors who discovered it, in compliment to their native town. The course now lay N.W., and next day the frigate's screw beat the waves of the Pacific Ocean.

"Keep your eyes open now," cried the sailors to each other. And they did very considerably.

Eyes and telescopes – somewhat dazzled, it is true, by the prospect of the $2,000 – rested not a minute. Day and night the ocean was scanned, and those who had night-glasses, whose facilities of seeing increased their opportunities fifty per cent., had a good chance of gaining the reward.

For myself, though the money was no attraction, I was not the least attentive of those on board. Giving but a few minutes to meals or repose, careless of the sun or wind, I scarcely quitted the deck. Sometimes perched in the nettings on the forecastle, sometimes on the poop-rail, I watched with anxious eyes the creamy wake of the frigate. And often have I partaken of the emotions of the officers and crew when some capricious whale elevated his black back above the surface of the waves. The deck of the frigate was crowded in an instant, officers and men came "tumbling up" from below, panting for breath, with restless eyes watched the course of the cetacean. I looked also, and became nearly blind over it, while Conseil, always so phlegmatic, would say calmly:

"If Monsieur would have the goodness to open his eyes a little less widely he would see very much better."

But all this excitement was to no purpose. The *Abraham Lincoln* would change her course and approach the animal signalled at the time, a whale or cachalot, which soon disappeared in the midst of a volley of curses.

Meantime the weather continued favourable, and the voyage

was proceeding under pleasant circumstances. It was then the winter season, for July in those latitudes corresponds to our January in Europe, but the sea remained calm, and could be observed for miles in every direction.

Ned Land still remained incredulous. He would not even pretend to examine the sea, save during his watch, except when a whale turned up; and, nevertheless, his wide range of vision would have rendered great service. But eight hours out of twelve this peculiar fellow was either reading or sleeping in his cabin. A hundred times I have expostulated with him.

"Bah," he would reply, "there is nothing at all, M. Aronnax, and if there were some animal what chance have we of seeing it? Are we not cruising at random? People have, they say, seen this now invisible beast in the Pacific; I admit it, but two months have passed since then, and your narwhal does not care to remain long in the same neighbourhood. It is gifted with great speed. Now you know as well as I, Monsieur, that nature would not have bestowed this attribute of speed upon the animal were it not for some useful purpose; so if the beast exist, he is far away from here by this time."

I had no reply to this. Evidently we were groping in the dark, but how else were we to proceed? So our chances of success were limited. However, no one despaired of ultimate success, and not a sailor on board had bet against the narwhal and his next appearance.

We crossed the tropic of Cancer in the 105° of longitude on the 20th July, and on the 27th of the same month we passed the equator on the 110° meridian. The frigate now directed her course towards the west, into the centre of the Pacific. Commodore Farragut thought, and with reason, that the monster would most likely frequent the deep waters at a distance from any land, which it feared to approach, "without doubt because there was not sufficient water for it", as the master remarked. The frigate passed by the Marquesas and the Sandwich Islands, crossed the tropic of Cancer at 132° longitude, and sailed towards the China seas.

We had at last reached the scene of the monster's latest gambols, and as a matter of fact, we lived for nothing else. Our hearts palpitated fearfully, and laid the foundation of future aneurism. The whole ship's company were suffering from a nervous excitement, of which I can give no idea. No one ate, no one slept. Twenty times a day a mistake or an optical delusion of some sailor perched upon the yards, gave rise to intolerable startings and emotions, twenty times repeated, which kept us in a state of "jumpiness", too violent not to bring upon us a reaction at no distant date.

And the reaction did not fail to set in. For three months – three months of which every day seemed a century – the *Abraham Lincoln* traversed the South Pacific, running up when a whale was signalled, making sudden turns, going first on one tack then on the other, stopping suddenly, "backing and filling", or reversing, and going ahead, in a manner calculated to put the engine altogether out of gear; and thus did not leave a point unexplored on the American side of the Japanese coast. And nothing – nothing after all was to be seen but the watery waste. No sign of a gigantic narwhal, nor a moving rock, nor of anything at all out of the common.

The reaction came. Discouragement seized upon all, and incredulity began to appear. A new feeling arose on board, which was composed of three-tenths shame and seven-tenths anger. They all felt very foolish, but were much more annoyed at having been taken in by a chimera. The mountains of argument which had been piled up for a year, crumbled away at once, and no one had any thought, except to make up for lost time, in the matters of food and sleep.

With the natural fickleness of the human mind, they went from one extreme to the other. The warmest adherents of the enterprise became, as a matter of course, the most ardent detractors. Reaction set in from the lowest ranks to the highest, and certainly had it not been for the firmness of Commodore Farragut, the frigate's head would have been put to the south again.

However, this useless search could not go on for ever. The *Abraham Lincoln* had nothing to reproach itself with, it had done its utmost to insure success. Never had ship or crew shown more patience or determination, the non-success could not be laid to their charge. Nothing now remained but to return home.

A representation to this effect was addressed to the Commodore. He was firm. The sailors did not conceal their disappointment, and the service was suffering accordingly. I do not mean to insinuate that there was a mutiny, but after a reasonable period, Farragut, like another Columbus, demanded three days more. If during that time the monster did not appear, the helmsman should have orders to put the ship about for American waters.

This promise was made upon the 2nd November. The result was to reanimate the failing courage of the crew. The ocean was scanned with fresh zeal. Everyone wished to give a last look in which memory might be summed up. Telescopes were used with a feverish activity. This was the last defiance hurled at the giant narwhal, and he could not in reason decline to reply to the challenge to appear.

Two days had passed. The *Abraham Lincoln* cruised about at half-speed. They employed a thousand means to awake the attention or to stimulate the apathy of the animal, in the hope that he was in the neighbourhood. Enormous quantities of lard were thrown over the stern, to the great satisfaction of the sharks, I may add. The boats pulled in all directions round the frigate, while she was hove-to, and did not leave any part unexplored. But the evening of the 4th of November arrived and nothing had been heard of the submarine mystery. On the following day, at noon, the three days' grace would expire. After that, Commodore Farragut, faithful to his promise, would give the order to "'bout ship", and abandon the Southern Pacific Ocean.

The frigate was then 31° 15′ N. lat. and 136° 42′ E. long. Japan was 200 miles to windward. Night came on. Eight bells was struck. Heavy clouds veiled the moon, then in her first quarter. The sea was calm, and rose and fell with a gentle swelling motion. At this time I was forward, leaning on the starboard nettings. Conseil, close to me, was looking ahead. The ship's company, perched in the shrouds, were scanning the horizon, which was darkened, and then lighted up occasionally. The officers, with their night-glasses, peered into the increasing obscurity. At times the dark sea scintillated under the moon's rays, which darted between the clouds: then all luminous effects would be again lost in the darkness.

Observing Conseil I fancied that he was yielding to the general influence. Perhaps, and for the first time, his nerves were moved by a sentiment of curiosity.

"Well, Conseil," said I; "here is our last opportunity to pocket $2,000."

"Monsieur must permit me to say that I have never counted upon winning this reward; and the Government of the Union might have promised $100,000 without being any the poorer."

"You are right, Conseil, this is a foolish business after all, and into which we rushed too hurriedly. What time has been lost! What useless worry! We might have been in France six months ago."

"In Monsieur's little apartment," replied Conseil, "in the museum. And I should have already classified the fossils, and the babiroussa would have been installed in his cage in the Jardin des Plantes, and been visited by all the curious people of Paris."

"Just so, Conseil, and no doubt they are all laughing at us."

"In reality," replied Conseil quietly, "I think that they do laugh at us, Monsieur. And— May I say it?"

"You may."

"Well, then, Monsieur has only got what he deserves."

"Indeed!"

"When one has the honour to be a *savant* like Monsieur, one does not make oneself conspicuous—"

But Conseil never finished his compliment. In the midst of the universal silence a voice was heard. It was Ned Land's voice, and Ned Land cried out:

"Hallo, there! There is our enemy, away on the weather beam!"

CHAPTER VI
FULL SPEED

AT THIS ANNOUNCEMENT the whole crew ran towards the harpooner – commodore, officers, mates, sailors, and boys; even the engineers left the engine-room, and the stokers the furnaces. The order to "stop her" was given, and the frigate now only glided through the water by her own momentum.

The darkness was profound: and the Canadian must have had very good eyes. And I wondered what he had seen, and how he had been able to see it. My heart was beating fast.

But Ned Land had not been mistaken, and we all perceived the object he indicated with his outstretched hand.

Two cables' lengths from the *Abraham Lincoln*, and on the

starboard quarter, the sea appeared to be illuminated from below. It was not a common phosphorescence, and could not be mistaken for it. The monster, some fathoms beneath the surface, gave forth this intense light, which had been referred to in the reports of many captains. This wonderful irradiation must have been produced by some tremendously powerful illuminating agent. The luminous part described an immense elongated oval upon the water, in the centre of which was condensed a focus of unbearable brilliancy, which radiated by successive gradations.

"It is nothing but an agglomeration of phosphorescent molecules," cried one of the officers.

"No, sir," I replied, firmly, "neither the pholades nor salpæ produce such a powerful light. This brilliancy is essentially electric. But look – look – it moves, it advances – it retreats – it is rushing towards us!"

A general cry arose.

"Silence," cried Farragut. "Put the helm up – hard! Turn astern!"

The sailors rushed to the wheel; the engineers to the engine-room. The engine was reversed, and the *Abraham Lincoln* payed off to larboard, and described a semi-circle.

"Steady!" – "Go ahead!" cried Commodore Farragut.

These orders were executed, and the frigate rapidly distanced the luminous object. I should have said, attempted to distance it, for the supernatural animal moved with twice the speed of the frigate.

We were speechless. Astonishment more than fear kept us silent and motionless. The animal gained upon us easily. He swam round the frigate, which was then going fourteen knots, and wrapped us in his electric beams like a luminous dust. He then went away for two or three miles, leaving a phosphorescent line behind him, like the volumes of steam left by the engine of an express train. All at once, from the dark limit of the horizon where he had gone to take his start, the monster launched himself suddenly against the *Abraham Lincoln* with fearful rapidity, stopped suddenly within twenty paces of the frigate, extinguished the light – not by plunging beneath the surface, since the gleam was not withdrawn by degrees – but suddenly, as if the source of the brilliant light had been suddenly dried up. It then reappeared at the other side of the frigate, so either it had turned, or the monster gone underneath it. At every moment a collision seemed imminent, and that would have been fatal to us.

Meantime, I wondered at the behaviour of the frigate. She was flying and not attacking. She was pursued, instead of being the pursuer, and I said so to Commodore Farragut. His usually impassible face betrayed the greatest astonishment.

"M. Aronnax," he replied, "I do not know with what formidable being I have to do – and I do not wish to risk my ship in this darkness. Besides, how can I attack it, or how defend myself from its attack? Let us wait for daylight and the sides will be changed."

"You have no doubt respecting the nature of the animal, commodore?"

"No, it is evidently a gigantic narwhal, but also an electric one."

"Perhaps," I added, "we should not approach it any more than a torpedo?"

"Quite so," replied the commodore, "and if it possess the power to emit a shock, it is the most terrible animal ever created. That is why, sir, I am on my guard."

The crew all remained on deck during the night. No one dared to sleep. The *Abraham Lincoln*, not being able to cope with the animal in speed, had moderated her pace, and was kept under easy steam. On his part the narwhal, imitating the frigate, lay rocking at the will of the waves, and appeared to have made up its mind not to abandon the struggle.

It disappeared, however, about midnight, or, to employ a better term, extinguished itself like an enormous glow-worm. Had it fled? We might fear, but could not hope so. But at seven minutes to 1 a.m. a deafening rushing noise was heard, like that produced by a column of water expelled with extreme violence.

Commodore Farragut, Ned Land, and I were then on the poop searching into the profound obscurity.

"Ned Land," asked the commodore, "you have often heard the blowing of whales?"

"Often, sir, but never of such whales, the sight of which has brought me $2,000."

"You have a right to the reward. But tell me is this noise the same as whales make in ejecting water from their 'blow-holes'?"

"The same noise, sir, but ever so much louder. One cannot mistake it. It is truly a cetacean which is here with us. With your permission," added the harpooner, "we will have a word or two with him to-morrow morning."

"If he will listen to you, Master Land," I said, in a sceptical tone.

"If I get within four harpoons' length of him," replied the Canadian, "I will engage that he will listen to me."

"But to approach him I must put a whale-boat at your disposal?" said the commodore.

"Certainly, sir."

"And by so doing risk the lives of my men?"

"And mine also," replied Land quietly.

About two o'clock a.m. the luminosity reappeared, not less intense, five miles to windward of the frigate. Despite the distance and the noise of the wind and waves, the sound made by the formidable beatings of the monster's tail could be distinctly heard, and even its hoarse respiration could be distinguished. It seemed that when this immense narwhal was breathing, that the air rushing from the lungs was like the steam from the cylinders of an engine of 2,000 horse-power.

"Hum," I muttered, "a whale with the force of a regiment of cavalry ought to be a fine one."

Everyone remained on the watch till daybreak, and prepared for the combat. The fishing material was arranged along the nettings. The mate had charge of those blunderbusses which can throw a harpoon to the distance of a mile, and the long duck-guns, with the explosive bullets, whose wound is mortal, even to the most powerful animals. Ned Land was content with his harpoon, which in his hands was a terrible weapon.

At six o'clock day began to dawn, and at the first beams of sunrise the narwhal's light was extinguished. At seven o'clock the light was sufficiently strong for our purpose, but a very thick mist hung around the horizon, and the best glasses could not pierce it. Much disappointment and anger was the result.

I ascended to the mizzen-yard. Several officers were already perched at the mast-head.

At eight o'clock the mist began to disperse slowly. The horizon gradually cleared. Suddenly the voice of Ned Land was heard,

"Here is the animal astern!"

Everyone looked in the direction indicated. There, about a

mile and a half from the frigate, a long black body raised itself about a yard above the waves. Its tail, which moved quickly, kept up a considerable agitation in the water; never had tail beaten the water with such force. An immense frothy wake marked the course of the animal, and described an extended curve.

The frigate approached the cetacean. I examined it carefully. The reports of the *Shannon* and *Helvetia* had exaggerated its dimensions a little, and I estimated its length at only 250 feet. As for its bulk, it could not be easily arrived at, but the animal appeared to me to be admirably proportioned throughout. While I was looking at this phenomenal creature, two jets of water and steam spurted from the blow-holes, up to a height of forty yards, which settled its manner of respiration in my mind. From that I concluded that the animal belonged to the vertebrates, class mammifer, sub-class mono-dolphins, pisciform group, cetacean order, and family— Here I was unable to pronounce an opinion. The cetaceans comprise three families: whales, cachalots, and dolphins; and it is with the last-named that narwhals are ranged. Each of these families is divided into several genus, each genus into species, each species into varieties. Varieties, species, genus, and family failed me here, but I did not doubt that I should be able to complete my classification with the assistance of heaven – and Commodore Farragut!

The crew were impatiently awaiting orders. The commodore, having attentively observed the animal, called the engineer. He came at once.

"Have you plenty of steam?"

"Yes, sir," replied the engineer.

"Good. Fire-up; and go a-head full speed."

Three cheers accompanied this order. The struggle had come. In a few moments after the frigate's chimneys poured forth their black smoke, and the deck shook with the action of the engines.

The *Abraham Lincoln*, impelled by her powerful screw, "went for" the strange animal direct. It permitted the frigate to approach to within half a cable's length, then, disdaining to dive, went on a little, and contented itself by keeping its distance. This manner of pursuit continued for about three-quarters of an hour, without the frigate having gained upon the cetacean. It became evident that if we kept thus we should never reach it.

Commodore Farragut got very angry. "Ned Land!" he cried.

The Canadian approached him.

"Well, Master Land, do you still advise me to launch a boat?"

"No, sir," replied Ned Land; "for this beast will not let you take him unless he please."

"What are we to do, then?"

"Keep up the highest possible pressure, and, if you will permit it, I will get under the bowsprit, and if I come within casting distance I will harpoon him."

"Go, Ned," replied the commodore. "Go a-head faster," he cried to the engineer.

Ned Land took up his position. The furnaces were coaled up, the screw made forty-three revolutions in the minute, and the steam went roaring through the safety-valves. They heaved the log, and found that the frigate was going at the rate of eighteen and a half miles an hour.

But the cursed animal also went at eighteen and a half miles an hour.

For an hour and a half the frigate went at this pace, without gaining a foot. This was rather humiliating for one of the swiftest vessels of the American navy. The ship's company got sulky. They reviled the monster, which did not condescend to reply. Commodore Farragut no longer twisted his chin-tuft – he bit it. The engineer was summoned once more.

"Are you going at your fullest possible pressure?"

"Yes, sir," replied the engineer.

"The valves are charged?"

"Up to two atmospheres and a half."

"Charge them up to ten," cried the commodore.

That was a true American order. It could not be surpassed on the Mississippi, to distance a rival steamer.

"Conseil," said I to my faithful servitor, who was near, "do you know where we are likely to go to?"

"Wherever Monsieur pleases," replied Conseil.

"Well, I confess I am not indisposed to take the chance," said I.

The steam-gauge went up; the furnaces were filled. The speed increased. The masts shook fearfully, and the chimneys seemed scarcely sufficient to permit the escape of the immense volumes of smoke.

They heaved the log again.

"What pace now, eh?" inquired the commodore.

"Nineteen and a quarter, sir."

"Press on more."

The engineer obeyed. The steam-gauge showed ten atmospheres' pressure. But the narwhal had also "fired-up", for it was now going at "nineteen and a quarter", also.

What a chase it was! I cannot describe my feelings. Ned Land was at his post – harpoon in hand. Many a time the animal permitted us to approach.

"We are gaining, we are gaining," cried the Canadian.

But at the moment he was prepared to strike, the cetacean went ahead with a speed of scarcely less than thirty miles an hour. And even at our greatest speed, it cruised round the frigate. A cry of fury then escaped from all.

At mid-day we were not more advanced towards the attainment of our object than we had been at eight o'clock.

Commodore Farragut then decided to employ more direct measures.

"Well," he said, "that animal can go faster than the *Abraham Lincoln*. We will see if he can distance a conical bullet. Gunner, get the forward gun ready for action."

The bow-gun was immediately loaded, pointed, and fired. The ball passed over the cetacean, now half a mile distant.

"Take better aim next time, you lubbers, and there's $5 to the man who puts a shot into the infernal beast."

An old gunner with a grey beard came forward, with a determined air and resolute eye. He pointed the gun and took a long steady aim. A loud detonation was heard amid the cheers of the crew.

The shot had hit the animal, but not fairly; it glanced off its smooth side, and fell into the sea two miles distant.

"Ah!" cried the gunner, angrily, "those kind of fellows are sheeted with six inches of iron, I suppose."

"Tarnation!" cried Commodore Farragut.

The chase recommenced, and the Commodore coming towards me, said:

"I will pursue that thing till the frigate blows up."

"Yes," I replied, "you are quite right."

But I could not but hope that the animal might become

exhausted, and not be so indifferent to fatigue as a steam-frigate. But it was no use. Time passed without the animal showing any signs of fatigue.

But I must confess that the *Abraham Lincoln* kept up the chase with great spirit. I do not think that we traversed less than 300 miles during that inauspicious 6th of November. Night came and enveloped the swelling ocean in its shadows.

I then began to believe that our expedition was at an end, and that we had seen the last of the fantastic monster. But I was mistaken. About 10 p.m. the electric gleam again appeared about three miles off, as clear and bright as upon the preceding night.

The narwhal was motionless. Perhaps, fatigued by its day's run, it was asleep, rocked by the billows. This was a chance by which Farragut determined to profit.

He gave orders that the frigate should be put at easy speed and advance cautiously towards its enemy. It was by no means an uncommon occurrence to meet sleeping whales at sea, when they have been successfully attacked, and Ned Land had frequently harpooned them under these circumstances. He took up his former position at the bows, while the frigate noiselessly approached the animal, and stopped the engines about two cables' length distant, merely advancing by its momentum. The crew were in a state of breathless attention. Profound silence reigned on deck. We were not a hundred paces from the light which flashed into our eyes.

At this moment I saw Ned Land beneath me, holding by one hand to the martingale, with the other brandishing his fatal harpoon. Scarcely twenty paces separated us from the sleeping monster.

Suddenly Ned launched his harpoon. I heard the blow with which it hit the prey; it sounded as if it had come in contact with a hard substance.

The electric gleam was suddenly extinguished, and two enormous columns of water were directed over the deck of the frigate, rushing like a torrent fore and aft, overturning the men, and breaking the seizings of the spars. A terrible shock was felt, and, thrown over the bulwark, before I had time to save myself, I was precipitated into the sea.

CHAPTER VII
AN UNKNOWN SPECIES OF WHALE

SO SURPRISED WAS I by my unexpected fall that I have but little recollection of my sensations at the time.

I was first dragged down about twenty feet. I am a good swimmer, not so good as Byron or Edgar Poe, and this plunge did not embarrass me. Two vigorous strokes brought me to the surface. My first care was to seek the frigate. Had the crew observed my fall? Had the *Abraham Lincoln* put about? Was the commodore sending a boat for me? Could I hope to be rescued?

The darkness was profound. I could perceive a black mass disappearing in the east, whose lights were extinguished by distance. It was the frigate. I felt I was lost!

"Help! help!" I cried, swimming in the direction of the *Abraham Lincoln* despairingly. My clothes weighed upon me heavily. The water glued them to my body; they paralysed my movements. I was dying; I was suffocating. "Help!"

This was the last cry I uttered. My mouth filled with water; I was overwhelmed – dragged beneath the surface.

Suddenly my clothes were seized by a strong hand. I was drawn up, and I heard – yes, heard these words:

"If Monsieur will have the great kindness to support himself upon my shoulder he will swim more easily."

I seized the arm of my faithful Conseil.

"Is it you?" I said; "*you!*"

"Myself," replied Conseil, "at Monsieur's orders."

"And you were thrown into the sea by that shock as well as I?"

"Not at all; but being in Monsieur's service I have followed him!" The worthy fellow saw nothing extraordinary in this.

"And the frigate?" I asked.

"The frigate," replied Conseil, turning on his back; "I think we had better not count upon her!"

"What!"

"I say, that as I jumped into the sea I heard the steersman cry, 'The screw and the helm are both broken!'"

"Broken!"

"Yes; by the teeth of that monster. It is the only damage the

Abraham Lincoln has suffered. But, unfortunately for us, she cannot steer."

"Then we are lost!"

"Perhaps so," replied Conseil calmly. "But we have still some hours before us, and a great many things may happen in that time."

The imperturbable coolness of Conseil reassured me. I swam more vigorously, but, impeded by my clothes, I found great difficulty in keeping afloat. Conseil perceived this.

"Will Monsieur permit me to make a little incision? There," said he; and with a quick movement he passed the blade of his knife from my back downwards. Then he slowly took off my garments, while I swam for both.

I, in my turn, then rendered him a like service; and we continued to swim close together.

Nevertheless, the situation was no less alarming. Perhaps our disappearance had not been remarked, and if it had the frigate could not return for us, being deprived of her rudder. We then could only count upon one of her boats to pick us up.

Conseil coolly reasoned upon this hypothesis, and made his arrangements accordingly. He was apparently quite at home.

We made up our minds that our only chance of safety lay in our rescue by the boats of the frigate, and we therefore ought to arrange so as to remain as long as possible above water. I resolved to divide our strength, so that we should not succumb simultaneously, and this is how we did it. While one lay upon his back, motionless, with folded arms and extended limbs, the other was to swim and push him along. The part of following in his companion's wake was not to last more than ten minutes, and by thus taking it in turn we might be able to swim for some hours, and perhaps until dawn.

It was but a chance, but hope is firmly anchored in the human breast. Then we were two. In fact, I declare, though it may appear improbable, if I tried to destroy all expectation, if I wished to despair, I could not have done so.

The collision between the frigate and the monster had occurred about 11 p.m. I counted upon eight hours' swimming until sunrise. This was very practicable by helping each other as explained. The sea, being smooth, did not trouble us much. Sometimes I tried to pierce the thick darkness, which was broken only by the phosphorescence created by our movements.

I kept looking at the luminous waves, which broke upon my hand, whose sparkling surface was spotted with bright bubbles. It looked as if we were swimming in a bath of mercury.

About one o'clock I began to feel very tired. My limbs were knotted with violent cramps. Conseil did his best to support me, and our preservation now depended upon his care. I soon heard the brave fellow gasping for breath. I understood that he could not hold out much longer.

"Let me go," I cried. "Leave me."

"Abandon Monsieur! Never!" he replied. "I am looking forward to drowning before him."

At this moment the moon broke through the clouds. The surface of the sea sparkled in its rays. This pleasant light re-animated our courage. I raised my head again and looked around the horizon. I saw the frigate five miles away – a black and scarcely distinguishable mass. But there were no boats!

I was about to cry out; but for what purpose at such a distance? My swollen lips refused to utter a sound. Conseil could articulate a little, and I heard him repeat many times, "Help, help!"

Suspending our movements for a moment, we listened. Was that a buzzing noise in the ear, or was it an answer to Conseil's cry for assistance?

"Did you hear that?" I murmured.

"Yes, yes!" and Conseil again cried for help despairingly.

This time there was no mistake. A human voice replied. Was it the voice of some unfortunate person, abandoned in the midst of the ocean – some other victim of that collision? or rather, was it a boat from the frigate hailing us in the darkness? Conseil made a last effort, and leaning on my shoulder, while I gave all the support of which I was capable, he raised himself half out of the water, and fell back exhausted.

"What have you seen?"

"I have seen," he murmured, "I have seen – but let us not talk, let us husband all our strength."

What had he seen? At that moment the monster came to my mind with all its old force. But there was the voice. The times were past for Jonahs to live in whales' bellies.

Nevertheless, Conseil pushed me forward once more. He raised his head at times to look before him, and uttered a cry, to which a voice replied nearer and nearer each time.

I could scarcely hear it. My strength was spent; my fingers were no longer at my command; my hands could no longer make the strokes; my mouth, convulsively opened, was filled with the salt water, and cold was seizing upon my limbs. I raised my head for the last time, and sank.

At that moment a hard substance struck me. I clung to it. It drew me upwards, and so soon as I regained the surface I fainted. I came to myself very speedily, thanks to the vigorous friction applied to my body. I opened my eyes.

"Conseil," I murmured.

"Did Monsieur call?" he asked.

The moon again burst forth, and by her light I recognized another figure beside Conseil.

"Ned!" I exclaimed.

"In person, sir, looking after his reward."

"You were also thrown into the sea by the collision, I presume?"

"Yes, sir," replied he; "but, more fortunate than you, I got upon a floating island at once."

"An island?"

"Yes; or rather upon our gigantic narwhal."

"Explain yourself, Ned."

"There is only this. I have discovered why my harpoon did not injure the creature, and was blunted by the hide."

"Why, Ned? Why?"

"Because this beast is clothed in sheet-iron."

It was now necessary for me to recover my spirits and collect my thoughts. The last words of the Canadian had produced a sudden change of thought. I pulled myself up to the top of the object or being upon which we had taken refuge. I kicked it. It was certainly a hard body, and not of the material of which immense marine mammifers are composed.

But this hard substance might be a bony covering like those possessed by some antediluvian animals; and I might be free to class it amongst amphibious animals – the tortoises and alligators. But the black surface that supported us was smooth and polished, not imbricated. It gave out a metallic sound when struck, and, incredible as it may appear, it seemed to me to be composed of riveted iron plates. No doubt about it. The animal, the monster, the phenomenon which had puzzled the entire scientific world, upset and mystified the minds of sailors in both hemispheres, was a greater wonder still – a phenomenon constructed by human agency.

I should not have been nearly so much astonished by the discovery of the most fabulous and mythological of animals. However extraordinary the being may be that is from the hands of the Creator, it can be understood; but to discover all at once, under one's very eyes, the human realization of the impossible, was sufficiently startling. But we must not hesitate. Here we were sitting upon the top of a species of submarine boat, which presented, so far as we could judge, the form of an immense fish of iron. This was Ned Land's opinion. Conseil and I could not classify it.

"But," said I, "he must contain within him the machinery for locomotion, and a crew to direct his course."

"Certainly," replied the Canadian; "and nevertheless, during the three hours I have been here, I have perceived no signs of life."

"The boat has not moved?"

"No, M. Aronnax; it has lain rocked by the waves, but has not otherwise moved."

"We know already that it possesses great speed. Now as there is a machine with this attribute, and a machinist to direct it, I conclude that we are safe."

"Hum," replied Ned Land, doubtfully.

At this moment, and as a commentary upon my remark, a disturbance arose at the stern of this strange vessel, whose mode of propulsion was evidently a screw, and it began to move. We had scarcely time to secure ourselves to the higher part, which was about a yard out of water. Fortunately the speed was not great.

"So long as it goes over the waves, I have no particular objection," said Ned Land. "But if it should take a dive, I would not give $2 for my skin."

The Canadian might have made even a lower estimate. But under the circumstances, it was necessary to communicate with the beings shut up in this machine. I looked for an opening – a panel – a "man hole", to use the technical term, but the lines of rivets solidly fixed upon the joinings of the iron plates were whole and regular.

Moreover, the moon deserted us, and left us in profound obscurity. We were, therefore, obliged to wait for daylight, to find means to penetrate into the interior of this submarine vessel.

Thus our safety depended entirely upon the caprice of the mysterious helmsman who guided this machine: if he descended we were lost. Unless this occurred, I had no doubt of being able to communicate with the crew. And indeed if they did not manufacture the air they breathed, they must come to the surface from time to time to replenish the supply. Thus the necessity for an aperture communicating with the outer air.

We had given up all hope of being rescued by Commodore Farragut. We were proceeding westwards, and I estimated our speed at twelve miles an hour. The screw revolved regularly, sometimes emerging and throwing phosphorescent jets of water to a great height.

About 4 a.m. the speed increased. We had some difficulty in resisting this giddy pace, as the waves beat upon us in full volume. Fortunately Ned felt a large ring, let in to the upper part of the iron back, and we fastened ourselves to it securely.

This long night at length came to an end.

My imperfect recollection cannot recall all the impressions of those hours. One detail comes to my mind. During certain lulls of the wind and waves, I fancied I could hear, vaguely, a sort of fugitive harmony, produced by distant chords. What was, then, this mystery of submarine navigation, of which the world was vainly seeking the key? What kind of beings inhabited this vessel? What mechanical agency permitted them to move at such a prodigious rate?

Daylight appeared. The morning mists wrapped us in their folds, but soon dispersed. I was making a careful survey of the hull, which formed, at its upper part, a sort of horizontal platform, when I found myself sinking by degrees.

"Eh! thousand devils," cried Ned Land, striking the iron a sounding blow with his foot. "Open, I say, you inhospitable travellers!"

But it was no easy matter to make them hear while the screw was working, Fortunately the descent was arrested.

Suddenly a noise, as of bars being pushed back within the boat, was heard. A plate was raised, a man appeared, uttered a singular cry, and immediately disappeared. Some time after, eight strong fellows, with veiled faces, silently rose up and pulled us into the formidable machine.

CHAPTER VIII
MOBILIS IN MOBILE

THIS MOVEMENT, THOUGH SO roughly executed, was performed with lightning rapidity. My companions and I had not time to look about us. I do not know that it was a great trial, our being thus introduced into the floating prison, but, for my own part, I must say that a rapid shudder went through me. With whom had we to do? Doubtless with some pirates, who were exploring the seas after their own fashion.

Scarcely had the narrow panel been closed than we were surrounded by thick darkness. My eyes coming from the daylight so suddenly could distinguish nothing. I felt that I was upon an iron ladder. Ned Land and Conseil, held tightly, followed me. At the bottom of the ladder a door was opened, and was shut upon us with a loud noise. We were left to ourselves. Where? I could not say – scarcely fancy. All around us was of such an absolute blackness that even after a time my eyes perceived none of those rays which are perceptible in the darkest nights.

Ned Land, furious at such treatment, gave free vent to his indignation.

"A thousand devils," he cried; "they call this hospitality. They only want to be cannibals to be perfect. I should not be surprised; but I will give them something before they make a meal of me!"

"Be quiet, friend Ned, keep quiet," said Conseil calmly. "Don't look too far ahead. We are not roasted yet."

"Roasted, no," replied Land; "but we are in the oven. It is as dark, at any rate. Fortunately, I have not lost my bowie-knife, and I can generally see well enough to use it. The very first of these robbers who lays a finger on me—"

"Don't put yourself out, Ned," I said; "we shall gain nothing by useless violence. Who can tell whether they can hear us? Let us rather endeavour to ascertain where we are."

I advanced with outstretched hands. After five paces I touched a wall of riveted iron plates. Returning, I ran against a wooden table, near which were some stools. The floor was covered with a thick matting, which deadened the sound of our footsteps. The bare walls had neither door nor window perceptible. Conseil, who had been making a tour in the opposite direction, rejoined me, and we came into the centre of this cabin, which appeared to be about twenty feet long and ten wide. Even Ned Land, with his great height to assist him, could not touch the ceiling.

After half an hour had passed in this way, our eyes were suddenly exposed to a violently brilliant light. Our prison was suddenly illuminated. In the whiteness and intensity of this gleam I recognized the electric light which produced the appearance of a magnificent phosphorescence round the submarine vessel. I was involuntarily obliged to close my eyes, and when I again opened them I found that the light had been placed in a ground-glass globe, which was fixed at the upper end of the cabin.

"At last we can see something," cried Ned Land, who, bowie-knife in hand, stood on the defensive.

"Yes," I replied, risking the antithesis, "but the situation is not the less obscure."

"If Monsieur will only have patience," said the impassible Conseil.

The sudden illumination of the cabin gave me the opportunity to examine it more minutely. It only contained a table and five stools. The invisible door was hermetically closed. No sound reached our ears. Everyone seemed dead on board. Whether it was still moving over the surface of the ocean, or plunged in its depths, I could not divine.

However, the lamp had not been lighted for nothing. So I was in hopes that the crew of the vessel would soon put in an appearance. When people wish to put an end to prisoners they do not illuminate the *oubliettes*.

I was not mistaken; the noise of withdrawing bolts was heard, the door opened, and two men entered.

One was rather short but strongly made, with immense breadth of shoulder, intellectual looking, with thick black hair and beard, piercing eyes, and with the vivacity which character-izes the provincial population of France.

Diderot has justly maintained that man's gesture is meta-phorical, and this little man was the living proof of that state-ment. One had a sort of feeling that his habitual discourse was made up of prosopopœia, metanymus, and hypallages. But I was not able to verify this, as he always used a peculiar and utterly incomprehensible idiom.

The second arrival deserves a more detailed description.

A pupil of Gratiolet or Engel would have read his face like a book. I can easily recall his characteristics. Confidence in himself, for his head rose nobly from the arc formed by the line of his shoulders, and his dark eyes regarded you with a cool assurance. He was composed, for his face, more pale than ruddy, betokened a dispassionate nature. Energy he possessed, as demonstrated by the rapid contraction of the eyebrows. Finally, he was courageous, for his deep breathing denoted great vitality.

I should add that this man was proud, his firm and composed look seemed to reflect elevated thoughts, and, added to all this, the homogeneity of expression in the movements of his body and face, according to the observation of physiognomists, resulted in an indisputable open-heartedness.

I felt myself involuntarily reassured in his presence, and I augured well of our interview. This person might have been any age between thirty-five and fifty. He was tall, a wide forehead, straight nose, a well-shaped mouth, beautiful teeth, long, thin, and very muscular hands, worthy to serve an elevated and passionate mind. This was certainly the most admirable type of individual that I had ever seen. To descend to detail, his eyes, set a little apart, could embrace nearly a quarter of the horizon.

This faculty, which came to my knowledge later, gave him a great advantage over the excellent sight of Ned Land. Whenever this unknown personage was looking intently at anything he frowned, his large eyelids contracted so as to conceal the pupils, and to considerably circumscribe his line of sight – and he *did* look! What a gaze that was, as if he was making distant objects larger, or penetrating your very soul by his gaze; as if he could pierce the depths of the waves, so opaque to our eyes, and could read the secrets of the sea.

The two strangers wore otter-skin caps and sea-boots of sealskin, and clothes of a peculiar texture, which sat loosely upon them, and allowed of great freedom in their movements.

The taller of the two – evidently the captain – regarded us with great attention, without speaking. Then turning to his companion, he conversed with him in a language I did not understand. The other replied by a nod, adding a few unintelligible words. Then with a glance he appeared to interrogate us personally.

I replied, in good French, that I did not understand his

language; but he did not appear to comprehend mine, and the situation became somewhat embarrassing.

"If Monsieur would relate our adventures," suggested Conseil, "perhaps the gentlemen would understand some of it."

I then commenced a recital of our experiences, distinctly dwelling upon all the words, and without omitting a single detail. I announced our names and station – then I presented in due form M. Aronnax – his servant Conseil, and Ned Land, the harpooner. The individual with the calm eyes listened quietly, even politely, and with great attention. But his face betrayed no sign that he understood a word. When I had finished, he remained perfectly silent.

There still remained the English language, as a last resource. Perhaps he would understand that almost universal tongue. I was acquainted with it, and with German sufficiently to read fluently, but not to speak it correctly. Now here it was absolutely necessary to be understood.

"Do you try," I said to the harpooner, "speak the best English ever heard, Master Land, and try to be more successful than I have been."

Ned made no objection, and repeated my recital, so as I could understand it pretty well. The issue was the same, but the form was different. The Canadian was more energetic. He complained bitterly at being imprisoned, against the rights of nations, demanded legal satisfaction for his detention, invoked the Habeas Corpus Act, threatened to prosecute those who had kept us prisoners unlawfully. He kicked about, gesticulated, cried out, and finally, by a most expressive pantomime, gave them to understand that we were almost dying of hunger.

This was true as a matter of fact, but we had nearly forgotten it.

To his intense surprise, the harpooner did not appear to have been more intelligible than I was. Our hosts did not move a muscle of their faces. It was evident that they understood neither the language of Arago nor Faraday. I was very much puzzled what to do next, when Conseil said:

"If Monsieur will permit me, I will speak to them in German."

"What! do you know German!" I cried.

"Like a Dutchman," replied he; "if Monsieur has no objection."

"I am much pleased. Go on my lad."

And Conseil recounted, for the third time, the various adventures we had met with. But notwithstanding the excellent accent and the elegantly-turned phrases of the speaker, German was not a success. At length, pushed to the very last position, I recalled all I could of my former studies, and essayed to tell the tale in Latin. Cicero would have stopped his ears, and declared it was "dog Latin", but, nevertheless, I went on. But with the same result!

This last attempt having miscarried, the two strangers exchanged some words in their incomprehensible language, and retired, without bestowing upon us even one of those signs which are universally understood. The door was again shut upon us.

"This is infamous," exclaimed Ned Land, who burst out for the twentieth time. "Why, we have spoken French, English, German, and Latin to those rascals, and they have not had the civility to reply."

"Calm yourself, Ned," said I to the angry harpooner; "anger will do no good!"

"But don't you know, sir, that we may die of hunger in this iron cage?"

"Bah!" said Conseil, with his usual philosophy, "we can hold out for some time yet."

"My friends," said I, "we must not despair. We have not come to the worst yet. Do me the favour to wait before you form an opinion respecting the captain and crew of this vessel."

"My opinion is already formed," replied Ned; "they are a set of rascals."

"Good; and of what country?"

"Of a rascally country."

"My brave Ned, that country is not clearly laid down upon the map of the world; and I confess that the nationality of these two strangers is difficult to determine. That they are neither English, French, nor German we can affirm. Now I am tempted to admit that they were born in lower latitudes. There is a southerly look about them; but whether they be Spaniards, Turks, Arabs, or Indians, their physical types do not enable me to decide. Their language is simply incomprehensible."

"There is the drawback of not knowing every language,"

replied Conseil, "and the disadvantage of not having a universal one."

"That would not help us at all," replied Ned Land. "Do you not understand that these fellows have got a language of their own, invented to drive to despair those brave people who ask for something to eat? But in any country in the world, if you open your mouth, move your jaws, smack your lips, would they not understand what you meant? Would not that be sufficient to indicate, equally in Quebec as in Pomaton, in Paris, or the antipodes, 'I am hungry; give me something to eat'?"

"Oh!" cried Conseil, "there are some natures so utterly stupid—"

As he spoke the door opened and a steward entered. He brought us clothing, vests and trousers, fit for sea wear, of a material with which I was unacquainted. I hastened to clothe myself; and my companions followed my example.

Meantime the steward – silent, perhaps deaf – had laid the table and set on three dishes.

"There is something satisfactory," said Conseil; "this promises well!"

"Bah!" cried the spiteful Canadian; "what the devil do you expect to get to eat here; tortoise livers, fillet of shark, or a slice from a sea-dog?"

"We shall soon see," replied Conseil.

The dishes, with their silver covers, were placed symmetrically upon the cloth, and we took our places. Decidedly we had to do with civilized beings; and were it not for the electric light which surrounded us, I should have fancied we were sitting in the Adelphi Hotel in Liverpool, or in the Grand Hotel in Paris. I must say that we had neither wine nor bread on this occasion. The water was pure and bright; but it was water, which was not acceptable to Ned Land. Amongst the meats served to us I recognized various kinds of fish very delicately cooked; but upon some of the dishes I could not pronounce an opinion, as I was perfectly unable to say to what kingdom, animal or vegetable, they belonged. The table-service was elegant, and in perfect taste. Every knife, fork, spoon, or plate, was marked with a letter surrounded by a motto, of which the following is a *facsimile*:

MOBILIS IN MOBILE
N

Mobile in a *mobile element*. This applied exactly to this submarine machine, if you translate the preposition "in" as "in", and not "upon". The letter N no doubt stood for the initial of the name of the eccentric individual who commanded.

Ned and Conseil did not waste much time in reflection. They began to eat, and I quickly followed their example. I was, moreover, now reassured as to our fate, and it was very evident that our hosts did not intend that we should die from inanition.

Everything must have an end in this world, and so must the appetites of people who have fasted for fifteen hours. The want of sleep now began to make itself felt – a natural reaction, after the long night during which we had struggled face to face with death.

"Faith, I shall sleep well," said Conseil.

"I am already asleep," replied Ned Land.

My companions lay down upon the floor, and were quickly in a profound slumber.

For my part I yielded less quickly to the drowsy god. A number of thoughts crowded my brain, insoluble questions pressed upon me, a troop of mental images kept my eyes open. Where were we? What strange power held us? I felt, or fancied I felt, the machine sinking to the bottom of the sea. Fearful nightmares beset me. I saw in mysterious passages the whole of the unknown animal kingdom, of which the submarine vessel appeared to be the congener, living, moving, and as formidable as they. Then my brain cooled, my imagination was steeped in sleep, and I soon fell into a peaceful slumber.

CHAPTER IX
NED LAND'S ANGER

HOW LONG WE slept I do not know, but it must have been some time, as we awoke completely refreshed. I was the first to awake. My companions had not stirred, and remained stretched in the corner like lifeless beings.

Scarcely had I got up from my hard bed, when I perceived that my brain was clear and my mind invigorated. I then began to re-examine our cell attentively.

Nothing had been altered in its arrangement. The prison was still a prison – the prisoners still prisoners. But the steward had cleared the table while we slept. There was no symptom of any approaching change for the better, and I began to wonder whether we were destined to live for ever in that cage.

This prospect was so much the more unpleasant, as, if my brain were clear, I felt my chest very much oppressed. My breathing had become difficult, the heavy air was not sufficient for the play of my lungs. The cell was certainly of large size, but it was evident that we had consumed the greater part of the oxygen it had contained. Each man breathes in an hour the amount of oxygen contained in 100 litres (22 gallons) of atmospheric air, and this air, then almost equal to carbonic acid gas, becomes insupportable.

It was, therefore, necessary to renovate the air of our prison, and, without doubt, also the atmosphere of our submarine boat.

Here was a puzzling question. How did the commander of the floating dwelling get on? Did he obtain air by chemical means, by disengaging the oxygen contained in chlorate of potash, and by absorbing the carbonic acid by the caustic potash? In this case he must keep up a communication with the earth to obtain a supply of these materials. Did he only take the precaution to store the air under great pressure in reservoirs, and free it again according to the requirements of the ship's company? Perhaps so. Or, what was a much easier method, more economical, and therefore more probable, was that he came up to the surface of the water to breathe, like a cetacean, and for twenty-four hours renew his supply of oxygen. However it might be, and by whatever means, it appeared to me prudent to employ it without delay.

In fact I was already obliged to breathe more quickly to extract what little oxygen the cell contained, when I was suddenly refreshed by a current of pure air, perfumed with the odour of the sea. It was the true sea-breeze vivified and charged with iodine. I opened my mouth wide. I was sensible of a rocking motion, a rolling of some extent, but perfectly determinable. The monster had evidently come up to the surface to breathe, after the fashion of the whale. The mode of ventilating the ship was now perfectly apparent.

While I was enjoying the pure air I looked for the medium of its introduction, and was not long in discovering it. Over the door was an aperture, through which the fresh air entered and renovated the vitiated atmosphere of the cabin.

I had got so far in my observations when Ned and Conseil woke almost at the same moment, under the influence of the fresh air. After sundry rubbings of the eyes and stretchings of the arms they got upon their feet.

"Has Monsieur slept well?" inquired Conseil, with his usual politeness.

"Very well indeed," I replied. "And you, Master Land?"

"Soundly," was the answer. "But – perhaps I am mistaken – I fancy I can detect the smell of the sea."

A sailor could make no mistake on this point, and I told the Canadian what had passed.

"That explains the roarings we heard when the supposed narwhal was near the *Abraham Lincoln*," said Ned.

"Quite so, Ned, that was its breathing."

"Only, M. Aronnax, I have no notion what time it is, unless it is dinner-time."

"Dinner-time, my worthy harpooner? say rather breakfast-time, for we are certainly in another day."

"Which shows that we have slept for twenty-four hours!"

"That is my opinion," I replied.

"I will not contradict you," replied Ned Land. "But dinner or breakfast, I shall be glad to see the steward, whichever he may bring."

"Both," said Conseil.

"Just so," replied Ned. "We are entitled to two meals, and, for my part, I could do justice to both."

"Listen, Ned," said I. "It is very evident that these people do not intend to starve us, else the dinner yesterday would have had no meaning."

"Unless they wanted to fatten us up a bit."

"I must protest against that," said I. "We have not fallen among cannibals."

"Once is not a custom," replied the Canadian seriously; "who can tell whether these people have not been deprived of fresh meat for some time? and, in that case, three such individuals as you, Monsieur, your servant, and I—"

"Banish such thoughts, Land," I said, "and above all things do not go out of your way to abuse our hosts – that will only make matters worse."

"In any case," said Ned, "I am as hungry as a thousand devils; dinner or breakfast, the meal is not here."

"We must conform to the regulations of the ship," I replied. "Possibly our appetites are in advance of the galley clock."

"And I suppose that is set correctly?" said Conseil calmly.

"That is so like you, friend Conseil," replied the impetuous Canadian. "You don't ever trouble yourself much, you are always calm. You are the kind of fellow to say grace before your *bene-dicite*, and die of hunger rather than complain."

"And what is the use of complaining?" asked Conseil.

"But it will do good. And if these pirates – I say 'pirates' with all respect, as the professor objects to my calling them cannibals, and I don't want to hurt his feelings – if these pirates imagine that they are going to keep me a prisoner in this stifling cage without hearing some pretty strong observations from me they are very much mistaken. Look here, M. Aronnax, tell me frankly, do you think we shall be kept long in this iron box?"

"To say the truth, I cannot tell any more than yourself."

"Well, but what do you think?"

"I imagine that chance has made us masters of an important secret. Now, if the crew of this submarine vessel are much interested in keeping it, and if such interest is as important as the lives of three men – I do think that we are in danger. But in the contrary case, the monster may put us ashore again amongst our species."

"Unless he enrol us with the crew," said Conseil, "and take care of his secret that way."

"Until some day," replied Ned, "when some frigate better 'found' and faster than the *Abraham Lincoln*, takes possession of this nest of robbers, and sends us and them to swing at the yard-arm."

"A good argument, Land," said I, "but nothing of all this has yet happened. It is useless to discuss what may happen, until the case arises. I repeat, let us wait and act according to circumstances. We need do nothing, because there is nothing to do."

"On the contrary, sir," replied the Canadian, who would not give in, "we ought to do something."

"Well, what?"

"Save ourselves – try to escape!"

"To escape from a prison on land is difficult; but to get out of a submarine prison, appears to me impracticable."

"Now, friend Ned," said Conseil, "what do you say to Monsieur? I cannot believe that an American is ever at a loss."

The harpooner, visibly embarrassed, was silent. Flight under the circumstances was out of the question. But a Canadian is half a Frenchman, and Master Land showed that by his reply.

"So, M. Aronnax," he said, after some minutes' consideration, "you do not know what people ought to do who cannot escape from their prison?"

"No, my friend."

"It is very simple – they ought to arrange in what manner they will remain."

"By Jove," said Conseil, "I think you are better inside than either above or below!"

"But having overcome gaolers, keys, and bolts?"

"What, Ned, is it possible that you are seriously contemplating escape from this vessel?"

"Very seriously, indeed," replied the Canadian.

"Impossible!"

"Why so, sir? Some favourable opportunity may arise; and I do not see why I should not profit by it. If there are not more than twenty men on board, they will not be able to resist two Frenchmen and a Canadian, I suppose?"

It was better to admit this proposition than to discuss it, so I contented myself by saying:

"Wait events, and see. But till the time comes pray curb your impatience. We cannot act except by stratagem, and it is not in our power to create opportunities. So promise me that you will take things as they come, quietly."

"I promise, sir," replied Ned, in a tone but little reassuring. "Not a coarse nor violent word shall pass my lips, not a gesture shall be perceived, even if the table be not served with desirable regularity."

"I have your promise, Ned," I replied.

Our conversation ceased, and each of us began to reflect. For myself, I confess, notwithstanding the assurance of the harpooner, I did not delude myself. I did not admit those favourable chances of which Ned had spoken. To be so well manœuvred, the submarine boat must be well manned and equipped, and consequently in the event of a dispute we should get the worst of it. Besides, above all it was necessary to be at liberty, and we were not. I did not perceive any means of flight from this close prison. And if the strange commander of this vessel had a secret to preserve – which was at least probable – he would not permit us to be at large on board. Now whether he would get rid of us by violence, or land us safely upon some corner of the earth, was the question. All these hypotheses appeared to me extremely plausible, and one needed to be a harpooner to hope to regain his liberty.

I comprehended, moreover, that Ned Land's intentions were by no means in keeping with his reflections. I heard him beginning to mutter strange oaths, and his gestures were becoming threatening. He got up and walked about like a wild beast in a cage, hitting and kicking the walls as he passed. By-and-by his anger evaporated, and hunger began to assail him cruelly, and yet the steward appeared not. Our position, as shipwrecked people, had been forgotten too long if they had really been well-intentioned towards us. Ned Land, really suffering from hunger, got more and more angry; and, notwithstanding his promise, I was afraid of an explosion should any of the crew enter our cabin. For two hours longer Ned's anger burned. He called, he shouted in vain. The walls were impervious to sound. I could not hear any sound within the boat. It was not moving, for we should in that event have felt the throbbings of the screw. Plunged in this state of uncertainty beneath the waves, we seemed to belong to earth no more. The death-like silence was appalling.

I did not dare to contemplate the chances of a lengthened abandonment and isolation in this cell. The hopes I had conceived after our interview with the commander faded by degrees. His kind expression of countenance, pleasant look, and nobility of mien all faded from my memory. I recalled this extraordinary personage, as he had now become, necessarily pitiless and cruel. I put him out of the pale of humanity, inaccessible to every sentiment of pity, the remorseless enemy of his fellow-creatures, against whom he had sworn an undying enmity.

But was this man, then, going to let us perish of hunger, incarcerated in an iron cell, at the mercy of those terrible temptations which assail men under the influence of extreme hunger? This fearful thought burnt itself into my brain, and imagination being at work, I felt myself becoming the prey of a maddening terror. Conseil was quite resigned. Ned was raging.

At this juncture a voice was heard outside, footsteps were heard on the iron flooring, the bolts were drawn back, and the steward appeared.

Before I could interpose to prevent him, the Canadian had thrown himself upon the unfortunate man, felled him to the ground, where he held him by the throat. The steward was strangling beneath that powerful grasp. Conseil had already attempted to loosen the deadly grasp of the harpooner, and I was about to assist, when I was glued to the spot by hearing a voice call out in French:

"Calm yourself, Master Land, and you also, professor, and be so good as to listen to me!"

CHAPTER X
THE MAN OF THE SEA

IT WAS THE COMMANDER of the vessel who had spoken.

At those words, Ned Land suddenly arose; the steward, half strangled, staggered out at a sign from his master; but such was the discipline enforced, that the man did not even by a gesture betray his resentment against the Canadian. Conseil was interested, in spite of himself, and I stood petrified with astonishment. We all awaited the *dénouement* in silence. The commander, leaning against the table, regarded us fixedly. Did he hesitate to speak, or was he regretting having addressed us in French? It might be so.

After a silence of some minutes, which none of us ventured to break:

"Gentlemen," said he, in a calm and penetrating tone, "I can speak French, English, German, and Latin with equal facility. I was therefore quite capable of replying to you at our first interview, but I wished to learn first, and reflect afterwards. Your respective accounts of your adventures agreeing in all important particulars assured me of your identity. I am now aware that chance has brought to me Monsieur Pierre Aronnax, Professor of Natural History in the museum at Paris, charged with a scientific mission; Conseil, his servant, and Ned Land, a Canadian by birth, harpooner on board the frigate *Abraham Lincoln*, of the United States Navy."

I bowed assent. There was no necessity for further reply. The man expressed himself with perfect ease, with no foreign accent. His phraseology was good, his words well chosen, his facility of speech remarkable. Nevertheless, I did not take to him as a countryman.

He continued:

"You have doubtless thought that I have been a long time in paying you a second visit. It was because, your identity once established, I wished to consider seriously how to act towards you. I hesitated for a long time. Unfortunate circumstances have brought you in contact with a man who has forsworn his fellow-creatures. You have come to disturb my existence—"

"Unintentionally," I put in.

"Unintentionally!" repeated the stranger, raising his voice. "Was it unintentionally that the *Abraham Lincoln* chased me through the ocean so long? Was it unintentionally that you came on board that ship? Was it unintentionally that your shot came hustling against the hull of my vessel? Was it unintentionally that Land here struck it with his harpoon?"

I perceived a subdued anger in these questions. But to all these recriminations I had a perfectly plain answer to make, and I made it.

"Monsieur," said I, "you are ignorant of the discussions which have arisen in Europe and America about you. You are not aware that the various collisions you have caused have evoked public observation in both continents. I spare you the numerous hypotheses by which people have endeavoured to explain the inexplicable phenomenon of which you alone possess the secret. But you must know that in pursuing you the *Abraham Lincoln*'s crew were under the impression that they were pursuing some powerful marine monster, of which it was necessary to rid the ocean at any cost."

A half-sigh parted the lips of the stranger; then, in a calmer tone he said:

"Monsieur Aronnax, can you affirm that your frigate would not have followed and fired at a submarine vessel as well as a monster?"

This question caused me some little embarrassment, for certainly Commodore Farragut had not hesitated. He would have deemed it his duty to destroy an apparatus of the kind as well as a gigantic narwhal.

"So you perceive, Monsieur," said the stranger, "that I have a right to treat you as enemies."

I did not reply, and for a good reason. Where was the use to answer a proposition, when force could overcome a thousand arguments.

"I have hesitated for a long time," said the commander. "There is no reason why I should extend my hospitality to you. If I leave you, I have no interest in seeing you again. If I replace you upon the platform outside, upon which you took refuge, I can sink beneath the surface and forget that you ever existed. Have I not this right?"

These thoughts chased rapidly across my mind while the strange personage was silent, absorbed, and plunged in thought. I was regarding him with a melancholy interest, much as Œdipus may have looked at the Sphinx. After a long silence the commander again spoke:

"I have waited before speaking," said he, "because I was thinking that my own interest may be in keeping with the natural consideration to which every human being has a right. You shall remain on board, since fate has thrown you in my way. You will be free here, and in exchange for this liberty, I will only impose one condition. Your word of honour that you agree to it will be sufficient."

"Speak, Monsieur," said I, "I have no doubt the condition is one that brave men may accept."

"Certainly, and this is it. It is possible that certain circumstances may compel me to confine you to your cabin for some hours, on some days. As I have no wish to use force, I expect from you, above all, the most passive obedience. In acting thus, I take all responsibility off your shoulders, and you are free; for it will be my business to see that you do not become acquainted with what it is inexpedient for you to know. Do you accept the condition?"

"We accept," I replied. "But I wish to ask one question – only one."

"Speak, Monsieur," he said.

"You have stated that we shall be free on board?"

"Entirely."

"I would ask what you mean by such freedom?"

"Permission to go and come and look about as you please, to see all that takes place here. In fact the same freedom as I and my companions enjoy."

"That is perhaps the right of a savage," I said, "but not of a civilized being."

"Monsieur, I am not, so to speak, a civilized being. I have broken with the world altogether, for reasons which I can alone appreciate. I obey no laws, and I recommend you never to put them in force against me."

This was sternly spoken. An angry and disdainful gleam shone in his eyes, and in this man's life I could discern a terrible past. Not only had he put himself out of reach of all human laws, but he was independent, free – in the largest acceptation of the term – beyond all reach.

Who would dare to pursue to the bottom of the sea a being, who at the surface baffled all efforts to overtake him? What ship could resist the shock of this submarine "ram"? What armour-plate could sustain his blows? None among men could demand an account of his actions. Providence, if he believed in Him; his conscience, if he had one, were the only judges before whom he could be brought.

It was evident that we did not altogether understand each other.

"I beg your pardon," I added, "but the liberty you would

accord is only that granted to a prisoner, to walk round his prison. That is not enongh for us."

"Well, it must suffice, nevertheless."

"What! You would debar us from ever seeing our friends, relatives, and our native land again?"

"Yes, Monsieur; but to renounce the insupportable yoke of earth which men call freedom, is not such a very great sacrifice as you imagine."

"Well," cried Ned, "I will never give my word of honour not to attempt to escape."

"I did not ask you for your word of honour, Master Land," replied the commander in a freezing tone.

"Sir," said I, carried away in spite of myself, "you take an unfair advantage of your position. It is cruel."

"No, sir; it is mercy. You are my prisoners of war. I take care of you, when, by a word, I could have you thrown into the sea. You have attacked me. You have come here, and have discovered a secret which no one in the world ought to know – the secret of my existence. And do you believe that I shall put you ashore upon that earth which shall know me no more? In keeping you here it is not you whom I take care of, it is myself."

These words indicated a resolution which no argument could overturn.

"Thus," I replied, "you give us simply a choice between life and death?"

"Exactly."

"My friends," said I, "to such a question there is no answer. But we are not bound to the master of the ship."

"Not at all," replied the captain. Then, in a more pleasant tone, he resumed: "Now permit me to finish what I have to say. I know you, M. Aronnax. You, personally, have not perhaps much reason to complain that you have cast in your lot with mine. You will find amongst the books which are my favourite studies your own work upon the greatest depths of the sea. I have often read it. You have extended your work as far as terrestrial science permitted. But you do not know everything, and have not seen everything. Allow me to tell you that you will not regret the time you may pass on board with me. You are about to sail through a world of wonders. Astonishment and stupefaction will be the prevailing feelings you will experience. You will not easily get tired of the never-ceasing spectacle before you. I am about to make a new tour of the submarine world – perhaps the last, who knows? – to study, as far as possible, at the bottom of those seas through which I have so frequently coursed, and you shall be my companion. From this day you will enter upon a new existence; you will see what no man has ever seen – for my companions and myself do not count – and our planet, thanks to me, shall yield its deepest secrets to you."

I could not deny it. The captain's words had a great effect upon me. I was assailed at my weak point, and forgot, at the moment, that the contemplation of these wonderful things could not compensate for my lost liberty. However, I counted upon the future to solve this question, so I answered:

"Monsieur, if you have quarrelled with humanity, I like to think that you have not renounced every human feeling. We are shipwrecked people, received charitably on board your vessel, we do not forget that. As for me, I am not sure but that, if the interests of science will permit me to forget the want of freedom, I can promise myself that our intercourse will be very pleasant."

I fancied that the commander would tender me his hand to ratify our agreement. He did not do so, and, for his sake, I was sorry for it.

"One last question," I said, as this strange individual was about to retire.

"Well, Monsieur?"

"By what name shall I address you?"

"Sir," he replied, "to you I am but Captain Nemo, and your companions and yourself are to me only passengers in the ship *Nautilus*."

Captain Nemo then called the steward, to whom he gave his orders in that strange language which I could not make out; then turning to Conseil and the Canadian he said to them:

"A meal awaits you in your cabin. Be so good as to follow that man."

"This is not to be refused," said the harpooner, and Conseil and he quitted the cell in which they had been interned thirty hours.

"Now, M. Aronnax, our breakfast is ready. Allow me to lead the way."

"At your orders, captain."

I followed Captain Nemo, and as soon as I had passed the door I entered a sort of corridor, illuminated by electric light, and resembling the waist of a ship. After proceeding a short distance a second door was opened before me.

I was ushered in a dining-room ornamented and furnished in perfect taste. Oaken shelves inlaid with ebony were erected at each end of this room, upon which were displayed, in varying order, china, earthenware, porcelain, and glass of inestimable value. The table-services glittered beneath the rays which extended to the ceiling, whose fine frescoes toned down the powerful light.

In the centre of the room was a splendidly-served table. Captain Nemo pointed out my place.

"Sit down," said he, "and eat like a man who is dying of hunger."

The meal was composed of a certain number of dishes which only the sea could have supplied, and some of which I was entirely ignorant. They were very good, but of curious flavour, to which, however, I speedily became accustomed. These various dishes were rich in phosphorus, and from this I argued that they were of oceanic origin.

Captain Nemo was looking at me. I asked him nothing, but he divined my thoughts, and replied voluntarily to the questions I was burning to address to him.

"The greater part of these dishes are unknown," said he; "but you may eat without fear. They are wholesome and nourishing. For years I have renounced all sustenance derived from the earth, and am none the worse. My crew, who are strong fellows, live as I do."

"All these things are produced in the sea, then?"

"Yes, the ocean furnishes me with all I require. Sometimes I spread my nets astern, and haul them in ready to break. Sometimes I go hunting in this element so inaccessible to man, and I take the game that inhabits the submarine forests. My flocks, like those of father Neptune, feed fearlessly in the submarine pastures, and share a vast estate which I cultivate myself, and which is always sown by the hand of the Creator of all things."

I gazed at Captain Nemo in astonishment, and replied:

"I can quite understand that your nets furnish you excellent fish, but I do not quite comprehend how you hunt the aquatic game in the submarine forests, and, least of all, why so small a portion of meat appears at your table."

"For the reason that I never consume the flesh of terrestrial animals."

"But this, now?" I retorted, pointing to a dish upon which some slices of a "fillet" were placed.

"That which you believe to be meat is nothing but tortoise fillet. Here is likewise some dolphin liver which you might take for pork. My cook is an experienced hand, and excels in preparing the various productions of the sea. Taste those. Here is a *conserve d'hololuries*, which Malais declared unrivalled. Here is a cream made of the milk from the breast of a cetacean, and sugar from the great fucus of the North Sea; and, finally, allow me to offer you these *confitures d'anemones*, which are equal to the most pleasant fruits."

I tasted them, more out of curiosity than hunger, while Captain Nemo amused me by his improbable tales.

"But this inexhaustible sea not only feeds but clothes me. That material you wear is made from the byssus of certain shell fish. They are coloured with the purple of the ancients, variegated with violet tints, which I extract from the aplysis of the Mediterranean. The perfumes you will find upon your dressing-table have been produced by the distillation of marine plants. Your bed is composed of the softest zostera of the ocean. Your pen is from the fin of a whale; your ink is the liquor secreted by the cuttle-fish. Everything now comes from the sea, and will return to it again some day."

"You are fond of the sea, captain."

"Yes; I love it. The sea is everything. It covers seven-tenths of the terrestrial globe. Its breathings are pure and healthy. It is an immense desert, in which man is never lonely, for life is spread around him. The sea is only the medium for a supernatural and wonderful existence; it is nothing but movement and affection; the living infinite, as one of the poets has said. In fact, nature is herein represented by all three kingdoms – the mineral, vegetable, and animal. The last is largely represented by the four groups of zoophytes, three classes of articulated animals, five classes of molluscs, three classes of vertebrates, the mammifers, reptiles, innumerable legions of fish, an infinite order of animals, which includes more than 13,000 species, of which only a tenth part inhabit fresh water. The sea is the vast reservoir of nature. It was by the sea that the world may be said to have commenced; and who knows whether it will not finish it also! There alone is perfect quiet. The sea is not for despots. At the surface it can still exercise its iniquitous rights; there it beats furiously and devours greedily; there it bears all earthly horrors. But at thirty feet below the surface its power ceases, its influence is extinguished, its strength dies out. Ah, Monsieur, live in the bosom of the waters. There alone you will find independence; there I recognize no master; there I am free!"

Captain Nemo suddenly stopped in the midst of his enthusiastic address. Had he been betrayed out of his habitual reserve? Had he said too much? For some time he walked about, evidently agitated. Then he became calmer; his face resumed its usual impassibility, and turning to me he said:

"Now, Monsieur, if you wish to inspect the *Nautilus*, I am at your service."

CHAPTER XI
THE *NAUTILUS*

CAPTAIN NEMO GOT up from his chair. I followed him. A double door at the end of the room was passed, and we entered a chamber of similar size to that we had just left.

It was a library. High ebony book-cases, inlaid with brass, contained a large number of books similarly bound. These followed the curvature of the walls, and terminated at their lower part in large sofas covered with maroon leather, which presented most comfortable resting-places. Light, moveable desks were attached thereto, adapted either for reading or writing. In the centre was a large table, littered with pamphlets, with here and there some old newspapers. The electric light fell upon all these from four swinging globular lamps fastened in the fluting of the ceiling. I gazed admiringly around me at this ingeniously-arranged room, and could scarcely believe my eyes.

"Captain Nemo," said I to my host, who had stretched himself upon a couch, "this library would do credit to a palace; and I am fairly astounded when I reflect that it can be equally available at the bottom of the sea."

"You can find true solitude and silence here," replied the captain. "I do not think that your study at the Museum can offer you such perfect quiet."

"No, indeed; and it will appear very poor after this. You must have 6,000 or 7,000 volumes on these shelves."

"Twelve thousand," replied Captain Nemo. "Those are the only things that bind me to the earth. The world was dead to me when my *Nautilus* plunged for the first time beneath the waves. Upon that day I purchased my last volumes, my last pamphlets, my last papers; and since then I wish to believe that the human race has neither thought nor written anything. These books are, however, quite at your disposal, and you may use them freely."

I thanked my host, and approached the shelves. There were books of science, and moral and literary subjects in every language; but I did not perceive any work upon political economy. One curious feature was that the books were mingled together, not arranged according to the language in which they were written; and this seemed to prove that the captain read whatever volumes came to hand.

Amongst the books I noticed the greatest works of ancient and modern celebrities, that is to say, all the finest works that humanity has produced. There was poetry, romance, and science represented, from Homer to Victor Hugo, from Xenophon to Michelet, from Rabelais to Madame Sand. But science composed the bulk of the works; books upon mechanics, ballistics, hydrography, meteorology, geography, geology, &c., held a no less important place than works on natural history, which I fancied was the captain's chief study. I perceived the complete writings of Humboldt, Arago, Foucault, Henry St. Claire Deville, Chasles, Milne-Edwards, Quatrefrages, Tyndall, Faraday, Berthelot, of the Abbé Secchi, Petermann, Commodore Maury, Agassiz, &c. The memoirs of the Academy of Science, the transactions of various geographical societies, &c., and, in a conspicuous position, those two volumes to which, perhaps, I was indebted for Captain Nemo's clemency.

Amongst the works of Joseph Bertrand, his book entitled "Les Fondateurs de l'Astronomie", gave me a fixed date, and as I knew that the book had appeared during the year 1865, I was enabled to arrive at the conclusion that the institution of the *Nautilus* had not been at a date more remote than that. Thus for three years or more Captain Nemo had led a submarine existence.

I was in hopes that more recent works would enable me to fix more definitely the exact period, but I had plenty of time before me, and did not wish to delay an exploration of the wonders of the *Nautilus*.

"I thank you," said I to the captain, "for having placed this library at my disposal. There are some treasures of scientific research which I shall be able to profit by."

"This is not only a library, it is also a smoking-room," said he.

"A smoking-room!" I exclaimed. "So you have some cigars on board?"

"Certainly."

"Then I am obliged to think that you must preserve relations with Havana."

"Not at all," replied the captain. "Try this cigar, and though it is very certain it never came from Havana, I think you will like the flavour."

I took the cigar, which was made like those sold in London, but it appeared to be composed of leaves of gold. I lit it at a little bronze brazier and inhaled its fragrance with all the gusto of a man who had not smoked for two days.

"It is excellent," I said, "but it is not tobacco."

"No," replied the captain, "that weed never grew in Havana nor the East. It is a kind of sea-weed, rich in nicotine, which the ocean supplies to me somewhat sparely. Do you regret your London cigar?"

"My dear sir, I shall despise them henceforth."

"Well, then, smoke as much as you like, and without thinking of the origin of the cigars. They bear the brand of no nation, but they are not the less good, I fancy."

"On the contrary."

Captain Nemo then opened a door opposite to that by which we had entered, and I passed into a large and brilliantly-lighted *salon*.

It was a large oblong with walls sloping inwards, ten yards long, six wide, and five high. The lighted ceiling, decorated by arabesques, distributed a clear and soft light upon all the marvels of this museum. For a museum it really was, in which an intelligent and prodigal mind had united all the treasures of nature and art, with a little of that "mixing" which distinguishes the "studio" of a painter. Thirty masterpieces in handsome frames ornamented the walls, covered with tapestry of chaste design.

Here I perceived pictures of the greatest value, which for the most part I had admired in private collections and exhibitions. The various schools of the old masters were represented by a "Madonna", by Raphael; a "Virgin", by Leonardo da Vinci; a "Nymph", by Correggio; a "Lady", by Titian; an "Adoration", by Veronese; an "Assumption", by Murillo; a portrait, by Holbein; a "Monk", by Velázquez; a "Martyr", by Ribeira; a "Kermesse", by Rubens; two Flemish landscapes by Teniers, three small pictures of the school of Gerard Dow, Metsu, and Paul Potter, two by Géricault and Prudhon, some sea views by Backuysen and Vernet. Amongst modern works were those of Delacroix, Ingres, Decamp, Troyon, Meissonnier, Daubigny, &c., and some admirable reductions from statues of the first models stood upon pedestals in the corners of this splendid museum.

The state of stupefaction predicted by the captain of the *Nautilus* had already taken possession of my mind.

"Monsieur," said the extraordinary man, "you will, I hope, excuse the informal manner in which I have received you, and the disorder of this room."

"Without seeking to know who you are, sir," I said, "I may remark that you are an artist."

"An amateur, no more; I like to collect these beautiful specimens of human workmanship. I was a great collector at one time, and have been able to obtain some works of great value. These are the last *souvenirs* of the earth which is now dead to me. To my eyes, your modern artists cannot compare with the old masters, who have two or three thousand years' existence, and I confuse them. They have no 'age'."

"And these musicians?" said I, pointing out works of Weber, Rossini, Mozart, Beethoven, Haydn, Meyerbeer, Herold, Wagner, Auber, Gounod, and others, scattered upon a piano-organ, which filled up one of the panels of the room.

"Those musicians," replied Captain Nemo, "are the contemporaries of Orpheus, for chronological difficulties are passed over in the memories of dead men; and I am dead, equally dead as any of your friends lying six feet under ground."

He ceased speaking, and appeared plunged in a profound reverie. I gazed at him with emotion, analysing his features in silence. Leaning against a beautiful Mosaic table, he was quite unconscious of my presence.

I respectfully recalled his attention, and we continued to inspect the curiosities of the *salon*.

After the works of art, the rare natural specimens held the most important position. They consisted chiefly of plants, shells, and other productions of the ocean, which Captain Nemo had himself picked up. In the centre of the room was a small jet of water, illuminated by the electric light, and falling into a simple tridone. This shell, produced by the greatest of acephalous molluscs, measured about six yards round the delicately-curved edge. It thus surpassed in size those that were presented to Francis I by the Republic of Venice, and of which the church of St. Sulpice in Paris has constructed two immense holy-water basins.

Around this vase were classed and ticketed the most precious productions of the sea that had ever gladdened the eyes of a naturalist. You can picture my delight.

The zoophytes presented most curious specimens of the two groups of polypes and echinodermes. In the first group, tubipores, gorgons displayed fan-wise, soft sponges from Syria, &c., and a series of those madrepores, which my master Milne-Edwards has so cleverly classed in sections. In fine, the whole represented a collection complete in individual specimens of the various groups.

The collection of shells was of inestimable value, and time would fail me in attempting to describe them all. Amongst them I well remember the elegant royal hammer-fish of the Indian Ocean, whose regularly-placed white spots showed out upon the red or brown beneath – an imperial spondyde of vivid colouring, bristling with spines, a rare specimen in European museums, and worth, I should say, 20,000 francs; a common specimen of hammer-fish from New Holland, where it is not easy to procure, however; "buccardia" of Senegal, fragile white bivalves, which one may blow away like a soap-bubble; a whole series of "trochi", some greenish brown, from American waters, some a reddish-brown, related to those of New Holland; the former from the Gulf of Mexico, remarkable for their imbricated shells; the latter, the stellaria, found in the South Seas, and rarest of all, the magnificent "spar" shell of New Zealand; and, in fine, ovula, oliva, buccini, voluta, harpa, cassis, cerethia, fissurella, patella, and other delicate and fragile shells, to which science has given most charming names.

Besides, and in special compartments, were displayed rows of pearls of great beauty, which the electric light tipped with little scintillations. Rose-pearls torn from the Red Sea; green pearls of the halistoid iris; yellow pearls, and blue, and black; curious products of various molluscs in every ocean, and in certain water-courses, besides many other specimens of immense value.

Some of these pearls surpassed a pigeon's egg in size, and were worth more than that which the traveller Tavernier sold to the Shah of Persia for three millions, and excelled that other pearl of the Imaum of Muscat, which I fancied without a rival in the world.

So to calculate the value of this collection was almost impossible. Captain Nemo must have spent millions on his specimens, and I was thinking how he could thus afford to gratify his tastes, when I was interrupted by his saying:

"You are examining my shells, Monsieur; they can interest a naturalist, but they have a greater charm for me, for I have collected them all myself, and there is not any part of the oceanic world that has escaped my search."

"I can quite understand," said I, "the pleasure of floating in the midst of such riches. You are one of those who have made their own fortune. No museum in Europe possesses such a collection as yours. But if I go on admiring these so much, I shall have no wonder left for the vessel that carries us. I do not wish to pry into your secrets, but I confess that the speed of the Nautilus, the machinery that guides her, the power that animates her, all have excited my curiosity to a very high pitch. I see hanging from these walls some instruments with whose uses I am unacquainted. May I know what they are?"

"M. Aronnax," replied the captain, "I have already told you that you are free on board my ship, and so no part of the Nautilus is forbidden you. You can go over her, and I shall be very happy to be your conductor."

"I really don't know how to thank you, Monsieur, but I will not abuse your confidence. I will only enquire the uses of those instruments."

"Similar instruments will be found in my room, and I will explain their uses there. But first come and see your own cabin. You ought to know how you are likely to be lodged on board the *Nautilus*."

I followed the captain, who, by one of the doors pierced in each side of the room, brought us back into the "waist" of the ship. He led the way forward, and there I found not merely a cabin, but an elegantly-fitted chamber, containing a bed, wardrobe, and other furniture.

I was not able to express my thanks to my host.

"Your room is contiguous to mine," said he, opening a door as he spoke, "and mine opens into the room we have just left."

I entered his room; it had an austere appearance almost monkish. An iron bedstead, a work-table, and some toilette furniture. The light was dim. There was nothing "cosy" about it; what was necessary was there, but nothing more.

Captain Nemo pointed to a seat.

"Won't you sit down," he said.

I sat down, and he addressed me as follows:

CHAPTER XII
ENTIRELY BY ELECTRICITY

"MONSIEUR," SAID HE, as he indicated the instruments suspended against the walls of the room, "there is the apparatus necessary for the navigation of the *Nautilus*. Here, as in the other room, I have them always under my eyes, and they point out to me my exact situation and direction in mid-ocean. Some of them are known to you, such as the thermometer, which tells me the temperature of the *Nautilus*; the barometer, which tells me the weight of the air, and predicts changes of weather; the hygrometer, which marks the dryness of the atmosphere; the stormglass, whose mixture decomposing, tells me of the approaching tempest; the compass, which guides me; the sextant, which, by the sun's altitude, tells me my latitude; the chronometers, which show my longitude; and finally, the day and night telescopes, by which I can scrutinize all parts of the horizon when the *Nautilus* comes up to the surface of the sea."

"These are the instruments in general use on board ship,"

I said, "and I know their uses. But there are some others, intended, no doubt, for the peculiar requirements of the *Nautilus*.
That dial-plate I see with the moveable needle. Is it a manometer?"

"It is a manometer, in fact. Placed in the water, of which it
indicates the exterior pressure, it gives me at the same time the
depth at which I am keeping my boat."

"And those novel sounding-lines?"

"They are the theometric 'leads', which inform me of the
temperature at various depths."

"And those instruments, with the use of which I am unacquainted?"

"On these points, I must give you some little explanation, if
you will listen to me."

After a short pause, he recommenced.

"There is an agent here, powerful, obedient, rapid in action,
natural, which adapts itself to everything on board. It does everything by itself. It gives me light, it warms me, it is the very soul
of my mechanical arrangements. This agent is electricity."

"Electricity!" I exclaimed.

"Yes, Monsieur."

"But," said I, "you move at a great pace, which is not in accord
with the power of electricity. So far as we know, its dynamic
power remains very limited, and is not able to produce any great
forces."

"Monsieur," replied Captain Nemo, "my electricity is not
that of the world in general, and that is all that I feel at liberty to
tell you."

"I will not insist upon it, of course, and will content myself
by being very much astonished at the result. One question
I would ask, to which, of course, you need not reply. Do not
the elements you employ soon expend themselves? Zinc for
instance. How can you replace it if you have no communication
with the land?"

"Your question shall have an answer," replied Captain Nemo.
"I may tell you, however, that mines of zinc, iron, silver, and gold,
all exist at the bottom of the sea, and the exploration of them is
surely practicable. But I am in no wise indebted to the minerals
of earth, and I only ask the sea to produce my electricity!"

"The sea!"

"Yes, and the means are these. I have been able to establish a circuit between the threads, cast in different depths, to obtain electricity by the difference of the temperature they underwent, but I prefer an easier plan."

"And that is?"

"You know the composition of sea-water. In 1,000 grammes there is $96\frac{1}{2}$ per cent. of water; two and one-third per cent. of chloride of sodium, then small quantities of chlorides of magnesium and potash, bromide of magnesium, sulphate of magnesia, sulphate and carbonate of lime. So you perceive that the chloride of sodium is present in a large proportion. Now, it is this sodium which I extract from the water, and of which I make my elements."

"The sodium?"

"Yes. Mixed with mercury it forms an amalgam, which takes the place of the zinc in the Bunzen elements. The mercury remains, the sodium only gives off, and the sea itself furnishes that. I may tell you, moreover, that the sodium battery may be considered as the most powerful, and the electric force is double that of the zinc battery."

"I quite understand the value of the sodium in the condition in which you find it. The sea contains it. So far so good. But still it is necessary to extract it. How do you do that? Your batteries could evidently be of use to extract it, but if I do not mistake, the expenditure of sodium, necessitated by the electric apparatus, exceeds the quantity extracted. So you would consume more of it than you could produce."

"But I do not extract it by the assistance of the battery. I simply employ the heat of pit-coal."

"Pit-coal?" I said, meaningly.

"Well, let us say sea-coal, if you prefer it," replied Captain Nemo.

"And can you dig out mines of sea-coal?"

"M. Aronnax, you shall see me work it. I only ask a little patience, since you have time to be patient. Only recollect this – I owe everything to the ocean. It produces electricity, and electricity gives the *Nautilus* heat, light, speed and, in a word, life!"

"But not the air you breathe!"

"Oh! I can make the air necessary for my use, but it is unnecessary, since I go up to the surface whenever I please. However, if electricity do not furnish me with air to breathe, it at least sets in motion some powerful pumps, which enable me to store in reservoirs for the purpose, sufficient to enable me to remain, at need, as long as I choose at the bottom of the sea."

"Captain Nemo," said I, "I can only admire you. You have discovered, what men will some day find out, the true dynamic power of electricity."

"I do not know if they will or not," replied Nemo, coldly. "However that may be, you already know the first application that I make of this precious agent. It gives us light with an equality and continuity equal to the sun. Now that clock is electric, and goes with a regularity that defies a thousand chronometers. I have divided it into twenty-four hours, like the Italian clocks, for, for me no night exists, and no day; nor sun, nor moon, but only this artificial light, which I produce from the depths of the sea. Look! at this moment it is 10 a.m."

"Just so!"

"Here is another application of electricity. That dial hanging before us indicates the speed of the vessel. An electric cord places it in communication with the screw's log, and the needle indicates the speed. Look here! at this moment we are going at the moderate speed of fifteen miles an hour."

"It is, indeed, marvellous; and I see that you are right to employ this agent, which is destined to supersede wind, water, and steam."

"We have not finished yet, M. Aronnax. If you like to follow me, we will go astern."

I already was acquainted with the forward portion of the ship, which was divided into two parts in the centre. The *salle-à-manger*, separated from the library by a watertight bulkhead; the library; the grand saloon, separated from the captain's room by another watertight partition; this room and mine and an air-reservoir composed the forward portion – in all thirty-five yards in length. The bulkheads were pierced with doors, which could be hermetically sealed, and assured the safety of the *Nautilus* in the event of any influx of water.

I followed Captain Nemo across the waist, and reached the centre. There was a sort of well, which opened between two bulkheads. An iron ladder led upwards. I asked the use to which this ladder was put.

"It leads to the 'launch'."

"What, have you a boat, too?"

"Certainly, and an excellent one – light, and impossible to sink; which serves for pleasure or fishing."

"But when you wish to embark in it you must surely go up to the surface of the sea?"

"By no means. This boat is fastened to the upper part of the hull of the *Nautilus*, and rests in a cavity prepared for it. It is decked, absolutely staunch, and kept secured by solid bolts. This ladder leads to a manhole in the hull of the *Nautilus*, which corresponds to another hole in the side of the launch. It is through these openings that I enter the boat. In shutting one I open the other, by pressure of a screw. I pull out the bolts, and the boat rises with great swiftness to the surface. I then open the deck-panel, hitherto carefully closed. I 'step' the mast, hoist my sail, or take to the oars and pull about."

"But how do you return on board?"

"I do not return; it is the *Nautilus* which comes up."

"At your order?"

"Yes. An electric cord is extended between us. I merely send a telegram, and that is sufficient."

"In fact," said I, intoxicated by these wonders, "nothing can be more easy."

Having passed the staircase leading to the platform, I saw a cabin in which Conseil and Ned Land had enjoyed an excellent meal. Thence a door opened into a kitchen, situated between the immense store-rooms.

There the electricity, more energetic and more obedient than gas, did all the cooking. The wires, passing into the fireplaces, communicated to the platinum sponges a heat which was evenly maintained. It equally heated the distilling apparatus, which, by vaporization, made a very drinkable water. From the kitchen opened a bath-room, comfortably arranged, and with hot and cold water laid on. Beyond the kitchen was the sailors' cabin. But the door was closed, and I was not able to inspect its arrangements, which might have given me some idea of the number of men required to navigate the *Nautilus*.

At the end another bulkhead separated this cabin from the engine-room. A door was opened, and I found myself in the compartment in which Captain Nemo, a most accomplished engineer, had arranged the machinery.

This engine-room, well-lighted, was of great extent. It was properly divided into two parts, one for the elements which produced the electricity, the other for the mechanism which moved the screw.

I was at first surprised by the smell – *sui generis* – which pervaded the room. Captain Nemo noticed my impressions.

"It is only an escape of gas produced by the use of the sodium – but it is not very unpleasant. Moreover, every morning we purify and ventilate the ship thoroughly."

But now I began to examine with a lively interest the engine of the *Nautilus*.

"You perceive," said the captain, "that I employ the Bunzen elements in preference to the Ruhmkorff, which did not answer. The Bunzen elements are fewer, but stronger, as experience has shown. The electricity produced goes to the stern of the vessel, where it acts by means of electro-magnets of great power upon a particular system of levers and gearing, which transmit the motion to the shaft of the screw. Thus, a diameter of six metres, and a pitch of seven and a half, can give me a hundred and twenty revolutions in a second."

"And you obtain from that?"

"A speed of fifty miles an hour."

There was some mystery here, but I did not insist upon an explanation. How could electricity yield such a force. Where did this illimitable force take its origin. Was it in the excessive tension obtained by a novel kind of bobbins? Was there in its transmission through the system of levers the power to increase it indefinitely? That was what I could not understand.

"Captain Nemo," said I, "I see the result, and I do not seek the explanation of the means. I have seen the *Nautilus* manœuvre before the *Abraham Lincoln*, and I know its speed. But speed is not everything. You must be able to see whither you are going. You must have the power to direct your course to the right or left – up or down. How do you reach the deeps, where you must support a pressure of hundreds of atmospheres? How do you rise to the surface of the ocean? Finally, how do you maintain your vessel halfway when it suits you to do so? Am I indiscreet in asking all these questions?"

"Not at all," replied the captain, after a little hesitation, "since you never are likely to quit this submarine vessel. Come into the saloon. It is our 'study', and there you shall be made acquainted with all you ought to know respecting the *Nautilus*."

CHAPTER XIII
A FEW FIGURES

WE WERE SOON seated in the saloon, enjoying our cigars. The captain placed a diagram in my hands, showing the sections and elevation of the *Nautilus*. He then commenced his description as follows:

"You perceive, M. Aronnax, that my boat is an elongated cylinder, pointed at the extremities. It is of much the same shape as a cigar, a form which has already been tried in England and several vessels. Its length is exactly seventy yards; its greatest breadth ten yards. It is not, you see, constructed exactly on the principle of your swift-going steamers, but its lines are sufficiently lengthened to permit the displacement of water to pass away easily, and to oppose no serious resistance to its progress.

"The above measurement will enable you to arrive at the displacement and weight of the *Nautilus*. Its surface measures $11,000\frac{45}{100}$ square metres, its volume $1,500\frac{2}{10}$ metres. So when completely immersed it displaces or weighs 1,500 cubic metres or tons.

"When I planned this vessel for submarine navigation, I intended that nine-tenths should be immersed, and one-tenth out of the water. Consequently, it would not displace more than nine-tenths of its volume, that is to say $1,356\frac{48}{100}$ square metres, or the same number of tons. I was therefore obliged not to exceed that weight in constructing it according to the following dimensions.

"The *Nautilus* is composed of two hulls, one within the other, fastened by T-shaped bolts, which give the vessel great strength. In fact, it has as much resistance in this form as a solid mass would possess. The bulwark cannot be broken, it adheres by itself, and is not riveted. The homogeneity of its construction and the joining of the materials enables it to defy the most violent seas.

"The two hulls are made of iron-plates, whose density with respect to the water is as $7\frac{8}{10}$. The first is not less than two-and-a-half inches thick, and weighs $364\frac{96}{100}$ tons. The second 'skin' includes the keel, twenty inches high and ten thick, which weighs by itself sixty-two tons; the engine, the ballast, the various accessories and gear, the compartments and supports of the interior, weigh $961\frac{62}{100}$ tons, which gives a total of $1,356\frac{48}{100}$ tons. Is that clear?"

"Perfectly!" I replied.

"Well," continued the captain, "when the *Nautilus* is in the sea, under these conditions, it emerges one-tenth. Now, I make the reservoirs of a capacity equal to this tenth, that is to say of $150\frac{72}{100}$ tons, and fill them with water; the vessel will then be completely immerged. That is the case. These reservoirs exist in the lower part of the *Nautilus*; I open the tops, the reservoirs are filled, and the boat sinks to a level with the surface of the water."

"Very good, captain, but now we have arrived at the real difficulty. I can understand that you can get level with the surface. But in going lower down in your submarine vessel, do you not encounter a pressure, and consequently endure a pressure, from below, which may be estimated at an atmosphere for thirty feet of water, or about 15 lbs. for every square inch?"

"Quite so."

"Then unless you fill up the *Nautilus* altogether, I do not see how you can get her down to the bottom of the sea."

"Monsieur," replied Captain Nemo, "you cannot confuse statics and dynamics without running the risk of grave errors. It gives me very little trouble to reach the depths of the ocean, for all bodies have a tendency to sink. Do you follow me?"

"I am listening, captain."

"When I wish to determine what increase of weight I must give the *Nautilus* to sink her, I have only to think of the reduction in the volume of sea water, according as we get lower and lower down."

"That is clear enough," I replied.

"Now, if water be not absolutely incompressible, it is nearly so. In fact, according to the latest calculations, it is only .000436 per atmosphere for each thirty feet of depth. If I want to descend 1,000 yards, I calculate the reduction of volume of a column of water of 1,000 yards – that is to say, under the pressure of 100 atmospheres. This reduction will then be 436 hundred-millionths. I must then increase the weight so as to sink, to $1,513\frac{77}{100}$ tons, instead of $1,507\frac{2}{10}$. The increase will consequently only be $6\frac{57}{100}$ tons."

"Is that all?"

"Yes, and the calculation can be easily verified. I have supplementary reservoirs capable of holding 100 tons. So I can descend to a very considerable depth. When I wish to come up again to the surface, I have only to eject the water in all the reservoirs, and the *Nautilus* will float with one-tenth emerged."

I could not object to these figures.

"I admit your calculations, captain," I replied, "and it would be very bad taste to dispute them, since experience has proved them right every day. But I confess to a difficulty."

"What is that?"

"When you are at a depth of 1,000 yards, the sides of the *Nautilus* support a pressure of 100 atmospheres. So then, at the time you employ your reservoirs for the purpose of rising to the surface, you must overcome by means of your pumps this pressure of 100 atmospheres which is 1,500 lbs. for a square inch. Such a power—"

"Electricity alone can give me," interrupted Captain Nemo. "I repeat that the dynamic power of my engines is almost infinite. The pumps have enormous power. For instance, look at the columns of water thrown like a torrent upon the deck of the *Abraham Lincoln*. Besides, I do not fill my supplementary reservoirs, except to reach moderate depths. But when the fancy seizes me to visit the very bottom of the sea, or two or three leagues below the surface, I employ other more complicated but not less certain measures."

"What are they?" I inquired.

"That naturally leads me to tell you how the *Nautilus* is worked."

"I am very anxious to know, I assure you."

"To steer her to larboard or starboard, to work her horizontally, in a word, I make use of an ordinary rudder, with a large blade fixed behind the stern post, and which a wheel and tackling puts in motion. But I can also move the *Nautilus* up or down vertically, by means of two inclined planes attached to her sides, at the centre of flotation. These are moveable, and fitted to take any position, and which are worked from inside by powerful levers. These are kept parallel to the vessel when she is moving horizontally; but if inclined upwards or downwards, the *Nautilus* follows the same direction, and by the power of her screw, plunges or rises at any angle I please. And even if I wish to return very rapidly to the surface, I ship the screw, and the pressure of the water sends the *Nautilus* vertically to the surface – as a balloon, filled with hydrogen, mounts into the air."

"Bravo, captain!" I cried; "but how can the steersman find the proper direction beneath the water?"

"The helmsman is placed in a glazed compartment, which opens upon the upper part of the vessel, which is fitted with lenticular glasses."

"Glasses capable of resisting so great a pressure."

"Certainly. Crystal, though fragile to a blow, will resist considerable pressure. In fishing experiences by electric light in the North Sea, in 1864, plates of this material, of only one-third of an inch in thickness, resisted a pressure of sixteen atmospheres, to say nothing of the heated rays which divided the heat unequally. Now the glasses I make use of are not less than twenty-one centimetres thick in the centre – that is to say, thirty times more than those."

"Admitted," said I; "but to be able to see the light you must overcome the obscurity of the water. How is that accomplished?"

"Behind the steersman a powerful electric light is placed, which lights up the sea for half a mile ahead."

"Well done, indeed, captain! I can now comprehend the phosphorescence of the pretended narwhal, which has puzzled all the 'knowing ones'. By, the way, may I ask if the collision between the *Nautilus* and the *Scotia* was purely accidental?"

"Entirely so. I was moving two yards under water when the collision occurred. I saw that it had no unpleasant result."

"None; but how about your meeting with the *Abraham Lincoln*?"

"I am very sorry, Monsieur, for one of the ships of the fine American navy; but she attacked me, and I only defended myself. Moreover, I was content to let the frigate off easily. They will have no difficulty to repair her in the nearest port."

"Ah!" I cried, with an air of conviction, "there is no doubt that your *Nautilus* is a wonderful vessel."

"Yes," replied Captain Nemo, with emotion, "indeed she is, and I love her as my own child. If all is danger upon one of your vessels launched upon the ocean, if upon the sea 'the first impression is of the gulf beneath' – as has been well said by Jansen – in the *Nautilus* a man has nothing to fear. No injury, for the double hull is as strong as iron can be; no inconvenience from rolling or pitching; no sails for the wind to carry away; no boilers to burst; no fire to fear, since the fittings are all iron; no coal to exhaust, because electricity is the motive power; no collisions need be feared, because we can traverse the very deeps of the ocean; no storm to brave, because at a few yards beneath the surface all is still. So there, Monsieur, there is *the* ship *par excellence*. And if it be true that the engineer has more confidence in the ship than the builder, and the builder more than the captain himself, you can understand how proud I am of my *Nautilus*, since I am constructor, engineer, and captain in my own person."

He spoke with a persuasive eloquence. The flashing eye, the passionate gesture, seemed to change him completely. Truly he loved his ship as a parent his child!

But another, perhaps an indiscreet question, naturally presented itself, and I risked it.

"You are an engineer, then, Captain Nemo?"

"Yes," he replied. "I studied in London, Paris, and New York."

"But how could you secretly construct such a vessel as the *Nautilus*?"

"Each part, M. Aronnax, reached me from a different part of the world, and under a false name. The keel was forged at Creusot; the screw-shaft by Penn & Co., London. The iron plates were made by Laird, of Liverpool; the screw was by Scott, of Glasgow. The reservoirs were constructed by Cail & Co., in Paris; the engine by Krupp, in Prussia; the 'spur', in the workshop of Motala, in Sweden; the instruments at Hart Brothers', New York; and each manufacturer received my plans under a different name."

"But when the parts were made it was necessary to put them together."

"I established my workshops in a desert island in the open sea. There my workmen – that is to say, the brave companions whom I have instructed and got together – and I built our *Nautilus*. When we had finished, we destroyed by fire every trace of our work. I would have destroyed the island had I been able."

"Then I may conclude that the price of the vessel was very great."

"M. Aronnax, a ship of iron costs 1,155 francs per ton. The *Nautilus* cost 1,500. That is, therefore, 1,687,000 francs cost. Allow two millions for the fittings, and four or five millions for the works of art and collections, and you have the total."

"A last question, Captain Nemo."

"What is it?"

"I suppose you are very rich?"

"Infinitely wealthy, Monsieur. I could without inconvenience pay the ten milliards of the French debt."

I looked steadily at this extraordinary individual as he spoke thus. Was he taking advantage of my credulity? The future will show!

CHAPTER XIV
THE BLACK RIVER

THE PORTION OF the terrestrial globe occupied by water is estimated at 80,000,000 of acres. This liquid mass includes 2,258,000,000 of cubic miles, and forms a sphere, of a diameter of sixty leagues, whose weight is three quintillions of tons. To understand this it must be stated that the quintillion is to the billion as the billion is to the unit; so there are as many billions in a quintillion as there are units in a billion. Now this mass of water is nearly as much as would flow through all the rivers in the world during a period of forty years.

During the geological epoch, when fire succeeded water, the ocean was universal. Then, by degrees, the summits of mountains appeared; islands emerged; disappeared again under partial floodings; reappeared; united themselves; formed continents; and, at length, the earth remained as we see it. The solid had gained from the liquid 37,000,657 square miles.

The configuration of the continents permits of the division of the waters into five great oceans: the Arctic and Antarctic, the Indian, the Atlantic, and the Pacific.

The Pacific Ocean extends from north to south, between the polar circles, and from west to east, between Asia and America, to a distance of 145° of longitude. It is the most tranquil of seas; its currents are wide and slow; its tides not excessive; its rains abundant. Such was the ocean which fate had destined me to traverse under such strange conditions.

"Professor Aronnax," said Captain Nemo to me, "let us endeavour to ascertain our true position, and fix the point of departure for this voyage. It wants a quarter to twelve noon. I am about to go up to the surface."

The captain pressed an electric bell three times. The pumps began to expel the water from the reservoirs; the needle of the manometer marked the ascent of the *Nautilus* by the different pressures. She stopped.

"We are at the surface," said the captain.

I advanced to the central staircase, which led to the platform, and by the open panel I reached the upper surface of the *Nautilus*.

The platform was not far above the water. The *Nautilus* was of the fusiform shape, which had been compared to a long cigar. I noticed that the iron plates, lightly imbricated, resembled the scales which clothe certain reptiles. I could then understand why this boat had always been taken for a marine animal, in defiance of the best glasses.

Towards the middle of the platform lay the launch, half buried in the hull of the ship. Fore and aft were two cages of medium height, with sloping sides, and partly closed by thick lenticular glasses. One of these cages was for the steersman, the other contained the electric light which lighted up the ship's course.

The sea was lovely, the sky clear. The long vessel scarcely rose to the lazy undulations of the ocean. A light breeze from the east ruffled the surface. The horizon was perfectly clear for observations. There was nothing in sight – not a rock, not an island. No more of the *Abraham Lincoln*!

Captain Nemo, furnished with his sextant, took the sun's altitude, which was to give him his latitude. For some minutes he waited till the level of the horizon was fixed. While he made his observations, not a muscle moved, and the instrument was as motionless as in a hand of marble.

"Now, professor," he said. "Now, if you are ready—"

I threw a last glance over the sea, and descended to the large saloon.

There the captain was making his longitude by chronometers altered in accordance with horal angles of his observations. Then he said: "We are 137° 5' west longitude."

"Of what meridian?" I asked, hoping from his reply to discover his nationality.

"Monsieur," said he, "I have chronometers regulated for the meridians of Paris, Greenwich, and Washington. But in your honour, I will use the Paris meridian."

I gained nothing from this reply. I bowed; he continued:

"Thirty-seven degrees fifteen minutes longitude west of Paris, and 30° 7′ north lat., so we are 300 miles from the Japanese coasts. So to-day, the 8th November, and at mid-day, we commence our exploration under the sea."

"May God preserve us!" I said.

"Now I must leave you to your studies," said the captain. "I have told them to proceed north-east about fifty metres down. There are maps on which you can trace the course. The saloon is at your service, but I must ask your permission to retire."

Captain Nemo saluted me, and withdrew. I remained absorbed in my reflections, which all turned to the commander. Should I never know to what nation this mysterious man belonged, who boasted that he was no longer of any? The hatred he had vowed against the human race, too, I wondered who had provoked that! Was he one of those misunderstood *savants*, a genius to whom all was bitterness – a modern Galileo – or even one of those scientific men like Commander Maury, whose career had been cut short by political revolutions? I could not then determine. He met me coolly, though he had taken me on board and treated me hospitably while my life was in his hands. But he had not accepted my extended hand, neither had he offered me his own.

For a whole hour I remained plunged in these reflections, seeking to pierce this mystery which interested me so deeply. Then my gaze became fixed upon the large map upon the table, and I placed my finger upon the very spot where the latitude and longitude lately arrived at, intersected.

The sea has its rivers as a continent. These are the special currents recognizable by their temperature and their colour, of which the most remarkable is the Gulf Stream. Science has determined the direction of five principal currents on the globe. One in the North Atlantic, one in the South Atlantic, a third in the North Pacific, a fourth in the South Pacific, and a fifth in the Southern Indian Ocean. It is even probable that a sixth current existed formerly in the Northern Indian Ocean, since the Caspian and Aral seas, united with the great Asian lakes, only formed one and the same sheet of water.

Now, at the point indicated on the map, one of these currents started – the Kuro Scivo, of the Japanese – the Black River, which, leaving the Bay of Bengal, warmed by a tropical sun, traverses the Strait of Malacca, extends along the coast of Asia, flows into the North Pacific near the Aleutian Islands, bearing trunks of the camphor-tree and other indigenous products, and contrasting the pure indigo of its warm waters with the waves of the ocean. This was the current that the *Nautilus* was about to follow. I traced it up and perceived that it was lost in the vastness of the Pacific, and I felt myself "carried away" by it, when Ned Land and Conseil appeared at the door of the apartment.

My two brave companions appeared petrified at the sight of the marvels presented to their gaze.

"Where are we?" cried the Canadian. "In the Quebec Museum?"

"If Monsieur has no objection, this may rather be the Musée du Sommerard!"

"My friends," I said, as I signed for them to enter, "you are neither in Canada nor France, but on board the *Nautilus*, at fifty yards beneath the surface of the sea."

"We must credit Monsieur if he says so," replied Conseil, "but this *salon* is enough to astonish even a Fleming like myself."

"Give rein to your astonishment then, and look around you; for, for a classifier of your reputation, there is something to do here."

I had not much need to encourage Conseil. The brave lad, bent over the cases, was already muttering "Class Gasteropods, family Buccinoids, genus Porcelain, species Cypræa Madagascariensis," &c.

Meantime, Ned Land, who was not much of a naturalist, was making inquiries respecting my interview with Captain Nemo. Had I found out who he was, whence he came, whither he was going, to what depths he was dragging us? and a thousand questions to which I had no time to reply.

I told him all I knew, or rather all that I did not know, on those points, and inquired what he had heard or seen on his side.

"Nothing at all," he replied; "not even the crew. I suppose they are not electric by any chance, are they, sir?"

"Electric!" I exclaimed.

"Faith, I am inclined to think so. But you, M. Aronnax," asked he, who had his own idea, "how many men do you think there are on board? Ten – twenty – fifty – a hundred?"

"I do not know how to answer, Ned," I said. "Moreover, take my advice, give up the idea of yours to seize the *Nautilus* and make your escape. This boat is one of the *chefs-d'œuvre* of modern industry, and I would have been sorry not to have seen it. Many people would accept the situation, if it were only to wander about amongst all these wonderful things. So keep quiet, and try to see what passes around us."

"See!" replied the harpooner; "there is nothing to see; one will see nothing in this iron prison. We are moving, we are sailing blindly—"

As Ned was speaking the light was suddenly extinguished, and a profound darkness supervened. So rapidly was the light withdrawn that my eyes retained an impression somewhat similar to that which is produced when darkness is suddenly illuminated.

We remained silent and motionless, not knowing what surprise, agreeable or otherwise, awaited us. A rustling noise was heard, as if the panels at the side were being moved.

"It is the end of the world," said Land.

"Order of Hydromedusæ," murmured Conseil.

Suddenly daylight appeared at each side of the room across two oblong openings. Liquid masses appeared vividly illuminated. Two crystal plates separated us from the sea. I shuddered at first at the thought that these fragile walls might give way; but the strong copper supports afforded them an almost infinite resistance against pressure.

The sea was distinctly visible in a radius of a mile around the *Nautilus*. And what a spectacle it was! What pen can describe it? Who could depict the effects of the light across these transparent waves, and the softness of the successive gradations to the upper or lower depths of the ocean.

The diaphonous quality of the sea is well known. We know that its clearness is superior to fresh water. The mineral and organic substances which it holds in suspension, even increase its transparency. In certain parts of the ocean – in the Antilles – the sand can be perceived at a depth of 145 yards; and the force of penetration of the solar rays seems to descend to a depth of 300 yards. But in the middle course of sea pursued by the

Nautilus, the electric light was produced in the very bosom of the deep. It was no more like a luminous ocean − it was a liquid light.

If we can admit Erhemberg's hypothesis, that there is a phosphorescent illumination at the bottom of the sea, then nature has certainly reserved for the inhabitants of the ocean one of its most wonderful sights, and I was able to judge of it here by the "play" of this light. Upon each side a window opened upon these unexplored abysses. The darkness of the room made the exterior more clearly visible, and we kept gazing as if the pure crystal was the glass case of an immense aquarium.

The *Nautilus* did not appear to move, because guiding-marks were absent. Sometimes the lines of water, divided by the "spur", passed before our eyes with wonderful rapidity. Perfectly amazed we were seated before these glasses, and no one spoke till Conseil said:

"You wanted to see something, friend Ned − do you see now?"

"Very curious indeed," exclaimed the Canadian, who, forgetful of his anger and his plans for flight, had submitted to the fascination; "and people would come from a very great distance to see such a sight as this!"

"Ah," I thought, "I understand the life of this man. He has made a world of his own, which reserves for him her most extraordinary wonders!"

"But the fish!" the Canadian cried; "I don't see any fish!"

"What does that matter," replied Conseil, "since you do not know them."

"I! why, I am a fisherman!"

And on this subject a discussion arose between the friends, for they knew the fish, but each in a different fashion.

Everybody knows that fishes form the fourth and last class of the vertebrate animals. They have been correctly defined as "vertebrates, with double circulation and cold blood, breathing by means of gills, and destined to live in water". They form two distinct series − that of osseous fishes (that is to say, those whose dorsal fin is made of osseous vertebræ, and the cartilaginous fishes, whose dorsal fin is composed of cartilaginous vertebræ. The Canadian may have been acquainted with this distinction, but Conseil knew a good deal more, and now, bound in friendship to Ned, he could not hint that he knew less than himself. So he said:

"Friend Ned, you are a killer of fish, and a very skilful fisherman. You have captured a great number of those animals. But I will bet that you do not know how they are classed."

"Indeed!" replied the harpooner. "They are classed as fish you may eat, and those you may not."

"That is merely the distinction of a *gourmand*," said Conseil. "But tell me if you know the difference between osseous and cartilaginous fishes."

"Perhaps so!" replied the Canadian.

"And the subdivision of these two great classes?"

"I have some doubt about it."

"Well then, friend Ned, listen and learn. The osseous fishes are subdivided into six orders. First, the 'acanthopterygians', whose upper jaw is complete and moveable, and whose gills somewhat resemble a comb. This order consists of fifteen families – that is to say, three-quarters of the known fishes. Type, the common perch."

"Not bad to eat," said Land.

"Secondly," continued Conseil, "the 'abdominal', which have the ventral fins suspended beneath the abdomen, and in rear of the pectoral fins, without being attached to the shoulder-bone; this order is divided into five families, and includes the greater part of the fresh-water fish. Type, the carp and the jack."

"Pooh!" said the Canadian, with contempt. "Fresh-water fish, indeed!"

"Thirdly," said Conseil, "the 'subrachians', whose ventral fins are fastened beneath the pectorals, and directly suspended from the bone of the shoulder. This order contains four families. Types, the plaice, dab, turbot, brill, soles, &c."

"Excellent, excellent!" cried Ned, who only looked at the fish from the gastronomic point of view.

"Fourthly," continued Conseil, without heeding the interruption, "the 'apodals', with long bodies, unprovided with ventral fins, and covered with a thick, and frequently slimy skin – an order which consists of only one family. Type, the eel."

"Middling, middling!" said Ned.

"Fifthly," said Conseil, "the 'lophobranchiata', which have

jaws complete and free, but whose gills are formed of little tufts, placed in pairs along the branchial arches. This order has only one family. Type, the sea-horse."

"Bad, bad!" replied the harpooner.

"Sixthly, and lastly," said Conseil, "are the 'plectognathes', whose maxillary bone is firmly fixed to the intermaxiliary, which forms the jaw, and of which the 'palatine anal' is connected by suture with the skull, which renders it immoveable – an order which has no true ventrals, and consists of two families. Type, the sun-fish."

"Would disgrace a copper," said Ned.

"Do you understand, friend Ned?" asked the learned Conseil.

"Not the least in the world, friend Conseil. But go on, for it is very interesting."

"The cartilaginous fishes," replied Conseil, "only include three orders."

"So much the better," said Ned.

"First come the cyclostomi, whose jaws are connected by a moveable ring, and the gills open in numerous holes – an order which includes only one family; type, the lamprey. Secondly, the selacians, with gills resembling those of the cyclostomi, but whose lower jaw is moveable. This order, which is the most important of its class, comprehends two families; types, the ray and the shark."

"What!" cried Ned, "rays and sharks in the same order! Well, in the interest of the rays, I do not advise you to put them in the same tank."

"Thirdly," said Conseil, "the sturiones, whose gills are open, as usual in fishes, but with a single aperture, provided with an operculum. This order includes four genera; type, the sturgeon."

"Ah, friend Conseil, you have kept the best to the last – in my opinion, at least. Is that all?"

"Yes, my brave Ned; and you may as well note, that when you know all this you know nothing at all; for the families are divided into genus, sub-genus, species, and varieties."

"Well, friend Conseil," said Ned, leaning against the glass, "look at the varieties passing."

"Yes; one could almost believe oneself in an aquarium."

"No," I said, "for an aquarium is a cage, and those fish are as free as a bird in the air."

"Come, now, name them, Conseil; name them," cried Ned Land.

"I," he replied; "I am not equal to that. You must ask my master."

In fact, Conseil, though an excellent classifier, was nothing of a naturalist; and I do not think he could tell the difference between a tunny and a bonito. He was just the opposite of the Canadian, who could name the fish without hesitation.

"A balista," I had said.

"And a Chinese balista," added Ned.

"Genus balista; family sclerodermes; order plectognathes," murmured Conseil.

The Canadian had not been mistaken. A shoal of balistas, with their flattened bodies and "grained" skin, armed with a prickly fin on the back, were playing around the *Nautilus*, moving the four ranges of spines, which bristled on each side of their tails. Nothing could be more beautiful than their skins, grey above and white underneath, the golden spots shining in the darkness of the waves. Amongst them rays were swimming, like a cloth undulated by the wind; and amongst them I could perceive, to my delight, the Chinese ray, yellow on the upper surface, light rose-colour underneath, and furnished with three spikes behind the eye; a very rare species this, and even doubtful in the time of Lacépède, who had never seen one, except in a collection of Japanese drawings.

For the space of two hours a regular aquatic army surrounded the *Nautilus*. In the midst of their gambols, in which they rivalled each other in beauty, speed, and agility, I distinguished the green wrass; the goby, with its rounded tail, white and violet tinted; the Japanese scomber, the beautiful mackerel of these seas, blue and white, the brilliant azure exceeding all description. The streaked sparus, with varied blue and yellow fins; the "fessy" sparus, relieved by a black band across the tail; the zonephorus sparus, elegantly streaked across the body; aulox-tones – the sea woodcocks, with regular beaks, some specimens attaining the length of nearly a yard; Japanese salamanders; eels six feet long, like serpents, with quick small eyes and large mouths bristling with teeth, &c.

Our wonder continued unabated. Exclamations of delight were frequent. Ned named the fish, Conseil classed, while I went into ecstasies before the vivacity of their movements and the beauty of their appearance. I had never had an opportunity to observe these animals living and in their native waters, till now. I will not mention all the varieties which passed before my dazed vision, this wonderful collection of the Japanese and China seas. These fishes were more numerous than are birds in the air, and were doubtless attracted by the electric light.

Suddenly light again appeared in the room – the panels were closed, and the enchanting vision disappeared. I thought of what I had seen for a long time, until my gaze fell upon the instruments suspended upon the wall The compass, I noticed, pointed N.N.E.; the manometer gave a pressure of five atmospheres, corresponding to a depth of fifty yards, and the electric gong indicated a speed of fifteen miles an hour.

I waited for Captain Nemo. He did not appear. It was five o'clock.

Ned and Conseil returned to their cabin, and I went to my room. There I found my dinner prepared. It was composed of turtle soup, mullet fillets, prepared from the "emperor holocanthus", the taste of which appeared to me to be superior to salmon.

I passed the evening in reading, writing, and reflection. Then sleep asserted its sway, and I retired to my grass couch and slept soundly, while the *Nautilus* skimmed across the rapid current of the black river.

CHAPTER XV
A NOTE OF INVITATION

WHEN I AWOKE next morning I found I had slept twelve hours. Conseil came as usual to inquire "how Monsieur had passed the night", and to offer his services. He had left the Canadian sleeping like a man who had never done such a thing in his life before.

I let Conseil chatter away, but did not reply. I was thinking of the absence of Captain Nemo, and I was hoping to see him again.

I was soon dressed in my garments of byssus, upon which Conseil commented freely. I informed him that the material was made from the silky fibres which attach the "jambouneaux" –

a sort of shell-fish very common in the Mediterranean – to the rocks. Formerly stockings and gloves were made of these filaments, and proved to be very warm and soft. The crew of the *Nautilus* could thus clothe themselves at will, independently of cotton, wool, or silkworms. When I was dressed I proceeded to the saloon. It was empty.

I plunged at once into conchology. I also inspected the large collection of aquatic plants of the rarest kinds, and which, although dried, still preserved their wondrous colourings. Amongst these beautiful hydrophytes I remarked the verticillated cledostephes, the vine-leaved caulupes, &c. – in fact, the whole series of sea-weeds.

The whole day passed without my receiving a visit from Captain Nemo. The panels did not open; perhaps he was afraid I should get tired of the sight.

The *Nautilus* still headed N.N.E.; the pace was sixteen miles an hour, and the depth sixty metres.

Next day (Nov. 10) there was the same freedom and the same solitude. I saw none of the ship's company. Ned and Conseil passed the greater part of the day with me. They were astonished at the inexplicable absence of the captain. Was he ill? Had he altered his plans concerning us?

After all, as Conseil remarked, we enjoyed complete freedom, and were well and abundantly fed. Our host observed the terms of the treaty; and, moreover, even the singularity of our situation had some real compensation, so that we had no right to find fault with him. Upon that day I commenced to write a record of our adventures, which has enabled me to relate them with such exactness; and I wrote upon a paper made from the sea-wrack.

Upon the 11th November, the influx of fresh air, very early in the morning, apprised us that we had risen to the surface to replenish the store of oxygen. I ascended the staircase, and passed out upon the platform.

It was six o'clock. The sky was cloudy, the sea looked grey, but calm; scarce a ripple ruffled the surface. I wondered whether Captain Nemo would appear. I expected to see him, but could only perceive the helmsman in the glass cage. I sat down upon the protuberance formed by the hull of the launch, and inhaled the delicious sea-breeze.

The mist gradually rose, under the influence of the rising sun, which soon flashed up over the eastern horizon, throwing a fiery track, like a lighted powder train, across the sea. The scattered clouds were tinged with bright and variegated colours, while the numerous "mares' tails" indicated a breeze.

But what did a storm matter to the *Nautilus*? I was admiring the beautiful sunrise, when I heard someone ascend to the platform. I expected to see Captain Nemo, but it was his mate, whom I had already met at the first interview with the captain. The mate came up, but did not seem to notice my presence, and he proceeded to "sweep" the horizon with his powerful glass. His observation having terminated, he approached the panel and pronounced the following sentence. I remember the exact terms, because every morning the same words were repeated under the same conditions. The sentence ran thus –

"Nautron respoc lorni virch."

What that meant, I cannot say.

Having pronounced those words, the mate descended, and I, fancying that the *Nautilus* would now resume her course, followed him, and returned to my room.

Five days passed in a similar manner. Every morning I ascended the platform. The same phrase was pronounced by the same person – but Captain Nemo never appeared.

I had made up my mind that I should see him no more, when, on the 16th November, as I entered my room with Conseil and Ned, I found a note on my table addressed to me.

I opened it quickly. It was written in a clear, bold hand, something of a German type was evident.

"To M. Aronnax,
    "On board the *Nautilus*,
        "16th November, 1867.

"Captain Nemo requests the pleasure of Professor Aronnax's society at a shooting party, to be held to-morrow morning, in the woods of the island of Crespo. Captain Nemo hopes that nothing will prevent M. Aronnax from attending, and will be pleased if his companions will also join the party."

"A shooting party!" cried Ned.

"And in his forests of Crespo!" added Conseil.

"But this particular gentleman must go ashore then!" said Ned.

"That is sufficiently clear from the note," I said, rereading it.

"Well, we must accept the invitation," said the Canadian.

"Once on shore we shall know what to do. Moreover, I shall not be sorry to have a little fresh meat."

Without stopping to reconcile the inconsistency of Captain Nemo, who, while professing horror of continents and islands, yet goes shooting in a wood, I merely accepted the invitation.

"Let us find where this island of Crespo is!"

I turned to the map, and at 32° 40′ N. lat., and 167°50′ E. long., I found the island discovered by Captain Crespo, in 1801. The old Spanish maps call it "Rocca de la Plata", or "Silver Rock". We were then about 1,800 miles from our starting-point, and the course of the *Nautilus* was now rather S.E.

I pointed out to my companions the little rock situated in the midst of the Pacific Ocean.

"If Captain Nemo is going to land at all," I said, "he has chosen the very smallest of desert islands."

Ned Land nodded without speaking, and then he and Conseil left me to myself. After supper, which was served by the silent and impassible steward, I retired – but much preoccupied.

Next morning I perceived that the *Nautilus* was stationary. I dressed hastily and proceeded to the saloon.

There I found Captain Nemo. He was awaiting me. He got up, saluted me, and asked whether it would suit me to accompany him.

As he made no allusion to his absence during the last eight days, neither did I, and merely replied that my companions and myself were ready to go with him.

"But, Monsieur," said I, "I must ask you a question."

"Ask it, M. Aronnax," said he, "and if I can reply to it, I will."

"How is it that you who have renounced all intercourse with the earth, can possess woods in the island of Crespo?"

"The woods I possess," he replied, "require no light nor heat from the sun. No lion, tiger, panther, nor any other quadruped inhabits them. They are known to me alone. They exist but for me. They are not terrestrial, but submarine forests."

"Submarine!" I exclaimed.

"Yes."

"And you ask me to go thither?"

"Precisely."

"On foot?"

"Yes, and dry-shod!"

"And shoot?"

"And shoot."

"With gun in hand!"

"Gun in hand."

I looked at the captain of the *Nautilus* with an air by no means flattering.

"He is evidently mad," I thought. "He has had an attack during the last eight days, which has not yet passed away. What a pity! I would rather see him eccentric than lunatic."

These ideas were clearly expressed by my countenance, but Captain Nemo merely invited me to follow him, and I did so. I was prepared for the worst.

We reached the dining-room, where breakfast was served.

"M. Aronnax," said the captain, "I beg you will partake of my breakfast, without any ceremony. We can talk while we are eating. But though I have promised you a 'turn' in the forest, I cannot promise you a *restaurant* there. So you had better breakfast like a man who will not dine till late."

I did honour to the meal, which was excellent. Captain Nemo at first ate without speaking, at length he said:

"Professor, when I first suggested your joining in a shooting-party in my forest in Crespo, you believed I was inconsistent. When I told you that these woods were under water, you thought I was a lunatic. You should never judge men hastily."

"But, captain—"

"Listen to me, if you please, and you will see whether I am to be accused of folly or inconsistency."

"I am listening."

"You are aware that man can live under water so long as he can carry with him a supply of atmospheric air. In all submarine works, the artisan is clothed with a waterproof dress, and his head is covered with a metal helmet. He receives the air by means of force-pumps and regulators of the supply."

"Like the diver's jacket," I said.

"Somewhat, but in those conditions the man is not free. He is attached to a pump by an india-rubber tube, a chain which binds him to the bank; and if we were thus tied to the *Nautilus*, we could not go far."

"And how do you obtain the desired freedom?" I asked.

"By employing the Rouquayrol-Denayrouze apparatus, invented by two of your countrymen, but which I have perfected for my own use, and which you may yourself make use of, without any inconvenience whatever. The apparatus is composed of a reservoir of sheet-iron, in which I store the air, under a pressure of fifty atmospheres. This reservoir is carried on the back, like a soldier's knapsack. The upper part forms a box, from which the air, restrained by a sort of bellows, cannot escape, except at the normal tension. In the Rouquayrol apparatus, as we employ it, two india-rubber tubes from this box open into a sort of respirator, which covers the head of the operator, one for the introduction and the other for the expulsion of the air, and the tongue closes one or the other, as the exigencies of inspiration and respiration demand. But I, who have to dare considerable pressure at the bottom of the sea, enclose my head in a helmet, as the divers do, and it is to this that the two tubes are attached."

"Excellent, Captain Nemo. But the air you carry must be quickly expended; and so soon as it contains more than fifteen per cent. of oxygen it ceases to be respirable."

"Certainly; but as I have said, the pumps of the *Nautilus* allow of the stowing of the air under a great pressure, and so the air in the reservoir will last for nine or ten hours."

"I have no objection to make," I said. "I only want to know how you can obtain light at the bottom of the ocean."

"By means of the Ruhmkorff apparatus. If the first be carried on the back, the other is fixed to the chest. It is composed of a Bunzen pile, which acts, not with bi-chromate of potash, but with sodium. An induction bobbin collects the electricity produced, and directs it towards a lamp of peculiar construction. In this lamp is a glass serpentine, which contains only a residuum of carbonic acid gas. When the apparatus is at work the gas becomes luminous, and gives forth a white and steady flame. Thus provided, I can both breathe and see."

"Captain Nemo, to all my objections you return such satisfactory replies, that I do not dare to express a doubt. But if I am obliged to accept the Rouquayrol and Ruhmkorff apparatus, I must make a reservation in regard to the gun with which you will arm me."

"But it is not an ordinary gun," replied the captain. "We do not use powder."

"It is an air-gun, then?"

"Certainly. How did you fancy I could make gunpowder on board, having neither saltpetre, sulphur, nor carbon."

"Besides," I said, "to fire under water in a surrounding medium, 855 times denser than the air, you must overcome a tremendous resistance."

"That need not affect the question. Certain cannons exist, improved upon Fulton's idea by the Englishmen Coles and Burley, by the Frenchman Farcy, and the Italian Laudi, which are made upon a particular system, and can be used under these conditions. But I repeat, that having no powder, I have to replace it by air at high pressure, which I can obtain in abundance by means of the pumps of the *Nautilus*."

"But this air must be rapidly expended."

"Well! have I not my Rouquayrol reservoir, which can furnish me with a supply at a pinch. A tap is sufficient. But you will see for yourself, M. Aronnax, that during our submarine shooting there is no great expenditure of air or bullets."

"Yet it seems to me that, in the semi-darkness, and in a medium much denser than the atmospheric air, the bullets would not travel far, and would not be frequently mortal."

"Monsieur, on the contrary, all hits made by this gun are mortal, and however lightly the animal may be struck, he falls dead."

"Why?"

"Because I do not use ordinary bullets – but little glass capsules, invented by the Austrian chemist Zeniebrock, and of which I have a large supply. These are covered with steel and weighted with lead – true Leyden jars in fact – in which electricity reaches a high tension. At the slightest resistance they burst, and the animal, however powerful he may be, falls dead. I may add that these capsules are no bigger than 'No. 4', and that six of them is the usual charge."

"I do not question it," I said, rising, "and I have no more to do than take my gun. So where you go – I go."

Captain Nemo then led me to the stern of the *Nautilus*, and as we passed the cabin where Ned and Conseil were seated, I called them to accompany us.

We all soon reached a small cabin near the engine-room, and in which we were to be fitted out for our expedition.

CHAPTER XVI
A WALK AT THE BOTTOM OF THE SEA

THIS LITTLE CABIN was, properly speaking, the arsenal and the vestry of the *Nautilus*. A dozen diving costumes hung upon the walls ready for use.

Ned Land, on seeing them, manifested a decided objection to adopt one.

"But," I said, "the forest of Crespo is under the sea, Ned."

"Ah," said the harpooner, disappointed as he saw his dream of fresh meat disappear. "And are you going to get into one of those dresses, M. Aronnax?"

"I must do so, Ned."

"Well, you are free to do so, of course," said he shrugging his shoulders; "but unless I am compelled to do so, I won't, I can tell you."

"No one will force you, Master Ned," said Captain Nemo.

"And is Conseil going to risk his life, too?"

"I go where Monsieur goes," replied Conseil.

At a sign from the captain two men came forward to assist us in donning the heavy waterproof dresses. They were like yielding suits of armour, and were composed of trousers and vest. The former terminated in a thick pair of leaden-soled boots. The vest was fastened by copper plates, which protected the chest against the pressure of the water, leaving the lungs free to act; the sleeves ended in flexible gloves, which did not interfere with the movements of the hands.

Captain Nemo, one of his crew – a perfect Hercules – Conseil, and I, were soon ready. It only remained for us to put on the helmet. But before I did so I asked the captain's permission to examine the guns.

I was handed an ordinary gun, the stock of which was made of sheet-iron, and hollow. It served as a reservoir for compressed air, which a valve, worked by a "tumbler", permitted to escape into the barrel. A box, hollowed out in the stock, contained twenty electric bullets, which the elasticity of the air placed in the barrel. So soon as one shot was discharged, the gun was again loaded automatically.

"Captain Nemo," I said, "this is a perfect weapon, and easily managed. I am anxious to try my skill. But how are we to reach the bottom of the sea?"

"At this moment the *Nautilus* is aground. We have not far to go."

"But how are we to get out?"

"You shall see."

Captain Nemo then put on his helmet. Conseil and I did likewise, not without bearing the Canadian's ironical wishes for "good sport".

The upper part of the vest was encircled by a copper collar with screws, to which the helmet was fastened. Three glazed apertures permitted us to see in all directions. So soon as we were ready, the Rouquayrol apparatus was placed upon our backs, and immediately began to act, so that I felt no inconvenience in breathing.

The Ruhmkorff lamp at my waist, and gun in hand, I declared myself ready to set out. But in those heavy garments and boots, I found it impossible to stir a step. This had been provided for, for I felt that I was carried into an adjoining chamber. My companions followed. I heard a door spring back, and darkness enveloped us. After some minutes, I heard a loud hissing noise – I am certain a sensation of cold rose from my feet to my chest. Evidently, the water had been admitted, and the chamber was filled. Then another door in the side of the *Nautilus* opened. A dim light was visible, and an instant afterwards, our feet touched the bottom of the sea.

And now, how can I recall the impressions which this expedition at the bottom of the sea has left upon me? Words are powerless to describe such marvels. Where the pencil cannot depict, how can the pen reproduce these wonders? Captain Nemo walked in front, his friend behind us, while Conseil and I remained together, as if any interchange of words were possible under the circumstances. I no longer felt the weight of my garments, or boots, or the reservoir of air; my head moved about in my helmet like a nut in its shell. All objects plunged into water lose a portion of their weight, equal to that of the water displaced, and I recognized that physical law discovered by Archimedes.

I was no longer an inert mass, but had considerable freedom of movement. The light, which illuminated the ground thirty feet below the surface, surprised me by its power. The solar rays easily penetrated this aqueous mass and dispersed its colouring. I could distinctly perceive objects 100 yards distant. Beyond, the depths toned down in fine gradations of ultramarine, then got bluer in the distance, and finally disappeared in a sort of undefined obscurity. The water around us was really but a kind of air, more dense than the terrestrial atmosphere, but almost as transparent. Above I could perceive the calm surface of the ocean.

We were walking upon a fine firm sand, not furrowed as that is upon which the waves leave their traces. This dazzling carpet, a true reflector, refracted the rays of the sun with surprising intensity. This is the cause of the tremendous reflection which penetrated all the liquid molecules. I should scarcely be credited, if I stated that, at this depth of thirty feet, I could see as plainly as in the daylight above – but it is a fact.

For a quarter of an hour we trod this glittering sand, composed of the impalpable dust of shells. The hull of the *Nautilus*, standing out like a rock, disappeared by degrees, but the light was burning to facilitate our return in the evening. It is difficult for those who have only seen the electric light on shore, to realize its vivid stream of brilliancy. There the dust which the air contains gives it the appearance of a luminous fog, while under the sea the light is transmitted with incomparable purity.

We kept going forward, and the plain of sand appeared boundless. I put by with my hands the liquid curtains which immediately closed behind me, while the pressure of the water obliterated our footsteps in the sand.

Some objects in the distance now attracted our attention. I recognized magnificent first formations of rocks covered with zoophytes of the most beautiful species, and I was struck with the peculiar effect of the sea at this depth.

It was ten o'clock. The sun's rays struck the water at a somewhat acute angle, and the light, decomposed by the contact as in a prism, flowers, rocks, plants, shells, polypes, were variegated with all the colours of the solar spectrum. It was wonderful, a perfect feast for the eyes. The mixture of colours and tones of colour formed a regular kaleidoscope of green, orange, yellow, violet, indigo, and blue; in a word, all the colours of the palette of an artist gone mad. How I longed to exchange with Conseil the sensations and ideas which possessed me! and I did not know even how to converse by signs as Captain Nemo and his companion did. So, as a last resource I talked to myself, and in so doing very likely used more air than was altogether desirable.

Conseil was equally delighted. He was evidently classing all these specimens of zoophytes and molluscs as hard as he could. Polypes and echinodermes abounded. The variegated "isis", the "cornulaires" which live by themselves, the clumps of virgin "ocularis" or white coral, the mushroom-like fungi, the anemones fixed by their muscular discs, formed quite a *parterre* of flowers, enamelled by the porpites dressed out in their necklaces of blue tentacles; the starfish, which shone upon the sand, and the "asterophytons", like beautiful lace, worked by naïads, moved in gentle undulations as our footsteps pressed upon the sand. It was a real sorrow to me to crush beneath my feet such splendid molluscs as lay around in thousands. But it was necessary to get along, and we went ahead, while above us the "physalides" waved their long tentacles over our heads; the umbrella-like medusæ with their opal and pink colouring surrounded by a scroll-work of azure, sheltered us from the sun's rays; and the pelagia panopyres, which, in the obscurity, sprinkled our path with phosphorescent light.

All these wonders were observed within the space of a quarter of a mile, and I scarcely stopped to observe them. Following Captain Nemo, who beckoned us onward, we found the nature of the ground began to change. To the plain of sand succeeded the viscous deposit termed "ooze", composed entirely of siliceous or calcareous shells. We then passed through a prairie of algæ – plants which the water had not disturbed, and whose growth was of a fungous nature. These grassy plants were soft to the feet, and rivalled in the softness of their texture the finest carpets ever made. A light arch of marine plants, also belonging to this extensive family of algæ, of which there are more than 2,000 known species, crossed the surface of the ocean. I could see, floating in long bands of *fucus*, some globular, some tubular, laurenciæ, cladostephi, the "palm" rhodymeniæ, like the fans of the cactus. I also observed that the green plants kept near the surface, while the red varieties grew lower down, leaving to the black and brown hydrophytes the formation of the lowest gardens of the sea.

These algæ are really wonderful. This "family" produces the largest, and at the same time the smallest vegetation in the world. While one may count forty thousand almost imperceptible plants in the space of a few square inches, one can collect *fucus* whose length exceeds many hundred feet.

We had been absent from the *Nautilus* about an hour and a half. It was nearly noon. I could see that the sun's rays were perpendicular, and did not refract. The magical appearance of the colours disappeared by degrees, and the shades of sapphire and emerald disappeared from our "sky". We proceeded at a steady pace, stepping together in a manner which resounded loudly from the ground. The slightest noises were transmitted with a clearness to which the ear on land is unaccustomed. Water is a much better conductor of sound than air, and the rapidity of the transmission of sounds is quadrupled in the former compound.

Now the ground descended steeply, and the light assumed a uniform tint. We had reached a depth of 100 yards, and under a pressure of ten atmospheres; but our divers' dresses were so constructed that we felt no inconvenience from the pressure. I only felt a little uncomfortable sensation in my fingers, which, however, quickly passed away. I felt no fatigue whatever, notwithstanding the unaccustomed "harness" I wore. My movements, assisted as they were by the water, were perfectly unconstrained.

At this depth of 300 feet I could still see the sun's rays, but feebly. To their intense brilliancy a crespucular ruddiness had succeeded a sort of twilight. We could, however, see sufficiently well to proceed, and the Ruhmkorff was not required.

Captain Nemo stopped here. He waited till I had rejoined him, and he then pointed to some mass, which formed a thick shade at a little distance.

"That is the Forest of Crespo," I thought; and I was not mistaken.

CHAPTER XVII
A SUBMARINE FOREST

WE HAD AT LENGTH reached the borders of this forest, without doubt one of the most beautiful in the extensive domains of Captain Nemo. He looked upon them as his own, and arrogated to himself the same rights as the first inhabitants in the world's infancy. Moreover, who would dispute with him the possession of this submarine domain? What other and more hardy pioneer would have come, hatchet in hand, to cut down these dark coppices.

This forest was composed of immense arborescent plants; and as soon as we had entered it I was struck by the peculiar disposition of their branches, such as I had not ever before observed. None of the grasses which carpeted the earth, nor any of the branches of the plants were curved, or crept along the ground; they all grew perpendicularly upward towards the surface. Not a filament nor a reed, thin and delicate as they were, but stood up straight as a rod of iron. The *fucus* and the bind-weeds grew rigid and perpendicular, sustained by the density of the element which gave them birth. So stiff were they that when put aside by the hand they sprang back into their former places. This was indeed a kingdom of uprightness!

I soon grew accustomed to this peculiarity, and also to the partial obscurity which surrounded us. The ground was encumbered with sharp blocks of stone, difficult to avoid. The submarine flora appeared to me to be as extensive, and even more rich, than under the tropical or arctic zones, where the productions are less numerous. But for some minutes I involuntarily confounded the zoophytes and hydrophytes, the animals and the plants.

And who would not have done so? so thickly are the flora and fauna of this submarine world interspersed. I observed that all these productions of the vegetable kingdom were only attached to the ground by a single superficial base. Deprived of roots, indifferent to a solid body, sand, shellfish, shells, or shingle, which supported them, they only asked a support, not life. These plants are born of themselves. The principle of their existence is the water, which nourishes and sustains them. The greater number of them, instead of leaves, possessed only capriciously-formed lamels, and were very limited in their scales of colour, which only included rose-carmine, green, olive, fawn-colour, and brown.

I perceived here – but not dried, as on board the *Nautilus* – the "peacock-padines", spread out in a fan-like form, as if to woo the breeze, and a number of other marine plants totally devoid of flowers. "A curious anomaly, a whimsical element," as has been said by a witty naturalist, "in which the animal kingdom flowers, and the vegetable kingdom does not flower at all."

Amongst the various shrubs, as large as in the trees of temperate zones, and under their damp shade, were massed, actual thickets of living flowers, hedges composed of zoophytes, upon which bloomed the striped and furrowed "encandrines", the yellow cariophylliæ, with their translucent tentacles, the gauzy tufts of "zoanthanes", and, to complete the illusion, the flying-fish darted between the branches like humming-birds, while the yellow lepisacanthi, with a bristling mouth and pointed scales, dactylopteri, and monocentrides rose under our feet like so many snipe.

In about an hour Captain Nemo signed to us to halt. I was not sorry for this, and we lay down under a canopy of alariæs, with long, arrow-like prongs.

The rest was most welcome to me. All we wanted was the charm of conversation. But it was impossible to speak. I put my great headpiece close to Conseil. I could perceive his eyes gleaming with happiness, and, as a token of his satisfaction, he moved himself in his heavy dress in a most comical manner.

After these four hours, I was astonished that I did not feel more hungry. Why I did not feel hungry, I do not know; but then, on the other hand, like all divers, I began to feel very sleepy. So my eyes soon closed behind the thick glass, and I fell into a deep sleep, which the action of walking had hitherto resisted. Captain Nemo and his robust companion, stretched in this liquid crystal medium, set us the example.

I do not know how long I slept, but when I woke, it appeared as if the sun were sinking towards the west. Captain Nemo had already risen, and I was beginning to stretch my limbs, when an unexpected sight caused me to spring nimbly to my feet.

A few paces off there was an enormous sea-spider, about three feet high, regarding me with its cross-squinting eyes, and ready to attack me. Although the diver's dress was sufficient to protect me from the bite of the animal, I could not restrain a movement of horror. Conseil and the sailor of the *Nautilus* now awoke; Captain Nemo pointed to the creature, and the sailor killed it by repeated blows with the stock of his gun, while I saw the terrible limbs of the monster twisting and curving in the agonies of death.

This meeting made me think of other and more dangerous animals which inhabited these dark depths, and against whose attacks my dress would be no protection. Up to this time I had not thought about such things, and I determined to be on my guard. I supposed also that this halt was to indicate the turning point of our expedition, but I was mistaken, for Captain Nemo continued his daring excursion.

The ground still fell away, and led us into very great depths. It was nearly three o'clock when we reached a narrow valley, hollowed out between two perpendicular walls, and at a depth of 150 yards. Thanks to the perfection of our dresses, we had exceeded by ninety yards the limit that nature appears to have hitherto put to man's sub-aqueous excursions.

I say 150 yards, although I had no instrument to measure the distance. But I know that in the clearest seas the solar rays cannot penetrate farther. Now the obscurity had become profound. Nothing was visible at a distance of ten paces. I was therefore obliged to grope my way, when I perceived a brilliant white light suddenly appear. Captain Nemo had put his electric apparatus into gear. His companion followed his example, and Conseil and I followed suit. I established the communication by turning a screw, and the sea, lit up by our four lamps, was illuminated to a distance of five-and-twenty yards.

Captain Nemo continued to plunge into the dark depths of the forest, in which the "copses" became fewer and fewer. I noticed that the vegetable disappeared more quickly than animal life. The aquatic plants had already quitted the inhospitable soil, while an immense number of animals, zoophytes, molluscs, fish, &c., were still visible.

All the time we were walking I thought that the lights we carried would probably attract some of the inhabitants of these gloomy depths. But if they did approach, they kept at a safe distance from our guns. Many times I saw the captain stop and bring up his gun, but after a pause he lowered it again and resumed his course.

At length, about four o'clock, the notable excursion reached its limit. A superb wall of rock, and of most imposing appearance, barred our passage. Enormous cliffs of granite, hollowed out into dark caves, presented no practicable breach. This was the shore of the island of Crespo – the earth itself.

Captain Nemo stopped at once. He signed to us to halt, and desirous as I was to cross the wall of rock, I was obliged to comply. Here Captain Nemo's territory ceased. He had no wish to go farther. Beyond that lay the portion of the globe which he never wished to tread.

The return journey was commenced. Captain Nemo re-assumed the lead, and proceeded without hesitation. We did not return by the same route as we had come. This new direction, very "stiff", and consequently very laborious, brought us rapidly to the surface of the ocean. Nevertheless, the ascent was not so steep as the descent had lately been, and which sudden changes lead to grave disorders, and are the cause of fatal internal injuries to divers. The light quickly reappeared and increased, the sun was already low in the sky, and the refraction again surrounded the various objects with a spectral halo.

At a depth of ten yards we met a crowd of little fishes of all kinds, more numerous and more active than birds in the air; but no aquatic "game" worthy of a bullet met our gaze. Just then I saw the captain shoulder his gun, and follow some moving object in the coppice. He fired; I heard a feeble hissing, and the animal fell dead a few paces off.

It was a magnificent sea-otter, the only exclusively marine animal. This was about four feet long, and would fetch a high price. Its skin, of a dark chestnut hue above, and silver below, would make one of those splendid furs so sought after in Russian and Chinese markets; the fineness and the lustre of the skin would make it worth 2,000 francs. I admired its rounded head, small ears, round eyes, its white "moustache", resembling that of a cat, its webbed feet, and tufted tail.

This valuable animal, hunted and trapped by fishermen, is becoming extremely rare, and it usually takes refuge in the southern portions of the Pacific, where, apparently, its species will soon become extinct. Captain Nemo's messmate shouldered the animal, and we resumed our route. For an hour the sand-plain extended round us. It ascended often to within six feet of the surface. I could at these times perceive our images clearly reflected upside down above us, and an identical party imitated all our gestures in every way like ourselves, except that their heads were at the surface, and their feet in the air. There was another effect to be noted. This was the passage of thick clouds,

which formed and vanished rapidly; but, as I reflected, I understood that these supposed clouds were only due to the varying
thickness of the long furrows at the bottom, and I could perceive
even the fleecy masses which their broken crests multiplied upon
the water. They were only the shadows of the great birds which
flew over our heads, and whose rapid skimming over the surface
I could not detect.

At this time I was witness to one of the most splendid shots
that ever thrilled a sportsman with delight. A large bird, with
immense spread of wing, was distinctly visible. Captain Nemo's
friend levelled and fired, when it was only a few yards above the
waves. The bird fell, and almost exactly at the feet of the keen
shot, who secured it. It proved to be an albatross of the most
beautiful species, a splendid specimen of sea-bird.

Our progress had not been interrupted by this incident. For
two hours we followed, sometimes a sandy plain, sometimes a
prairie of wrack, very difficult to cross. Frankly, I could not have
accomplished much more, when I distinguished a vague gleam,
which broke the obscurity, about half-a-mile distant. It was the
lantern of the *Nautilus*. In less than twenty minutes we should be
on board, and there I should be able to breathe more at ease, for
it appeared to me that the air supplied by my reservoir was
deficient in oxygen. But I did not count upon an incident which
delayed our arrival. I was about twenty paces behind the others,
when Captain Nemo hurriedly returned towards me. He dragged me to the ground by main force, while his companion did
the same to Conseil. I did not know what to make of this sudden
attack, but was somewhat reassured to perceive that the captain
lay down close beside me, and remained motionless.

I was stretched upon the ground, under the shade of a clump
of sea-wrack, when, as I raised my head, I saw some enormous
masses pass noiselessy by, emitting a phosphorescent gleam as
they went.

My blood ran cold. I recognized the shark. They were two
terrible specimens, with enormous tails, a dull and glassy stare,
and they gave forth a phosphorescent matter from the holes
pierced near the muzzles. Their enormous fiery mouths could
engulf a man whole within those fearful teeth. I do not know
whether Conseil amused himself in classifying them, but, for my
own part, I regarded their shining bellies, and their formidable

throats, bristling with teeth, in a very unscientific manner, and more from a victim's than from a naturalist's point of view.

Fortunately, these voracious animals cannot see very distinctly. They passed without noticing us, although they almost brushed us with their black fins, and we escaped as by a miracle from this encounter, even more dangerous than an encounter with a tiger in a jungle.

Half-an-hour later, guided by the electric light, we reached the *Nautilus*. The outside door was still open, Captain Nemo closed it when we had entered. He then pressed a spring. I heard the pumps working, and felt the water subsiding around me. In a few moments the cell was quite emptied. Then the inner door was opened and we stepped into the "vestry".

There our divers' dresses were doffed, but not without difficulty; and worn out, giddy from the want of food and rest, I regained my chamber, quite knocked up by this most extraordinary excursion to the bottom of the sea.

CHAPTER XVIII
FOUR THOUSAND LEAGUES BENEATH THE PACIFIC

I HAD QUITE recovered from my fatigue on the next day (18th Nov.), and, as usual, ascended to the platform, just as the mate of the *Nautilus* was giving his daily report. It occurred to me that this was to announce the appearance of the sea, or rather that it signified "no vessel in sight".

As a fact the ocean was perfectly clear. The Isle of Crespo had disappeared. There was not a sail to be seen. The sea, which absorbed all the prismatic colours, except the blue rays, reflected them in all directions, and bore a beautiful indigo tint. It appeared like a broadly-striped watered silk.

I was admiring its beauties when Captain Nemo appeared. He took no notice of my presence, and busied himself with astronomical observations. He then seated himself upon the lantern-cover, and gazed abstractedly at the ocean.

Meantime, twenty sailors, all strong and wiry fellows, had reached the platform. They came to draw the nets they had "shot" during the night. The crew seemed to be of all nations, but the

European types were predominant. I recognized, if I was not much mistaken, Irish, French, Sclaves, a Greek, a Candian. They were chary of speech, and only conversed in that strange idiom, the origin of which I could not determine; so I gave up my idea of questioning them.

The nets were hauled on board, and appeared to be like those in use on the Normandy coast; vast pockets, kept open by a large piece of wood and a chain fixed in the lower meshes. These nets, dragged upon iron fittings, swept the bottom of the ocean, and picked up everything in their way. Upon that occasion they brought to light many curious specimens of fish; lophies, whose comical movements reminded one of actors; black commersons, balistæ, tetrodons, some lampreys, trichures, whose electric power is equal to that of the electric eel or torpedo, many varieties of gobies, and some extremely large fish; a cavanx, with its very prominent head, about a yard long, some beautiful scombres, laced with blue and silver, and three splendid tunny-fish, whose rapid swimming could not save them from the net.

I estimated the take at about 1,000 lbs. of fish, which was a good but not a surprising quantity. These nets might be kept at the bottom of the sea for many hours, and would then enclose specimens of the whole marine world. It was evident there would be no stint of excellent food, and the rapidity of the *Nautilus*, and the attraction of its electric light, could always insure us a new supply at any time.

The various productions were immediately sent down to the store-rooms; some for use while fresh, the other to be pickled.

Now that the fishing was over and the supply of air renewed, I thought that the *Nautilus* would resume her submarine voyage, and I was preparing to go below when Captain Nemo addressed me suddenly as follows:

"Is not that ocean endowed with real life? Has it not its angry and its tender moments? Yesterday it slept like ourselves, and now it is awake after a peaceful night."

No salutation had passed between us. Would not one have thought that this strange captain was only continuing a conversation.

"Do you see," he continued, "it has awakened under the sun's caresses. It will live anew its daily life. It is an interesting study to

follow the play of its organism. It has a pulse, arteries, it has its
spasms too, and I agree with Maury, who has discovered in it a
circulation, as real as the circulation of the blood in animals."

It is certain that Captain Nemo expected no reply from me,
and it appeared useless to throw in the "evidentlys", "certainlys",
and "quite rights". He seemed to be talking rather to himself
than to me, and paused between each sentence. He was thinking
aloud!

"Yes," he continued, "the ocean possesses a real circulation,
and to excite it, it is only necessary that the Creator should
increase its temperature, the salt, and the animalcules. Heat causes
different densities, which bring about currents and counter-
currents. Evaporation, which is *nil* in extremely cold latitudes, is
very active in tropical zones, and constitutes a regular change
between the tropical and polar waters. Further, I have detected
currents from beneath the sea to the surface, and *vice versa*, which
constitute the true breathings of the ocean. I have seen the mol-
ecule of sea-water warmed at the surface, redescend towards the
depths, attain its maximum of density at 2° below zero, and then
freezing once more become lighter, and mount upwards again.
At the poles, you will perceive the consequences of this phenomenon, and you can understand why, by this law of all-provident
nature, congelation can only be produced at the surface of water."

While Captain Nemo was speaking, I was thinking.

"The pole! is it possible that he intends to visit such latitudes!"

The captain was again silently regarding the element he had
so completely studied, and yet was incessantly studying. He
resumed.

"Salts," he said, "are in the sea in large quantities, and if you
could take all that it holds in solution, you would form a mass of
4,500,000 cubic leagues, which, spread out upon the globe,
would reach to a height of more than ten yards. Do not imagine,
either, that the presence of these salts is only due to nature's
caprice. Not at all. They make the water less liable to evaporate,
and prevent the winds from raising too much vapour, which,
in again resolving, would drown the temperate zones. There is
a great part played by the sea, it possesses great weight in the
interior economy of the globe!"

Captain Nemo stopped speaking, took a few turns up and
down, and again approaching me, said: –

"As regards the *infusoria*, the milliards of animalcules which exist by millions in every drop of water, and of which 800 weigh about the thousandth part of a grain, their part is not less important. They absorb the marine salts, they assimilate the more solid elements of the water, and the true constructors of calcareous lands, they make the corals and the madrepores. And then the drop of water deprived of its mineral nourishment gets lighter and ascends to the surface. It there absorbs the salts set free by evaporation, which makes it heavier and it descends, and carries new elements of absorption to the animalcules below. So there is a double current, ascending and descending, ever moving, ever living. A life more exuberant, more infinite, and more intense than that of earth, spreading out in every part of the ocean, the element of death to mankind, an element of life to myriads of other animals, and to me."

While Captain Nemo thus spoke his whole countenance was lighted up, and he produced an extraordinary impression upon me.

"Besides," he added, "this is life indeed. And I can imagine the establishment of nautical towns and groups of submarine houses, which, like the *Nautilus*, might come up every morning to the surface to breathe. Free towns, so to speak, independent cities! And yet, who knows but some despot—"

Captain Nemo accompanied this speech with a violent gesture. Then addressing himself directly to me, like one who would get rid of an uncomfortable thought –

"Monsieur Aronnax," he said, "do you know the depth of the ocean?"

"I, at least, know the principal soundings that have been obtained," I replied.

"Can you quote them so that I may correct them if necessary?"

"These are some," I replied, "that I can remember. If I mistake not, an average depth of 8,200 yards in the North Atlantic, and 2,500 yards in the Mediterranean. The most remarkable soundings have been made in the South Atlantic, near the 35th degree, which have given 12,000 yards, 14,091 yards, and 15,149 yards. To sum up, it has been estimated that if the bottom of the sea were levelled it would give a depth of about five miles and a-half."

"Very good, professor," said Captain Nemo; "but we will

show you something better than that, I hope. I may tell you that the average depth of this part of the Pacific is but 4,000 yards."

As he spoke, Captain Nemo advanced to the panel and descended, and I regained the saloon. The screw was set in motion, and we proceeded at twenty miles an hour.

During the days and weeks that passed I saw very little of Captain Nemo. The mate made the direction regularly, which I found entered on the map, so that I could always tell the route of the *Nautilus*.

Conseil and Land passed the days with me. The former had related the marvellous incidents of our expedition, and the Canadian regretted that he had not accompanied me. But I hoped that another occasion might arise to visit the sub-oceanic forests.

Each day, for some hours, the panels of the saloon were drawn back, and our eyes were by no means fatigued.

The *Nautilus* was kept in a south-easterly course, and at about 150 yards below the surface. One day, however, for some reason, she descended diagonally by means of the inclined planes, to a depth of 2,000 feet. The thermometer indicated 4.25 centigrade, a temperature that at this depth appears to be common to all latitudes.

On the 26th November, at 3 a.m., the *Nautilus* crossed the tropic of Cancer at 172° longitude. On the 27th we passed the Sandwich Islands, where the illustrious Captain Cook met his death, on the 14th February, 1779. We had then made 4,860 leagues from our starting-point. In the morning, when I came up on the platform, I perceived, about two miles to windward, the island of Hawaii, the largest of the seven composing the group. I could distinctly perceive its cultivated borders, the chains of mountains parallel to the coast, and the volcanoes, of which Mouna Rea is the highest, rising 15,000 feet above the level of the sea. Amongst other souvenirs of these regions, the nets pulled in some polyps peculiar to this part of the ocean.

The *Nautilus* still ran south-east. We passed the equator on the 1st December, in 142° longitude, and on the fourth of the same month, after a rapid passage, but devoid of incident, we reached the Marquesas Isles. I perceived three miles away, in 8° 57′ south latitude, and 139° 32′ longitude, Point Martin, in Nouka-Hiva, the principal of the group which belongs to France. I could only distinguish the wooded hills, for Captain Nemo did not like to hug the shore. Here the nets secured some splendid fish, the choryphenes, with blue flesh and golden tail, the flesh being unrivalled; hologymnoses, nearly scaleless, but of exquisite flavour; ostorhinques, with bony jaws; and the yellow thasards, which are equal to the bonita. All these fish were worthy of being "classed" in the kitchen.

Quitting these beautiful islands in the interval between the 4th and 11th December, the *Nautilus* ran about 2,000 miles. This part of the voyage was marked by one meeting with an immense shoal of calmars, a curious mollusc, very like the cuttle-fish. The French fishermen call them "horned" calmars, and they belong to the class of cephalopodes and the family of di-branchia, which includes likewise the cuttle and the argonaut. These animals were studied particularly by the naturalists of old, and furnished numerous metaphors to the orators, at the same time that they supplied an excellent dish to wealthy citizens – that is, if we may believe Athene, a Greek doctor, who lived before Galen.

It was during the night, 9–10th December, that the *Nautilus* encountered this army of nocturnal molluscs. They could be reckoned by millions. They emigrate from the temperate to the warmer zones, and follow the same mode of travelling as the herring and the sardine. We watched them through the thick crystal plates, swimming backwards with extreme rapidity, moving by means of their tubular locomotive power, and pursued by fish and molluscs, eating the smaller ones and being eaten by the larger, and moving to and fro in indescribable confusion the ten legs that nature had fixed upon their heads like a wreath of pneumatic serpents. The *Nautilus*, notwithstanding her speed, kept meeting these animals for many consecutive hours, and the nets brought in an innumerable quantity – when I recognized the nine species that d'Orbigny has classed for the Pacific Ocean.

During this voyage the sea displayed her marvels with a prodigal hand, and with an infinite variety. She changed her decorations and *mise en scène* at our will apparently, and we were permitted to observe, not only the works of the Creator in mid-ocean, but even to penetrate the most hidden mysteries of the sea.

During the 11th December I was engaged reading in the saloon. Ned and Conseil were watching the glittering waters through the panels. The *Nautilus* was at rest. Her reservoirs were full, and she lay at a depth of 1,000 yards, a somewhat uninhabited level, in which large fish were very seldom seen.

I was reading a very interesting book by Jean Macé, entitled "Les Serviteurs de l'Estomac", and I was relishing its ingenious teaching when Conseil interrupted my reading.

"Will Monsieur come here for a moment?" he said in a peculiar tone.

"What is it, Conseil?"

"Monsieur will see."

I got up, sat before the sheet of glass, and looked out.

In full glare of the electric light was an immense black mass, suspended in mid sea. I looked at it attentively, seeking to recognize the nature of such an enormous cetacean. Suddenly a thought flashed into my mind.

"It is a ship!" I cried.

"Yes," replied the Canadian, "an abandoned vessel which has sunk."

He was right. It was a ship before us, the shrouds cut and hanging down as they had fallen. The hull appeared to be in good condition, and yet her wreck was not of yesterday. Three stumps, broken about two feet above the deck, indicated that her masts and rigging had been cut away. But she lay, full of water, heeling over to port. A sad spectacle, indeed, was this noble vessel beneath the waves; but a far sadder sight were the dead bodies, still held by the cords lying as they had been entangled. I counted four – four men, of whom one was still at the tiller – then a young woman, half hanging from the sky-light in the poop, holding a child in her arms. I could plainly see, by the light of the *Nautilus*, the features not already decomposed. In the supreme moment she had held the infant above her head, who – poor little thing! – was clasping its mother's neck with its tiny arms. The attitude of the four sailors appeared terrible to me – tortured in their convulsive efforts to release themselves from the cordage that bound them helpless. Alone, more calm, with a quiet, grave face, his grey hair pressed down over his forehead, and with one shrivelled hand still grasping the tiller, the steersman appeared to be still guiding his shipwrecked vessel amidst the depths of the ocean.

What a spectacle! We sat dumb with beating hearts before this shipwreck, taken in the fact, as it were, and photographed at the last moment. And I could see already advancing, with fiery eyes, the enormous sharks attracted by this bait of human flesh.

But the *Nautilus* moved, and as we turned round the stern of the wreck, I read the name, "Florida, Sunderland".

CHAPTER XIX
VANIKORO

THAT TERRIBLE SIGHT inaugurated the series of maritime catastrophes which the *Nautilus* encountered. Since we had been passing through more frequented seas we often noticed ship-wrecked vessels decaying in mid-sea depths, and, deeper down, the cannons, anchors, chains, cannon-balls, and a number of other things that were being devoured by rust.

Still going forward in this *Nautilus*, in which we existed like an isolated set of beings, as we were, we entered the archipelago of Pomotou on the 11th December. This was the group of "dangerous isles" in ages past, and extend across a space of five hundred leagues from E.S.E. to W.N.W., between 13° 30′ and 23° 50′ S. lat., and 125° 30′ and 151° 30′ W. long., from the Isle Ducie to the Isle Lazareff. This archipelago covers an area of 370 square leagues, and is composed of sixty groups of islands, amongst which is the Gambier group under French protection. These isles are coralaginous. A very gentle but surely building-up process by the polypes will some day form a communication between them. Then the new island will (later on) become united to neighbouring islands, and a fifth continent will extend from New Zealand and New Caledonia to the Marquesas.

When I suggested this to Captain Nemo, he coldly replied:

"It is not new continents that are required, but new inhabitants of the old ones."

The chances of navigation had conducted the *Nautilus* towards the island of Clermont-Tonnerre, one of the most curious of the group which was discovered in 1822 by Captain Bell of the *Minerva*. I was thus able to study the system by which islands are formed in this ocean by madrepores.

The madrepores, which must not be confounded with the coral, have a tissue enclosed in a calcareous crust, and the modi-fications of the structure have enabled Mr. Milne-Edwards, my

illustrious master, to class them in five sections. The tiny animalcules which secrete this polypary live in thousands of millions at
the bottom of the little cells. These are the calcareous depôts
which become rocks, reefs, islets, islands. Here they form a ring,
enclosing a lagoon or interior lake, in which an opening permits
communication with the sea. There they construct reefy barriers
like those which exist on the coasts of New Caledonia and the
various islands of Pomotou. In other places, like Reunion and
Maurice, they build fringed reefs, high upright walls, alongside
which the sea is extremely deep.

At a few cables' lengths from the shore of the island of
Clermont-Tonnerre I inspected the work done by those microscopic workers. These walls were exclusively the work of madrepores known as "millepores", "porites", "astrea", and
"meandrines". These polypes are chiefly developed at the moving and higher beds of the ocean, and consequently it is their
upper parts which commence these works, and which are buried
by degrees with the *débris* of the secretions which support them.
This, at least, is the theory of Mr. Darwin, who thus explains the
theory of "atolls". A better theory, as I think, is that the madrepores have as a basis the summits of mountains or volcanoes upon
which to work, and which are at some distance below the surface.

I was enabled to observe these curious walls very closely, for
in perpendicular depth the soundings gave more than 300 yards,
and our electric light made these brilliant calcareous masses
gleam again.

Replying to a question of Conseil's, respecting the time these
barriers had taken to construct, I astonished him somewhat by
telling him that *savants* estimated the progress at the eighth of an
inch in a hundred years.

"Then to build up these walls," he said, "it must have taken—"

"One hundred and ninety-two thousand years, my brave
friend, which lengthens the Biblical days. Moreover, the formation of the pit-coal – that is to say, the mineralization of the forests
buried by the deluge – has required a much longer time. But I may
add that the Biblical days are not the epochs, and not the interval
of time between sunrise and sunrise; for, according to the Bible
itself, the sun was not made upon the first day of the creation."

While the *Nautilus* remained at the surface of the sea, I was able
to inspect, in all its development, this small and wooded island of

Clermont-Tonnerre. Its madreporical rocks were evidently fertilized by water-spouts and tempests. One day some corn, carried by a hurricane from neighbouring islands, fell upon its calcareous formation, mixed with the detritus which forms the vegetable mould, and which is made of decomposed fish and marine plants. A cocoa-nut, impelled by the waves, reaches this new coast. The germ takes root, the tree grows, absorbs the watery vapour. The stream is born, vegetation increases apace. Animalcules, worms, insects, arrive upon these island beginnings. Turtles come and lay their eggs there. The birds build their nests in the young trees. In this way animal life is developed, and attracted by the verdure and fertility, man appears. Thus these islands are formed, the vast works of microscopic animals.

Towards evening Clermont-Tonnerre disappeared in the distance, and the course of the *Nautilus* was sensibly diverted. After touching the Tropic of Capricorn at the 130° degree of longitude, she turned to the W.N.W., ascending towards the intertropical zone. Although the summer sun was extremely powerful, we did not suffer from the heat, for at thirty or forty yards below the surface the temperature did not increase more than ten or twelve degrees.

On the 15th December we passed the Society Isles and Tahiti, the queen of the Pacific. In the morning I perceived the elevated summits of the mountains of that island. Its waters supplied us with some excellent fish – mackerel, bonita, albicoras, and a variety of sea-serpent, called "muneoplies". The *Nautilus* had accomplished 8,100 miles: 9,720 miles were recorded on the log when we passed the archipelago of Tonga-Tabou, where the *Argo*, the *Port au Prince*, and the *Duke of Portland* were lost; and the Navigator Isles, where Captain Langle, the friend of La Perouse, was killed. Then we came to the Fiji Islands, where the savages murdered the sailors of the ship *Union*, and Captain Bureau, of Nantes, of the *Aimable Josephine*. This archipelago extends 100 leagues to the north and south, and 90 leagues from east to west, and is comprised between 6° and 2° S. lat., and 174° and 179° W. long. It is composed of islands, islets, and rocks, amongst which are the islands of Viti-Levou, Vanona-Levou, and Kandubon.

Tasman discovered this group in 1643, the same year that Toricelli invented the barometer, and in which Louis XIV ascended the throne. I leave my readers to reflect which of these facts has proved most useful to mankind.

After Tasman, Cook, in 1714, Entrecasteaux, in 1793, and, finally, Dumont d'Urville, in 1827, came to clear up the obscurity of these regions. The *Nautilus* now approached the Bay of Wailea, the scene of the terrible adventures of Captain Dillon, who was the first to clear up the mystery connected with the shipwreck of La Perouse.

This bay, dredged many times, furnished us with abundance of oysters. We ate quantities of them, opening them at our own table, as recommended by Seneca. These belonged to the species known as the ostre lamellosa, which is very common in Corsica. That the bank of Wailea will become of great extent, is certain; and if destructive agencies be not increased, the quantities of oysters will soon fill up the bay, as we counted 2,000,000 of eggs in a single oyster. And if Master Ned Land did not repent of his gluttony in this respect, it was because the oyster is the only thing that does not cause indigestion. In fact it would necessitate the consumption of sixteen dozen oysters to furnish the 315 grammes of azote substance necessary to nourish one man. On the 25th December the *Nautilus* sailed into the midst of the group of the New Hebrides, discovered by Quiros, in 1606, which Bongainville explored in 1768, and to which Captain Cook gave its name in 1773. This group is composed principally of nine large islands, and forms a band of 120 leagues from N.N.W. to S.S.E., included between 15° and 2° S. lat., and 164° and 168° long. We also passed close to the island of Auron, which at midday appeared to be a mass of green woods, commanded by a mountain of immense height.

This was Christmas Day, and Ned Land appeared to regret keenly the usual celebration of the day – the family gathering in which some people are so fanatical.

I had not seen Captain Nemo for eight days, when, on the 27th, very early in the morning, he entered the saloon, having as usual the air of a man who had left you but five minutes before. I was engaged in tracing our course upon the map. The captain approached, placed his finger upon a spot in the map, and uttered the single word, "Vanikoro!"

The word was magical. It was the name of the island where the ships of La Perouse were lost. I rose up suddenly.

"Is the *Nautilus* carrying us to Vanikoro?" I said.

"Yes," replied the captain.

"And can I explore those islands upon which the *Boussole* and the *Astrolabe* were lost?"

"If you wish to do so," was the reply.

"When shall we reach Vanikoro?"

"We are there now, professor."

Following the captain, I ascended to the platform, and eagerly scanned the horizon.

In the north-west, two volcanic islands of unequal size showed themselves; they were surrounded by a coral reef of forty miles in circumference. We were close to the island of Vanikoro, properly so called, which Dumont d'Urville designated the "Isle of Research", and immediately opposite the small harbour of Vanou in 16° 4′ S. lat., 164° 32′ E. long. The island appeared covered with verdure from shore to summit, and was dominated by Mount Kapogo, 2,856 feet high.

The *Nautilus*, having cleared the outward rocks through a narrow passage, was safely within the line of breakers in a depth of thirty to forty fathoms. Beneath the mangroves I distinguished some savages, who appeared much astonished at our appearance. In the long black mass moving along the surface of the water, they probably only recognized some formidable cetacean, which they were bound to challenge.

Captain Nemo now asked me what I knew of the shipwreck of La Perouse.

"What everyone else does," I replied.

"And can you tell me what everyone else knows about it?" he asked, with a touch of irony.

"Very easily."

And I then recounted to him what the last works of Dumont d'Urville had made known, of which the following is a very succinct account.

La Perouse, and his mate, de Langle, were despatched by Louis XVI, in the year 1785, to circumnavigate the world. They embarked in the *Boussole* and *Astrolabe*, which never again returned.

In 1791, the French Government, naturally uneasy respecting the fate of these vessels, fitted out two large store-ships, the *Recherche* and *Espérance*, which left Brest on the 28th September,

commanded by Bruni d'Entrecasteaux. Two months after it
became known by the deposition of a certain Captain Bowen, of
the *Albemarle*, that the remains of some wrecked vessels had been
seen upon the coast of New Georgia. But Entrecasteaux, ignorant of this, and equally uncertain, moreover, sailed towards the
Admiralty Isles, described in the report of a Captain Hunter, as
being the scene of the shipwreck of La Perouse.

Entrecasteaux's search was fruitless. The *Espérance* and the
Recherche even passed Vanikoro without stopping, and the voyage
altogether was most disastrous, as it cost the lives of Entrecasteaux, two of his lieutenants, and many of his crew.

An old hand, one Captain Dillon, was the first to discover
some traces of the shipwrecks. On the 15th of May, 1824, his
vessel, the *Saint Patrick*, passed close to the island of Tikopia, one
of the New Hebrides. There a Lascar, who sold him the silver
hilt of a sword, stated that six years previously, during his stay at
Vanikoro, he had seen two Europeans who had belonged to the
ships wrecked many years before upon the reefs of that island.
Dillon suspected that the man was referring to the ships of La
Perouse, whose disappearance had interested the entire civilized
world. He wished to reach Vanikoro, where, according to the
Lascar, he would find many traces of the wrecked vessels; but the
winds and opposing elements prevented him.

Dillon returned to Calcutta. There he made known his
discovery to the Asiatic Society and to the East India Company.
A vessel, to which they gave the name of the *Research*, was placed
at his disposal, and he sailed on the 23rd of January, 1827, accompanied by a French agent.

The *Research*, having touched at several ports in the Pacific,
anchored before Vanikoro on the 7th of July, 1827, in the same
harbour of Vanou in which the *Nautilus* is now lying.

There they picked up many relics of the wrecks: iron utensils,
anchors, block-strops, swivel-guns and shot, astronomical
instruments, a part of the taffrail, and a bronze timepiece, with
the inscription, *Bazin m'a fait* marked by the manufactory at
Brest, 1785. Doubt was no longer possible.

Dillon remained at the ill-fated spot to complete his arrangements. In October he quitted Vanikoro, and sailing towards New
Zealand, reached Calcutta on 7th April, 1828. He then proceeded to France, where he was kindly received by Charles X.

But meantime Dumont d'Urville, ignorant of what Dillon had accomplished, had sailed to discover the scene of the shipwreck. He had learnt from a whaler that a medal and cross of St. Louis had been seen in the hands of savages in New Caledonia.

D'Urville then put to sea, and, two months after Dillon had quitted Vanikoro, he anchored before Hobart Town. There he heard of Dillon's success, and further he learned that a certain James Hobbs, mate of the *Union*, of Calcutta, had landed on an island situated in 8° 18' south lat., and 156° 30' east long., and had remarked the iron bars and the red stuffs which were in use by the aborigines.

Dumont d'Urville was much perplexed, and did not know whether he could believe these reports, so he finally decided to follow Dillon's tracks.

On the 10th February, 1828, the *Astrolabe* appeared before Tikopia, and, taking on board as guide a deserter who had taken up his abode in the island, he made Vanikoro on the 12th February, and anchored in the harbour of Vanou.

On the 23rd, many of the officers explored the island and brought back a few unimportant relics. The natives, by denials and evasions, refused to lend them assistance in discovering the locality of the disaster. This suspicious conduct gave the French reason to believe that the natives had maltreated the shipwrecked crews, and, in fact, they appeared to be fearful that d'Urville would avenge La Perouse and his unfortunate companions.

However, on the 26th, by presents, &c., the natives were induced to believe that there was nothing to fear, and they conducted the mate, M. Jacquinot, to the scene of the wreck.

There, in three or four fathoms of water, between the Pacon and Vanou reefs, lay anchors, cannon, pig-iron, and lead, embedded in the calcareous secretions. The long boat and the whaler of the *Astrolabe* were sent to the spot, and after much labour they returned with an anchor, a cannon, some pig-lead, and two brass swivel-guns.

Dumont d'Urville, by interrogating the natives, also discovered that La Perouse, after having lost his ships, had constructed a smaller vessel, in which he was again lost – where they did not know.

The commander then caused a cenotaph to be erected to the memory of the bold navigator and his companions. It was a simple quadrangular pyramid erected on a basis of coral, and in which was no ornamentation likely to excite the cupidity of the natives.

D'Urville then wished to return home, but fever and malaria had attacked his crews, and even he himself was very ill. He was not able to get away before the 17th March.

Meantime, the French Government, fearing that Dumont d'Urville had not followed Dillon's route correctly, sent the corvette *Bayonnaise*, commanded by Legoarant de Tromelin, which was stationed on the west coast of America. The *Bayonnaise* arrived at Vanikoro some months after the departure of the *Astrolabe*, and did not find anything further, but took note that the mausoleum had been respected by the natives.

That is the substance of the narrative I told Captain Nemo.

"So," said he, "nobody knows yet what became of the third ship, constructed by the shipwrecked sailors on the island of Vanikoro."

"No one."

Captain Nemo made no reply, but signed to me to follow him into the saloon. The *Nautilus* was then at some distance below the surface, and the panels were opened.

I hurried to the glass, and beneath the workings of the coral, clothed with fungi, and amid hundreds of beautiful fish, I recognized certain *débris* which the drags had not been able to recover, such as iron "stirrups", anchors, cannon-balls, cannon, capstan and bars, the stern of a vessel, all belonging to the shipwrecked vessels, and now strewn upon that living floor.

While I was looking at these desolate waifs and strays, Captain Nemo said gravely:

"The commander, La Perouse, left on the 7th December, 1785, with the *Bussole* and the *Astrolabe*. He touched first at Botany Bay, visited the Friendly Isles, New Caledonia, sailed thence towards Vera-Cruz, put into Namonka, one of the Hapaï group. His ships then arrived at the unknown Vanikoro reefs. The *Bussole*, which was in advance, struck them on the south side; the *Astrolabe* went to her assistance, and shared her fate. The former vessel was soon entirely knocked to pieces, but the latter, being to leeward, lasted some days. The natives treated the crews kindly. They lodged them on the island, and there they built a smaller vessel from the timbers of the ships. Some sailors elected to remain at Vanikoro. The rest, weak and ill, accompanied La Perouse. He made for the Solomon Isles, and there the adventurers all perished upon the western side of the principal island, between capes Deception and Satisfaction."

"And how do you know all this?" I exclaimed.

"See what I found at the scene of the last shipwreck."

Captain Nemo then showed me a tin box stamped with the French arms, but much corroded by the salt water. I opened it, and within I found a bundle of yellow, but still readable, papers.

They were the actual instructions issued by the Minister of Marine to La Perouse, and were annotated in the margin by Louis XVI himself.

"Ah! it was a fine death for a sailor," said Captain Nemo. "The coral is a peaceful resting-place and constitutes the only heaven for me and my companion."

CHAPTER XX
TORRES STRAIT

DURING THE NIGHT of the 27th December the *Nautilus* quitted Vanikoro, and resumed her voyage at a great speed. We sailed S.E., and in three days had cleared the 750 leagues which divide the Isles of La Perouse from the S.E. point of Papua.

Very early in the morning of the 1st January, 1863, Conseil joined me on the platform.

"Monsieur," said he, "Monsieur will allow me to wish him a happy new year."

"What, Conseil! Just as if I were in my study at the Jardin des Plantes at Paris? I accept your good wishes, and thank you heartily. But I would ask you what you mean by the happy new year under present circumstances? Will the year put an end to our imprisonment, or see the end of this strange voyage?"

"Faith," replied Conseil, "I do not know what to say to Monsieur. It is certain that we have seen some curious things, and for two months have not found our sojourn tiresome. The last marvel is always the greatest, and if we go on at this rate I do not know what we shall eventually arrive at. My opinion is that we shall never have such another experience."

"Never, Conseil."

"Besides this Captain Nemo, who fully justifies his Latin name, as he is not any more trouble than if he never existed."

"Just so, Conseil."

"I think, therefore, if Monsieur has no objection, that a happy new year will be one which may permit us to see everything—"

"To see everything! Why, that will take a very long time. What does Ned Land say?"

"Ned Land is of the exactly opposite opinion," replied Conseil. "He has certainly an obstinate brain and a powerful appetite. Look at the fish he is always eating, and is never satisfied. The want of wine, bread, and meat does not agree with a worthy Saxon, to whom beef-steaks are familiar, and who is not alarmed at brandy and gin."

"So far as I am concerned, Conseil, that is not the point that troubles me. I can get on very well with the supplies on board."

"So can I," replied Conseil. "So I think as much about stopping here as Master Land does of escaping. Therefore, if the new year is not good for me, it may be so for him, and *vice versâ*. In this way somebody is sure to be satisfied. So, in conclusion, I wish Monsieur whatever pleases him best."

"Thank you, Conseil; but I must ask you to remit, for the present, the question of New Year's gifts; and, meantime, accept a shake of the hand; I have nothing else to offer."

"Monsieur has never been so generous," said Conseil.

And the brave lad descended.

On the 2nd January we had made 11,340 miles, or 5,250 leagues from our starting-point in the Japanese seas. In front now extended the dangerous coral-reefs of the north-east coast of Australia. We skirted this wonderful bank (on which Cook's vessels were lost in 1770) for a distance of many miles. The ship which carried Cook ran upon a rock, and that it did not sink was owing to the fact that a piece of coral, detached by the blow, remained fast in the hole it had made in the ship's hull.

I wished very much to visit this reef, which is 360 leagues in length, and against which the sea, always rough, breaks with a roar like thunder. But at this moment the inclined planes of the *Nautilus* directed us to a very great depth, and I could see nothing of these high walls of coral. So I was obliged to content myself with various specimens of fish, brought up in the nets. I remarked, amongst others, the germons, a sort of large scombre, as large as tunny-fish, with bluish sides, and striped transversely. These stripes faded at the death of the animal. These fish accompanied us by hundreds, and furnished us with excellent dishes. We caught, also, a large number of sparus vertor, tasting like a John Dory, and the flying pyrapeds, true sea-swallows, which, in dark nights, illuminate the air and water alternately with their phosphorescent glimmerings. Amongst the molluscs and the zoophytes I found in the meshes of the nets, were various species of alcyoniares, sea-hedgehogs, "cadrans", "hammers", acrites, and hyattæ.

The flora were represented by beautiful floating algæ laminariæ and macrocystes impregnated with the mucilage which exuded from their pores, and amongst them I found a splendid Nemastoma Geliniaroïde, which was placed amongst the natural curiosities in the museum.

Two days after crossing the coral sea, on the 4th of January, we made the Papuan coast. The captain then informed me of his intention to gain the Indian Ocean by Torres Strait. His communication was limited there. Ned hailed with delight the prospect of approaching European waters. Torres Strait is no less dangerous by reason of the rocks with which it abounds, than on account of the savage races on its coasts. It separates New Holland from the large island of New Guinea, or Papua.

New Guinea is 400 leagues in length, and 130 in breadth, and has a superficies of 40,000 geographical miles. It is situated between 0° 19' and 10° 2' S. lat., and 128° 83' and 146° 15' long. At mid-day, while the mate was taking an observation, I discerned the summits of Mount Arpalx rising into sharp peaks.

This land, discovered in 1511 by the Portuguese Serrano, was visited successively by Don José de Menesis in 1526; by Grijalva, in 1527; by the Spanish general, Alvar de Saavedra, 1528; by Juigo Ortez, in 1545; by Shonten, in 1616; by Nicholas Srinck, in 1753; by Tasman, Dampier, Furnel, Carteret, Edwards, Bougainville, Cook, Forrest, MacCluer, and Entrecasteaux, in 1792; by Dupeney, in 1823; and by Dumont d'Urville, in 1827. "It is the worst passage of all in the Malayan Archipelago," as M. de Runzi has said, and I had little doubt that this hazardous bit of navigation would bring us to the celebrated Andaman Islands.

The *Nautilus* was then at the entrance of the most dangerous strait in the globe, and one which the hardiest sailors scarcely dare to traverse, and which Louis Paz de Torres braved in returning from the south into the Malaynesia, and in which the ships of Dumont d'Urville were nearly lost. The *Nautilus* itself, superior to all the perils of the sea, was nevertheless obliged to exercise great caution amongst those coral reefs.

Torres Strait is about thirty-four leagues wide, but it is obstructed by innumerable islands, and islets, shoals, rocks, &c., which render navigation almost impracticable. Consequently Captain Nemo took all necessary precautions. The *Nautilus*, floating at the surface, proceeded at a moderate pace. The screw beat the water slowly, like the tail of a cetacean.

Profiting by these circumstances, my two companions and I took up our position on the platform. Before us rose the steersman's cage, and I believe Captain Nemo was also there directing the *Nautilus* himself.

I had the excellent maps of Torres Straits designed and drawn up by the hydrographical engineers, Vincendon Dumoulin and Lieutenant Coupvent Desbois, who is now an admiral, who formed part of the staff of Dumont d'Urville during his last voyage of circumnavigation. These are, with those of Captain King, the best maps, and which unravel the intricacies of this narrow passage; therefore I studied them attentively.

The sea broke furiously around the *Nautilus*. The current ran from south-east to north-east, at a rate of two and a half miles an hour, and broke in foam against the coral-reefs, which rose at frequent intervals.

"That is a nasty sea," I said to Ned Land.

"This lunatic captain of ours must be very sure of his course," replied the Canadian, "for I can see some reefs there which would splinter this vessel if she touched them."

The situation was really perilous, but the *Nautilus* appeared to glide magically between these foaming rocks. She did not follow the route of the *Astrolabe* and the *Zélée*, which was fatal to Dumont d'Urville, but took a more northerly course, coasting Murray Island and turning to the south-east, towards Cumberland Passage. I really did think we should be wrecked when, bearing to the north-west, we passed amid a quantity of unknown islets towards the island of Tounel and the Dangerous Passage.

I was already reflecting whether Captain Nemo, imprudent even to foolhardiness, wished to bring his ship into this passage where the corvettes of Dumont d'Urville had been lost, when, changing his course a second time and bearing westward, he made for the island of Gueberoar.

It was then 3 p.m. The waves raged. It was almost high water. The *Nautilus* approached the island, which I could see scarcely two miles distant. Suddenly a shock threw me down. The *Nautilus* had struck upon a rock, and remained immoveable, with a gentle "list" to port.

When I got up again I noticed Captain Nemo and the mate on the platform. He was examining the situation of the vessel, and they exchanged a few words in their extraordinary dialect.

We were about three miles to windward of the island of Gueberoar, whose shore trended from north to west like an immense arm. Towards the south and east some coral-reefs were already being uncovered by the ebb tide. We were, in truth, stranded; and in a sea where the tides are never high – an unfortunate circumstance with reference to the refloating of the *Nautilus*. However, the vessel had not suffered at all, as the hull was so solidly built. But if it could neither float nor be opened there was a great chance that we should be stuck here for ever, and then there would be an end of Captain Nemo's submarine vessel. I was thinking of all this when the captain, calm and cool as ever, neither appearing to be excited nor depressed, approached.

"An accident has happened?" I said.

"No, an incident," he replied.

"But an incident which may oblige you to return to that earth you wish to avoid," I replied.

Captain Nemo gazed at me with a curious expression, and made a sign in the negative, thereby intimating that nothing would induce him ever to become an inhabitant of the continent again. Then he said:

"However, M. Aronnax, the *Nautilus* is not lost. It will yet carry you into the midst of the ocean marvels. Our voyage has scarcely begun, and I do not wish to deprive myself of the honour of your company so soon."

"But, captain," I replied, without noticing these ironical expressions, "the *Nautilus* is stranded at this moment in the open sea. Now the tides are not high in the Pacific, and if you cannot lighten the *Nautilus* – which appears to me impossible – I do not see how you can get her off."

"You are right about the tides, professor, but in Torres Strait there is still a difference of a yard and a half between high and low water. To-day is the 4th January, and in five days there will be a full moon. Now I shall be much surprised if this complaisant planet does not raise the water sufficiently to render me a service which I do not wish to owe to anyone but her."

As he spoke, Captain Nemo, followed by the mate, descended. The ship never moved, and remained as motionless as if the coral polyps had enclosed her in their indestructible cement.

"Well, sir?" said Ned Land, who came up to me after the captain had left.

"Well, Ned, we must wait patiently for the tide of the 9th, for it appears that the moon will be good enough to float us again."

"Without assistance?"

"Yes."

"And is not the captain going to try to warp her off?"

"Not if the sea will be sufficient," said Conseil.

The Canadian looked at Conseil, and shrugged his shoulders – the sailor in him had spoken.

"Monsieur," said he, "you would not believe me when I told you that this bit of metal would not travel either above or below the ocean. It is no good, except to sell for the iron. I think, therefore, that the time has come to part company with Captain Nemo."

"Friend Ned," I replied, "I do not despair, as you do, and in four days we shall know to what we have to trust to. And your suggestion as to flight would be opportune were we in sight of the coast of England or France, but in the Papuan Archipelago it is a different thing; and we can always fall back upon it if the Nautilus is not floated, which I look upon as a very serious question."

"But may we not go ashore at least. Here is an island, and there are trees. Beneath those trees are animals in which are cutlets and steaks, to which I would gladly introduce my teeth."

"Now here Ned is right," said Conseil, "and I agree with him. Cannot Monsieur obtain permission to land, so that we may not lose the habit of walking on dry land altogether?"

"I could ask him," I said, "but he will refuse."

"Well, Monsieur, risk it, and we shall then know how far we may count upon the captain's good nature."

To my great surprise, Captain Nemo made no objection, and accorded his permission in a most polite and gracious manner, without even exacting any promise of return. But a walk in New Guinea was somewhat dangerous, and I would have advised Ned Land not to attempt it. Better be a prisoner on board the *Nautilus* than fall into the hands of the natives.

The launch was placed at our disposal for the next morning. I did not inquire whether Captain Nemo would accompany us. I thought that none of the crew would be "told off", and that Ned Land would be sufficient to steer the boat. Moreover, the land was only two miles off, and it was only "child's play" for the Canadian to steer a boat amongst the reefs so fatal to large vessels. Next morning the boat was launched by two men. The oars were in the boat, and we had only to take our places.

At eight o'clock, armed with guns and hatchets, we left the *Nautilus*. The sea was calm, but there was a slight land-breeze. Conseil and I took the oars and pulled vigorously, and Ned steered. The boat was well managed, and went at a good pace.

Ned Land was unable to restrain his exultation. He was like an escaped prisoner, and did not think it was by any means necessary to return to prison.

"Aha, meat!" he cried, "we shall now eat some meat; and what meat? Game. No bread, perhaps. I am far from saying that fish is not a very good thing; but you may have too much of it; and a bit of venison grilled on the hot embers will be an agreeable variety."

"*Gourmand!*" cried Conseil; "you make my mouth water."

"We do not yet know whether there is any game in these woods," said I, "or whether the game is not such as is more likely to hunt the hunter than to be hunted itself."

"Very good, M. Aronnax," said Ned, whose teeth must have been lately sharpened; "then I will eat the sirloin of a tiger if there be no other quadruped in the island."

"Ned is getting alarming," said Conseil.

"Come what will," said Ned, "the first animal on four legs, without feathers; or the first on two legs, with feathers, shall be saluted by a shot from my gun, I assure you."

"Now," said I, "Master Land's imprudence is beginning to manifest itself."

"Don't you be alarmed, M. Aronnax," replied the Canadian,

"and pull strong. I only ask for twenty-five minutes to offer you a meal of my providing."

At half-past eight the launch ran gently upon a sandy beach, having safely traversed the coral-studded sea which washes the island of Gueberoar.

CHAPTER XXI
SOME DAYS "ASHORE"

I WAS MUCH IMPRESSED upon landing. Ned trod the ground as if he had come to take possession. We had been two months "passengers in the *Nautilus*", to use Captain Nemo's expression – that is to say, prisoners of the commander.

We were soon at gun-shot distance from the shore. The soil was almost entirely madreporic, but some dry beds of torrents, scattered with granite *débris*, betokened the primal formation of the island. The horizon was completely hidden by the woods. Enormous trees, nearly 200 feet high, intertwined by bind-weed of the tropics, formed actual hammocks, which were rocked by the gentle breeze. There were mimosas, figs, teaks, hibiscas, palms, in mingled profusion; and beneath their verdant shade the orchids, both vegetable and ferny, were growing. But without noticing the beautiful flora, the Canadian abandoned the agreeable for the useful. He perceived a cocoa-nut tree. He knocked down a nut, broke it, and we drank the milk; we ate the kernel with a satisfaction which was a mute protest against the *Nautilus* dinners.

"Excellent," said Ned.

"Exquisite," replied Conseil.

"And I did not think that your Nemo would object to our expedition if he saw the prospect of a cargo of cocoa-nuts," said Ned.

"I do not believe so myself, but he will not want to taste them," said I.

"So much the worse for him," said Conseil.

"And the better for us," replied Ned. "There will be more left."

"Just one word, Master Land," said I, as he was preparing to attack another tree; "the cocoa-nut is a very good thing, but before we fill the launch with them let us see whether the island does not produce something equally useful. Fresh vegetables will be welcome in the store-rooms of the *Nautilus*."

"Monsieur is right," said Conseil; "and I propose to have three divisions in the boat – one for fruit, one for vegetables, and one for venison, of which we have hitherto had not the slightest trace."

"Conseil, you must never despair of anything," said Ned.

"Let us get on," I said; "but keep a sharp look-out. Although the island appears to be uninhabited, it may contain some individuals who would be less hard to please as to the quality of 'game'."

"Ha, ha!" laughed Ned Land, as he moved his jaws significantly.

"Well, Ned?" cried Conseil.

"Faith," he replied, "I am beginning to understand the charms of anthropophagy."

"Ned, Ned, what are you saying? You a cannibal! I shall not be safe so near you in the cabin now. Suppose I should wake up some fine morning, half eaten?"

"Friend Conseil, I like you very much, but not enough to eat you, unless under the pressure of necessity."

"I am not proud," replied Conseil. "Let us go on. We must kill some game to satisfy this cannibal, or one of these mornings Monsieur will only have the fragments of a servant to wait on him."

All this time we were penetrating into the wooded glades of the forest. We looked through it in every way.

Chance brought about what we desired in this search for vegetables, and one of the most useful products of tropical regions furnished us with an article of food much needed on board. I mean the bread-fruit, which is very plentiful in the island of Gueberoar, and I there noticed the variety without grains, which in Malaya is entitled "rima".

This tree is distinguished from others by its upright stem, which is about forty feet high. The top is gracefully rounded, and is composed of large multilobed leaves, known to naturalists at once by this "artocorpus". From this green mass the fruit detaches itself. It is nearly four inches long, and of hexagonal form. A most useful vegetable supplied by nature to countries where corn does not grow, and which, without any cultivation, yields its fruit during eight months of the year.

Ned Land was well acquainted with this fruit; he had eaten

them on former occasions, and he knew how to prepare them. Thus the sight of them excited a desire to possess them, and he did not long delay the attempt.

"Monsieur," he said, "I shall die if I do not taste a little of this bread-fruit."

"Eat at your leisure, Ned," I replied. "'We are here to experimentalize. Get them down."

"That will not take long," replied the Canadian; and, armed with a match, he lit a fire of dead wood, which crackled joyously. Meantime, Conseil and I chose the best fruits. Some had not yet reached maturity, and their thick skin was covered over with a white fibrous pulp. In other places great numbers, yellow and gelatinous, had not waited to be gathered.

These fruits do not contain noyau. Conseil brought a dozen to Ned Land, who placed them on the fire, after cutting them in thick slices. In so doing he kept saying:

"You will see how good the bread will be."

"Particularly as we have been so long deprived of it," said Conseil.

"It is even better than bread," added the Canadian. "It is like fine pastry. Have you ever eaten it, Monsieur?"

"No, Ned."

"Well, then, prepare yourself for something very nice; and if you do not enjoy it, I am no longer the king of harpooners."

In a few moments the part of the fruit exposed to the fire was completely baked. The interior appeared like a white dough, like the crumb of bread; the taste was something like the artichoke.

It must be admitted that the bread was excellent, and I ate it with much gusto.

"Unfortunately," said I, "it will not keep fresh, and it seems to me useless to attempt to lay in any store of it on board."

"Indeed, Monsieur!" cried Ned. "But you speak as a naturalist; now I speak as a baker. Conseil, collect a quantity of those fruits for us to carry on board."

"And how will you prepare them?" I asked.

"By making a fermented paste with their pulp, which will keep it sweet for an indefinite period. When I want to use the bread I have only to cook it on board, and, notwithstanding a slightly acid taste, you will find it excellent."

"Then, Master Ned, I see that the bread will be all right."

"If," replied the Canadian, "we had some fruit and vege-tables."

"Let us look for them."

When our search was ended we set about completing our dinner.

Our efforts were not fruitless, and towards mid-day we had laid in a quantity of bananas. These delicious products of the torrid zone ripen all the year round, and the Malays, who call them "pisang", eat them raw. We also found some enormous "jaks", somewhat "strong" in their flavour, savoury mangoes, and ananas of an immense size. But this collecting took up a long time, which, however, we did not regret.

Conseil kept his eyes upon Ned. The harpooner marched in front, and as he went through the forest he collected with unerring skill the fruit we required.

"Well, now," said Conseil, "you want nothing more, eh?"

"Hum," replied the Canadian.

"What! not satisfied?"

"Vegetables and fruit alone do not constitute a meal," said Ned. "They come in at the end like dessert. Where is the soup and the joint?"

"In fact," I said, "Ned has promised us cutlets, and they appear to me doubtful."

"Monsieur," replied Ned, "not only has our hunting not finished, but it has not even commenced. Patience. We are sure to meet some feathered or hairy animal – if not in this spot, some-where else."

"And if not here to-day it will be here to-morrow," added Conseil, "for it cannot be far off. I vote we return to the boat."

"What, already?" exclaimed Ned.

"We ought to be back before night," I said.

"But what time is it now?" asked Ned.

"About two o'clock," replied Conseil.

"How quickly time passes on firm ground," said Ned Land with a sigh.

"Let us return," said Conseil.

We again passed through the forest, and completed our supply of provisions by making a raid upon the cabbage-palms, which we had to climb up to obtain the fruit; some small beans, which I recognized as the "abrou" of the Malays; and some excellent yams.

We were overloaded when we reached the launch; nevertheless, Ned still found the supply insufficient. But fortune favoured him. As we were embarking he caught sight of some trees which appeared to be a species of palm. These trees are justly reckoned amongst the most useful of the Malayan products. They were sago trees. They grew naturally without culture, and were reproduced, like the mulberry, by their shoots and seeds.

Ned Land knew how to treat them. He seized a hatchet, and, working with great determination, he soon felled two or three sago trees, whose maturity he recognized by the white dust powdering their leaves.

I watched him from a naturalist's point of view, rather than as a hungry man. He began by raising a strip of bark, about an inch thick, from each tree, which covered a network of long fibres, forming inextricable knots, which were cemented together by a sort of gummy farine. This was the sago which forms a principal article of food amongst the Malays. Ned Land, for the moment, only cut the trees in pieces as for firewood, intending to extract the sago later by separating it from the fibrous ligatures, evaporating the water by the sun's heat, and leaving it to harden in the moulds.

At length, about 5 p.m., laden with our treasures, we quitted the island, and half an hour later climbed on board the *Nautilus*. No one was to be seen. The vessel appeared deserted. We embarked our provisions. I descended to my room, where I found my supper prepared. I ate it and went to bed.

Next morning, the 6th January, nothing new appeared on board. No sound was heard, not a sign of life. The launch lay alongside as we had left it. We resolved to return to the island. Ned Land was hoping to be more successful as a hunter than he had been the day before, and wished to visit another portion of the forest.

At sunrise we were *en route*. The boat, assisted by the tide, soon reached the island.

We disembarked, and thinking it better to trust to the instinct of the Canadian, we followed Ned Land, whose long legs threatened to distance us.

He took his course towards the west, then finding some torrents, he gained the high ground, which is surrounded by beautiful woods. Some kingfishers darted along the water-courses, but would not allow us to approach them. Their caution was to me evidence that they were acquainted with mankind; and if the island was not actually inhabited, it was frequently visited by human beings.

Having crossed an immense grass prairie, we reached the edge of a little wood, which resounded with the songs and rustlings of a quantity of birds.

"They are nothing but birds," said Conseil.

"But there is something to be eaten," replied the harpooner.

"Not at all," replied Conseil, "for I can see nothing but parrots."

"Friend Conseil," said Ned, gravely, "a parrot becomes a pheasant to those who have nothing but parrots to eat."

"And I will add," said I, "that, nicely prepared, they are worth eating."

A whole race of parrots were flitting from branch to branch, beneath the thick foliage of this wood, and only required a little careful teaching to be able to speak. They chattered with paroquets of all colours, grave cockatoos, which seemed to be considering some problem; the loris, of a beautiful scarlet, darted like a bit of stamen carried by the wind; and every variety of bird, beautiful to behold, but not usually good to eat.

Nevertheless, there was one bird wanting, which never passes the limits of the Aroo and the Papuan Islands. But fate had decreed that I should admire it before long.

We crossed through a thicket, and found ourselves on a plain sprinkled with clumps of bushes. I then saw get up some beautiful birds, whose long feathers obliged them to fly against the wind. Their undulating flight, their graceful curves in their aerial course, the varying play of colour, attracted and charmed the eye. I had no difficulty to recognize them.

"These are birds of paradise!" I cried.

"Order, sparrows; section, clystomores," said Conseil.

"Family partridges?" inquired Ned Land.

"I do not know, Master Land. Nevertheless, I count upon your skill to procure one of them."

"I can try, though I am more accustomed to handle a harpoon than a gun."

The Malays, who drive a great trade in these birds with the Chinese, have various methods of catching them, which we could not employ. Sometimes they fix snares at the top of the high trees, for which the birds of paradise have a preference. Sometimes they secure them with a kind of bird-lime. They sometimes even poison the pools where the birds drink. But we were reduced to taking flying shots at them, which left us little chance of success; and in fact we did expend some of our ammunition in vain. Towards eleven o'clock we had crossed the hills which rise in the centre of the island, and had hitherto killed nothing. Hunger began to attack us.

The sportsmen had trusted to the produce of their skill, and had been mistaken. Fortunately Conseil, to his own great amazement, fired "right and left", and secured our breakfast. He killed a white pigeon and a wood-pigeon, which quickly were plucked, and, suspended to a stick, were roasted over a fire of dead wood. While these interesting fowls were cooking, Ned prepared the bread-fruit. Then the pigeons were eaten, the bones picked, and the meal declared excellent. The nutmeg, upon which they feed, perfumes their flesh and gives it a pleasant flavour.

"It is as if the fowls had been fed upon 'trouffles'," said Conseil.

"Now Ned, what do you want?" I said.

"Some four-footed game, M. Aronnax," he replied. "All these pigeons are only side-dishes, and whets for the appetite. So until I have killed some animal available for cutlets, I shall not be satisfied."

"Nor shall I, Ned, unless I catch a bird of paradise."

"Let us go, then," replied Conseil, "but in the direction of our boat. We have reached the first mountains, and I think it will be better to re-enter the forest."

This was sensible advice, and was followed. After an hour's walking, we reached a regular forest of sago-trees. Some harmless serpents fled at our approach. The birds of paradise disappeared, and I was beginning to despair of getting a specimen, when Conseil, who was ahead, stooped suddenly, uttered a triumphant cry, and came back to me carrying a magnificent bird of paradise.

"Bravo, Conseil!" I cried.

"Monsieur is very good," replied Conseil.

"Not at all, my lad. You have made a master-stroke, to catch one of those birds alive in your hand!"

"If Monsieur will examine it more nearly, he will see that there is nothing very wonderful in it after all."

"Why, Conseil?"

"Because the bird is as drunk as an owl!"

"Drunk!"

"Yes, sir: intoxicated with the nutmegs under the tree, where I took him. Just see, friend Ned, the terrible effects of intemperance!"

"A thousand devils!" exclaimed the Canadian, "it is rather hard to reproach me with intemperance – I, who have not tasted spirits for two months!"

Meanwhile I was examining this curious bird. Conseil was right. The bird of paradise, intoxicated by the "heady" juice, had become helpless. It could not fly, scarcely walk. But that did not trouble me at all, and I let it "get over it".

This bird belongs to the most beautiful of the eight species which are found in Papua and the neighbouring islands. This was the "Emerald" bird of paradise – one of the rarest. It measures nearly a foot in length. Its head is relatively small. Its eyes are placed near the opening of the beak, and are likewise small. But it presents a wonderful combination of colour; the beak is yellow, the feet and claws brown; hazel wings, tipped with purple at their extremities; pale yellow on the head and behind the neck; throat emerald green, and the chest and stomach is a fine maroon. Two curved and soft feathers growing above the tail, and prolonged in beautiful light and lengthy plumes of admirable softness, complete the *ensemble* of this wonderful bird, which the natives call the "bird of the sun".

I was very anxious to bring back this lovely specimen to Paris, and to present it to the "Jardin des Plantes", where there was not a living one.

"Is it, then, so very uncommon?" asked the Canadian, in the tone of a hunter who did not regard game from the artistic point of view.

"Very rare, indeed, and, above all, very difficult to catch alive; and even dead these birds are the object of much business traffic. So the natives have conceived the idea of 'making them up', as people might imitate diamonds or pearls."

"What!" exclaimed Conseil, "fabricate birds of paradise?"

"Yes, Conseil."

"Can Monsieur explain the process?"

"Certainly. During the east monsoon these birds lose their

magnificent plumage, which surrounds the tail. These are the feathers which are collected by the false traffickers in birds, and which they fix cleverly into some unfortunate paroquet, previously mutilated for the purpose. Then they dye the suture, varnish the bird, and export to the museums and amateurs in Europe – the result of their industry."

"Well, at any rate," said Ned, "if you have not got the bird you have got his feathers; and so long as you don't want to eat the animal it is no great matter."

But if my wishes were satisfied in the possession of the bird of paradise, Ned's were not so. Happily, during the afternoon he shot a magnificent wild pig, which the natives call "bari-outang". This animal came in very opportunely, and was welcomed accordingly. Ned Land was very proud of his shooting. The pig, touched by the electric bullet, had fallen dead on the instant.

The Canadian prepared him in workmanlike manner, after having taken some cutlets from him for our evening meal. Then the chase was resumed, which was further distinguished by the exploits of Conseil and Ned Land.

These two, by beating, roused a herd of kangaroo, which bounded away as actively as usual. But they did not fly so rapidly as the electric bullets, which checked their bounding career.

"Aha! Professor!" cried Ned, into whose head the sportsman's passion for killing had mounted, "what excellent game, particularly stewed. What a provision for the *Nautilus*. Two, three, five head. And when I think that we are eating all this fresh meat, and the idiots on board have not a crumb—"

In the excess of his joy the Canadian, if he had not talked so much, would have slain the whole herd. But he was content with a dozen of these marsupials, "which form the first order of aplacentary mammifers", as Conseil told us.

These animals were small. They were a species of the "rabbit kangaroo", which live in the trees, and whose rapidity of movement is extreme; but if only of medium height they furnish excellent food.

We were very well pleased with the results of our "hunting". The delighted Ned proposed to return again upon the following morning, with the view to depopulate all the game. But he was reckoning "without his host".

At 6 p.m. we arrived at the shore. Our boat was as we had

left it. The *Nautilus*, like a great rock, rose up from the waves about two miles off. Ned Land at once occupied himself respecting the important question of dinner. He understood the cooking part of this very well. The cutlets, grilled upon the wood embers, soon spread a delicious odour around us.

And I perceived that I was following Ned in this. Here was I delighted at the prospect of pork chops. I trust I may be forgiven, even as I forgave Master Land, and for the same reason.

In fact the dinner was a success. The pigeons wound up this (to us) extraordinary meal. The sago *pâté*, the bread fruit, some mangoes, half-a-dozen bananas, some fermented cocoa-nut milk put us in good trim. I really believe that the ideas of my worthy companions were not altogether so clear as they might have been.

"Suppose we do not return to the *Nautilus* to-night?" said Conseil.

"Suppose we don't return to the *Nautilus* at all?" added Ned Land.

At this moment a large stone fell at our feet, and cut short the harpooner's suggestions.

CHAPTER XXII
CAPTAIN NEMO'S LIGHTNING

WE TURNED TOWARDS the forest without getting up. My hand was arrested in the act of putting a morsel in my mouth. Ned did not stop his hand.

"A stone does not fall from heaven," said Conseil, "unless it be an aërolite."

A second stone, well aimed, which knocked a savoury bit of pigeon out of Conseil's hand, gave a point to the remark.

We all rose, shouldered our rifles, and were ready to repulse any attack.

"Are they apes?" said Ned.

"Nearer relatives," said Conseil. "They are savages."

"Let us gain the boat," I cried, retreating towards the shore.

We were obliged to retreat fighting, for twenty natives, armed with bows and spears, appeared at the edge of a coppice which lay to the right, scarcely a hundred paces distant.

Our launch was sixty yards away.

The savages approached steadily, but very demonstrative in their hostility. Stones and arrows whistled round us.

Ned Land had no intention to abandon his provisions, and, despite our danger, with the pig in one hand and the kangaroos in the other, he retired at a moderate pace.

In two minutes we had reached the shore. To throw ourselves into the boat with our arms and provisions, push off, and man the oars, was the work of a moment. We had scarcely gained two cables' length when a hundred savages, shouting and gesticulating, ran into the water up to their waists in pursuit. I looked to see whether anyone was on the deck of the *Nautilus*. But no, the enormous machine appeared absolutely deserted.

Twenty minutes later we were on board. The panels were open. We pulled up the launch, and entered the *Nautilus*.

I descended to the saloon, whence I heard music. Captain Nemo was there, seated at the organ, and plunged in a musical reverie.

"Captain," I said.

He did not hear me.

"Captain," I repeated, touching him as I spoke.

He started, and turned round.

"Ah, professor; is it you?" said he. "Well, have you had good sport; have you had success in your botanizing?"

"Yes, captain. But we have unfortunately met with some bipeds, whose near neighbourhood makes me uneasy!"

"What bipeds?"

"Savages!"

"Savages!" repeated Captain Nemo ironically. "And are you astonished at meeting savages anywhere on the earth? Savages! Where are they not? And are these savages worse than any others?"

"But, captain—"

"For my part," he said, "I have met them everywhere."

"Well," said I, "if you do not wish to receive them on board you had better take some precautions."

"Be at ease, professor. There is nothing to worry about."

"But these natives are numerous."

"How many did you reckon them to be?"

"A hundred at least."

"M. Aronnax," replied Captain Nemo, who again turned to

the instrument, "if all the natives of Papua were assembled on this coast, the *Nautilus* would have nothing to fear."

The captain's fingers ran over the notes, and I remarked that he only played the black keys, which gave his melodies an essentially Scotch tone. He soon forgot my presence, and was again plunged in the reverie from which I had aroused him, and which I did not again venture to disturb.

I remained alone for some hours, sometimes thinking of the savages, but not fearing them, as the confidence of the captain inspired me; sometimes forgetting them, to admire the beauties of the tropical night. My thoughts turned to France, following those zodiacal stars which would shine over it in a few hours. The moon shone brilliantly amidst the northern constellations.

I wondered whether this complaisant planet would raise the waters for us to-morrow and float the *Nautilus*. Towards midnight, seeing that all was quiet around us, I retired and slept quietly. The night passed without incident. The Papuans were afraid, no doubt, even at the view of the monster stranded in their bay, for the panels had been left open, and access to the *Nautilus* was easy.

At six o'clock the next morning I ascended to the platform. The morning mists were rising. The island, its shores and mountains, would soon be distinctly visible.

The natives were still there, and in greater numbers than before — five or six hundred, perhaps. Some of them advanced over the coral-reefs — the tide being out — to within two cables' length of the *Nautilus*. I could distinguish them plainly. They were of the true Papuan type — tall, athletic men, high foreheads, large noses, not flattened, and white teeth. Their long hair, tinted red, fell over their shoulders, and their skin was as black and glossy as that of the Nubian. The lobes of their ears, cut and distended, were hung with bone ornaments. The men were naked, as a rule. Amongst them there were a few women, clothed from waist to knee in a regular crinoline of grassy texture, sustained by a girdle of bark. Some of the chiefs had ornamented their necks with a painted crescent, and with rows of red and white beads. They were nearly all armed with bows and arrows and shields, while over the shoulder they wore a kind of net, in which they carried the round stones which they sling with much accuracy of aim.

One of the chiefs approached the *Nautilus* pretty closely, and examined it attentively. He appeared to be a "mado" of high rank, for he was dressed in a mat of banana leaves, fringed at the edges, and trimmed up with bright colours.

I could easily have shot this fellow, who was so unguardedly gazing at us, but I thought it better to wait the actual commencement of hostilities. Between Europeans and savages it is always better to let the latter commence an attack.

So long as the tide was low these natives prowled around the *Nautilus*, but they were not demonstrative. I heard them frequently repeat the "assai", and by their gestures they invited me to go ashore, an invitation which I felt myself obliged to decline.

All that day, therefore, the launch did not leave the ship, much to Land's disappointment, as he wished to complete his stock of provisions. The "handy" Canadian, however, occupied himself in preparing the food and vegetables we had brought on board. The savages returned to *terra firmâ*, as the tide rose about eleven o'clock, but their numbers still kept increasing considerably on the shore. It is probable that they came from the neighbouring islands, but I had not yet perceived any of the native canoes.

Having nothing better to do, I thought I would "drag" the clear water, in which numbers of shell-fish could be distinctly seen, as well as zoophytes and marine plants. This was, moreover, the last day which the *Nautilus* was to pass in this place, if it was to be again afloat the next day, according to Captain Nemo's promise.

I called to Conseil to bring me a light chag-net, something like those which are used in oyster dredging.

"If Monsieur is not displeased at my remark, I would say that these savages are very wicked; are they?" asked Conseil.

"They are at any rate cannibals, my friend."

"Still they can be cannibals and brave men too," replied Conseil; "just as one may be a *gourmand* and an honest man. The one does not exclude the other."

"Well, Conseil, I grant you that there may be honest cannibals, who honestly devour their captives. However, as I do not wish to be eaten, even honestly, I will be upon my guard; for it seems that the captain of the *Nautilus* is taking no precaution whatever. Now let us get to work."

We fished for two hours, without pulling up anything extra-ordinary. We caught some "Ears of Midas", some "harpes", some "holotures", some pearl oysters, and a dozen little turtles, which we handed over to the cook. But at a moment when I was least attentive, I lighted upon a wonderful specimen – I might almost say a natural deformity – very rarely met with. Conseil dragged the net, and it came up filled with a number of ordinary specimens; when suddenly I plunged my hand quickly into the net and pulled out a shell-fish, and uttered the cry of a con-chologist, which is the most piercing cry that the human throat can produce.

"What is the matter?" asked Conseil, in surprise. "Has Mon-sieur been bitten?"

"No, but nevertheless my finger has paid for my discovery."

"What discovery?"

"This shell," I said, displaying it.

"It is only an olive porphyry – genus, olive; order, pectini-branchal; class, gasteropodes; branch, mollusc."

"Yes, Conseil; but instead of curving from right to left, this 'olive' turns from left to right."

"Is it possible!" exclaimed Conseil.

"Yes, my lad."

"A 'sinister' shell!"

"Look at the spiral."

"Ah Monsieur," said Conseil, "I can believe it; but I have never had such an experience before."

There was, after all, something to excite surprise. Everyone is aware that nature, as a rule, works as it were from right to left. The planets and stars, in their movements, go from right to left. Man-kind use the right hand more than the left, and consequently all his instruments, &c., are made with the view of being employed as from right to left. Nature has generally carried out this prin-ciple in the "whorl" of shells. With very rare exceptions, they all have the spiral from right to left, and when by chance a "left-handed" whorl is discovered, it is worth its weight in gold.

Conseil and I were engaged in the contemplation of our treas-ure, and I was anticipating its presentation to the museum, when a stone, only too well directed by a native, shivered the precious object in Conseil's hands.

I uttered a cry of despair. Conseil seized my gun and levelled

it at a savage who was swinging his sling about a dozen yards off.
I tried to stop him, but he fired, and struck the bracelet of beads
which was hanging from the arm of the savage.

"Conseil!" I cried, "Conseil!"

"Well, did not Monsieur see that the cannibal began the
attack?"

"A shell is not worth a man's life," I said.

"Ah, the blackguard!" cried Conseil; "I would rather he had
broken my shoulder."

Conseil was sincere, but I did not agree with him. However,
the situation had altered during the last few minutes, and we had
not perceived the change. Twenty canoes now surrounded the
Nautilus. These canoes, hollowed out from trunks of trees, are
long and narrow, and well put together for speed, and kept in
equilibrio by double sets of bamboo poles, which floated on the
surface of the water. They were worked by skilful hands, and it
was not without some misgivings that I perceived their approach.
It was evident that the Papuans had already been in communication with Europeans, and that they knew their ships. But this
long cylinder of iron, without masts or chimney, what could they
make of it? Nothing very pleasant apparently, as they kept at a
respectful distance. However, seeing it motionless, they regained
confidence by degrees, and sought to make themselves acquainted with the *Nautilus*.

Now it was precisely this familiarity that it behoved us to
check. Our arms, which gave no report, only produced a slight
effect upon the natives, who respected loud-mouthed guns.
People are not so much frightened by lightning when unaccompanied by thunder, although it is really the lightning, and not the
thunder, which constitutes the danger.

At this moment the canoes approached the *Nautilus*, and a
shower of arrows struck it.

"The devil!" cried Conseil; "here is a regular hail-storm; and
perhaps the hail is poisoned too."

"We must acquaint Captain Nemo," I said, entering the panel
as I spoke.

I descended to the saloon; no one was there. I ventured to
knock at the door which opened into the captain's room.

A "Come in" answered me, and I found the captain immersed
in algebraical calculations.

"I am disturbing you, I fear," I said politely.

"Well, yes, M. Aronnax; but I daresay you have very good reasons for so doing."

"I have indeed. We are surrounded by canoes filled with the natives, and in a short time we shall be attacked by hundreds of savages."

"Ah!" said Captain Nemo quietly; "so they have come in their canoes, eh?"

"Yes."

"Well, we have only to close the panel."

"Precisely; I came to tell you so."

"Nothing can be easier," was the reply; and pressing an electric bell, it gave the order.

After a pause, he said:

"That is done. The launch is in its place, and the panels are closed. You have no fear, I suppose, that these gentlemen outside will break the walls which the shot from your frigate could not hurt?"

"No, captain; but there is still danger."

"In what way?"

"To-morrow we must open the panels again for fresh air."

"Certainly; we breathe like cetaceans, you know."

"If at this moment the savages were on the outer platform, I do not see how you could prevent their entrance."

"Then you suppose they will get on board?"

"I am sure of it."

"Well, let them if they like. I see no reason to prevent them. After all, they are but poor devils, these Papuans, and I do not wish that my visit to the isle of Gueberoar should cost one of them his life."

At that I rose to retire, but Captain Nemo detained me, and invited me to sit beside him. He questioned me with much interest respecting our excursions to the island, and our hunting, and did not appear to understand the Canadian's desire for fresh meat. The conversation then became more lively, and without being too communicative, Captain Nemo displayed great amiability.

Amongst other things, we spoke of the position of the *Nautilus*, stranded upon the precise spot where Dumont d'Urville was so nearly lost. Speaking of this the captain said:

"He was one of your greatest and best sailors. He was the French Captain Cook. Unfortunate man! Having braved the icebergs of the southern polar regions, the coral-reefs of the ocean, and the cannibals of the Pacific, to perish miserably in a railway train. If this majestic man was able to reflect during the last moments of his existence, you can imagine what his thoughts may have been."

Captain Nemo appeared to be moved, and I gave him credit for the feeling.

Then, maps in hand, we traced the discoveries of this bold navigator, his voyages round the world, his two attempts to reach the South Pole, which resulted in the discovery of "Adélie" and "Louis Philippe", and finally his hydrographical survey of the principal oceanic islands.

"What your d'Urville did at the surface, I have done beneath," said Captain Nemo, "and more easily and completely than he. The *Astrolabe* and *Zélée*, continually knocked about by the winds and waves, were not as good as the *Nautilus*, where there is a quiet 'study', and really motionless in the water."

"Nevertheless, there is one point of resemblance between the ships of Dumont d'Urville and the *Nautilus*."

"What is that?"

"That the *Nautilus* has stranded, just as they did."

"The *Nautilus* has not stranded," replied Captain Nemo coldly. "The *Nautilus* is merely reposing on the bed of the ocean, and the persistent labour and work which D'Urville had to refloat his vessels will not be necessary with us. The *Astrolabe* and the *Zélée* ran a great risk of being lost, but we are in no danger. To-morrow, the day named, and at the time I mentioned, the tide will raise us quietly, and we shall resume our voyage."

"Captain," I said, "I have no doubt about it."

"To-morrow," added he, rising, "to-morrow, at 2.40 p.m., the *Nautilus* will float, and leave Torres Strait uninjured."

These words were spoken quickly, and Captain Nemo reseated himself and bowed slightly. This was the signal for my departure, and I regained my room.

There I found Conseil, anxious to hear the result of my interview with the captain.

"My lad," I replied, "when I fancied his *Nautilus* was threatened by these Papuans, he replied to my fears in a bantering tone.

I have but one thing to say – have confidence in him, and go to sleep in peace."

"Monsieur does not want me?"

"No. What is Ned Land doing?"

"Monsieur will excuse me, but Ned is making kangaroo pie, which will be a great success."

I was left alone, and I went to bed, but slept badly. I heard the savages trampling overhead, and uttering discordant yells. The night passed in this manner, and none of the crew seemed to be in the least disturbed about it. They no more disturbed themselves about these cannibals, than in an iron battery they would trouble about the ants crawling on it.

At six o'clock I got up. The panels had not been opened. The air in the interior had not therefore been renewed, but the reservoirs, which were destined to act under such circumstances, forced fresh oxygen into the vitiated atmosphere within the *Nautilus*.

I worked in my room up to mid-day, without even having a glimpse of Captain Nemo. There did not appear any preparation for departure.

I waited some time longer, then went into the saloon. The clock showed it was half-past two. In ten minutes the tide would have attained its maximum height, and if Captain Nemo had not made a rash promise, the *Nautilus* would be soon at liberty again. If not, then several months must elapse before we could quit this coral bed.

However, some little vibrations began to be felt in the hull, and I could hear the coral grinding beneath the weight of the ship.

At 2.35, Captain Nemo appeared.

"Well!" said I.

"I have given orders to have the panels opened."

"And the Papuans—?"

"The Papuans!" he exclaimed, shrugging his shoulders.

"Will they not penetrate into the interior of the *Nautilus*?"

"How?"

"Through the panels you have just opened!"

"M. Aronnax," replied Captain Nemo, calmly, "they will not enter, even though the panels be open."

I looked at the captain.

"You do not understand?" he said.

"Not at all."

"Well, then, come and see for yourself."

I accompanied him to the centre staircase. There I found Ned Land and Conseil very much puzzled to see the crew open the panels, while cries and shouts of rage resounded outside.

The mantelets were beaten down, and twenty horrible figures appeared. But, the first of the natives who placed his hand upon the balustrade of the staircase was hurled backwards by some invisible force; and he fled, uttering terrified yells, and executing most extraordinary antics.

Ten of his companions succeeded him, but all met the same fate.

Conseil was delighted. Ned Land, carried away by his impetuosity, advanced to the staircase; but so soon as he had touched the balustrade, he was upset bodily in his turn.

"A thousand devils!" he cried; "I am struck by lightning."

That one word explained everything. It was not a balustrade, but a metal cable charged with electricity, and whoever touched it immediately received a fearful shock, which would have been fatal if Captain Nemo had permitted the full power to be used. One could truly say that between himself and his assailants he had drawn an electric chain which none could pass. Meanwhile the astonished Papuans had beaten a retreat, quite overcome with terror. We, half laughing, consoled and rubbed the unfortunate Ned Land, who kept swearing like a trooper.

But now the *Nautilus*, raised by the last waves of the high tide, left her bed of coral, and at the exact moment predicted by Captain Nemo. The screw slowly beat the ebbing waters. Her speed increased by degrees, and sailing upon the surface of the sea, she quitted the dangerous Torres Straits safe and sound.

CHAPTER XXIII
ÆGRI SOMNIA

ON THE FOLLOWING day, 10th January, the *Nautilus* resumed her course beneath the waves at a speed which surprised me, and which could not have been less than thirty-five miles an hour. The revolutions of her screw were too rapid to admit of being reckoned.

When I thought of this marvellous electric agency, which gave light, heat, and movement to the *Nautilus*, protected her from attack, and transformed it into an ark, into which no one could enter without running the risk of death by lightning, my admiration knew no bounds; the machine was worthy of the hand that made it.

We proceeded due west, and on the 11th of January we doubled Cape Wessel (situated in 135° E. long, and 10° N. lat.), which forms the eastern point of the Gulf of Carpentaria. The reefs were numerous, but easily distinguished, and shown upon the map with great accuracy. The *Nautilus* easily avoided the breakers of Money to larboard and the Victoria reefs to starboard, situated in 130° long., and on the tenth parallel, which we steadily followed.

On the 13th of January, Captain Nemo reached the Timor Sea, and sighted the island of that name in 122° long. This island is ruled by the Radjahs. These princes call themselves the "sons of crocodiles"; that is to say, descended from the highest rank to which human nature can lay claim. So these scaly ancestors abounded in the streams, and were the object of peculiar veneration. The people protected them, petted them, worshipped them, and fed them, even giving them their young children to eat; and woe to the stranger who raised his hand against these sacred lizards.

But the *Nautilus* had nothing to do with these horrible animals. Timor was only visible for a moment at mid-day, while the mate made the observations. And equally I could only catch a glimpse of the little island of Rotti, which made one of the group, the women of which bear a high reputation for beauty in the Malayan markets.

The *Nautilus* now went south-west, and bore up for the Indian Ocean. Whither was Captain Nemo taking us? Was he about to run up the Asian coasts, and towards Europe? This was not likely to be the idea of a man who kept aloof from inhabited continents. Would he descend to the southward, double the Cape of Good Hope and Cape Horn, and advance to the Antarctic regions? Or would he return to the Pacific, where the *Nautilus* found easy and independent navigation? Time would show.

Having skirted the rocks of Cartier, Hibernia, Seringapatam, and Scott – the last barriers of the land against the water – on the

14th January we were beneath all lands. The speed of the *Nautilus* was slackened, and she became very capricious in her movements, sometimes sailing beneath and sometimes at the surface of the water.

During this portion of the trip Captain Nemo made some very interesting observations respecting the temperature of the sea at different depths. Under ordinary circumstances the results are obtained by means of complicated instruments, and are at least doubtful as regards theometric soundings, as the glasses frequently break under the pressure of the water, or of those appearances based upon the principle of the variation of the resistance of metals to the electric currents. The results thus obtained cannot be really depended upon.

Captain Nemo, on the contrary, went down to ascertain the temperature in those depths, and his thermometer, put in communication with the various zones of liquid, gave him surely and immediately the looked-for temperature. Thus it was, whether in filling the reservoirs, or in descending obliquely by means of the "inclined planes", the *Nautilus* attained successively the depths of 3,000, 4,000, 5,000, 7,000, 9,000, and 10,000 yards, and the definite result of these experiences was that the sea gave a permanent temperature of $4\frac{1}{2}°$ at a depth of 1,000 yards* in all latitudes. I followed his experiments with the greatest interest. Captain Nemo was passionately fond of this work. I often wondered what was the use of all these observations. Was it for the benefit of his fellow-creatures? This was not likely, for some day or other his work would perish with him in some unknown sea. It was not likely that he destined them for me, as that would be to admit that my strange voyage would have an end; and this termination I did not yet perceive.

However, Captain Nemo made me equally acquainted with himself with various results obtained by him, and which established the agreement of the densities of the water in the principal seas. From this communication I drew a personal lesson, which had nothing scientific about it.

On the morning of the 15th January the captain, with whom I was walking on the platform, asked me if I knew the different

* Metres.

densities of sea-water. I replied in the negative, and I added that exact observations on the subject had not been recorded.

"I have made such observations, and I can vouch for their accuracy," said the captain.

"Very good," said I, "but the *Nautilus* is a world in itself, and the secrets of its wise men have not reached *terra firmâ*."

"You are right, professor," he replied after a pause. "It is a world apart. It is as great a stranger to the earth as the planets which accompany the globe round the sun; and the earth does not yet know the secrets of the *savants* in Saturn and Jupiter. However, since chance has thrown us together, I will tell you the result of my observations."

"I am all attention, captain."

"You know," said Captain Nemo, "that salt water is more dense than fresh water, but this density is not uniform. For example, if I represent the density of fresh water by 1, I find $1\frac{23}{1000}$ as the density of the Atlantic, $1\frac{26}{1000}$ that of the Pacific, $1\frac{30}{1000}$ that of the Mediterranean—"

"Ah!" thought I, "he has sailed in the Mediterranean."

"In the Ionian Sea $1\frac{18}{1000}$, and $1\frac{29}{1000}$ in the Adriatic."

The *Nautilus* certainly did not avoid the crowded seas of Europe, and I judged from this that it would carry us, perhaps before very long, towards the more civilized lands. I fancied that Ned Land would appreciate this very highly.

For a long time the days passed in experiments of all kinds, to ascertain the saltiness of the sea-water at different temperatures – its electrization, its colouration, its transparency; and under all circumstances Captain Nemo displayed an ingenuity which was only equalled by his great politeness to me. Then for many days I did not see him, and I remained almost isolated on board.

On the 16th January the *Nautilus* appeared to sleep at a few metres only beneath the surface. The electric apparatus was not at work, and the screw being immoveable, she drifted at the will of the currents. I supposed that the machinery was being repaired, such a course being necessary after the late violent working.

My companions and I were witnesses of a curious spectacle that day. The side panels of the saloon were open, and as the lamp of the *Nautilus* was not alight, a vague obscurity reigned in the water. The stormy and clouded sky could give but little light even to the first beds of the waters.

I was observing the sea under these conditions, and the largest fish only appeared like indistinct masses, when the *Nautilus* was suddenly in a bright zone of light. I at first believed that the electric light had been set going, and was thus illuminating the surrounding sea; but I was mistaken, and soon perceived my error.

The *Nautilus* was floating in the midst of a phosphorescent zone, which in the prevailing obscurity became dazzling. This was produced by myriads of luminous animalcules, whose sparkling increased as they glided against the metallic hull of the vessel. I could perceive spots of light in the midst of this luminous sheet, like the lumps of iron in a furnace when the metal is at a white heat; and sometimes, on the contrary, certain luminous portions would become dark in the midst of the brilliant mass, from which all shade had apparently been banished. No, this was not the calm irradiation of our usual light. There was a vigour and an unwonted movement in it all. It was a living light.

In fact, it was an innumerable collection of pelagian infusoria of noctiluqueous glands, regular globules of diaphanous jelly, provided with a filiform tentacle; and of which animals there are about 25,000 in thirty cubic centimetres of water. And their light was doubly increased by the gleams of the medusæ, the asteroids, and other phosphorescent zoophytes impregnated with the oily substance of organic matter decomposed in the sea, or, perhaps, with the mucus secreted by the fish. For a long time the *Nautilus* continued to float in these brilliant waves, and our admiration was increased at perceiving great marine animals disporting themselves like salamanders. I saw in that fire which did not burn the elegant and rapid porpoise, indefatigable clown of the sea, and sword-fish three yards long, those intelligent prophets of storms, whose formidable weapons now and then struck the glass of the saloon panels. Smaller fish also appeared, which flashed amidst the luminous waters.

There was a fascination in this dazzling spectacle. Perhaps some atmospherical condition increased the brilliancy of the phenomenon. Some storm perhaps, from which the *Nautilus*, so low down, was secure, and so lay peacefully in the midst of calm waters.

Thus we proceeded, incessantly being charmed by some new marvel. Conseil observed and classed the zoophytes, the articulates, the molluscs, and fish. The days passed rapidly away, and

I no longer took note of them. Ned, as usual, employed himself in finding out some additions to our table. Like snails, we were fastened to our shell; and I can state that it is not difficult to become a perfect snail.

Therefore this life appeared to us easy and natural, and we were no longer thinking of a different existence on land, when an event suddenly recalled us to the strangeness of our position.

On the 18th January the *Nautilus* was in long. 105° and 15° S. lat. The weather was threatening, the sea rough, and the wind blew strongly from the east. The barometer had for some days predicted an approaching storm.

I was on the platform when the mate was taking the usual angles. I was awaiting, as usual, for the customary sentence to be pronounced, but that morning another phrase, equally incomprehensible, was uttered. Almost immediately I saw Captain Nemo approach, and direct his glass towards the horizon.

For some minutes the captain remained motionless, without taking his eyes from the telescope. He then dropped the glass and exchanged a few words with the mate. He appeared to be the prey of an irrepressible emotion; but Captain Nemo, more master of himself, remained cool and collected. He seemed, moreover, to be making certain objections, to which the mate responded by formal assurances. So at least I fancied, judging from their voices and gestures. I had been carefully looking in the direction indicated without discovering anything. The sea and sky met without any intervening object to break the continuity.

Meanwhile, Captain Nemo walked up and down the platform without noticing me, perhaps without being aware of my presence. His step was firm, but less regular than usual. Sometimes he stopped, folded his arms across his chest, and gazed fixedly at the sea. What could he be seeking in that immense expanse? The *Nautilus* was then some hundreds of miles from the nearest land.

The mate had taken up the glass and swept the horizon, going and coming, stamping his feet, and contrasting generally with his chief in the nervous agitation of his manner.

However, the mystery was about to be cleared up, and before long, for by the captain's order the screw was set going at a great rate.

At this moment the mate again attracted the captain's attention. Captain Nemo stopped in his walk and levelled his glass in the direction indicated. He gazed for a long time steadily. I was now somewhat disturbed, and descending to the saloon, brought up an excellent telescope which I was in the habit of using. Then resting the glass upon the cage forward, I disposed myself to observe the sea and sky. But scarcely had I applied my eye to the telescope when it was snatched from my grasp. I turned round. Captain Nemo stood before me, but I scarcely recognized him. His face was completely altered. His eyes, flashing with a lurid light, glanced at me beneath his frowning brows. His mouth was half open, his body was rigid, his hands clenched, his head bowed between his shoulders – all bearing testimony to the violent emotion that possessed him. He did not move an inch. My glass, fallen from his hand, rolled to his feet. What had happened that I had thus unwittingly provoked his anger? Did he imagine that I had discovered some secret interdicted from the guests of the *Nautilus*?

No. I was not the object of his hatred, for he was not looking at me, but gazing steadily on the particular portion of the horizon.

At length he became calm, his face and figure resumed their usual impassibility. He spoke some words to the mate in the unknown tongue, and he then turned to me.

"M. Aronnax," said he, in a somewhat haughty tone, "I would recall your attention to one of the conditions I imposed upon you."

"What is the question, captain?"

"You and your companions must be content to be incarcerated until I shall judge it desirable to release you."

"You are master here," I replied, looking at him steadily. "But may I ask you a question?"

"No, Monsieur."

There was no disputing this. I had not to discuss, but to obey. Any resistance was impossible.

I descended into the cabin occupied by Conseil and Ned, and told them of the captain's resolve. I will leave you to imagine how my tidings were received by the Canadian. However, there was no time for explanations. Four of the crew appeared at the door and conducted us to the cell in which we had passed our first night on board the *Nautilus*.

Ned Land wished to expostulate, but the door was shut upon him for all reply.

"Will Monsieur tell me what all this means?" asked Conseil.

I related all that had passed. They were as much astonished, but no more enlightened than I was. I fell into a reverie, and the strange expression of fear in Captain Nemo's face haunted me. I was quite incapable of putting two logical ideas together, and I had lost myself in the most absurd hypotheses, when I was aroused by Ned saying:

"Hullo! Breakfast is served."

And as a fact the table was prepared. Captain Nemo had evidently given this order at the time he directed the increase of the speed.

"Will Monsieur permit me to recommend him some thing?"

"Yes, Conseil," I replied.

"Well, then, I recommend that Monsieur eat his breakfast. It is prudent, for we do not know what may happen."

"You are right, Conseil."

"Unfortunately," said Ned, "they have only given us ship's fare."

"Friend Ned," said I, "what would you have done had there been no breakfast at all?"

This remark put an end to the harpooner's grumbling. We sat down and ate in silence. I ate little; Conseil forced himself to eat, as a matter of prudence; and Ned Land, nevertheless, did not lose a mouthful. Then, breakfast over, we rested on the table as we sat.

Just then the luminous globes were extinguished, and we were left in utter darkness. Ned Land went to sleep on the spot, and to my astonishment Conseil also yielded to a heavy drowsiness. I was wondering what had caused this sudden accession of sleep in him when I felt my brain affected by a drowsy feeling. My eyes closed in spite of all my efforts to the contrary. I became a prey to a terrible hallucination. Evidently some soporific had been mixed with the food we had eaten. It was therefore not enough to imprison us to prevent the betrayal of Captain Nemo's secret — it was necessary to drug us as well.

I heard the panels shut. The undulation of the water ceased. The *Nautilus* had then quitted the surface of the ocean. Was she again descending to the motionless zones of the seas?

I tried to resist sleep; it was impossible. My breathing became weaker; I felt a death-like chill extend over my frame. My eyelids fell over my eyes like lumps of lead; I could not raise them.

A morbid trance, and full of fancies, took possession of my whole being. Then the visions disappeared, and left me completely prostrated.

CHAPTER XXIV
THE REALMS OF CORAL

NEXT DAY I awoke, and my head was wonderfully clear. To my great surprise I was in my own room. My companions doubtless had been taken to their cabin without being more aware of the transfer than I was. They were quite as ignorant as I was respecting the occurrences of the night, and I could only hope that chance would develop the mystery at some future time. I then thought I would leave my chamber; but was I free, or still a prisoner? Free. I opened the door and went out upon the central staircase. The panels were now open. I reached the platform.

Ned Land and Conseil met me there. I questioned them; they knew nothing. Wrapped in such a heavy slumber that they remembered nothing, they had been much surprised to find themselves in their cabin.

All this time the *Nautilus* was as quiet and mysterious as ever. It floated at the surface and progressed slowly. Nothing was changed on board. Ned Land kept his eyes fixed upon the sea; it was deserted. The Canadian signalled nothing new – no land, not even a sail. The west wind blew stiffly, and the long waves gave a perceptible motion to the *Nautilus*.

After the air had been renewed, we descended to a depth of fifteen metres, so that we might quickly return to the surface. This operation, contrary to custom, was often performed during the day. The mate then ascended to the platform, and the usual phrase was transmitted to the interior of the vessel.

Captain Nemo did not appear. Of all the ship's company, I only saw the impassible steward, who waited on me with his usual punctuality and silence.

About two o'clock I was in the saloon arranging my notes, when the captain entered. I saluted him. He acknowledged my greeting in an almost imperceptible manner, but did not speak. I resumed my occupation, hoping that he would offer some explanation of the events of the preceding night. He said nothing. I looked at him attentively. He appeared fatigued – his eyes had not been refreshed by sleep, and his face expressed a deep sadness, a real sorrow. He moved about, seated himself, then got up again, took up any book that came to hand, threw it down again immediately, looked at his instruments vacantly, and appeared thoroughly restless.

At length he came to me and said:

"Are you a doctor, M. Aronnax?"

I paused a little at this unexpected question.

"Are you a doctor?" repeated Captain Nemo. "Many of your colleagues have studied medicine – Gratiolet, Moquin-Tandon, and others."

"Well, in fact," I said, "I am a doctor, and a house-surgeon. I practised many months before I entered the museum."

"Good," was the reply.

My answer evidently satisfied the captain. But not knowing what might come of it, I waited for further questions, resolving to reply according to circumstances.

"M. Aronnax," said the captain, "will you extend your skill to one of my men?"

"There is an invalid on board, then?"

"Yes."

"I am ready."

"Come with me."

I confess that my heart was beating. I do not know why I perceived some connection between this patient and the events of the preceding day, and the mystery troubled me at least as much as the sick man.

Captain Nemo led me abaft, into a cabin close to the men's quarters.

There lay a man about forty years old, a determined face too – a regular Anglo-Saxon.

I knelt beside him. He was not only a sick, but a wounded man. His head was wrapped in blood-stained bandages, and lay on a double pillow. I took off the bandages, and the wounded man, gazing at me with his great round eyes, made no sign and uttered no complaint. The wound was fearful. The skull, fractured by some blunt instrument, had laid the brain bare, and the cerebral substance had suffered complete attrition. Some clots of blood had formed within the mass, which was like the dregs of wine. There was a contusion and concussion of the brain here. The breathing of the patient was laboured, and spasmodic movements agitated his features. The cerebral phlegmasia was complete, and induced paralysis both of body and mind.

I felt the sick man's pulse. It was intermittent. The extremities were already cold, and I could perceive that death was approaching without any possibility of my staying its approach. Having dressed his wounds I readjusted the bandages, and, turning to Captain Nemo, said:

"How did this man come by this hurt?"

"What matters?" he replied evasively. "The *Nautilus* struck, and broke one of the levers of the engine, which struck this man. But what is your opinion?"

I hesitated.

"You may speak fearlessly, he does not understand French."

I looked again steadily at the wounded man.

"He will not live two hours longer," I said.

"Can nothing save him?"

"Nothing."

Captain Nemo clenched his hand, and tears glittered in his eyes, which I did not think were made to weep.

For some minutes I kept looking at the dying man as his life ebbed away. His paleness appeared more ghastly beneath the electric light that illuminated his death-bed. I looked at that intellectual head, and the face seemed furrowed by premature wrinkles, which sin, or perhaps trouble, had placed there long ago. I endeavoured to learn the secret of his life from the last words that escaped his lips.

"You can retire, M. Aronnax," said the captain.

I left him in the cabin of the dying man, and regained my own room very much impressed by the scene I had witnessed.

All day I was haunted by sinister presentiments. At night I slept little, and amid my frequently interrupted dreams I fancied I heard distant sighings and the sound of a funeral hymn. Was it the prayer for the dead, uttered in that language which I did not understand.

Next morning I went on deck. Captain Nemo was there before me. So soon as he saw me he approached and said:

"Would it be convenient for you to make a submarine excursion to-day?"

"With my friends?" I asked.

"They can go if they like."

"We are at your orders, captain."

"Will you, then, put on your divers' dresses, please?"

There was no question of the dying or the dead. I told Conseil and Ned Land what Captain Nemo had suggested.

Conseil was anxious to go, and the Canadian appeared very willing to accompany him.

It was eight o'clock, a.m. At half-past eight we were equipped for our expedition, and furnished with the lighting and breathing apparatus. The double door was opened, and, accompanied by the captain and followed by a dozen of the crew, we trod, at a depth of ten yards, upon the ground where the *Nautilus* was firmly reposing.

A gentle slope led us to a bottom much furrowed, and about fifteen fathoms down. This ground was very different from that which we had first met with beneath the Pacific Ocean. Here was no fine sand, no submarine prairies nor forests. I immediately recognized that wonderful region of which Captain Nemo did the honours. It was the Kingdom of Coral.

In the branch of zoophytes, and in the class of alayonnares, we remarked the order of gorgonares, which includes the three groups of gorgonians, the insidians, and the corallines. It is to the last named that the coral is attributed – a curious substance, which has been classed by turns in the animal, mineral, and vegetable kingdoms. A remedy with the ancients, an ornament in modern days, it was only in 1694 that Peysonnel classed it definitely in the animal kingdom.

Coral is a conglomeration of animalcules, united on a natural, brittle, and stony polypary. These polypes have a single generator, which produces them by a budding process; they have a separate existence, while participating in a common life. It is a kind of natural solecism. I had read the latest works upon this curious zoophyte which mineralizes itself in growing like a tree, following the very just observation of naturalists, and nothing could be more interesting to me than a visit to one of these petrified forests which nature has planted at the bottom of the sea.

The Ruhmkorff apparatus were set going, and we followed a coral bank in course of formation, which in time will form a barrier to this part of the Indian Ocean. The way was by the side of inextricable thickets, formed by the entanglement of the branches which covered the little starry flowers with white rays, only, inverse to the plants of earth, those fixed to the rocks all grew downwards.

The lights we carried produced a thousand beautiful effects amid those coloured branches. It appeared to me that the membranous and cylindrical tubes trembled at the undulation of the water. I was tempted to collect some of these beautiful fresh corals with such delicate tentacles, some newly opened, some just sprouting, which the fish, with rapid fins, moved as they passed, as a bird might move the twigs of the trees. But as my hand approached these living flowers, these sensitive plants, all were immediately on the alert. The white corals retired into their red cases, the flowers disappeared from my sight, and the "coppice" was changed into a block of stony hills.

Chance put me in possession of the most valuable specimens of this zoophyte. The coral is equal to that found in the Mediterranean, on the French, Italian, and Barbary coasts. It fully justifies its names of "Fleur de sang" and "Écume de sang", which trade has bestowed upon the most beautiful kinds. Coral is sold at 500 francs the kilogramme; and in this spot the beds would have made the fortunes of a thousand fishers. This valuable material, often mixed with other polypes, forms the compound called "Macciota", and amongst which I remarked some splendid specimens of rose coral.

But the "bushes" soon became smaller, and the tree growths increased. A petrified underwood and long fantastic arches opened before us. Captain Nemo penetrated beneath a dark gallery, whose gentle descent led us to a depth of 100 yards. The lights at times produced magical effects, and caught the angles and projections of these natural arcades, until they appeared tipped with fire. Amidst the branching corallines I noticed other polypes no less curious — melites, articulated iris; some tufts of corallines — some red, some green, true algæ, crusted in their calcareous salts, which naturalists, after much discussion, have definitively ranged in the vegetable kingdom. But in the words of a deep thinker, "perhaps the real point to get at is where the life obscurely rises from the stony sleep, without being yet detached from this rude starting-point".

After about two hours' walking, we attained a depth of about three hundred yards, that is to say, the extreme limit at which coral begins to form. But here was no thicket nor modest bush, but an immense forest of coral, enormous petrified trees. We passed freely underneath the high branches which were lost in the shade of the waves, while at our feet the tubipores, meandrines, fungi, &c., formed a flowing carpet, sprinkled with sparkling gems.

It was an indescribable sight. Oh, that we could have exchanged confidences. Why were we imprisoned in this head-piece of metal and glass? Why could we not speak to each other? Why could we not live like the fish, or even like the amphibious animals, which for hours can roam at will in the domains of the land or water?

Meantime Captain Nemo had stopped. We all followed his example, and turning round, I perceived that the men had formed themselves in a semi-circle round their chief. And looking more closely, I perceived that four of them carried something on their shoulders. We had arrived at a large open space in the coral forest. Our lamps threw around this clearing a sort of twilight, which cast long shadows on the ground. Beyond the reach of our lamps the darkness was profound, and only here and there a gleam fell upon the points of the coral.

Ned Land and Conseil were close to me. We looked on, and it appeared to me that I was about to take part in a very curious drama. On examining the ground I saw that it was heaped up in places, and these heaps were disposed with a regularity which betrayed man's handiwork.

In the midst of the clearing, upon a pedestal of rocks piled up to a great height, was a cross of coral, and its long, extended arms looked almost like petrified blood. At a sign from Captain Nemo one of the men advanced, and at some paces from the cross he began to dig a hole with a pick-axe which he detached from his girdle.

I understood it all. This clearing was a cemetery, this hole a grave, that long object the body of the man who had died during the night. Captain Nemo and his men had come hither to bury their companion in this their common resting-place at the bottom of the ocean.

Never had my mind been so impressed. Never had more impressive thoughts crowded my brain. I did not wish to see what was being enacted before me.

Meanwhile the grave was being slowly excavated. The fish fled hither and thither. I heard the iron ring upon the calcareous ground, and sometimes a spark would break forth as the pick came in contact with some lost piece of silex. The hole extended and widened, and was soon sufficiently large to receive the body.

The bearers then approached. The corpse, wrapped in white byssus, was laid in its damp tomb. Captain Nemo, with folded arms, and all the friends of the dead man, knelt down; I and my companions knelt also.

The grave was then covered with the *débris*, which had been dug out, and which thus formed a slight mound.

When this had been done, Captain Nemo and his men rose up, and approaching the grave all bent the knee once more, and waved a last adieu to their dead friend.

The funeral procession then returned to the *Nautilus*, repassing in its way beneath the arcades and the long bush-like formations of the coral.

At length the light appeared burning on board. The long gleam led us to the *Nautilus*. At one o'clock we had regained the ship.

As soon as I had changed my dress, I ascended to the platform, and beset by a crowd of mingled feelings, I sat down near the lighting apparatus.

Captain Nemo joined me. I got up and said:

"So, as I warned you, the man died during the night?"

"Yes, M. Aronnax," he replied.

"And he now rests among his companions in the cemetery of coral."

"Yes, forgotten by all – except by us. We have dug his grave, and the polypes will take care to seal up our dead for ever." And hiding his face in his hard hands, the captain tried in vain to conceal a tear. Then he added:

"It is our most peaceful burying-ground, some hundreds of feet beneath the surface of the waves."

"Your dead sleep there tranquilly at least; out of reach of sharks."

"Yes," replied the captain, gravely, "out of the reach of sharks – and men."

 END OF PART I

PART II

CHAPTER I
THE INDIAN OCEAN

WE NOW COMMENCE the second part of the voyage under the sea. The first ended with that sad scene at the cemetery of coral, which left a deep impression on my mind. Thus, then, in the bosom of the deep sea the life of Captain Nemo was entirely passed, and he had even prepared his last resting-place in the most impenetrable of its abysses. There no ocean monster will ever disturb the last sleep of these companions of the *Nautilus*, of those friends united in death as in their lives. "Nor will any man, for ever," the captain had added — always the same strange implacable defiance towards mankind! For my part I was not any more contented by the hypothesis which satisfied Conseil. He persisted in taking the commander of the *Nautilus* for one of those mistaken *savants* who return man's indifference by dislike. So to Conseil the captain was an eccentric genius, who, disgusted by the falseness of earthly things, had been obliged to take refuge in the inaccessible seas where he could exercise his tastes freely. But in my opinion this idea only explained one of the sides of Captain Nemo's character. In fact, the mystery of the night during which we had been imprisoned and drugged, the precaution so violently taken by Captain Nemo to snatch the telescope from my grasp, the mortal wound inflicted upon the sailor by some unexplained collision of the *Nautilus* — all these things led me into a new vein of thought. No; Captain Nemo did not content himself by merely avoiding mankind. His formidable apparatus not only served his tastes, but for some terrible vengeance.

At this time nothing is clear to me. I can only grope in the dark, and only write, so to speak, under the dictation of events.

Furthermore, nothing binds us to Captain Nemo. He knows that escape from the *Nautilus* is impossible. We are not even prisoners on parole. No promise binds us. We are merely captives — prisoners, called guests by courtesy. Ned Land has never given up the idea of recovering his liberty. He will surely take advantage of the very first opportunity that chance may throw in his way.

I shall do the same. Nevertheless, it will not be without a sense of regret that I shall carry away with me all the mystery of the *Nautilus* that the captain's kindness has permitted me to penetrate. For, after all, was he a man to be hated or admired? Was he a victim or an executioner? And then, to be frank, I would like, before I quitted the vessel for ever, to finish this tour of the submarine world whose opening scenes are so splendid. I should like to see the marvels scattered beneath the seas, to behold what man never yet has seen, even if I pay by my life for this insatiable desire for knowledge. What have I discovered so far? Nothing, or scarcely more than nothing, since we have only travelled 6,000 leagues across the Pacific. Still, I know very well that the *Nautilus* is approaching some inhabited land, and that if chance befriend us it would be cruel to sacrifice my companions to my passion for discovery. I must follow – perhaps lead them. But would the opportunity ever present itself? Then man, forcibly deprived of his liberty, wishes for it; the connoisseur – the *savant* fears it.

On the 21st January, 1868, at mid-day, the mate came up to take the sun's altitude. I was on the platform, and, lighting a cigar, I watched the operation. It seemed evident to me that this man did not understand French, for I often spoke my thoughts aloud, and the very words would have drawn from him some involuntary sign of attention if he had understood the language, but he remained impassible and silent.

While he was taking the observation, one of the sailors – the same who had accompanied us in our first excursion to the island of Crespo – came to rub up the lantern glasses. I then examined the fixing of this apparatus whose power is multiplied by lenticular rings arranged as in lighthouses, and which keep the light in the horizontal plane. The electric lamp was so arranged as to yield all its illuminating power. The light was produced in a vacuum, so the regularity and intensity were assured at the same time. By these means the points of graphite between which the light was developed were economized. This economy was very important for Captain Nemo, who could not easily renew the points. But under these conditions the expenditure was almost insensible.

So soon as the *Nautilus* was ready to recommence her submarine journey, I descended to the saloon. The panels were shut down and the course directed to the west.

We skimmed through the waves of the Indian Ocean, a vast

liquid plain containing five hundred and fifty millions of hectares,* and the water is so transparent as to make those giddy who lean over them. The *Nautilus* usually floated at a depth of between 100 and 200 yards (metres). So we passed many days. To any one but myself, who is so passionately fond of the sea, the hours would have appeared, no doubt, long and wearisome; but the daily walks upon the platform, where I was able to drink in the healthy sea-air, the sight of the teeming waters through the crystal side-panels of the saloon, the books, the editing of my memoirs, engaged all my time, and did not leave me a moment for lassitude or *ennui*.

The health of the whole ship's company was still extremely good. The food suited us perfectly, and, for my own part, I could well have dispensed with the variations which Ned Land, in his spirit of protestation, studied hard to supply. Besides, in this even temperature we had no fear of catching cold, while the Madrepore dendrophylle, known in Provence as the "Sea-fennel", and of which a supply remained on board, furnished us by the melted flesh of its polyps with an excellent remedy against coughs.

We saw great numbers of aquatic birds as we proceeded; there were palimpeds, sea-mews and gulls, some of which we shot, and prepared in a particular way, furnished us with an acceptable supply of "water game". Amongst the larger birds which had flown long distances and were resting upon the water, I perceived a magnificent albatross, whose discordant cry is not unlike a donkey's bray. It belongs to the family of "longipennes". The family of totipalmes was represented by the frigate birds, which rapidly brought the fish to the surface, and by a number of "phaetons", or tropic birds, some as large as a pigeon; and of this kind, the red-tipped variety, the white plumage is shaded with rose-colour, which sets off the dark tints of the wings.

The nets captured many sorts of marine tortoise of the convex-backed genus, the shell of which is much sought after. These reptiles, which dive easily, can remain a long time under water by shutting the valve of flesh situated at the external orifice of the nose. Some of them when taken were still asleep beneath the marine animals. The flesh of these tortoises was generally only "middling", but their eggs were most excellent.

* A hectare is 2 acres, 1 rood, 35 perches.

The fish continually roused our admiration as we watched them through the open side-panels of the vessel. I remarked here many species that I had not seen before.

I will notice principally the ostraceans native to the Red Sea, to the Indian Sea, and to that portion of the ocean which washes the coasts of equatorial America. These fish, like the tortoise, the turtle, the echinus, the crustacea, are protected by a cuirass which is neither cretaceous nor stony, but actually bony. Sometimes this covering takes the form of a triangular solid, sometimes of a quadrilateral form. Amongst the former kind I noticed some of the length of an inch and a half, the flesh most wholesome and of pleasant taste. The tail was brown, fins yellow; and I recommend the acclimatization of these fishes in fresh water, to which some sea fish soon accustom themselves. There were also quadrangular ostraceans, bearing four large tubercles on the back; the spotted ostraceans, with white spots on the belly, which grow as tame as birds; the trigons, provided with prickles formed by the prolongation of their bony covering – these fish have been dubbed "sea-pigs", on account of the singular grunting noise they emit; then there were "dromedary" fish, with large humps, whose flesh is hard and coarse.

I also extract from the notes daily taken by Conseil certain fish of the tetrodon genus peculiar to these seas with red backs and white bellies, which are marked by three longitudinal rows of filaments; and electric eels seven feet in length, adorned with most beautiful colours.

Then, as specimens of other genus, there were ovoïds like a brownish-black egg, striped with white bands, and tailless; disdons, regular sea-porcupines, furnished with quills, and able to swell themselves out so as to present the appearance of a ball bristling with spikes. The sea-horses common to all oceans; the flying pegasus, with long snouts and with their pectoral fins so elongated and disposed in the form of wings that they can almost fly – at least rise into the air; pigeon-spatulæ, whose tails are covered with numerous scaly rings; macrognathes, with long jaws – excellent fish, twenty-five centimetres long, and shining with various colours; pale calliomores, with reddish heads; myriads of blennies, striped with black, and shooting to the surface with prodigious velocity, aided by their long pectoral fins; the trichopteres, whose wings are formed of filaments;

trygles, whose liver is considered poison; bodians, which wear a moveable blinker on the eyes; and, finally, the blow-fish, or chætodons, having a long tubular snout; fly-catchers, armed with a gun which neither chassepots nor Remingtons can beat, and which kill the insects by shooting a drop of water at them.

In the eighty-ninth genus of fishes classed by Lacépède, which belongs to the second sub-class of Ossians, characterized by an operculum and a bronchial membrane, I remarked the scorpena, the head of which is furnished with spikes, and which only possesses a single dorsal fin; these animals are supplied with or deficient of little scales according to the sub-genus to which they belong. The second sub-genus gives us specimens of didactyles, thirteen or fourteen inches in length, striped with yellow, with very odd-looking heads. The first sub-genus furnishes many specimens of a curious fish justly named the "sea-frog". It is a large-headed fish, sometimes shrunken, sometimes puffed out, bristling with spines, and sprinkled with tubercles; it has irregular and ugly horns, its tail and body are furnished with a hard skin, its prickles inflict dangerous wounds, and it is altogether horrible and repugnant.

From the 21st to the 23rd of January, the *Nautilus* steamed at the rate of 250 leagues in twenty-four hours; that is to say, 540 miles, or twenty-two miles an hour.

Any fish we recognized on the passage were those which were attracted by our electric light; the greater number were speedily distanced, but some managed to keep up with the *Nautilus* for a time.

On the morning of the 24th, in S. lat. 12° 5′, long. 94° 33′, we sighted the isle of Keeling, planted with magnificent cocoa-nut trees. It was formed by the madrepores, and was visited by Mr. Darwin and Captain Fitzroy. The *Nautilus* gave the shores of this desert island a wide berth. We brought up in the drags numerous specimens of polypi and echinodermes, and some curious shells of molluscs. Some beautiful specimens of the delphinale species were added to Captain Nemo's treasures, to which I contributed an Astræa punctifera, a sort of polype parasite often fixed upon a shell.

Keeling Island soon disappeared, and we steered N.W. towards the southern point of Hindostan.

"Some civilized territory," said Ned, "would be better than

these islands, where there are more savages than goats. In India, sir, there are roads, railways, towns inhabited by English, French, and Hindoos; one could not go for five miles without meeting a fellow-countryman. Is not this the time to stir up Captain Nemo's sense of politeness?"

"No, Ned," I replied, in a determined tone. "Let us go on as we are. The *Nautilus* is approaching habitable continents. We are returning towards Europe. Once arrived in our own seas we shall see what prudence suggests as best to be done. Besides, I do not suppose that Captain Nemo would permit us to go ashore to hunt upon the coasts of Malabar or Coromandel, as we did in the forests of New Guinea."

"Well, but cannot we go without leave?"

I made no reply, for I did not wish to discuss this point. At heart I was ready to go through the adventure to the end.

After leaving Keeling Island our progress was slower and more erratic, leading us at times to great depths. The inclined planes were often used, and which levers within the vessel placed obliquely to the line of flotation. We went in this manner for about two miles, but without ever reaching the enormous depths of the Indian Sea, in which sounding lines of 7,000 fathoms have not touched bottom. The temperature of the low zones is always four degrees above zero. I observed, however, that in the upper zones the water was always colder in the high levels than in the open sea.

On the 25th January the ocean was absolutely deserted, the *Nautilus* passed the whole day at the surface, knocking up great waves with her powerful screw. Who would not, under these circumstances, have mistaken her for an enormous cetacean? I passed the greater portion of the day upon the platform, looking at the sea. There was nothing in sight till about 4 p.m. we saw a large steamer running westward, on the opposite tack. Her masts were for an instant visible, but she could not perceive the *Nautilus*, which was so low in the water. I fancied that this steamer belonged to the Peninsular and Oriental Company, plying between Ceylon and Sydney, touching at King George's Point and Melbourne.

At 5 p.m., before the quickly-passing twilight, which joins day and night in tropical countries, Conseil and I were astonished by a very curious sight.

It was a pretty animal we saw, the appearance of which, according to the ancients, betokened good luck. Aristotle, Pliny, &c., had studied its habits and exhausted in respect of it all the poetry of the *savants* of Greece and Italy. They called them Nautilus and Pompylius; but modern science has not endorsed these appellations, and the mollusc is now known as the argonaut.

If anyone had consulted Conseil, he would have told them that the molluscs are divided into five classes; that the first class, that of the cephaloids, are shell-less sometimes, sometimes tentacular, and include two families – the dibranchiæe and the tetrabranchiæ. The former family includes three genus – the argonaut, the calmar, and the "seiche", while the other has only one genus – the nautilus. If, after this distinction, anyone confuses the argonaut, which is a cetabulifer, or air-carriers, with the nautilus, which is tentaculifer, or carrying tentacles, there can be no excuse for him.

Now this was a shoal of argonauts which were sailing along. We could reckon them by hundreds; they belonged to the tubercular argonauts, which are peculiar to the Indian seas.

These graceful molluscs moved backwards by means of expelling the water they had aspired. Of their eight tentacles, six long and thin floated in the water, while the others, rolled up in a rounded, flattened form, were extended to the wind, and acted as sails. I could easily see the spiral and undulating shells, which Cuvier justly compared to an elegant boat. A boat indeed, for it bears the animal without the animal being fixed to it.

"The argonaut is free to quit its shell," I said to Conseil, "but it does not do so."

"Just like Captain Nemo," replied Conseil, judiciously. "Perhaps it would be better to have called this vessel the *Argonaut*."

For about an hour the *Nautilus* was surrounded by this shoal of molluscs. Suddenly they took alarm, I know not why. At a signal all the sails were furled, the arms were folded, the bodies contracted; the shells, turning over, changed the centre of gravity, and the whole fleet disappeared beneath the waves. It was instantaneous, and no ships in the navy could execute a manœuvre with greater smartness.

Night now fell, and the waves, scarcely ruffled by the breeze, rolled quietly alongside the *Nautilus*.

The following day we crossed the equator at the eighty-second meridian, and passed into the northern hemisphere.

During the day a formidable tribe of sharks kept us company. Terrible animals they are, and render these seas very dangerous. These were the "Phillipi" species, with brown backs and whitish bellies, having eleven rows of teeth; the "eyed" sharks, which have a great black patch surrounded by white on their backs, which resembles an eye; and the "Isabelle" sharks, their round backs spotted with black. These powerful animals often struck the glass panels of the saloon with a violence that was rather alarming. At those times Ned Land got very impatient; he wanted to go up to the surface and harpoon some of the monsters; and some, whose mouths were studded with teeth, disposed like a mosaic, and enormous tiger-sharks, five yards long at least, provoked him incessantly. But the *Nautilus* increased her speed, and soon left the most rapid of the sharks astern.

On the 27th January, opening up the Bay of Bengal, we repeatedly encountered a horrible sight – viz., dead bodies, which were floating at the surface. These were the dead from the Indian towns on the Ganges, and which the vultures, the only scavengers of the country, had not been able to devour. But the sharks had no need of assistance in their horrid banquet.

About 7 p.m. the *Nautilus*, half emerged, was ploughing through a sea of milk. As far as one could see the ocean appeared to be covered with milk. Was this the effect of the lunar rays? No, for the moon was scarcely two days old, and was still below the horizon. The whole sky, although illuminated by the sheen of the stars, appeared dark in contrast with the whiteness of the sea.

Conseil could not believe his eyes, and inquired the cause of this singular phenomenon. Fortunately I was able to answer.

"It is what is called a 'milk sea'," I replied, "a vast expanse of white waves, which is frequently observed upon the coasts of Amboyna and in these latitudes."

"But," said Conseil, "Monsieur will perhaps inform me what is the cause of this, for I do not imagine that the sea is changed to milk."

"No, my lad, this whiteness which astonishes you is due to the presence of myriads of infusoria, a kind of luminous worm, gelatinous and colourless, about as thick as a hair, and not more than $\frac{7}{1000}$ of an inch in length. Some of these animals adhere to each other for many leagues."

"For many leagues!" exclaimed Conseil.

"Yes, and do not seek to ascertain the number of these infusoria. You will never arrive at it, for, if I do not mistake, people have sailed through these milk seas for more than forty miles."

I do not know whether Conseil attended to my advice, but he seemed to be deep in thought, seeking, no doubt, to calculate how many $\frac{7}{1000}$ths of an inch were contained in forty square miles. I continued to observe the phenomenon. For many hours the *Nautilus* drove through these white waves, but towards midnight the sea resumed its usual appearance, but behind us, as far as we could see, the sky, tinged by the reflection from the waves, seemed to be covered with the indistinct gleams of the aurora borealis.

CHAPTER II
A NOVEL PROPOSITION OF CAPTAIN NEMO

ON THE 28TH FEBRUARY, when the *Nautilus* came up to the surface, in 9° 4′ N. lat., we were in view of land about eight miles westward. I noticed first a range of mountains about 2,000 feet high, whose forms were very uneven. After our position had been ascertained and reported, I found that we were close to Ceylon, the pearl which hangs from the lobe of the Indian peninsula.

I searched in the library for some book about this island, which is one of the most fertile in the world. I found a volume entitled, "Ceylon and the Cingalese".

At that moment Captain Nemo appeared with the mate. The captain cast a hasty glance at the map, then turning to me, he said:

"Ceylon is celebrated for its pearl fisheries. Would you like to visit one of them?"

"Very much indeed, captain," I replied.

"Well then, that is easily managed. Only, if we go to the fishery, we must go as fishermen. The annual search has not yet commenced, but never mind. I will give orders to 'pull up' in the Gulf of Manaar, where we shall arrive during the night."

The captain then said something to the mate, who went out

immediately. The *Nautilus* soon descended again, and remained at a depth of about thirty feet.

Map in hand I searched for the Gulf of Manaar. I descried it in the 9th parallel on the N.E. coast of Ceylon.

"Professor Aronnax," said Captain Nemo, "pearls are found in the Bay of Bengal, in the Indian Ocean, in Japanese and Chinese seas, in the South American waters, in the gulfs of Panama and California, but it is at Ceylon that this fishery obtains the best results. We shall soon get there. The divers only assemble in March in the Gulf of Manaar, and there for thirty days their 300 boats reap a glorious harvest. Each boat is fitted for six rowers and six divers. These in two parties descend alternately to a depth of more than 150 feet by means of a heavy stone, which they retain between their feet, and which is fastened to the boat by a rope."

"This," said I, "was the primitive method. Is it still used?"

"Yes," replied the captain, "even now when the fisheries belong to the English, to whom they were ceded by the Treaty of Amiens in 1802."

"It seems to me, captain, that the diver's dress you have would suffice in this expedition."

"Yes, for the poor fishers cannot remain long under water. Perceval, an Englishman, in his 'Travels in Ceylon', spoke highly of a Caffre, who remained for five minutes under water, but I can scarcely credit it. I know that some divers can stay for fifty-seven seconds, and very skilful ones for eighty-seven, which is very seldom done, and when they return to the boat, these unfortunate fellows bleed from the nose and ears. I believe the average time these divers can exist under water to be thirty seconds, during which time they detach all the pearl oysters they can seize, but these men do not live long as a rule; they are weakened, ulcers form in their eyes, sores come upon their bodies, and they are frequently seized with apoplexy at the bottom of the sea."

"Yes," I replied, "it is an unpleasant avocation, and only to satisfy a caprice. But what number of oysters can a boat capture during the day?"

"From 40,000 to 50,000. It is said that in 1814 the English Government, having taken the fishing on its own account, the divers, during twenty days' working, brought up 76,000,000 of oysters."

"Well, at any rate these fishers are well paid?"

"Not at all. In Panama they make only one dollar a week. More frequently they receive a halfpenny for every pearl oyster; and how many do they bring up which contain no pearl!"

"A halfpenny for these poor people who enrich their masters! It is iniquitous."

"Well, Monsieur, you and your companions shall visit the Manaar Bank, and if by chance we find some early fisher there we will see him at work."

"That's a bargain, captain."

"By-the-by, M. Aronnax, are you afraid of sharks?"

"Sharks!" I exclaimed.

This appeared a somewhat difficult question, to me at least.

"Well?" asked the captain.

"I must confess," I said, "that I am not yet very familiar with that genus."

"Well, we people here are accustomed to them, and so will you be in time. Besides, we are armed, and as we go along we may perhaps have a shark hunt. It is a very interesting occupation. So to-morrow, Monsieur; and very early."

And saying this in an airy manner, Captain Nemo quitted the saloon.

If you were invited to a bear hunt on the Swiss mountains what would you say? "Well, to-morrow we will go bear-hunting." If asked to hunt lions on the plains of the Atlas, or the tiger in an Indian jungle, you would reply, "All right. It seems we are going to hunt the lion or the tiger (as the case may be)." But if you were asked to hunt the shark in his native element, you would, perhaps, request a little time to consider before accepting the polite invitation.

I passed my hand over my forehead as I mused, and found it covered with a cold perspiration.

"Let us think over this," I said to myself; "and take our time. To hunt otters, as we did, in the forest of the Isle of Crespo is one thing, but to go down to the bottom of the sea where one is nearly certain to encounter sharks is another. I know very well that in some places – the Andaman Islands, for instance – the negroes do not hesitate to attack the sharks, a dagger in one hand a lasso in the other, but I also am aware that many of the venture-some individuals never return. Besides, I am not a negro; and even if I were, I do not think a little hesitation would be at all out of place under the circumstances."

And so I dreamt of sharks, and of their vast jaws armed with rows of teeth capable of snapping a man in half. I already began to experience a curiously unpleasant sensation about the waist. But I could not understand the easy way in which the captain had given this deplorable invitation; he had said it in much the same way as one would ask you to go fox-hunting.

"However," I thought, "Conseil will not want to go, and that will give me an excuse to let the captain go without me."

As for Ned Land, I was obliged to confess that I was not so sure of his sagacity. Any peril, however great, had always an attraction for his bellicose nature. So I returned to my book on Ceylon, but between the lines I could perceive the formidable jaws opening still.

At this moment Conseil and Ned returned with quite a cheerful air; they little knew what was in store for them.

"Faith, Monsieur! your Captain Nemo – may the devil take him – has made us a very nice offer."

"Ah!" I exclaimed, "you know—"

"If Monsieur has no objection," replied Conseil, "the captain has asked us to accompany Monsieur to the magnificent pearl fisheries of Ceylon. He made the suggestion like a gentleman."

"He said nothing more than that?"

"Nothing," replied Ned, "except that he had spoken to you on the subject."

"So, in fact, he gave you no details?"

"None. You will accompany us, won't you?"

"I? Certainly. I perceive you like the idea, Master Land."

"Yes, it is curious, very curious!"

"A little dangerous, perhaps?" I insinuated.

"Dangerous?" exclaimed Ned. "A little excursion on an oyster-bank – dangerous?"

It was evident that Captain Nemo had decided that it would be useless to awake the idea of sharks in the minds of my companions. I already looked upon them with a pitying glance, as if they had lost a limb. Ought I to warn them? Yes, doubtless, but I did not quite know how to set about it.

"Monsieur," said Conseil, "will Monsieur tell us how they set about this oyster fishing."

"The fishing itself, or the incidents connected with it?"

"About the fishing," said the Canadian. "Before getting to the ground, we ought to know something of it."

"Well, then, if you will sit down, I will tell you all I have read upon the subject."

Ned and Conseil took their seats, and suddenly the Canadian asked:

"What is a pearl?"

"My brave Ned," I replied, "to a poet a pearl is a tear of the sea; to the Orientals it is a solidified dew-drop; to ladies it is a jewel of oblong shape, of a material like mother-of-pearl, which they wear on the finger, the neck, or ears; for the chemist it is a mixture of the phosphate and the carbonate of lime with a little gelatine; and, finally, for naturalists it is merely a morbid secretion of the organ which produces the mother-of-pearl in some bivalves."

"Branch of mollusca – class acephali; order testacea," said Conseil.

"Precisely, Professor Conseil. Now amongst these testacea, the sea-ear iris, the turbot, the tridanæ, and all those which secrete the mother-of-pearl – that is to say, that blue, bluish-violet, or white substance which lines the interior of their shells – are not unlikely to produce pearls."

"And mussels also?" asked the Canadian.

"Yes, mussels in certain districts of the coast of Scotland, Wales, Ireland, Saxony, Bohemia, and France."

"Ah! in future I will pay them a little attention," replied Ned.

"But I said the mollusc that really forms the pearl is the pearl-oyster – the Meleagrina margaritifera pintadines. The pearl is only a nacreous concretion which is disposed in a globular shape. It adheres to the oyster-shell, or encrusts itself in the body of the animal. Upon the shells the pearl adheres, in the flesh it is loose; but in any case it possesses a little hard nucleus, which may be a barren-egg – a grain of sand around which the nacreous matter has been disposed, during many years, by delicate and concentric layers."

"Are many pearls found in one oyster?" asked Conseil.

"Yes; there are certain 'pintadines' which form a regular casket of pearls. I have heard of an oyster – though I rather doubt the story – which contained no less than 150 sharks!"

"A hundred and fifty sharks!" exclaimed Ned.

"Did I say sharks?" I cried quickly, "I meant pearls; sharks would be absurd."

"Of course," said Conseil. "But Monsieur has not yet told us how the pearls are obtained."

"In many ways, and frequently when the pearls adhere to the shells, the divers tear them with pincers. But more commonly the 'pintadines' are extended on the esparto fibres which are laid on the banks. They then die in the open air, and at the end of ten days they are in a satisfactory state of putrefaction. They are then thrown into large reservoirs of salt water, and are then opened and washed. At this period the real labour of the sorters begins. First they separate the layers of mother-of-pearl, known in commerce as *franche argentée*, bastard whites and bastard blacks, which are sent off in cases of 200 or 300 pounds each. The 'parenchyma' of the oyster is then raised, boiled, and sifted for the pearls."

"I suppose pearls vary in price according to size?" said Conseil.

"Not only according to size, but according to shape and the 'water', or colour, and their 'orient', that is the 'shot' coloured hue which is so beautiful. The most beautiful are called virgin pearls, or paragons; they form only in the tissue of the mollusc. They are white, often opaque, but sometimes of an opaline clearness, and more usually oval or rounded. The spherical pearls are made into bracelets, the oval into pendants, and, being the most valuable, they are sold singly. The other pearls adhere to the oyster-shell, and, not being so good, are sold by weight. Finally, in the inferior class come the small pearls, known as 'seed-pearls', which are sold by the measure, and are chiefly used to embroider church furniture."

"But is it a long or difficult job to separate the pearls according to size?" asked Ned.

"No; this work is performed by means of sieves or screens of various meshes. The pearls that remain in the largest sieves are reckoned of the first class, those that do not pass through the medium screens are counted in the second class, and those are called 'seed-pearls', for which the smallest sieves, pierced with 900 to 1,000 holes, are used."

"It is ingenious, but I see the classing of pearls is only a mechanical operation," said Conseil. "But can Monsieur tell us what the cultivation of oyster-beds yields to the owner?"

"According to my information, the annual value of the Ceylon fisheries is three millions of sharks."

"Of francs, I suppose," said the Canadian.

"I mean francs – three millions of francs. But I do not think the fisheries yield as much as formerly. It is the same with the American beds, and in fact we may estimate nine millions as the whole value of the pearl fisheries."

"But are there not some celebrated pearls which command a very high price?"

"Yes, my lad. They say Cæsar offered Servillia a pearl estimated at 120,000 francs of our money."

"I have even heard it stated that some woman of antiquity used to drink pearls dissolved in vinegar," said Ned.

"Cleopatra," replied Conseil.

"That must have been very unpleasant," added Ned.

"Detestable, friend Ned; and a little glass of vinegar that cost 1,500,000 francs *was* dear!"

"I am sorry I didn't marry that woman," said the Canadian, raising his arm in a menacing manner.

"Ned Land Cleopatra's husband!" exclaimed Conseil.

"But I ought to marry, Conseil, and it is not my fault that the business has not come off. I have even purchased a necklace of pearls for Kate Tender, my *fiancée*, who, meanwhile, married somebody else; the necklace cost only a dollar and a half, and yet, if Monsieur will believe me, the pearls would not have passed through the biggest sieve."

"My good Ned," I said, laughing, "they were artificial pearls, simple glass drops filled with essence of orient."

"Is that expensive?" asked the Canadian.

"Not at all. It is only the silvery substance of the scales of the bleak collected in the water and preserved in ammonia. It has no value."

"Perhaps that is the reason why Kate married the other fellow," said Ned, philosophically.

"But," said I, "to return to our high-priced pearls. I do not believe any sovereign ever possessed any so valuable as those Captain Nemo has."

"This?" said Conseil, indicating a splendid one in a glass case.

"Certainly. I do not think I am wrong in estimating it as worth two millions of—"

"Francs!" said Conseil, quickly.

"Yes, two millions of francs; and I daresay that sum would not repay the captain for the trouble of obtaining it."

"Eh!" said Ned; "but who knows that we may not get such another to-morrow."

"Bah!" said Conseil.

"Why not?"

"What would be the use of millions to us here?"

"On board, no. But otherwise—"

"Oh! otherwise," echoed Conseil, with an upward toss of his head.

"Master Land is right, though," said I, "and if we could bring back to Europe a pearl worth a few millions there will be at once a proof of the truth and success of our expedition."

"I believe it," said the Canadian.

"But," said Conseil, who always came back to the instructive side of things, "is this pearl-fishing dangerous?"

"No," said I quickly, "not if you take proper care."

"What risks do you run?" asked Ned. "The taste of some mouthfuls of sea water?"

"Just so, Ned. By-the-by, are you afraid of sharks?"

I asked this in as airy a tone as I could assume.

"I?" exclaimed Ned. "A harpooner by profession? Why I laugh at them!"

"But," said I, "it is not the question of fishing for them, hauling them on board ship, and cutting them up, and throwing the heart into the sea."

"Then it is—"

"Yes, exactly."

"In the water?"

"Yes, in the water."

"Faith, with a stout harpoon, I don't know. You understand that these sharks are very ill-made beasts. They must turn on their backs to snap you up, and meantime—"

Ned's way of pronouncing "snap you up" made my blood run cold.

"Very well. And, Conseil, what do *you* think of the sharks?"

"I will be frank with Monsieur," he said.

"So much the better," I thought.

"If Monsieur will encounter the sharks, his faithful servant will also encounter them by his side."

CHAPTER III
A PEARL OF TEN MILLIONS

NIGHT CAME. I went to bed, but slept badly. The sharks played an important part in my dreams. I was awakened by the steward at four o'clock. I got up at once, and, dressing quickly, passed into the saloon.

There Captain Nemo was waiting for me.

"M. Aronnax," said he, "are you ready to start?"

"I am."

"Will you follow me, please?"

"And my companions also, captain?"

"They have gone, and are waiting for us."

"Shall we not put on our diving dresses?" I asked.

"Not yet. I have not permitted the *Nautilus* to come very close to the shore, and we are still at some distance from the Manaar Bank; but the launch is ready to take us to the exact spot, and will save us a long way. It has the apparatus on board, and we can put our dresses on at the moment we commence our submarine journey."

Captain Nemo then led the way towards the central staircase to the platform. There we found Ned and Conseil, delighted at the "pleasure party" in prospect. Five sailors were resting on their oars in the boat alongside.

Day had not yet appeared. The sky was cloudy, and but few stars were visible. I looked towards the land, but could descry nothing but a dark line across the horizon from S.W. to N.W. The *Nautilus*, having run up the western side of Ceylon during the night, was west of the bay, or rather of the gulf formed between the "main island" and the island of Manaar. There, beneath the dark waters, lay the bank of pintadines, an inexhaustible pearl-field twenty miles in length. Captain Nemo, Ned Land, and I took our places in the stern-sheets of the launch. The coxswain took the tiller, the sailors were ready, the "painter" was "cast-off", and we started.

The course was to the south; the rowers did not hurry. I noticed that, while they pulled strongly, they rested for about ten seconds between each stroke, like man-o'-war's men. As the boat proceeded the bubbles broke crisply upon the dark waves like drops of molten lead. A slight swell rolling in from the offing gave some motion to the boat, and broke beneath the bows in curling waves.

We were all silent. What was Captain Nemo thinking about? Perhaps of the land we were approaching, and which was too near for him, as it was still too far for the Canadian. As for Conseil, he was with us merely as a spectator. About half-past five the first tints on the horizon showed the coast-line more clearly. It appeared to be somewhat flat on the east side, but became more undulating towards the south. We were still five miles away, and the coast was not very distinctly seen, owing to the mist. Between us and the shore nothing was to be seen. Not a diver nor his boat. A death-like silence reigned in this trysting-place of pearl-fishers. So, as Captain Nemo had said, we had arrived a month too soon.

At six o'clock the day broke with that suddenness peculiar to tropical climes. The sun's rays pierced the bank of clouds on the eastern horizon, and the orb ascended rapidly in the heavens. I could now see the land distinctly, with the trees scattered here and there upon it.

The launch approached the island of Manaar, which trended to the south. Captain Nemo rose from his seat, and gazed over the sea.

At a sign from him the anchor was let go, and the chain ran out; but not far, for the depth was not much more than a yard; and just here was the highest portion of the pearl-oyster-beds. The launch immediately swung to the ebb-tide.

"Well, here we are, M. Aronnax," said the captain. "You see this bay is well enclosed. Here, in a month's time, will assemble numerous fishing-boats, and in these waters the divers will go boldly to work. This bay is wonderfully formed for this kind of fishing. It is protected from the strongest winds, and the sea is never very high, which is a favourable circumstance for the divers. We will now put on our dresses, and commence our excursion."

I made no reply, and, all the time gazing at the "suspected" sea of sharks, I was assisted into my dress by one of the sailors. Captain Nemo and my companions were also inducted into their habiliments. None of the sailors of the *Nautilus* were to go with us.

We were soon clothed up to the neck in the india-rubber garments, and the air apparatus was fastened to our shoulders by braces. There was no necessity to use the Ruhmkorff lighting apparatus. Before putting on my helmet I spoke to the captain about it.

"They would be useless," he said, "as we shall not go to any great depth, and the sunlight will suffice for us. Besides, it would not be very prudent to carry an electric lamp under these waters. The light might attract some dangerous inhabitants inopportunely."

As Captain Nemo spoke, I turned towards Ned and Conseil. They had already put on their helmets, and could neither hear nor reply.

One last question I must address to the captain.

"Our arms," I said; "what about our guns?"

"Guns, for what?" he said. "Do not mountaineers attack bears with daggers? and is not the steel more certain than lead? Here is a true bit of steel for you. Stick it in your waist-belt and let's go."

I again looked at my friends. They were also furnished like ourselves, and besides the dagger, Ned Land brandished an enormous harpoon, which he had placed in the boat before we left the *Nautilus*. Then following the captain's example, I put on my head-piece, and the air-reservoirs immediately began to act.

An instant after the sailors let us gently down into the water, and at about ten yards from the surface we touched a fine sand.

Captain Nemo signed to us; we followed him, and descending a gentle slope, we disappeared under the waves.

Once beneath the water, the fearsome ideas I had hitherto indulged disappeared, and I was quite calm. The ease with which I was able to move, gave me confidence, and the unusual sights around me captivated my imagination.

The sun already gave us sufficient light. The smallest objects were perceptible. After walking for ten minutes, we were about six yards beneath the surface, and the sand became more level.

Shoals of fish, as we advanced, rose up before us like snipe in a bog. These fish were of the monoptera genus, having no other fin than the tail. I recognized the Javanese, a true serpent, about three feet long, which might easily be mistaken for the conger, without the line of gold on his sides. Amongst the stromatas, whose bodies are very compressed and oval-shaped, I observed "parus" of brilliant colours, with scythe-like dorsal fin, an eatable fish, and which, when dried and salted, makes an excellent food called *karawade*; there were tranquebars that belong to the apsiphoroïdes, the bodies of which are covered with a scaly protection.

Meantime the light increased as the sun rose higher in the heavens. The nature of the ground changed by degrees. A regular causeway succeeded to the fine firm sand, and the stones were clothed with a carpet of molluscs and zoophytes. Amid the specimens of these two branches, I remarked the placenes, with thin and unequal shells, a sort of ostracea peculiar to the Red Sea and the Indian Ocean; some orange lucinæ with orbicular shells, and many other interesting varieties, panopines, oculines, &c. In the midst of these living plants, and beneath the hydrophytes, lay legions of articulates, chiefly the *raniæ dentalæ*, the carapace of which make a slightly rounded triangle. A hideous animal, and one I have encountered many times, was the enormous crab observed by Mr. Darwin, on which nature has bestowed the instinct and strength necessary to live upon cocoa-nuts. It ascends the trees on the beach, knocks off the nuts, which are cracked by the fall, and it then "prises" them open with its powerful claws. Here beneath these transparent waves this animal moves with incredible velocity. Towards seven o'clock we reached the oyster-beds, on which the pearl-oysters reproduce themselves by millions. These valuable molluscs adhere to the rocks and are there strongly attached by the byssus which will not allow them to move. In this respect, the oyster is inferior to the lowly mussel, to which nature has granted certain powers of locomotion.

Captain Nemo indicated a prodigious number of pintadines, and I could understand that the supply was really inexhaustible, for the creative power of nature is beyond man's destructive tastes. Ned Land, faithful to his instinct, hastened to fill his net with the best oysters he could gather.

But we could not stay, we were obliged to follow Captain Nemo, who appeared to be striking out paths known to him alone. The ground was getting higher evidently, and sometimes my arm, when held up, was above the surface of the water. The levels of the beds were very irregular, we often turned high rocks worn into pyramid shape. In their gloomy fissures enormous crustacea, standing on their long limbs like war-machines, looked at us with fixed eyes, while beneath our feet were many others.

A large grotto now opened before us, excavated amid a pictur-esque mass of rock, covered with thick submarine flora. The grotto at first sight seemed very dark indeed. The sun's rays seemed to be extinguished gradually, and the vague transparency might fitly be termed "drowned light".

Captain Nemo entered it, however; we all followed him. My eyes soon got accustomed to the gloom. I perceived that the springings of the arches were irregular, and supported by natural pillars standing on broad granite bases like Tuscan columns. Why did our guide lead us into this submarine crypt? I was to know ere long.

Having descended a somewhat steep decline, we reached a kind of circular pit. Here Captain Nemo stopped and pointed out to us something I had never seen before.

It was an oyster of most extraordinary size, a gigantic tridacne, a shell which would have held a lake of holy water, a vase whose breadth was more than two and a half yards, and, therefore, larger than that which was in the saloon of the *Nautilus*.

I approached this enormous mollusc. It was fixed to a granite slab, and there it grew by itself beneath the calm waters of the grotto. I estimated its weight at 600 pounds. Now an oyster like this would contain about thirty pounds' weight of meat, and one must have the stomach of a Gargantua to swallow a few dozen of such "natives".

The captain was aware of the existence of this bivalve; evi-dently it was not the first time he had visited it, and I thought that in coming hither he had only wished to show us a natural curiosity. I was mistaken. Captain Nemo had a personal interest in ascertaining the actual condition of this tridacne.

The shells were open. The captain thrust his dagger between them so as to prevent them shutting again. He then raised the membraneous tissue with its fringed edges which formed the covering of the oyster. There, between the plaits, I saw a loose pearl of the size of a small cocoa-nut. Its globular form, its perfect transparency, the splendid "water", stamped it as a jewel of in-estimable price. Actuated by an impulse of curiosity, I extended my hand to seize it and weigh it, but the captain stopped me, shook his head, and, withdrawing his dagger, permitted the shells to close suddenly.

I then understood his motives. By leaving this pearl hidden

within the tridacne, he allowed it to grow insensibly. With each year of existence the mollusc added new concentric rings. The captain alone was acquainted with this grotto, in which this admirable fruit of nature was ripening; he alone would reap it, so to speak, for his famous museum. Perhaps, after the fashion of the Chinese and Indians, he had brought the pearl into existence, by introducing into the folds of the mollusc a piece of glass or iron, which became covered by the nacreous substance by degrees. In any case, comparing this pearl to those which I already knew, and to those which glittered amid the captain's collection, I should say its value was ten millions of francs at least (£400,000). It was a magnificent natural curiosity, and not a jewel, for there are no ladies' ears capable of sustaining such a weight.

Our visit to this "aristocrat" tridacne was over. Captain Nemo left the grotto, and we remounted to the oyster-beds into those clear waters not yet disturbed by divers.

We walked singly, in an easy sort of way, stopping or advancing as suited our respective fancies. For my part I had no thought for the dangers I had previously conjured up. We were advancing sensibly towards the surface, and my head soon rose high above it as I stood in less than four feet of water. Conseil drew near me, and, putting his helmeted head close to mine, "made eyes" at me in the most friendly manner. But this high ground did not extend for any great distance, and we soon were below the surface of our *element*. I believe I am entitled to say so now!

Ten minutes after, Captain Nemo stopped suddenly. I fancied he had only halted in order to retrace his steps. No. By a gesture he directed us to crouch near him, at the bottom of a large fissure. He pointed towards a particular spot. I looked steadily at it. About six yards off a shadow appeared and fell on the ground. The nervous idea of sharks crossed my mind. But I was wrong, and this time we had not to encounter these ocean monsters. It was a man – a living man, an Indian: a poor devil of a diver, no doubt, who came to glean before the corn was cut. I could perceive his canoe anchored some feet above his head. He dived and ascended again; a stone which he held between his feet (a cord that secured him to the boat) was sufficient to cause him to descend rapidly. This was his whole apparatus. As he reached the bottom he fell upon his knees and filled his net with pinta-dines, collected indiscriminately. He then ascended, emptied the net, replaced the stone, and recommenced his operations, which never exceeded thirty seconds' duration.

The diver did not perceive us. The shadow of the rock hid us; and, besides, how could this poor Indian suppose that beings like himself would be there under water watching his movements, not losing a detail?

Many times he ascended and dived again. He did not bring up more than ten oysters at a time, for he was obliged to tear some away by main force; and how many of these oysters had no pearls, for which he was risking his life!

I was watching him with fixed attention; his movements were regular, and during half an hour no danger threatened him. I was getting accustomed in watching this interesting fishing, when suddenly, as the Indian was kneeling on the ground, I saw him make a gesture of terror, rise up, and spring for his boat.

I understood the position. A gigantic shadow appeared above the terrified diver. It was a shark of the largest size, which was swimming diagonally – eyes flaming, and with extended jaws.

I was petrified with horror.

The voracious fish, by a vigorous stroke of his fins, darted towards the Indian, who threw himself aside, and avoided the open jaws of the shark, but not the stroke of his tail, for he received a blow in the chest which stretched him on the ground. This was the work of a few seconds. The shark came again to the attack, and, turning on his back, seemed about to cut the Indian in two, when Captain Nemo jumped up, poniard in hand, and, rushed straight at the monster, ready for a "hand-to-hand" encounter.

The shark perceived this new adversary just as he was about to snap up the unfortunate diver, and, turning on his belly, he went for the captain.

I can still see Captain Nemo, as he stood.

With wonderful self-possession he coolly waited the attack of this enormous shark, and, when it rushed at him, the captain, jumping aside with surprising dexterity, avoided the contact and plunged his dagger into the belly of the animal. But all was not over. A terrible fight ensued.

The shark seemed to roar, as it were. The blood poured in torrents from the wounds. The sea was tinged with red, and through this opaque liquid I could not perceive how the fight was waging.

I saw nothing more until the moment when, as the ensan-guined waves cleared away, I perceived the undaunted captain holding to one of the shark's fins, and dealing him blow after blow, but unable to deal a mortal one at the heart. The shark in its struggles so agitated the water that I could scarcely keep my position.

I wished to get to the captain's assistance, but I was nailed by horror to the spot.

I looked on with haggard eye. I saw the varying fortunes of the combat. The captain fell upon the ground, overturned by the enormous mass that weighed upon him. Then the shark's jaws opened like enormous shears, and would have made an end of the captain, had not Ned Land, quick as thought, precipitated himself, harpoon in hand, upon the shark, and driven the terrible weapon into his side.

The waves were immediately a mass of blood, and rolled in large billows as the shark beat them in his struggles. Ned Land had struck home; this was the monster's last gasp. Pierced to the heart, he beat out his life in spasmodic writhings, the shock of which upset Conseil.

Meantime, Ned Land had gone to the captain's assistance, and he, again on his feet, hastened to the Indian, cut the cord which fastened the stone, and, taking him in his arms, by a vigorous stroke ascended to the surface. We all followed, and, in a few minutes, most miraculously preserved from death, we reached the diver's boat.

Captain Nemo's first care was to restore this unfortunate man to life. I was afraid he would not succeed – I hoped he would, for the poor man's immersion had not lasted long – but the blow from the shark's tail might have been fatal.

Happily, by vigorous rubbing, I perceived the diver regaining consciousness. He opened his eyes, and great was his astonish-ment to perceive four great copper-helmeted heads leaning over him.

And still greater must have been his surprise, when Captain Nemo, taking a string of pearls from his dress, placed them in his hand. This munificent present from the man of the seas to the poor Cingalese was accepted with trembling hands. His startled eyes showed that he did not know to what superhuman beings he owed at once his fortune and his life.

At a sign from the captain we regained the oyster-beds, and retracing our steps, we reached the anchor of the launch in about half an hour. Once again on board, we with the sailors' assistance took off our dresses.

Captain Nemo's first words were addressed to the Canadian.

"Thank you, Master Land," he said.

"It was only a 'return match'," said Ned. "I owed you that."

A wan smile flitted across the captain's features, and that was all.

"To the *Nautilus*," he cried.

The boat flew over the waves. Some minutes later we encountered the dead body of the shark floating on the surface.

In its black marking at the extremities of the fins, I recognized the terrible melanopteron of the Indian Seas, sharks properly so called. Its length was twenty-five feet, its enormous mouth occupied a third of its body. It was a full-grown specimen, as we could perceive by the six rows of teeth, disposed in the form of an isosceles triangle in its upper jaw.

Conseil regarded it from an entirely scientific point of view, and I am sure he classed it, and not without reason, amongst the cartilaginous animals – order of chondropterygians with fixed gills, family selacian – genus sharks.

While I was looking at it, a dozen of its voracious relatives appeared close by; but, without noticing us, they threw themselves upon the corpse, and fought for the fragments.

At half-past nine we were on board the *Nautilus* again.

There I began to reflect upon the incidents of our excursion to the Manaar Bank. Two reflections suggested themselves at once. One was the unparalleled bravery of Captain Nemo; the other, his devotion to a human being, a representative of the race he shunned. Whatever he might hint to the contrary, I was persuaded that this extraordinary man was not entirely devoid of heart.

When I said as much to him he replied, with some little emotion, "That Indian, Monsieur, is an inhabitant of an oppressed country. I am, and shall be to my last day, such an one myself!"

CHAPTER IV
THE RED SEA

DURING THE DAY the island of Ceylon disappeared from view, and the *Nautilus* steamed at about twenty miles an hour into the labyrinth of canals that separate the Maldive from the Lacadive Isles. We skirted the island of Kitlan, of madreporic formation, which was discovered by Vasca de Gama in 1499, and is one of the nineteen large islands of the Lacadive group, situated between 10° and 14° 30′ N. lat. and 69° and 50° 72′ E. long. We had now made 16,220 miles, or 7,500 leagues, since our departure from Japan.

Next day, 30th January, when the *Nautilus* rose to the surface, no land was in sight. We steered N.N.W. towards the Sea of Oman, between Arabia and Hindostan, and which is the mouth of the Persian Gulf.

There was evidently no egress. Whither was Captain Nemo leading us? I could not say. This did not satisfy Ned, who asked me where we were going.

"We are going," said I, "whither the captain's fancy leads us."

"This fancy will not lead us very far, then. There is no other outlet to the Persian Gulf, and if we enter it we shall soon have to retrace our steps."

"Well, then, we must come back again, Master Land; and if, after the Persian Gulf, the *Nautilus* chooses to visit the Red Sea, the Strait of Bab-el-Mandeb is always free to us."

"I need scarcely tell you, sir," replied Ned Land, "that the Red Sea is closed equally with the Gulf, since the Isthmus of Suez is not yet cut through; and if it were, a mysterious vessel like ours would not risk herself in a canal intersected with sluices. So the Red Sea is not our road to Europe."

"But I have not said that we were going back to Europe."

"What do you think, then?"

"I suppose that, after having seen the curious localities of Arabia and Egypt, the *Nautilus* will go back into the Indian Ocean again, perhaps through the Mozambique Channel, perhaps outside Madagascar, so as to gain the Cape of Good Hope."

"And when we have reached the Cape?" asked the Canadian, with peculiar insistence.

"Well, then we shall explore that part of the Atlantic we do not yet know. Ah! friend Ned, you are getting tired of this submarine travelling. You are *blasé* with the incessant wonders of the sea, varied though they be. For my own part, I shall be sorry to come to the end of a voyage such as is given to few men to enjoy."

"But are you aware that we have been shut up in the *Nautilus* nearly three months?"

"No, Ned, I did not know it. I do not wish to – and I reckon neither hours nor days."

"But what is the end to be?"

"The end will come in good time. Besides, we can do nothing, and there is no use talking about it. If you should come to me and say: 'I see a chance of escape for us,' I would go into the question with you; but that is not the case now, and I tell you frankly I do not think that Captain Nemo will ever venture into European waters."

By this short conversation you will perceive that I was almost as much attached to the *Nautilus* as its commander. Ned Land brought the interview to a conclusion by the following muttered words:

"That is all very well, but in my opinion, when one is tired of the thing, there is no fun in it."

For four days the *Nautilus* explored the Sea of Oman at various depths, and with varying speed. We appeared to be sailing at random, as if there were some hesitation respecting our route, but we did not pass the Tropic of Cancer.

As we left this sea we caught a glimpse of Muscat, the most important town of the Oman territory. I admired its strange aspect in the midst of the black rocks surrounding it, and against which the white houses and forts stood out in strong relief. The round domes of the mosques, the tapering points of the minarets, the fresh green terraces, were all before us. But it was only a fleeting vision, for the *Nautilus* again plunged under Oman's green water.

We afterwards coasted the Arabian shore for six miles, and its line of undulating mountains dotted with ancient ruins.

On the 5th of February we entered the Gulf of Aden, a regular funnel introduced into the neck of Bab-el-Mandeb, which serves as the entrance for the waters of the Indian Ocean to the Red Sea.

Next day the *Nautilus* lay off Aden, which is perched up upon a promontory united to the mainland by a narrow isthmus – a miniature Gibraltar, the fortifications having been built by the English in 1839. I could see the octagon minarets of the town, which was formerly one of the richest commercial stations on the coast.

I was certain that Captain Nemo would now retrace his steps, but, to my surprise, he did nothing of the kind.

On the 7th we entered Bab-el-Mandeb, which in Arabic signifies "Gate of Tears". The strait is twenty miles wide and about thirty long, and, for the *Nautilus* at full speed, the passage was accomplished in less than an hour. But I saw nothing, not even the island of Perim, by which the British Government has strengthened the position of Aden. Too many steamers of all nations passed this strait for the *Nautilus* to venture to show herself, so we prudently kept under water. At noon we were in the Red Sea. This sea, celebrated in Bible history, is scarcely refreshed by rain, nor is it supplied by any important river; it is subject to an excessive evaporation, and loses each year a layer of water about two yards high. A singular gulf, which, enclosed, and under similar conditions to a lake, would be dried up, and in this respect inferior to its neighbours the Caspian or the Dead Sea, the levels of which have only descended to the points where their evaporation exactly equals the amount of water received by them.

The Red Sea is between 1,500 and 1,600 miles long, and about 150 miles in width. At the time of the Ptolemys and the Roman Empire, it was the great commercial artery of the world; and the cutting of the Suez Canal will restore it to its former importance, a result that the railway has already partly brought about.

I did not even seek to understand the caprice of the captain, which had decided him to enter the Red Sea; but I quite approved of this course. He went at less speed, sometimes at the surface, sometimes plunging down to escape observation; and I was able to notice both the upper and lower parts of this curious sea.

On the 8th of February, at dawn, we sighted Mocha, a town now ruined; whose walls would fall down at the report of a single cannon. It was formerly an important city, enclosing six public markets, twenty-six mosques, and the walls, defended by fourteen fortresses, were more than two miles in circumference.

The *Nautilus* approached close to the African side, where the depth of water is greater. There, in a medium as clear as crystal, we were able to gaze upon the beautiful corals and the enormous masses of rock covered with algæ and fuci. It was indescribable! What a variety of landscapes there were among those rocks and islands which border on the Libyan coasts. But it was on the eastern side that these appeared in full beauty, and the *Nautilus* was not long in reaching them. This was on the Tehama coast, for there not only did the expanse of the zoophytes flourish below the level of the sea, but they entwined themselves picturesquely some feet above the surface. These were more extensive but less beautiful than those which were kept fresher by the surrounding vitality of the waters.

How many pleasant hours I passed at the open panels of the saloon. What numbers of specimens of submarine flora I admired by the gleam of the electric light. Mushroom-shaped fungi, red-coloured sea-anemones, amongst others, the *thalassianthus aster*; tubipores like flutes, which only waited the breath of the "great god Pan"; shells peculiar to this sea, which were resting in the holes made by the madrepores, and the bases of which were turned in a short spiral; and finally, what I had never seen in its natural polype state – the common sponge.

The class of sponges, first in the group of polypi, has been precisely created by this curious product, the uses of which are indisputable. The sponge is not a vegetable, as some naturalists think it, but an animal of the lowest order, a polype inferior to the coral. There is no doubt of its being an animal, and one cannot even adopt the classification of the ancients, who put it between the plants and animals. I ought to mention that naturalists do not agree respecting the mode of organization of the sponge. Some say it is a polypus; others, such as Mr. Milne-Edwards, that it is an isolated species, and unique.

The class of sponges include about 300 species, which are met with in many seas, and even in water-courses, where they received the name of "fluviatiles". But they are chiefly found in the Mediterranean, in the Grecian Archipelago, on the coasts of Syria, and in the Red Sea. There the softest and most beautiful sponges grow, and rise to a value of six pounds sterling, such as the white Syrian sponge, Barbary sponge, &c. But as I could not hope to study these zoophytes in the Levant, from which we were separated by the Isthmus of Suez, I was obliged to content myself by examining them in the Red Sea.

I called Conseil to me while the *Nautilus* slowly passed by the beautiful rocks of the eastern coast at about ten yards below the surface.

Sponges of all shapes and sizes were there, pediculated, foliated, globulous, and digital. They justified the appellations of baskets, vases, distaffs, elk-horns, lion's feet, peacock-tail, Neptune's glove, which have been bestowed upon them by the fishermen, more poetical than naturalists. From the fibrous tissue coated with a semi-gelutinous substance, a thread of water is incessantly escaping, which, having carried life into each cell, is expelled by a contractile movement. This substance disappears after the death of the polypus, which, when putrifying, disengages ammonia. Nothing is then left but the horny or gelutinous fibres, forming the domestic sponge, which takes a russet tinge, and is used in various ways, according to its elasticity, permeability, or resistance to maceration.

These polypes adhere to rocks, to shells of molluscs, and even to the stalks of hydrophytes. They garnish the smallest crevices, some extending outwards, others close or hanging down like corals. I told Conseil that these sponges are fished for in two ways, by a drag or by hand. The latter method is preferable, for the divers take care of the tissue of the polype, and this gives the commodity greater value.

The other zoophytes which live near the sponges are chiefly medusæ of a beautiful species. Molluscs were represented by the varieties of calmar, which, according to Orbigny, are peculiar to the Red Sea, and the reptiles by the *virgata* turtle belonging to the Cheloniæ genus, which furnishes our table with such delicate and wholesome food.

The fish were numerous and often remarkable. The nets of the *Nautilus* were frequently drawn, and we found rays of a reddish brick colour, mullet, gobies, blennies, balista, hammer-fish, and a thousand other fish common to the oceans which we had already traversed. On the 9th of February the *Nautilus* was in the broadest part of the Red Sea, which is between Souakin on the west and Quonfodah on the east coast, a distance of ninety miles.

At noon Captain Nemo came upon the platform, where he found me. I determined not to allow him to go away without having at least given me some hint as to his future proceedings. He approached as soon as he saw me, and offered me a cigar.

"Well, Monsieur," he said, "does the Red Sea please you? Have you sufficiently examined the wonders it contains – its fish and zoophytes, its sponges and corals? Have you seen the towns on the coast?"

"Yes, Captain Nemo," I replied, "and the *Nautilus* is wonderfully fitted for such studies. It is a very cleverly-designed vessel."

"Yes, sir; clever, fearless, and invulnerable. It neither fears the tempests of the Red Sea, its currents, nor its rocks."

"In fact," said I, "this sea is quoted as being one of the worst, and, if I do not mistake, its reputation in ancient times was very bad indeed."

"Detestable, M. Aronnax. The Greek and Latin writers do not speak well of it, and Strabo says that it is particularly dangerous during the season of the Etesian winds and in the rainy season. The Arab historian, Edrisi, who has described it under the name of the Gulf of Colzoum, relates that ships have perished in great numbers on its sand-banks, and that no one would venture to navigate it during the night. It was, he states, subject to terrific hurricanes, and interspersed with barren islands, and 'had nothing good in it', either above or below. Such, indeed, was the opinion of Arrian, Agatharchides, and Artemidorus."

"One can very easily perceive that these historians never navigated it in the *Nautilus*," said I.

"Exactly," replied the captain, smiling; "and in this respect the moderns are not much more advanced than were the ancients. It has taken many centuries to develop the mechanical powers of steam. Who knows but that in a hundred years they may see another *Nautilus*. Progress is slow, M. Aronnax."

"It is true," said I, "that your vessel is a century, many centuries perhaps, in advance of its time. What a pity it is that the secret should die with its inventor."

Captain Nemo made no answer. After a pause he said: "We were speaking of the opinions of the ancient historians respecting the dangers of the Red Sea."

"Yes," I said, "but were not their fears exaggerated?"

"Well, yes – and no, M. Aronnax," replied the captain, who seemed to have physically and morally gone deeply into the Red Sea. "That which is not dangerous for a modern ship, well found and solidly built, and, thanks to steam-power, master of its course, would offer considerable danger to ancient galleys. We must consider these first navigators in their roughly-built vessels. They had not any instruments to take bearings, and they sailed at the mercy of almost unknown currents. Under such conditions shipwrecks were, as might be expected, frequent. But in our time the steamers that perform the service between Suez and the Southern Seas have nothing to fear in this sea, despite of monsoons even. Captains and passengers do not offer propitiatory sacrifices before starting, and when they return they do not carry gilded ornaments and fillets as thank-offerings to the gods."

"I agree with you," I said; "and steam appears to have killed thankfulness in the hearts of sailors. But, captain, as you appear to have made this sea your study, can you tell me the origin of its name?"

"Numerous explanations exist. Should you like to know the opinion of a chronicler of the fourteenth century?"

"Very much indeed."

"This writer pretends that the name was bestowed upon it after the passage of the Israelites, when Pharaoh perished at the closing in of the waters:

> "As sign of miracle so dread,
>   The waves became a rosy red.
>   And since by ages handed down.
>   As the Red Sea the gulf is known."*

"A poetical explanation, captain," I replied, "but I cannot accept that reason. I should like your own opinion."

"You shall have it. In my opinion, M. Aronnax, the name Red Sea is a translation from the Hebrew word 'Edrom', and if the ancients gave it that name, it was in consequence of the peculiar colouring of its waters."

"Till now, nevertheless, I have observed nothing but clear water, without any peculiar tint whatever."

"No doubt, but towards the end of this gulf, you will perceive

---

* The original is as follows:

> En signe de cette merveille,
>   Devint la mer rouge et vermeille.
>   Non puis ne surent la nommer,
>   Autrement que la rouge mer.

this singular appearance. I remember having seen it in the Bay of Tor, perfectly red, like a lake of blood."

"And this colour you attribute to the presence of microscopic algæ?"

"Yes – it is a purple mucilaginous sea-weed, produced by the plants known as trichodesmia, and of which it requires forty thousand to occupy a space of a surface about .04 of an inch square. Perhaps at Tor we may meet them."

"I perceive, captain, that this is not the first time you have traversed the Red Sea."

"No."

"Well, as you were speaking just now of the passage of the Israelites, and the destruction of the Egyptians, I would ask if any submarine traces of this fact have been discovered?"

"No, Monsieur, and for a very excellent reason."

"What is that?"

"Because the spot where Moses crossed over with his people is now so silted up that camels can scarcely bathe their limbs there. Even my *Nautilus* could not float in that spot."

"And where is the place?"

"It is situated a little below the Isthmus of Suez, in the arm that formerly formed a deep estuary at the time when the Red Sea extended to the Salt Lakes. Now, whether this passage was miraculous or not, the Israelites did not the less pass there to gain the Promised Land, and the army of Pharaoh perished at that identical spot. I think, therefore, that excavations into these sands would be successful in discovering a quantity of ancient Egyptian arms and accoutrements."

"No doubt," I replied, "and it is to be hoped, for archæologists, that these excavations will be made when towns shall be built upon the isthmus after the construction of the Suez Canal. A very useless canal for such a ship as the *Nautilus*."

"I daresay; but very useful to the world in general," replied Captain Nemo. "The ancients understood the utility of establishing a water communication between the Red Sea and the Mediterranean, but they did not think of cutting a canal direct, and they took the Nile as the intermediary route. Very probably the canal which united the Nile to the Red Sea was commenced under Sesostris, if tradition may be accepted. It is certain, however, that in 615 B.C., Necos undertook the excavation of an 'alimentary' canal across the plain of Egypt opposite Arabia. This canal might be ascended in four days, and its width was that of two triremes abreast. It was continued by Darius, the son of Hydaspes, and probably completed by Ptolemy the Second. Strabo saw it in use for vessels, but the very slight 'fall' between its point of departure near Bubastes to the Red Sea rendered it navigable only for a few months in the year. This canal served for commerce up to the age of Antoninus, when it was abandoned, then silted up, but restored by the Caliph Omar. It was finally filled in in 761 or 762 by the Caliph Al-Mensor, who wished to prevent food from reaching Mohammed-Ben-Abdullah, who had revolted against him. During Napoleon's expedition to Egypt, the traces of the work were discovered in the desert of Suez, and, surprised by the tide, the French were nearly lost some distance from Hadjaroth, the same place where Moses had encamped three thousand years before."

"Well, captain, if the ancients failed to make this canal, which would shorten the distance from Cadiz to India by water by nearly 6,000 miles, M. de Lesseps has done it, and before long he will have changed Africa into an immense island."

"Yes, M. Aronnax; and you have reason to be proud of your countryman. He is a greater hero to a nation than a great general. He began, like many others, under slights and rebuffs, but he has triumphed, for he has brain and good will. It is sad to think that this undertaking, which ought to have been international, and is sufficient to add lustre to any reign, was only successful owing to the energy of one man. So all honour to M. de Lesseps!"

"Yes, all honour to this great citizen!" I replied, surprised by the manner in which Captain Nemo spoke.

"Unfortunately," he said, "I cannot take you up the Suez Canal, but the day after to-morrow you will see the long piers of Port Saïd, when we shall be in the Mediterranean."

"In the Mediterranean?" I exclaimed.

"Yes. Does that astonish you?"

"Yes, it does. The idea that we shall be there the day after to-morrow!"

"Really!"

"Yes, captain. Although I confess I ought not to be surprised at anything while on board your vessel."

"But why are you surprised?"

"Because I think of the awful speed you must make to double the Cape of Good Hope, go round Africa, and enter the Mediterranean the day after to-morrow."

"And who told you that I am going to double the Cape and go up the African coast, eh?"

"Well, you will admit that even the *Nautilus* cannot sail on dry land, across the Isthmus of Suez."

"Nor beneath it, M. Aronnax?"

"Beneath it?" I echoed.

"Certainly," replied the captain, calmly. "Nature long ago made, underneath, what mortals have only to-day completed on the surface."

"What do you say? A passage exists?"

"Yes, a subterranean passage does exist. I call it the Arabian Tunnel; it commences underneath Suez and ends in the Gulf of Pelusium."

"But the isthmus is only composed of shifting sand!"

"To a certain depth – yes. But at about sixty yards down there is a solid rock."

"And did you discover this passage by chance?"

"By chance and reason, professor; and by reason even more than chance."

"Captain Nemo, I hear you, but my ears can scarcely take it all in."

"Ah, Monsieur, *aures habent et non audient* is a motto for all ages. Not only does this passage exist, but I have often taken advantage of it. Were it not for it, I should not have come into the Red Sea at all just now."

"May I ask how you discovered the tunnel?"

"Monsieur," replied the captain, "there is no reason to keep any secret between people who will never be separated."

I did not notice the insinuation, and waited for the captain's explanation.

"M. Aronnax," said he, "it was the simple reasoning of a naturalist that led me to the discovery of this passage, with which I alone am acquainted. I had remarked that in the Red Sea and in the Mediterranean there existed a number of fish identical in every respect. Once certain of this fact, I began to consider whether there might not be some communication between the two seas. If such existed, the subterranean current would flow

from the Red Sea to the Mediterranean by the simple difference
of level. I then caught a quantity of fish off Suez; I placed on
their tails brass rings, and let them go. Some months later, on the
Syrian coasts, I pulled up some specimens of fish which were
decorated with brass rings on their tails. Thus the communication between the seas was demonstrated. I made search with
the *Nautilus*, I discovered the passage, I ventured into it, and
before long, sir, you will also have passed the Arabian Tunnel."

CHAPTER V
THE ARABIAN TUNNEL

THAT DAY I REPORTED to Conseil and Ned Land such portions
of my conversation with Captain Nemo as directly interested
them. When I told them that in two days we should be in the
Mediterranean, Conseil clapped his hands, but the Canadian
shrugged his shoulders.

"A submarine tunnel!" he cried. "A communication between
the seas! Who ever heard of such a thing?"

"Friend Ned," replied Conseil, "had you ever heard of the
Nautilus? No, but it nevertheless is a fact. Therefore, do not shrug
your shoulders so quickly, and do not disbelieve things because
you have never heard of them."

"Well, we shall see," said Ned, nodding his head. "After all,
I desire nothing better than to make this passage into the
Mediterranean."

The same evening, in 21° 30′ N. lat., the *Nautilus* approached
the Arabian coast. I could see Djeddah, an important "exchange"
of Egypt, Syria, Turkey, and the Indies. I could distinguish
clearly its houses, the vessels alongside the quays; and those
anchored farther out. The setting sun fell full upon the houses,
making them appear so very white, while farther off some cabins
of wood or reeds indicated the Bedaween quarter.

Djeddah was soon lost in the gloom, and the *Nautilus* descended beneath the phosphorescent water.

Next day, February 10th, many vessels appeared to windward.
The *Nautilus* resumed her submarine navigation; but at mid-day,
at the time for taking "bearings", the sea was clear of ships as we
came to the surface again. Accompanied by Ned and Conseil,

I sat down upon the platform. The coast on the east side was half hidden by a thick mist.

Leaning against the launch, we were chatting on various topics, when Ned, extending his hand, said:

"Do you see anything over there, sir?"

"No, Ned," I replied, "my eyes are not so good as yours."

"Look steadily," replied Ned, "a little above the lanthorn to starboard. Don't you see something moving?"

"In fact," I said, after gazing attentively in the direction indicated, "I do believe there is a long black body at the surface of the water."

"Another *Nautilus*?" suggested Conseil.

"No," said the Canadian; "if I mistake not, it is some marine animal."

"Are there any whales in the Red Sea?" asked Conseil.

"Yes," I replied, "they are sometimes met with."

"It is not a whale," said Ned, who still kept his gaze fixed upon the object. "Whales and I are such old acquaintances, that I cannot mistake them."

"Let us wait," said Conseil. "The *Nautilus* is going in that direction, we shall soon see what it is."

The black object was soon within a mile of us. It looked like a great sandbank. What could it be? I was not able to decide.

"Aha! it moves, it dives!" cried Ned. "Thousand devils! what can it be? Its tail is not divided like the whales' and cachalots', and its fins look as if they had been cut."

"But then—"

"Look there!" cried the Canadian, "it is on its back!"

"It is a siren, a true siren," cried Conseil. "If Monsieur has no objection."

The term "siren" gave me a hint, and I perceived at once that this animal belonged to that order of marine animals which are fabulously called sirens – half-female, half-fish.

"No," I said to Conseil, "it is not a siren, but a very curious being of which very few specimens exist in the Red Sea; it is a dugong."

"Order, sirens; group, pisciform; sub-class, monodolphin; class, mammifer; branch, vertebrates," replied Conseil.

When Conseil had said this there was nothing to add.

Meanwhile Ned kept his eyes fixed on the dugong, and they

shone with expectation. His hand seemed ready to grasp his harpoon, and one would have said that he only awaited the proper moment to throw himself into the sea and attack the animal in his native element.

"Oh, Monsieur!" he said, in a voice trembling with eagerness, "I have never killed one of that kind."

All the harpooner was in these words.

Just then the captain appeared. He noticed the dugong. Understanding the attitude of the Canadian, he at once addressed him:

"If you had a harpoon in your hand just now, Master Land, it would burn your palm, would it not?"

"Quite true, sir."

"And it would not displease you to return to your former avocation for a day, and to add yonder cetacean to the list of your victories?"

"It would not displease me in the least."

"Well, then, you can try."

"Thank you, sir," replied Ned Land, with kindling eyes.

"Only, I advise you not to miss that creature, for your own sake."

"Is the dugong a very dangerous animal to attack?" I asked, notwithstanding Ned's shrug of the shoulders.

"Sometimes," replied Captain Nemo, "the animal will turn and attack its assailant; but, with Master Land, this danger is not to be apprehended. His eye is quick, his arm sure. If I recommended him not to miss his stroke, it was because I look at it as fine game, and I know Master Land has no objection to tid-bits."

"Ah!" cried Ned, "so he is good to eat, is he?"

"Yes, his flesh is held in high estimation, and the Malays universally reserve it for the tables of their princes. Indeed, they hunt the animal so persistently that, like its relation the manatee, it has become very scarce."

"Then, Monsieur," said Conseil to the captain, "if that dugong be the last of his race, would it not be better to spare him, in the interests of science?"

"Perhaps so," replied Ned, "but in the interests of cookery it will be better to give him chase."

"Well, go ahead, Master Land," cried Captain Nemo.

Now seven of the crew, silent as ever, appeared upon the

platform. One of them carried a harpoon and line similar to those used in whaling. The boat was lowered. Six rowers took their places, and the coxswain seized the tiller. Ned, Conseil, and myself sat in the stern-sheets.

"Are you not coming, captain?"

"No, professor, but I wish you good sport."

The boat shoved off and, impelled by six sturdy rowers, rapidly approached the dugong.

We slacked speed a few cables' length from the creature, and pulled silently. Ned Land, harpoon in hand, took up his position in the bows. The usual whaling harpoon is attached to a long cord, which is paid out when the animal dives; but in this instance there were only about twelve fathoms of line, and at the end of this a barrel was fastened so as to indicate the course of the dugong in the water.

I got up and took a good look at the enemy. The dugong – also known as the halicore – is very much like the manatee, or lamantine. Its body is terminated by a long tail, and its lateral fins by fingers. The difference between the dugong and manatee consists in the former being armed with two long and pointed teeth in the upper jaw, which form a defence for each side.

This was the animal that Ned was about to attack; its length was about twenty-four feet. It did not move, and appeared to be sleeping, which circumstance would render its capture more easy. The launch approached cautiously to within three fathoms. The oars were eased. I half raised myself. Ned Land, his body thrown back a little, brandished his harpoon.

Suddenly a hissing noise was heard, and the dugong disappeared. The harpoon, forcibly cast, had only struck the water apparently.

"Thousand devils!" cried Ned furiously. "I have missed it."

"No," I said, "the animal is wounded, look at the blood, but the weapon did not stick in the body."

"My harpoon, my harpoon!" cried Ned.

The sailors pulled and the coxswain steered for the barrel. The harpoon was picked up, and the chase recommenced. The dugong came up to the surface to breathe occasionally. The wound had not disabled him, for he swam with great rapidity. The boat, impelled by vigorous arms, flew upon his track. Many times we were close to him, and the Canadian was prepared to strike, but the dugong plunged suddenly, and it was impossible to reach it.

You may imagine Ned Land's indignation. He heaped the most energetic forms of expression upon the unhappy animal. For my part, I was annoyed to see the dugong escape us.

We pursued it steadily for an hour, and I was beginning to believe that its capture would be a very difficult operation, when the animal was suddenly seized with the idea of retaliation (of which we had cause to repent later), and came to attack the boat.

This manœuvre did not escape the Canadian.

"Look out, men!" he cried.

The coxswain addressed his crew in his peculiar tongue and no doubt put them on their guard.

Arrived at twenty feet from the boat, the dugong pulled up. He sniffed the air with his immense nostrils, pierced in the upper part of the muzzle, then with a spring he threw himself upon us.

The boat could not avoid the shock. It was nearly upset, and took in a couple of tons of water, which it was necessary to get rid of. But, thanks to the coxswain, we received the blow sideways, and we were not upset.

Ned Land, holding on tightly in the bows, struck blow after blow at the gigantic animal, which, having fastened its teeth in the gunwale, nearly lifted the boat out of the water. We were thrown all together in a heap, and I do not know how the adventure would have terminated, had not the Canadian sent a lucky blow direct to the creature's heart.

I heard its teeth grinding upon the gunwale, and the animal disappeared, taking the harpoon with him. But the barrel soon came to the surface again, and a few minutes afterwards, the body of the dugong appeared floating on its back. We pulled towards it, took it in tow, and returned to the *Nautilus*.

It was necessary to employ some very strong tackle to hoist the dugong on board. It weighed more than four tons. It was cut up under the superintendence of the Canadian, and the same afternoon the steward served me with slices of the excellent flesh. I found it very good, superior to veal, if not to beef.

Next day our larder was again enriched by some choice game. A flock of sea-swallows alighted on the *Nautilus*. They were a species of *Sterna milotica* peculiar to Egypt; the beak is white, the head grey and pointed; the eyes are surrounded by white spots; the back, wings, and tail are greyish, the belly and throat white; the feet are red. We also captured some dozen Nile ducks, wild birds of a high flavour.

The speed was then lowered. We strolled along, so to speak. I noticed that the water of the Red Sea became less and less salt as we approached Suez.

About 5 p.m. we sighted the Cape of Ras Mohammed. This cape forms the extremity of Arabia Petræa, which is included between the gulfs of Suez and Acabah. The *Nautilus* entered the Jubal Straits, which lead to the Gulf of Suez. I could distinctly see a high mountain rising up between the two gulfs. It was Mount Horeb, at the summit of which Moses met God face to face in the midst of the fiery bush.

At six o'clock the *Nautilus* passed Tor at some distance; at the end of the bay, the waters appeared red as Captain Nemo had stated. Night fell, and the deep silence was sometimes broken by the cry of the pelican or some night birds, and by the noise of the waves, or the distant beat of the paddles of a steamer.

From eight to nine o'clock the *Nautilus* remained some yards below the surface. As far as I could judge, we were very close to Suez. Through the windows of the saloon I could perceive the adjacent rocks lighted up by our electric gleam. The straits seemed to be getting narrower and narrower.

At a quarter-past nine we rose to the surface. I went upon the platform. I was very impatient to go through Captain Nemo's tunnel. I could not keep quiet, and I sought the fresh air.

Very soon I perceived a pale light breaking through the gloom, and half discoloured by the surrounding fog. It appeared to be shining about a mile off.

"A floating lighthouse," said some one close to me.

I turned round and recognized the captain.

"It is the Suez floating light," he said; "we shall not be long ere we reach the entrance to the tunnel."

"The entrance is not very easy, I suppose?"

"No; and therefore I am in the habit of taking the helm myself as we go through. Now, M. Aronnax, if you will be so good as to go below, the *Nautilus* will do the same, and not return to the surface until she has cleared the Arabian Tunnel."

I followed the captain; the panels were closed; the reservoirs of water filled, and the vessel descended for a distance of forty feet, or so.

Just as I was about to enter my room, Captain Nemo stopped me.

"Would you like to come with me to the pilot-house?" he asked.

"I scarcely dared to ask you," I said.

"Come along; you will see all that can be seen at once beneath the earth and under water."

Captain Nemo led the way to the central staircase. Half-way up he opened a door and reached the pilot-cage, which was, as may be remembered, at the extremity of the platform.

It was a cabin measuring about six feet square, and somewhat like those occupied by pilots in the Mississippi and Hudson steamers. A wheel, vertically placed, occupied the centre, and chains connected it with the rudder astern. Four "ports" gave sufficient light to the man at the wheel to see all around him.

The cabin was dark, but my eyes soon accustomed themselves to the gloom, and I saw the pilot, his hands resting upon the spokes of the wheel. Outside the sea appeared vividly illuminated by the lamp which was burning behind us at the other end of the platform.

"Now," said Captain Nemo, "let us look for our passage."

Electric wires connected the helmsman's cage with the engine-room, and the captain could communicate at the same time the necessary speed and direction of his vessel. He pressed a button, and the speed was sensibly diminished.

I gazed in silence at the high perpendicular wall alongside of which we were running at that moment, the unyielding foundation of a sandy coast. We proceeded thus for an hour at a few yards' distance only. Captain Nemo never took his eyes from the compass suspended in the cabin. By a gesture he indicated to the steersman the proper directions.

I was placed on the port-side, and could perceive the magnificent formations of coral; the zoophytes, algæ, and crustacea moving their enormous claws which were extended from the holes in the rocks.

At a quarter-past ten Captain Nemo himself took the helm. A large black gallery opened before us; the *Nautilus* entered it boldly. An unusual rushing sound of water accompanied us; this was caused by the waters of the Red Sea which the incline of the tunnel sent rushing to the Mediterranean. The *Nautilus* was borne upon the torrent like an arrow notwithstanding that the screw was reversed to counteract the speed.

Upon the walls of the tunnel I could distinguish nothing but brilliant rays, lines of fire traced by the speed of our electric light; my heart beat fast and I put my hand to my chest.

At 10.35 Captain Nemo gave up the wheel to the helmsman, and, turning to me, said:

"The Mediterranean!"

In less than twenty minutes the *Nautilus*, carried along by the current, had passed beneath the Isthmus of Suez!

CHAPTER VI
THE GRECIAN ARCHIPELAGO

AT DAWN NEXT day (February 12) the *Nautilus* came up to the surface again. I ran up to the platform. Three miles to the south-ward I could see the outline of Pelusium. A torrent had carried us from sea to sea. But the tunnel, though easy to descend, seemed to me impossible to ascend.

About 7 a.m. Ned and Conseil joined me. These two "insép-arables" had been calmly sleeping, without troubling themselves about the exploits of the *Nautilus*.

"Well, sir," asked the Canadian, in a bantering tone, "and how about this Mediterranean?"

"We are floating on its surface, friend Ned!"

"What," said Conseil, "last night—"

"Yes, last night, in a few minutes, we cleared the Isthmus of Suez."

"I don't believe a word of it," said Ned.

"Well, you are wrong, Master Land. That low coast trending to the south is Egypt."

"Or some other," replied the infatuated Canadian.

"But since Monsieur says it is so," says Conseil, "you must believe him."

"Besides, Ned, Captain Nemo showed me the tunnel. I was close to him in the pilot-house while he steered the *Nautilus* through the passage."

"Do you hear, Ned?" asked Conseil.

"And since you have such good eyes, Ned," I added, "you can perceive the piers of Port Saïd."

The Canadian looked attentively at them.

"Well," he said, "you are right, sir, and this captain is a wonderful fellow. We are in the Mediterranean. Good. We may talk of our own little business if you please, but so that we may not be overheard."

I saw very well what the Canadian was driving at. In any case I thought it better that he should talk, since he wanted to do so, and we all sat down by the lamp, where we were less likely to be subject to the spray.

"Now, Ned, we are listening," said I. "What have you to tell us?"

"It is not much," he replied; "we are in Europe, and before Captain Nemo's vagaries plunge us into the Polar Seas, I vote we quit the *Nautilus*."

This style of conversation always embarrassed me. I did not wish to be any tie upon my friends, and at the same time I did not want to leave Captain Nemo. Thanks to him and his vessel, I was day by day increasing my studies, and I was rewriting my book respecting the submarine depths in those very depths themselves. Should I ever have such another chance to observe the wonders of the ocean? Certainly not; and I could not bear to leave the *Nautilus* before our round of exploration was completed.

"Friend Ned," I said, "answer me frankly. Are you tired of being on board? Do you regret the fate that placed you in Captain Nemo's hands?"

The Canadian did not reply immediately; then folding his arms, he said:

"Frankly, then, I do not regret this voyage. I am very glad to have made it, but to have made it, it must have an end. That is my opinion."

"It will come to an end, Ned!"

"When and where?"

"Where, I cannot say; when, I do not know; but I suppose it will end when we can learn nothing more from the sea. Everything must have an end in this world."

"I agree with Monsieur, that when we have been all round the world, Captain Nemo will give us our liberty."

"We have nothing to fear from the captain," I said, "but I do not so far agree with Conseil's ideas. We are master of the secret of the *Nautilus*, and I cannot expect that the captain will take the risk of releasing us and letting his secrets be known."

"Then what do you expect?" inquired Ned.

"That circumstances may occur by which we may and ought to profit as well six months hence as now."

"All very well, but where shall we be six months hence?"

"Here perhaps, or in China. You know the *Nautilus* is a rapid sailer. It can cross the seas as a swallow the air, or like an express train on land. It does not fear frequented seas. Who can tell whether we may not close with the coasts of France, England, or America, when an attempt to escape might be made with at least as much hope of success as now."

"M. Aronnax," said Ned Land, "your arguments won't hold water. You speak of the future. We shall be here or there. But I speak of the present. We are here, let us profit by the opportunity."

I was hit hard by Ned's logic, and felt beaten. I had no other argument to advance.

"Sir," replied Ned, "let us suppose, as an impossibility, that Captain Nemo were to offer you liberty to-day – would you accept it?"

"I am not sure," I replied.

"And were he to say that he would not renew his offer, would you then accept it?"

I did not answer.

"And what do you think of it, friend Conseil?" demanded Ned.

"Friend Conseil!" replied that worthy, "friend Conseil has nothing to say on the subject. He is absolutely disinterested. As the master, and as is Ned, he is a single man. No wife, children, nor parents await his return. He is in his master's service. He thinks and speaks as his master does; and, to his great regret, you must not count on him for a casting-vote. There are only two persons here – my master on one side, Ned Land on the other. So Conseil listens, and will mark the points for you."

I could not repress a smile to see how completely Conseil annihilated his personality. The Canadian ought to have been delighted at not having him against him.

"Then, Monsieur, since Conseil does not exist, the discussion is confined to us two. I have spoken, what is your reply?"

The thing must be settled once for all, and evasion was distasteful to me.

"Friend Ned," I said, "here is my answer. You have had the best of it, and my arguments have not been able to stand against yours. We must not count upon the goodwill of Captain Nemo. The most common prudence would prevent him from releasing us. On the other hand, prudence bids us to take advantage of the first opportunity to quit the *Nautilus*."

"You speak wisely, M. Aronnax."

"But just one observation," said I. "The occasion must be a good one, for our first attempt will surely be our last; and, if retaken, Captain Nemo will not forgive us."

"Quite right," replied the Canadian, "but your remark applies to all attempts at flight – in two years' time, or two days. Now the question is this: If a favourable occasion present itself, we must seize it."

"Quite so. And now, Ned, what do you consider as a favourable occasion?"

"When, some dark night, the *Nautilus* is not far from some European coast."

"And you will endeavour to save yourself by swimming?"

"Yes, if we are not too far from the beach, and if the ship be on the surface. Not if we were far away or under water, of course."

"And in that case?"

"In that case I would endeavour to get out the launch; I know how to work it. We should have to get inside it and draw the bolts, when we should come to the surface without even the steersman, who is forward, being aware of our flight."

"Good, Ned! Look out for the opportunity, and remember that a hitch in the arrangements will be fatal."

"I will not forget, sir," replied Ned.

"Now, Ned, would you like to hear my opinion of your project?"

"Gladly, M. Aronnax."

"Well, I think – I do not say hope – I think that this occasion will never present itself."

"Why not?"

"Because Captain Nemo cannot hide from himself the idea

that we hope to recover our liberty some day, and he will be on his guard; particularly in European waters, and in sight of European coasts."

"I agree with Monsieur," said Conseil.

"We shall see," replied Ned, nodding his head in a determined manner.

"And now, Ned Land," said I, "let the matter rest thus as it is. Not a word of all this. When you are ready, let us know, and we will follow you. I leave the matter entirely to you."

So this conversation, which was destined to lead to grave results, terminated here. I ought to mention that the facts appeared to confirm my predictions, to the Canadian's despair. Did Captain Nemo distrust us while in these crowded seas, or did he only wish to conceal his ship from the numerous vessels that sailed the Mediterranean? I cannot say, but we certainly were more often underneath the water, and at a greater distance from the coast, than formerly. When the *Nautilus* emerged, nothing was visible but the pilot's house, and we went to great depths also; for between the Grecian Archipelago and Asia Minor we found more than a thousand fathoms of water.

I only knew we were near the island of Carpathos, one of the Sporades, by Captain Nemo quoting me Virgil's lines, as he placed his hand on the map:

> Est in Carpathio Neptuni gurgite vates
> Cœruleus Proteus—

This was the ancient residence of Proteus, the shepherd of Neptune's flocks – now the Isle of Scarpanto, situated between Rhodes and Crete – but I saw nothing but the granitic foundations from the windows of the saloon.

Next day, the 14th of February, I made up my mind to devote a few hours to the study of the fish of the Archipelago, but for some reason the panels remained closed. Upon taking the course of the *Nautilus*, I perceived that we were approaching Candia – the ancient Crete. When I had embarked on board the *Abraham Lincoln*, I had heard that the inhabitants of this island had revolted against the Turks, but how the insurrection had prospered since that time I was absolutely ignorant, and Captain Nemo could not, of course, give me any information on this point.

I made no allusion to it when in the evening I was alone with

him in the saloon. Besides, he seemed to be taciturn and pre-
occupied. Then, contrary to his usual custom, he ordered the
panels of the saloon to be opened, and he watched the water
attentively from one or the other. What his purpose was in so
doing, I could not divine, and I amused myself by watching
the fish.

I remarked the gobies mentioned by Aristotle, and vulgarly
called sea-loaches, which are chiefly found in the salt water about
the Delta of the Nile. Near these were a semi-phosphorescent
bream, a sort of sparus which the Egyptians hold sacred, and the
arrival of which in the Nile announces a rich overflow, and is
celebrated by religious ceremonies. I also saw some cheilones, a
bony fish with transparent scales, which are great devourers of
marine plants, are most excellent to eat, and were much prized
by the epicures of ancient Rome.

Another inhabitant of these seas attracted my attention, and
renewed all my recollections of antiquity. This was the remora,
which travels fixed upon the belly of the shark. According to the
ancients, this little fish fastened to the keel of a ship could stop
its course, and one of them in this way kept back the galley of
Antony at the battle of Actium, and thus facilitated the victory
of Augustus. On how little the destinies of nations hang! I also
noticed some beautiful anthiæ which belong to the lutjan order,
a fish sacred to the Greeks, who attribute to them the power to
chase marine animals from the waters they frequent. Their name
means *flower*, and is justified by their colours, which comprise
every shade of red, from the rose to the ruby-tint. I was gazing
earnestly at these marvels of the sea, when an unexpected apparition appeared.

A man appeared suddenly – a diver, carrying at his waist a
leathern purse. He was not shipwrecked, but a vigorous swimmer, disappearing occasionally to breathe, and then returning
immediately.

I turned to Captain Nemo and exclaimed: "Here is a shipwrecked man, we must save him at all hazards."

The captain made no answer, but approached the window.

The diver came near, and putting his face against the glass he
looked at us.

To my utter astonishment Captain Nemo made a sign to him.

The diver waved his hand; at once ascended, and did not again appear.

"Don't alarm yourself," said Captain Nemo. "It is only Nicholas, of Cape Matapan, surnamed Pesca. He is well known in the Cyclades. A daring diver, water is his element, he lives in it more than on land, passing between the islands even as far as Crete."

"You know him, captain?"

"Why not, M. Aronnax?"

As he said this, he advanced towards a cabinet placed near the left window of the saloon. Near to this I saw a coffer bound with iron, on the cover of which was a plate of copper, engraved with a representation of the *Nautilus*, and the motto *Mobilis in Mobile*.

The captain opened the chest, which held a quantity of ingots.

Golden ingots! Whence could he have collected this enormous sum of money? What was he going to do with it?

I did not speak. I looked on. Captain Nemo took these ingots and placed them mathematically one by one in the chest, which he filled completely. I estimated that there must have been 4,000 lbs. weight of gold – five millions of francs (£200,000).

The chest was securely fastened down, and the captain wrote upon the lid an address, in characters which appeared to me to be modern Greek.

That done, the captain pressed a button communicating with the men's quarters. Four men appeared, and without any trouble they pushed the chest out of the saloon. Subsequently I could hear them hauling it up the iron staircase.

Captain Nemo then turned to me and said: "You were saying—?"

"I was saying nothing," I replied.

"Then, sir, you will allow me to bid you good night," and he quitted the saloon.

I returned to my room much exercised in my mind.

I tried in vain to sleep. I sought some connection between the appearance of the diver and the chest of gold. I soon perceived by the motion of the *Nautilus* that we were ascending to the surface.

Then I heard some noise on the platform, I fancied that they were launching the boat; it struck the side and all was quiet.

Two hours later the same noise and movement were repeated;

the boat was hoisted up and secured, and the *Nautilus* plunged once again beneath the waves. So the millions had been forwarded to their destination; but on what part of the continent. Who was Captain Nemo's correspondent?

Next day I related all I had seen to Conseil and Ned. My companions were not less astonished than I had been.

"But where does he take his millions to?" asked Ned Land.

This we could not answer. After breakfast I went into the saloon and sat down to work. Till 5 p.m. I was arranging my notes, when I suddenly felt a great heat, and I was glad to take off my outer garment of byssus. This heat was extraordinary in effect, for we were not in tropic latitudes; and, besides, the *Nautilus* being under water, would not be affected in any case. I looked at the manometer; we were at a depth of sixty feet, to which the heat of the air could not reach. I continued to work, but the heat became intolerable.

"Is the ship on fire?" I thought.

I was about to leave the saloon when Captain Nemo entered. He looked at the thermometer and, turning to me, said:

"Forty-two degrees."

"So I see, captain; and if the heat increases we shall not be able to bear it."

"It will not get hotter if we do not like it."

"You can reduce it, then, if you wish, captain?"

"No, but I can go farther from the cause of it."

"Is it, then, outside the ship?"

"Certainly; we are floating in a current of boiling water."

"Is it possible?" I exclaimed.

"Look!"

The panels were opened, and I could perceive that the sea was quite white around the *Nautilus*. A sulphurous vapour rolled amid the waves, which boiled like water in a copper. I placed my hand against one of the windows, but the heat was so great I had to withdraw it.

"Where are we?" I asked.

"Close to the island of Santorin," replied the captain, "and in the canal which separates Nea-Kamenni from Palea-Kamenni. I wished to let you see a submarine eruption."

"I thought that this formation of new islands had ceased," I said.

"Nothing is ever at an end in volcanic localities," replied Captain Nemo; "and the globe is always being moved by these subterranean fires. According to Cassiodorno and Pliny, a new island – Thera (the divine) – appeared in the very place in which these islands have been formed, about the nineteenth year of our era. Then they sank, to rise again in 69, and again disappeared. Since then, to our time, this Plutonian work has been suspended. But on the 3rd of February, 1866, a new island, called George Island, rose near Nea-Kamenni, and disappeared upon the 6th of the same month. Seven days after, the island of Aphroessa appeared, leaving a passage about twelve yards wide between it and Nea-Kamenni. I was in these seas when it happened, and was able to observe the phases. The island of Aphroessa, of a rounded form, measured 300 feet across and 30 feet in height. It was composed of a black and vitreous lava, mingled with felspar. Finally, on the 10th of March, a smaller island called Reka arose close to Nea-Kamenni, and since these three islands have been united."

"And the canal in which we now are?" I asked.

"There it is," replied Captain Nemo, indicating it on a map of the Archipelago. "You see that I have put down all the newest islands."

"But this canal will some day be filled up, surely?"

"Very likely, M. Aronnax, for since 1866 eight little islands of lava have risen opposite the harbour of St. Nicholas, in Palea-Kamenni. It is, therefore, evident that Nea and Palea will be joined together some day. If in the Pacific there are infusoria, which form continents, here it is by eruptive phenomena. You can see, sir, what work is being done beneath the waves."

I turned to the window. The *Nautilus* was not going fast. The heat became almost unbearable. The white appearance of the sea had given place to a red tinge, which colour was due to salts of iron. Notwithstanding the hermetic ceiling of the saloon, an almost insupportable smell of sulphur was present, and I could perceive that the bright red of the flames completely overcame the electric light.

I felt in a bath. I was choking. I was almost broiled. I really did feel as if I were cooking!

"We cannot remain in this boiling-water any longer," I said.

"No," replied the captain, calmly, "it would be scarcely prudent."

An order was passed along – the *Nautilus* went about, and soon left the furnace at a distance. A quarter of an hour later, we were breathing at the surface of the sea.

It occurred to me, that if Ned Land had selected those places to make his escape in, we should never emerge alive from the fiery sea!

The following day (February 16th) we left the basin between Rhodes and Alexandria, which can boast of a depth of about 4,500 yards, and the *Nautilus* giving Cerigo a wide berth, doubled Cape Matopan, and left the Greek Archipelago astern.

CHAPTER VII
THE MEDITERRANEAN IN FORTY-EIGHT HOURS

THE MEDITERRANEAN: the blue sea *par excellence*. The "great sea" of the Hebrews, "*The* sea" of the Greeks, the "Mare Nostrum" of the Romans, bordered by orange-trees, aloes, cactus, pines, perfumed with myrtle, enclosed by rude mountains, enveloped with a pure and transparent atmosphere, but ever worked by the earth's fires, is the regular battle-field of Neptune and Pluto disputing for the empire of the world. It is here on its banks as on its waters, says Michelet, that man acquires new vigour, in one of the most wonderful climates in the world!

But beautiful though it be, I could only indulge in a very hasty glance. The personal experience of Captain Nemo failed me here, for that extraordinary personage did not appear once during the passage through, which we made at full speed. I estimated the distance that the *Nautilus* ran under the water was about 600 leagues, and she performed it in eight-and-forty hours. We left the Grecian Archipelago on the 16th of February, and on the 18th, at sunrise, we had passed the Strait of Gibraltar.

It was evident to me that Captain Nemo did not like being surrounded by these countries he wished to avoid. The winds and waves carried too many *souvenirs* – if not regrets to his mind. Here he did not possess the same liberty of motion as in the ocean, and his *Nautilus* was in a Strait, so to speak, between Europe and Africa.

Our speed was about twenty-five miles an hour.

It is needless to say that Ned Land, to his great disappointment, was obliged to renounce his plan of escape. It was of no use to think of launching the boat at the pace we were travelling. To leave the *Nautilus* under these circumstances was like jumping out of a train at full speed, which is not the most prudent thing to do at any time. Besides, the ship only came to the surface during the night to renew the air, and was solely guided by the compass and the log.

Therefore I saw no more of the Mediterranean than a traveller by an express can see of the country through which he passes. Nevertheless, Conseil and I were able to note some of the Mediterranean fish, whose swimming powers enabled them to keep alongside the *Nautilus* for a few moments. My notes enable me to reproduce some account of the ichthyology of this sea.

Of the many fish inhabiting it I saw some, and only caught a glimpse of others; so I must class them in a somewhat fantastic manner.

Amongst those surrounded by our light were lampreys about three feet long, which are common to all seas, oxyrhinchia, a kind of ray, about five feet wide, with white belly, spread out like shawls carried along by the current. Other rays passed so quickly that I could not ascertain whether they were the "eagles" of the Greeks, or the "rat", "frog", and "bat", which modern fisher-men have dubbed them. Sea-foxes, several feet long, and gifted with acute scent came along like great blue shadows. Dorades got up in blue and silver, sacred to Venus, the eyes chased with a gold pencilling; a precious species, but suited to either salt or fresh water, living in all climates and all temperatures, and though belonging to the geological era, have preserved all their pristine beauty. Magnificent sturgeons, ten or eleven yards long, of great speed, and knocking their powerful tails against the windows of the saloon, showed their bluish backs spotted with brown. They are like sharks, though inferior in strength, and are found in all seas. In the spring they like to ascend great rivers like the Volga, the Danube, the Po, the Rhine, the Loire, and Oder, living on herrings, mackerel, &c. But of the various inhabitants of the Mediterranean those which I could see best were of the sixty-third genus of osseous fishes. These were tunny, with blue-black backs. They are stated to follow ships in search of the refreshing shade from the fiery tropical sky, and they certainly proved the saying, for they followed the *Nautilus* just as they followed the ships of La Pérouse. For hours they emulated the speed of our ship. I could not help admiring them, they seemed so built for speed; small head, lissome body, fins of great power, and forked tails. They swam in a triangle, as some birds fly. But with all their speed they do not escape the Provençals, and these blind and stupid yet precious creatures throw themselves by millions into the nets of the Marseillaises.

I could quote numbers of other fish – gymnotes, congers of four yards length, trygles, red mullet, the ocean "bird of Paradise"; and if I do not put down balista, tertodrons, hippocampus, blennies, and numerous others, it is because the speed of the *Nautilus* made it impossible to note them accurately.

I fancied I saw at the entrance to the Adriatic two or three cachalots, some dolphin of the genus globicephali, peculiar to the Mediterranean, the back of the head being variegated with small lines; and some seals known as "Monks", and which have really something of the appearance of a Dominican.

Conseil thought he saw a tortoise six feet wide. I was sorry I had not noticed it, for, from Conseil's description, I believed it to be the "luth", which is very rare. I only remarked a few caconans, with elongated shell coverings.

As regards zoophytes, I was able to admire for some minutes an admirable orange-coloured galcolaria, which had attached itself to the panel on the port side. I, unfortunately, was unable to secure this splendid specimen; and perhaps no other Mediterranean zoophytes would have presented themselves if the *Nautilus*, during the evening of the 16th, had not unexpectedly slackened speed, under the following circumstances.

We were passing between the coasts of Sicily and Tunis. In this narrow space, between Cape Bon and the Strait of Messina, the bottom of the sea rose very suddenly. A regular reef had formed, above which there was not sixty feet of water. The *Nautilus* had therefore to move very carefully, so as not to knock against the reef.

I pointed out to Conseil the position of the reef on the chart.

"But, if Monsieur has no objection, this is a regular isthmus, uniting Europe to Africa."

"Yes," I replied, "it is a perfect bar to the Libyan Straits, and the soundings of Smith have proved that those continents were formerly united between Cape Boco and Cape Furnia."

"I can easily believe it," replied Conseil.

"I may add that a similar reef exists between Ceuta and Gibraltar. These bars, in the geological epoch, completely shut in the Mediterranean."

"Ah!" said Conseil, "and suppose some volcanic action should raise these reefs again?"

"That is scarcely probable."

"At least, if Monsieur will allow me to finish; if this should happen, it will be very awkward for M. de Lesseps, who has taken so much trouble to cut the Suez Canal."

"I agree with you, Conseil; but I repeat I do not think it likely to happen. The violence of the subterranean forces is always diminishing. The volcanoes, so common in early ages, are now comparatively few; the interior heat is dying out, the temperature of the earth's strata is being lowered appreciably every century, and to the detriment of our globe, for this heat is life."

"Yet the sun—"

"The sun is not enough, Conseil. Can it warm a corpse?"

"No, I should say not."

"Well, my friend, the earth will one day become a cold body; it will become uninhabitable and uninhabited; like the moon, which has long ago lost its vital heat."

"In how many centuries?" asked Conseil.

"In some hundreds of thousands of years."

"Then," said Conseil, "we have still time to complete our voyage, if Ned Land does not interrupt us."

And Conseil, reassured, applied himself to the study of the high bank that the *Nautilus* was skirting at a moderated pace.

There, beneath a rocky and volcanic soil, was outspread a living flora of sponges, holotines, cydippes, ornamented with ruddy foliage, which emitted a slight phosphorescence; heroës, commonly known as sea-cucumbers, and bathed in glittering light of a solar spectrum; walking comatula a yard long, whose purple hue coloured the water.

Conseil occupied himself chiefly in observing the molluscs and the articulates. Time failed him to complete the crustacea by the examination of the stomapodes, the amphipodes, the homopodes, the trilobites, the branchiapodes, the ostracods, and the entomostaces. But the *Nautilus* having passed the high bank on the right of the African coast, redescended into deep water, and

proceeded at her full speed. No more molluscs, no more articulates, no more zoophytes. Only a few large fish passed us, like
great shadows.

During the night of the 16–17th February we entered the
second Mediterranean basin, whose greatest depth is 3,000 yards.
The *Nautilus* descended almost to the very bottom.

There, in default of natural wonders, the great mass of waters
offered me very moving and terrible scenes. We were then
traversing that portion of the Mediterranean so fertile in shipwrecks. From the Algerine coast to Provence what vessels have
disappeared! The Mediterranean is but a lake compared to the
Pacific, but it is a capricious and changeful lake: to-day smiling
and beautiful, to-morrow raging, roaring, and swept by furious
winds, disabling the finest vessels, and smashing them against its
precipitous rocks.

So in this rapid transit, at these immense depths, I could
perceive anchors, cannon, cannon-balls, iron utensils, threads of
screws, pieces of the engines, cylinders, boilers, hulls floating
mid-way, some upright, some overturned!

Of these shipwrecked vessels, some had been injured by collision, others from striking on the rocks. I saw some which had
gone down "all standing". They looked as if they were at anchor
in a foreign harbour, and were waiting the signal to depart. When
the *Nautilus* passed between them and wrapped them in the
electric light, it seemed as if these ships were going to salute
the flag and hoist their numbers. But no! nothing but the silence
of death reigned in this scene of a great catastrophe.

I noticed that towards Gibraltar these sinister traces became
more numerous. The coasts of Europe and Africa get closer here,
and the meetings were more frequent. I perceived numerous iron
hulls, remains of steamers, some careened over, some upright,
like some formidable animals. One of these vessels presented a
terrible spectacle. How many had gone down with her, who of
all those on board had survived to tell the tale, or did the waves
still guard this terrible secret? I do not know why, but it occurred
to me that this was the *Atlas*, which had disappeared about
twenty years ago, and of which no one had ever since heard. Ah!
what fearful history might be written about these depths, this vast
mortuary of the Mediterranean, where so much wealth has been
lost, and where so many victims have found death!

But the *Nautilus*, indifferent to this, continued her rapid course amid all this ruin. On the 18th of February, about 3 a.m., she entered the Straits of Gibraltar.

Here two currents exist; the upper long known, which takes the water from the ocean into the Mediterranean, the other in the opposite direction of which reason has proved the existence. In fact, the bulk of the Mediterranean waters, incessantly increased by the Atlantic, and by the rivers it receives, would rise each year to the level of the sea, for its evaporation is not sufficient to establish the equilibrium. Now, it is not so, and the existence of an under-current is only natural, and this current empties the surplus water of the Mediterranean into the Atlantic through the Straits of Gibraltar. This is a fact, and the *Nautilus* took advantage of this current. It rapidly advanced. For an instant I caught sight of the beautiful ruins of the temple of Hercules (according to Pliny and Avienus), buried with the island that supported it, and a few moments later we were floating in the waves of the Atlantic Ocean.

CHAPTER VIII
VIGO BAY

THE ATLANTIC! A vast expanse of water, whose superficial area covers 25,000,000 of square miles, is 9,000 miles long, and has an average breadth of 2,700 miles. This enormous ocean was almost unknown to the ancients, unless the Carthaginians perhaps, who in their commercial progression followed the coasts of Europe and Africa. An ocean whose winding and parallel shores embrace an immense area; supplied by the largest rivers in the world – the St. Lawrence, the Mississippi, the Amazon, La Plata, Orinoco, Niger, Senegal, Elbe, Loire, Rhine, which bear their waters to it through the most civilized, and also through the most barbarous countries. A magnificent sheet of water ploughed by vessels over which the flag of every nation waves, and which is bounded by those two points, so terrible to sailors, the Cape Horn and the "Cape of Storms".

The *Nautilus* was cutting her way through these waters, having made 10,000 leagues in three months and a half – a distance greater than one of the earth's great circles. Whither were we now bound, and what had the future in store for us?

The *Nautilus* having cleared the straits, kept well in the offing. We came to the surface, and our daily airings on the platform were resumed.

I ascended at once, accompanied by Conseil and Ned Land. Cape St. Vincent appeared about twelve miles away. The wind was blowing stiffly from the south, the sea was very rough indeed, and the *Nautilus* rolled tremendously. It was almost impossible to stand upon the platform, which was swept by the waves almost every instant. We descended, therefore, after having taken in a few mouthfuls of fresh air.

I retired to my room, Conseil went to his cabin also, but the Canadian, who appeared preoccupied, followed me. Our rapid passage through the Mediterranean had not permitted him to put his design into execution, and he did not conceal his disappointment. When he had closed the door he sat down and contemplated me in silence.

"Friend Ned," I said, "I understand you, but you have nothing to reproach yourself with. Under the circumstances in which the *Nautilus* was worked, it would have been utter folly to have attempted to leave it."

Ned made no reply, his compressed lips and lowering brow showed how deeply the idea of escape possessed him.

"But," said I, "we will not despair. We are coasting up by Portugal. France and England are not far off, where we may easily find refuge. If the *Nautilus* had gone southwards after clearing the straits we should have been again carried away into mid-ocean, and I should have shared your uneasiness, but we know that Captain Nemo does not fear these frequented seas, and in a few days I believe we shall be in safety."

Ned Land gazed at me still more intently, and at length opening his lips, said:

"It is for this evening."

I jumped up. I was, I confess, unprepared for such a communication. I could not reply.

"It was arranged to wait an opportunity. It is at hand. This evening we shall be only a few miles from the Spanish coast. The night will be dark. The wind is high. You promised, M. Aronnax, and I depend upon you."

As I still was silent the Canadian rose and came towards me.

"To-night at nine o'clock," said he. "I have warned Conseil.

At that time Captain Nemo will be shut in in his own room, and most likely asleep. Neither the engineers nor the crew will be able to see us. Conseil and I will gain the centre staircase. You, M. Aronnax, can remain in the library close by till I give the signal. The oars, mast, and sail are in the launch; I have even succeeded in laying in some provisions, and I have got an English 'key' to undo the bolts which fasten the boat to the *Nautilus*. You see all is prepared. This evening, mind."

"The sea is very rough," I said.

"I know that," replied the Canadian, "but we must risk it. Our freedom is worth a little danger. But the boat is strong, and a few miles with a favourable wind is nothing after all. Who knows, by to-morrow we may be a hundred leagues away. If only fate be propitious, by ten or eleven to-night we shall have landed some-where or be dead. Therefore, until the evening, adieu."

The Canadian retired, leaving me speechless. I had fancied that, the chance once gone, I should have had time to reflect or discuss the point. My obstinate companion would not allow this; but, after all, what could I have said? Ned Land was right – a hundred times right. Here was a chance of an opportunity, and he was taking advantage of it. Could I retract my prom-ise, and assume the responsibility to compromise my companions by my selfishness? To-morrow Captain Nemo might take us out to sea again.

At this moment a loud hissing noise made me aware that the reservoirs were filling, and the *Nautilus* was descending beneath the Atlantic waves.

I remained in my room. I wished to avoid the captain, to hide from him the emotion that overcame me. I passed a very weary-ing day, and left my submarine studies, as I was balanced between the desire for liberty and my regret at quitting the *Nautilus*. To quit this ocean – "my Atlantic", as I liked to call it – without having visited its greater depths, without having gained its secrets, while the Indian and Pacific Oceans had yielded theirs! My romance fell from my hand at the first volume; my dream was interrupted at the most pleasant moment! What unhappy hours I passed thus! Sometimes picturing myself and my companions in safety; sometimes hoping, against my own reason, that some-thing would prevent Ned Land's project from being carried out.

Twice I came into the saloon. I wanted to look at the compass.

I wished to see in what direction the *Nautilus* was going; whether bringing us nearer to, or taking us farther from the coast. But there was no change, we continued in Portuguese waters.

I must therefore make up my mind to depart. My baggage was not excessive – only my notes!

I wondered what Captain Nemo would think of our flight. What unhappiness, what evil might it not bring upon him; and how would he act in either event – on success or failure? I had certainly no cause to complain of his conduct – on the contrary – he was hospitality itself. But in leaving the ship I could not be taxed with ingratitude; I was bound by no oath. He depended on circumstances, and not upon any promise, to keep us with him. But this claim, which openly avowed his intention to keep us prisoners for ever, quite justified our attempt to escape.

I had not seen the captain since our visit to the island of Santorin. Would chance bring us together before we escaped? I desired, and yet feared, the meeting. I listened to hear if he were walking up and down in his room. I heard no sound; the room must be empty! Then I began to wonder whether he were on board. Since the evening that the boat had left the *Nautilus*, on some mysterious service, my ideas had been slightly modified concerning him. I fancied, and I wish I could say so, that Captain Nemo still kept up some communication with the earth. Would he never leave the *Nautilus* altogether? Weeks had passed without our meeting. What did he do in that time? And, while I believed him a prey to misanthropy, might he not be at a distance, carrying out some secret plans?

All these and a thousand similar ideas crowded my brain. Conjecture could be infinite under such circumstances. I was terribly uneasy. The day appeared interminable. The hours struck too slowly for my impatience. My dinner was served as usual in my room. I ate little, I left the table at seven o'clock. One hundred and twenty minutes more separated me, from the moment I was to join Ned Land. My agitation increased: my pulse beat violently, I could not rest a moment. I moved about, in the hope to calm my mind by so doing. The idea of non-success was the least painful of my cares, but the thought of having our enterprise discovered before we quitted the ship; of being arraigned before Captain Nemo, irritated, or what would be even worse, sad at my abandonment of him, made my heart beat painfully.

I wished to take a last look at the saloon. I gazed at all its riches, and treasured specimens, like one on the brink of exile, and who was never to see these things again. Those marvels of Nature, the masterpieces of Art, amongst which my life had moved on for so long – was I about to abandon them for ever! I wished to take a glance through the windows across the Atlantic waves, but the panels were closed, and an iron cloak separated me from the ocean which I should no longer know.

As I wandered round the saloon, I reached a door that opened into the captain's room. To my great surprise it was ajar. I drew back involuntarily. If Captain Nemo were in his room, he would see me. However, not hearing any noise, I approached the room – it was empty. I pushed the door and entered. All was still, and plain of aspect as ever.

Just then some engravings, which I had not noticed in my previous visit, attracted my attention. They were portraits of men renowned in history, whose existences have been devoted to some grand aim. Kosciusko, the Pole; Botzaris, the Leonidas of modern Greece; O'Connell, the Irish Patriot; Washington, the founder of the American Republic; Mauin, the Italian Patriot; Lincoln, who fell by the assassin's bullet; and finally that martyr to the freedom of the black races – John Brown, depicted on the gibbet, as drawn with such terrible truthfulness by Victor Hugo.

What fellow-feeling existed between these heroic souls and the mind of Captain Nemo? Could I now unravel the mystery of his existence! Was he a champion of an oppressed people – the liberator of a race of slaves? Had he taken part in the later political and social commotions of the century? Was he one of the heroes of that terrible, lamentable, yet glorious American war?

The clock struck eight. The sound of the first stroke roused me from my dreaming. I trembled as if some invisible eye had read my most secret thoughts, and I hurriedly left the room.

In the saloon my eye fell upon the compass. We were still going north. The log indicated a moderate speed, the manometer gave a depth of about sixty feet. These circumstances were favourable for the Canadian's plan.

I regained my room. I clothed myself warmly, sea-boots, a cap of otter-skin, a coat of byssus, lined with seal-skin – I was ready – waiting. The vibrations of the screw alone broke the profound

silence that reigned throughout the ship. I listened most attentively. Would no uproar tell me that Ned Land had failed? A mortal uneasiness was upon me. I in vain endeavoured to assume my
usual coolness.

It was nearly nine o'clock; I put my ear close to the door of
the captain's room. No sound whatever! I left my room and
entered the saloon, which was rather dark, but quite deserted.

I opened the door communicating with the library. The same
semi-obscurity reigned here, but there was sufficient light.
I placed myself close to the door opening to the central staircase.
Here I awaited Ned Land's signal.

At this moment the beatings of the screw diminished sensibly,
then ceased altogether. Why this change in the pace of the
Nautilus? Whether this stoppage would facilitate or prevent
the designs of Ned Land, I could not imagine.

I could hear no sound but the throbbing of my heart. Suddenly
a slight shock was felt, and I perceived that the *Nautilus* had
grounded at the bottom of the ocean. My uneasiness increased,
the Canadian made no sign. I had a great mind to join Ned Land,
and induce him to forgo his attempt to escape; I felt that our progress was no longer being made under ordinary conditions.

The door of the saloon now opened, and Captain Nemo
appeared. He perceived me, and without preamble, addressed me.

"Ah! professor, I was seeking you. Do you know your Spanish
history?"

One might know the history of one's own country perfectly,
while, under the conditions in which I then was – mind upset,
and head in a whirl – one could not recall a fact.

"Well," repeated Captain Nemo, "did you hear my question?
Do you know Spanish history?"

"Not very well," I replied.

"There are *savants* then," replied the captain, "who know!
Well, sit down, for I am going to relate to you a curious episode
in this history."

The captain lay down upon a sofa; mechanically I sat beside
him.

"Listen attentively, Monsieur, if you please," he said. "This
history will interest you, for it will answer a question you have,
no doubt, not yet been able to solve."

"I am listening, captain," I replied, not knowing what he was leading up to, and whether he was about to touch upon our projected escape.

"If you have no objection," said Captain Nemo, "we will go back to the year 1702. You are aware that at that time your King Louis XIV, thinking that his gesture was enough to bring the Pyrenees into his kingdom again, imposed his grandson, the Duke of Anjou, on the Spaniards. This prince, who reigned more or less badly under the name of Philip V, had to do with a strong party abroad.

"In fact, in the preceding year Holland, Austria, and England had concluded a treaty of alliance at the Hague with the view to snatch the crown from Philip V, and bestow it upon an archduke whom they prematurely designated Charles III.

"Spain felt she ought to resist this, but she was almost deprived of soldiers and sailors. However, money would be forthcoming if only all those galleons laden with gold and silver could arrive from America. Now, towards the end of 1702, the Spaniards awaited a rich convoy which France was escorting by a fleet of twenty-three ships under the command of Admiral Chateau-Renaud, for the combined fleets were already in the Atlantic.

"This convoy was to arrive at Cadiz, but the admiral, hearing that the English fleet was cruising in the neighbourhood, resolved to enter a French port. The Spanish officers protested against this. They wanted to be conducted into a Spanish port – if not Cadiz, Vigo, situated on the N.E. coast of Spain, and which was not blockaded.

"Admiral Chateau-Renaud was weak enough to comply, and the galleons entered Vigo Bay. Unfortunately this bay forms an open roadstead which could not be defended. It was then necessary to hurry on the discharge of the galleons before the arrival of the hostile fleet, and plenty of time was available for the operation had not a petty question of precedence arisen.

"You are following the facts?" asked Captain Nemo.

"Perfectly," I said; not knowing how all this was to be applied to me.

"Well, then, this is what occurred, the Cadiz merchants had a privilege according to which they were to receive all merchandise which came from the West Indies. Now, to disembark ingots at Vigo was against their privileges. They, therefore, lodged a complaint at Madrid and obtained from the weak

Philip V permission for the convoy to remain in sequestration in the roadstead of Vigo until the hostile fleet had disappeared from the neighbourhood.

"But while this decision was being arrived at, the English fleet appeared in Vigo Bay. Admiral Chateau-Renaud, notwithstanding his inferior force, gave them battle. But when he saw that the convoy was likely to fall into the enemies' hands, he burnt and sunk the galleons, which went to the bottom with the immense treasure on board."

Captain Nemo paused; I could not yet perceive how this history could interest me.

"Well?" I said.

"Well, sir," replied Captain Nemo, "we are now in Vigo Bay, and, if you please, you can penetrate its mysteries."

He rose and begged me to accompany him. I had had time to recover myself. I obeyed. The saloon was dark, but the sea scintillated before the windows; I looked out.

All round the *Nautilus*, to a distance of perhaps half a mile, the sea appeared to be illuminated by electric light. The sandy bottom was clear and distinct. Some of our crew in their diving-dresses were engaged in clearing rotten barrels and empty chests from the wrecks. From these barrels and cases ingots of gold and silver were escaping, cascades of money and jewels. They were piled up on the sand. Then, laden with their booty, the men returned to the *Nautilus*, and, depositing their loads, went back for another haul in this inexhaustible fishery of silver and gold.

I understood it all. This was the scene of the battle of the 22nd October, 1702. It was here that the galleons, laden for the Spanish Government, had been sunk. Here Captain Nemo was enabled to secure, as he chose, millions to ballast the *Nautilus*. 'Twas for him, and him alone, that America had yielded that precious metal. He was the sole heir to these treasures, torn away from Incas, and from the conquered people of Ferdinand Cortez.

"Were you ever aware that the sea contained such riches, professor?"

"I have heard that the silver in suspension in these waters has been estimated at two millions."

"No doubt; but to extract this silver, the expenses would carry away all profit. Here, on the contrary, I have only to collect what has been lost; and not only here, but at the scenes of a thousand other shipwrecks, which I have noted on the chart. Now do you perceive why I am so rich?"

"Yes, captain; but allow me to inform you that, in exploring the Bay of Vigo, you are only a little ahead of a rival."

"What is that?"

"A society has received from the Spanish Government the privilege to search for these sunken galleons. The shareholders are attracted by the promise of a large booty, for they value the contents of these ships at five hundred millions."

"They were five hundred millions," replied Captain Nemo, "but they are not so now."

"In fact, then," said I, "a warning to these shareholders would only be a charitable action. But how would it be received? That which gamblers regret above all, usually, is less the loss of their money than that of their foolish expectations. I pity them less, after all, than the numbers of unhappy people to whom so much treasure, well bestowed, would have been a boon; while they will be for ever useless to them."

No sooner had I made this remark than I felt it had wounded Captain Nemo.

"Useless!" he said, with animation. "Do you imagine, Monsieur, that these treasures are lost because I gather them? Is it for myself – as you imagine – that I give myself all this trouble to collect this wealth? Who has told you that I do not make a good use of it all? Do you think I do not know that suffering people and oppressed races exist on the earth – unhappy ones to console and victims to avenge? Do you not understand—"

Captain Nemo checked himself, regretting, perhaps, that he had said so much. But I had guessed. Whatever the motives that had forced him to seek freedom on the ocean, after all he was a man at heart. His bosom throbbed for the sufferings of mankind, and his unlimited charity was extended to oppressed races, as well as to individuals.

And I understood then to whom these millions were forwarded by Captain Nemo, when the *Nautilus* was cruising in the neighbourhood of the Crete insurgents.

CHAPTER IX
A SUBMERGED CONTINENT

THE NEXT MORNING (19th February) Ned Land entered my room. I rather expected him. He wore a very disappointed look.

"Well, Monsieur," he said.

"Well, Ned, fate was adverse yesterday."

"Yes, because that damned captain stopped exactly at the hour we were about to get into the boat."

"Yes, Ned; he had some business to transact with his banker."

"His banker!"

"Or rather, I should say his banking-house. I mean by that this ocean, in which his treasures are more safe than in the coffers of a state."

I then narrated the occurrences of the previous evening, in the secret hope to bring him back to the idea not to abandon the captain, but my recital had no other result than to cause him to regret, in the most energetic manner of which he was capable (which was something), of not having been able to make a little excursion on his own account into the "battle-field" of Vigo.

"However," he said, "all is not lost yet. It is only a 'cast' lost. We will recoup ourselves another time, and this evening—"

"How is the ship's head?" I asked.

"I do not know," he replied.

"Well, to-morrow at noon we shall see the observations."

The Canadian returned to Conseil. So soon as I was dressed I entered the saloon. The compass did not give us any hope, the course was S.S.E. We were turning our backs on Europe.

I waited with some impatience till the bearings were taken. About half-past eleven the reservoirs were emptied, and we mounted to the surface of the ocean.

I hastened up to the platform, Ned Land had anticipated me.

Land was no longer in view. Nothing was to be seen but the expanse of ocean. There were a few sails on the horizon seeking at Cape St. Roque favourable winds to double the cape. The weather was overcast, a storm was brewing.

Ned, in rage, attempted to pierce the misty horizon. He was in hopes still that behind all this cloud there might be some land for which he was so anxious.

At mid-day the sun showed himself for an instant. The mate profited by this burst to take the elevation. Then the sea got up again, we descended accordingly, and the panels were closed.

An hour afterwards, when I was looking at the chart, I saw that the position of the *Nautilus* was 16° 17′ long. and 33° 22′ lat., about 150 leagues from the nearest shore. There was no chance even to think of escape, and I may fairly leave you to guess the feelings of Ned Land when he fully recognized the situation of things.

I did not worry myself particularly. I felt in a manner relieved from a weight that had oppressed me, and I was able to return to my usual occupations with some degree of calmness.

About 11 p.m. I received a very unexpected visit from Captain Nemo. He inquired very politely whether I felt fatigued by my exertions of the preceding evening. I replied in the negative.

"Then, Monsieur, I will suggest a very interesting excursion."

"By all means, captain," I said.

"Hitherto you have only visited the ocean depths by day and with the light of the sun. Should you like to see them on a dark night?"

"Very much, indeed."

"I warn you the excursion will be tiring. We shall have to walk for a long distance and scale a mountain. The roads are not very well marked."

"What you say only redoubles my curiosity. I am quite ready to accompany you."

"Come along, then," replied the captain, "let us put on our diving-dresses."

As we reached the room in which the dresses were kept, I perceived that none of the crew, nor had either of my companions, been selected to follow us on this excursion. Captain Nemo had not proposed my taking either Conseil or Ned.

We were ready in a few minutes. We shouldered a reservoir of air each, but the electric lamps were not prepared; I called the captain's attention to this.

"They would be of no use," he said.

I fancied I was mistaken, but I could not repeat the suggestion, for the captain had already put on his helmet. I managed to equip myself, and I felt somebody put an iron-pointed stick into my hand, and some moments later we touched the bottom of the Atlantic, at a depth of three hundred yards.

Midnight was at hand. The water was very dark, but Captain
Nemo pointed to a reddish gleam in the distance, a sort of
extended light, which burned at about two miles distant from
the *Nautilus*. What this fire was, how it was fed, why and how it
burned amid the waters, I could not hazard a conjecture. In any
case it gave us light, vaguely 'tis true, but I soon became accustomed to the peculiar obscurity, and I understood the inutility
of the Ruhmkorff apparatus under the circumstances.

We advanced side by side directly towards the fire. The flat
ground mounted gradually. We made very long strides, assisted
by our sticks, but still our progress was not rapid, for our feet
often sank into a sort of ooze.

But, still advancing, I heard a sort of pattering noise overhead.
This sometimes increased until it sounded like a hailstorm. I soon
understood the cause; it was the raindrops falling upon the
surface of the waves. Instinctively I had an idea that I should get
very wet. Wetted by rainwater in the middle of the sea! I could
not refrain from a quiet chuckle inside my helmet at the idea;
but, as a fact, in the thick diver's dress one does not feel the water,
and can fancy oneself in an atmosphere only a little more dense
than the terrestrial atmosphere, that's all.

After half-an-hour's walking the ground became stony.
Medusæ, small crustacea, &c., lit up with their light phosphorescent gleams. I caught glimpses of piles of rocks covered with
millions of zoophytes and algæ. My foot often slipped upon the
viscous carpet of varech, and had it not been for my *bâton* I should
have fallen more than once. When I turned round I could see the
white lamp of the *Nautilus*, though paling a little, in the distance.

These stony heaps of which I have spoken were disposed at
the bottom of the ocean with a degree of regularity which I could
not explain. I saw gigantic furrows which lost themselves in the
obscurity, and whose length exceeded all computation. Other
curious experiences presented themselves. It appeared to me that
my heavy leaden soles crushed a litter of bony fragments which
cracked with a loud noise. What was this vast plain which I was
treading? I should have liked to ask the captain, but his language
of signs, which permitted communication with his companions
when they accompanied him in his submarine excursions, was
utterly incomprehensible to me.

Meanwhile, the flame which guided us increased, and lighted

up the horizon. The existence of this fire beneath the ocean puzzled me considerably. Was it electric? Was I about to become acquainted with a natural phenomenon hitherto unknown? Or had the power of man aught to do vith this? Were men fanning this flame? Was I about to meet in these depths friends and companions of Captain Nemo, living like him this strange life, and whom he was about to visit? Should we find here below a colony of exiles, who, tired of earth and its troubles, had sought and found independence in the lowest depths of the ocean? These foolish and utterly absurd ideas pressed upon me, and in my condition of mind, over-excited by the wonders I beheld at every step, I should not have been very much astonished to enter, at the bottom of this ocean, one of those submarine towns of which Captain Nemo dreamed.

Our route got more and more illuminated. The white gleam radiated from a mountain about 800 feet in height. But what I could see was only a reflection thrown up by the crystal of the sea depths. The fire, the original cause of this extraordinary illumination, lay at the opposite slope of the hill.

Captain Nemo advanced amid the rocky masses without the least hesitation. He evidently was acquainted with this dark road. He had doubtless frequently traversed it, and would not lose his way. I followed him in full confidence. He seemed to me like one of those genii of the sea, and as he walked in front, I admired his lofty stature, which was thrown out in strong relief against the luminous horizon.

It was 1 a.m. We reached the first slopes of the mountain, but to cross them we were obliged to attempt a difficult path in a vast thicket. Yes, a thicket of dead trees, trees mineralized by the action of the water, with here and there a gigantic pine dominating them. It was like a standing coal-pit, whose ramifications, like cuttings upon black paper, stood out clearly against the watery ceiling. It was like a submerged forest of the Hartz, clinging to the mountain sides. The paths were encumbered with algæ and fucus, amongst which crawled a whole colony of crustacea. I went on jumping over the rocks, striding over the tree-trunks, breaking away the bind-weed that extended from branch to branch, and frightening the fish. Carried onward, I felt no weariness. I followed my guide, who knew no fatigue.

And what a sight it was! How can I reproduce it? How can

I depict the aspect of those trees and rocks in this liquid medium, the black foundations, while red-tinged tops glowed in the light, which was doubled by the reflecting powers of the water? We clambered up rocks which gave way as we passed, and fell with the roar of an avalanche. Right and left there were long dark galleries. In other places were vast clear spaces, apparently man's handiwork, and I wondered whether some inhabitant of these submarine districts would not suddenly appear!

Captain Nemo still kept ascending, and I could not stay. I followed him boldly. My *bâton* was of great assistance; a false step would have been dangerous on those narrow places, but I walked carefully, and without feeling giddy. Sometimes I was obliged to jump a crevasse, the depth of which would have repelled me on land; sometimes I ventured across the unsteady trunk of a tree, thrown over an abyss; and without looking to my feet, for my eyes were fully occupied in admiring the wild scenery. Monumental-like rocks, perched upon irregular bases, here seemed to defy all laws of equilibrium. Between their stony embraces trees sprang up, like a jet under the influence of great pressure, and sustained those which sustained them in turn. Then natural towers and escarpments which inclined at an angle that gravitation would never have permitted on land.

I, myself, felt the influence of the great density of the water, for, notwithstanding my heavy clothing, I was able to scale these stiff ascents with the lightness and ease of a chamois.

In thus narrating my expedition under water, I am aware that it may appear incredible. I am merely the historian of things apparently impossible, but none the less real and incontestible. I did not dream all these things; I saw, and came in contact with them.

Two hours after leaving the *Nautilus*, we had cleared the line of trees; and the mountain, a hundred feet above us, threw a long shadow upon the opposite slope. Some petrified trees appeared to move in fantastic zigzags. Fishes rose in masses under our feet, like frightened birds in the long grass. The massive rocks were seamed with immense fissures; deep grottos, unfathomable holes, in which formidable creatures were moving about. The blood went back to my heart when I perceived an enormous antenna blocking up the way, or a frightful claw shutting with a loud noise in the depths of the caverns. Thousands of luminous points glittered in the darkness. These were the eyes of enormous crustacea; giant lobsters, holding themselves upright like so many halberdiers, and moving their claws with a clanking sound; titanic crabs, and fearful octopi, waving their arms like a nest full of serpents. What was the extraordinary world which hitherto I had never known? To what order did these articulates belong, for whom the rocks formed a second carapace? Where had nature discovered the secret of their vegetative life, and how long – how many centuries – had they lived thus in the lowest depths of the ocean?

But I was unable to halt. Captain Nemo, evidently familiar with these terrible creatures, paid no heed to them; so we reached the first platform, where there were other surprises in store for me. There were scattered ruins which betrayed the hand of man, not of the Creator. Amongst the piles of stones, rose the vague forms of chateaux and temples, clothed with zoophytes in full flower; and over which, like ivy, the algæ and fucus threw a thick vegetable mantle.

I would have fain asked Captain Nemo for an explanation of all this, but, not being able to do so, I stopped and seized his arm; but he shook his head and, pointing to the last peak of the mountain, motioned me onward. I followed, and in a few minutes we gained the top, which, in a circle of ten yards, commanded the whole of the rocky expanse beneath.

I looked down the ascent we had just climbed. The mountain was only about 700 feet high from that plain we had left, but on the other side it looked down twice the height to the depths of the Atlantic. My gaze roamed over a vast space, lighted up by a violent conflagration. The mountain was, in fact, a volcano. Fifty feet below the summit a large crater was vomiting torrents of lava in the midst of a rain of stones and scoriæ; the volcano lit up the plain below like an immense torch, even to the limits of the horizon.

I have said that the volcano cast up lava but no flames. To have flame oxygen of the air is necessary, and flame cannot be developed under water, but lava possesses in itself the principle of incandescence, and reaches a white heat, and, in contact with the liquid element, gains the upper hand and vaporizes it. Rapid currents, carrying all the gases in diffusion, and the lava torrents, flowed to the base of the mountain, like the eruptions of Vesuvius upon another *Torre del Greco*.

In fact, beneath my eyes, ruined and destroyed, appeared the remains of a town, its roofs open, its temples fallen, its architecture gone, and, in the columns still remaining, the Tuscan style could be recognized.

Further on were the traces of a gigantic aqueduct, and again the base of an Acropolis, with the dim outlines of a Parthenon. Here were vestiges of a quay, as if an ancient harbour had been existent, and had sunk, with its merchantmen and ships of war, to the bottom. At a greater distance still were long lines of sunken walls and streets – a Pompeii engulfed in the ocean.

Where was I? I was determined to know at any hazard. I wished to speak, and would have taken off my helmet had not Captain Nemo stopped me by a gesture. He then picked up a piece of chalky stone, and, advancing towards a black rock, he wrote the single word –

ATLANTIS

A sudden light flashed through my mind. Atlantis! The ancient Meropis of Theopompus! The Atlantis of Plato! The continent whose existence was denied by Origen, Porphyrus, Jambilicus, D'Anville, Malte-Brun, and Humboldt, who ranked its disappearance amongst the old legends. Admitted by Passidonius, Pliny, Tertullian, Engel, Sherer, Tournefort, Buffon, d'Avezac, there it was now before my eyes, bearing witness to the catastrophe. The region thus engulfed lay astride Europe, Asia, and Africa; beyond the Pillars of Hercules, in which lived a people – the powerful Atlantides – against whom was waged the first battles of ancient Greece.

Plato, himself, is the historian who has recounted the events of the heroic times.

"One day Solon was conversing with some aged sages of Saïs, a town then 800 years old, as its graven annals bear witness. One of the old men was narrating the history of another town more ancient still. This first Athenian city, 800 years old, had been attacked and partly destroyed by the Atlantides. These people occupied an immense continent, greater than Africa and Asia put together, which covered a surface between the 12° to 14° N. lat. Their domination extended even to Egypt, and they wished to conquer Greece also, but were repulsed by the indomitable resistance they met with. Centuries rolled on. A cataclysm occurred – inundations and earthquakes. A night and a day sufficed for the destruction of the Atlantis; the highest summits – Madeira, the Azores, the Canaries, and the Cape Verd Islands – only remaining above water."

Such were the historical souvenirs which Captain Nemo's inscription called up in my mind. Thus, led by the strangest destiny, I was standing upon one of the mountains of that continent; I was touching these ruins, a thousand centuries old, and of the geological epoch; I was walking in the places where the contemporaries of the first man had walked; I was crushing under foot the skeletons of animals of a fabulous age, which the trees, now mineralized, once covered with their shade.

Ah! If time had not failed me, I should have descended those steep hills and explored the whole continent – which, no doubt, unites Africa to America – and visited the grand antediluvian cities. Here lived those gigantic races of old, who were able to move those blocks which still resisted the action of the water. Some day, perhaps, a convulsion of nature will heave these ruins up again. Many submarine volcanoes have been reported in this portion of the ocean; and many ships have felt extraordinary shocks in passing over these disturbed depths. The whole of the soil, to the equator, is still rent by these Platonian forces; and who knows but that at some distant day the summits of these volcanic mountains will appear once more above the surface of the Atlantic!

As I was musing thus, and endeavouring to fix the details on my memory, Captain Nemo remained immoveable, and as if petrified. Was he thinking of those former generations, and endeavouring to elucidate the secret of human destiny. Was it to this place he came to revel in historical memories, and to revive the ancient life – he to whom a modern one was distasteful. What would I not have given to have known his thoughts, to share them, to understand them!

We remained in the same place for a whole hour, contemplating the vast plain by the gleam of the lava, which at times glowed with intense brilliancy. Loud noises were clearly transmitted by the water, and were echoed with majestic fulness of sound.

The moon now appeared across the waters, and threw her pale rays over the engulfed continent. It was but a gleam, but it had a wonderful effect. The captain rose, threw a last look at the immense plain, and then signalled to me to return.

We rapidly descended the mountain. The mineral forest once passed, we could perceive the lantern of the *Nautilus* shining in the distance like a star. The captain made directly for it, and we got on board just as the first rays of dawn were brightening the surface of the ocean.

CHAPTER X
THE SUBMARINE COAL-FIELDS

I AWOKE VERY LATE next morning, the 20th February. I dressed quickly, and hastened to ascertain the course of the *Nautilus*. The instruments indicated a southerly direction at a speed of twenty miles, and at 100 yards below the surface.

Conseil entered. I related to him the incidents of our nocturnal excursion, and the panels being open, we could catch a glimpse of the sunken continent.

In fact, the *Nautilus* was only about ten yards from the bottom of the Atlantic, and skimmed along like a balloon, hurried across terrestrial prairies, but it would be more correct to say that we were apparently in a saloon carriage of an express train. The first objects that we passed were fantastically splintered rock forests which had been changed from the vegetable to the animal kingdom, and whose immoveable outline was shadowed beneath the waves. Stony masses hidden beneath a carpet of axidies and anemones, bristling with long vertical hydrophytes, and strangely twisted blocks of lava, which attested the fury of the eruptions.

While these strange things were clearly observable under our electric light, I made Conseil acquainted with the history of the Atlantides; which, from a purely imaginative point of view, inspired Bailly with material for many charming pages. But Conseil appeared somewhat indifferent to my wish to discuss those questions respecting ancient Atlantis, and his indifference was soon explained.

So many fish passed before him, and when fish were in the way Conseil plunged into the depths of classification, and went out of the world altogether. In this case I could only yield, and study with him.

The fish in the Atlantic, as a rule, do not differ much from those we have already noticed. There were gigantic rays, various kinds of sharks, a glaucus about fifteen feet long, with sharp triangular teeth, brown sagre, humanteris sturgeons, trumpet syngnathes, about a foot and a half long, without teeth or tongue, which swam like beautiful and lissome serpents.

Amongst the bony fishes, Conseil noted the black mokairas, nine feet long, and armed with a long sharp "sword" in the upper jaw; other coloured animals known in the days of Aristotle, as the sea-dragon, whose spikes and sharp dorsal fin make it dangerous to grasp with the bare hand, coraphines whose brown backs were prettily striped with blue and surrounded by a golden edging; beautiful dorades also, and troops of enormous sword-fish, fierce animals, some of them more than twenty-four feet in length. They are more herbivorous than carnivorous, and the males obeyed the slightest gesture of the female fish, as well-trained husbands should do.

But all this time I did not fail to examine the long plains of Atlantis. Sometimes the nature of the bottom obliged the *Nautilus* to slacken speed, and it glided with the dexterity of a cetacean amongst the scattered hillocks. If the labyrinth appeared inextricable the vessel rose like a balloon, and the obstacle overcome it resumed its course at the lower level. An admirable and charming way of sailing which recalled a balloon voyage with the difference that the *Nautilus* always obeyed the hand of the steersman.

About 4 p.m. the appearance of the soil, hitherto composed of thick mud and petrified wood, began to change. It was more stony now, and sprinkled with conglomerate and basaltic lumps, with lava and sulphurous obsidian. I fancied that a mountainous region would soon succeed the plains, and at a movement of the *Nautilus* I perceived the southern horizon was barred by a high wall which appeared to block all further progress. The summit of this was evidently above the sea level. It must be a continent or an island, perhaps one of the Canaries, or Cape Verd islands. The observations not having yet been taken, perhaps designedly omitted, I was ignorant of our position. At any rate this wall appeared to me to mark the limit of Atlantis, only a very small portion of which we had traversed after all.

Night put an end to my observations. I was left alone. Conseil had retired to his cabin. The *Nautilus* slackened speed, sometimes it passed over high ground, sometimes it almost touched bottom, and at times it rose capriciously to the surface of the ocean.

I could have remained much longer at the window but the panels were closed. The *Nautilus* had now reached the high wall. What would be done now? I regained my room; the *Nautilus* did not move. I went to sleep with the determination to wake after an hour or two.

But it was eight o'clock next morning when I re-entered the saloon. I perceived by the manometer that the *Nautilus* was floating on the surface. Besides, I could hear a noise upon the platform. Nevertheless, no rolling motion betokened that we were lying at the surface of the water.

I ascended to the deck panel. It was open. But instead of the daylight I expected, all around was dark. Where were we? Had I made a mistake and it was still night? No, not a star glittered, and no night is so absolutely dark.

I did not know what to think of this when a voice close to me said:

"Ah, professor, is that you?"

"Oh, Captain Nemo," I cried, "where are we?"

"Under ground!" he replied.

"Under ground, and the *Nautilus* afloat, too!"

"It always does float," replied the captain.

"I do not understand," I said.

"Wait a minute or two and you will. Our lantern will soon be lighted, and if you like light you will then be satisfied."

I accordingly waited. The darkness was so thick that I could not even see Captain Nemo. Nevertheless, just exactly overhead I fancied I could detect a glimmer of twilight coming through a circular hole.

At this moment the lamp was lighted, and its strong light quite extinguished the gleam overhead.

I looked round me so soon as I could accustom my eyes to the sudden change from the darkness. The *Nautilus* did not move. It was floating alongside a mountain like an enormous quay. The water in which it floated formed a lake enclosed within a circle of rocky walls about two miles in diameter. The level indicated by the manometer was only that of the exterior sea-level, for a communication, of course, existed between the lake and the ocean. The high rocks leant over and united in a vaulted roof about 500 or 600 yards above us. At the top was a circular hole, through which I had caught that glimpse of daylight.

"Where are we?" I asked.

"In the heart of an extinct volcano," replied the captain; "a volcano to which the sea was admitted by some great natural convulsion. While you were asleep the *Nautilus* entered this lagoon by a canal which opens about ten yards below the surface of the ocean. This is our harbour of refuge, sure, safe, commodious, and mysterious, perfectly sheltered. Can you find me any harbour in the world so completely out of the reach of all storms?"

"You are certainly in perfect safety here, captain – who could reach you in the centre of a volcano? But is there not an opening at the top?"

"Yes, the crater, which now gives passage to the air we breathe."

"But what is this volcano?"

"It belongs to one of the numerous islands scattered in this sea. A rock for all vessels save mine, for us an enormous cavern. I discovered it by chance, and in that fate befriended me."

"But can no one descend through the crater?" I asked.

"No more than I can ascend it. For a hundred feet up the interior base of the mountain is practicable, but above the cliffs are perpendicular, and they cannot be scaled."

"I see, captain, that Nature helps you everywhere, and in everything. You are in perfect safety here, and no one can intrude in these waters. But what is the good of it, after all? The *Nautilus* does not require a harbour."

"No, but it requires electricity to move it, and the elements to make the electricity; sodium to supply those elements, carbon to make the sodium, and coal to extract the carbon. In this very spot the sea covers entire forests which were embedded during the geological period, now mineralized and become coal, an inexhaustible mine for me."

"Your crew become miners here, then, captain."

"Certainly. These mines extend beneath the waves, like the Newcastle collieries. Here in their divers' dresses, with pick and shovel, my men dig the coal out, which I do not ask from terrestrial mines. When I burn it to make sodium, the smoke escapes by the crater, which makes the mountain appear as an active volcano."

"Shall we see your companions at work?" I asked.

"Well, not this time, for I am in a hurry to continue our voyage. So I will only draw the sodium from my reserves. We only allow a day to put it on board; so if you wish to see the cavern and make a tour of the lagoon you had better take advantage of that day, M. Aronnax."

I thanked the captain and sought my companions, who had not yet left their cabin. I invited them to accompany me, but did not tell them where we were.

They ascended to the platform. Conseil, who was never astonished at anything, looked upon it as quite a natural thing to wake up in the centre of a mountain, having gone to sleep while under water. But Ned Land thought of nothing but of finding an exit.

After breakfast – about six o'clock – we landed.

"Well, here we are on land again," said Conseil.

"I don't call this land," replied Ned. "And, besides, we are not on land, we are underneath it."

Between the mountain side and the lake ran a sandy ridge about 500 feet wide at its greatest breadth. We could easily walk round the lake upon this shore. At the base of the rocks was a rough soil, upon which, in picturesque confusion, lay volcanic blocks and enormous pumice boulders. All these masses, polished as they were by the action of fire, shone under the gleam of our electric lamps. The micacious dust flew around like sparks.

The ground ascended as we left the margin, and we soon arrived at long inclined planes or slopes, but we were obliged to step carefully amongst those loose conglomerates, upon which the feet often slipped.

The truly volcanic nature of the place was everywhere observable, and I pointed it out to Ned and Conseil.

"Can you imagine," I asked, "what this crater must have been when choked with boiling lava, and when the level of the boiling liquid rose to the aperture of the mountain?"

"I can imagine quite well," replied Conseil. "But will Monsieur tell me why the Great Founder has suspended this operation, and how it is that the furnace is filled by the tranquil waters of a lake?"

"Most likely," I replied, "because some convulsion of nature produced the opening through which the *Nautilus* entered. The waters of the Atlantic then deluged the interior of the mountain.

It must have been a terrible struggle between the two elements, but Neptune gained the day. Many ages have elapsed since then, and the submerged volcano is now a peaceful grotto."

"All right, sir!" said Ned, "I will accept the explanation, but I should have preferred, for our sakes, that the opening of which you speak had been above the sea level."

"But, friend Ned," replied Conseil, "if the passage were not submarine, the *Nautilus* would not have been able to enter it."

"And I may add that, if the water had not rushed in under the mountain, the volcano would have remained in activity. So your regrets are altogether superfluous."

We continued to ascend. The slopes became more and more narrow and perpendicular. There were many deep crevasses which we were obliged to cross. Overhanging rocks had to be turned. We crawled on our knees and even on our stomachs; but Conseil's skill and Ned's strength succeeded in surmounting all obstacles.

At a height of about ninety feet, the nature of the ground underwent an alteration, though it became no more practicable for us. Black basalt succeeded to the conglomerates and trachytes; the former in an extended surface, sprinkled with bubbles; the latter in prisms, placed like a colonnade, an admirable specimen of nature's architecture. Amongst the basalt wound streams of cold lava, incrusted with bituminous rays; and in places there were quantities of sulphur. A stronger gleam entered by the crater, and lit up vaguely the eruptive remains buried for ever in the bosom of the mountain.

But our ascent was soon arrested at a height of about 250 feet. A vault overhung our heads, and our ascent gave way to a circuitous walk. Here the vegetable kingdom struggled with the mineral. Some shrubs and even a few trees appeared in the fissures. I saw some euphorbias with the caustic juice exuding from them; some heliotropes – quite unable to justify their name, since the sun never reached them – drooped their flowers, both scent and colour being half gone. A few chrysanthemums gushed their timid way up at the stems of the aloes, with their sad and sickly leaves. But, amid the lava, I perceived some little violets, still scented, and I confess that I inhaled their perfume with delight. Perfume is the soul of a flower, and sea flowers – the splendid hydrophytes – have no souls.

We had reached some fine dragon trees, which had thrust away the stones by their strong roots, when Ned said:

"Look here! Here's a hive – a hive!"

"A hive?" I exclaimed, incredulously.

"Yes, a hive; and the bees humming around it, too."

I approached, and was bound to confess the fact. There it was, in a hole in the dragon tree, inhabited by some thousands of bees so common in the Canary Isles, where their produce is held in particularly high estimation.

The Canadian naturally wished to lay in a stock of honey, and I was loth to prevent him. He soon got together some leaves, and with a quantity of sulphur he began to fumigate the bees. The humming gradually subsided, and the hive yielded several pounds of excellent honey, which Ned placed in his haversack.

"When I have mixed the honey with a paste of artocarpus," he said, "I shall be ready to offer you an excellent cake."

"By Jove!" said Conseil, "that will be like gingerbread."

"Bother the gingerbread!" I said. "Let us continue our excursion."

At various turns of the path we had the view of the lake from end to end. The lantern lit up the whole of the unruffled surface. The *Nautilus* was perfectly motionless. The crew were at work at the side of the mountain and upon the platform, like black shadows, clearly defined against the light.

At this time we were rounding the highest crests of the most elevated of the first pillars of rock supporting the vaulted roof. I then saw that the bees were not the only representatives of animal life in the volcano. Birds of prey flew hither and thither in the obscurity, or rose from their nests on the pinnacles of rock. There were sparrow-hawks and kestrels. Several bustards scampered down the slopes. You can imagine how Ned's mouth watered at the sight of this game, and how he regretted he had no gun with him. He endeavoured to make up for the absence of lead with stones and, after several misses, he did manage to disable a splendid bustard. It is only right to say that he risked his life twenty times in his endeavours to secure it, but he succeeded, at length, in pouching the bird along with the honey.

We had to descend towards the shore, for the crest had become impracticable. Overhead the crater gaped like a great pit shaft, and we could see the sky distinctly, and the clouds flying to the eastward, leaving mist on the mountain as they passed.

Half an hour later we gained the inner shore. Here the flora were represented by marine crystal, a little umbelliferous plant very good for pickling, and also known as sea-fennel. Conseil picked some. The fauna were represented by thousands of crustacea of all kinds, lobsters, crabs, spider-crabs, &c., &c.

Here we lighted upon a beautiful grotto. We stretched ourselves gladly upon the smooth, fine sand. Ned Land amused me by sounding the rocky sides with the view to ascertain their thickness. The conversation turned upon the everlasting project of escape, and I believed I was justified, without stating so absolutely, to give Ned hope by telling him that Captain Nemo had only come down south to renew his supply of sodium. I hoped that now he would return to the European and American coasts and give the Canadian the opportunity to put his scheme into execution with success.

We stayed in the grotto for more than an hour, but as the conversation languished, sleep stole over us. We slept, and I dreamt that I was a mollusc, and that the grotto formed the two valves of my shell. Suddenly I was awakened by Conseil.

"Get up, get up!" he cried.

"What is the matter?" I said, sitting up.

"The water is rising!"

I jumped up. The sea was rushing into the grotto like a sluice, and as we were not really molluscs, it was advisable to save ourselves.

In a few moments we were safe at the summit of the grotto.

"What is the cause of that; some new phenomenon?" asked Conseil.

"Oh, no," I replied, "it is only the tide that has surprised us, like Walter Scott's hero. The ocean has risen, and, of course, this lake must rise to the same level. We have escaped with a little wetting only. Let us go on, we can change on board."

Three-quarters of an hour later we had finished our circular tour and got back to the *Nautilus*. The crew had finished embarking the sodium, and the *Nautilus* could start at once. However, the captain gave no order to that effect. Perhaps he wished to wait till nightfall, and pass secretly through the secret canal.

Whatever his reason was, the next day the *Nautilus* was clear of her harbour and, far from land, was skimming along some yards beneath the surface of the Atlantic.

CHAPTER XI
THE SARGASSO SEA

NO ALTERATION WAS made in the course of the *Nautilus* and all hope of gaining European waters was now gone. Where Captain Nemo was hurrying I could not imagine.

That day we crossed a curious portion of the Atlantic. Everyone is acquainted with the existence of the great warm current called the Gulf Stream. Leaving Florida it flows towards Spitzbergen. But before entering the Gulf of Mexico, about the 44° N. lat., the current divides, one branch going towards the Irish coast and up to Norway while the other trends southwards up to the Azores, then touching the coast of Africa, and describing a long oval, it turns again towards the Antilles.

Now, this second arm (or rather collar), surrounds with its warm water the portion of the cold ocean denominated the Sargasso Sea, a veritable lake in the open Atlantic, and it takes the great current no less than three years to encircle it.

The Sargasso Sea, properly speaking, covers the submerged Atlantis. Certain authors have even admitted that the herbs with which it is strewn have been torn from the fields of that ancient continent. It is more probable, however, that these algæ and fucus, loosed from the coasts of Europe and America, are carried hither by the Gulf Stream.

This was one of the reasons why Columbus believed in the existence of a new world. When this hardy navigator arrived in the Sargasso Sea the ships sailed with difficulty in the midst of the herbs, to the terror of the crews, and it took three long weeks to get through them.

Such was the region the *Nautilus* entered, a regular prairie, a carpet of sea-weed, fucus, and berries, so thick and compact that a vessel could hardly make way through it. Captain Nemo, not wishing to get the screw entangled in the weeds, kept the *Nautilus* at some distance beneath the surface.

This name of Sargasso is derived from the Spanish word "Sargazzo", signifying sea-wrack. This wrack or varech is the principal constituent of this immense bank. And the following is the reason, according to Maury, why hydrophytes unite in this peaceful basin in the Atlantic.

"The only possible explanation," says Maury, "seems to me the result of a world-wide experience. If you place in the centre of a vase some fragments of cork or other floating substance, and give to the water a circular motion, the fragments will unite in the centre, in the least agitated part. In the phenomenon we are considering the vase is the Atlantic, the Gulf Stream is the circular current, and the Sargasso Sea the central point where the floating bodies unite."

I agree with Maury, and was enabled to study the phenomenon in the very centre where ships but rarely penetrate. Overhead floated all kinds of products, trunks of trees torn from the Andes or Rocky Mountains, and floated out to sea by the Amazon or the Mississippi; numerous wrecks, keels, and hulls, and planks so heavy with shells and barnacles as to be unable to float on the surface. And time will justify Maury in his other opinion, that these accumulations of centuries will petrify and form inexhaustible coal-fields; a valuable reserve which Nature is preparing for the time when continental coal-mines shall be exhausted.

In the midst of this tangled mass of plants and fucus, I noticed some beautiful rose halcyus trailing their long tentacles, and green, red, and blue medusæ, particularly the great rhizostoms of Cuvier, the blue "umbrella" of which is bordered by a violet fringe.

We passed the whole of the 22nd of February in the Sargasso Sea, where the fish, great admirers of marine plants and crustacea, found abundant food. Next day the ocean had assumed its usual appearance.

For the next nineteen days the *Nautilus* kept in mid-Atlantic. We proceeded steadily, at the rate of 100 leagues in the twenty-four hours. Captain Nemo was evidently determined to carry out his programme, and I had no doubt that he intended, when he had doubled Cape Horn, to return to the South Pacific.

Ned Land had therefore some cause for alarm. In these immense expanses of sea, with but few islands, it would not do to think of escape, nor were there any means to oppose Captain Nemo's wishes. We could only submit, but we might gain by diplomacy what we could not attain by force or stratagem. Once the voyage was over, would not Captain Nemo restore us our liberty, under an oath never to betray him. Now could I claim this liberty? He had declared that the secret of his life entailed in return our lasting incarceration on board the *Nautilus*, and would not my silence for four months look like a tacit acceptation of the conditions? In fact I was forced to confess that our chances of seeing our relatives again diminished more and more from the day Captain Nemo went south again.

During the nineteen days I have referred to, no incident of any note occurred. I saw but little of the captain. He was at work. In the library I often found his books upon natural history left open.

At this part of our voyage we often sailed for whole days at the surface. The sea was, as it were, deserted. A few sailing vessels bound to India, *via* the Cape, were all we perceived. One day we were pursued by the boats of a whaler, who no doubt took us for some valuable whale. But Captain Nemo was unwilling that these brave fellows should lose both time and trouble, and so he plunged incontinently into the depths. This incident appeared to interest Ned Land mightily. I rather think he regretted that our iron cetacean had not been captured by the fishermen.

The fish we observed here were not greatly different from those we had previously noticed; the principal specimens were various kinds of sharks.

We also saw tremendous dog-fish, about which many extravagant stories are related by fishermen, one of which was reported to have swallowed two pickled tunnies and a sailor, clothes and all, another a soldier fully equipped, and, a third, a cavalier and his horse complete. But I do not think we can rank the credit of these tales among our articles of faith. At any rate we caught none, so I could not verify even one story.

Troops of dolphins accompanied us for whole days at a time, and I noticed also some curious specimens of the fish of the acanthopterigian order of the family of scienoïdes.

Some authors, chiefly poets, pretend that these fish sing, and their voices form quite a concert, to which human voices cannot compare. I do not deny this, but at any rate we were not serenaded by them, and I am sorry for it.

We also saw quantities of flying-fish. Nothing can be more curious than to see the dolphins giving chase with such wonderful precision. No matter how the unfortunate fish flew, or what course he took, even across the *Nautilus*, he always dropped into the mouth of his pursuer.

Up to the 13th of March our voyage continued like this. On that day we took some soundings, which interested me particularly.

We had made nearly 13,000 leagues since our departure from the Pacific high seas. The bearings we took gave us 45° 37′ S. lat. and 37° 53′ E. long. We were in the same locality where Captain Denham, of the *Harold*, gave out 14,000 yards of line without touching bottom. There, also, Lieutenant Parker, of the American frigate *Congress*, did not find soundings at 15,140 yards.

Captain Nemo resolved to bring down the *Nautilus* to the greatest depth, to test these different soundings. I made preparation to note the results. The panels were opened and we set about reaching the depths of the ocean.

One might imagine that to dive it was only a question of filling the reservoirs. But perhaps they would not be sufficient. On the other hand, perhaps the pumps were not sufficiently powerful to overcome the exterior pressure.

Captain Nemo resolved to get to the bottom by a long diagonal by means of the inclined planes at the side being placed at an angle of 45°. Then the screw was worked at full speed, and it beat the waves with tremendous violence.

Under this tremendous pressure the *Nautilus* quivered like a chord, and descended straightway into the water.

The captain and I, posted in the saloon, followed the movements of the manometer, which moved rapidly. We soon passed the habitable zone in which the greater number of fish live. I asked Captain Nemo whether he had ever observed fish at a very great depth.

"Very seldom," he said; "but what does science say?"

"It is known," I replied, "that towards the very low depths vegetable life disappears more quickly than the animal; and it is known that where even animated beings are met with no vegetation is observable but hydrophyte. It is known that pelerines and oysters live at 2,000 yards under water, and that Captain McClintock, the Polar hero, has brought up a living star-fish from a depth of 2,500 yards. The nets of the *Bulldog* of the Royal Navy fished up an asteroid from 2,620 fathoms. But, Captain Nemo, perhaps you will say they know nothing about it."

"No, professor; I should not be so rude. And, moreover,

I should like you to explain how these things are able to live at such great depths."

"I can give you two reasons," I replied. "First, because the vertical currents, determined by the difference in the saltness and density of the water, produce a movement which is sufficient to give a rudimentary life on the ecrines and asteroids."

"Quite so," replied the captain.

"Secondly, because, if oxygen be the basis of life, we know that the quantity of oxygen contained in the sea increases with the depth, instead of diminishing, and that the pressure helps to compress it."

"Ah! they know that," said the captain, in a light tone of surprise. "Well, they are right. I will add that the swimming-bladders of fish contain more azote than oxygen when the animal is near the surface, and more oxygen than azote when at a great depth. That gives your system probability. But let us continue our observations."

My gaze was fixed on the manometer. The instrument indicated a depth of 6,000 yards. We had been immersed for an hour, and the *Nautilus* was still descending. The water was beautifully clear. An hour later we had reached 13,000 yards – about three and a quarter leagues – and the bottom of the ocean had not yet been attained.

At 14,000 yards I saw some black peaks rising up; but these summits appeared to be those of mountains as high as the Himalayas or Mont Blanc, or higher, and the depths appeared as far off as ever.

The *Nautilus* still descended, notwithstanding the tremendous pressure. I felt it tremble, and the bolts seemed to start; the partitions groaned, and the windows of the saloon seemed to "cave in" with the enormous pressure. And the whole thing would have given way, had it not been, as the captain had said, capable of resisting any possible pressure, like a solid block of iron.

The last remnants of animal life soon disappeared, and at three leagues down the *Nautilus* had passed the limits of submarine existence. We had attained a depth of 16,000 yards – four leagues – and the sides of the *Nautilus* bore the pressure of 6,000 atmospheres, or 2,000 lbs. (about) for each two-fifths of an inch square of its surface.

"What a position!" I cried. "Sailing through these profundities, where human kind has never been. Look at those splendid rocks, captain! those uninhabited grottos, the last receptacles of the earth, where life is impossible! What unknown sites are here, and how impossible it is that we should retain any souvenir of them!"

"Would it please you to have a souvenir of them?" asked Captain Nemo.

"What do you mean?"

"I mean that nothing is easier than to take a photograph of this submarine view."

I had no time to express my surprise, for at a summons from Captain Nemo the apparatus was brought in. The water was electrically illuminated, and the perfectly distributed light could not have been surpassed by the sun's rays. The *Nautilus*, under the pressure of her screw, and overcome by the inclined planes, remained steady. The camera was fixed, and in a few seconds we had obtained a beautiful "negative".

I can only give the "positive proof" here. The primitive rocks which have never met heaven's light, the lower granite strata which form the foundations of the earth, the deep grottos included in the stony masses, those clear profiles with black edges. Then, beyond a horizon of mountains, an admirable undulating line, which makes the perspective of the picture. I cannot describe this assemblage of smooth, black, and polished rocks, and of the strange forms which glittered beneath the gleam of our electric light.

When Captain Nemo had finished, he said:

"Let us ascend again now. We must not go too far: nor expose the *Nautilus* to such a pressure."

"Ascend again?" I said.

"Hold tight, I advise you," said he.

I had no time to understand this caution, when I was thrown upon the floor.

The screw was hauled in, the inclined planes pointed upwards, and the *Nautilus*, carried up like a balloon, rose with fearful rapidity. It cut through the waters with a roar. Nothing whatever was visible as we ascended. In four minutes we had passed the four leagues which lay between us and the surface, and after emerging from the water like a flying-fish, we fell back to float upon the waves, making the billows rise to a prodigious height as we did so.

CHAPTER XII
CACHALOTS AND WHALES

DURING THE NIGHT of the 13th March the *Nautilus* steered towards the south. I thought that when Captain Nemo had got to the latitude of Cape Horn he would put the helm up for the Pacific, and complete his tour of the world. But he did not, and still kept his southerly course. Whither was he bound? To the Pole? That was madness! I really began to think that the captain's rashness sufficiently justified the apprehensions of Ned Land.

The Canadian had not spoken to me respecting his plans of escape for some time. He had become less communicative – almost silent. I perceived how this long imprisonment preyed upon him. I felt that he was "bottling up" his indignation. Whenever he met the captain his eyes gleamed with a fierce light, and I was always fearful that his violent temperament would impel him to some rash action. On that day, the 14th March, Conseil and he came to see me in my room. I inquired the object of this visit.

"To ask a simple question, Monsieur," replied the Canadian.

"Speak, Ned."

"How many men do you think there are on board the *Nautilus*?"

"I cannot tell you, my friend," I replied.

"It seems to me," said Ned, "that she does not require a large crew to work her."

"As a matter of fact, under present circumstances, ten men would suffice," I replied.

"Well, why should there be any more?" said Ned.

"Why?" I asked.

I looked steadily at Ned, whose ideas were not difficult to fathom.

"Because," I continued, "if my presentiments are correct, and I have understood the captain, the *Nautilus* is not merely a ship – it is a refuge for those who, like its commander, have broken all worldly ties."

"Perhaps so," replied Conseil, "but it can only contain a certain number of men, and Monsieur can give us the maximum."

"How so, Conseil?"

"By calculation. Given the capacity of the vessel, which Monsieur knows, and consequently the quantity of air it can contain, and knowing, also, how much each individual would require for respiration; and, by comparing the result with the recurring necessity for returning to the surface for air every twenty-four hours."

I saw at once what Conseil meant.

"I understand," I said, "but such a calculation could give but an uncertain result."

"Never mind," insisted Ned Land.

"Well, this is the calculation," I said. "Every man in one hour consumes the oxygen contained in 100 litres (twenty gallons) of air, so in twenty-four hours that would be 480 gallons. We must now endeavour to find out how many times 480 gallons of air are contained in the *Nautilus*."

"Exactly," said Conseil.

"Now," I continued, "the capacity of the *Nautilus* is 1,500 tons, and that of a ton is 200 gallons; the *Nautilus*, therefore, contains 300,000 gallons of air, which, divided by 480, gives 625. So the air contained in the *Nautilus* would suffice for 625 men for twenty-four hours."

"Six hundred and twenty-five!" repeated Ned.

"But you may take for granted that, including ourselves, crew, and officers, there is not a tenth part of that number on board."

"But there are still too many for three men," muttered Conseil.

"Therefore, my poor Ned," I said, "I can only advise you to be patient."

"And what is better, be resigned," said Conseil. Conseil had used the right word.

"After all," he resumed, "Captain Nemo cannot always keep going to the south. He must stop somewhere, and return into more civilized seas. It will then be time to put Ned Land's plans in action."

The Canadian shook his head, passed his hand over his forehead, and went out, but did not answer.

"Will Monsieur permit me to make an observation," said Conseil. "Poor Ned is ever wanting what he cannot have. All his past life returns to him. He regrets everything that is forbidden to us. Old memories oppress him, and he has a large heart. We must try to understand him. What has he to do here? Nothing.

He is not a *savant*, and cannot take the same pleasure in admiring the sea as we do. He would risk all he possesses to be able to enter an inn in his own country again."

It is certain the monotony of ship-life had become insupportable to the Canadian, used to an active existence. Events which could rouse him up were rare. However, an incident happened that day, which recalled bright days to the harpooner.

About 11 a.m., being at the surface, the *Nautilus* fell in with a school of whales, at which I was not surprised, as I knew that the creatures, hunted to death, seek refuge in the high latitudes.

The part played by the whale in the marine world, and its influence upon geographical discovery, has been considerable. It is the whale that successively induced the Basques, the Asturians, the English, and the Dutch to accustom themselves to the dangers of the sea, and has led them from one end of the earth to the other. Whales frequent the Arctic and the Antarctic Seas. Ancient stories say that these cetaceans have brought fishers to within seven leagues of the North Pole. If this be not true, it soon will be, and in their chase of the whale, men will reach this unknown point of the globe.

We were sitting upon the platform – the sea was calm. But October of these latitudes gave us some lovely autumnal days. The Canadian – he could not err – signalled a whale on the horizon to the east. As we gazed attentively, we could distinguish his black back rising and falling with the sea, about five miles from us.

"Ah!" cried Ned, "if I were only on board a whaler, there is an encounter that would do me good. It is a splendid animal. Look with what force he is 'spouting'. Why am I bound to this iron plate?"

"What, Ned," said I, "then you have not forgotten your old tastes?"

"Can a whale-fisher ever forget his trade, sir? Can the excitement incident to such a chase ever die out?"

"You have never fished in these seas I suppose?"

"Never, sir, only in the north, in Behring's and Davis' Straits – about equally."

"Then the whale of the southern seas is unknown to you. You have hitherto only hunted the Greenland whale, which would not pass the warm waters of the equator."

"Ah, Monsieur! What do you mean?" cried Ned, in a some-what incredulous tone.

"I am stating a fact."

"Well, now, for instance; I, myself, in 1865, that is two years and a half ago, fell in with a whale near Greenland, which carried another harpoon in his side; a harpoon marked as belonging to a Behring whaler. Now I ask you how, having been struck on the west side of America, the animal could come up to be killed in the east, unless he had doubled the Cape, and crossed the equator?"

"I agree with you, Ned," said Conseil, "and should like to have an explanation."

"Whales are localized," I replied, "according to their species, in certain seas which they do not leave; and if one of them did pass from Behring's to Davis' Strait, it is simply because some passage must exist beneath Asia or America."

"Must we believe that?" asked the Canadian, with a wink.

"We must believe Monsieur," said Conseil.

"All right, then," said Ned; "and as I have never fished in these seas, I do *not* know the species of whale that frequents them."

"I have told you so, Ned."

"All the more reason why we should make their acquaint-ance," replied Conseil.

"Look, look!" cried Ned, excitedly, "it is coming nearer; it is aggravating; it knows that I cannot get at it."

Ned stamped his foot. His hand shook as if he were brandish-ing a harpoon.

"Are these cetaceans as big as those of the North seas?" he asked.

"Very nearly," I replied.

"I have seen whales 100 feet long, and I am told that, at the Aleutian Islands, they have been known to exceed 150 feet in length."

"That seems an exaggeration," I replied. "These animals are only baleninopterous, provided with dorsal fins, and, like the cachalots, are usually smaller than the Greenland species."

"Ah!" said the Canadian, whose eyes never left the sea, "it is approaching nearer still"; then, resuming the conversation, he said: "You speak of the cachalot as a small animal, but enormous specimens have been known. They are intelligent cetaceans;

some of them, it is said, cover themselves with sea-weed, and are sometimes mistaken for islands; then people land and encamp, light a fire—"

"And also build houses on them," added Conseil.

"Yes, you joker," replied Ned. "Then at last, some fine day, the animal takes it into his head to dive, and drowns all the inhabitants."

"That is like the 'Travels of Sinbad the Sailor'," I said, laughing.

"Ah! Master Land, it appears you are fond of extravagant tales. 'Very like a whale' your cachalot! I hope you do not believe it."

"Monsieur," replied the Canadian, seriously, "we must believe anything about whales. (Look how that fellow is going along!) People say that these animals can go round the world in fifteen days."

"I do not assert the contrary."

"But you are doubtless aware, M. Aronnax, that at the creation whales swam even more rapidly."

"Indeed, Ned; why was that?"

"Because they then had their tails like fishes, vertically, placed so that they struck the water from left to right, and from right to left. But the Creator, perceiving that they moved too quickly, altered the tail so that it now beats the water upwards and downwards to the detriment of great speed."

"Good, Ned," I replied; but, borrowing his own expression, I added, "Must we believe that?"

"Not unless you like," said he, "and not any more than if I told you that there exist whales 300 feet long, and 100,000 pounds weight."

"Well, that is something," I said. "Nevertheless, it must be admitted that some cetaceans reach an enormous size, since they furnish, it is said, nearly 120 tuns of oil."

"I have seen as much," said the Canadian.

"I willingly believe it, Ned, as I believe that some whales equal 100 elephants in size. Judge of the effect which would be produced by such a mass coming in contact with a vessel!"

"Is it true that vessels are wrecked by them?" asked Conseil.

"No," I replied, "I do not believe ships are. But a tale is told that in the year 1820, in these very seas, a whale launched itself against the Essex, and 'rammed' her backwards at the rate of four yards in a second. The waves entered over the stern, and the vessel sank almost immediately."

Ned looked at me quizzically.

"I have received a blow from the tail of a whale," he said, "in my boat, of course. My companions and I were flung six or seven yards into the air. But, beside your animal, sir, mine was but a baby."

"Do those animals live long?" asked Conseil.

"A thousand years," replied Ned.

"How do you know that, Ned?"

"Because I have been told so."

"And why did they tell you so?"

"Because they knew it."

"No, Ned," I said, "they do not know it, they only supposed so. Four hundred years ago, when whale-fishing first began, these animals were larger than they are at present. Therefore people suppose that the smaller size is due to the fact that they have not had time to grow to their full bulk. That caused Buffon to state that whales lived a thousand years. Do you see?"

Ned Land neither heard nor understood. The whale was approaching, and he was devouring him with all his eyes!

"Ah!" he exclaimed, "it is not one whale, there is a whole school. And I unable to do anything, tied here hand and foot."

"But, friend Ned," said Conseil, "why do you not ask permission to hunt them?"

Scarcely were the words uttered, than Ned Land had descended in search of the captain. In a few moments they appeared together.

Captain Nemo looked at the whales, which were spouting about a mile away.

"They are the southern whales," he said, "and would make the fortune of a whaling fleet."

"Well, then, Monsieur, may we not chase them, if it be for nothing else than to keep my hand in."

"For what object," replied the captain, "simply for the sake of killing? We have no use for oil on board."

"Nevertheless, in the Red Sea you permitted us to kill the dugong."

"It was then with a view to procure fresh meat for my crew. Here it is only killing for killing's sake. I know very well it is

man's privilege, but I do not like killing for pastime. In destroy-
ing the southern whales – like the Greenland whale, inoffensive
and useful animals – people like you, Master Land, are very culp-
able. They have already decimated them in Baffin's Bay, and a
class of useful animals is being annihilated. Leave these poor cetaceans alone. They have plenty of natural enemies – cachalots,
sword-fish, and saw-fish – without you."

I leave you to imagine what a figure the Canadian cut during
this homily. To talk like that to a hunter was to throw words away.
Ned gazed at the captain, and evidently did not understand him.
Nevertheless the captain was right. The barbarous and indis-
criminate fishing will soon clear off all the whales from the ocean.

Ned Land whistled "Yankee Doodle", thrust his hands into
his pockets, and turned his back on us.

Captain Nemo continued to watch the cetaceans, and turning
to me, said,

"I was right in saying that, without counting man, whales had
enemies enough. Those will have enough to occupy them soon.
Do you see those black moving spots about eight miles to leeward,
M. Aronnax?"

"Yes," I replied.

"Those are cachalots – terrible animals, too. I have sometimes
met them in 'schools' of two hundred or three hundred at a time.
They are cruel creatures, and one will do well to kill *them*."

The Canadian turned quickly –

"Well, captain, there is still time, even in the interest of the
whales."

"It is no use to expose one's self. The *Nautilus* will suffice to
disperse them. It is armed with a steel spur as good as Ned Land's
harpoon, I imagine."

The Canadian did not even trouble to shrug his shoulders.
Who had ever heard of attacking cetaceans with a spur!

"Wait, M. Aronnax," said the captain, "and you will see a
novel chase. We need not pity these ferocious beasts, they are
only mouth and teeth."

All mouth and teeth! No better description of the macro-
cephalous cachalot could have been given. It is sometimes
seventy-five feet in length. Its enormous head is fully one-
third of its body. It is better armed than the whale, whose upper
jaw is only furnished with whalebone, while the cachalot has

twenty-five large teeth about eight inches long, round, and pointed at the top, weighing about 2 lbs. each. In the upper part of the enormous head, the valuable spermaceti is found in large quantities. The cachalot is a very disagreeable animal, more tadpole than fish, according to Frédol; it is very badly made (so to speak), and one side is quite a failure, for it can only see with the right eye.

Meanwhile, this 'school' of monsters was approaching. They had perceived the whales, and hastened to attack them. One could predict victory for the cachalots, not only because they were better fitted for the encounter than their defenceless adversaries, but also because they could remain longer beneath the waves without rising to breathe.

There was scarcely time to go to the assistance of the whales. The *Nautilus* went under water. Conseil, Ned and I, took our places at the windows of the saloon. Captain Nemo stood by the helmsman, so as to work the vessel like an engine of destruction. I soon heard the beating of the screw, and our speed increased.

The fight had already commenced when the *Nautilus* arrived on the scene. We steered so as to divide the cachalots. They at first appeared little impressed at the sight of the new monster which had come to take part in the battle. But very soon they had to guard its attack.

What a struggle it was! Ned Land, very quickly excited, clapped his hands. The *Nautilus* was like a tremendous harpoon brandished in the captain's hand. He turned it against the thick, fleshy masses, cutting them asunder, leaving the quivering portions of the animal in the wake.

We did not feel the furious blows applied to the sides of the *Nautilus*, nor the shocks they produced, to any great extent. One cachalot slain, we rushed at another; backing, going ahead or astern, under water, or remounting to the surface, and then striking it full or diagonally; cutting or tearing in every direction, at all paces, piercing them with the terrible "spear".

It was a massacre. The noise was prodigious. The hissing and snorting of the enraged animals was deafening. In these usually calm waters there were enormous waves.

For an hour this Homeric massacre continued. The cachalots could not get away. Frequently ten or a dozen would get together and attempt to crush the *Nautilus* beneath their weight. We could see from the window their enormous throats lined with teeth, and their formidable eyes. Ned Land threatened and cursed them alternately. We could feel them fasten upon the hull and "worry" it like wild dogs their prey. But the *Nautilus*, putting on the steam, would carry them along, either up or down, without heeding their enormous bulk, or their tremendous "pull" on the vessel.

At length the cachalots fled. The sea became calm again. We ascended to the surface; the panels were opened; we hastened to the platform. The ocean was covered with mutilated bodies. A tremendous explosion could not have had more terrible effects. We were floating surrounded by gigantic corpses. Some cachalots were visible on the horizon in full retreat. The waves were tinged with red for several miles, and we appeared to be sailing in a sea of blood.

Captain Nemo now joined us.

"Well, Master Land!" he said.

"Well, sir!" replied the Canadian, whose ardour had some-what abated. "It is really a terrible spectacle; but I am not a butcher, myself; I am merely a hunter, and this has been butchery."

"It was only a massacre of mischievous animals," replied the captain; "and the *Nautilus* is not a butcher's knife."

"I prefer my harpoon," replied Ned.

"Everyone to his own weapon," replied the captain, looking steadily at the Canadian.

I was afraid the latter would give way to some violence, which would have deplorable consequences. But his wrath was turned aside by the sight of a whale, which the *Nautilus* had just reached. The animal had not escaped scot-free from the jaws of the cachalots. I recognized the southern whale by its black and flattened head. Anatomically it is distinguished from the white and the North Cape whales by the joining of the seven cervical vertebræ, and it possesses two more ribs than the others. This unhappy specimen was lying upon its side, the belly bitten to pieces, quite dead. From a mutilated fin still hung a young whale, which the poor animal could not save from the massacre. The water flowed in and out of its open mouth with a sound like waves breaking on the shore.

Captain Nemo guided the *Nautilus* close to the body. Two

men then mounted it, and with no little astonishment I saw them draw all the milk from the breasts, about two or three tuns.

The captain offered me a glass of the still warm liquid. I could not conceal my repugnance, but he assured me it was excellent, and could not be in any way distinguished from cows' milk.

I tasted it, and found he was right. This, therefore, gave us a very useful supply, for cheese and butter would improve our table.

From that day I noticed that Ned Land grew more and more badly disposed towards the captain, and I resolved to keep a strict watch on the sayings and doings of the Canadian.

CHAPTER XIII
THE ICEBERGS

THE *NAUTILUS* STILL continued her southerly course. Was it Captain Nemo's wish to reach the Pole? I did think so, for hitherto all such attempts had signally failed. Besides, the season was too far advanced, as the 13th of March, in those latitudes, corresponds to the 13th of September in northern climates, when the equinoctial period commences.

Upon the 14th of March, I perceived ice floating in latitude 55°, merely field ice, in patches twenty to twenty-five feet long, upon which the waves broke. The *Nautilus* remained at the surface. Ned Land, having fished in Arctic seas, was familiar with icebergs. Conseil and I admired them for the first time.

Towards the southern horizon, in the air, lay extended a white band of dazzling appearance. This is what English whalers have called the "ice-blink". No matter how thick the clouds, they cannot obscure its rays. It betokens the near approach to a pack or floe of ice.

And, sure enough, blocks of considerable size soon began to make their appearance, whose brilliancy was modified by the caprice of the fogs. Upon some of these masses we could trace green veins, as if caused by sulphate of copper. Others appeared like immense amethysts, through which the light penetrated.

Some reflected the rays from the thousand facets of their crystals, while others, clouded with vivid calcareous reflections, would have passed for a town of marble.

The further we got southward the greater became the size and frequency of the icebergs. Polar birds built in them by thousands. Petrels, damiers, and puffins deafened us with their screams. Some of these birds, taking the *Nautilus* for the dead body of a whale, came to rest upon it and pecked the iron skin.

During our progress through the ice, Captain Nemo kept upon the deck. He took note of these desolate places. I perceived his calm face light up now and then. Was he thinking how much at home he was in these polar seas, denied to other men? Perhaps so; but he did not speak. He piloted the *Nautilus* with consummate skill, avoiding skilfully any encounter with those masses, some of which were many miles long, and of a height varying from 200 to 250 feet. The horizon often appeared entirely shut in. At the 60° of latitude all passage seemed barred, but the captain, after a careful search, found a narrow opening, through which he glided boldly; knowing very well, however, that it would close in on his wake.

Thus the *Nautilus*, skilfully steered, passed all this ice, classed, with a precision that delighted Conseil, according to their form or size – icebergs or mountains; ice fields, or united and apparently boundless expanses; drift ice or packs, when circular called *palchs*, or streams when they are lengthened out.

The temperature was very low; the thermometer marked 2° to 3° below zero in the open air. But we were warmly clad in furs, at the cost of the seal and sea-bear. The interior of the *Nautilus*, warmed by the electric apparatus, defied the most intense cold. Besides, we had only to go under water a few yards to find a comfortable temperature.

Two months earlier we should have enjoyed perpetual day in these latitudes, but now we had three or four hours' night; and, later six months' darkness would envelop these circumpolar regions.

On the 15th March we passed the latitude of the islands of New Zealand and the South Orkneys. The captain informed me that at one time quantities of seals inhabited those islands, but the English and American whalers, in their zeal for killing, massacred males and females indiscriminately; and, where once life had been, after their departure was the silence of death.

On the 16th March, about 8 a.m., the *Nautilus* crossed the Antarctic Circle. Ice lay all round us and closed in upon the horizon; nevertheless the captain still kept on towards the Pole.

"But, where can he be going?" I said to Conseil.

"Ahead," he replied; "and when he cannot get any farther he will stop."

"I wouldn't swear to that," I said.

And, to tell the truth, I was not displeased at this adventurous kind of life. I cannot express the degree of pleasure I experienced in these novel regions. The ice assumed the most impressive and beautiful forms. Here was an oriental town with innumerable mosques and minarets; there a city thrown headlong to the ground by some natural convulsion. These appearances were continually varied by the oblique rays of the sun, or lost amid the grey mists in hurricanes of snow. On all sides were the detonations and the sounds of the falls of great masses of ice, which changed the aspect at once, like the passing scene of a diorama.

Whenever these falls took place while the *Nautilus* was under water, the noise was astounding to our ears, and the waves were moved even to the lowest depths. At these times the *Nautilus* rolled and pitched like an abandoned vessel at sea.

On several occasions, as I could not discover any exit, I thought we were actually hemmed in by the ice; but as if it were by instinct Captain Nemo would always hit upon a passage. He was never mistaken when he could see the little blue rivulets trickling through the field-ice. I had now no doubt that he had already ventured into these Antarctic seas.

However, on the 16th March, the ice stopped us completely. Not icebergs, but vast ice-fields. This could not stop the captain, however, and he rushed into the ice with tremendous speed. The *Nautilus* penetrated like a wedge into this brittle mass, dividing it with loud cracking. It was like the old "battering-ram" impelled with tremendous power. The fragments of ice thrown high in the air fell round us like hail. By its own impulsive force the *Nautilus* made a channel through it. Sometimes carried forward by its impetus it rose over the ice and crushed it beneath its weight, sometimes when beneath the ice-field it broke it up by a simple pitching movement.

All this time we encountered violent squalls, and thick fogs prevented us seeing from one end of the platform to the other. The wind blew sharply from all round the compass, and the snow lay so thickly that we had to break it up with pickaxes. The temperature was steady at 5° below zero, and the *Nautilus* was completely covered with ice. An ordinary vessel could not have worked her way through, as the rigging would have been frozen in the blocks and pulleys. Such a ship as ours was had the only chance of success.

Under these circumstances the barometer kept very low; it fell even to 73° 5′. The compass gave us no guarantee. The erring needles marked contrary directions as we approached the south meridianal pole, which must not be confounded with the South Pole of the earth. According to Hausten this pole is situated close to 70° lat. and 130° long., and, according to the observations of Duperrey, in 135° long. and 70° 30′ lat. We were, therefore, obliged to make numerous observations and move the compasses from place to place in the ship to get a meridian. But frequently they trusted to the reckoning to make out the course we had run, a very unsatisfactory method in the midst of these winding passes, in which the "landmarks" were constantly changing.

At length the *Nautilus* was actually blocked on the 18th March. There were no longer streams, packs, nor fields, but an immoveable, interminable, barrier formed by mountains of ice wedged together.

"An iceberg," said Ned Land to me.

I knew that to Ned Land, like all other navigators, this was insurmountable. The sun appeared at noon for an instant, and Captain Nemo obtained an observation which gave our position as 51° 30′ long. and 67° 39′ south lat. We were now a point more advanced in the Antarctic regions. We were unable to obtain even a glimpse of sea. Before the *Nautilus* lay a vast confused plain, heaped with ice blocks, with all the capricious "pell-mell" confusion which characterizes the surface of a river before the ice thaws on it, but on an immense scale. Here and there sharp peaks and delicate needle-points raised themselves to a height of 200 feet; farther on was a long line of cliffs hewn out into great peaks, and of greyish tint – vast mirrors which reflected the half-obscured sunbeams. The dread silence was scarcely disturbed by the flapping of the sea-birds' wings. Everything – even the noise – seemed frozen up.

The *Nautilus* was obliged to halt in her adventurous course in the midst of the ice-field.

"Monsieur," said Ned Land to me one day, "if this captain of yours goes any farther—"

"Well?"

"He will be something very wonderful."

"Why, Ned?"

"Because no one ever crossed an iceberg. Captain Nemo is powerful, but, confound him, he is not stronger than Nature, and where she has placed bounds he must stop willy-nilly!"

"Just so, Ned, and I should like to know what is behind this iceberg. A wall, that is what irritates me more."

"Monsieur is quite right," said Conseil. "Walls are only invented to irritate *savants*. There never ought to be any walls."

"Well," said the Canadian, "they know very well what is behind this iceberg."

"What?"

"Ice, nothing but ice."

"You appear certain about that, Ned," I replied, "but I am not at all sure, and that is why I want to see."

"Then, sir, you may relinquish the idea. You have reached the iceberg, which is quite enough, and neither you, nor Captain Nemo, nor his *Nautilus* will go any farther. And, whether he will or no, we must go northwards again, that is to say, amongst honest people."

Notwithstanding all our efforts, notwithstanding the most powerful means employed to break up the ice, the *Nautilus* remained motionless. Usually, in like cases, when progress is impossible, the return path is open, but in this case to return was as impracticable as to advance, for all passages were closed astern, and if our vessel remained stationary for a little it would be at once blocked up. This actually happened about two o'clock p.m., and the young ice formed round us with surprising rapidity.

I was obliged to confess that Captain Nemo had been more than imprudent. I was on the platform at the time.

The captain, who had been taking in the situation for some time, said to me:

"Well, professor, what do you think of this?"

"I think we are prisoners, captain."

"Prisoners! How do you make that out?"

"I mean, as we can neither move backwards or forwards, nor to either side. That is being a prisoner – at least, in civilized countries it is so considered."

"So, M. Aronnax, you think that the *Nautilus* cannot get away?"

"It will be very difficult, at least, for the season is already too far advanced to give you any hope of a temporary break-up of the ice."

"Ah, M. Aronnax!" replied the captain, in an ironical tone of voice, "you will always be the same. You see nothing but obstacles and difficulties in the way; now, I not only assert that the *Nautilus* will disengage herself, but that she will go farther on."

"Further south?" I asked, gazing at the captain.

"Yes, she will go to the Pole."

"To the Pole?" I exclaimed, incredulously.

"Yes," the captain replied, coldly, "to the Antarctic Pole; to that unknown point from which every meridian of the earth springs. You are aware that I can do as I please with the *Nautilus*?"

Yes, I did know that! I knew this man was bold to recklessness; but, to overcome the obstacles surrounding the South Pole – more inaccessible than the North Pole, which had not yet been discovered by the most hardy explorers – was to carry out a mad idea, and one which only the mind of a madman could conceive.

It then occurred to me to ask Captain Nemo whether he had already discovered "the Pole", which had never yet been touched by human foot.

"No, professor," he replied, "we will discover it together. Where other people have failed, I shall not fail. I have never, hitherto, driven my *Nautilus* so far over the southern seas; but, I repeat, we shall go farther still."

"I wish to believe you, captain," I replied, with a playful irony; "I do believe you. Let us get on; there is nothing to hinder *us*. Let us smash up this iceberg; blow it to pieces if it resist. Let us give the *Nautilus* her wings to fly over it."

"Over it, professor?" said the captain, calmly. "Not *over* it – *under* it!"

"Under it?" I exclaimed.

A sudden revelation of the captain's plans flashed into my mind. I understood it all. The wonderful qualities of the *Nautilus* were once again to serve in a superhuman enterprise.

"I perceive we are beginning to understand each other, professor," said the captain, smiling. "You already see the possibility, nay, the success of our attempt. What to an ordinary vessel is impracticable, to the *Nautilus* is easy of accomplishment. If a continent is around the Pole, we must stop at the continent, but if, on the contrary, the open sea laves it, we shall run up to the Pole itself."

"In fact," I said, quite carried away by the captain's reasoning, "if the surface of the sea be solidified by ice, the lower depths are free, in consequence of the natural law that has fixed the maximum density of salt water at one degree higher than freezing point; and if I am right, the submerged portion of this iceberg is to the part out of the water as four to one."

"Very nearly, professor, for for one foot of iceberg above the water there are, as a rule, three below. Now, since these icy mountains are never more than 300 feet high, they are not more than 900 feet below; and what is a depth of 900 feet to the *Nautilus*?"

"Nothing at all."

"We could even seek, at a greater depth, the equable temperature of sea water, and disdain the 30° or 40° of surface cold."

"Quite so," I assented.

"The only difficulty for us," said Captain Nemo, "will be to remain many days under water without renewing our supply of fresh air."

"Oh, is that all!" I cried. "Why the *Nautilus* has immense reservoirs, and they can supply us with all the oxygen we shall require."

"Happy thought, M. Aronnax," replied the captain, smiling; "but as I do not want you to think me reckless, I will submit to you my objections in advance."

"Have you any more?"

"Only one. It is possible that if there be sea around the South Pole, it may be frozen, and in that case we should not be able to return to the surface at all."

"Very well. But you forget that the *Nautilus* is armed with a sharp spur; and cannot we cut our way diagonally through the ice, which would give way before us?"

"Certainly, professor, you are brilliant to-day."

"Besides, captain," I added enthusiastically, "why may we not find the sea free at the South Pole as well as at the north? The ice-poles and the earth's poles are not the same in either hemisphere; and, until there is proof adduced to the contrary, we may fairly assume that there is a continent or an ocean free from ice at these extremities of the globe."

"I agree with you, M. Aronnax," replied the captain. "I would hint to you, however, that after first making all kinds of objections to my plan, you are now overwhelming me with arguments in favour of it!"

Captain Nemo only spoke the truth. I had been "out-Heroding Herod". It was I who was taking him to the Pole. I was going ahead of him altogether. But no, poor fool! Captain Nemo knows better than you the *pros* and the *cons* of this question, and it only amused him to see you carried away by visions of the impossible!

All the same, he had not lost a minute. At a signal the mate appeared. These two then conversed rapidly in their incomprehensible language, and whether the mate had been previously warned, or whether he believed the project practicable, he at any rate showed no surprise.

But, impassible as he was, he did not come up to Conseil in that respect, for when I announced to him our intention to reach the South Pole, he merely said, "Just as Monsieur pleases"; and I had to be content with that. As for Ned Land, if ever shoulders were lifted they were those of the Canadian.

"Look here, sir," said Ned Land, "I pity you and your captain."

"But we are going to the Pole, Master Ned."

"Well, you may go there, but you will never come back again."

And Ned Land went to his cabin, "so as not to make a disturbance", he said as he left me.

Meanwhile the preparations for this rash expedition were commenced. The powerful pumps filled the reservoirs with air, and stowed it at a high pressure. About four o'clock Captain Nemo informed me that the panels on the platform were about to be closed. I took a last look at the thick iceberg which we were about to penetrate. The weather was fine, the atmosphere clear, the cold piercing – 12° below zero; but as there was no wind this cold was bearable.

A dozen men, armed with axes, cut away the ice around the *Nautilus*. This was soon done, and the young ice was still thin. We all descended into the interior. The usual reservoirs were filled with water, and the *Nautilus* quickly sank.

I sat with Conseil in the saloon. Through the open window

we could inspect the lower beds of the Southern Ocean. The thermometer rose. The needle of the manometer deviated on the dial-plate. At about 300 yards down, as the captain had anticipated, we were floating below the moving icebergs. But the *Nautilus* went lower still. It reached 800 yards depth. The temperature of the water was 12° at the surface, down here it was only 10°. Two degrees had been already gained. Of course the temperature of the *Nautilus* was maintained at a higher level by one degree by its heating apparatus. All its movements were executed with wondrous precision.

"If Monsieur please, I think we shall get through," said Conseil.

"I quite expect so," I replied in a tone of conviction.

In this open water the *Nautilus* steered direct for the Pole without quitting the 52nd meridian. From 67° 30' to 90°, $23\frac{1}{2}$° of latitude remained to be got over, or a little more than 500 leagues. The average speed was twenty-eight miles an hour. At this rate we should reach the Pole in forty hours.

For a portion of the night the novelty of the situation kept us at the windows of the saloon. The sea was lit up by the electric lamp, but it was deserted. Fish could not live in those prison-waters. They would only find a passage here from the Antarctic Ocean to the open Polar Sea. Our progress was rapid, as we could feel by the quivering of the hull.

About two o'clock a.m. I retired to snatch some sleep, and Conseil did likewise. On my way I did not meet Captain Nemo. I suppose he was in the pilot-house.

Next morning, 19th of March, I again took my place at the window. The speed of the *Nautilus* had been diminished. We were ascending, prudently emptying the reservoirs, but slowly. My heart beat fast. Were we about to emerge and breathe fresh air around the Pole?

No. A shock told me that the *Nautilus* had struck the underside of the iceberg, still very thick, judging from the sound. We had "touched bottom", to use a sea-term, but in the inverse sense, and at a thousand feet below. This would give us 2,000 feet of ice above us, of which 1,000 feet were above the sea level. So the iceberg must be thicker now than when we started, which was not a very cheerful conclusion to arrive at.

Many times during the day the *Nautilus* tried the ice, and

always with the same success. At certain times it encountered this icy ceiling at a depth of 900 yards, which gave a thickness of 1,000 yards in all, 200 being above the sea level. The ice was double the thickness at the surface now than it had been when we first plunged beneath it.

I noted these different depths carefully, and thus obtained a submarine profile of this chain of mountains, as it were developed under water.

By the evening no change had taken place. Ice everywhere, between 400 and 500 yards deep. The thickness was diminishing, but what a depth yet remained between us and the surface of the ocean! It was eight o'clock. At four o'clock the air of the *Nautilus* should have been renewed as usual. However, I did not suffer much, though no demand had been made on the reservoirs for a supply of oxygen. I slept but little that night. Hope and fear assailed me by turns; I got up many times. The *Nautilus* continued to "tap" the ice. Towards 3 a.m. I noticed that the lower surface of the iceberg was only fifty yards down. Only 150 feet now separated us from the surface. The iceberg was rapidly becoming an ice-field. The mountain was dropping to a plain. My eyes never left the manometer. We kept ascending steadily and diagonally. The surrounding surfaces glittered beneath our electric light. The ice was getting thinner both above and below, mile after mile. At length, at 6 o'clock a.m. on this memorable 19th March, Captain Nemo opened the door of the saloon and said:

"We are in open water!"

CHAPTER XIV
THE SOUTH POLE

I HURRIED TO THE platform. Yes, the sea was clear of ice, with the exception of a few scattered pieces and moving icebergs – in the distance a long extent of open sea. Birds filled the air, fish crowded the sea which, according to its depth, varied from an intense blue to an olive green. The thermometer marked 3° (centigrade) below zero. This was, comparatively speaking, spring, shut up behind the icebergs whose distant masses were visible on the northern horizon.

"Are we at the Pole?" I asked, with a beating heart.

"I do not know," he said; "I will take the bearings at noon."

"But shall we be able to see the sun through the fog?" I asked, looking at the dull grey sky.

"If he shine out ever so little it will suffice," said the captain.

Ten miles to the southward, a solitary islet rose to a height of 200 yards. We advanced towards it cautiously, for it might have been surrounded by shoals. An hour later we had reached it; two hours after that we had explored it; it was between four and five miles in circumference. A narrow canal separated it from a large tract of land of which I could not see the whole extent. The existence of this land appeared to confirm Maury's theory. That ingenious American has stated that between the South Pole and the sixtieth parallel the sea is covered with floating ice of great size, which is never met with in the North Atlantic. From this fact he has deduced the conclusion that the Antarctic Circle encloses large tracts of land, since the icebergs cannot form in the open sea, but only on a coast. According to his calculations the mass of ice surrounding the South Pole forms an enormous cap, extending about 2,400 miles.

Meanwhile the *Nautilus*, for fear of striking, stopped at three cables' length from a beach crowned by a splendid mass of rock. The boat was launched. The captain, two men carrying the instruments, Conseil, and I, embarked. It was ten o'clock. I had not seen Ned Land. He probably did not wish to stultify himself in the presence of the South Pole.

A few strokes brought us to land. Conseil was about to jump ashore, but I restrained him.

"Sir," said I to Captain Nemo, "to you belongs the honour of first landing on this ground."

"Yes," replied the captain, "and if I do not hesitate to tread this polar soil it is because no man has ever landed here before."

As he ceased speaking, he leaped lightly ashore. His heart was beating with strong emotion. He climbed a rock which terminated in a little promontory, and there, with folded arms, with eager look, motionless and silent, he seemed to take possession of those southern regions. After five minutes he returned to us.

"Now, professor, when you please!" he cried.

I then disembarked, followed by Conseil, leaving the two sailors in the boat.

For some distance the soil appeared to be composed of tufa of a reddish colour, something like powdered bricks, Scoriæ, lava streams, and pumice-stone covered it. We could not mistake its volcanic origin. In some places arose a light smoke which emitted a smell of sulphur, thereby attesting that the subterranean fires had lost none of their expansive power. However, having ascended a high pinnacle of rock, I could perceive no volcano. We know that in these regions James Ross discovered the craters of Erebus and Terror in full activity in the 167th meridian, in latitude 77° 32' south.

The vegetation appeared very limited. Some lichens of the *Unsnea melanoxantha* kind, spread over the black rocks. Some microscopic plants, rudimentary diatomas, a kind of cells placed between two quartz shells, the long purple and scarlet fucus supported by their little swimming-bladders which the surf carried to the shore, composed all the meagre flora of this region.

The beach was covered with molluscs, small mussels, limpets, smooth heart-shaped buccards, and particularly clios with oblong and membraneous bodies, whose heads are formed of two rounded lobes. There were myriads of northern clios about an inch long, of which a whale would swallow a world at one gulp. These charming pteropods, perfect sea-butterflies, gave animation to the shore.

Amongst other zoophytes appeared, in the higher levels, some arborescent corals of the species which, according to James Ross, live in the Antarctic seas at a thousand feet deep. Then there were little alcyores, belonging to the species *Procellaria pelagica*; and also a number of asteroids peculiar to these climates, and star-fish.

But it was in the air that life was so prolific. Thousands of birds flew and wheeled around us, deafening us with their cries. Others crowded upon the rocks and watched us pass without fear, and even came close to our feet. There were penguins, so agile in the water that they have been mistaken for the active bonitos, and yet so very heavy and clumsy on shore. They uttered harsh cries, and formed a numerous assemblage, quiet in their movements, but wonderful as to clamour.

Amongst the birds I recognized the "chionis" of the family of waders. It is as large as a pigeon, white, with a short and pointed beak, with a red circle round the eye. Conseil laid in a stock of these, for, properly prepared, these birds are very good to eat. Albatrosses flew about, the width of their expanded wings being fully twelve feet. They are rightly called the ocean vultures. Gigantic petrels, amongst others the *Quebrante huesas*, with curved wings. These birds are great eaters of seals. Some damiers, a kind of small duck, the upper part of whose bodies is black and white, a quantity of petrels, some white with brown-bordered wings, some blue, peculiar to the Antarctic seas, and so full of oil, I told Conseil, that the inhabitants of the Faroe Isles have only to insert a wick in their bodies before lighting them.

"A very little more and they would be perfect lamps," replied Conseil. "So we can scarcely expect nature to have furnished them with wicks at first."

After half a mile the ground was riddled with ruff's nests. It was a laying-ground, and from which many birds were escaping. Captain Nemo caused some hundreds to be hunted down, for their flesh is tasty. They uttered a cry something similar to the bray of an ass. They are about as large as a goose; body of a slaty colour, white underneath, and with a yellow ring round the neck. They were killed with stones without making any attempt to escape.

All this time the fog hung over us, and at 11 a.m. the sun had not shone out. His absence caused me some uneasiness, for without his appearance we could get no observations. How, then, could we ascertain whether we had reached the Pole?

When I rejoined Captain Nemo I found him leaning against a rock, gazing at the sky. He seemed impatient – worried. But what was to be done? He could not command the sun like the sea.

Mid-day arrived, and the sun had not appeared for a moment. We could not even see its position through the fog, and the fog soon turned to snow.

"To-morrow," the captain said calmly, and we returned to the *Nautilus*. During our absence the nets had been drawn, and I noticed with much interest the fish that had been captured, which were chiefly migrates from less elevated zones. I tasted some of them subsequently, and found them insipid, notwithstanding Conseil's opinion, for he liked them.

The snow-storm continued till next day. It was impossible to remain on the platform. Even in the saloon, where I stayed to make notes of the excursion, I could hear the cries of the petrels and albatrosses sporting in the storm. The *Nautilus* did not remain at anchor, but went down the coast about ten miles to the south in the midst of the twilight left by the sun as it touched the horizon.

Next day, 20th of March, the snow had ceased to fall. The cold was rather more intense; the thermometer was 2° below zero. The mists were lifting, and I was in hopes that to-day we should be able to take the observation.

Captain Nemo not having yet appeared, the boat took Conseil and myself ashore. The soil was of the same nature – volcanic. All round were traces of lava, scoriæ, and basalt, although I could see no crater. Here, as lower down, myriads of birds enlivened the scene. But their dominion was here divided with troops of marine mammifers, which gazed at us from their soft eyes. There were various species of seals, some extended on the ground, others on the ice, many plunging in and emerging from the water. They did not move at our approach, never having before encountered man; and I calculated that there were sufficient to fill hundreds of ships.

"Faith," said Conseil, "it is a very good thing that Ned Land did not come with us."

"Why, Conseil?"

"Because he would have killed all these."

"All of them? That is saying a great deal. But I do not think we should have been able to prevent our Canadian friend from harpooning some of these splendid cetaceans. That would have annoyed Captain Nemo, for he does not spill the blood of inoffensive animals wantonly."

"He is quite right."

"Certainly, Conseil; but tell me, have you not already classed these magnificent specimens of marine fauna?"

"Monsieur knows," replied Conseil, "that I am not well up in it. When Monsieur has told me the names of the animals—"

"They are seals and morses," said I.

"Two genus which belong to the family of pinnipeds," said Conseil; "order, carnivorous; group, unguiculus; sub-class, monodelphians; class, mammifer; branch, vertebrates."

"Good, Conseil," I replied; "but these two genus are divided into species, and, if I am not mistaken, we shall here have the opportunity to observe them. Let us go on."

It was now 8 a.m. We had four hours before the sun could be

observed with advantage. I therefore advanced towards a large bay, which had hollowed itself out in the granite cliffs.

There, as far as we could see, the earth and ice fragments were absolutely covered with marine mammifers, and I looked involuntarily for Proteus, the mythological shepherd, who guarded Neptune's immense flocks. The seals were most numerous. They formed distinct groups, males and females, the fathers watching the family, the mother suckling the young, some of which were sufficiently strong to walk a little. When any of the animals wished to move they went along by little jumps, due to the contraction of the body; and they helped themselves along awkwardly enough by means of their fin, which, as in the lamantine, their congener, forms a perfect fore-arm. In the water – their element – the spine is mobile, and they are admirably adapted for swimming, the skin being smooth and the feet webbed. When resting upon the ground their attitudes are extremely graceful. So the ancients, observing their expressive faces, soft looks, which even a beautiful woman cannot surpass, the clear and limpid eyes, their charming positions, and the poetry of their manners, metamorphosed the males into tritons and the females into sirens.

I called Conseil's attention to the great development of the brain-lobes of these interesting animals. No mammal, except man, has such a development of cerebral material. Thus seals are capable of receiving a certain amount of education; they are easily domesticated, and I agree with some naturalists that, if properly taught, they could be easily utilized as fishing dogs.

The greater number of the seals were asleep on the rocks or on the sand. Amongst the seals proper, which have no external ears, in which they differ from the others whose ears are prominent, I observed several varieties of the stenorhynchi, about nine feet long, white, with "bull-dog" heads, armed with ten teeth in each jaw, four incisors above and below, and two great canine teeth, shaped like a fleur de lis.

Amongst them, sea-elephants moved about. They are a kind of seal, having short flexible trunks; and the giants of the species measured twenty feet round, and more than thirty feet long. They did not move as we appoached them.

"Are these creatures dangerous?" asked Conseil.

"Not if they are not molested," I replied. "When a seal is

obliged to defend her young, her rage is terrific, and they frequently break the fishing-boats to pieces."

"And quite right, too," replied Conseil.

"I will not contradict you."

Two miles farther we were stopped by a promontory which sheltered the bay from the south winds. It fell perpendicularly to the sea, which foamed round the base in surf. Beyond it we heard loud bellowings.

"Halloa!" cried Conseil, "there is a concert of bulls."

"No," said I, "it is a morse concert."

"Are they fighting?"

"Either that or playing."

"I should like to see them," said Conseil.

"We must have a look at them, Conseil, certainly."

We commenced our ascent of the black rocks, and got many a tumble over the slippery stones. More than once I rolled over, and to the detriment of my ribs. Conseil, more prudent or more steady, did not fall, and was ready to help me up, saying:

"If Monsieur would take longer steps he would keep his balance better."

When we arrived at the upper ridge of the promontory, I perceived a vast white plain quite covered with morses. They were frisking about; so what we had heard were bellowings of joy, not anger.

The morses resemble seals in form and the arrangement of their members, but the canine and incisor teeth are wanting in the lower jaw, and the superior canines are two long tusks. These teeth are of ivory, harder than that of the elephant, and less likely to become yellow, and are much sought after. So morses are an object for the hunter, and they will soon be exterminated, as the fishers kill indiscriminately, females and young, upwards of four thousand every year.

We passed close to these curious animals, and I was enabled to examine them at leisure. Their skins are thick and rugged, of a fawn-colour, tending to red; the hair is short and scanty. Some of them were twelve feet long. Quieter and less timid than their northern relatives, they did not post sentinels to warn them of approaching danger.

Having examined this city of morses, I thought it time to retrace my steps. It was eleven o'clock, and, if Captain Nemo could find a favourable moment for his observations, I wished to be present at the time. However, I had little hope of the sun showing that day; the clouds, heaped up above the horizon, hid him from our sight. It seemed as if the jealous orb did not wish to reveal to human beings this inaccessible portion of the globe.

Nevertheless, I made up my mind to return. We followed a narrow track which ran along the top of the cliff. At half-past eleven we reached the landing-place. The canoe was drawn up and had landed the captain and his instruments; I saw him standing upon a block of basalt. His instruments were ready at hand; his gaze was fixed upon the northern horizon, near which the sun was then describing a long curve.

I took my place beside him, and waited without speaking. Twelve o'clock came, and, as on the previous day, no sun was visible.

It was fatality. The observation could not be made. If it could not be accomplished to-morrow, we must entirely give up the idea of knowing our situation.

We were now at the 20th March; the morrow, the 21st, was the equinox – refraction not counted. The sun would then disappear behind the horizon for six months, and, at his departure, the long polar night set in. Since the September equinox it had risen above the horizon, rising in elongated curves daily till the 21st December; at that time – the summer solstice of northern latitudes – it began to descend; and, on the 21st March, it would pour out its last rays.

I made known my observations and fears to Captain Nemo.

"You are right, M. Aronnax," he replied. "If to-morrow I do not obtain the height of the sun, I cannot repeat my attempt here for six months. But, also, precisely because the chances of my sailing have led me to these seas on the 21st March, my object will be all the easier to attain, if, at mid-day, the sun will only show himself."

"Why, captain?"

"Because, when the orb describes such lengthened curves, it is difficult to measure exactly its height above the horizon, and the instruments are not unlikely to return erroneous results."

"But how do you intend to proceed?"

"I shall only use my chronometer," replied the captain. "If to-morrow, 21st March, at noon, the disc of the sun – taking account for refraction – is exactly divided by the northern horizon, I shall know we are at the South Pole."

"Quite so," said I; "but, nevertheless, this conclusion is not mathematically correct, since the equinox does not necessarily commence at mid-day."

"No doubt, but the difference will not be a hundred yards, and we do not want anything more than we shall get. Till to-morrow, then."

Captain Nemo returned on board. Conseil and I remained until nearly five o'clock, surveying and studying the shore. I did not pick up any curious thing except a penguin's egg of enormous size, for which a collector would have paid a thousand francs. Its isabelle colour, its lines, and the characters which ornamented it like so many hieroglyphics, made it quite a curiosity. I put it into Conseil's hands, and this prudent and sure-footed lad, holding it like a precious bit of china, carried it in safety on board the *Nautilus*. I placed the specimen in one of the glass cases of the saloon, and after an excellent supper of seal's liver, I went to sleep, first invoking the favour of the sun like a Hindoo.

Next morning at five o'clock I ascended to the platform, and there found Captain Nemo.

"The weather is clearing a little," he said. "I begin to hope. After breakfast we will land to select a post of observation."

This point settled, I went to find Ned Land. I wished him to come with me, but he refused, and I perceived that his sullenness increased every day. After all I did not regret his decision under the circumstances. There were a number of seals on shore, and it was needless to submit the harpooner to such temptation.

After breakfast we went ashore. The *Nautilus* had worked up the coast a few miles during the night. We were in the offing quite a league from the shore, which was commanded by a high peak about 1,500 feet high. The boat carried, besides myself and Captain Nemo, two men and the instruments, viz., a chronometer, a field-glass, and a barometer.

During our row I noticed numbers of the three austral species of whale, viz., the "right whale" of the English fishers, which has no dorsal fin; the hump-back, or "balænopteron", with creased belly and large white fins, which, notwithstanding its name, do not form wings; and the fin-back, a brownish-yellow creature, the most lively of all cetaceans. This powerful animal can be heard at a great distance when he throws to a great height columns of air and vapour, which resemble clouds of smoke. These mammals disported themselves in the quiet sea, and I saw that the basin of the South Pole now served as a place of refuge for these cetacea too closely pressed by fishermen.

At nine o'clock we landed. The sky was clearing. The clouds were flying to the south, and the fogs rose.

Captain Nemo directed his steps to the peak, whence he wished to make his observation, no doubt. It was a rough ascent over the sharp lava blocks and pumice stones, amid an atmosphere saturated with sulphurous exhalations. The captain, for a man unaccustomed to walk on land, ascended the steep and difficult slopes with an activity and agility I could not emulate, and which a chamois-hunter would have envied.

We had two hours to wait at the summit. From thence we commanded an extensive prospect of sea, which towards the north was clearly defined against the horizon. At our feet lay snow fields of dazzling whiteness. Over head was the pale blue sky. In the north, the sun's disc, like a ball of fire, already "horned" by the cutting of the horizon. Magnificent jets of water rose by hundreds from the bosom of the ocean, and in the distance the *Nautilus* lay like a sleeping whale. Behind us, to the south and east, extended an immense tract of land, a chaotic mingling of rock and ice without visible boundary.

Captain Nemo having reached the very top of the peak, carefully took the mean elevation of the barometer, for that he would have to take into account in his observation. At a quarter to twelve the sun, seen only by refraction, showed itself like a disc of gold, and threw its last rays upon this desolate continent, and those seas which man had never yet entered.

The captain, furnished with a reticulated glass, which, by means of a mirror, corrected refraction, began to observe the sun, which was sinking slowly below the horizon in a long diagonal. I held the chronometer. My heart beat loudly. If the disappearance of half the disc coincided with noon on the chronometer, we were at the Pole itself.

"Twelve o'clock!" I cried.

"The South Pole," replied the captain, in a grave tone, and handing me the glass, I perceived the orb of day precisely bisected by the horizon.

I looked at the last rays tipping the peak, and watched the shadows creeping up by degrees.

At that moment Captain Nemo turned to me and said:

"Professor – in the year 1600 the Dutchman Gheritk, driven by currents and storms, reached 64° of S. lat., and discovered New Shetland. In 1773, on the 17th of January, the illustrious Cook, following the 38th meridian, reached 67° 30′, and in 1774, on the 109th meridian, he got to 71° 15 S. lat. The Russian, Bellinghausen, in 1819, found himself on the 69th parallel, and in 1821 on the 66th parallel in 110° W. longitude. In 1820, the Englishman, Brunsfield, stopped at the 65th degree. The same year Morel, an American, whose narratives are dubious, mounted to the 42nd meridian, discovered the open sea in 70° 14′ S. lat. In 1825, Powell, an Englishman, was not able to get beyond the 62nd degree. The same year a simple seal-fisher, Weddel, an Englishman, reached as far as 74° 15′ on the 36th meridian. In 1829, Foster, his countryman, captain of the *Chanticleer*, took possession of the Antarctic continent, in 63° 26′ S. lat., and 66° 26′ long. In 1831, Biscoe, upon the 1st of February, discovered the land he called 'Enderby', in lat. 68° 50′; in 1832, on the 5th February, 'Adelaide', in lat. 67°; and on 21st February, 'Graham's Land', in lat. 64° 45′. In 1838, the French explorer, Dumont d'Urville, stopped by ice in lat. 62° 57′, found the territory 'Louis Philippe'; two years later, in a new place to the south, on the 24th January, he named 'Adelie', in 66° 30′; and eight days later, in 64° 40′, the Clarie coasts. In 1838, Wilkes, an Englishman, advanced as far as the 69th parallel on the 100th meridian. In 1839, Ballerny, an Englishman, also discovered 'Sabrina Land', on the edge of the polar circle. Finally, in 1842, James Ross, mounting 'Erebus' and 'Terror', on the 12th January, in 76° 56′ lat., and 171° 7′ E. long., discovered Victoria Land. On the 23rd of the same month he reached the 74th parallel – the highest point attained to that time. On the 27th day he was in 76° 8′, on the 28th at 77° 32′, on the 2nd February in 78° 4′, and in 1842 he reached the 71st degree, which he could not pass. So then, I, Captain Nemo on this 21st March, 1868, have reached the South Pole, on the 90th degree; and I take possession of this part of the globe – equal to one-sixth of the known continents."

"In whose name, captain?"

"In my own!" he replied.

As he spoke he unfurled a black flag embroidered with an "N" in gold. Then, turning to the sun, whose last rays were tinting the waves on the horizon, he exclaimed:

"Adieu, oh, sun! Disappear, radiant orb! Sleep beneath this open sea, and leave a long night of six months' duration to extend its shadow over my new dominion!"

CHAPTER XV
ACCIDENT OR INCIDENT?

NEXT MORNING, AT six o'clock, the preparations for our departure commenced. The last hours of twilight were buried in the night. The cold was intense. The stars shone with wonderful brilliancy, and in the zenith glittered the Southern Cross, the "polar star" of the Antarctic regions.

The thermometer marked 12° below zero, and when the wind got up it "bit" shrewdly. The ice-blocks increased upon the ocean. Numerous black patches spread themselves over the surface, and announced the formation of the young ice. Evidently the southern basin, frozen during the six months of winter, was absolutely inaccessible. What became of the whales during that period? Doubtless they went below the icebergs to seek more open seas. As for the seals and morses, accustomed to live in the most icy climates, they remained where they were. The instinct of these animals bids them to cut holes in the ice, and keep them always open. They come to these holes to breathe, and when the birds, chased away by the cold, have migrated to the north, the mammals are the sole occupants of the polar continent.

However, the reservoirs were filled, and the *Nautilus* slowly descended. At a depth of 1,000 feet it stopped. The screw beat the water, and it went right away towards the north at a rate of fifteen miles an hour. Towards evening we floated beneath the immense icebergs.

The saloon panels had been closed as a matter of prudence, for the *Nautilus* might strike some immersed block of ice. So I employed myself during the day putting my notes in order. My mind was fully occupied in recollections of the Pole. We had reached the hitherto inaccessible point without fatigue or danger, as if our floating waggon had run along a line of railway.

And now our return had actually begun. Had Captain Nemo any more such wonders in store? What a series of submarine wonders had I witnessed during the five months I had been on board! We had sailed 14,000 leagues, and incidents of the most curious or terrible nature had given a charm to our journey. The chase in the Isle of Crespo, the threading of Torres Strait, the coral cemetery, the Ceylon fisheries, the Arabian tunnel, the fires of Santorin, Vigo Bay, Atlantide, and the South Pole. During the night all these reminiscences prevented my sleeping.

At 3 a.m. I was disturbed by a violent shock. I sat up and listened, when I was roughly thrown into the middle of the room. The *Nautilus*, having struck, had rebounded violently. I groped my way to the saloon, which was lighted from the ceiling. The furniture was upset. Happily the glass cases were firmly fixed, and had not given way. The pictures on the starboard side – the vessel being no no longer upright – were hanging close to the paper, while those opposite were a foot from the wall. The *Nautilus* was lying on the starboard side motionless. I could hear a noise of footsteps and hurried voices, but Captain Nemo did not appear. Just as I was about to leave the saloon Ned and Conseil entered it.

"What is the matter?" I asked.

"We came to ask Monsieur—" said Conseil.

"Thousand devils! I know what it is very well," said the Canadian; "the *Nautilus* has struck, and, judging from the 'heel' she has, I do not think she will recover as easily as she did in the Torres' Strait."

"But, at least," said I, "we shall go up to the surface."

"We do not know," replied Conseil.

"We can easily find out," I said.

I consulted the manometer: to my great surprise it indicated a depth of 11,000 feet.

"What is the meaning of this?" I cried.

"We must ask Captain Nemo," said Conseil.

"But where will you find him?" said Ned.

"Follow me," I said.

We quitted the saloon. There was no one in the library, no one at the central staircase. I fancied that the captain was in the pilot-house, so it was better to wait; we therefore returned to the saloon.

I pass over the recriminations of the Canadian; I let him exhaust his ill-humour at his ease without replying.

We remained thus for twenty minutes, endeavouring to catch the slightest noise, when Captain Nemo entered.

He did not appear to see us; he showed signs of uneasiness; he examined the compass and manometer in silence, and placed his finger on a point on the map of the Southern Seas.

I did not like to interrupt him, but, as he leaned towards me, I made use of the expression he had used in Torres' Strait.

"An incident, captain?"

"No, sir," he replied; "an accident this time."

"Serious?"

"Perhaps."

"Is there immediate danger?"

"No."

"The *Nautilus* is stranded, I suppose?"

"Yes."

"And how has it occurred?"

"From a caprice of Nature, not from our ignorance. No mistake has been made in our course. But we cannot prevent the effects of the laws of equilibrium. We may brave human laws, but not those of Nature."

This was a curious moment for Captain Nemo to select to give vent to this philosophical reflection; and, on the whole, I got little from his reply.

"May I know how this accident has come about?" I asked.

"A whole mountain of ice has turned over," he replied. "When icebergs get undermined, either by warmth or repeated shocks, the centre of gravity ascends. Then they topple over. That is what has occurred. One of these blocks, as it fell, struck the *Nautilus* under water; then, gliding beneath the hull, it raised it with irresistible force, and forced us into thinner ice, where the *Nautilus* now lies on her side."

"But cannot we empty the reservoirs, and get her off by those means?"

"That is now being done. You can hear the pumps at work. Look at the manometer. It shows that the *Nautilus* is rising, but the block of ice is rising with it, and, until its progress is stopped, our situation will be practically the same."

In fact the *Nautilus* now gave a bound to leeward. She would right herself, no doubt, when the ice-block was separated from her. But at that moment we could not tell whether we might not be crushed up against the iceberg, and crushed between the blocks.

I kept thinking of the consequences of the situation. Captain Nemo never took his gaze from the manometer. The *Nautilus*, since the fall of the iceberg, had risen about 150 feet, but at the same angle as before.

Suddenly a slight movement was felt. The vessel was evidently righting a little. The objects suspended in the saloon appeared to be recovering their normal position. The sides got more upright. No one spoke a word. With beating hearts we watched, and felt the ship recovering herself. The floor was at length horizontal. Ten minutes elapsed.

"At length we have righted!" I cried.

"Yes," said the captain, as he advanced to the door.

"But are we floating?" I asked.

"Certainly," he replied, "since the reservoirs are not empty. When they are empty we shall rise to the surface again."

The captain went out, and I soon found that the ascent of the *Nautilus* had been stopped. We should soon have struck against the bottom of the iceberg had we gone up, and it was more prudent to remain beneath the waters.

"We have escaped very well," said Conseil.

"Yes, indeed. We might have been crushed between the blocks of ice, or at any rate imprisoned. And, then, in the absence of opportunity to renew the air—! Yes, we *have* escaped very well."

"If it is all over," murmured Ned.

I did not wish to enter on a useless discussion with the Canadian, so I did not reply. Besides, the panels were just then opened, and the exterior light entered.

We were in open water, as I have said; but, at about six yards on each side of the *Nautilus*, rose a dazzling wall of ice. Above and below it was the same. Above us the lower surface of the iceberg covered us like an immense ceiling, while below, the overturned iceberg having slipped a little, had found a rest upon the two lateral walls which kept it in that position. The *Nautilus* was thus imprisoned in a regular ice-tunnel, about twenty yards in length, and filled with still water. It was, therefore, easy to get out of it by going backwards or forwards, and afterwards make, at some hundred yards lower down, a free passage beneath the iceberg.

The ceiling light had been extinguished, and, nevertheless, the saloon was brilliantly illuminated. This was the powerful reflection from the glass partitions, caused by the intense light of the electric lamp. I cannot describe the effect of the voltaic rays upon the capriciously-shaped ice blocks; each angle, ridge, and facet threw off a different gleam according to the vein of the ice. A sparkling mine of gems, and particularly of sapphires, which crossed their blue rays with the green of the emerald. There were also opal shades of infinite softness coursing amidst brilliant diamond-points of fire, whose intense brilliancy the eye could not sustain. The power of the lantern was increased a hundred-fold, like a lamp through the lenticular sheets of a large lighthouse.

"Is it not beautiful?" cried Conseil.

"Yes," I said, "it is a magnificent sight, is it not, Ned?"

"Yes, confound it, yes it is," replied Ned Land. "It is superb. I am angry at being forced to admit it. Nothing to equal it has ever been seen. But this sight may cost us dear. And if I must say all I think, I believe that we are now looking at things which God never intended man to see."

Ned was right. It was too beautiful. Suddenly a cry from Conseil made me turn.

"What is the matter?" I cried.

"I am blinded, I believe!"

I turned involuntarily to the window. The vessel was going at a great pace now. I understood what had happened. All the quiet glittering of the icy walls was now changed into flashing lightning. The glare of these myriads of diamonds was absolutely blinding. The *Nautilus* was sailing through a stream of lightning.

The panels were closed. We held our hands before our eyes, still affected by the intense glare. It was some time before our eyes recovered their usual power. At length we removed our hands.

"I should scarcely believe such a thing," said Conseil.

"I do not believe it now," replied the Canadian.

"When we return to earth," added Conseil, "satiated with all the wonders of nature, what shall we think of the miserable continents and the petty efforts of men? No, the habitable world is not enough for us."

To hear such a speech from the impassible Fleming was a proof that some degree of excitement had increased our enthusiasm. But the Canadian did not fail to throw cold water on it.

"The inhabited world!" cried he, nodding his head. "Be easy on that score, friend Conseil; we shall never get there again."

It was then 5 a.m. We suddenly felt a shock. I understood that the spur of the *Nautilus* had struck a block of ice. This must have been caused by a false movement; for the submarine tunnel, encumbered as it was with ice-blocks, did not offer very good navigation. I thought, therefore, that Captain Nemo, by changing his course, would turn these obstacles, or follow the windings of the tunnel. In any case, our advance could not be entirely stopped. But, contrary to my expectations, the *Nautilus* went astern again.

"We are going back," cried Conseil.

"Yes," I replied; "I suppose that there is no outlet this way."

"And then?"

"Then," I said, "the plan is very simple: we must retrace our steps, and get out by the south end, that is all."

I spoke thus, so as to appear more confident than I really felt. Meantime the *Nautilus* retired at a greater pace, and soon at a very high speed.

"This will be a drawback, indeed," said Ned.

"What can a few hours matter, more or less," I said, "provided we get out at last."

"Yes," said Ned, "provided we *do* get out at last."

For a short time I walked from the saloon to the library. My companions sat down in silence. I soon threw myself upon a couch, and took up a book, which I began to read mechanically.

After the lapse of a quarter of an hour Conseil approached and said:

"Is that book interesting to Monsieur?"

"Very interesting indeed," I replied.

"I can quite believe it," he said. "It is Monieur's own work that he is reading!"

"My book!" I exclaimed.

But so it was. I was reading the "Great Submarine Depths". I had not the slightest idea of it. I closed the book and resumed my walk. Ned and Conseil got up to go.

"Stay here, my friends, let us wait together till we are clear of this ice."

"Just as Monsieur pleases," said Conseil.

Some hours passed. I often consulted the instruments hanging in the saloon. The manometer showed that the *Nautilus* maintained an uniform depth of 300 yards; the compass showed her on a southerly course; the log that we were going at twenty miles an hour, a great speed in such a confined space. But Captain Nemo knew what he was about, and every minute was worth a century to us.

At 8.25 a second shock occurred, astern this time. I turned pale. My companions approached me. I seized Conseil's hand. We looked at each other, and our looks interpreted our thoughts better than words could have done.

At that moment the captain entered. I went up to him.

"Our course southward is barred?" I asked.

"Yes; the iceberg in turning over has closed every outlet."

"We are blocked up then?" I said.

"Yes."

CHAPTER XVI
WANT OF AIR

SO AROUND THE *Nautilus*, above and below, was an impenetrable wall of ice. We were imprisoned in the iceberg. The Canadian struck the table with his heavy fist. Conseil said nothing. I looked at the captain. His face wore its usual look. He was standing with his arms crossed, lost in thought. The *Nautilus* did not move.

The captain roused himself and said, in a calm tone, "Gentlemen, there are two ways for us to die under present circumstances." – He spoke as if he were a professor of mathematics, delivering a lecture to his pupils. – "The first is to be crushed up, the other is to die by suffocation. I do not speak of the possibility to die of hunger, for the supplies on board will last longer than we can. Let us therefore calculate our chances of being crushed or suffocated."

"As far as suffocation goes, captain," I replied, "there is not much fear of that, for our reservoirs are filled."

"Quite so," replied the captain, "but they only give us two days' supply. Now we have been under water six-and-thirty hours, and the atmosphere here requires renovating already. In forty-eight hours our reserve will be exhausted."

"Well, captain, we shall be free before that."

"We will try at any rate, by piercing the walls around us."

"Which side?" I asked.

"The sound must guide us. I will run the *Nautilus* on the lower bank, and my men in their divers' dresses must attack the iceberg at the thinnest spot."

"Can they open the windows of the saloon?"

"Easily, we are moving no longer."

The captain went out. A hissing noise soon told me that the water was entering the reservoirs. The *Nautilus* sank slowly, and rested on the ice at a depth of 350 yards, at which distance the lower pack of ice was immersed.

"My friend," said I, "the case is serious, but I count on your courage and energy."

"Monsieur," said the Canadian, "I am not going to weary you with complaints at such a time as this. I am ready to do anything for the common safety."

"Thank you, Ned," I replied, extending my hand to him.

"I may add that I am as handy with a pick as with a harpoon, so if I can be of any use to the captain, I am at his disposal!"

"He will not refuse your assistance, Ned. Come."

I conducted the Canadian to the room where the crew were putting on their diving dresses. I mentioned Ned's suggestion to the captain, who accepted it. The Canadian then put on the dress, and was ready as soon as the rest. Each one carried on his back the Ronquayrol apparatus, which furnished a reservoir of pure air. A considerable but necessary deduction had been made from the supply on board. The Ruhmkorff lamps were not necessary.

When Ned was dressed I returned to the saloon, the windows of which were now open, and with Conseil examined the ambient beds which supported the *Nautilus*.

Some moments after we saw a dozen of the crew on the bank of ice. Ned Land was with them, distinguishable by his great height. Captain Nemo also accompanied the party.

Before digging into the ice he sounded it, so as to be certain of the best direction in which to work. Sounding-lines were let into the side walls, but the lead stopped after fifteen yards. It was useless to attack the ceiling, since the iceberg was more than 1,200 feet high. Captain Nemo then sounded the lower part. Ten yards of ice separated us from the water. That, then, was the thickness of the ice-field. It was therefore necessary to cut out a piece equal to the *Nautilus'* line of flotation. There were thus about 6,000 cubic yards to detach, so as to give us an opening to descend to the ice-field.

The work was at once commenced and vigorously prosecuted. Instead of cutting close around the *Nautilus*, which would have been a difficult operation, Captain Nemo determined to describe an immense trench round it, at about eight yards from the starboard side. Then the men worked with "borers" at several points of the circumference, and the picks soon went to work, and immense blocks were detached. By the curious effect of specific gravity, these blocks, lighter than water, flew, so to speak, to the top of the tunnel; which got as much thicker above as it got thinner underneath.

After two hours' hard work Ned Land gave in. His companions and he were replaced by new hands, to whom we were allied. The mate superintended us.

The water appeared to me to be very cold, but I soon warmed myself at work. I could move freely, although under a pressure of thirty atmospheres.

When I entered the *Nautilus* – after two hours' work – to get some food and repose, I perceived a great difference between the air on board and what had been supplied by the apparatus. The air in the *Nautilus* had not been renewed for forty-eight hours, and its vivifying qualities were considerably weakened. But, after a lapse of twelve hours, we had only raised a block of ice a yard thick, on the marked portion, which was about 600 cubic yards. At this rate, we should take five nights and four days to finish the task.

"Five nights and four days," I said to my companions; "and we have but two days' supply of air in the reservoirs."

"Without counting," added Ned, "that, if we ever do get out of this damned prison, we shall still be under the iceberg, and without communication with the open air."

It was quite true. Who could foresee the minimum of time necessary for our deliverance? Might not we be suffocated before the *Nautilus* had time to reach the surface again? Were we doomed to perish in this tomb of ice which shut us in? The situation was terrible! But every one looked it in the face, and all were determined to do their duty to the end.

As I had foreseen, another block, a yard square, was raised during the night. But in the morning when, clothed in my diving dress, I explored the water in a temperature of 6° or 7° below zero, it seemed to me that the lateral walls were coming closer! The water at a distance from the trench – not warmed by the presence of the workers – had a tendency to solidify. Our chances of escape were diminished by this discovery. And how were we to stop the solidification of the surrounding water, which, when frozen, would crack the *Nautilus* like glass?

I did not point out this new danger to my companions, for what good was there to diminish their energy in the hard efforts to escape? But when I returned on board I told Captain Nemo my fears.

"I know it," he said, in that calm tone of his which the gravest danger could not alter; "it is only one danger more, and I do not see any way to avoid it. The only chance of safety is to work quicker than the solidification. We must be first, that's all."

We must be first! I had become accustomed to his manner of speech by this time.

During that day I wielded a pick vigorously for many hours. This toil sustained me. Besides, to work was to quit the *Nautilus* and to breathe the pure air supplied by the apparatus, to abandon a vitiated atmosphere.

Another yard was dug out by evening. When I returned on board I was almost choked by the carbonic acid gas with which the air was saturated. If we had only some chemical appliances with which to get rid of this deleterious gas! We had no want of oxygen. The water contained a very large quantity, and by decomposition we might restore the air. I had thought about it, but it was of no use to attempt it, as the carbonic produced by our respiration had permeated the vessel. To absorb it we must have some caustic potash, and work it about incessantly. Now we had none of this on board, and nothing else would do.

In the evening Captain Nemo let some fresh air escape from his reservoirs, and without it we certainly should not have lived.

Next day (March 26) I resumed my work in taking out the fifth yard. The sides and the upper ice began to thicken visibly. It was evident they would join together before the *Nautilus* could escape. Despair seized upon me for a moment, and my pickaxe fell from my grasp. What was the use of cutting away the ice if we were to be suffocated and crushed by the rapidly-petrifying water! This was a punishment that even savages had never invented. It seemed to me that we were between the jaws of a monster which were irresistibly approaching. At that moment, Captain Nemo, directing and working by turns, passed near me. I touched his arm, and pointed to the side walls of our prison. The wall on the port side had advanced to within four yards from the *Nautilus*.

He understood and made me a sign to follow him.

We returned on board. I took off my dress and accompanied him into the saloon.

"M. Aronnax," he said, "we must try something desperate, or we shall be sealed up as in cement."

"Yes," said I, "but what can we do?"

"Ah! if the *Nautilus* were only strong enough to resist the pressure!"

"Well?" I said, not catching the idea.

"Do you not understand," he continued, "that this freezing of the water would help us. It would burst through the ice that imprisons us. It can burst the hardest stones when it freezes. We have therefore an agent of safety, not of destruction."

"Yes, perhaps so, but the *Nautilus* could never hold out against this terrible pressure, it would be flattened like an iron plate."

"I know it," replied the captain; "so we must only trust to ourselves. We must oppose this solidification. Not only are the lateral walls closing in on us, but there do not remain ten feet of water either before or behind us. The congelation is gaining on all sides."

"How long," I asked, "will the air in the reservoirs permit us to breathe?"

The captain looked at me steadily.

"After to-morrow," he said, "the reservoirs will be empty!"

A cold sweat came over me. And yet I ought not to have been surprised at his reply. On the 22nd of March the *Nautilus* went under water at the Pole. We had now reached the 26th. We had lived for five days upon the reserve on board, and what air remained respirable must be kept for the working parties. Even now the impression is still so vivid that an involuntary fear seizes me, and my lungs seem to want air.

Meanwhile Captain Nemo was reflecting in silence, and motionless. An idea had apparently occurred to him, but he seemed to reject it. At length he said:

"Boiling water."

"Boiling water!" I exclaimed.

"Yes, we are shut up in a space relatively small. Would not streams of boiling water, constantly injected by pumps of the *Nautilus*, raise the temperature of the water and retard the congelation?"

"We must try it," I said resolutely.

"Let us do so, professor."

The thermometer showed 7° outside. Captain Nemo led me to the "galley", where the vast apparatus for distilling drinking water by evaporation were at work. They were filled with water, and the whole power of the electric heat was directed through the serpentines immersed in the liquid. In a few moments it had reached 100°. It was sent to the pumps while fresh supplies came in proportion. The heat was so great that the cold water drawn from the sea after having only passed through the apparatus came boiling to the pumps.

The pumping commenced, and in three hours the thermometer marked 6° below zero. We had gained a degree. Two hours after the thermometer marked 4°.

"We shall succeed," said I to the captain, having most carefully watched the progress of the operation.

"I think so," he said. "We shall not be crushed, and so have only suffocation to fear."

During the night the temperature of the water rose to one degree below zero. The injections could not carry it any higher. But as the congelation of the sea water is only produced at 2°, I was reassured against solidification.

The following day, 27th March, eighteen feet of ice had been cut away. Twelve feet only remained. We had still forty-eight hours to work in. The air could not be renewed in the interior of the *Nautilus*, so this day would make it worse still. An intolerable weight pressed upon me. About 3 p.m. this feeling of distress affected me in a violent degree. I yawned enough to dislocate my jaws. I panted in endeavouring to inhale the burning fluid so necessary to respiration, and which became more and more rarefied. A mortal torpor oppressed me. I was powerless, almost unconscious. My brave Conseil, similarly affected, and suffering as I did, never quitted my side. He took my hand, he gave me encouragement, and I heard him murmur:

"Ah, if I were not obliged to breathe I should be able to leave more air for Monsieur." Tears came to my eyes at hearing him speak thus.

If our situation all round was so intolerable on board, you can imagine how willingly we donned our diving-dresses for work. The blows of the pickaxes resounded on the frozen ice-beds. Our arms were aching, the skin was peeling from our hands, but what was fatigue? what did wounds matter? We had air for our lungs, we breathed – we breathed!

Nevertheless, no one prolonged his turn under water beyond his allotted time. His task finished, each one handed to a companion the reservoirs that supplied him with vital air. Captain Nemo set the example, and was the first to submit to this severe discipline. As the time came round he handed his dress to another, and returned to the vitiated atmosphere on board, calm as ever, without a murmur, unflinchingly.

On that day our usual work was accomplished with more than usual vigour. Six feet only remained to be raised. Only two yards separated us from the open sea. But the air reservoirs were almost empty. What little remained must be kept for the working parties. Not an atom for the *Nautilus*.

When I returned on board I felt half suffocated. What a night I passed! I do not know how to describe it.

Such sufferings are better untold. Next day my breathing was oppressed. A sensation of dizziness oppressed my brain, and I went about like one intoxicated. My companions were affected in the same way, and some of the crew had rattling in the throat.

This, the sixth day of our imprisonment, Captain Nemo, thinking the work progressed too slowly with mattock and pick, resolved to crush the bed of ice that separated us from the open water. He had preserved his coolness and energy throughout. He overcame physical pain by moral force. He deliberated, he combined his reasonings, and acted.

By his order the *Nautilus* was lightened, that is to say, raised

from the ice-bed by an alteration in the specific gravity. So soon
as it floated it was towed over the top of the circumference of the
trench, which had been excavated according to its line of flotation. Then the reservoirs of water were filled, it descended, and
was engulfed in the hole.

Then all the crew came aboard and the door of communication was shut. The *Nautilus* was then resting upon a bed of ice,
which was about a yard in thickness, and pierced in a thousand
places.

The reservoirs were then opened, and 300 cubic feet of water
admitted, increasing the weight of the vessel to about 1,800 tons.

We waited, we listened, all suffering forgotten in the tension
of those moments, hoping still. We had thrown our last stake for
safety.

Notwithstanding the buzzings that filled my brain, I soon
heard groanings beneath the hull of the *Nautilus*. The ice cracked
in a curious manner, with a sound like the tearing of paper, and
the *Nautilus* broke through.

"We have passed it," muttered Conseil in my ear.

I was not able to reply. I seized his hand, and pressed it
convulsively.

The *Nautilus*, carried down by the enormous weights within,
sank like a stone. Then all the electric force was put on the pumps
to clear the water out, and in a few minutes our fall was checked.
Soon after the manometer indicated an ascensional movement.
The screw going at full speed made the vessel tremble, even to
its bolts, and we "steamed" to the north. But how long was this
progress beneath the ice to last? Another day? I shall be dead
before that!

I lay half-suffocated upon the divan in the library. My face was
blue, my faculties suspended. I saw and heard nothing. All idea
of time had left me. My muscles refused to contract.

Suddenly I came to myself. Some breaths of air seemed to
penetrate my lungs. Had we gained the surface? Had we cleared
the iceberg?

No, it was Ned and Conseil, my two brave friends, who were
sacrificing themselves to save me. Some molecules of air still
remained in some of the apparatus, and instead of respiring
them they had preserved them for me, and though almost
suffocating, they gave it to me drop by drop. I wished to push

the apparatus away. They held my hands, and for a few moments I respired voluptuously.

My eyes turned to the clock. It was 11 a.m. It was then the 28th March. The *Nautilus* was speeding at forty miles an hour, tearing through the water. Where were Captain Nemo and his companions? Had they all succumbed?

At this moment the manometer indicated that we were only twenty feet from the surface. A simple layer of ice separated us from the atmosphere. Could we not break through it?

Perhaps so. In any case the *Nautilus* would try. I could feel it assume an oblique position, and elevate its spur. The introduction of water was sufficient for this change. Then, impelled by the powerful screw, it attacked the ice-field like a formidable battering ram. It broke it by degrees, by retiring and then attacking it with renewed force against the ice-field, which gave way, and at last, carried upwards by its impetus, it crushed down upon the icy fragments, which it splintered beneath its weight.

The panels were opened – torn open I may say – and fresh pure air from the sea permeated all parts of the *Nautilus* once again.

CHAPTER XVII
FROM CAPE HORN TO THE AMAZON

HOW I GOT UP to the platform I have not a notion. Perhaps the Canadian carried me thither. But I breathed, I inhaled the life-restoring sea air. Close to me my two companions were drinking in the fresh molecules. Men deprived of food for a long time must not too suddenly partake of nourishment. We, on the contrary, had no necessity to limit ourselves; we could inspire to our lungs' content the blessed air, and the breeze alone gave us this delightful sensation of mental intoxication.

"Ah!" cried Conseil, "how pleasant the oxygen is, and Monsieur need not fear to breathe it. There is enough for us all!"

Ned Land did not speak, but he opened his jaws wide enough to astonish a shark. And what breaths he took! The Canadian "drew" like a furnace in full blast.

Strength quickly returned, and when I looked round me I saw that we were the only occupants of the platform. Not one of the crew was there. Not even Captain Nemo. The strange sailors of the *Nautilus* contented themselves with the air circulating in the interior. Not one of them had come to imbibe the fresh air.

My first words were of thanks and gratitude to my two companions. Ned and Conseil had prolonged my existence for the last hours of this long agony. All my thanks could not repay such devotion.

"Oh!" said the Canadian, "it is not worth speaking about. What merit is there in what we did? None at all. It was only a question of arithmetic. Your life was worth more than ours, therefore it was necessary to preserve it."

"No, Ned," I replied, "it was not worth so much. No one is superior to a good and generous man, and you are that."

"All right, all right!" repeated the Canadian in an embarrassed manner.

"And you, my brave Conseil, you have also suffered."

"But nothing compared to Monsieur; I certainly did want air, but I believe that I did right. Besides, I looked at Monsieur, who was fainting, and that gave me no encouragement to breathe."

"My friends," I replied, much agitated, "we are bound to one another for ever, and I am under great obligations to you."

"I shall take advantage of that," replied the Canadian.

"How?" asked Conseil.

"Yes," replied Ned: "I claim the right to take you with me when I leave the *Nautilus*."

"But are we going in the right direction?" said Conseil.

"Yes," I replied, "since we follow the sun, and here the sun is in the north."

"Certainly," replied Ned; "but it remains to be seen whether we reach the Pacific or the Atlantic, that is to say a frequented or a deserted ocean."

I could not reply to this, and I was afraid that Captain Nemo would carry us rather towards the vast ocean which washes the shores of Asia and America. He would thus complete his tour round the world, and return to the seas where the *Nautilus* found the greatest liberty. But if we should return to the Pacific, what would become of all the projects of Ned Land?

This important point ought to be fixed before long.

The *Nautilus* was going at a great rate. The polar circle was soon cleared, and our course made for Cape Horn. We were off that point of America on March 31st, at seven o'clock p.m.

Then all our past sufferings were forgotten. The remembrance of our icy imprisonment melted away. We only thought of the future. Captain Nemo appeared neither on the platform nor in the saloon. The mark upon the chart each day showed me the position of the *Nautilus*. Now, that evening, to my great satisfaction, it was evident that we were returning to the north by the Atlantic.

I apprised Conseil and the Canadian of this.

"Good news," said the latter, "but whither is the *Nautilus* bound?"

"That I cannot say, Ned."

"Does the captain wish, having seen the South Pole, to discover the North Pole too, and return to the Pacific by the celebrated North-West passage, I wonder?"

"I should not be surprised." said Conseil.

"Well," said the Canadian, "we shall have given him the slip first."

"At any rate we must acknowledge that Captain Nemo is a first-rate fellow, and we do not regret having made his acquaintance," said Conseil.

"Particularly when we have left him," said Ned.

Next day (April 1st) the *Nautilus* came up to the surface. Some minutes before noon we noticed land to the westward. This was Terra del Fuego, which was so named by early navigators from the quantity of smoke arising from the native huts. It is a vast agglomeration of islands extending for a length of thirty, and a breadth of eighty leagues. The coast seemed low, but in the distance high mountains appeared. I believe I saw Mount Sarmiento, which is more than 6,000 feet high, a pyramidical block of schist with a very peaked top, "which, according as it is clouded or clear, announces bad or fine weather", Ned Land told me.

"A capital barometer, my friend."

"Yes, a natural one, and which was always right all the time I passed in the Straits of Magellan."

On this occasion the top was clearly defined against the heavens. So fine weather was in store for us, and we enjoyed it too.

The *Nautilus* again descended and coasted along. From the saloon windows I could see long sea-weeds and gigantic fucus, and the varech, of which the Polar Seas contain many specimens, with their viscous and polished filaments; they measured nearly

300 yards in length, regular cables, thicker than the thumb and very tough, they often served to fasten ships by. Another plant called "velp", with leaves four feet in length, enclosed in the corralous concretions, carpeted the depths. They served as nests and food for myriads of crustacea. There the seals and otters "lived in clover", mingling the flesh of fish with the vegetables of the sea, in English fashion!

The *Nautilus* passed rapidly over these luxuriant regions. Towards evening we neared the Malouine Isles, whose summits I could see the following day. The sea was of medium depth. I thought, and not unreasonably, that these two large islands, surrounded by a number of small ones, were formerly part of the land of Magellan. The Malouines were probably first discovered by John Davis, who called them "Davis' Southern Isles". Later, Richard Hawkins called them the Maiden, or Virgin Islands, and afterwards they were named Malouines, at the beginning of the eighteenth century by the St. Malo fishers, and finally designated Falkland Isles by the English, to whom they now belong.

In these places the nets brought up some beautiful specimens of algæ, and particularly a certain fucus, whose roots contained some mussels, which are the best in the world. Geese and ducks fell upon the platform in dozens, and were soon in the larder. Amongst the fish I noticed the gobies and "bouberots", spotted yellow and white. There were also numerous medusæ, and the chrysanes, which are peculiar to those regions. They sometimes appeared like an enormous umbrella, streaked with reddish-brown lines, and terminating in a dozen regular festoons. Sometimes like an inverted cap, from which large leaves and long red twigs escaped in graceful curves. They swam by moving their four foliaceous arms, and letting their long curling tentacles drift behind them. I wished to preserve some specimens, but they evaporate when out of their native element like shadows or apparitions.

When the Falklands had disappeared beneath the horizon the *Nautilus* plunged down about twenty-five yards and followed the American coast. Captain Nemo did not appear. We did not leave the Patagonian coast till April 3rd, and were sometimes above sometimes under water. We passed the large estuary formed by the La Plata, and on the 4th were opposite Uruguay, but at a distance of fifty miles from land. We still steered north, and followed the trendings of the American coast. We had now made 16,000 leagues since our departure from the Japanese seas.

We crossed the Tropic of Cancer on the 37th meridian about 11 a.m., and passed Cape Frio. To Ned Land's disgust Captain Nemo did not hug these Brazilian shores, and we went at a great pace. Not a bird nor fish, however rapid, could keep up with us, and all natural curiosities escaped me.

This pace was sustained for several days, and on the 9th April, in the afternoon, we sighted Cape Roque, the most easterly point of South America. But here the *Nautilus* altered her course again, and sought the deeps of a submarine valley, which extends between this cape and Sierra Leone. This valley bifurcates as high up as the Antilles and ends at the north in a tremendous dip of 2,700 feet. In this place the geological cutting of the ocean forms a perpendicular cliff of three and a half miles as far as the Lesser Antilles; and at the Cape Verd Islands is another wall no less considerable, which thus shuts in the whole of the submerged continent of Atlantis. The bottom of this immense valley is sprinkled with mountains, which gives some picturesqueness to these sub-oceanic depths. I am speaking from information derived from the charts of the *Nautilus* – charts which Captain Nemo had laid down after personal inspection.

For two days we visited the deep and deserted waters. But on the 11th of April we rose suddenly to the surface, and descried the land at the mouth of the Amazon, an estuary large enough to freshen the sea-water for several leagues.

We crossed the equator. The Guianas, a French settlement, lay twenty miles to the west, and on which we could have found refuge easily. But the wind was blowing fearfully, and the waves were so high, that no ordinary boat could live in them. Ned Land saw that, no doubt for he made no remark to me. For my part I made no allusion to his plans, for I did not wish to urge him to make an attempt which could only end in failure.

I amused myself very easily in the interval, by interesting studies. During the 11th and 12th April, the *Nautilus* remained at the surface, and the nets brought in a miraculous draught of zoophytes, fish, and reptiles. Some zoophytes had been dragged up by the chain – these were chiefly phyctallines belonging to the actinedian family, and amongst other species were the *Phyctalis protexta*, a native of this part of the ocean, a little cylindrical trunk striped with vertical lines and studded with red dots, which cover a marvellous show of tentacles. The molluscs consisted of those I have already mentioned, such as turntillas, olive prophyras, pteroceras, like petrified scorpions; and cuttle fish, which are very good to eat.

I noted various species of fish on these shores, which I had not hitherto studied. Amongst the cartilaginous specimens were the petromyzous-pricka, a kind of eel, fifteen inches in length, greenish head, fins violet, the back a bluish-grey colour, the belly is brown, of a silvery hue and speckled, the pupils of the eyes are surrounded with a golden circle. A curious animal this, which the current of the river Amazon had carried out to sea – for it is a fresh-water fish. There were "tubercular" rays, with pointed nose, a long and loose tail, armed with a long toothed sting; little sharks, about three feet long, commonly known as pantouffles; lophic-vespertilios, a sort of reddish isosceles triangle, half a yard long, which look like bats, owing to the prolongation of their pectoral fins, but the horny appendage placed near the nostrils has caused them to be denominated sea-unicorns; finally some specimens of balistæ, the curassavian, spotted with brilliant gold dots, the capriscus, of pure violet, with varying colours of the pigeon's throat.

I will end this somewhat dry (but exact) catalogue, with a series of osseous fishes that I observed; the passans, belonging to the apternotes, with blunt snow-white noses, the body is of a beautiful black, furnished with a long, slender, fleshy stripe; odontagnathes, with spikes; immense sardines, glittering with silver scales; mackerel, provided with two anal fins; black centro-notes, for which they fish with torches – these fish are about two yards in length, fat, with white firm flesh, when fresh they taste like eels, when dried, like smoked salmon; and labres, covered with scales at the bases of the anal and dorsal fins; chrysoptera, in which gold and silver scales blend in brightness; anableps, of Surinam, &c. But this "et cetera" must not prevent me from mentioning another fish, which Conseil for a long time kept in remembrance, and with good reason.

One of our nets had hauled up a kind of ray-fish, very flat, which with its tail cut off would have formed a perfect disc, and which weighed nearly forty pounds. It was white underneath, red above, with large round spots of blue, surrounded with black and very smooth skin. It struggled as it lay upon the platform, and endeavouring to turn itself, making so many efforts, that it nearly fell back into the sea. But Conseil, wishing to keep it, threw himself upon it, and before I could prevent him, had seized it with both hands. He was immediately knocked down, his legs high in the air, with half his body paralysed – and he cried out:

"Oh, master, master, come to me!"

This was the first time he had not addressed me in the third person.

The Canadian and I raised him up, we rubbed his paralysed arms, and when this inveterate classifier recovered his senses he murmured:

"Class, cartilaginous; order, chondropterygians; sub-order, selacians; family, rays; genus, torpedos."

"Yes, my friend," I replied; "it is a torpedo that has knocked you over in this way."

"Ah, Monsieur may believe me, I will be revenged on that animal."

"How?"

"By eating him."

Which was done that same evening, but in pure reprisal, for, to tell the truth, he was very tough.

The unfortunate Conseil had been attacked by a torpedo of the most dangerous species – the cumana. This curious animal in a medium conductor like water can give a shock to fish at several yards distance, so great is its power in the electric organs, the two principal surfaces of which measure twenty-seven square feet at least.

During the following day, the 12th April, the *Nautilus* approached the Dutch coast near the mouth of the Maroni. There were several herds of lamantins here; they were manatees, which, like the dugong and the stellera, belong to the syrenian order. These beautiful animals, peaceable and inoffensive, measured between eighteen and twenty-one feet in length, and weighed at least three tons (4,000 kilos). I told Ned Land and Conseil that Nature had assigned a very important part to these mammals. They, like the seals, are intended to feed upon the submarine prairies, and so destroy the accumulations of plants which block the mouths of tropical rivers.

"And do you know," I added, "what has happened since men

have almost entirely destroyed this useful race? The grasses have putrified and poisoned the air, and that has given rise to yellow fever, which has laid waste beautiful districts. Poisonous vegetation multiplies in these tropical seas, and the evil is irresistibly developed from the mouth of the La Plata to Florida."

And, if we can credit Toussenel, this plague is nothing at all to what will happen to our descendants when the seas become depopulated of whales and seals. Then, infested with cuttles, medusæ, and calmars, the waves will become vast hot-beds of infection, since they will no longer possess those "vast stomachs that God has commanded to scour the surface of the seas".

But, without disputing this theory, the crew of the *Nautilus* caught half a dozen manatees. They did so to provision the ship with excellent meat, superior to beef or veal. The capture was not interesting. The manatees permitted themselves to be killed without resistance. Many thousand pounds weight of meat destined to be dried was stored on board.

This day a tremendous haul of fish increased the reserves of the *Nautilus*; the seas are so very rich. The net brought up a number of fish whose heads terminated in an oval plate with fleshy edges. These were echeneïdes of the third family, of the sub-brachian malacopterygians. This was the *Echeneide osteocher*, peculiar to those seas. When taken, the sailors put them in buckets filled with water.

When the fishing was over, the *Nautilus* approached the coast. A number of tortoises were sleeping on the surface; otherwise it would have been difficult to capture them, for the least noise awakens them, and their shells are proof against the harpoon. But the echeneïde captured them with extraordinary precision. This animal is, in fact, a living fish-hook, which would make a tyro's fortune.

The sailors tied to the tail a ring sufficiently large not to encumber its movements, and to this ring was fastened a long cord fastened to the *Nautilus*.

The echeneïde, thrown into the sea, fixed themselves to the breastplates of the tortoises. Their tenacity was so great that they suffered themselves to be torn to pieces rather than let go. They were hauled on board with the tortoises to which they had attached themselves.

Several caconanes were also taken, weighing 400 lbs. Their

shells, covered with horny plates – thin, brown, and transparent – fetch a high price. They are also excellent eating – like the fresh turtles. This fishing brought our sojourn at the Amazon to a close, and, as night fell, the *Nautilus* steered for the open sea.

CHAPTER XVIII
THE OCTOPUS

FOR SOME DAYS the *Nautilus* gave the American coast a wide berth. Captain Nemo evidently did not wish to encounter the waves of the Gulf of Mexico or of the Antilles Seas. There was no want of water there, for the average depth is about 1,800 yards; but probably the islands, with which the seas are studded, did not recommend them to the captain.

On the 16th April we sighted Martinique and Guadeloupe at thirty miles distance. I saw the high peaks for a moment.

The Canadian, who had counted upon putting his plans of escape into execution in the Gulf – either by landing on some island, or by hailing one of the numerous vessels which ply from one island to another – was very much put out.

Flight would have been practicable had Ned been able to get possession of the boat without the captain's knowledge; but, in the open sea, it was useless to think of it.

Ned, Conseil, and I had a long conversation on this subject. We had now been six months on board the *Nautilus*, we had sailed 17,000 leagues, and, as Ned remarked, it was time to put an end to it. He suggested that we should go and put the question boldly to Captain Nemo whether he intended to keep us on board for ever? But to this I would not agree. We had nothing to hope from the captain, we must trust to ourselves. Besides, for some time he had become gloomy, reserved, and unsociable. He seemed to avoid me; I only encountered him at rare intervals. Formerly he seemed pleased to be able to explain the wonders of the sea; now he left me to my studies in the saloon.

What change was come upon him, and why? I had no reason to reproach myself. Perhaps our presence on board worried him. Nevertheless, I did not think he would give us our liberty.

I therefore begged Ned to pause before acting. If this attempt had no result it would only revive his suspicions, and render our position unpleasant, and injurious to the projects of the Canadian. I will add that I could adduce no argument on the score of health. If I except the rough experience beneath the iceberg, we had never been better in our lives. The healthy food, the pure air, and regularity of our lives, with the uniformity of temperature, gave illness no chance, and for a man who did not regret the world, or – like Captain Nemo, who was at home, who went where he chose – I could understand the pleasure of such an existence. But for us, we had not broken with mankind. I did not wish to bury with me my curious and novel studies. I had now the right to write a true book of the sea, and I wished sooner or later to have it published.

Then again, in the waters of the Antilles, at ten yards beneath the surface, by the open panels, what interesting objects had I to note daily! Here, amongst other zoophytes, were those known as *Physalis pelagica*, like large oblong bladders with mother-of-pearl rays, lifting their membranes to the breeze, and letting their long blue tentacles float like silken threads, beautiful medusæ to look at, but regular nettles to touch, and distilling a corrosive liquid. Among the articulates were annelides a yard and a half in length, armed with a rose-coloured horn, and furnished with 1,700 organs of locomotion, which twined about in the water and reflected all the colours of the solar spectrum. Amongst the fish were, Malabar-rays – enormous cartilaginous fish, ten feet long and 600 lbs. weight, a triangular pectoral fin on a lumpy back, eyes fixed beyond the head at the extremities of the face, and which floated like wreckage, and appearing sometimes like a shutter before our window. There were the American balistæ, dressed by Dame Nature in black and white, gobies, mackerel of enormous size, of the albicore species. Then we had grey mullet in shoals, striped with gold from head to tail, moving their resplendent fins, which shone like a masterpiece of jewellers' workmanship; these were formerly consecrated to Diana, and were particularly sought after by rich Romans, and of which the proverb states, "who takes them does not eat them". Lastly, pomacanthe dorys, ornamented with emerald bands, dressed in silk and velvet, passed like Veronese lords. What a number of other specimens I might have noted had not the *Nautilus* dived to the lowest depths! Here animal life is not represented except by ecrines, starfish, pentacrines, medusæ-heads, troques, and such like.

On the 20th April we had risen to a medium height of 1,500 yards. The nearest land was the Bahamas, lying like a number of paving-stones at the surface of the sea. High cliffs rose up, perpendicular walls, rough blocks placed in long layers, amongst which were deep holes to the end of which our electric light could not penetrate. These rocks were clothed with immense sea-grasses and weeds, hydrophytes worthy of a Titan world.

From speaking of enormous plants Ned and Conseil naturally turned to gigantic animals in the sea. The former were evidently intended to nourish the latter; while from the windows of the saloon I did not see any but the principal articulates of the division of brachiousa, long-footed lampreys, violet crabs, and clios, peculiar to the Antilles.

About 11 a.m. Ned Land directed my attention to the extraordinary amount of movement going on amongst the algæ.

"Well," I said, "they are the regular caves of cuttle-fish, and I should not be surprised to see one of those monsters."

"What!" cried Conseil, "calmars, simple calmars, of the class of cephalopods?"

"No," I replied, "but cuttle-fish of enormous size. But perhaps friend Ned is mistaken, for I can perceive none of them."

"I am sorry for it. I should like to see one of those 'porpoises' of which I have heard, which are able to drag ships under water. They are called krak—"

"It *is* a regular 'cracker', altogether, I should think," said Ned; "'cracker' will do!"

"Krakens!" replied Conseil, having got out the word without noticing his companion's "chaff".

"You will never make me believe that such animals exist," said Ned.

"Why not?" exclaimed Conseil, "you believed Monsieur's narwhal."

"We were wrong, Conseil."

"No doubt, but other people believe it still."

"It is probable, Conseil; but I have made up my mind not to admit the existence of these monsters till I have dissected them myself," said I.

"So," replied Conseil, "Monsieur does not believe in these gigantic octopi?"

"Why, who the devil *has* ever believed in them?" asked Ned.

"Lots of people, friend Ned."

"No fishermen – *savants* perhaps may!"

"Excuse me, Ned, both fishermen and *savants*."

"But," said Conseil, with the most serious air in the world, "I perfectly remember to have seen a large ship pulled down beneath the waves by one of the arms of a cuttle."

"You have seen that!" exclaimed the Canadian.

"Yes, Ned."

"With your own eyes?"

"With my own eyes."

"And where, if you please?"

"At St. Malo," replied the imperturbable Conseil.

"In the harbour, I suppose," said Ned, ironically.

"No, in a church."

"In a church!" exclaimed Ned.

"Yes, there is a picture there, representing the cuttle."

"Capital!" cried Ned, laughing. "Conseil did puzzle me a bit."

"As a fact, he is quite right," I said. "I have heard of that picture, but the subject is taken from a legend, and you know what to think of legends, when applied to natural history. Besides, when monsters are in question, the imagination is apt to run wild a little. Not only has it been stated that these cuttles can drag ships down, but a certain Olaüs Magnus speaks of a cephalopod a mile long, which was more like an island than an animal. It is also recounted that the Bishop of Nidros one day built an altar upon an enormous rock. Mass concluded, the rock got up and departed to the sea. The rock was a cuttle!"

"Is that all?" said Ned.

"No; another bishop, Pontoppidan de Berghem, also speaks of a cuttle upon which he could exercise a regiment of cavalry!"

"They said something besides their prayers, did those bishops," replied Ned.

"Finally, the ancient naturalists quote monsters whose throats were like gulfs, and which were too large to get through the Straits of Gibraltar."

"Oh! go ahead!" said the Canadian.

"But now, what is the truth of all this?" asked Conseil.

"Nothing, my friends – nothing at least but which passes the limits of truth and reaches legend or fable. Still, there is at any rate some ground or pretext for this play of the imagination of story-tellers. One cannot deny that cuttles and calmars of great size do exist, but they are not so large as cetacea. Aristotle mentioned a calmar of five cubits, nearly ten yards in length. Fishermen have often met with them more than four feet long. The museums of Trieste and Montpellier have skeletons of poulpes measuring two yards. Besides, according to the calculation of naturalists, one of these animals, measuring six feet only, has tentacles twenty-seven feet in length. That would be a formidable monster!"

"Do they fish for them at present?" asked Ned Land.

"If they do not fish for them, sailors see them. One of my friends, Captain Paul Bos, of Havre, has often told me that he met an enormous cuttle in the Indian seas. But the most astonishing incident, and one that will not allow us to deny the existence of these animals, happened in 1861."

"How was that?" asked Ned.

"In 1861, at the north-east of Teneriffe, not far from where we are now, the crew of the despatch-vessel, *Alecto*, perceived an enormous cuttle. Captain Bonguer approached it, and attacked it with harpoons and guns, without any marked success, for both bullets and harpoons recoiled from its flesh, which is like soft jelly. After many attempts they succeeded in fastening a rope round the animal's body. The noose slipped to the caudal fins, and there it stopped. They then attempted to haul the monster on board, but his weight was so enormous that the tail was separated from the body, and, deprived of this ornament, the cuttle disappeared beneath the waves."

"At length we have a fact," said Ned Land.

"An indisputable fact. So it was proposed to name the poulpe the 'Bonguer cuttle-fish'."

"How long was it?" asked the Canadian.

"Did it not measure about six yards?" said Conseil, who was posted at the window, watching the fissures in the cliffs.

"Precisely," I replied.

"Was not its head crowned with eight tentacles, which moved about in the water like a nest of serpents?"

"Quite so," I replied.

"Were not the eyes placed at the back of the head and very large?"

"Yes, Conseil."

"And was its mouth like a parrot's beak, but a very terrible one?"

"Quite true, Conseil."

"Well, then, if Monsieur pleases," replied Conseil, quietly, "if yonder is not Bonguer's cuttle-fish, it is one of the family."

I gazed at Conseil. Ned Land rushed to the window.

"The horrible beast!" he cried.

I in my turn came to look, and could not repress a shudder of disgust. Before my eyes was a fearful monster, worthy to figure in legends of the marvellous.

It was a cuttle of enormous dimensions, eight yards long. It moved sideways with extreme velocity in the direction of the *Nautilus*. It gazed at us with its enormous staring sea-green eyes. Its eight arms, or rather its eight feet, were fixed to its head, which gives these animals the name of cephalopods – were double the length of its body, and turned about like the head-dress of the furies. We could distinctly see the 250 air-holes on the inner side of the "arms", shaped like semi-spherical capsules. Sometimes these air-holes fastened against the window, and thus emptied themselves. The monster's mouth, a horny beak like that of a parrot, opened vertically. Its horny tongue, itself armed with many ranges of sharp teeth, came quivering from out those veritable shears. What a freak of Nature this – a bird's beak on a mollusc! Its body shaped like a spindle, and swollen in the middle, formed a fleshy mass which must have weighed 40,000 or 50,000 lbs. Its colour changed with great rapidity, according to the irritation of the animal, passing successively from a livid grey to a reddish-brown tinge.

What irritated the mollusc? No doubt the presence of the *Nautilus*, more formidable than itself, and on which its beak and tentacles had no effect. What monsters these cuttles are, what vitality they possess, what vigour they must have in their movements, since they have three hearts!

Chance had brought us in contact with this octopus, and I did not wish to lose the opportunity to study the specimen carefully. I overcame the horror with which its appearance inspired me, and, seizing a pencil, I commenced to make a sketch of it.

"Perhaps this is the same that the *Alecto* encountered," said Conseil.

"No," said the Canadian, "because this one is complete; the other fellow had lost a tail."

"This is no reason," I replied; "these animals can reform their arms and tail by redintegration, and in seven years the tail of Bonguer's cuttle, no doubt, has had time to grow again."

"Besides," replied Ned, "if this be not the one, it may be one of those others."

As he spoke other cuttles appeared at the window. I counted seven of them. They attended on the *Nautilus*, and I heard the grinding of their beaks on the iron hull. We had enough now at any rate.

I continued my work. The monsters kept their places with such precision that they appeared immoveable, and I was able to draw them foreshortened on the glass; besides, we were not going fast.

Suddenly the *Nautilus* stopped. A shock was felt all through her frame.

"What have we struck?" I exclaimed.

"In any case we are free, for we are floating," said the Canadian.

The *Nautilus* was floating, certainly, but it was not moving. The screw was not going. A minute passed, when Captain Nemo and his mate entered.

I had not seen the captain for some time; he seemed pre-occupied. Without speaking, perhaps without seeing us, he went to the panel, looked at the cuttle-fish, and said something to the mate.

The latter went out; the panels were soon closed, and the ceiling was lighted. I approached the captain.

"A curious collection of cuttles," I said, in the easy way a person might speak of them in an aquarium.

"Yes, indeed, professor, and we are going to fight them hand to hand."

I looked at the captain, not thinking I had heard aright.

"Hand to hand?" I repeated.

"Yes, the screw is stopped; I think one of their horny beaks has seized it. That is why we cannot move."

"And what are you going to do?"

"Rise to the surface and kill the vermin."

"Rather difficult, won't it?"

"Yes, indeed, for the electric bullets do not meet with sufficient resistance in their pulpy bodies to take effect."

"But we shall attack them with hatchets."

"And a harpoon," suggested the Canadian, "if you will accept my assistance."

"I do, Master Land."

"We will accompany you," I said; and, with Captain Nemo, we advanced to the staircase.

There a dozen men, armed with boarding hatchets, were in readiness for the attack. Conseil and I armed ourselves likewise. Ned Land seized a harpoon.

The *Nautilus* now floated at the surface. One of the sailors, placed on the top of the ladder, unscrewed the bolts of the panel. But the screws were scarcely loosened when the panel was wrenched violently open, evidently drawn in by the suckers of an octopus.

Immediately one of the long arms glided through the aperture, and twenty others were moving above. With a single blow Captain Nemo cut off this formidable tentacle, which slid writhing down the ladder.

As we were pressing forward together to reach the platform, two other arms, circling in the air, fell upon a sailor who was in front of Captain Nemo, and raised him up with irresistible power.

Captain Nemo uttered a shout, and rushed in front; we followed.

What a sight it was! The unhappy sailor, seized by the tentacle and fixed upon the sucker, was balanced in the air by this enormous "trunk". He gasped; he was almost stifled; and cried out "Help, help!" These words, *pronounced in French*, astonished me greatly. I had a fellow-countryman on board – several perhaps. I shall hear that heart-rending appeal all my life.

The poor fellow was lost! Who could tear him from such a grasp as that? Nevertheless Captain Nemo threw himself upon the octopus, and cut off one arm at a blow. The mate waged a terrible fight with others, which were assailing the sides of the *Nautilus*. The ship's company fought with hatchets. The Canadian, Conseil, and I wearied our arms hacking at these fleshy masses. A strong odour of musk pervaded the air. The scene was horrible.

For a moment I hoped that the unfortunate sailor seized by the octopus would be released. Seven of the eight arms had been cut off. Only one, now brandishing like a feather twined aloft. But as Captain Nemo and his mate both rushed at the animal it ejected a column of black liquid, secreted in a bag near the abdomen, at them. They were blinded, and when they recovered the octopus had disappeared with our unfortunate friend.

Enraged against the monsters, we rushed pell-mell amongst ten or a dozen which had now gained the platform and sides of the *Nautilus*, which were soon covered with waves of inky blood. The viscous tentacles seemed to spring up like hydra heads. Ned Land, at each thrust of his harpoon, blinded the great staring eyes. But my companion was suddenly overturned by the tentacles of a monster that he had not been able to avoid. My heart beat wildly. The beak of the octopus was extended over Ned Land. He would be cut in half. I rushed to his assistance. But Captain Nemo anticipated me. He flung his hatchet between the enormous mandibles, and the Canadian, miraculously rescued, plunged his harpoon into the triple heart of the octopus.

"I owe myself that revenge," said the captain to Ned Land.

Ned bowed, but made no reply.

The fight had lasted a quarter of an hour. The monsters, conquered, mutilated, beaten to death, left us at last, and disappeared.

Captain Nemo, red with blood, stood motionless near the lantern, gazed into the sea which had swallowed up one of his companions, and great tears stood in his eyes.

CHAPTER XIX
THE GULF STREAM

NONE OF US will ever forget that terrible scene of the 20th April. I have written the account of it under excitement. But since I have revised the description, and read it to Ned and Conseil. They found it quite correct as to fact, but wanting in effect. To describe such incidents properly one must have the pen of the most illustrious of our poets – the author of the "Toilers of the Sea".

I have stated that Captain Nemo was much affected while regarding the waves. His grief was intense. This was the second companion he had lost since our arrival on board. What a death too! A friend stifled, crushed, and bruised in the formidable arms of an octopus, and pounded between his iron mandibles, could never repose with his messmates in the peaceful waters of the coral cemetery.

The cry of despair uttered by the unhappy sailor was still ringing in my ears. This poor Frenchman, oblivious of his conventional dialect, was constrained to speak his mother-tongue in a last appeal for help. Amongst the crew of the *Nautilus*, linked body and soul with Captain Nemo, flying with him any contact with mankind, I had had a fellow-countryman. Was he the only representative of France in this mysterious association evidently composed of individuals of different nationalities? This was one of those unsolvable problems that were continually agitating my mind.

Captain Nemo entered his own room, and I did not see him again for some days. But that he was ill and careless and irresolute I could perceive, as the ship of which he was the soul received all its impressions from him. The *Nautilus* did not maintain the fixed direction. It moved and floated like a corpse tossed by the waves. The screw had been disconnected, and so was no use. We steered at random, and could not get away from the neighbourhood of our late encounter, from those very waves that engulfed our friend.

Ten days passed in this manner, and the 1st of May arrived ere the *Nautilus* actually resumed her old course, having sighted the Bahamas. We then followed the current of the greatest river of the sea, which has its own banks, its fish, and temperature. I mean the Gulf Stream.

It is, in fact, a river which runs freely to the middle of the Atlantic, and whose waters do not mingle with any ocean waves. It is a salt river, more salt than the sea surrounding it. Its average depth is 3,000 feet; its average breadth, sixty miles. In certain places the current runs at the rate of nearly three miles an hour. The unvarying volume of its waters is greater than that of all the rivers of the globe.

The true source of the Gulf Stream, discovered by Commander Maury – its point of departure, if you prefer the term – is in the Gulf of Gascony. There its waters, feeble in colour and temperature, commence to form. It descends to the south by equatorial Africa, warms itself in the rays of the torrid zone, crosses the Atlantic, touches Cape San Roque on the Brazilian coast, and divides – one branch goes to be again warmed by the waters of the Antilles. Then the Gulf Stream, charged to re-establish the temperature, and to mingle the waters of the tropics with the northern seas, commences to play its part of inter-mediary. Warmed to a great heat in the Gulf of Mexico, it runs along the American coast nearly to Newfoundland; deviates under pressure from a cold current from Davis' Straits; resumes the ocean route, following the loxodromic line – one of the great circles of the globe; divides into two branches about the 43rd degree. One arm, assisted by the north-east trade-wind, returns to the Gulf of Gascony and to the Azores; while the other, having laved the coasts of Ireland and Norway, flows as far as Spitzbergen, where its temperature falls to 4°, to form the open Polar Sea.

It was this ocean river that the *Nautilus* then entered. At the mouth of the Bahama Canal, about fourteen leagues out, and 350 yards deep, the Gulf Stream flows at the rate of five miles an hour. This pace decreases regularly in proportion as it advances towards the North, and it is to be hoped that this regularity may continue, for if its direction and pace undergo any alteration, the disturbances to European climates would involve very serious consequences.

Towards noon, I was with Conseil upon the platform. I gave him some particulars relative to the Gulf Stream; when I had finished, I suggested his putting his hand into the water. He did so, and was surprised not to perceive any sensation either of heat or cold.

"That is," I said, "because the temperature of the waters of the Gulf Stream, when leaving the Gulf of Mexico, is very little different from that of the blood. This Gulf Stream is a vast conductor of warmth, which clothes the coasts of Europe with verdure. And if we may credit Maury, the aggregate temperature of its waters would supply sufficient heat to hold in fusion a river of molten iron, as large as the Amazon or the Missouri."

At this time the speed of the Gulf Stream was 2.25 yards per second. Its current is so distinct from the surrounding sea, that its compressed waters mingle with the ocean waves. Darker than the others and richer in saline matter, the waves of the Gulf

Stream trace their course in pure indigo, amid the green waters around them. Such is the distinctness of the line of demarcation, that the *Nautilus*, at the latitude of the Carolines, separated the waters of the Gulf Stream with her prow, while the screw revolved in those of the ocean.

The current carried with it all kinds of living things. Argonauts, so common in the Mediterranean, were here sailing in fleets. Amongst cartilaginous fishes, the most remarkable were the rays, the slender tails constituting nearly one-third of their bodies, and looked like large lozenges twenty-five feet long. Small sharks, a yard in length, large heads, muzzles short and rounded, pointed teeth arranged in several rows, and very scaly bodies.

Amongst the bony fishes I noted the gray goby, peculiar to this region; the black "gilt head", the eyes of which sparkled like fire; sirenes, a yard long, with large mouths filled with little teeth (these fish uttered low cries); blue coryphenes, striped with gold and silver; "parrot" fish – true ocean rainbows – which could rival the most splendid tropical birds in colours; triangular-headed blennies, blue rhombs, denuded of scales; batrachoïdes, covered with yellow transversal bands, something like the Greek letter *T*; little gobies, in crowds; dipterous, with silvery heads and yellow tails; salmon; mugilomores, slender and shining with a soft radiance, which Lacépède consecrated to his amiable wife; and finally a large fish, called the "American chevalier", which, decorated with many orders and covered with ribands, frequents the coasts of that great nation where "ribands" and "orders" are so very lightly esteemed.

I may add that during the night the phosphorescent waters of the Gulf Stream rivalled our own electric light, particularly during stormy weather.

On the 8th May we passed Cape Hatteras. The width of the Gulf Stream is here seventy-five miles, its depth 210 yards. The *Nautilus* still sailed at random; all supervision seemed suspended on board. I began to consider that, under these circumstances, escape was possible. The inhabited coasts offered us easy refuge. Steamers from New York or Boston were continually passing on their way to the Gulf of Mexico; and, night and day, pretty little schooners were darting from point to point of the American coast. We might really hope to be picked up. This was therefore a favourable occasion, notwithstanding the thirty miles of water that separated the *Nautilus* from the United States.

But an untoward circumstance baulked the plans of Ned Land. The weather was very bad. We were approaching latitudes where storms are frequent – the district of waterspouts and cyclones, engendered by the current of the Gulf Stream. To launch upon a tempestuous sea in a frail boat was to court certain destruction. Ned Land even confessed as much. So he fretted himself into a regular attack of home-sickness, which flight only could cure.

"Monsieur," said he one day, "this must come to an end some-how. I wish to make a clean breast of it. Your Nemo is quitting land and going north; but I declare that I had enough of the South Pole, and I will not go up to the North Pole as well."

"But what are we to do, Ned, since flight, at present, is im-practicable?"

"I come back to my original notion; we must speak to the captain. You said nothing when we were in your national seas; I wish to speak now that we are in mine. When I consider that in a few days the *Nautilus* will be close to Nova Scotia, and near Newfoundland is a large bay into which the St. Lawrence flows, and that the St. Lawrence is my river – the river of Quebec, my native town! – when I think of all this, I get angry, it makes my hair stand on end with rage, and I would rather throw myself into the sea than stay here."

The Canadian was fast losing patience. His vigorous manhood could not brook this prolonged imprisonment. His appearance was daily altered, his temperament became morose. I knew what he was suffering, for I began to have a touch of that home-sickness. Nearly seven months had elapsed, and we had had no news from earth. Further, the isolation of Captain Nemo, his changed habits, particularly since our encounter with the cuttle-fish, his taciturnity gave all things a very different appearance. I no longer looked at things with my former enthusiasm. One must be a Fleming, like Conseil, to adapt oneself to the present circum-stances in this water, reserved for cestacea and suchlike animals. Indeed, had Conseil been furnished with gills, instead of lungs, I believe he would have taken a high position amongst fishes.

"Well, sir?" said Ned, perceiving I did not reply.

"Well, do you wish me to ask Captain Nemo what are his intentions concerning us?"

"Yes, sir."

"Even though he has already made them known?"

"Yes, I should like the matter to be decided. Speak for me in my name only, if you prefer to do so."

"But I so seldom meet him. He even avoids me!"

"All the greater reason to go and see him."

"I will ask him, Ned."

"When?"

"Whenever I meet him."

"M. Aronnax, shall I go and see him myself?"

"No, let me do it; to-morrow—"

"To-day," said Ned.

"Well, then, to-day be it. I will go and see him," I replied.

Had the Canadian gone and got angry, everything would have been compromised.

I was alone. As it had been decided I was to ask, the sooner it was done the better. I entered my own room, whence I meant to go to Captain Nemo's cabin. I must not permit this opportunity to escape. I knocked. No answer being given, I knocked again; then I turned the handle and entered.

The captain was in his room. Bending over his work, he had not heard me. Determined not to leave without asking him the question, I approached him. He raised his head suddenly, frowned, and said, in a rude tone:

"You here! What do you want?"

"To speak to you, captain."

"But I am engaged – I am at work. You can be private if you choose, cannot I have the same privilege?"

This reception was not very encouraging, but I was determined to hear all, to answer all.

"Yes," said I, coldly; "I have to speak to you of a matter that will not admit of delay."

"What is that?" said he ironically. "Have you made some discovery that has escaped me? Has the sea revealed any new secret to you?"

We were at cross purposes. But before I could reply he said gravely:

"M. Aronnax, here is a MS., written in several languages. It contains the 'digest' of ray studies beneath the sea, and, please goodness, it will not perish with me. This MS., signed by me, completed by the history of my life, will be enclosed in a small unsinkable case. The last survivor of all of us on board the *Nautilus* will throw this into the sea, and it will go whithersoever the waves may carry it."

The name of this man, his history written by himself! The mystery shall then be dissolved some day. But at the moment I only saw in this communication an opening to my business.

"Captain," I replied, "I can but approve your resolve. It is not right that the result of your studies should be lost. But the means you intend to employ are primitive. Who knows where the wind may carry your work, or into whose hands it may fall? Cannot you devise something better? Cannot you or one of your—"

"Never, sir!" he cried, hastily interrupting me.

"But I and my companions are willing to take care of this MS., and if you set us at liberty—"

"At liberty!" exclaimed Captain Nemo, rising.

"Yes; and it is upon this subject I came to speak to you. For seven months we have been on board, and I ask to-day, in my companions' names, as well as my own, whether you intend to confine us here for ever?"

"M. Aronnax, I will reply to you to-day as I replied to you seven months ago. Whoever enters the *Nautilus* must never leave it."

"But this is slavery you would impose!"

"You may give it any name you please."

"But in every country a slave reserves the right to regain his liberty by whatever means he can."

"And who has denied you this right? Have I ever bound you by any oath?" and the captain, folding his arms, regarded me steadfastly.

"Captain Nemo," said I, "to revert to this subject will not be to the taste of either of us, but as we have once entered upon it, let us go through with it. I repeat, it is not only for myself; for my studies are a relaxation, a passion that swallows up all other thoughts. Like yourself, I am one to live unnoticed, obscure, in the distant hope of bequeathing the results of my work to a future age. In a word, I can admire you – you have taken up a line that I can understand in certain points; but there are other aspects to your life surrounded by mysteries and complications in which I and my companions can take no part. And even when our hearts have been moved by your sorrow, or excited by your acts of genius or courage, we have been obliged to repel any expression of sympathy, however small, which is born at the sight of brave or good actions in a friend or enemy. Well, this feeling that we are strangers to every thing about you, makes our position unacceptable, impossible even for me, and above all for Ned Land. Every man, worthy of the name of man, deserves consideration. Have you ever told yourself that love of liberty, hatred of servitude, can give rise to projects of revenge in such a nature as the Canadian's, that he can think, attempt, put in execution—"

I was silenced by the captain, who rose and said:

"Ned Land may think, attempt, or put in execution what he pleases – what does it matter to me? It was not I who sought him. It is not for my pleasure that he remains on board. You, M. Aronnax, are one of those who can understand everything, even silence. I have no more to say. This is the first time you have spoken on this subject to me – let it be the last; for I will not even listen to a second attempt."

I retired. Our situation henceforth was critical. I related the conversation to my two companions.

"We now know," said Ned, "that we have nothing to hope for from him. The *Nautilus* is approaching Long Island. Let us make our escape, no matter what the weather may be."

But the sky became more and more threatening. Signs of a hurricane were not wanting. The atmosphere became white and misty. Delicate *cirri* clouds were succeeded on the horizon by heavy *cumuli*. The lower clouds passed overhead very rapidly. The sea got up, and rolled in long swelling waves. Birds, with the petrels, disappeared. The barometer fell rapidly, and indicated extreme tension of vapours. The mixture in the storm-glass melted under the atmosphere, now sub-charged with electricity. The strife of the elements was at hand!

During the 18th May the storm burst, just as the *Nautilus* was off Long Island, some miles from New York. I am able to describe the tempest, for by some unaccountable whim Captain Nemo determined to brave it at the surface of the ocean, instead of going beneath the waves.

The wind was south-west, first pretty "fresh", that is to say, about fifteen yards in a second, which increased to a rate of twenty-five yards a second about 3 p.m.

Captain Nemo, unmoved by the squalls, had taken his place on the platform. He was lashed round the waist to prevent his being carried away by the enormous waves. I managed to hoist myself up also, and made myself secure, dividing my admiration between the storm and the incomprehensible man who encountered it.

The raging sea was swept by great ragged clouds which dipped into the waves. I could not perceive any of those small waves which are formed at the bottom of the great hollows of the billows. Nothing but long rolling compact waves, which did not break. The *Nautilus*, sometimes on her side, and sometimes almost upright, rolled and pitched fearfully.

About five o'clock rain fell in torrents, but neither the wind nor the sea abated. The hurricane blew at the rate of more than forty-five yards a second, or about forty leagues an hour.

Houses are overturned by such gales as this, and cannon are frequently dismounted, but the *Nautilus*, in the midst of the tempest, justified the saying of a certain engineer, viz.: "there is no well-built hull that cannot defy the sea". She was not a resisting mass, which the waves might have overcome; she was a steel spindle, obedient, mobile, without masts or rigging, and which braved the fury of the waves.

I studied these billows attentively. They measured nearly forty-five feet in height, and from 150 to 175 feet in length, and the rate at which they travelled – less than the wind – was about fifteen yards in a second. Their volume and force increased with the depth of water. I now understood the mission of these waves, which carry a quantity of air in their sides, and carry it to the bottom of the sea, where the oxygen it contains gives life. Their extreme forces have been calculated at 6,000 lbs. on the square foot. Such waves as these at the Hebrides have displaced a block weighing 80,000 lbs.; and, in the tempest on the 23rd December, 1864, overturned part of the town of Yeddo, in Japan, and going at the rate of about 500 miles an hour, broke the same day upon the shores of America.

The storm with us increased during the night. The barometer fell $\frac{7}{10}$. In the evening I perceived a large ship on the horizon labouring painfully. She appeared to be lying-to under half steam, and was probably one of the New York steamers from Liverpool or Havre. Darkness soon hid her from our sight.

At 10 p.m. the sky was regularly on fire with lightning. I could

not support the glare, while Captain Nemo as he gazed at it
seemed imbued with the spirit of the storm. A mingled and
terrible noise of the surging of the waves, the roaring of the
wind, and the crashing of the thunder filled the air. The wind
seemed to blow from all quarters, and the cyclone first from the
east, "backed" round again to it by the north, west, and south, in
the inverse direction adopted by circular storms in southern seas.

Ah! the Gulf Stream well deserves its name of the king of
tempests! These violent storms are caused by the difference of
the temperature between the air and its current.

The rain had been succeeded by a fiery shower. The drops
seemed changed into lightning points. Captain Nemo seemed
determined to court death by lightning, a worthy end for such a
man! In its violent pitching the *Nautilus* would raise the steel
"spur" like a lightning conductor, and long sparks were given
out by it.

Bruised and exhausted, I crawled to the panel and descended
to the saloon. The storm was then at its height, and it was impossible to stand up in the *Nautilus*.

Captain Nemo came down about midnight. I heard the reservoirs filled, and the *Nautilus* sank slowly beneath the waves. From
the saloon windows I could perceive great fish passing in the
briny water, quite terrified; while some were actually struck by
the lightning as I gazed.

The *Nautilus* continued to descend. I fancied we could have
reached calm water at a depth of sixteen yards; but, no; the upper
waters were too rough, and we had to go down to a depth of fifty
yards to seek repose.

But, what quiet, what peace and tranquillity reigned there!
Who could have imagined that such a fearful hurricane was raging
at the surface of the ocean overhead?

CHAPTER XX
FROM LATITUDE 47° 24′ TO LONGITUDE 17° 28′

THE TEMPEST HAD driven us to the east. All hope of landing at
New York or on the shores of the St. Lawrence had fled. Poor
Ned Land, in despair, kept aloof, like Captain Nemo; but
Conseil and I were together continually.

It would be more correct to state that the *Nautilus* had been carried to the north-east by the storm. For some days we wandered at the surface, sometimes beneath it; surrounded, when above, by those fogs so dreaded by sailors. The fogs are chiefly owing to the melting of the ice, which causes great moisture in the atmosphere. What ships are lost in these latitudes when attempting to ascertain their whereabouts on this dangerous coast! Numerous accidents are due to these thick fogs. The noise of the wind drowns the breaking of the surf; and ships go ashore helplessly. Collisions, in spite of whistles and fog-bells. The bottom of these seas looks like a battle-field, where the conquered ones of ocean still lie as they fell. Some old, and already covered up; some young and bright, reflecting the light of our lantern from bolts and copper sheathings.

What a number of ships have been lost, with all hands, off Cape Race, St. Paul Island, Straits of Belle-isle, and in the estuary of the St. Lawrence! The *Solway*, the *Isis*, the *Paramatta*, the *Hungarian*, the *Canadian*, the *Anglo-Saxon*, the *Humboldt*, the *United States*, all foundered. The *Arctic*, the *Lyonnais* sprung leaks; the *President*, the *Pacific*, and the *City of Glasgow* disappeared from causes unknown – a funeral line along which the *Nautilus* glided as if it were holding a review of the dead.

On the 16th of May we reached the southern end of the Bank of Newfoundland. This bank is composed of organic matter, alluvial deposits, brought from the equator by the Gulf Stream, or from the North Pole by the counter cold-water current that washes the American coast. There, also, are formed those erratic blocks, drifted along with the broken-up ice. There is also a vast charnel-house of fish, molluscs, or zoophytes, which perish by hundreds of millions.

The depth of the sea is not great off Newfoundland. A few hundred fathoms only. But towards the south it dips suddenly to three thousand yards. There the Gulf Stream widens out, it loses speed and temperature, but becomes a sea.

Amongst the fish I noted the cyclopterus, the murnack of large size and excellent taste, karacks with large dog-like eyes, blennies, gobies, &c., &c.

The nets brought up a very hardy, bold, and vigorous fish, armed with spikes and prickly fins; a sea scorpion about nine feet long, the determined enemy of blenny, gads, and salmon. We had some difficulty to lay hold of this aninial, which, thanks to the formation of its opercules, prevents its respiratory organs from the drying contact of the atmosphere, and can live for some time out of water; and I must not omit the cod-fish, in its favourite waters on the inexhaustible Bank of Newfoundland. One may say that these cod are mountain-fish, for Newfoundland is nothing but a submarine mountain.

When the *Nautilus* cut her way through their thick masses, Conseil could not help saying, "Ah, cod! I always fancied that cod were flat-fish like dabs or soles."

"Stupid," I said. "Cod are only flat at the fishmongers', where they are displayed opened and spread out. In the water they are rounded like mullet, and constructed perfectly for swimming."

"I daresay," replied Conseil, "but what a quantity there are!"

"And there would be a great many thousands more, but they have enemies – fishes and men. Do you know how many eggs there are in a female cod?"

"Let me give a good guess," said Conseil. "Five hundred thousand!"

"Eleven millions, my friend!"

"Eleven millions!" exclaimed Conseil. "I cannot believe that unless I count them myself."

"Well count, Conseil. But the fish is taken in thousands by the French, English, Americans, Danes, and Norwegians. They all consume enormous quantities, and were it not for the fecundity of these animals, the sea would soon be cleared of them. Thus, England and America alone have 5,000 ships, manned by 75,000 sailors employed in the cod-fishery. Each ship takes 40,000 at least, which gives a total of 25,000,000. It is the same on the coast of Norway."

"Well," said Conseil, "I agree: and I will not count them."

"Count what?"

"The eggs – the eleven millions? But I will make a remark."

"What is it?"

"Merely that if all the eggs were hatched, four cod would be sufficient to supply England and America."

During our inspection of the Banks of Newfoundland I could distinguish the long fishing lines, armed with 200 hooks, which every boat throws over by dozens. The *Nautilus* had some trouble to escape this submarine network.

However, we did not remain long in these crowded places. We went up to the 42nd degree of latitude, as high as St. John's and Heart's Content, where the Atlantic cable emerges.

The *Nautilus*, instead of continuing to the north, turned in an easterly direction, as if it wished to follow up the plain upon which the telegraphic cable is laid. It was on the 17th May, about 500 miles from Heart's Content, at a depth of 2,900 yards, that I perceived the cable lying on the ground. Conseil, whom I had not told of it, took it for a large sea-serpent, and was about to "class" it as usual. But I undeceived him, and, to console him, gave him some particulars concerning the laying of the cable.

The first cable was established during the years 1857 and 1858, but, after having transmitted about 4,000 telegrams, it stopped working. In 1863 another was constructed, over 2,000 miles long, and weighing 4,500 tons, which was shipped in the *Great Eastern*. This attempt did not succeed.

Now, the *Nautilus*, on the 25th May, was on the exact spot at which the breakage occurred which ruined the enterprise. It was 638 miles from the Irish coast. At 2 p.m. they perceived that the communication was interrupted. The electricians determined to cut the cable before fishing for it, and at 11 p.m. they found the damaged part. They spliced it and resank it, but some days later it broke again, and, in such deep water, that it could not be recovered.

The Americans were not discouraged. The brave Cyrus Field, the promoter of the undertaking, who had embarked all his fortune in it, started another subscription. It was well responded to. Another cable was made on better principles. The wires were wrapped in gutta percha, protected by a covering of hemp, and surrounded by a metallic skin. The *Great Eastern* sailed with it on the 13th July, 1866.

The operation proceeded successfully, but an incident happened. It was remarked that nails were frequently found inserted in the cable with a view to injure it. Captain Anderson, his officers, and the scientific men held a consultation, and a notice was promulgated that, if anyone were discovered as the author of such an action, he would be incontinently flung into the sea. No further attempt to spoil the cable was made.

On the 23rd July the *Great Eastern* was only about 500 miles from Newfoundland, when a telegram from Ireland apprised those on board of the armistice between Prussia and Austria after Sadowa. On the 27th, in thick fogs, they reached Heart's Content. The enterprise had fairly and happily succeeded, and the first telegram young America sent to Mother England were the grand words so rarely comprehended:

"Glory to God in the highest; peace on earth, goodwill towards men."

I did not expect to find the electric cable in the same state as when it left the manufactory. The long "serpent", covered with the *débris* of shells, was encased with a strong coating, which protected it against boring molluscs. It lay undisturbed by the motion of the sea, and under favourable pressure for the transmission of the electric spark, which passes from America to Europe in .32 of a second. The duration of this cable will be almost indefinite, for the gutta percha is improved by the salt water.

Besides, on this well-selected level, the cable is never so deeply immerged as to break. The *Nautilus* went to its lowest depth, situated 4,431 yards (metres), and there it lay without any distention; we then arrived at the spot where the accident of 1863 happened.

The ocean bed forms a large valley, upon which Mont Blanc might be placed, without the top appearing above the water. This valley is enclosed on the east by a perpendicular wall, more than 2,000 yards high. We arrived there on the 28th May, and the *Nautilus* was then only 120 miles from the Irish coast.

Did Captain Nemo wish to reach the British Isles? No. To my great surprise he again turned southward, and to European seas. In rounding the "Emerald Isle", I perceived Cape Clear for a moment, and the Fastnet lighthouse, which guides the thousands of ships bound for Liverpool and Glasgow.

An important question presented itself to my mind. Did the *Nautilus* dare to enter the English Channel? Ned, who had reappeared since we sighted land, did not cease to inquire. How could I reply. Captain Nemo was still invisible to us. Having permitted the Canadian a glimpse of America, perhaps he was going to give me a look at France!

But we went south still. On the 30th May we passed the Land's End, leaving the Scilly Isles to starboard. If Captain Nemo wished to enter the English Channel, he must now go east, but he did not.

During the whole of the 31st, the *Nautilus* described a series of circles in the sea, which puzzled me greatly. It seemed as if search were being made to find a spot difficult to hit on. At midday Captain Nemo came up on the platform to take the position himself. He did not speak a word, and seemed more reserved than ever. What had made him so sad? Was it the proximity of the European shores? Had he some remembrances of his abandoned native land? This thought haunted me, and I began to think that I should soon, by a happy chance, discover the captain's secrets.

Next day, the 1st of June, the *Nautilus* continued her manœuvres. It was evident some precise spot was wanted. Captain Nemo came up, as on the previous day. The sea was calm, the sky clear. Eight miles off a great steamer trailed a line of smoke across the horizon. She showed no colours, and I could not ascertain her nationality.

Captain Nemo took his sextant and began to observe the sun, some minutes before it reached the meridian. The absolute calm assisted this operation. The *Nautilus* did not move at all.

I was on the platform at that time. When the observation had been completed, Captain Nemo merely said:

"Here it is!" and descended to his room.

Had he seen the ship, which had changed her course and now approached us? I could not tell.

I returned to the saloon. The panel was shut. I heard the water entering the reservoirs. The *Nautilus* sank direct, for the screw did not move.

A few minutes later we were aground at 835 yards. The ceiling was lighted up, the windows were opened, and I could watch the sea, brilliantly illuminated by our electric lamp for half a mile round.

To port there was nothing but the watery expanse; but to starboard appeared a large mass which riveted my attention. It was like a ruin buried beneath white shells, as under a mantle of snow. Examining it attentively, I fancied I could distinguish a vessel, mastless, which must have foundered. The wreck must be an old one; many years must have passed for it to have become so encrusted with the lime of the ocean.

What was this ship? Why should the *Nautilus* visit its tomb? Was it a shipwreck in the ordinary sense?

I did not know what to think, when suddenly close by me I heard the captain's voice.

"That vessel," he said slowly, "was formerly called the *Marseillais*. She carried seventy-four guns, and was launched in 1762. In 1778, commanded by La Poype-Vertrieux, she fought the *Preston*. On 4th July, 1779, she was at the taking of Grenada, with the fleet of Admiral Estaing. On 5th September, 1781, she took part in the action in Chesapeake Bay. In 1794 her name was changed by the French Republic. On the 16th April of the same year she joined the fleet of Villaret-Joyeuse, at Brest, charged to escort a convoy of corn to come from America, under the command of Admiral Van Stabel. On the 11th and 12th Prairial of year II, the squadron encountered the English fleet. To-day, Monsieur, is the 13th Prairial, the 1st June, 1868. Seventy-four years ago this day, in this place, in 47° 24′ lat. and 17° 28′ long., this ship, after a gallant fight, dismasted, with a leak sprung, a third of her crew disabled, preferred to sink with her 356 sailors than to surrender; and, nailing their colours to the poop, they disappeared beneath the waves, crying '*Vive la République*'."

"The *Vengeur*!" I exclaimed.

"Yes, Monsieur, the *Vengeur*. A good name," muttered the captain as he folded his arms.

CHAPTER XXI
A HECATOMB

THE STYLE OF ADDRESS, the unexpected scene, this history of a ship of my country – so coldly told at first – then the emotion with which the strange individual had pronounced the last words, the significance of the name, *Avenger*, were all impressed deeply upon my mind. My gaze did not quit the captain. He, with outstretched hands, was watching with glittering eyes the glorious wreck. Perhaps I should never know who he was, whence he came, or whither he went; but I know that the man disengaged himself from the *savant*. It was no ordinary misanthropy that had caused Captain Nemo to hide himself, with his companions, in the *Nautilus*; but a hatred, whether monstrous or sublime, that time could not enfeeble.

Did this hatred still demand vengeance? The future would disclose this.

Meanwhile the *Nautilus* rose slowly, and the confused forms of the *Avenger* disappeared by degrees. A slight rolling motion indicated our arrival at the surface.

At that moment a dull roar was heard. I looked at the captain; he did not stir.

"Captain!" I said. He did not reply, so I left him and mounted to the platform. Conseil and the Canadian had preceded me.

"What is the meaning of that sound?" I asked.

"It was a cannon-shot," replied Ned Land.

I looked towards the ship I had seen before. It had approached the *Nautilus*, and was coming at high speed. It was six miles away.

"What ship is that, Ned?"

"Judging by her rigging and spars, I should say she is a man-o'-war. I hope she may come up with us, and, if possible, sink this damned *Nautilus*."

"Friend Ned!" said Conseil. "What harm can she do the *Nautilus*? Can she attack us under water?"

"Tell me Ned," I said, "can you see to what nation this vessel belongs?"

The Canadian frowned, lowered his eyelids, and gazed for some seconds at the vessel earnestly.

"No," he replied, at length, "I do not know to what country she belongs. Her ensign is not at the peak; but I can swear she is a man-of-war, because of the pennant at the main."

For a quarter of an hour we continued to gaze at the approaching ship. I could not quite believe that she could have distinguished the *Nautilus* at such a distance, still less have guessed that she was a submarine engine.

The Canadian soon informed me that the new-comer was a large man-o'-war, a two-decked, ironclad ram. A thick, black smoke escaped from her two funnels. Her sails were furled; she had no ensign. The distance prevented our distinguishing the colours of the pennant, which blew out like a long ribbon.

She rapidly approached us. If Captain Nemo remained apathetic here was our chance of escape.

"Monsieur," said Ned Land to me, "when this vessel is a mile distant I will throw myself into the sea, and I should suggest your doing the same thing."

To this I made no reply, but continued to look at the vessel, which became rapidly more distinguishable. French, English, American, or Russian, she would receive us hospitably if we could only get on board.

"Monsieur will remember," said Conseil, "that we have some little experience of swimming; he can rest upon me if he decide to follow Ned Land."

I was about to reply, when a puff of white smoke burst from the man-of-war. Some seconds later the water was splashed up by the fall of a heavy shot astern of the *Nautilus*. A little later the report came to our ears.

"Hullo! they are firing at us," I exclaimed.

"Good men," murmured the Canadian.

"They evidently do not take us for shipwrecked sailors," said I.

"If Monsieur has no objection— Good," said Conseil, as another shot ploughed up the water close to us. "If Monsieur has no objection, I think they have recognized the narwhal, and are cannonading it."

"But they ought to see that there are human beings in question," I said.

"Perhaps that is why they fire," said Ned, looking at me.

A sudden idea struck me. No doubt they had formed their own conclusions respecting the pretended monster. Doubtless, on board the *Abraham Lincoln*, when the Canadian struck the narwhal with the harpoon, Commodore Farragut had perceived that it was in reality a submarine vessel more dangerous than a supernatural cetacean.

Yes, this must be it, and in every sea they were now pursuing this engine of destruction.

It was indeed terrible if, as we thought, Captain Nemo used the *Nautilus* in a scheme of vengeance. Did he not attack some ship that night in the Indian Ocean when we were imprisoned? Had not that man who was buried in the coral cemetery fallen a victim to the attack provoked by the *Nautilus*? Yes, it must be so. One portion of Captain Nemo's mysterious existence was developing itself. And if his identity were not established, at least the several nations had banded against him, and now hunted him, not as a chimera, but as a man who had vowed an implacable hatred against them.

All the terrible past rose up before me. Instead of meeting

friends on board the attacking vessel, we should only find pitiless enemies.

Meantime the cannon-shot kept flying about our ears. Some striking the water, ricochetted, and sank at a great distance. But none of them hit the *Nautilus*.

The ironclad was then only three miles away. But notwithstanding the tremendous cannonade, Captain Nemo did not appear on the platform, and yet had one of these conical shot struck the *Nautilus* it would have been fatal. The Canadian then said:

"Ought we not to endeavour to get out of this scrape? Let us make signals, they will perhaps understand that we are honest people."

Ned Land took his handkerchief to wave to them, but scarcely had he opened it than he was struck down by an iron hand, and, notwithstanding his great strength he fell upon the deck.

"Wretch," cried Captain Nemo, "do you wish to be immolated on the spur of the *Nautilus* before it is hurled against yonder ship?"

Captain Nemo, terrible to hear, was still more terrible to see. His face was pale as death, from a spasm of the heart, which had for an instant ceased to beat. The pupils of his eyes were contracted. His voice did not sound – it was almost a roar that issued from his throat as he grasped the Canadian's shoulder. Then he turned from Ned towards the man-of-war from which the shot showered round him.

"Ah, you know who I am, you ship of a cursed race," he cried in his powerful tones. "I don't want to see your colours to recognize your breed. Look here, I will show you mine!"

And he displayed a black flag similar to that which he had planted at the South Pole.

At that moment a shot struck the *Nautilus* obliquely, and without damaging her flew close by the captain and fell into the sea.

He shrugged his shoulders, then addressing me said:

"Go below, you and your companions."

"Monsieur," I cried, "do you intend to attack that ship?"

"Monsieur, I am going to sink her."

"You will not do that, surely."

"I will," replied Captain Nemo coldly; "and I advise you not to pass judgment upon me. Fate has shown you what you ought not to have seen. The attack has begun. The reprisal will be terrible! Go down."

"What ship is this?" I asked.

"Do you not know? So much the better. Her nationality at least is a secret to you. Go down."

The Canadian, Conseil, and I had no choice. Fifteen sailors surrounded the captain, and seemed to regard the approaching vessel with intense hatred. We felt that the same spirit of revenge animated them all.

I descended, and at that moment another shot hulled the *Nautilus*. I heard the captain cry out:

"Strike, you mad vessel; let fly your useless shot. You shall not escape the *Nautilus*. But you shall not perish here. Your wreck shall not mingle with that of the *Avenger*!"

I regained my cabin. The captain and the mate were still on the platform. The screw was put in motion. The *Nautilus* distanced her pursuer very quickly, and was soon out of range. But the chase continued, and Captain Nemo contented himself with keeping his distance.

About 4 p.m., I could not restrain the impatience and restlessness that was consuming me; I went to the foot of the staircase; the panel was open. I ventured upon the platform. The captain was walking up and down in a very excited manner. He kept looking at the man-of-war to leeward, about five or six miles away. He was sailing round it, and drawing the pursuit towards the east. But he did not attack it. Perhaps he hesitated to do so after all.

I wished to intercede once again. But I had hardly opened my mouth to Captain Nemo, when he silenced me.

"I am the law here; I am justice. I am the oppressed and yonder is the oppressor. Through him I have lost everything I loved, cherished, venerated: country, wife, children, father, mother. I have seen them all perish. All I hate is there. Be silent."

I took a last look at the man-of-war now steaming at high pressure, and then I rejoined Conseil and Ned.

"We will fly this," I exclaimed.

"Good," said Ned. "But what ship is it?"

"I do not know," I replied, "but whatever it be it will be sunk during the night. Better perish with it than be accomplices in a war of reprisal of which we do not understand the justice."

"That is my opinion," replied Ned. "Let us wait till night."

Night came. A deep silence reigned on board. The compass indicated that the *Nautilus* still held her course. I heard the rapid throbbings of the screw. We were still at the surface, and a slight roll affected the *Nautilus*.

My companions and I had determined to escape so soon as the ship was sufficiently near to make ourselves heard or seen, for the moon, which was nearly at the full, shone brightly. Once on board the other ship, we could prevent the attack that threatened her, or at least do all that the circumstances admitted. Many times I thought that the *Nautilus* was ready to attack, but Captain Nemo was contented to let the chase approach nearer, and then the *Nautilus* would again increase her distance.

The first part of the night passed without incident. We watched our opportunity. We spoke little, being too much excited to talk. Ned Land wanted to throw himself into the sea, but I persuaded him to wait. I thought the *Nautilus* would attack the ironclad at the surface of the sea, and then it would be not only possible but easy to escape.

At three o'clock, being restless, I ascended to the platform. Captain Nemo had not quitted it. He was standing up at the "bow", near his flag, which was waving in the breeze over his head. He did not lift his eyes from the ship; his look was one of extraordinary attention, and appeared to attract, to fascinate, and to draw the pursuer along as if it were being towed.

The moon was passing to the meridian. Jupiter was rising in the east. Amid this peace, heaven and the ocean rivalled each other in tranquillity, and the sea offered to the stars as lovely a mirror as had ever been presented for their reflection. And when I considered this holy calm of the elements, compared to the passions raging in the *Nautilus*, I felt chilled to the heart.

The man-of-war was within two miles of us. It was approaching nearer and nearer to that phosphorescent gleam which betrayed the whereabouts of the *Nautilus*. I saw the lights – green and red – and the white lamp suspended to the mizzen "stay". A sort of vibration seemed to make the rigging quiver, which indicated a very high pressure of working. Sparks flew up from the funnels, and shone in the air like stars.

I remained thus till 4 a.m., without Captain Nemo having perceived me. The ship was now a mile and a half away, and at dawn the cannonade recommenced. The moment could not be far distant when, as the *Nautilus* attacked the ship, we could make our escape.

I was about to descend, when the mate appeared upon the platform. Several sailors accompanied him. Captain Nemo either did not see, or did not wish to see them. Certain preparations for action were made. They were very simple. The railing round the platform was removed; in the same way the lantern and pilot cages were lowered to a level with the deck. The surface of the long cigar-shaped vessel did not offer a single obstruction to its free manœuvring.

I returned to the saloon, the *Nautilus* still on the surface. The morning rays were beginning to penetrate the water. As the waves undulated, the gleam of the rising sun illuminated the windows. This terrible 2nd of June dawned!

At 5 a.m. I perceived that the speed had moderated. I understood that the vessel was to be permitted to approach. Besides, the guns were heard more distinctly, and the shot hissed strangely through the morning air.

"My friends," said I, "the time has come. A grasp of the hand, and may Heaven preserve us!"

Ned Land was resolute; Conseil calm; I was nervous, and could scarcely control myself. We passed into the library. As I pushed open the door leading to the central staircase, I heard the upper panel shut sharply. The Canadian hurried up the steps. I stopped him. A well-known hissing sound informed me that the water was coming into the reservoirs; and in fact in a few minutes the *Nautilus* had sunk some yards under water.

I understood it all. It was too late to act now. The *Nautilus* did not dare to attack the ironclad, except below the water-line, where there were no iron plates to offer any resistance.

We were again imprisoned, unwilling witnesses of the tragedy about to be performed. We had scarcely time to reflect even. Shut in my room, we gazed at each other without speaking. A profound stupor had settled upon my spirits. All thought appeared to be arrested in my mind. I was in that state of tension which precedes some expected explosion. I waited, I listened, every sense concentrated in the ear.

The speed of the *Nautilus* increased; the rush was coming, the whole fabric trembled.

Suddenly I uttered a cry. There was a shock, but comparatively gentle. I felt the penetrating force of the steel spur. I heard a scraping noise. But the *Nautilus*, carried onward by her immense power of propulsion, passed through the vessel like a needle through canvas.

I could contain myself no longer. I rushed madly out of my room into the saloon. Captain Nemo was there, silent, gloomy, and implacable; he was looking through the port panel. An enormous mass overshadowed the water, and, so as to lose nothing of the death agony, the *Nautilus* slowly sank to the abyss beside the ironclad. Ten yards off was the wounded vessel, into which the waves were pouring like a sluice, and beyond a double tier of guns and nettings. The deck was covered with moving black shadows.

The water rose higher. The unhappy victims crowded into the shrouds, ascended the masts, or struggled in the pitiless water. Paralysed with anguish, my hair grew stiff with terror, my eyes dilated, I could not breathe; and there, breathless, voiceless, I was glued to the spot, and gazed at the sight in horror.

The enormous vessel sank slowly. The *Nautilus* following, watched all her movements. Suddenly an explosion occurred. The confined air had blown up the decks as if by gunpowder. The agitation of the water heeled the *Nautilus* over.

Then the ill-fated vessel sank more rapidly. Her topmasts, covered with victims, appeared before us; then the yards, bending beneath the weight of the crew; at length the main-topgallant-mast came in sight. Then the dark mass disappeared, and with it the drowned ship's company, dragged underneath by the powerful eddy.

I turned to Captain Nemo. That terrible executioner, a true archangel of hate, kept steadily regarding his handiwork. When all was over, he went to his own room. I looked after him.

On the wall, beneath the portraits of his heroes, I perceived the likeness of a young woman with two little children. Captain Nemo looked at them for some minutes, extended his arms to them, and, falling upon his knees, burst into a passion of sobs.

CHAPTER XXII
THE LAST WORDS OF CAPTAIN NEMO

THE PANELS HAD been shut upon the dreadful spectacle, but no light had been given to the saloon.

Darkness and silence now reigned in the *Nautilus*. We were leaving the desolation behind us at a tremendous rate, but whither were we flying? North or south? Did that man wish to escape the horrible reprisal?

I re-entered my room, where I found Conseil and Ned sitting in silence. I experienced an insurmountable disgust for Captain Nemo. No matter how much he had suffered from mankind, he had no right to act as he had done. He had made me, if not an accomplice, a witness to his vengeance. It was too much!

At eleven o'clock light was given us. I entered the saloon; it was empty. I inspected the various instruments. We were going north at twenty-five miles an hour, sometimes at the surface, sometimes thirty feet beneath the waves.

Taking the bearings on the chart, I saw that we were passing the mouth of the British Channel, and were advancing rapidly towards the Northern seas. I could scarcely see the various fish we passed; but it was not now a question of studying and classifying.

In the evening we had crossed 200 leagues of the Atlantic. Evening came, and the sea would be dark till the moon rose. I regained my room. I could not sleep long, I suffered from nightmare. The horrible scene I had witnessed kept recurring to my mind. Who could now tell to what part of the North Atlantic Captain Nemo would take us. We still were travelling at speed, and, in the midst of northern fogs. Should we go up to Spitzbergen or Nova Zembla, or explore those unknown seas, viz., the White Sea, the Sea of Kara, the Gulf of Obi, the Archipelago of Liarrov, and the equally strange coasts of the Asiatic continent? I could not tell. The clocks on board had been stopped, so we could no longer judge the flight of time; it seemed that day and night, as in polar regions, no longer followed in regular rotation. I felt I was being dragged into that wild region where the imagination can run riot as in the mysterious tales of Edgar Poe. At each moment I expected to see, like the fabulous Gordon

Pym, that veiled figure, of a size exceeding all inhabitants of earth, thrown across the cataract that defends the approach to the Pole.

I estimated (though, perhaps, I was mistaken) that this wild course of the *Nautilus* lasted fifteen or twenty days, and how much longer it might have continued I do not know, had not a catastrophe brought our voyage to a conclusion. Neither Captain Nemo, the mate, nor any of the sailors ever appeared now. The *Nautilus* was almost always beneath the water. When it did rise to the surface to replenish the air the panels opened automatically. The reckoning was no longer marked on the chart; I could not tell where we were.

Moreover, the Canadian, who had come to an end of his strength and patience, kept aloof also. Conseil could not induce him to speak, and fearing, in an excess of delirium, and under the influence of the terrible home-sickness that devoured him, he would kill himself, he watched him untiringly. One can understand that, under all the circumstances, the situation was scarcely bearable.

One morning – I do not know the date – I was sleeping heavily towards dawn, when I awoke and found Ned Land leaning over me, and he said in a low tone: "We are going to escape!"

I sat up at once.

"When?" I asked.

"To-night. All *surveillance* on board the *Nautilus* seems over; they all appear stupefied. You will be ready, sir?"

"Yes. Whereabouts are we?"

"In sight of land, which I observed through the fog this morning, twenty miles to the east."

"What land is it?"

"I do not know; but whatever land it may be, we will escape thither."

"Yes, Ned, we will fly to-night, even should the sea swallow us up."

"The sea is high and the wind is strong, but twenty miles in that light boat does not frighten me. I have succeeded in putting on board some food and water."

"I will follow you," I said.

"But," said the Canadian, "if I am surprised I will fight, and they will perhaps kill me."

"We will die together, Ned."

I had decided. The Canadian left me. I gained the platform, upon which I could scarcely withstand the shock of the waves. The sky was threatening, but as we were so near land we were obliged to make our escape. We must not lose a day, not an hour.

I returned to the saloon, both hoping and fearing to meet Captain Nemo – wishing, and yet not wishing to see him. What had I to say to him? Could I hide the horror with which he inspired me? No! Better not to find myself face to face with him; better to forget him entirely; and, nevertheless—

What a long day this was – the last that I was to pass on board the *Nautilus*. I remained by myself. Ned and Conseil did not speak to me, for fear of betraying themselves.

I dined at six o'clock, but I had no appetite. I forced myself to eat, so as to keep up my strength.

At half-past six Ned Land entered my room, and said: "We shall not meet again before we leave. At ten o'clock the moon will not be up; we will take advantage of the darkness. Come to the boat, and Conseil and I will await you there."

The Canadian went out, without giving me time to reply.

I wanted to verify the course of the *Nautilus*. I went into the saloon. We were running N.N.E. with tremendous speed, at a depth of rather more than fifty yards.

I took a last look at all the marvels of nature around, the art-riches heaped up in this museum, on this unrivalled collection destined to perish some day at the bottom of the sea which had yielded it up. I wished to fix the impression upon my mind. I remained thus for an hour, beneath the light of the luminous ceiling, and, passing in review those beautiful specimens in the glass cases, then returned to my room.

I then donned some stout sea-clothing, and collected my notes and secured them carefully about my person. My heart beat loudly; I could not help it. My trouble and agitation would certainly have betrayed me to Captain Nemo.

What was he doing at that moment? I listened at the door of his room; I could hear footsteps. Captain Nemo was there, and had not retired to rest. At every movement it seemed to me as if he were about to appear and ask me why I was going to escape. I was nervously sensitive. My imagination magnified everything around me. This impression became so vivid that I began to think whether it would not be better to go into the captain's room, see him face to face, and "beard the lion in his den".

This was madness; fortunately I restrained myself, and lay down on my bed to cool my agitation. My nerves became more calm by degrees, but my brain was at work, and I seemed to see all over again the pleasant and unpleasant incidents that had happened since our disappearance from the *Abraham Lincoln* – the submarine shooting-party, Torres' Strait, the Papuan savages, our stranding, the coral cemetery, the Suez passage, the island of Sautorin, the Cretan diver, Vigo Bay, Atlantis, the iceberg, the South Pole, the imprisonment in the ice, the octopus-fight, the tempest in the Gulf Stream, the *Avenger*, and the last horrible scene of the vessel sent to the bottom with all hands.

All these events passed before my mental vision like the scenes at a theatre. Then Captain Nemo seemed to increase in size tremendously in this strange medley. His apparition forced itself in, and took superhuman proportions. He was no longer my equal, he was the man of the waters – the genius of the seas.

It was then half-past nine. I held my head between my hands to still its throbbing. I shut my eyes, and tried not to think. Another half-hour – a half-hour of nightmare would drive me mad.

At that moment I fancied I heard the distant notes of the organ, a sad harmony, like the wail of a soul which longed to break its earthly bonds. I listened intently, scarcely breathing, plunged, like Captain Nemo, in one of those musical ecstasies which lead one beyond the limits of this world!

Then a sudden idea terrified me. Captain Nemo had left his room. He was in the saloon, and I must cross it to escape. There I might meet him for the last time. He would see – would speak to me, perhaps. A gesture of his could annihilate me; a word, chain me to the ship for ever!

It was on the stroke of ten! The moment had come to leave my room and join my friends.

It would not do to hesitate, for fear that Captain Nemo should anticipate me. I opened the door of my room carefully, and yet it seemed to make a great noise as I opened it; perhaps this noise only existed in my imagination.

I then crept along the dark passage, pausing at each step to still the beating of my heart. I reached the door of the saloon, and opened it very gently. The room was perfectly dark: the organ sounded faintly. Captain Nemo was there and had not seen me. I really believe that had there been light in the room, he would not have noticed me, so absorbed was he in his music.

I crept along the carpet, avoiding the least contact that would have betrayed my presence. It took me fully five minutes to gain the door, which opened into the library. I was about to open it, when a deep sigh from Captain Nemo glued me to my place. I could perceive that he was rising from the instrument, for some rays of light filtered into the room. He came towards me with folded arms, silent, gliding like a ghost, rather than walking. His bosom heaved with sobs, and I heard him murmur these words – the last I ever heard him speak:

"Enough, enough! Oh! Almighty God, enough!"

Was this the effect of remorse which thus escaped from the over-laden conscience of the man?

In a sort of despair I precipitated myself into the library and rushed up the central staircase, and, following the upper turn, reached the boat. I entered it by the opening which had already given ingress to my two companions.

"Let us be off! let us go!" I cried.

"In one second," replied the Canadian.

The opening in the *Nautilus* was first closed and secured by Ned Land by means of a key he had discovered. The opening in the boat was likewise fastened, and then the Canadian began to release the screws which held us to the *Nautilus*.

Suddenly a noise within the vessel was heard. Voices replied loudly. What had happened? Had our flight been discovered? I felt Ned Land slip a poniard into my hand.

"Yes," I murmured, "we can die like men."

The Canadian ceased working. But a word, repeated twenty times, a terrible word revealed to me the cause of the agitation within the *Nautilus*. The crew were not troubling themselves about us at all.

"The Maëlstrom! the Maëlstrom!" cried Ned.

The Maëlstrom! No more terrible word, and no more horrible situation than ours could be conceived. We were, then, in close proximity to the dangerous Norwegian coast. Had the *Nautilus* been drawn into the whirlpool just as our boat was about to quit the ship?

It is well known that at flood-tide the waters pent up between the Loffoden and the Feroë Islands are precipitated together with tremendous violence, and form a whirlpool from which no ship can escape. On every side of us huge waves were rearing their crests and forming a gulf, which has been rightly called the "navel of the ocean", whose power of attraction extends to a distance of about twelve miles round.

There, not vessels only, but whales, and even white bears from the northern regions, meet their doom.

It was to this terrible fate that the *Nautilus*, whether designedly or not, was rushing. It was describing a circle, the circumference of which was gradually lessening, and the boat, which was attached to the side, was thus carried along with appalling speed. I got giddy. I felt that sensation which is produced by turning round for a long time rapidly. We were dreadfully alarmed, horror had reached its limit, circulation had ceased, our nervous force was annihilated; we were bathed in a cold perspiration of agony. What a noise rose round us – roarings which the echoes repeated several miles away. The noise of the waves breaking upon the sharp rocks below, where the stoutest bodies are broken to pieces, where trunks of trees are worn away, and become "like fur", to use the Norwegian term.

What a situation it was! We were tossed about like a cork. The *Nautilus* defended herself like a human being, the steel muscles were strained. Sometimes it rose upright, and we along with it.

"We must hold on tightly," said Ned, "and see about the bolts. If we stand by the *Nautilus* we may be saved yet."

He was still speaking when a crashing noise was heard. The screws gave way, and the boat was hurled like a stone from a sling into the very centre of the whirlpool.

My head was struck by a piece of iron, and the violence of the blow deprived me of consciousness.

CHAPTER XXIII
CONCLUSION

THERE WAS AN end to our voyage under the sea. What passed
during the night, and how the boat escaped from the terrible
jaws of the Maëlstrom – how Ned Land, Conseil, and I ever came
out of the gulf alive – I cannot tell.

When I came to myself, I was lying in a fisherman's hut in
the Loffoden Islands. My two companions, safe and sound, were
beside me, holding my hands in theirs.

We embraced each other joyfully.

We had no chance to return to France then. Communication
between the north of Norway and the southern ports is rare.
I was therefore obliged to wait for the starting of the steamboat
which plies bi-monthly from the North Cape.

So, now, amongst the kind-hearted people who have rescued
us, I am revising these notes of our adventures. It is quite true.
Not a fact has been omitted; not a detail exaggerated. It is the
faithful narrative of this incredible expedition beneath the element inaccessible to mankind, but which progress will one day
open up.

Shall I be credited! I do not know. After all it matters little.
What I now declare is that I have a right to speak of those seas
beneath which I have traversed twenty thousand leagues in less
than ten months in a submarine tour of the world, which has
revealed to me the wonders of the Pacific, the Indian Ocean, the
Red Sea, the Mediterranean, the Atlantic, the Southern and
Northern Polar Seas.

But what became of the *Nautilus*? Did it resist the Maëlstrom?
Is Captain Nemo still living? Does he still exact his terrible
reprisals, or did he cease for ever after that last hecatomb?
Will the waves one day bring to land that manuscript which
contains the whole history of his life? Shall I ever know the name
of the man, or will the missing vessel tell us by the fact of its
nationality, that of Captain Nemo?

I hope so, and I also trust that his powerful ship has overcome
the Maëlstrom, and that the *Nautilus* survives where so many
vessels have perished. If it be so, if Captain Nemo still inhabits
the ocean – his adopted country, so to speak – may the hatred of

that savage breast be appeased! May the contemplation of so many wonders calm the spirit of revenge in him: may the judge disappear, and the *savant* continue his peaceful exploration of the sea. If his fate be a strange one, there is something sublime in it also.

Have I not comprehended it myself – have I not lived for ten months of that unnatural existence? So, to the question propounded three thousand years ago by Ecclesiastes – "Who has ever sounded the depths of the abyss?" – two men only of all the world have the right to reply – CAPTAIN NEMO AND MYSELF!

ROUND THE
WORLD IN
EIGHTY DAYS

CONTENTS

CHAPTER I

IN WHICH PHILEAS FOGG AND PASSE-PARTOUT ACCEPT, RELATIVELY, THE POSITIONS OF MASTER AND SERVANT

IN THE YEAR of grace One thousand eight hundred and seventy-two, the house in which Sheridan died in 1816 – viz. No. 7, Saville Row, Burlington Gardens – was occupied by Phileas Fogg, Esq., one of the most eccentric members of the Reform Club, though it always appeared as if he were very anxious to avoid remark. Phileas had succeeded to the house of one of England's greatest orators, but, unlike his predecessor, no one knew anything of Fogg, who was impenetrable, though a brave man and moving in the best society. Some people declared that he resembled Byron – merely in appearance, for he was irreproachable in tone – but still a Byron with whiskers and moustache: an impassible Byron, who might live a thousand years and not get old.

A thorough Briton was Phileas Fogg, though perhaps not a Londoner. He was never seen on the Stock Exchange, nor at the Bank of England, nor at any of the great City houses. No vessel with a cargo consigned to Phileas Fogg ever entered the port of London. He held no Government appointment. He had never been entered at any of the Inns of Court. He had never pleaded at the Chancery Bar, the Queen's Bench, the Exchequer, or the Ecclesiastical Courts. He was not a merchant, a manufacturer, a farmer, nor a man of business of any kind. He was not in the habit of frequenting the Royal Institution or any other of the learned societies of the metropolis. He was simply a member of the "Reform", and that was all!

If anyone ever inquired how it was that he had become a member of the club, the questioner was informed that he had been put up by the Barings, with whom he kept his account, which always showed a good balance, and from which his cheques were regularly and promptly honoured.

Was Phileas Fogg a rich man? Unquestionably. But in what manner he had made his money even the best-informed gossips could not tell, and Mr. Fogg was the very last person from whom one would seek to obtain information on the subject. He was never prodigal in expenditure, but never stingy; and whenever his contribution towards some good or useful object was required he gave cheerfully, and in many cases anonymously.

In short, he was one of the most uncommunicative of men. He talked little, and his habitual taciturnity added to the mystery surrounding him. Nevertheless, his life was simple and open enough, but he regulated all his actions with a mathematical exactness which, to the imagination of the quidnuncs, was in itself suspicious.

Had he ever travelled? It was very probable, for no one was better informed in the science of geography. There was apparently no out-of-the-way place concerning which he had not some exclusive information. Occasionally, in a few sentences, he would clear away the thousand-and-one rumours which circulated in the club concerning some lost or some nearly-forgotten traveller; he would point out the true probabilities; and it really appeared as if he were gifted with second sight, so correctly were his anticipations justified by succeeding events. He was a man who must have been everywhere – in spirit at least.

One thing at any rate was certain, viz. that he had not been absent from London for many a year. Those with whom he was on a more intimate footing used to declare that no one had ever seen him anywhere else but on his way to or from his club. His only amusement was a game of whist, varied by the perusal of the daily papers. At whist, which was a game peculiarly fitted to such a taciturn disposition as his, he was habitually a winner; but his gains always were expended in charitable objects. Besides, it was evident to everyone that Mr. Fogg played for the game, not for the sake of winning money. It was a trial of skill with him, a combat; but a fight unaccompanied by fatigue, and one entailing no great exertion, and thus suiting him "down to the ground!"

No one had ever credited Phileas Fogg with wife or child, which even the most scrupulously honest people may possess; nor even had he any near relatives or intimate friends, who are more rare in this world. He lived alone in his house in Saville Row, and no one called upon him, or at any rate entered there. One servant sufficed for him. He took all his meals at his club, but he never shared a table with any of his acquaintance, nor did he ever invite a stranger to dinner. He only returned home to sleep at midnight precisely, for he never occupied any one of the comfortable bedrooms provided by the "Reform" for its members. Ten hours of the four-and-twenty he passed at home, partly sleeping, partly dressing or undressing. If he walked, it was in the entrance-hall with its mosaic pavement, or in the circular gallery beneath the dome, which was supported by twenty Ionic columns. Here he would pace with measured step. When he dined or breakfasted, all the resources of the club were taxed to supply his table with the daintiest fare; he was waited upon by the gravest black-coated servants, who stepped softly as they ministered to his wants upon a special porcelain service and upon the most expensive damask. His wine was contained in decanters of a now unobtainable mould, while his sherry was iced to the most excellent point of refrigeration of the Wenham Lake.

If existence under such circumstances be a proof of eccentricity, it must be confessed that something may be said in favour of it.

The house in Saville Row, without being luxurious, was extremely comfortable. Besides, in accordance with the habits of the tenant, the service was reduced to a minimum. But Phileas Fogg exacted the most rigid punctuality on the part of his sole domestic – something supernatural in fact. On this very day, the 2nd of October, Fogg had given James Forster notice to leave, because the fellow had actually brought up his master's shaving-water at a temperature of eighty-four instead of eighty-six degrees Fahrenheit; and Phileas was now looking out for a successor, who was expected between eleven and half-past.

Phileas Fogg was seated in his arm-chair, his feet close together at the position of "attention"; his hands were resting on his knees, his body was drawn up; with head erect he was watching the clock, which, by a complexity of mechanism, told the hours, minutes, seconds, the days of the week, and the month and year. As this clock chimed half-past eleven, Mr. Fogg, according to custom, would leave the house and walk down to his club.

Just then a knock was heard at the door of the room, and James Forster, the outgoing servant, appeared and announced, "The new young man" for the place.

A young fellow of about thirty entered and bowed.

"You are a Frenchman, and your name is John, eh?" inquired Phileas Fogg.

"Jean, sir, if you have no objection," replied the newcomer.

"Jean Passe-partout, a surname which clings to me because I have a weakness for change. I believe I am honest, sir; but to speak plainly, I have tried a good many things. I have been an itinerant singer; a rider in a circus, where I used to do the trapeze like Leotard and walk the tight-rope like Blondin; then I became a professor of gymnastics; and, finally, in order to make myself useful, I became a fireman in Paris, and bear on my back to this day the scars of several bad burns. But it is five years since I left France, and wishing to enjoy a taste of domestic life I became a valet in England. Just now being out of a situation, and having heard that you, sir, were the most punctual and regular gentleman in the United Kingdom, I have come here in the hope that I shall be able to live a quiet life and forget my name of Jack-of-all-trades – Passe-partout!"

"Passe-partout suits me," replied Mr. Fogg. "I have heard a very good character of you, and you have been well recommended. You are aware of my conditions of service?"

"Yes, sir."

"Very well. What o'clock do you make it?"

"Twenty-two minutes past eleven," replied the valet, as he consulted an enormous silver watch.

"You are too slow," said Mr. Fogg.

"Excuse me, sir, that is impossible!"

"You are four minutes too slow. Never mind, it is enough to note the error. Now from this moment, twenty-nine minutes past eleven o'clock in the forenoon upon this 2nd of October, 1872, you are in my service!"

As he spoke, Phileas Fogg rose from his chair, took up his hat, put it on his head as an automaton might have done, and left the room without another word.

Passe-partout heard the street-door shut; it was his new master who had gone out. Shortly afterwards he heard it shut again – that was his predecessor, James Forster, departing in his turn.

Passe-partout was then left alone in the house in Saville Row.

CHAPTER II

PASSE-PARTOUT IS CONVINCED THAT HE HAS ATTAINED THE OBJECT OF HIS AMBITION

"FAITH," MUTTERED PASSE-PARTOUT, who for the moment felt rather in a flutter; "faith, I have seen creatures at Madame Tussaud's quite as lively as my new master."

Madame Tussaud's "creatures" are all of wax, and only want the power of speech.

During the short period that Passe-partout had been in Mr. Fogg's presence, he had carefully scrutinized his future master. He appeared to be about forty years of age, with a fine face; a tall and well-made man, whose figure was not too stout. He had light hair and whiskers, a clear brow, a somewhat pale face, and splendid teeth. He appeared to possess in a very marked degree that attribute which physiognomists call "repose in action", a faculty appertaining to those whose motto is "Deeds, not words". Calm and phlegmatic, with a clear and steady eye, he was the perfect type of those cool Englishmen whom one meets so frequently in the United Kingdom, and whom Angelica Kauffmann has so wonderfully portrayed. Mr. Fogg gave one the idea of being perfectly balanced, like a perfect chronometer, and as well regulated. He was, in fact, the personification of exactness, which was evident in the very expression of his hands and feet; for amongst men, as amongst the lower animals, the members are expressive of certain passions.

Phileas Fogg was one of those mathematical people who, never in a hurry, and always ready, are economical of their movements. He never made even one step too many; he always took the shortest cut; he never wasted a glance, nor permitted himself a superfluous gesture. No one had ever seen him agitated or moved by any emotion. He was the last man in the world to hurry himself, but he always arrived in time. He lived quite alone, and, so to speak, outside the social scale. He knew that in life there is a great deal of friction; and as friction always retards progress, he never rubbed against anybody.

As for Jean, who called himself Passe-partout, he was a Parisian of the Parisians. He had been for five years in England, and had taken service in London as a *valet-de-chambre*, during which period he had in vain sought for such a master as Mr. Fogg.

Passe-partout was not one of those Frontii or Mascarilles, who, with high shoulders and snubbed noses, and plenty of assurance, are nothing more than impudent dunces; he was a good fellow, with a pleasant face, somewhat full lips, always ready to eat or to kiss, with one of those good round heads that one likes to see on the shoulders of one's friends. He had bright blue eyes, was somewhat stout, but very muscular, and possessed of great strength. He wore his hair in a somewhat tumbled fashion. If sculptors of antiquity were aware of eighteen ways of arranging the hair of Minerva, Passe-partout knew but one way of doing his, namely, with three strokes of a comb.

We will not go as far as to predict how the man's nature would accord with Mr. Fogg's. It was a question whether Passe-partout was the exact sort of servant to suit such a master. Experience only would show. After having passed his youth in such a vagabond manner, he looked forward to some repose.

Having heard of the proverbial method and coolness of the English gentleman, he had come to seek his fortune in England; but up to the present time fate had been adverse. He had tried six situations, but remained in none. In all of them he had found either a whimsical, an irregular, or a restless master, which did not suit Passe-partout. His last master, the young Lord Longsferry, M.P., after passing the evening in the Haymarket, was carried home on the policemen's shoulders. Passe-partout, wishing above all things to respect his master, remonstrated in a respectful manner; but as his expostulations were so ill received, he took his leave. It was at that time that he heard Phileas Fogg was in search of a servant, and he presented himself for the situation. A gentleman whose life was so regular, who never stayed away from home, who never travelled, who never was absent even for a day, was the very master for him, so he presented himself and was engaged, as we have seen.

Thus it came to pass that at half-past eleven o'clock, Passe-partout found himself alone in the house in Saville Row. He immediately commenced to look about him, and search the house from cellar to garret. This well-arranged, severe, almost puritanical house pleased him very much. It appeared to him like the pretty shell of a snail; but a snail's shell lighted and warmed with gas would serve for both those purposes. He soon discovered the room he was to occupy, and was quite satisfied. Electric bells and india-rubber speaking-tubes put him into communication with the rooms below. Upon the chimney-piece stood an electric clock, which kept time exactly with that in Phileas Fogg's bedroom.

"This will suit me exactly," said Passe-partout to himself.

He also remarked in his room a notice fixed above the clock. It was the programme of his daily duties. It included the whole details of the service from eight o'clock in the morning, the hour at which Mr. Fogg invariably arose, to half-past eleven, when he left the house to breakfast at the Reform Club. It comprised everything – the tea and toast at twenty-three minutes past eight, the shaving-water at thirty-seven minutes past nine, and his attendance at his master's toilet at twenty minutes to ten, and so on. Then from half-past eleven a.m. until midnight, when the methodical Fogg retired to bed, everything was noted down and arranged for. Passe-partout joyfully set himself to study the programme and to master its contents.

Mr. Fogg's wardrobe was well stocked and wonderfully arranged. Every pair of trousers, coat, or waistcoat bore a number, which was also noted in a register of entries and exits, indicating the date on which, according to the season, the clothes were to be worn. There were even relays of shoes and boots.

In fact, in this house in Saville Row, which had been a temple of disorder in the days of the illustrious but dissipated Sheridan, cosiness reigned supreme. There was no library and no books, which would have been useless to Mr. Fogg, since there were two reading-rooms at the Reform Club. In his bedroom was a small safe, perfectly burglar and fire proof. There were no fire-arms nor any other weapons in the house; everything proclaimed the owner to be a man of peaceable habits.

After having examined the house thoroughly, Passe-partout rubbed his hands joyously, a genial smile overspread his rounded face, and he muttered:

"This suits me completely. It is the very thing. We understand each other thoroughly, Mr. Fogg and I. He is a thoroughly regular and domestic man, a true machine. Well, I am not sorry to serve a machine."

CHAPTER III
IN WHICH A CONVERSATION ARISES WHICH IS LIKELY
TO COST PHILEAS FOGG DEAR

PHILEAS FOGG LEFT home at half-past eleven, and having placed his right foot before his left exactly five hundred and seventy-five times, and his left foot before his right five hundred and seventy-six times, he arrived at the Reform Club in Pall Mall, and immediately went up to the dining-room and took his place at his usual table, where his breakfast awaited him. The meal was composed of one "side-dish", a delicious little bit of boiled fish, a slice of underdone roast beef with mushrooms, a rhubarb and gooseberry tart, and some Cheshire cheese; the whole washed down with several cups of excellent tea, for which the Reform Club is celebrated.

At forty-seven minutes after twelve he rose from table and went into the drawing-room; there the servant handed him an uncut copy of *The Times*, which Phileas Fogg folded and cut with a dexterity which denoted a practised hand. The perusal of this journal occupied him till a quarter to four, and then *The Standard* sufficed till dinner-time. This repast was eaten under the same conditions as his breakfast, and at twenty minutes to six he returned to the saloon and read *The Morning Chronicle*.

About half an hour later, several of Mr. Fogg's friends entered the room and collected round the fire-place. These gentlemen were his usual partners at whist, and, like him, were all inveterate players.

They comprised Andrew Stuart, an engineer; the bankers, John Sullivan and Samuel Fallentin; Thomas Flanagan, the brewer; and Gauthier Ralph, one of the directors of the Bank of England; – all rich, and men of consequence, even in that club which comprised so many men of mark.

"Well, Ralph," asked Thomas Flanagan, "what about this robbery?"

"The bank must lose the money," replied Stuart.

"On the contrary," replied Ralph, "I am in hopes that we shall be able to put our hand upon the thief. We have detectives in America and Europe, at all the principal ports, and it will be no easy matter for him to escape the clutches of the law."

"Then you have the robber's description, of course," said Andrew Stuart.

"In the first place he is not a thief at all," replied Ralph seriously.

"What do you mean? Is not a man a thief who takes away fifty-five thousand pounds in bank-notes?"

"No," replied Ralph.

"He is then a man of business, I suppose?" said Sullivan.

"The *Morning Chronicle* assures me he is a gentleman."

This last observation was uttered by Phileas Fogg, whose head rose up from the sea of papers surrounding him, and then Phileas got up and exchanged greetings with his acquaintances.

The subject of conversation was a robbery, which was in everyone's mouth, and had been committed three days previously – viz. on the 29th of September. A pile of bank-notes, amounting to the enormous sum of fifty-five thousand pounds, had been stolen from the counter at the Bank of England.

The astonishing part of the matter was that the robbery had been so easily accomplished, and as Ralph, who was one of the deputy-governors, explained, that when the fifty-five thousand pounds were stolen, the cashier was occupied in carefully registering the receipt of three shillings and sixpence, and of course could not have his eyes in every direction at once.

It may not be out of place here to remark, which in some measure may account for the robbery, that the Bank of England trusts greatly in the honesty of the public. There are no guards, or commissionaires, or gratings; gold, silver, and notes are all exposed freely, and, so to speak, at the mercy of the first-comer. No one's honesty is suspected. Take the following instance, related by one of the closest observers of English customs. This gentleman was one day in one of the parlours of the bank, and had the curiosity to take up and closely-examine a nugget of gold weighing seven or eight pounds, which was lying on the table. Having examined the ingot, he passed it to his neighbour, he to the next man; and so the gold went from hand to hand quite down to the dark entry, and was not returned for quite half an hour, and all the time the bank official had not raised his head.

But on the 29th of September things did not work so nicely; the pile of bank-notes was not returned; and when the hands of the magnificent clock in the drawing-office pointed to the hour of five, at which time the bank is closed, the sum of fifty-five thousand pounds was written off to "profit and loss".

When it was certain that a robbery had been committed, the most skilful detectives were sent down to Liverpool and Glasgow and other principal ports, also to Suez, Brindisi, New York, &c., with promises of a reward of two thousand pounds, and five per cent. on the amount recovered. In the meantime, inspectors were appointed to observe scrupulously all travellers arriving at and departing from the several sea-ports.

Now there was some reason to suppose, as *The Morning Chronicle* put it, that the thief did not belong to a gang, for during the 29th of September a well-dressed gentlemanly man had been observed in the bank, near where the robbery had been perpetrated. An exact description of this person was fortunately obtained, and supplied to all the detectives; and so some sanguine persons, of whom Ralph was one, believed the thief could not escape.

As may be imagined, nothing else was talked about just then. The probabilities of success and failure were warmly discussed in the newspapers, so it was not surprising that the members of the Reform Club should talk about it, particularly as one of the deputy-governors of the bank was present.

Ralph did not doubt that the search would be successful because of the amount of the reward, which would probably stimulate the zeal of the detectives. But Andrew Stuart was of a different opinion, and the discussion was continued between these gentlemen during their game of whist. Stuart was Flanagan's partner, and Fallentin was Fogg's. While they played they did not talk; but between the rubbers the subject cropped up again.

"Well," said Stuart, "I maintain that the chances are in favour of the thief, who must be a sharp one."

"But," replied Ralph, "there is no place a fellow can go to."

"Oh, come!"

"Well, where can he go to?"

"I can't tell," replied Stuart; "but the world is big enough, at any rate."

"It used to be," said Phileas Fogg, in an undertone. "Cut, if you please," he added, handing the cards to Flanagan.

Conversation was then suspended, but after the rubber Stuart took it up again, saying:

"What do you mean by 'used to be'? Has the world grown smaller, then?"

"Of course it has," replied Ralph. "I am of Mr. Fogg's opinion; the world has grown smaller, inasmuch as one can go round it ten times quicker than you could a hundred years ago. That is the reason why, in the present case, search will be more rapid, and render the escape of the thief easier."

"Your lead, Mr. Stuart," said Fogg.

But the incredulous Stuart was not convinced, and he again returned to the subject.

"I must say, Mr. Ralph," he continued, "that you have found an easy way that the world has grown smaller, because one now goes round it in three months."

"In eighty days only," said Phileas Fogg.

"That is a fact, gentlemen," added John Sullivan. "You can make the tour of the world in eighty days, now that the section of the Great Indian Peninsular Railway is opened between Rothal and Allahabad, and here is the estimate made by *The Morning Chronicle*:

"London to Suez, by Mont Cenis and Brindisi, Rail and Steamer	7	days
Suez to Bombay, by Steamer	13	,,
Bombay to Calcutta, by Rail	3	,,
Calcutta to Hong Kong, by Steamer	13	,,
Hong Kong to Yokohama, by Steamer	6	,,
Yokohama to San Francisco, by Steamer	22	,,
San Francisco to New York, by Rail	7	,,
New York to London, Steam and Rail	9	,,
Total	80	days."

"Yes, eighty days!" exclaimed Stuart, who, being absorbed in his calculations, made a mis-deal; "but that estimate does not take into consideration bad weather, head-winds, shipwreck, railway accidents, &c."

"They are all included," remarked Fogg, as he continued to play, for this time the conversation did not cease with the deal.

"Even if the Hindoos or Indians take up the rails? Suppose

they stop the trains, pillage the baggage-waggons, and scalp the travellers?"

"All included," replied Fogg quietly. "Two trumps," he added, as he won the tricks.

Stuart, who was "pony", collected the cards, and said: "No doubt you are right in theory, Mr. Fogg, but in practice—"

"In practice too, Mr. Stuart."

"I should like to see you do it."

"It only rests with you. Let us go together."

"Heaven forbid," cried Stuart; "but I will bet you a cool four thousand that such a journey, under such conditions, is impossible."

"On the contrary, it is quite possible," replied Mr. Fogg.

"Well, then, why don't you do it?"

"Go round the world in eighty days, do you mean?"

"Yes."

"I will."

"When?

"At once; only I give you warning I shall do it at your expense."

"Oh, this is all nonsense," replied Stuart, who began to feel a little vexed at Fogg's persitence; "let us continue the game."

"You had better deal, then; that was a mis-deal."

Andrew Stuart took up the cards, and suddenly put them down again.

"Look, here, Mr. Fogg," he said; "if you like, I will bet you four thousand."

"My dear Stuart," said Fallentin, "don't be ridiculous; it is only a joke."

"When I say I will bet," said Stuart, "I mean it."

"All right," said Mr. Fogg; then turning towards the others, he said: "I have twenty thousand pounds deposited at Baring's. I will willingly risk that sum."

"Twenty thousand pounds!" exclaimed Sullivan; "why, the slightest accident might cause you to lose the whole of it. Anything unforeseen—"

"The unforeseen does not exist," replied Fogg simply.

"But, Mr. Fogg, this estimate of eighty days is the very least time in which the journey can be accomplished."

"A minimum well employed is quite sufficient."

"But to succeed you must pass from railways to steamers, from steamers to railways, with mathematical accuracy."

"I will be mathematically accurate."

"Oh, this is a joke!"

"A true Englishman never jokes when he has a stake depending on the matter. I bet twenty thousand against any of you that I will make the tour of the world in eighty days or less; that is to say, in nineteen hundred and twenty hours, or a hundred and fifteen thousand two hundred minutes. Will you take me?"

"We do," replied the others, after consultation together.

"Very well, then," said Fogg, "the Dover mail starts at 8.45; I will go by it."

"This evening?" said Stuart.

"Yes, this evening," replied Fogg. Then, referring to a pocket almanack, he added: "This is Wednesday, the 2nd of October; I shall be due in London, in this room, on Saturday, the 21st of December, at a quarter to nine in the evening, or, in default, the twenty thousand at Baring's, to my credit, will be yours, gentlemen. Here is my cheque for that sum."

A memorandum of the conditions of the bet was made and signed by all parties concerned. Phileas Fogg was as cool as ever. He had certainly not bet to win the money, and he had only bet twenty thousand pounds, half of his fortune, because he foresaw that he would probably have to spend the other half to enable him to carry out this difficult if not actually impossible feat. His opponents appeared quite agitated, not on account of the value of their stake, but because they had some misgivings and scruples about betting under such conditions.

Seven o'clock struck, and it was suggested that the game should stop, while Mr. Fogg made his preparations for the journey.

"I am always ready," replied this impassible gentleman, as he dealt the cards. "Diamonds are trumps," he added; "your lead, Mr. Stuart."

CHAPTER IV
IN WHICH PHILEAS FOGG ASTONISHES PASSE-PARTOUT

AT TWENTY-FIVE MINUTES past seven, Phileas Fogg, having won twenty guineas at whist, took leave of his friends and left the club. At ten minutes to eight he reached home.

Passe-partout, who had conscientiously studied his programme, was astonished to see Mr. Fogg appear at such an unusual hour, for, according to all precedent, he was not due in Saville Row till midnight.

Phileas Fogg went straight up to his room and called for Passe-partout.

Passe-partout did not reply. It was evident this could not refer to him, it was not time.

"Passe-partout," cried Mr. Fogg again, but without raising his voice; "this is the second time I have called you," said Mr. Fogg.

"But it is not midnight," replied Passe-partout, producing his watch.

"I know that," replied Fogg, "and I do not blame you. We start for Dover and Calais in ten minutes."

A sort of grimace contracted the Frenchman's round face; he evidently did not understand.

"Are you going out, sir?" he asked.

"Yes," replied his master; "we are going around the world."

Passe-partout at this announcement opened his eyes to their greatest extent, held up his arms, and looked the picture of stupefied astonishment.

"Around the world!" he muttered.

"In eighty days," replied Mr. Fogg; "so we have not a moment to lose."

"But the luggage," said Passe-partout, who was wagging his head unconsciously from side to side.

"We want no luggage; a carpet-bag will do. Pack up two night-shirts and three pairs of socks, and the same for yourself. We will buy what we want as we go along. Bring my mackintosh and travelling-cloak down with you, and a couple of pairs of strong boots, although we shall have little or no walking. Look alive."

Passe-partout wished to speak, but could not. He left his

master's bedroom, and went upstairs to his own, fell into a chair, and exclaimed:

"Well, this is coming it pretty strong, and for me too, who wanted to be quiet!"

Mechanically he set about making preparations for departure. Around the world in eighty days! Had he engaged himself with a maniac? No, – it was only a joke. But they were going to Dover and to Calais. So far so good. After all, he did not object to that very much, for it was five years since he had seen his native land. Perhaps they would even go on to Paris, and he would be delighted to see the capital again. No doubt a gentleman so economical of his steps would stop there; but on the other hand, this hitherto very domestic gentleman was leaving home. That was a fact.

At eight o'clock Passe-partout had packed the small bag which now contained his master's luggage and his own, and in a very troubled frame of mind he quitted his room, closed the door carefully, and went downstairs to Mr. Fogg.

That gentleman was quite ready. Under his arm he carried a copy of "Bradshaw's Continental Guide". He took the small bag from Passe-partout, opened it, and placed therein a bulky roll of bank-notes, which will pass in any country.

"You are sure you have not forgotten anything?" he asked.

"Quite sure, sir."

"You have my mackintosh and travelling-cloak?"

"Here they are, sir."

"All right, take the bag"; and Mr. Fogg handed it back to the man. "You had better take care of it," he added, "there are twenty thousand pounds in it."

Passe-partout nearly let the bag fall, as if it were weighted with the twenty thousand pounds in gold.

Master and man went downstairs together; the door was shut and double-locked. Phileas called a cab from the bottom of Saville Row, and drove to Charing Cross Station. It was twenty minutes past eight when they reached the railway. Passe-partout jumped out. His master followed, and paid the cabman. At this moment a poor beggar-woman, carrying a baby, looking very miserable with her naked feet and tattered appearance, approached Mr. Fogg, and asked for alms.

Mr. Fogg draw from his waistcoat pocket the twenty guineas

he had won at whist, and handing them to the beggar-woman, said: "Take these, my good woman. I am glad I have met you." He then entered the station.

This action of his master brought the tears into Passe-partout's susceptible eyes. Mr. Fogg had risen in his estimation. That eccentric individual now told him to take two first-class tickets for Paris, and as he turned round he perceived his five friends from the Reform Club.

"Well, gentlemen, you see I am about to start, and the *visas* on my passport on my return will convince you that I have performed the journey."

"Oh, Mr. Fogg," replied Gauthier Ralph politely, "that is quite unnecessary. We believe you to be a man of your word."

"All the better," was Fogg's reply.

"You won't forget when you have to come back," observed Stuart.

"In eighty days," replied Mr. Fogg. "On Saturday, the 21st day of December, 1872, at forty-five minutes past eight in the evening. *Au revoir*, gentlemen."

At twenty minutes to nine Phileas Fogg and his servant took their places in the train. At 8.45 the engine whistled and the train started.

The night was dark, and a fine rain was falling. Mr. Fogg was comfortably settled in his corner, and did not say a word. Passe-partout, still rather in a state of stupefaction, mechanically gripped the bag with the bank-notes.

But scarcely had the train rushed through Sydenham, than Passe-partout uttered a cry of despair.

"What is the matter with you?" asked Mr. Fogg.

"Oh dear me! In my hurry I quite forgot—"

"What?"

"I forgot to turn the gas off in my room!"

"Very well, my lad," replied Mr. Fogg coolly, "then it must burn while we are away – at your expense."

CHAPTER V

IN WHICH A NEW KIND OF INVESTMENT APPEARS ON THE STOCK EXCHANGE

WHEN PHILEAS FOGG quitted London, he had no doubt that his departure would create a great sensation. The report of the bet spread from the club to outsiders, and so to all the newspapers in the United Kingdom.

This question of going round the world in eighty days was commented upon, discussed, and dissected, and argued as much as the Alabama Claims had been. Some agreed with Phileas Fogg, but the majority were against him. To accomplish the tour in fact was an impossibility, under the present system of communication. It was sheer madness.

The Times, The Standard, The Morning Chronicle, and twenty other respectable journals gave their verdict against Mr. Fogg. *The Daily Telegraph* was the only paper that to a certain extent supported him. Phileas Fogg was generally looked upon as a maniac, and his friends at the Reform Club were much blamed for having taken up the wager, which only betrayed the want of brain of its proposer.

Extremely passionate but logical articles were written upon the question. We all know the interest that the English take in any geographical problem, and readers of every class devoured the columns in which Mr. Fogg's expedition was debated.

For the first few days some bold spirits, principally women, espoused his cause, particularly when *The Illustrated London News* published his portrait, and certain gentlemen went so far as to say: "Well, why should he not after all? More extraordinary things have happened." These were chiefly readers of *The Daily Telegraph*, but they very soon felt that that journal itself began to waver.

On the 7th of October a long article appeared in the proceedings of the Royal Geographical Society, the writer of which treated the question from all points of view, and clearly demonstrated the futility of the enterprise. According to that article, everything was against the traveller – all obstacles material and physical were against him. In order to succeed, it was necessary to admit miraculous concordance in the hours of the arrival and departure of trains and ships – a concordance which could not and did not exist. In Europe perhaps he might be able to reckon upon the punctuality of trains, but when three days are occupied in crossing India, and seven in traversing the American continent, how was it possible that he could count upon absolute success? Were not accidents to machinery, runnings off the rails, collisions, bad weather, or snowdrifts all against Phileas Fogg? On board ship in winter-time he would be at the mercy of hurricanes or contrary winds. Even the best steamers of the transoceanic lines experience a delay of sometimes two or three days. Now, if only one such delay occurred, the chain of communication would be irreparably severed. If Phileas Fogg lost a steamer by only a few hours, he would be obliged to wait for the following boat; and that fact alone would imperil the success of the whole undertaking.

This article made a great sensation. It was copied into almost all the papers, and the "shares" of Phileas Fogg fell in proportion.

For the first few days after his departure a good deal of money was laid on the success or failure of the enterprise. Everyone knows that people in England are great gamblers; it comes natural to them. So the public all went into the speculation. Phileas Fogg became a sort of favourite, as in horse-racing. He was of a certain value on the Stock Exchange. Fogg bonds were offered at par or at a premium, and enormous speculations were entered into. But five days after his departure, subsequently to the appearance of the article above quoted, the bonds were at a discount, and they were offered to anybody who would take them.

One supporter was still left to him, and that the paralytic Lord Albemarle. This worthy gentleman, who was unable to leave his chair, would have given his whole fortune to have made the tour of the world, even in ten years, and he had laid fifty thousand pounds on Phileas Fogg; and when people explained to him at the same time the folly and uselessness of the expedition, he would merely reply: "If the thing can be done, the first man to do it ought to be an Englishman."

Now as things were, the partisans of Phileas Fogg were becoming fewer by degrees and beautifully less. Everybody, and not without reason, was against him. People would only take fifty or even two hundred to one, when, seven days after his departure, a quite unexpected incident deprived him of support at any price. In fact, at nine o'clock on the evening of the seventh day, the Chief Inspector of Metropolitan Police received the following telegram:

"From Fix, Detective, Suez,

To Rowan, Commissioner of Police, Scotland Yard.

"I have traced the bank-robber, Phileas Fogg. Send immediately authority for arrest to Bombay. – Fix."

The effect of this despatch was immediately apparent. The honourable man gave place to the "bank-robber". His photograph, deposited in the Reform Club with those of other members, was narrowly scrutinized. It appeared to be, feature by feature, the very man whose description had been already furnished to the police. People now began to recollect Fogg's mysterious manner, his solitary habits, and his sudden departure. He must be the culprit, and it was evident that under the pretext of a voyage round the world, under shelter of a ridiculous bet, he had no other end in view but to throw the detectives off the scent.

CHAPTER VI
IN WHICH FIX, THE DETECTIVE, BETRAYS SOME NOT UNNATURAL IMPATIENCE

THE CIRCUMSTANCES UNDER which the foregoing telegram had been despatched were as follows:

On Wednesday, the 29th of October, the Peninsular and Oriental Company's steamer *Mongolia* was being anxiously expected at Suez. This vessel made the passage between Brindisi and Bombay through the Suez Canal. She is one of the swiftest of the Company's vessels, and her usual speed is ten knots an hour between Brindisi and Suez, and nine and a half between Suez and Bombay, and sometimes even more.

Pending the arrival of the *Mongolia*, two men were walking together up and down the quay in the midst of the crowd of natives and visitors who thronged the little town, which, thanks to the enterprise of M. de Lesseps, was becoming a considerable place. One of these men was the British Consular Agent at Suez, who, in spite of the prophecies of the English Government, and the unfavourable opinion of Stephenson the engineer, beheld daily English ships passing through the canal, thus shortening by one-half the old route to India round the Cape.

The other was a small thin man with a nervous intelligent face. Beneath his long eyelashes his eyes sparkled brightly, and at that moment he was displaying unquestionable signs of impatience, moving hither and thither, quite unable to keep still for one moment.

This man was Fix, the English detective, who had been sent out in consequence of the bank robbery. He carefully scrutinized every traveller, and if one of them bore any resemblance to the culprit he would be arrested. Two days previously, Fix had received from London the description of the criminal. It was that of the well-dressed person who had been observed in the bank.

The detective was evidently inspired by the hope of obtaining the large reward offered, and was awaiting the arrival of the *Mongolia* with much impatience accordingly.

"So you say that the steamer is never behind its time," remarked Mr. Fix to the Consul.

"No," replied the other. "She was signalled off Port Said yesterday, and the length of the Canal is nothing to such a vessel as she is. I repeat that the *Mongolia* has always gained the twenty-five pounds allowance granted by the Government for every advance of twenty-four on the regulation time."

"Does she come from Brindisi direct?" asked Fix.

"Yes, direct. She takes the Indian mails on board there. She left on Saturday afternoon at five o'clock. So be patient. She will not be late. But I really do not see how you will be able to recognize your man from the description you have, even supposing he be on board."

"One knows him by instinct more than by feature," replied Fix; "by scent, as it were, more than sight. I have had to do with more than one of these gentlemen in my time, and if the thief be on board I guarantee he will not slip through my fingers."

"I hope you will catch him – it is a big robbery."

"First-rate," replied Fix enthusiastically; "fifty-five thousand pounds. We don't often have such a windfall as that. These sort of fellows are becoming scarce. The family of Jack Sheppard has died out – people get 'lagged' now for a few shillings."

"You speak like an enthusiast, Mr. Fix," replied the Agent, "and I hope you will succeed, but I fear under the circumstances you will find it very difficult. Besides, after all, the description you have received might be that of a very honest man."

"Great criminals always do resemble honest men," replied the detective dogmatically. "You must understand that ruffianly-looking fellows would not have a chance. They must remain honest or they would be arrested at once. It is the honest appearance that we are obliged to unmask; it is a difficult thing, I confess, and one that really is an art."

It was evident that Mr. Fix thought a good deal of his profession.

Meanwhile the bustle on the quay increased. Sailors of all nations, merchants, porters, and fellahs were crowding together. The steamer was evidently expected shortly.

It was a beautiful day and the east wind cooled the air. The rays of the sun lighted up the distant minarets of the town. Towards the south the long jetty extended into the roadstead. A crowd of fishing-boats dotted the waters of the Red Sea, and amongst them one could perceive some ships of the ancient build of galleys.

Fix kept moving about amongst the crowd, scrutinizing professionally the countenances of its component members.

It was half-past ten o'clock.

"This steamer is not coming," he said, as he heard the clock strike.

"It can't be far off," said the Consul.

"How long will she stop at Suez?" said Fix.

"Four hours, to take her coal on board. From Suez to Aden it is thirteen hundred and ten miles, so she is to take in a good supply."

"And from Suez the boat goes directly to Bombay?" asked Fix.

"Direct, without breaking bulk."

"Well," said Fix, "if the thief has taken this route, and by this steamer, it will no doubt be his little game to land at Suez, so as to reach the Dutch or French possessions in Asia by some other route. He must know very well that he would not be safe in India, which is British territory."

"I don't think he can be a very sharp fellow," replied the Consul, "for London is the best place to hide in, after all."

The Consul having thus given the detective something to think about, went away to his office close by. The detective, now alone, became more and more impatient, as he had some peculiar presentiment that the robber was on board the *Mongolia*; and if he had left England with the intention to gain the new world, the route *via* India, being less open to observation, or more difficult to watch than the Atlantic route, would naturally be the one chosen.

The detective was not left long to his reflections. A succession of shrill whistles denoted the approach of the steamer. The whole crowd of porters and fellahs hurried towards the quay in a manner somewhat distressing for the limbs and clothes of the lookers-on. A number of boats also put off to meet the *Mongolia*.

Her immense hull was soon perceived passing between the banks of the Canal, and as eleven o'clock was striking she came to an anchor in the roadstead, while a cloud of steam was blown off from her safety-valves.

There were a great number of passengers on board. Some of them remained upon the bridge, admiring the view, but the greater number came ashore in the boats, which had put off to meet the vessel.

Fix carefully examined each one as they landed. As he was thus employed, one of the passengers approached him, and vigorously pushing aside the fellahs who surrounded him, inquired of the detective the way to the British Consul's office; at the same time, the passenger produced his passport, upon which he desired, no doubt, to have the British *visa*.

Fix mechanically took the passport, and mastered its contents at a glance. His hand shook involuntarily. The description on the passport agreed exactly with the description of the thief.

"This passport does not belong to you?" he said to the passenger.

"No," replied the man addressed; "it is my master's."

"And where is your master?"

"He is on board."

"But," replied the detective, "he must come himself to the Consul's office to establish his identity."

"Oh, is that necessary?"

"Quite indispensable."

"Where is the office?"

"In the corner of the square yonder," replied the detective, indicating a house about two hundred paces off.

"Well then, I will go and fetch my master; but I can tell you he won't thank you for disturbing him."

So saying, the passenger saluted Fix, and returned on board the steamer.

CHAPTER VII
WHICH ONCE MORE SHOWS THE FUTILITY OF PASSPORTS WHERE POLICEMEN ARE CONCERNED

THE DETECTIVE QUICKLY traversed the quay once more in the direction of the Consul's office. At his particular request he was at once ushered into the presence of the official.

"I beg your pardon," he said to the Consul abruptly, "but I have great reason to believe that my man is really on board the *Mongolia*." And then Mr. Fix related what had passed between him and the servant.

"Good," replied the Consul; "I should not be sorry to see the rascal's face myself; but perhaps he will not present himself here if the case stands as you believe it does. No thief likes to leave a trace behind him; and moreover, the *visa* to the passport is not necessary."

"If he is the sharp fellow he ought to be, he will come," replied Mr. Fix.

"To have his passport examined?"

"Yes. Passports are no use, except to worry honest people and to facilitate the escape of rogues. I have no doubt whatever that this fellow's passport will be all right; but I hope you will not *visé* it all the same."

"Why not? If the passport is all regular I have no right to refuse my *visa*," replied the Consul.

"Nevertheless, I must keep the fellow here until I have received the warrant of arrest from London."

"Ah, Mr. Fix, that is *your* business," said the Consul; "for my part I must—"

The Consul did not conclude the sentence. At that moment a knock was heard, and the servant introduced two strangers, one of whom was the servant who had lately interviewed the detective on the quay. The new-comers were master and servant. The former handed his passport to the Consul, and laconically requested him to attach his *visa*.

The Consul took the passport and examined it narrowly, while Fix from a corner devoured the stranger with his eyes. When the Consul had perused the document, he said:

"You are Phileas Fogg?"

"Yes," replied that gentleman.

"And this man is your servant?"

"Yes; he is a Frenchman named Passe-partout."

"You have come from London?"

"Yes."

"And you are bound – whither?"

"To Bombay."

"Very well, sir. You are aware, perhaps, that this formality is unnecessary, even useless. We only require to see the passport."

"I know that," replied Fogg; "but I want you to testify to my presence at Suez."

"Very well, sir, so be it," replied the Consul, who thereupon attested the passport. Mr. Fogg paid the fee, and bowing formally, departed, followed by his servant.

"Well, what do you think, sir?" said the detective.

"I think he looks a perfectly honest man," replied the Consul.

"That may be," said Fix; "but that is not the point. Do you not perceive that this cool gentleman answers in every particular to the description of the thief sent out?"

"I grant you that; but you know all descriptions—"

"I will settle the business," replied Fix. "It strikes me that the servant is more get-at-able than the master. Besides, he is a Frenchman, and cannot help chattering. I will return soon, sir." As he finished speaking, the detective left the Consul's office in search of Passe-partout.

Meanwhile, Mr. Fogg, having left the Consul's house, proceeded down to the quay. There he gave his servant some instructions, and then put off in a boat to the *Mongolia*, and descended to his cabin. Taking out his notebook, he made the following entries:

Left London, Wednesday, 2nd October, at 8.45 p.m.
Reached Paris, Thursday, at 8.40 a.m.

Arrived at Turin, *viâ* Mont Cenis, Friday, 4th October,
    6.35 a.m.
Left Turin, Friday, at 7.20 a.m.
Arrived at Brindisi, Saturday, 5th October, 4 p.m.
Embarked on *Mongolia*, Saturday, 5 p.m.
Reached Suez, Wednesday, 9th October, 11 a.m.
Total of hours occupied in the journey, $158\frac{1}{4}$, or $6\frac{1}{2}$ days.

Mr. Fogg made these entries in a journal ruled in columns, commencing on the 2nd of October, and so on to the 21st of December, which indicated respectively the month, the day of the month, and the day of the week, as well as the days at which he was due at the principal places *en route* – as, for instance, Paris, Brindisi, Suez, Bombay, Calcutta, Singapore, Hong Kong, Yokohama, San Francisco, New York, Liverpool, London. There was also a column in which the gain or loss upon the stipulated time could be entered against each place. This methodical arrangement of dates showed Mr. Fogg whether he was in advance or behindhand, and contained all necessary information.

So on that occasion, Wednesday, the 9th of October, was recorded as the day of his arrival at Suez, and he perceived at a glance that he had neither gained nor lost so far.

He then had his luncheon sent into his cabin. It did not occur to him to go and look at the town; he was one of those gentlemen who are quite content to see foreign countries through the eyes of their servants.

CHAPTER VIII
IN WHICH PASSE-PARTOUT TALKS A LITTLE MORE
THAN HE OUGHT TO HAVE DONE

IT WAS NOT very long before Fix rejoined Passe-partout on the quay. The latter was looking about him, as he did not feel he was debarred from seeing all he could.

"Well, my friend," said Fix, as he came up to him, "has your passport been *viséd* all right?"

"Ah! it is you," replied the valet. "I am much obliged to you. Yes, everything was in order."

"And now you are seeing something of the place, I suppose?"

"Yes, but we are going on so fast that it seems to me like a dream. And so we are in Suez, are we?"

"Yes, you are."

"In Egypt?"

"In Egypt, most decidedly."

"And in Africa?"

"Yes, in Africa."

"Well now," replied Passe-partout, "I could scarcely believe it. In Africa, actually in Africa. Just fancy. I had not the slightest idea that we should go beyond Paris, and all I saw of that beautiful city was from 7.20 a.m. to 8.40, between the terminus of the Northern Railway and the terminus of the Lyons line, and this through the windows of a fiacre as we drove through the rain. I am very sorry for it. I should like to have seen Père La Chaise and the Circus in the Champs Elysées again."

"You are in a very great hurry then?" said the detective.

"No, I am not in the least hurry," replied Passe-partout. "It is my master. By-the-way, I must buy some shirts and a pair of shoes. We came away without any luggage except a small carpet-bag."

"I will take you to a bazaar where you will find everything you want."

"Really, sir," replied Passe-partout, "you are extremely good-natured."

So they started off together, Passe-partout talking all the time.

"I must take very good care I do not lose the steamer," said he.

"Oh, you have plenty of time," replied Fix; "it is only twelve o'clock."

Passe-partout drew out his great watch. "Twelve o'clock," said he. "Nonsense. It is fifty-two minutes past nine."

"Your watch is slow," replied Fix.

"Slow, my watch slow; why this watch has come to me from my grandfather. It is an heirloom, and does not vary five minutes in a year. It is a regular chronometer."

"I see how it is," replied Fix; "you have got London time, which is about two hours slower than Suez time. You must take care to set your watch at twelve o'clock in every country you visit."

"Not a bit of it," said Passe-partout, "I am not going to touch my watch."

"Well, then, it won't agree with the sun."

"I can't help that. So much the worse for the sun; it will be wrong then." And the brave fellow put his watch back in his pocket with a contemptuous gesture.

After a few minutes' pause, Fix remarked, "You must have left London very suddenly?"

"I believe you. Last Wednesday evening at eight o'clock, Mr. Fogg came home from his club, and in three-quarters of an hour afterwards we started."

"But where is your master going to?"

"Straight ahead – he is going round the world."

"Going round the world!" exclaimed Fix.

"Yes, in eighty days. He says it is for a wager, but between ourselves, I don't believe a word of it. It is not common-sense. There must be some other reason."

"This master of yours is quite an original, I should think."

"Rather," replied the valet.

"Is he very rich?"

"He must be; and he carries a large sum with him, all in new bank-notes. He never spares expense. He promised a large reward to the engineer of the *Mongolia* if he reached Bombay well in advance of time."

"Have you known your master long?"

"Oh dear no," replied Passe-partout. "I only entered his service the very day we left."

The effect which all these replies had upon the suspicious nature of the detective may be imagined.

The hurried departure from London, so soon after the robbery, the large sum in bank-notes, the haste to reach India, under the pretext of an eccentric bet, all confirmed Fix, and not unnaturally, in his previously conceived ideas. He made up his mind to pump the Frenchman a little more, and make certain that the valet knew no more concerning his master than that he lived alone in London, was reported to be very rich, though no one knew from whence his fortune was derived, and that he was a very mysterious man, etc. But at the same time, Fix felt sure that Phileas Fogg would not land at Suez, and would really go on to Bombay.

"Is Bombay far off?" asked Passe-partout.

"Pretty well. It is ten days' steaming from here."

"And whereabouts is Bombay?"

"It is in India."

"In Asia?"

"Naturally."

"The devil! I was going to say that there is something on my mind, and that is my burner."

"What burner?"

"Why, my gas-burner, which I forgot to turn off when I left London, and which is still alight at my expense. Now I have calculated that I lose two shillings every four-and-twenty hours, which is just sixpence more than my wages. So you see that the longer our journey is—"

It is not very likely that Fix paid much attention to this question of the gas; he was thinking of something else. The pair soon reached the bazaar, and leaving his companion to make his purchases, Fix hastened back to the Consul's office, and now that his suspicions were confirmed he regained his usual coolness.

"I am quite certain now," he said to the Consul, "that this is our man. He wishes to pass himself off as an eccentric person who wants to go round the world in eighty days."

"He is a very sharp fellow, and he probably counts on returning to London, after having thrown all the police off the scent."

"Well, we shall see," replied Fix.

"But are you sure you are right?" asked the Consul once more.

"I am sure I am not mistaken."

"Well then, how do you account for the fellow being so determined upon proving he had been here by having his passport *viséd*?"

"Why— Well, I can't say," replied the detective; "but listen a moment." And then in as few words as possible he communicated the heads of his conversation with Passe-partout.

"Well, I must confess that appearances are very much against him," replied the Consul. "Now what are you going to do?"

"I shall telegraph to London, with a pressing request that a warrant of arrest may be immediately transmitted to Bombay. I shall then embark in the *Mongolia*, and so keep my eye on my man till we reach Bombay, and then, on English ground, quietly arrest him."

As he coolly finished this explanation, the detective bowed to the Consul, walked to the telegraph-office, and there despatched the message we have already seen.

A quarter of an hour later, Mr. Fix, carrying his light baggage and well furnished with money, embarked on board the
Mongolia. In a short time afterwards the vessel was ploughing her
way at full speed down the Red Sea.

CHAPTER IX

IN WHICH THE RED SEA AND THE INDIAN OCEAN
FAVOUR THE PROJECTS OF PHILEAS FOGG

THE DISTANCE BETWEEN Suez and Aden is exactly three hundred and ten miles, and the steamers are allowed one hundred
and thirty-eight hours to do it in. The *Mongolia*, however, was
going at a speed which seemed likely to bring her to her destination considerably before time.

The majority of the passengers from Brindisi were bound for
India, some for Calcutta, some for Bombay; and since the railway
crosses the peninsula it is not necessary to go round by Ceylon.

Amongst the passengers were many military officers and civil
servants of every degree. The former included officers of the
regular as well as the Indian army, holding lucrative appoint-
ments, for the sub-lieutenants get two hundred and eighty;
brigadiers, two thousand four hundred; and generals, four thousand pounds a year.

Society, therefore, on board the *Mongolia* was very pleasant.
The purser feasted them sumptuously every day. They had early
breakfast, then tiffin at two o'clock, dinner at half-past five, and
supper at eight; and the tables groaned beneath the variety of
dishes. The ladies on board changed their toilettes twice a day,
and there was music and dancing when the weather was sufficiently favourable to admit of those amusements.

But the Red Sea is very capricious; it is frequently very rough,
like all long and narrow gulfs. When the wind blew broadside
on, the *Mongolia* rolled fearfully. At these times the ladies went
below, the pianos were silent, singing and dancing ceased. But
notwithstanding the wind and the sea, the vessel, urged by her
powerful screw, dashed onward to the straits of Bab-el-Mandeb.

And what was Phileas Fogg doing all this time? Perhaps it may
be supposed that he was anxious and restless, thinking of the
contrary winds and the speed of the ship, which was likely to be

retarded by the storm, and so compromise the success of his undertaking. At any rate, whether he did or did not concern himself with these things, he never betrayed the least anxiety on the subject. He was as taciturn and impassible as ever; a man whom no eventuality could surprise. He did not appear to be any more interested than one of the ship's chronometers. He was rarely seen on deck. He troubled himself very little about the Red Sea, so full of interest, the scene of some of the greatest incidents in the history of mankind. He never cared to look at the towns standing out in relief against the sky. He had no fear of the dangers of the Arabian Gulf, of which ancient writers, Strabo, Arian, Artemidorus, etc., have always written with horror, and upon which sailors of those days never dared to venture without first making a propitiatory sacrifice.

How then did this eccentric gentleman occupy his time, cooped up in his cabin? In the first place he regularly ate his four meals a day, for neither pitching nor rolling had the least effect upon his appetite. And he played whist, for he had made the acquaintance of some lovers of the game as enthusiastic as himself, a collector of revenue *en route* to Goa, a clergyman, the Rev. Decimus Smith, returning to Bombay, and an English general officer bound for Benares. These three were as madly devoted to whist as Mr. Fogg himself, and they spent whole days silently enjoying it.

As for Passe-partout, he had also escaped sea-sickness, and ate his meals with pleasing regularity and in a conscientious manner, worthy of imitation. The voyage after all did not displease him; he had made up his mind; he gazed at the scenery as he went along, enjoyed his meals, and was fully persuaded that all this absurd business would come to an end at Bombay.

The day after their departure from Suez, viz. the 10th of October, Passe-partout was by no means ill-pleased to meet upon deck the person who had been so civil to him in Egypt.

"I'm sure I cannot be mistaken," he said. "Have I not the pleasure of meeting the gentleman who was so polite to me at Suez?"

"Ah yes, I remember you now. You are the servant of that eccentric Englishman."

"Exactly. Mr. —"

"Fix," replied the detective.

"Mr. Fix," continued Passe-partout, "I am delighted to find you on board. Whither are you bound?"

"Like yourself, to Bombay."

"All the better. Have you ever made this voyage before?"

"Frequently. I am an agent of the P. and O. Company."

"Oh, then you know India very well, no doubt?"

"Well, yes," replied Fix, who did not wish to commit himself. "It is a curious part of the world, isn't it?"

"Very much so. There are mosques, minarets, temples, fakirs, pagodas, tigers, serpents, and dancing-girls. It is to be hoped that you will have time to see the country."

"I hope so too, Mr. Fix. You must be aware that a man can hardly be expected to pass his whole existence in jumping from the deck of a steamer into a train, and from the train to another steamer, under the pretence of going round the world in eighty days. No; all these gymnastics will end at Bombay, I trust."

"Is Mr. Fogg quite well?" asked Fix, politely.

"Quite well, thank you. So am I. I eat like an ogre. I suppose that is the effect of the sea-air."

"I never see your master on deck."

"No, he has no curiosity whatever."

"Do you know, Mr. Passe-partout, that I fancy this pretended journey round the world in eighty days is only a cover for a more important object, a diplomatic mission perhaps?"

"Upon my word, Mr. Fix, I know nothing about it, I declare; and what is more, I would not give half-a-crown to know!"

After this, Passe-partout and Fix frequently chatted together; the detective doing all in his power to draw the valet out, whenever possible. He would offer the Frenchman a glass of whisky or bitter beer, which the latter accepted without ceremony, and pronounced Fix a perfect gentleman.

Meantime the steamer plunged and ploughed on her way rapidly. Mocha was sighted on the 13th, surrounded by its ruined walls, above which some date-palms reared their heads. Beyond extended immense coffee plantations. Passe-partout was delighted to gaze upon this celebrated town, and fancied that it and its ruined walls bore a great resemblance to a gigantic cup and saucer.

During the following night the *Mongolia* cleared the strait of Bab-el-Mandeb, which means the Gate of Tears, and the following day they came to Steamer Point, to the N.W. of Aden harbour, where the supply of coal was to be shipped.

It is no light task to provide the steamers with coal at such a distance from the mines, and the P. and O. Company expend annually no less a sum than eight hundred thousand pounds on this service. Depôts have to be established at distant ports, and the coal costs more than three pounds a ton.

The *Mongolia* had still sixteen hundred and fifty miles to run before she could reach Bombay, and she was therefore obliged to remain four hours at Steamer Point to complete her coaling. But this delay was not at all detrimental to the plans of Phileas Fogg. It had been foreseen. Besides, the *Mongolia*, instead of reaching Aden on the 15th, had made that port on the evening of the 14th, so there was a gain of about fifteen hours.

Mr. Fogg and his servant went ashore. The former wished to have his passport *viséd*. Fix followed him unnoticed. The formality of the *visé* having been accomplished, Phileas Fogg returned on board to his game of whist.

Passe-partout, as usual, lounged about amongst the mixed races which make up the inhabitants of Aden. He admired the fortifications of this eastern Gibraltar, and the splendid tanks at which the British engineers were still at work, two thousand years after Solomon's craftsmen.

"Very curious, very curious indeed," thought Passe-partout, as he returned on board. "It is worth travelling if one can see something new each time."

At six p.m. the *Mongolia* weighed anchor, and made her way across the Indian Ocean. She had now one hundred and sixty-eight hours in which to make the passage to Bombay. The weather was good, with a pleasant nor'-west wind; so the sails were hoisted to aid the screw.

The ship being thus steadied, the lady passengers took the opportunity to reappear in fresh toilettes, and dancing and singing were again indulged in. The voyage continued under most favourable conditions. Passe-partout was delighted that he had such a pleasant companion as Fix.

On Sunday, the 20th of October, about mid-day, they sighted the coast of Hindostan. Two hours later the pilot came on board. A long range of hills cut the sky-line, and soon palm-trees began to show themselves. The mail steamer ran into the roadstead formed between the islands of Salsette, Colaba, Elephanta, and Butcher, and at half-past four o'clock the vessel came alongside the quay.

Phileas Fogg was just finishing his thirty-third rubber for that day. His partner and he had succeeded in scoring a "treble", and thus terminated the voyage with a stroke of luck.

The *Mongolia* was not due at Bombay until the 22nd of October; she had actually arrived on the 20th; so Mr. Fogg had really gained two days upon the estimated period, and he entered the "profit" accordingly in the column of his diary set apart for that purpose.

CHAPTER X
IN WHICH PASSE-PARTOUT THINKS HIMSELF LUCKY IN ESCAPING WITH ONLY THE LOSS OF HIS SHOES

EVERYBODY IS AWARE that the peninsula of Hindostan has a superficial area of one million four hundred thousand square miles, in which the unequally distributed population numbers one hundred and eighty millions. The British Government rules absolutely over the greater portion of this immense tract of country. The Governor-General resides at Calcutta, and there are also governors of presidencies at Madras and Bombay, and a deputy-governor at Agra, as well as a governor for Bengal.

British India proper only includes an area of seven hundred thousand square miles, and a population of one hundred to one hundred and ten millions; so there is still a large portion of India independent, and, in fact, there are rajahs in the interior who wield absolute authority.

From the year 1756 to the great Sepoy Mutiny, the East India Company was the supreme authority in British India; but now the country is under the rule of the English Crown. The manners and customs of India are in a continual state of change. Till lately, travelling was only by antiquated modes of conveyance, but now steamers cover the Ganges, and the railways have opened up the country, and one can go from Bombay to Calcutta in three days. But the railroad does not cut the peninsula in a direct line. As the crow flies, the distance from Calcutta to Bombay is only about eleven hundred miles, and the trains would not occupy three days in accomplishing that distance; but the journey is lengthened at least one-third of that distance by the loop the line describes up to Allahabad.

The Great Indian Peninsula Railway line is as follows: leaving Bombay Island, it crosses Salsette, reaches the mainland at Tannah, crosses the Western Ghauts, thence runs north-east to Burhampoor, skirts the independent territory of Bundelcund, ascends to Allahabad, and then, turning eastward, meets the Ganges at Benares then, quitting it again, the line descends in a south-easterly direction, by Burdivan and Chandernagore, to the terminal station at Calcutta.

It was half-past four p.m. when the Bombay passengers landed from the *Mongolia*, and the train for Calcutta was timed to start at eight o'clock.

Mr. Fogg took leave of his colleagues of the whist-table, and going ashore, gave his servant orders concerning a few necessary purchases, enjoining him to be at the railroad station before eight o'clock, and then, at his own regular pace, he started for the Consul's office.

He saw nothing of the sights of Bombay – the town-hall, the magnificent library, the forts, the docks, the cotton market, the bazaars, mosques, &c., were all disregarded. Elephanta was ignored, and the grottos of Salsette unexplored by Phileas Fogg.

After leaving the consulate, he walked calmly to the railroad station and dined. The proprietor of the hotel particularly recommended "a native rabbit". Phileas accepted the dish as put before him, but found it horrible.

He rang the bell. The landlord was sent for.

"Is that a rabbit?" inquired Mr. Fogg.

"Yes, my lord, a jungle rabbit."

"Has that rabbit never mewed, do you think?"

"Oh, my lord, a jungle-rabbit mew! I swear—"

"Don't swear," said Fogg calmly, "and remember that formerly cats were sacred animals in India. These were happy days."

"For the cats, my lord?"

"And perhaps for travellers too," said Fogg, as he proceeded with his dinner.

Soon afterwards Mr. Fix landed, and his first act was to go to the police-office. He said who and what he was, and stated his business and how matters stood regarding the robbery. Had any warrant been forwarded? No, nothing of the kind had been received, and of course it could not have reached Bombay, as it was despatched after Fogg's departure.

Fix was disappointed. He wanted the Commissioner to grant him a warrant on the spot, but the request was refused. The business was the Home Government's affair, not his, and he could not issue the warrant. This red-tapeism is quite British style. Fix of course did not insist, and made up his mind to await the arrival of the warrant. But he resolved not to lose sight of the robber meanwhile. He had no doubt whatever that Fogg would remain some time in Bombay – we know that was also Passe-partout's notion – and the warrant would probably arrive before the criminal left the town.

But it was now evident to Passe-partout that his master intended to push on from Bombay as rapidly as he had left Paris and Suez; that the journey was not to end at Bombay, it was to be continued to Calcutta at any rate, and perhaps even farther still. Passe-partout then began to think that perhaps the bet was really the object, and that fate had indeed condemned him, with all his wish for rest, to journey around the world in eighty days.

However, having purchased some necessary articles, he walked about the streets of Bombay. There were a great number of people about – Europeans of all nationalities; Persians, wearing pointed caps; Buntryas, with round turbans; Scindees, with square caps; Armenians, in their flowing robes; Parsees, with black mitres. It was a Parsee festival that day.

These Parsees are followers of Zoroaster, and are the most industrious, most intelligent, and most civilized of the native races, and to which the majority of the Bombay merchants belong. On that occasion a sort of religious carnival was being held; there were processions, and numbers of dancing-girls clad in gauzy rose-coloured garments, who danced modestly and gracefully to the sound of the tom-tom and viols.

Passe-partout, as may be imagined, drank in all these sights and sounds with delight; and his expression at the unusual spectacle was that of the greatest astonishment.

Unfortunately, his curiosity very nearly compromised the object of his master's journey. He wandered on, after watching the carnival, on his way to the station, but seeing the splendid pagoda on Malabar Hill, he thought he would like to go in.

He was quite unaware of two things: first, that certain pagodas are closed to all Christians, and even the believers can only obtain admittance by leaving their shoes or slippers at the doors of the temple. The British Government, respecting the native creed, severely punishes anyone attempting to violate the sanctity of the native mosques or temples.

But Passe-partout, innocent of harm, tourist-like, went in, and was admiring the pagoda and the lavish ornamentation of the interior, when he suddenly found himself sprawling on his back on the pavement. Over him stood three angry men, who rushed upon him, tore off his shoes, and began to pommel him soundly, uttering savage cries as they did so.

The agile Frenchman was quickly upon his feet again, and with a couple of well-directed blows of his fists upset two of his adversaries, who were much encumbered in their long robes; then, rushing out of the temple, he quickly distanced the remaining Hindoo and evaded him in the crowd.

At five minutes to eight he presented himself at the railroad station, without his hat and shoes and minus the parcel in which all his purchases were wrapped. Fix was there on the platform. Having tracked Fogg, he perceived that that worthy was about to leave Bombay at once. Fix made up his mind to go with him as far as Calcutta, and even beyond if necessary. Passe-partout did not notice the detective, who kept in the shade; but the policeman heard the recital of the valet's adventures, which Passe-partout told to his master in a few sentences.

"I trust this will not happen again," replied Fogg, quietly, as he took his seat in the carriage.

The poor lad, quite upset and minus his hat and shoes, took his place also without replying.

Fix was getting into another compartment, when suddenly a thought struck him, and he muttered:

"No, I will remain. An offence has been committed upon Indian ground. I've got my man!"

At that moment the engine uttered a piercing whistle, and the train moved out into the night.

CHAPTER XI
SHOWING HOW PHILEAS FOGG PURCHASED A "MOUNT" AT A FABULOUS PRICE

THE TRAIN STARTED punctually, carrying the usual complement of travellers, including officers of the civil and military classes and merchants. Passe-partout was seated near his master, a third traveller had secured a corner opposite.

This gentleman was General Sir Francis Cromarty, one of Mr. Fogg's whist-party on board the *Mongolia*, who was *en route* to take up his command at Benares.

Sir Francis was a tall fair specimen of the British officer, about fifty years old. He had greatly distinguished himself during the Mutiny. He had been in India almost all his life, and only paid occasional visits to his native country. He was a well-informed man, and would willingly have imparted any information he possessed, had Phileas Fogg chosen to apply to him. But the latter did nothing of the kind. He never travelled. He merely made a track across country. He was a heavy body, describing an orbit around the terrestrial globe, according to certain mechanical laws. At that time he was actually engaged in calculating how many hours had passed since he left London, and he would have rubbed his hands joyfully, had he been one of those people who indulge in these needless enthusiastic demonstrations.

Sir Francis Cromarty had already noticed the eccentricity of his companion while at whist, and had questioned seriously whether a human heart actually beat beneath that cold envelope of flesh, whether Fogg really possessed a soul alive to the beauties of nature, and subject to human failings and aspirations. That was what puzzled the gallant soldier. None of the many original characters which it had been his fortune to encounter had, in any way, resembled this product of the action of exact science upon humanity.

Phileas Fogg had not concealed from Sir Francis the object of his journey round the world, nor the conditions under which he had undertaken it. The general saw nothing in this wager but the eccentricity of its surroundings, and the want of *transire benefaciendo* which ought to guide any reasonable man. If this extraordinary man went on in this manner all his life, he would finally quit the world, having done absolutely nothing for his own benefit or for that of others.

An hour after leaving Bombay, the train crossed the viaduct carrying the line from Salsette to the mainland. At Callyan station they left the branch-line to Kandallah and Poona on the right, and proceeded to Panwell. Here they traversed the gorges of the Western Ghauts, composed of trap and basaltic rocks, the highest summits of which are crowned with thick trees.

Sir Francis Cromarty and Phileas Fogg occasionally exchanged a few words, and at one time the general picked up the thread of conversation by remarking:

"A few years ago, Mr. Fogg, you would have experienced a considerable impediment to your journey here, and would most likely have compromised your success."

"How do you mean, Sir Francis?"

"Because the railway did not go beyond the base of these mountains, and it was then necessary to make the journey in palanquins or on ponies as far as Kandallah on the opposite slope."

"Such an interruption would not in any way have disarranged my plans," replied Mr. Fogg. "I have taken precautions against certain obstacles."

"Nevertheless, Mr. Fogg, you very nearly had an awkward bit of business on hand in consequence of yonder fellow's adventure."

Passe-partout was fast asleep, with his feet well muffled up in the railway-rug, and was quite unconscious that he was the subject of conversation.

"The British Government is extremely strict, and with reason, upon any such offences," continued Sir Francis. "Above everything, it considers that the religious feelings of the native races should be respected, and if your servant had been arrested—"

"Well," interrupted Mr. Fogg, "well, Sir Francis, suppose he had been taken and condemned and punished, he might have returned quietly to Europe afterwards. That would not have been a reason for stopping his master."

And then the conversation again languished. During the night the train crossed the mountains, passed Nassik, and next day, the 21st October, it traversed a comparatively flat district of Kandish. The well-cultivated country was sprinkled with villages, above which the minarets of the pagodas took the place of the English church-spires. Numerous tributaries of the Godavery watered this fertile territory.

Passe-partout awoke and looked about him. He could not at first believe that he actually was crossing India in a carriage upon the G.I.P. Railway. It appeared quite incredible, but it was none the less real. The locomotive, driven by an English engineer and fed with English coal, puffed its steam over coffee, cotton, clove, and pepper plantations. The smoke curled around the palm-trees, amid which picturesque bungalows were frequently visible, and "viharis", a sort of abandoned monasteries, as well as a few temples enriched with wonderful Indian architecture, were here and there apparent. Farther on, they passed immense tracts of land extending as far as the eye could reach, and jungles in which serpents and tigers fled scared at the roar and rattle of the train; then succeeded forests through which the line passed, the abode of elephants which, with pensive gaze, watched the speeding train.

During the forenoon our travellers traversed the blood-stained district beyond Malligaum, sacred to the votaries of the goddess Kâli. Not far from this arose the minarets of Ellora and its pagodas, and the famous Aurungabad, the capital of the ferocious Aurung-Zeb, now the chief town of one of the detached kingdoms of the Nizam. It was in this country that Feringhea, chief of the Thugs – the King of Stranglers – exercised sway. These assassins, united in an invisible and secret association, strangled, in honour of the goddess of death, victims of every age without shedding blood, and in time there was scarcely a place where a corpse was not to be found. The English Government has succeeded in checking very considerably these wholesale massacres, but Thugs still exist and pursue their horrible vocation.

At half-past twelve the train stopped at Burhampore, and Passe-partout succeeded in obtaining a pair of slippers decorated with false pearls, which he wore with evident conceit.

The passengers ate a hurried breakfast, and the train again started for Assinghur, skirting for a moment the river Tapy, a small stream which flows into the Gulf of Cambay, near Surat.

It may now not be out of place to record Passe-partout's reflections. Until his arrival at Bombay he had cherished the idea that the journey would not be continued farther. But now that he was being carried across India he saw things in a different light. His old love of wandering returned in full force. The fantastic ideas of his youthful days came back to him again; he took his master's projects quite seriously; he began to believe in the wager, and consequently in the tour of the world to be completed in that maximum of eighty days which must not on any account be exceeded. Even now he was beginning to feel anxious about possible delays and accidents *en route*. He felt interested in winning, and trembled when he considered that he had actually compromised the whole thing by his stupidity on the previous day. So he was much more restless than Mr. Fogg, because he was less phlegmatic. He counted over and over again the days that had already passed since he had started, cursed at the stoppages at stations, found fault with the slow speed, and in his heart blamed Mr. Fogg for not having "tipped" the engine-driver. He quite overlooked the fact that, though such a thing was possible on board a steamer, it was out of question on a railroad where the time of the trains is fixed and the speed regulated.

Towards evening they penetrated the defiles of the mountains of Sutpoor, which separate the territory of Khandeish from that of Bundelcund.

Next day, the 22nd, Passe-partout replied, to a question of Sir Francis Cromarty, that it was three a.m., but, as a matter of fact, this wonderful watch was about four hours slow, as it was always kept at Greenwich time, which was then nearly seventy-seven degrees west, and the watch would of course get slower and slower.

Sir Francis corrected Passe-partout's time, respecting which he made a remark similar to that made by Mr. Fix. He endeavoured to convince the valet that he ought to regulate his watch by each new meridian, and as he was still going east the days became shorter and shorter by four minutes for every degree. But all this was useless. Whether the headstrong fellow understood the general or not, he certainly did not alter his watch, which was steadily kept at London time. At any rate it was a delusion which pleased him and hurt nobody.

At eight o'clock in the morning the train stopped about fifteen miles from Rothal, at a place where there were many bungalows and huts erected. The guard passed along the line, crying out, "All change here!"

Phileas Fogg looked at Sir Francis Cromarty, who did not appear to understand this unexpected halt.

Passe-partout, not less astonished, leaped down, and in a moment or two returned, exclaiming, "There is no railway beyond this place, sir."

"What do you mean?" inquired Sir Francis.

"I mean that the train does not go any farther."

The general immediately got out. Phileas Fogg followed quietly. Both these gentlemen accosted the guard.

"Where are we?" asked Sir Francis.

"At the village of Kholby, sir," replied the guard.

"Why do we stop here?"

"Because the line is not finished beyond."

"Not finished! How is that?"

"There are about fifty miles yet to be laid between this point and Allahabad, where we take the train again."

"The papers announced the line complete."

"I cannot help that, sir; the papers were mistaken."

"But you book people 'through' from Bombay to Calcutta," persisted Sir Francis, who was waxing angry.

"Certainly we do; but it is an understood thing that the passengers provide their own conveyance between Kholby and Allahabad."

Sir Francis was furious. Passe-partout would have liked to have knocked the guard down, if he had been able. He did not dare to look at his master.

"We had better get on, Sir Francis," said Mr. Fogg; "we must get to Allahabad somehow; let us see how we can do so."

"It strikes me that this delay will upset your arrangements considerably, Mr. Fogg," replied Sir Francis.

"Oh dear no! all this has been discounted," replied Fogg.

"What! did you know that the line was unfinished?"

"No; but I was quite sure that some obstacles would crop up to retard me. Nothing is yet lost. I have two days in reserve. The steamer does not leave Calcutta for Hong Kong until the 23rd, at mid-day. This is only the 22nd, and we shall reach Calcutta in good time even now."

What could be urged against such an assured reply as this? It was only too evident that the railway ceased at that point. Newspapers are so fond of anticipating, and in this case they had been decidedly premature in announcing the completion of the line. The majority of the passengers had been made aware of the existing state of things, and provided themselves with conveyance accordingly, whatever they could obtain – "palkigharies" with four wheels, waggons drawn by zebus, a sort of brahma ox, palanquins, ponies, &c. So it happened that there was nothing left for Mr. Fogg and Sir Francis Cromarty.

"I shall walk," said Phileas Fogg.

Passe-partout, who was close to his master, made a very expressive grimace when he gazed at his elegant but very thin slippers. Fortunately he had made a discovery, but hesitated a little to announce it.

"Sir," he said at length, "I think I have found means for our transport."

"What is it?"

"An elephant. It belongs to a native who lives close by."

"Let us go and see this animal," said Mr. Fogg.

Five minutes later Sir Francis and Mr. Fogg, accompanied by Passe-partout, reached the hut, which was surrounded by a palisade. In the hut resided the native; inside the palisade the elephant lived. The former introduced the new arrivals to the latter, at their particular request.

They found that the animal was half domesticated; it had originally been purchased for a fighting elephant, not for carrying purposes. With this end in view, the owner had begun to alter the naturally placid disposition of the beast by irritating him, and getting him gradually up to that pitch of fury called "mutsh" by the Hindoos, and this is done by feeding the elephant on sugar and butter for three months. This at first sight would appear scarcely the treatment likely to conduce to such an object, but it is successfully employed.

Fortunately, however, for Mr. Fogg, the elephant in question had not been subjected to this treatment for a very long time, and the "mutsh" had not appeared.

Kiouni – for so was the animal called – was no doubt quite competent to perform the journey required, and in the absence of other conveyance, Phileas Fogg determined to hire him.

But elephants in India are dear, for they are becoming somewhat scarce. The males, which only are suited to the circus training, are much in request. They seldom breed when in a domesticated state, so they can only be procured by hunting. They are, therefore, the objects of much solicitude, and when Mr. Fogg asked the owner what he could hire his elephant for, the man declined point-blank to lend him at all.

Fogg persisted, and offered ten pounds an hour for the beast! It was refused. Twenty? Still refused. Forty? Declined with thanks. Passe-partout actually jumped at each "bid". But the native would not yield to the temptation.

Nevertheless the price tendered was a handsome one. Supposing that the elephant took fifteen hours to reach Allahabad, the price would amount to six hundred pounds!

Phileas Fogg, without betraying the least irritation, then proposed to the owner that he should sell the animal outright, and offered one thousand pounds for him.

But the Hindoo declined; perhaps he thought he would make more by so doing.

Sir Francis Cromarty then took Mr. Fogg aside, and requested him to reflect ere he bid higher. Mr. Fogg replied that he was not in the habit of acting on impulse, that a bet of twenty thousand pounds depended upon the accomplishment of the journey, that the elephant was absolutely necessary, and if he paid twenty times the value of the animal, it must be had.

So Mr. Fogg returned to the Indian, who perceived it was only a question of asking. Phileas offered in quick succession twelve hundred, fifteen hundred, eighteen hundred, and finally two thousand pounds. Passe-partout, usually so ruddy, was now pale with emotion.

At two thousand pounds the native yielded.

"I declare by my slippers, that's a pretty price for an elephant!" exclaimed Passe-partout.

This business over, there was nothing but to obtain a guide. That was easily done. A young and intelligent-looking Parsee offered his services. Mr. Fogg engaged him, and promised him a good reward, which would naturally increase his intelligence.

The elephant was got ready without delay. The Parsee was quite skilled in the business of a "mahout". He placed a sort of saddle on the elephant's back, and at each end of it he fixed a small howdah.

Mr. Fogg paid the native the two thousand pounds in bank-notes, which he took from the inexhaustible carpet-bag. Passe-partout writhed as they were paid over. Then Mr. Fogg offered Sir Francis Cromarty a seat on the elephant, which the general gratefully accepted. One traveller more or less would not signify to such an animal.

Provisions were purchased. Sir Francis and Mr. Fogg each occupied a howdah, while Passe-partout sat astride between them. The Parsee seated himself upon the elephant's neck, and at nine o'clock they quitted the village, the elephant taking a short cut through the thick palm-forest.

CHAPTER XII
SHOWING WHAT HAPPENED TO PHILEAS FOGG AND HIS COMPANIONS AS THEY TRAVERSED THE FOREST

THE GUIDE, HOPING to shorten the journey, kept to the left of the railroad line, which would be carried in a circuitous manner through the Vindhia Mountains when completed. The Parsee, who was well acquainted with all the byways, declared that twenty miles would be saved by striking directly across the forest; so the party yielded.

Sir Francis and Mr. Fogg, buried up to their necks in the howdahs, got terribly shaken by the rough trotting of the elephant, which was urged by the driver. But they put up with the inconvenience with true British self-restraint; they spoke but seldom and scarcely looked at each other.

Passe-partout was obliged to be very careful not to keep his tongue between his teeth, else it would have been bitten off, so unmercifully was he jogged up and down. The brave fellow, sometimes thrown forward on the animal's neck, sometimes upon the croup, performed a series of vaulting movements something like a circus clown on the "spring-board". But all the time he joked and laughed at the somersaults he performed so involuntarily; occasionally he took out a lump of sugar from his pocket and handed it to Kiouni, who took it in his trunk without slackening his pace for a second.

After proceeding thus for a couple of hours, the driver called a halt and gave the elephant an hour's rest. The animal ate all the branches and shrubs in the vicinity, as soon as he had quenched his thirst at a neighbouring spring. Sir Francis did not complain of this delay; he was terribly bruised. Mr. Fogg did not appear any more discomposed than if he had only got out of bed.

"He is a man of iron!" exclaimed the general, as he gazed at his companion admiringly.

"Of hammered iron," replied Passe-partout, who was preparing a hasty breakfast.

At noon the driver gave the signal for departure. The country soon became very wild. The dense forest was succeeded by groves of dates and palms; then came extensive arid plains dotted here and there with bushes, and sprinkled with immense blocks of syenite. The whole of this region of Bundelcund, which is seldom traversed, is inhabited by a fanatical people inured to the most fearful practices of the Hindoos. The English Government has scarcely yet entirely obtained the control over this region, which is ruled by rajahs, who are very difficult to bring to book from their almost inaccessible mountain fastnesses. Many times the travellers noticed bands of fierce natives, who gesticulated angrily at perceiving the swift-footed elephant pass by; and the Parsee took care to give them all a wide berth. They encountered very few wild animals; even monkeys were not numerous, and they fled away with grimaces and gestures, which amused Passe-partout very much indeed.

One reflection, however, troubled Passe-partout exceedingly, and that was how would his master dispose of the elephant when they reached Allahabad? Would he take it on with him? That was scarcely possible. The price of conveyance, added to the purchase-money, would be ruinous. Would he sell the beast or set him free? No doubt the animal deserved some consideration. Suppose Mr. Fogg made him, Passe-partout, a present of the elephant? He would feel very much embarrassed. So these considerations worried the valet not a little.

At eight o'clock they had crossed the principal heights of the Vindhia chain, and at a ruined bungalow upon the southern slope of the mountains our travellers halted again.

The distance traversed was about twenty-five miles, and they had still as far to go to reach Allahabad. The night was quite chilly. A fire lighted by the Parsee was very acceptable, and the travellers made an excellent supper of the provisions they had purchased at Kholby. The intermittent conversation soon gave way to steady snoring. The guide kept watch by the elephant, which slept outside, supported by the trunk of an enormous tree.

Nothing happened to disturb the party during the night. Now and then the growls of wild animals, or the chattering of monkeys, broke the silence, but nothing more terrible was heard, and the larger animals did not disturb the occupants of the bungalow. Sir Francis Cromarty "lay like a warrior taking his rest". Passe-partout, in a restless sleep, appeared to be practising the gymnastics he had executed on the elephant's back. As for Mr. Fogg, he slept as peacefully as if he were in his quiet bed in Saville Row.

At six o'clock they resumed their journey. The guide hoped to reach Allahabad that evening. In that case Mr. Fogg would only lose a portion of the eight-and-forty hours already saved since the commencement of the trip.

They descended the last slopes of the Vindhias. The elephant resumed his rapid pace. Towards mid-day the guide passed round the village of Kallenger on the Cani, one of the small affluents of the Ganges. He appeared to avoid all inhabited places, feeling more secure in the deserted tracts. Allahabad was thence only a dozen miles off in a north-easterly direction. They halted once more under a banana-tree, the fruit of which, as wholesome as bread and "as succulent as cream", as they said, was highly appreciated by our travellers.

At two o'clock they entered a dense forest, which they had to traverse for some miles. The guide preferred to travel in the shade of the woods. So far at any rate they had encountered nothing unpleasant, and there was every reason to suppose that the journey would be accomplished without accident, when the elephant, after a few premonitory symptoms, stopped suddenly.

It was then four o'clock in the afternoon.

"What is the matter?" asked Sir Francis Cromarty, putting his head up over the top of his howdah.

"I don't know, sir," replied the Parsee, listening intently to a confused murmuring sound which came through the thickly-interlacing branches.

Soon the sound became more defined. One might have fancied it was a concert at a great distance; composed of human voices and brass instruments all performing at once. Passe-partout was all eyes and ears. Mr. Fogg waited patiently without uttering a word.

The Parsee leaped down, fastened the elephant to a tree, and plunged into the thick underwood. In a few moments he came back, exclaiming: "A procession of Brahmins is coming this way! Let us hide ourselves if we can."

As he spoke he loosed the elephant and led him into a thicket, bidding the travellers to stay where they were. He was ready to remount should flight be necessary, but he thought that the procession would pass without noticing the party, for the thick foliage completely concealed them.

The discordant sounds kept approaching – a monotonous kind of chant, mingled with the beating of tom-toms and the clash of cymbals. The head of the procession soon became visible beneath the trees about fifty paces off, and Mr. Fogg and his party easily distinguished the curious individuals who composed it.

The priests, wearing mitres and long robes trimmed with lace, marched in front. They were surrounded by a motley crowd of men, women, and children, who were chanting a sort of funeral hymn, broken at intervals by the sound of the various instruments. Behind these came, on a car (the large wheels of which, spokes and all, were ornamented with the similitude of serpents), a hideous figure drawn by four richly-caparisoned zebus. This idol had four arms, the body was painted a dusky red, with staring eyes, matted hair, a protruding tongue, and lips tinted with henna and betel. Round its neck was hung a necklace of skulls, and it was girt with a zone of human hands; it stood upright upon the headless trunk of a giant figure.

Sir Francis Cromarty recognized the idol at once.

"That is the goddess Kâli," he whispered; "the goddess of love and of death."

"Of death I can understand, but not of love," muttered Passepartout; "what a villainous hag it is!"

The Parsee signed to him to hold his tongue.

Around the idol a number of fakirs danced and twirled about. These wretches were daubed with ochre, and covered with wounds, from which the blood issued drop by drop; absurd idiots, who would throw themselves under the wheels of Juggernaut's chariot had they the opportunity.

Behind these fanatics marched some Brahmins, clad in all their oriental sumptuousness of garb, dragging a woman along, who faltered at each step.

This female was young, and as white as a European. Her head, neck, shoulders, ears, arms, hands, and ankles were covered with jewels, bracelets, or rings. A gold-laced tunic, over which she wore a thin muslin robe, revealed the swelling contours of her form.

Behind this young woman, and in violent contrast to her, came a guard, armed with naked sabres and long damascened pistols, carrying a dead body in a palanquin.

The corpse was that of an old man clothed in the rich dress of a rajah; the turban embroidered with pearls, the robe of silk tissue and gold, the girdle of cashmere studded with diamonds, and wearing the beautiful weapons of an Indian prince.

The musicians brought up the rear with a guard of fanatics, whose cries even drowned the noise of the instruments at times. These closed the *cortège*.

Sir Francis Cromarty watched the procession pass by and his face wore a peculiarly saddened expression. Turning to the guide, he said:

"Is it a suttee?"

The Parsee made a sign in the affirmative, and put his fingers on his lips. The long procession wended its way slowly amongst the trees, and before long the last of it disappeared in the depths of the forest. The music gradually died away, occasionally a few cries could be heard, but soon they ceased, and silence reigned around.

Phileas Fogg had heard what Sir Francis had said, and as soon as the procession had passed out of sight, he said:

"What is a suttee?"

"A suttee," replied the general, "is a human sacrifice – but a voluntary one. That woman you saw just now will be burned to-morrow morning at daylight."

"The scoundrels!" exclaimed Passe-partout, who could not repress his indignation.

"And that dead body?" said Mr. Fogg.

"Is that of her husband – a prince," replied the guide. "He was an independent rajah in Bundelcund."

"Do you mean to say that these barbarous customs still obtain in India – under British rule?" said Mr. Fogg, without betraying any emotion whatever.

"In the greater portion of India," replied Sir Francis

Cromarty, "these sacrifices do not take place; but we have no authority in the savage districts, one of the principal of which is Bundelcund. The entire district north of the Vindhia range is the theatre of pillage and murder."

"Poor creature," exclaimed Passe-partout; "burned alive!"

"Yes," continued the general, "burned alive; and if she was not, you have no idea to what a wretched condition she would be reduced by her relatives. They would shave off her hair, feed her very scantily upon rice, and hold no communication with her, for she would be regarded as unclean, and would die like a dog. The prospect of such treatment, even more strongly than affection or religious fanaticism, often urges the widows to submit themselves to suttee. Sometimes, however, the act is really voluntary, and energetic interference by the Government is necessary to prevent it. Some years ago, when I was in Bombay, a young widow asked the governor's leave to be burned with her late husband's body. As you may imagine, he refused her request. Then the disconsolate widow left the town, took refuge with an independent rajah, and burned herself, to the satisfaction of all concerned."

As the general proceeded, the guide nodded in assent to the truthfulness of the relation, and when the speaker had finished, the Parsee said:

"But the suttee to take place to-morrow is not voluntary."

"How do you know?"

"Everyone in Bundelcund knows that," replied the guide.

"Yet the unfortunate woman offered no resistance," said Sir Francis Cromarty.

"Because she was drugged with hemp and opium," replied the Parsee.

"But whither are they taking her?"

"To the Pagoda of Pillaji, two miles away from here. There she will pass the night, and wait for the hour appointed for the sacrifice."

"And the sacrifice will take place?

"At dawn to-morrow."

As he spoke, the guide led forth the elephant and clambered up to his seat on its neck; but just as he was about to whistle to the animal to proceed, Mr. Fogg stopped him, and said to Sir Francis Cromarty, "Suppose we save this woman?"

"Save her!" exclaimed the general.

"I have still twelve hours to spare," continued Fogg; "I can devote that time to the purpose."

"Well, I declare you are a man with a heart in the right place," cried Sir Francis.

"Sometimes it is," replied Mr. Fogg, smiling grimly, "when I have time!"

CHAPTER XIII
SHOWING HOW PASSE-PARTOUT PERCEIVES ONCE AGAIN
THAT FORTUNE FAVOURS THE BRAVE

THE PROJECT WAS a difficult one and a bold, almost impossible to carry out. Mr. Fogg was about to risk his life, or at least his liberty, and consequently the success of his undertaking; but, nevertheless, he hesitated not a moment. Besides, he found in Sir Francis Cromarty a sturdy ally. Passe-partout also was at their disposal; he was quite ready, and his opinion of his master was rising every moment. He possessed a heart, after all, beneath that cold exterior. Passe-partout was beginning to love Mr. Fogg.

The guide remained. What course would he take in this business? He would probably side with the natives. At any rate, if he would not assist, his neutrality must be assured.

Sir Francis put the question to him plainly.

"Your honour," replied the man, "I am a Parsee. The woman is a Parsee also. You may dispose of me as you wish."

"Good," replied Sir Francis.

"But," continued the guide, "you must remember that not only do we risk our lives in this affair, but we may be horribly tortured if we are taken alive. So take care."

"We have made up our minds to run the risk," said Mr. Fogg. "I think we had better wait till nightfall before we act."

"I think so too," said the guide, who then proceeded to give his employers some information respecting the lady. He said she was a Parsee, a celebrated Indian beauty, daughter of one of the richest merchants in Bombay. She had received a complete English education; her manners and tastes were all European. Her name was Aouda. She was, moreover, an orphan, and had been married against her will to the rajah. She had only been three months wed. Knowing the fate that awaited her, she had attempted to escape, but was immediately retaken; and the rajah's relatives, who were desirous, from motives of interest, for her death, had devoted her to the suttee, which now appeared inevitable.

These particulars only served to confirm Mr. Fogg and his companions in their generous resolve. It was then decided that the guide should take them as near to the pagoda as possible without attracting attention.

In about half an hour the elephant was halted in the brushwood about five hundred yards from the temple, which was not visible; but the shouts of the fanatics were distinctly audible.

The best manner of releasing the intended victim was then discussed. The guide was acquainted with the pagoda in which he declared the young woman was imprisoned. Was it possible to enter by one of the doors, when all the band of priests, etc., were wrapped in a drunken sleep? or, should they enter through a hole in the wall? This could only be decided when they reached the pagoda. But one thing was very certain, and that was that the deed must be done at night, and not at daybreak, when the victim was being led to the sacrifice. Then human aid would be powerless to save her.

So the party waited till night. At about six o'clock in the evening it would be dark, and then they would make a reconnaissance. The last cries of the fakirs would by that time be hushed. The Hindoos would by that time, according to custom, be wrapped in the intoxicating arms of "bang" – liquid opium mixed with hemp; and it would be possible to glide past them into the temple.

The whole party, guided by the Parsee, then advanced stealthily through the forest. After ten minutes' creeping beneath the branches of the trees, they reached a rivulet, whence, by the glare of the torches, they were enabled to distinguish the funeral pyre, composed of the fragrant sandal-wood, and already saturated with perfumed oil. Upon this pile lay the dead body of the deceased prince, which was to be burned with his widow. A hundred paces from the pyre was the pagoda, the minarets of which uprose beyond the tops of the surrounding trees.

"Come on," whispered the guide.

With increasing caution the Parsee, followed by his companions, glided silently amongst the tall grasses. The murmur of the breeze through the trees was the only sound that broke the silence.

The Parsee soon halted on the border of the clearing. Some torches lit up the space. The ground was covered with groups of tipsy sleepers, and bore a great resemblance to a battle-field strewn with dead bodies. Men, women, and children lay all together. Some drunken individuals still staggered about here and there. In the background the temple loomed amid the thick trees. But greatly to the disappointment of the guide, armed rajpoots kept watch by torchlight upon the doors, in front of which they paced up and down with naked swords. No doubt the priests within were equally vigilant.

The Parsee advanced no farther. He perceived at once that it was impossible to force an entrance to the temple, and he led his companions back again. Sir Francis and Mr. Fogg also understood that no more could be done in that direction. They stopped and consulted together in undertones.

"Let us wait a little," whispered the brigadier. "It is only eight o'clock. Those sentries may go to sleep later."

"That is possible, certainly," said the Parsee.

So they all lay down under the trees and waited.

The time passed very slowly. At intervals the guide would go forward and reconnoitre. But the guards were always there; the torches burned brightly still, and an uncertain glimmer penetrated through the windows of the temple from the inside.

They waited until nearly midnight. There was no change in the situation. The sentries were sleepless, and it became evident that they intended to keep watch all night. They were probably quite sober. It now became necessary to try another plan and to cut through the walls of the pagoda. There was then the chance of finding the priests awake inside, watching their intended victim as closely as the soldiers guarded the door.

After a final consultation, the guide expressed himself ready to proceed. Mr. Fogg, Sir Francis, and Passe-partout followed. They made a long detour with the intention of approaching the pagoda from behind. About half-past twelve they gained the walls without having encountered anyone. Evidently no watch was kept at the side, but it was equally evident that there was neither window nor door at the back.

The night was dark. The moon, then in her last quarter, appeared scarcely above the horizon, and was covered frequently by thick clouds. The trees also served to render the darkness more profound. It was enough to have reached the wall, an opening must be discovered or made. To accomplish this, Mr. Fogg and his companions had nothing but their pocket-knives. Fortunately, the temple walls were only composed of bricks and wood, which would not be very hard to cut through. Once the first brick had been taken out, the rest was easy.

They set about the work immediately, and as noiselessly as possible. The Parsee and Passe-partout worked away to loosen the bricks in a space about two feet wide. The labour was continued, and they were getting on capitally, when a cry was heard from the interior of the temple, and was immediately succeeded by others from the outside. Passe-partout and the guide ceased working. Had they been heard, and had the alarm been given? Common prudence necessitated a retreat, which was effected in company with Six Francis Cromarty and Phileas Fogg. They ensconced themselves again beneath the trees to wait until the alarm, if it were an alarm, had subsided, and ready in that event to resume their operations. But, alas! the guards now completely surrounded the pagoda and prevented all approach. It would be difficult to depict the disappointment of these four men at this unfortunate *contretemps*. As they were prevented from approaching the victim, how could they hope to save her? Sir Francis Cromarty clenched his hands, Passe-partout was almost beside himself, and even the guide had some difficulty in preserving his self-restraint. The impassible Phileas Fogg alone preserved his equanimity.

"I suppose we may as well go away now?" whispered Sir Francis Cromarty.

"That's all we can do," the guide assented.

"Don't be in a hurry," said Mr. Fogg. "It will suit me well enough if we reach Allahabad at mid-day."

"But what do you expect to do if we remain here?" said Sir Francis. "It will be daylight in a couple of hours, and——"

"We may get a chance at the last moment."

The brigadier would have liked to have been able to read the expression of Mr. Fogg's face. What was he thinking about, this cool-headed Englishman? Would he, at the last moment, throw himself upon the burning pile, and snatch her from the clutches of her executioners openly?

Such a proceeding would have been the height of folly, and no one could for a moment imagine that Mr. Fogg was so fool-hardy as that. Nevertheless, Sir Francis consented to wait the *dénouement* of this terrible scene. But the guide led the party to the edge of the clearing, where, from behind a thicket, they could observe all the proceedings. Meanwhile, Passe-partout had been hatching a project in his busy brain, and at last the idea came forth like a flash of lightning. His first concepion of the notion he had repudiated as ridiculously foolish, but at length he began to look upon the project as feasible. "It is a chance," he muttered, "but perhaps the only one with such bigoted idiots." At any rate he wriggled himself to the end of the lowest branch of a tree, the extremity of which almost touched the ground.

The hours passed slowly on, and at length some faint indications of day became visible in the sky. But it was still quite dark in the neighbourhood of the pagoda.

This was the time chosen for the sacrifice. The sleeping groups arose as if the resurrection had arrived. The tom-toms sounded. Chants and cries were once more heard. The sublime moment had come!

Just then the doors of the pagoda were opened, and a strong light flashed out from the interior. The victim could be perceived being dragged by two priests to the door. It appeared to the spectators that the unhappy woman, having shaken off the effects of her enforced intoxication, was endeavouring to escape from her executioners. Sir Francis Cromarty was deeply agitated, and seizing Mr. Fogg's hand convulsively he perceived that the hand grasped an open knife.

The crowd now began to move about. The young woman had been again stupefied with hemp-fumes, and passed between the lines of fakirs who escorted her, uttering wild cries as they proceeded.

Phileas Fogg and his companions followed on the outskirts of the crowd. Two minutes later they reached the bank of the stream, and stopped about fifty paces from the funeral pyre, upon which the corpse was extended. In the dim religious light, they could perceive the outline of the victim close beside her deceased husband.

A lighted torch was then quickly applied to the pile of wood, which, saturated with oil, was instantly in a blaze. Sir Francis Cromarty and the guide had to exert all their strength to restrain Mr. Fogg, who, in his generous indignation, appeared about to rush upon the blazing pile.

But just as Phileas Fogg had succeeded in throwing them off, a change came o'er the scene. A cry of terror rose from the natives, and they bowed themselves to the earth in indescribable terror.

The old rajah was not dead after all; there he was standing upright upon the fiery funeral pile, clasping his young wife in his arms; ready to leap from amid the smoke into the midst of the horror-stricken crowd. The fakirs, the guards, the priests were all seized with superstitious fear, and lay, faces to the earth, not daring to lift their eyes to behold such a stupendous miracle.

The resuscitated man was thus practically quite close to the place where Phileas Fogg and Sir Francis Cromarty were standing with the guide.

"Let us be off," exclaimed the "spectre".

It was only Passe-partout, who had, unperceived, gained the pyre under cover of the smoke, and had rescued the young lady from certain death. It was Passe-partout himself who, thanks to his happy audacity, was enabled to pass unharmed through the terrified assemblage.

In an instant the four friends had disappeared in the woods, and the elephant was trotting rapidly away. But very soon the loud cries and the clamour that arose told them that the trick had been discovered, and a bullet whizzed by as an additional confirmation. For there upon the blazing pile lay the rajah's corpse; and the priests quickly understood that a rescue had been so far successfully accomplished. They immediately dashed into the forest, accompanied by the soldiers, who fired a volley; but the fugitives had got away, and in a few moments more were out of reach of arrows and bullets both.

CHAPTER XIV

IN WHICH PHILEAS FOGG DESCENDS THE CHARMING VALLEY OF THE GANGES, WITHOUT NOTICING ITS BEAUTIES

THE RASH ATTEMPT had proved successful. An hour later, Passe-partout was laughing at the result of his venturous plan. Sir Francis Cromarty had shaken hands with him. His master had said, "Well done!" which from him was high commendation indeed. To which expressions of approbation, Passe-partout had replied that all the credit of the affair belonged to his master. His own share in it had been an absurd notion after all; and he laughed again when he thought that he, Passe-partout, the ex-gymnast, ex-sergeant of the fire brigade, had actually played the part of spouse of a beautiful young lady, the widow of an embalmed rajah!

As for the young lady herself, she was still insensible, and quite unconscious of all that was passing or had lately passed. Wrapped up in a railroad-rug, she was now reclining in one of the howdahs.

Meanwhile the elephant, guided with unerring care by the Parsee, was progressing rapidly through the still gloomy forest. After an hour's ride, they arrived at an extensive plain. At seven o'clock they halted. The young lady was still quite unconscious. The guide poured some brandy down her throat, but she remained insensible for some time afterwards. Sir Francis Cromarty, who was aware that no serious evil effects supervened from the inhalation of the fumes of hemp, was in no way anxious about her.

But if her restoration to consciousness was not a subject of anxiety to the brigadier, he was less assured respecting her life in the future. He did not hesitate to tell Mr. Fogg that if Madame Aouda remained in India, she would sooner or later be taken by her would-be executioners. Those fanatics were scattered everywhere through the peninsula, and there was not a doubt that, despite the English police, the Hindoos would claim their victim, no matter in what presidency she might endeavour to take refuge. And in support of his assertion, Sir Francis instanced a similar case which had recently taken place. His opinion, therefore, was that she would only be in absolute safety when she quitted India for ever.

Mr. Fogg replied that he would consider the matter, and give his opinion later.

About ten o'clock the guide announced that they were close to Allahabad. Then they would be able to continue their journey by the railroad, and in about four-and-twenty hours they would reach Calcutta. Phileas Fogg would in that case be in time to catch the Hong Kong steamer, which was to sail at noon on the 25th of October. The young woman was safely bestowed in a private waiting-room, while Passe-partout was hurriedly despatched to purchase various necessary articles of clothing, etc., for her use. His master supplied the funds for the purpose.

Passe-partout hastened away, and ran through the streets of Allahabad – the City of God – one of the most sacred cities of India, inasmuch as it is built at the junction of the two holy streams of the Ganges and the Jumna, whose waters attract pilgrims from every part of the peninsula. We are also told that the Ganges has its source in heaven, whence, owing to the influence of Bramah, it condescends to earth.

While he made his purchases diligently, Passe-partout did not forget to look about him and see something of the city. It was at one time defended by a splendid fort, which has since become the State prison. Commerce and business no longer occupy their former places in Allahabad. Vainly did the worthy European seek for such emporiums as he would have met in Regent Street; he could find nothing better than the shop of an old Jew clothesman – a crusty old man he was too. From him he purchased a tweed dress, a large cloak, and a magnificent otter-skin pelisse which cost seventy-five pounds. With these garments he returned in triumph to the railway station.

Mrs. Aouda had by that time partly recovered consciousness. The influence of the drug administered by the priests was passing away by degrees, and her bright eyes were once again resuming their soft and charming Indian expression.

The poet-king, Uçaf Uddaul, celebrating the charms of the Queen of Ahundnagara, thus sings:

"Her shining locks, parted in the centre of her forehead, set off the harmonious contours of her white and delicate cheeks, all glowing in their freshness. Her ebon brows have the shape and power of the bow of Kama, the god of love; and beneath her silken lashes, her dark eyes swim in liquid tenderness, as in the sacred lakes of the Himalayas is reflected the celestial light. Her glittering, even, pearl-like teeth shine between the smiling lips as the dewdrops in the half-closed petals of the passion-flower. Her tiny ears, with curves divine, her small hands, her little feet, tender as the buds of lotus, sparkle with the pearls of Ceylon and the dazzling diamonds of the famed Golconda. Her rounded, supple waist, which hand may circle round, displays the curving outline of the hips, and swelling bosom, where youth in all its loveliness expands its perfect treasures. Beneath the tunic-folds the limbs seem formed within a silver mould by the god-like hand of Vicvarcarnia, the immortal sculptor."

Without exactly comparing Mrs. Aouda with the foregoing description, it may be stated that she was a most charming woman, in the fullest acceptation of the term. She spoke English with fluency and purity, and the guide had only stated the truth when he had averred that the Parsee lady had been transformed by her education.

The train was about to start; Mr. Fogg was paying the Parsee guide his hire as agreed – not a farthing in excess. This business-like arrangement rather astonished Passe-partout, when he recalled all they owed to the guide's devotion. In fact, the Parsee had risked his life voluntarily by engaging in the affair at Pillaji, and if he should be caught by the Hindoos he would very likely be severely dealt with. There was still Kiouni, however. What was to be done with the elephant, which had cost so much? But Phileas Fogg had already made up his mind on that point.

"Parsee," said he to the guide, "you have been most useful and devoted to us. I have paid for your services, but not for your devotion. Would you like to have the elephant? If so, he is yours." The eyes of the guide sparkled.

"Your honour is giving me a fortune!" he exclaimed.

"Take him," replied Mr. Fogg, "and then I shall still be in your debt."

"Hurrah!" cried Passe-partout; "take him, my friend. Kiouni is a fine animal"; and going up to the beast, he gave him some pieces of sugar, saying, "Here, Kiouni, take this, and this."

The elephant gave vent to some grunts of satisfaction, and then seizing Passe-partout by the waist with his trunk, he lifted him up. Passe-partout, not in the least afraid, continued to caress the animal, which replaced him gently on the ground, and to the pressure of the honest Kiouni's trunk, Passe-partout responded with a kindly blow.

Some short time after, Phileas Fogg, Sir Francis Cromarty, and Passe-partout were seated with Mrs. Aouda, who occupied the best place in a comfortable compartment of the train, which was speeding towards Benares. This run of eighty miles from Allah-abad was accomplished in two hours, and in that time the young lady had quite recovered from the drugs she had inhaled.

Her astonishment at finding herself in the train, dressed in European garments, and with three travellers utterly unknown to her, may be imagined.

Her companions in the first place showed her every attention, even to the administration of a few drops of liqueur, and then the general told her what had happened. He particularly dwelt upon the devotedness of Phileas Fogg, who had risked his life to save hers, and upon the termination of the adventure, of which Passe-partout was the hero. Mr. Fogg made no remark whatever, and Passe-partout looked very bashful, and declared it was not worth speaking of.

Mrs. Aouda thanked her deliverers effusively by tears at least as much as by words. Her beautiful eyes even more than her lips expressed her gratitude. Then her thoughts flew back to the suttee, and as she remarked she was still on Indian territory, she shuddered with horror. Phileas Fogg, guessing her thoughts, hastened to reassure her, and quietly offered to escort her to Hong Kong, where she could remain till the affair had blown over. This offer the lady most gratefully accepted, for – curiously enough – a relative of hers, a Parsee like herself, was then residing at Hong Kong, and was one of the principal merchants of that British settlement.

At half-past twelve the train stopped at Benares. Brahmin legends state that this town is built upon the site of the ancient Casi, which was at one time suspended between heaven and earth, like Mahomet's coffin. But in these practical days, Benares, which orientals call the Athens of India, rests prosaically upon the ground, and Passe-partout caught many a glimpse of brick houses and numerous clay huts, which gave the place a desolate appearance, without any local colour.

Sir Francis Cromarty had now reached his destination; the troops he was to command were encamped a few miles to the north of the town. He took farewell of Phileas Fogg, wished him every success, and expressed a hope that he would continue his journey in a more profitable and less original manner. Mr. Fogg gently pressed his companion's hand. Mrs. Aouda was more demonstrative; she could not forget what she owed to Sir Francis Cromarty. As for Passe-partout, he was honoured with a hearty shake of the general's hand, and was much impressed thereby. So they parted.

From Benares the railway traverses the valley of the Ganges. The travellers had many glimpses of the varied country of Behar, the hills covered with verdure, and a succession of barley, wheat, and corn fields, jungles full of alligators, neat villages, and thick forests. Elephants and other animals were bathing in the sacred river, as were also bands of Hindoos of both sexes, who, notwithstanding the advanced season of the year, were accomplishing their pious ablutions. These devotees were declared enemies of Buddhism, and were strict Brahmins, believing in Vishnu, the sun god; Shiva, the personification of nature; and Brahma, the head of priests and rulers. But how do Brahma, Shiva, and Vishnu regard India, now completely Anglicized, with hundreds of steamers darting and screaming along the holy waters of the Ganges, frightening the birds and beasts and faithful followers of the gods dwelling along the banks?

The landscape passed rapidly by, and was occasionally hidden by the stream. The travellers could now discern the fort of Chunar, twenty miles south-west of Benares; then Ghazipore and its important rose-water manufactories came in sight; then they caught a glimpse of the tomb of Lord Cornwallis, which rises on the left bank of the river; then the fortified town of Buxar; Patna, the great commercial city and principal opium-market of India; Monghir, an European town, as English as Manchester or Birmingham, with its foundries, factories, and tall chimneys vomiting forth volumes of black smoke.

Night fell, and still the train rushed on, in the midst of the roaring and growling of wild animals, which fled from the advancing locomotive. Nothing could of course then be seen of those wonders of Bengal, Golconda, the ruins of Gom, and Morschabad, Burdwan, the ancient capital, Hooghly, Chandernagore, in

French territory, where Passe-partout would have been glad to see his country's ensign.

At last, at seven o'clock in the morning, they reached Calcutta. The steamer for Hong Kong was not to leave till mid-day, so Phileas Fogg had still five hours to spare.

According to his journal, he was due at Calcutta on the 25th October – twenty-three days from London; and at Calcutta he was as arranged. He had neither gained nor lost so far. Unfortunately, the two days he had had to spare he spent as we have seen while crossing the peninsula; but we must not suppose that Phileas Fogg regretted his actions for a moment.

CHAPTER XV
IN WHICH THE BAG OF BANK-NOTES IS LIGHTENED
BY SOME THOUSANDS OF POUNDS MORE

PASSE-PARTOUT WAS the first to alight from the train; Mr. Fogg followed, and helped out his fair companion. Phileas had counted upon proceeding directly to the steamer, so as to settle Mrs. Aouda comfortably on board. He was unwilling to leave her so long, as she was on such dangerous ground.

As Mr. Fogg was leaving the station a policeman approached him, and said, "Mr. Phileas Fogg, is it not?"

"It is," replied Phileas.

"And this is your servant?" continued the policeman, indicating Passe-partout.

"Yes."

"Will you be so good as to follow me?"

Mr. Fogg did not appear in the least degree surprised. The policeman was a representative of the law, and to an Englishman the law is sacred. Passe-partout, like a Frenchman, wanted to argue the point, but the policeman touched him with his cane, and his master made him a sign to obey.

"This young lady can accompany us?" said Mr. Fogg.

"Certainly," replied the policeman.

Mr. Fogg, Mrs. Aouda, and Passe-partout were then conducted to a "palkighari", a sort of four-wheeled carriage, holding four people, and drawn by two horses. They drove away, and no one spoke during the twenty minutes' drive.

The carriage passed through the "Black Town", and then through the European quarter, which, with its brick houses, well-dressed people, and handsome equipages, presented a marked contrast to the native town. The carriage stopped before a quiet-looking house, which, however, did not appear to be a private mansion. The policeman directed his prisoners – for so we may term them – to alight, and conducted them to a room, the windows of which were barred.

"At half-past eight," he said, "you will be brought before Judge Obadiah." He then went out and locked the door.

"So we are prisoners," exclaimed Passe-partout, dropping into a chair.

Mrs. Aouda, turning to Mr. Fogg, said tearfully: "Oh sir, pray do not think of me any longer. It is on my account that you have been arrested. It is for having saved me."

Phileas Fogg calmly replied that such a thing was not possible. It was quite out of the question that they could be arrested on account of the suttee. The complainants would not dare to present themselves. There must be some mistake, and Mr. Fogg added that in any case he would see the young lady safe to Hong Kong.

"But the steamer starts at twelve o'clock," said Passe-partout.

"We shall be on board before that," replied the impassible Fogg.

This was said so decidedly that Passe-partout could not help muttering, "That's all right then, we shall be on board in time no doubt." But in his soul he was not so very certain of it.

At half-past eight the door opened, the policeman entered, and conducted the friends into an adjoining room. This was the court, and was pretty well filled by Europeans and natives. The three companions were allotted seats on a bench facing the magistrate's desk. Judge Obadiah, followed by the clerk, entered almost immediately. He was a fat, round-faced man. He took down a wig from a nail and put it on.

"Call the first case," he began, but immediately putting his hand to his head he said, "This is not my wig."

"The fact is, your honour, it is mine," replied the clerk.

"My dear Mr. Oysterpuff, how can you expect a judge to administer justice in a clerk's wig?"

The exchange was made. All this time Passe-partout was boiling over with impatience, for the hands of the clock were getting on terribly fast towards noon.

"Now, then, the first case," said the judge.

"Phileas Fogg," called out the clerk.

"Here I am."

"Passe-partout."

"Here."

"Good," said the judge.

"For two days we have been awaiting you."

"But of what do you accuse us?" cried Passe-partout impatiently.

"You are going to hear," said the judge quietly.

"Your honour," said Mr. Fogg, "I am a British citizen, and I have the right—"

"Have you not been properly treated?" asked the judge.

"Oh yes, but—"

"Very well, then. Call the plaintiffs."

As the judge spoke the door opened, and three Hindoo priests were introduced by an usher.

"It is that, after all," muttered Passe-partout. "Those are the fellows that wanted to burn our young lady."

The priests stood erect before the judge, and the clerk read aloud the complaint of sacrilege against Phileas Fogg and his servant, who were accused of having defiled a place consecrated to the Brahmin religion.

"You hear the charge," said the judge to Phileas Fogg.

"Yes, your honour," replied the accused, looking at his watch, "and I confess it."

"You admit it?"

"I admit it, and I wait to see what these priests in their turn will confess respecting their doings at the Pagoda of Pillaji."

The priests looked at each other. They evidently did not understand the reference.

"Of course," cried Passe-partout impetuously, "at the Pagoda of Pillaji, where they were about to burn their victim."

The priests looked stupefied, and the judge was almost equally astonished.

"What victim?" he asked. "To burn whom? In Bombay?"

"Bombay!" exclaimed Passe-partout.

"Of course. We are not talking of the Pagoda of Pillaji, but of the Pagoda of Malabar Hill at Bombay."

"And as a proof," added the clerk, "here are the shoes of the profaner of the temple"; and he placed a pair of shoes upon the desk as he spoke.

"My shoes!" exclaimed Passe-partout, who was surprised into this incautious admission.

One can imagine the confusion which ensued. The incident at the pagoda in Bombay had been quite forgotten by both master and man, and it was on account of that that they were both detained.

The detective Fix had seen at once the advantage he could derive from that *contretemps*; so, delaying his departure for twelve hours, he consulted with the priests at Malabar Hill and had promised them a large reward, knowing very well that the English Government would punish with extreme severity any trespass of such a description. Then he had sent the priests by train on the track of the offenders. Owing to the time spent by Phileas Fogg and his party in releasing the young widow from the suttee, Fix and the Hindoo priests had reached Calcutta first, but in any case Mr. Fogg and his servant would have been arrested as they left the train in consequence of a telegraphic despatch which had been forwarded to Calcutta by the authorities. The disappointment of Fix may be imagined when he heard on his arrival that Fogg had not reached Calcutta. He thought that his victim had stopped at one of the intermediate stations, and had taken refuge in the southern provinces. For four-and-twenty hours Fix had restlessly paced the railway station at Calcutta. What was his joy when that very morning he perceived his man descending from the train in company with a lady whose presence he could not account for. He had immediately directed a policeman to arrest Mr. Fogg, and that is how the whole party came to be brought before Judge Obadiah.

If Passe-partout had been less wrapped up in his own business he would have noticed the detective seated in the corner of the court, watching the proceedings with an interest easy to be understood, for at Calcutta, as heretofore, he still wanted the warrant to arrest the supposed thief.

But Judge Obadiah had noticed the avowal, which Passe-partout would have given the world to recall.

"So the facts are admitted," said the judge.

"They are," replied Fogg coldly.

"Well," continued the judge, "inasmuch as the English law is intended to protect rigorously, and without distinction, all religions in India, and as this fellow, Passe-partout, has confessed his crime, and is convicted of having violated with sacrilegious feet the Pagoda of Malabar Hill at Bombay during the day of the 20th of October, the said Passe-partout is condemned to fifteen days' imprisonment and to pay a fine of three hundred pounds."

"Three hundred pounds!" exclaimed Passe-partout, who was scarcely conscious of anything but the amount of the fine.

"Silence!" shouted the usher.

"And," continued the judge, "seeing that it is not proved that this sacrilege was connived at by the master, but as he must be held responsible for the acts and deeds of his servant, the said Phileas Fogg is sentenced to eight days' imprisonment and a fine of one hundred and fifty pounds. Usher, call the next case."

Fix, in his corner, rubbed his hands to his satisfaction. Phileas Fogg detained eight days at Calcutta! This was fortunate, by that time the warrant would have arrived from England. Passe-partout was completely dumbfoundered. This conviction would ruin his master. His wager of twenty thousand pounds would be lost; and all because he, like an idiot, had gone into that cursed pagoda.

But Phileas Fogg was as cool and collected as if he were in no way concerned in the matter. At the moment the usher was calling on the next case, Phileas rose and said, "I offer bail."

"That is within your right," said the judge.

Fix's blood ran cold; but he revived again, when he heard the judge say, that as the prisoners were strangers, a bail of a thousand pounds each would be necessary. So it would cost Mr. Fogg two thousand pounds, if he did not put in an appearance when called upon.

"I will pay the money now," said that gentleman; and from the bag which Passe-partout still held, he drew bank-notes for two thousand pounds, and placed them on the clerk's desk.

"This sum will be restored to you, when you come out of prison," said the judge. "Meantime you are free on bail."

"Come along," said Phileas Fogg to his servant.

"But I suppose they will give me back my shoes?" said Passe-partout angrily.

They gave him back his shoes. "They have cost us pretty dearly," he muttered, "more than one thousand pounds apiece, without counting the inconvenience to myself"; and with the most hang-dog appearance, Passe-partout followed his master, who had offered his arm to the young lady. Fix was still in hopes that his prey would not abandon such a sum as two thousand pounds; so he followed Mr. Fogg closely.

Phileas took a fly, and the whole party were driven down to the quays. Half-a-mile from the pier the *Rangoon* was moored, the "blue-peter" at the mast head. Eleven o'clock was striking, so Mr. Fogg had an hour to spare. Fix saw him put off in a boat, with Mrs. Aouda and his servant. The detective stamped with rage.

"The rascal!" he exclaimed; "he is going then. Two thousand pounds sacrificed. He is as reckless as a thief. I will follow him to the end of the world, if necessary; but at the rate he is going, the stolen money will soon be spent."

The detective was not far wrong. In fact, since he had left London, what with travelling expenses, "tips", the money paid for the elephant, in fines, and in bail, Phileas Fogg had already disbursed more than five thousand pounds, so that the percent-age upon the sum likely to be recovered by the detective (as he imagined) was growing small by degrees and beautifully less.

CHAPTER XVI

FIX DOES NOT AT ALL UNDERSTAND WHAT IS SAID TO HIM

THE *RANGOON*, ONE of the P. and O. Company's vessels, plying between India, China, and Japan, was an iron screw steamer of about one thousand seven hundred and seventy tons, with engines of four hundred horse-power. She was as fast but not so comfortable as the *Mongolia*, and Mrs. Aouda was scarcely as well accommodated as Phileas Fogg would have wished. But as the voyage was only three thousand five hundred miles, that is to say eleven or twelve days' steaming, and the young lady was not difficult to please, it was no great matter.

During the first portion of the voyage she became well

acquainted with Phileas Fogg, and gave expression to her great gratitude on every occasion. That phlegmatic gentleman listened to her protestations with the most unmoved exterior, not an expression, not a movement evidenced the slightest emotion; but he took care that the young lady should want for nothing. He saw her at certain hours every day, if not to talk, at least to listen to her conversation; he exhibited towards her the greatest politeness, but the politeness of an automaton. Mrs. Aouda did not know what to think of him, though Passe-partout had given her a few hints about his eccentric master, and had told her of the wager about going round the world. Mrs. Aouda had rather ridiculed the idea, but after all did she not owe him her life? And Mr. Fogg would not lose by being regarded through the glasses of gratitude.

Mrs. Aouda confirmed the Parsee guide's explanation of her past history. She was, in fact, of the highest native caste.

Many Parsee merchants had made great fortunes in cotton in India. One of them, Sir Jamsetjee Jejeebhoy, has been made a baronet by the English Government, and Mrs. Aouda was connected with this personage, who was then living in Bombay. It was a cousin of his whom she hoped to join at Hong Kong, and with whom she trusted to find protection. She could not say whether she would be received or not; but Mr. Fogg told her not to trouble herself, as all would come mathematically square. These were the words he used. It was uncertain whether the young lady quite understood him. She fixed her great eyes – "those eyes as limpid as the sacred lakes of the Himalayas" – upon him; but Mr. Fogg was as impassive as ever, and did not show any disposition to throw himself into those lakes.

The first portion of the voyage passed very pleasantly. Everything was favourable. The *Rangoon* soon sighted the great Andaman, with its picturesque mountain called Saddle Peak, two thousand four hundred feet high, a landmark for all sailors. They skirted the coast, but they saw none of the inhabitants. The appearance of the islands was magnificent. Immense forests of palm, teak, and gigantic mimosas (tree-ferns), covered the foreground of the landscape, while at the back rose the undulating profile of the hills. The cliffs swarmed with that species of swallows which build the edible nests so prized in China.

But the islands were soon passed, and the *Rangoon* rapidly

steamed towards the Straits of Malacca, which give access to the Chinese Sea.

Now what is Fix doing all this time? Having left instructions for the transmission of the warrant to Hong Kong, he had embarked on board the *Rangoon* without being perceived by Passe-partout, and was in hopes to be able to keep out of sight until the steamer should have reached her destination. In fact, it would be difficult to explain his presence on board without awakening the suspicions of Passe-partout, who thought him in Bombay. But fate obliged him to resume acquaintance with the lad, as we shall see later.

All the aspirations and hopes of the detective were now centred in Hong Kong, for the steamer would not stop at Singapore long enough for him to do anything there. It was at Hong Kong that the arrest must be made, or the thief would escape, and, so to speak, for ever.

Hong Kong, in fact, was English territory, but the last British territory which they would see on the route. Beyond that, China, Japan, and America would offer an almost secure asylum to Mr. Fogg. If they should find the warrant of arrest at Hong Kong, Fix could hand Fogg over to the local police, and have done with him. But after leaving the island a simple warrant would not be sufficient; a warrant of extradition would be necessary, which would give rise to delays of all kinds, and of which the criminal might take advantage and escape; so if he did not arrest him at Hong Kong, he might give up the idea altogether.

"Now," said Fix to himself, "either the warrant will be at Hong Kong, and I shall arrest my man, or it will not be there; and this time I must delay his departure at any cost. I have failed both at Bombay and Calcutta, and if I make a mess of it at Hong Kong, my reputation is gone. I must succeed, at any cost; but what means shall I adopt to stop him if the worst comes to the worst?"

Fix then, as a last resource, made up his mind to tell Passe-partout everything, and what sort of a man his master was, for he was not his accomplice evidently. Passe-partout would no doubt under those circumstances assist him (Fix). But in any case this was a dangerous expedient, and one not to be employed except under pressure. A hint from Passe-partout to his master would upset the whole thing at once.

The detective, therefore, was very much embarrassed, and the presence of Mrs. Aouda on board gave him more food for thought. Who was this woman? and how did it happen that she was in Fogg's society? They must have met between Bombay and Calcutta, but at what place? Was it by chance, or had he purposely gone to seek this charming woman? for she was charming no doubt – Fix had seen as much in the court at Calcutta.

He was puzzled, and began to think that perhaps there had been an elopement. He was certain of it. This idea now took complete possession of Fix, and he began to think what advantage he could gain from the circumstance: whether the young lady was married or not, there was still the elopement; and he might make it so unpleasant for Mr. Fogg at Hong Kong that he would not be able to get away by paying money.

But the *Rangoon* had to get to Hong Kong first, and could he wait? for Fogg had an unpleasant habit of jumping from one steamer to another, and might be far away before anything had been settled. The thing to do, therefore, was to give notice to the English authorities, and to signal the *Rangoon* before she arrived. This was not difficult, as the steamer stopped at Singapore, and he could telegraph thence to Hong Kong.

In any case, before taking decisive action, he determined to question Passe-partout. He knew it was not difficult to make the lad talk, and Fix decided to make himself known. There was no time to lose, for the steamer would reach Singapore the following day.

That afternoon, therefore, Fix left his cabin, and seeing Passe-partout on deck, the detective rushed towards him, exclaiming:

"What, you on board the *Rangoon*?"

"Mr. Fix, is it really you?" said Passe-partout, as he recognized his fellow-voyager of the *Mongolia*. "Why, I left you at Bombay, and here you are on the way to Hong Kong. Are you also going round the world?"

"No," replied Fix, "I think of stopping at Hong Kong for a few days, at any rate."

"Ah!" said Passe-partout, "but how is it I have not seen you on board since we left Calcutta?"

"The fact is I have not been very well, and obliged to stay below. The Bay of Bengal does not suit me as well as the Indian Ocean. And how is your master, Mr. Phileas Fogg?"

"Oh, quite well, and as punctual to his time as ever; but Mr. Fix, you do not know that we have got a young lady with us."

"A young lady?" repeated the detective, who pretended not to understand what was said.

Passe-partout nodded, and immediately proceeded to give him the history of the business at the pagoda, the purchase of the elephant, the suttee, the rescue of Aouda, the judgement of the Calcutta court, and their release on bail. Fix, who was quite familiar with the last incidents, pretended to be ignorant of all, and Passe-partout was quite delighted to have such an interested listener.

"But," said Fix, when his companion had ceased, "does your master wish to carry this young lady to Europe?"

"By no means, Mr. Fix, by no means. We are simply going to Hong Kong, to place her under the care of a relative of hers, a rich merchant there."

"Nothing to be done on that line," said the detective to himself, as he concealed his disappointment. "Come and have a glass of gin, monsieur."

"With all my heart, Mr. Fix; the least we can do is to have a friendly glass to our meeting on board the *Rangoon*."

CHAPTER XVII
WHAT HAPPENED ON THE VOYAGE BETWEEN SINGAPORE AND HONG KONG

AFTER THAT, PASSE-PARTOUT and the detective met frequently, but the latter was very reserved and did not attempt to pump his companion respecting Mr. Fogg. He only encountered that gentleman once or twice, for he kept very much in the cabin, attending on Mrs. Aouda, or engaged in a game of whist.

As for Passe-partout, he began to meditate seriously upon the curious chance which had brought Mr. Fix once again on his master's track, and it certainly was somewhat astonishing. How was it that this amiable, good-natured gentleman, whom they had met first at Suez, and on board the *Mongolia*, who had landed at Bombay, where he said he was going to remain, was now on board the *Rangoon* bound for Hong Kong, and, in a word, following Mr. Fogg step by step – that was the question? It certainly was a most extraordinary coincidence, and what did Fix want? Passe-partout was ready to wager his Indian shoes, which all this time he had carefully preserved, that this man Fix would leave Hong Kong with them, and probably on board the same steamer.

If Passe-partout had worried his head for a hundred years, he never would have hit upon the real object of the detective. It would never have occurred to him that Phileas Fogg was being tracked round the globe for a robbery. But as it is only human nature to find some explanation for everything, this is how Passe-partout interpreted Fix's unremitting attention, and after all it was not an unreasonable conclusion to arrive at. In fact, he made up his mind that Fix was an agent sent after Mr. Fogg by the members of the Reform Club, to see that the conditions of the wager were properly carried out.

"That's it," repeated Passe-partout to himself, very proud of his shrewdness. "He is a spy these gentlemen have sent out. It is scarcely a gentlemanly thing to do, Mr. Fogg is so honourable and straightforward. Fancy sending a spy after us! Ah, gentlemen of the Reform Club, this shall cost you dearly."

Passe-partout, quite delighted with the discovery, determined to say nothing to his master on the subject, lest he should be very justly offended at his opponents' distrust, but he determined to chaff Fix at every opportunity without betraying himself.

On Wednesday, the 30th of October, the *Rangoon* entered the Straits of Malacca, which separate that peninsula from Sumatra, and at four o'clock the next morning the *Rangoon*, having gained half a day in advance of time, anchored at Singapore to coal.

Phileas Fogg having noted the gain in his book, went ashore accompanied by Mrs. Aouda, who expressed a wish to land for a few hours.

Fix, who was very suspicious of Fogg's movements, followed without being noticed; and Passe-partout, who was secretly amused at the detective's manœuvres, went about his usual business.

The island of Singapore, though not grand or imposing, still has its peculiar beauties. It is a park traversed by pleasant roads. A well-appointed carriage took Phileas Fogg and Aouda through palm-groves and clove-plantations, various tropical plants per-fumed the air, while troops of monkeys gambolled in the trees; the woods, also, were not innocent of tigers, and to those travellers who were astonished to learn why these terrible animals were not destroyed in such a small island, the reply would be that they swam across from the mainland.

After a couple of hours' drive, Mr. Fogg and Aouda returned to the town and went on board ship again, all the time followed by the detective. Passe-partout was awaiting them on deck; the brave fellow had purchased some beautiful mangoes, and was enabled to offer them to Mrs. Aouda, who received them gracefully.

At eleven o'clock the *Rangoon* resumed her voyage and a few hours later Malacca had sunk below the horizon. They had about thirteen hundred miles to traverse to reach Hong Kong, and Phileas Fogg hoped to get there in six days, so as to be able to catch the steamer for Yokohama on the 6th of November.

The weather, which had hitherto been very fine, changed with the last quarter of the moon. There was a high wind, fortunately favourable, and a very heavy sea.

The captain set the sails at every opportunity, and the *Rangoon*, under these circumstances, made rapid progress. But in very rough weather extra precautions were necessary, and steam had to be reduced. This delay did not appear to affect Phileas Fogg in the least, but it worried Passe-partout tremendously. He swore at the captain, the engineers, and the company, and consigned all concerned to a warmer climate than Hong Kong. Perhaps the thought of the gas that was still burning in his room in London may have had something to do with his impatience.

"You seem in a great hurry to reach Hong Kong," said Fix to him one day.

"I am," replied Passe-partout.

"You think Mr. Fogg is anxious to catch the steamer for Yokohama?"

"Very anxious indeed."

"You believe in this journey round the world, then?"

"Most decidedly; don't you?"

"Not a bit of it."

"You are a sly one," replied Passe-partout with a wink.

This remark rather disturbed Fix, without his knowing why. Could the Frenchman have discovered who he was? He did not know what to do. But how could Passe-partout have found out his real object? And yet in speaking as he did, Passe-partout must certainly have had some ulterior motive.

On a subsequent occasion the valet went still further, and said, half maliciously:

"Well, Mr. Fix, shall we be so unfortunate as to lose the pleasure of your society at Hong Kong?"

"Well," replied Fix, somewhat embarrassed, "I am not quite sure. You see—"

"Ah," said Passe-partout, "if you would only come with us I should be so delighted. An agent of the company cannot stop halfway, you know. You were only going to Bombay, and here you are almost in China. America is not far off, and from America to Europe is but a step."

Fix looked very hard at his companion, whose face was perfectly innocent, and laughed too. But Passe-partout was in the humour for quizzing, and asked him if he made much by his present business.

"Yes and no," replied Fix, without flinching. "We have our good and bad times, but of course I do not travel at my own expense."

"Of that I am quite sure," said Passe-partout, laughing.

Fix then returned to his cabin, where he remained deep in thought. Somehow or another the Frenchman had found him out, but had he told his master? Was he his accomplice or not? And must the whole thing be given up? The detective passed many hours considering the matter in all its bearings, and was as undecided at the end as he had been at the beginning.

But he retained his presence of mind, and resolved at length to deal frankly with Passe-partout, if he could not arrest Fogg at Hong Kong. Either the servant was an accomplice, knowing everything, and he would fail; or the servant knew nothing, and then his interest would be to quit the service of the criminal.

Such was the state of affairs, and meantime Phileas Fogg appeared perfectly indifferent to everything. But nevertheless there was a disturbing cause not far off, which might be able to produce an influence on his heart; but no, Mrs. Aouda's charms had no effect, to the great surprise of Passe-partout.

Yes, it certainly was a matter of astonishment to that worthy man, who every day read the lady's gratitude to his master in Mrs. Aouda's eyes. Phileas Fogg must certainly be heartless; brave he was no doubt, but sympathetic, no. There was no proof that the incidents of the journey had wakened any feelings in his breast, while Passe-partout was continually indulging in reverie.

One day he was contemplating the working of the machinery, when a pitch of the vessel threw the screw out of the water. The steam roared through the valves, and Passe-partout exclaimed, indignantly: "The escape valves are not sufficiently charged! We make no way! That is English all over. Ah! if this were only an American ship – we might blow up, perhaps, but at any rate we should go quicker meantime."

CHAPTER XVIII

IN WHICH PHILEAS FOGG, PASSE-PARTOUT, AND FIX SEVERALLY GO EACH ABOUT HIS OWN BUSINESS

DURING THE LATTER part of the voyage the weather was very bad; the wind was blowing freshly – almost a gale – right in the teeth of the *Rangoon*, which rolled considerably, and disturbed the passengers very much. In fact, on the 3rd and 4th of November there was quite a tempest, and the *Rangoon* was obliged to proceed slowly. All the sails were furled, and the captain was of opinion that they would be twenty hours late at Hong Kong, or perhaps more, if the storm lasted.

Phileas Fogg gazed at the turbulent sea as coolly as ever; he betrayed no impatience, even though twenty hours' delay would upset his calculations, by causing him to lose the Yokohama steamer. It seemed almost as if the storm were part of his programme, and Mrs. Aouda, who sympathized with him, was surprised to find him quite unmoved.

But Fix did not look upon these things with unconcern; he was very glad that the storm had happened, and would have been delighted if the *Rangoon* had been obliged to scud before the tempest. All these delays were in his favour, because they tended towards detaining Mr. Fogg at Hong Kong; he did not mind the sea-sickness he suffered, and while his body was tortured, his spirit was exultant.

But Passe-partout was very much annoyed by this bad weather. All had gone well till now. Everything had appeared to favour his master, hitherto. Steamers and railways obeyed him; wind and steam had united to assist him. Was it possible that the hour of misfortune had struck? Passe-partout felt as if the wager of twenty thousand pounds was to come out of his own purse. The storm exasperated him, the wind made him furious, and he would like to have whipped this disobedient sea. Poor fellow! Fix all the time carefully concealed his personal satisfaction, for had Passe-partout perceived it, Fix would have had a bad time.

Passe-partout remained on deck as long as the storm lasted, for it was quite impossible for him to go down below. He assisted the crew in every way in his power, and astonished the sailors by his activity. He questioned the captain, the officers, and the men hundreds of times as to their progress, and got laughed at for his pains. He wanted to know how long the tempest would last, and was referred to the barometer, which had evidently not made up its mind to rise; even when Passe-partout shook it, it would not change its mind.

At last the storm subsided, and the wind veered round to the south, which was in their favour. Passe-partout regained his serenity as the weather improved. Sails were once more set on the *Rangoon*, and she resumed her route at great speed, but she could not make up for lost time. It could not be helped, however, and land was not signalled till five o'clock on the morning of the 6th of November. The itinerary of Phileas Fogg showed that they ought to have arrived the day before, so they were twenty-four hours behindhand, and the Yokohama steamer would be missed.

At six o'clock the pilot came on board. Passe-partout longed to ask the man if the Yokohama steamer had sailed, but he preferred to nurse his hopes till the last moment. He had confided his troubles to Fix, who, sly fellow as he was, pretended to sympathize with him, and told him he would be in time if his master took the next steamer, a remark which put Passe-partout into a violent rage.

But if he did not like to ask the pilot, Mr. Fogg, having consulted his Bradshaw, did not hesitate to inquire when the steamer left for Yokohama.

"To-morrow, at the morning's flood-tide," replied the pilot.

"Ah, indeed," said Mr. Fogg, without manifesting any emotion.

Passe-partout could have embraced the pilot for this information, while Fix would gladly have twisted his neck.

"What is the name of the steamer?" asked Mr. Fogg.

"The *Carnatic*," replied the pilot.

"Ought she not to have sailed yesterday?"

"Yes; but one of her boilers required repairing, so she will not start till to-morrow."

"Thank you," replied Mr. Fogg, as he descended quietly to the cabin.

Passe-partout wrung the pilot's hand, exclaiming, "Well, you are a good fellow."

Probably to this day the pilot has not the slightest idea of what Passe-partout was driving at. He merely whistled, and went back to his station on the bridge to guide the steamer through a flotilla of junks, tankas, and fishing-boats, and a crowd of other vessels which encumbered the waters of Hong Kong.

At one o'clock the steamer was alongside the quay, and the passengers went ashore.

On this occasion it must be confessed that fortune had singularly favoured Phileas Fogg. But for the necessary repairs to her boilers, the *Carnatic* would have sailed on the 5th, and the travellers bound for Japan would have been obliged to wait for eight days for the next steamer. Mr. Fogg, it is true, was twenty-four hours behindhand, but this would not seriously affect his journey.

In fact, the steamer which plied from Yokohama to San Francisco was connected with the Hong Kong boat, and would not start till the arrival of the latter; so, if he were twenty-four hours late at Yokohama, he would make it up in crossing the Pacific. At present, however, Phileas Fogg found himself twenty-four hours late during the thirty-five days since he quitted London.

The *Carnatic* would sail the next morning at five o'clock, so Mr. Fogg had still sixteen hours to devote to Mrs. Aouda. He landed with the young lady upon his arm, and conducted her to the Club-house Hotel, where apartments were engaged for her accommodation. Mr. Fogg then went in search of her relatives, telling Passe-partout to remain until his return, so that the young lady might not feel herself quite alone.

Mr. Fogg made his way to the exchange, for he rightly conjectured that such a rich man as Jejeeb would be most likely heard of in that direction.

The broker to whom Mr. Fogg addressed himself knew the

man for whom he was inquiring, but he had left China two years before, and gone to live in Holland, he thought; for he had principally traded with Dutch merchants.

Phileas Fogg returned to the hotel, and informed Mrs. Aouda that her cousin had left Hong Kong, and had gone to live in Holland.

Mrs. Aouda made no reply for a moment; she passed her hand across her brow, and appeared lost in thought. At length, in a gentle voice, she said, "What ought I to do, Mr. Fogg?"

"Your course is simple enough," he replied; "come on to Europe."

"But I cannot intrude upon you."

"You do not intrude in the least. Passe-partout."

"Sir."

"Go to the *Carnatic* and secure three berths."

Passe-partout was delighted to think that the young lady was going to continue her journey with them, for she had been very kind to him. He accordingly quitted the hotel to execute his master's orders cheerfully.

CHAPTER XIX
SHOWING HOW PASSE-PARTOUT TOOK TOO GREAT AN INTEREST IN HIS MASTER, AND WHAT CAME OF IT

HONG KONG IS only an island, which fell into the possession of the English by the Treaty of Nankin, in 1843. In a few years the colonizing enterprise of the British made of it an important city and a fine port – Victoria. The island is at the mouth of the Canton river, sixty miles only from Macao, upon the opposite bank. Hong Kong has beaten the other port in the struggle for commercial supremacy, and the greater traffic in Chinese merchandise finds its way to the island. There are docks, hospitals, wharfs, warehouses, a cathedral, a Government house, macadamized roads, &c., which give to Hong Kong as English an aspect as a town in Kent or Surrey, which had by some accident fallen to the antipodes.

Passe-partout, with his hands in his pockets, wandered towards Port Victoria, gazing at the people as they passed, and admiring the palanquins and other conveyances. The city appeared to him like Bombay, Calcutta, and Singapore; or like any other town colonized by the English.

At the port situated at the mouth of the Canton river was a regular confusion of ships of all nations, commercial and war-like: junks, sempas, tankas, and even flower-boats, like floating garden-borders. Passe-partout remarked several of the natives, elderly men, clothed in nankeen; and when he went to a barber's to be shaved, he inquired of the man, who spoke pretty good English, who they were, and was informed that these men were all eighty years of age, and were therefore permitted to wear the imperial colour, namely yellow. Passe-partout, without exactly knowing why, thought this very funny.

After being shaved, he went to the quay from which the *Carnatic* was to start, and there he found Fix walking up and down, in a very disturbed manner.

"Ho, ho!" thought Passe-partout, "this does not look well for the Reform Club"; and with a merry smile he accosted the detective without appearing to have noticed his vexation. Fix had indeed good reasons for feeling annoyed. The warrant had not arrived. No doubt it was on its way, but it was quite impos-sible it could reach Hong Kong for several days, and as this was the last British territory at which Mr. Fogg would touch, he would escape if he could not be detained somehow.

"Well, Mr. Fix," said Passe-partout, "have you decided to come to America with us?"

"Yes," replied Fix, between his clenched teeth.

"Come along, then," said Passe-partout, laughing loudly; "I knew you could not leave us. Come and engage your berth."

So they went to the office, and took four places. But the clerk informed them that the *Carnatic*, having had her repairs com-pleted, would sail that evening at eight o'clock, and not next morning, as previously announced.

"Very good," said Passe-partout, "that will suit my master exactly. I will go and tell him."

And now Fix determined to make a bold move. He would tell Passe-partout everything. This was perhaps the only way by which he could keep Phileas Fogg at Hong Kong.

As they quitted the office, Fix offered his companion some refreshment, which Passe-partout accepted. They saw a tavern close by, which they entered, and reached a large well-decorated room, at the end of which was a large camp-bedstead furnished with cushions. On this lay a number of men asleep. About thirty people were seated at small tables drinking beer, porter, brandy, or other liquors; and the majority of drinkers were smoking long pipes of red clay filled with little balls of opium steeped in rose-water. From time to time a smoker would subside under the table, and the waiters would carry him and place him on the bed at the end of the room. There were about twenty of these stupe-fied smokers altogether.

Fix and Passe-partout perceived that they had entered a smoking-house, patronized by those wretched idiots devoted to one of the most injurious vices of humanity – the smoking of opium, which the English merchants sell every year to the value of one million four hundred thousand pounds. The Chinese Government has vainly endeavoured by stringent laws to remedy the evil, but in vain. The habit has descended from the rich to the poorest classes, and now opium is smoked everywhere at all times by men and women, and those accustomed to it cannot do without it. A great smoker can consume eight pipes a day, but he dies in five years.

It was to one of these dens that Fix and Passe-partout had come for refreshment; the latter had no money, but accepted his companion's treat, hoping to return the civility at some future time. Fix ordered two bottles of port, to which the Frenchman paid considerable attention, while Fix, more cautious, watched his companion narrowly. They talked upon many subjects, and particularly respecting Fix's happy determination to sail in the *Carnatic*, and that put Passe-partout in mind that he ought to go and inform his master respecting the alteration in the time of the steamer's departure, which, as the bottles were empty, he proceeded to do.

"Just one moment," said Fix, detaining him.

"What do you want, Mr. Fix?"

"I want to speak to you seriously."

"Seriously!" exclaimed Passe-partout. "Well, then, let us talk to-morrow, I have no time to-day."

"You had better wait," said Fix; "it concerns your master."

Passe-partout looked closely at his companion, and as the expression of his face was peculiar he sat down again.

"What have you got to say to me?" he said.

Fix placed his hand on his companion's arm, and said, in a low voice, "You have guessed who I am, eh?"

"Rather," replied Passe-partout.

"Well, then, I am going to tell you everything."

"Yes, now that I know everything, my friend. That's pretty good. However, go on; but first let me tell you that those gentlemen have sent you on a wild-goose chase."

"It is evident that you do not know how large the sum in question is," said Fix.

"Oh yes, but I do," said Passe-partout, "it is twenty thousand pounds."

"Fifty-five thousand," replied Fix, shaking the Frenchman's hand.

"What!" exclaimed Passe-partout, "has Mr. Fogg risked fifty-five thousand pounds? Well, then, all the more reason we should not lose any time," he added, as he rose from his chair.

"Fifty-five thousand pounds," continued Fix, pressing his companion into his seat again, as a flask of brandy was placed before them; "and if I succeed I shall get a percentage of two thousand pounds. If you will assist me I will give you five hundred."

"Assist you!" exclaimed Passe-partout, as he stared wildly at the detective.

"Yes, assist me to keep Mr. Fogg here for some hours longer."

"What is that you say?" said Passe-partout. "Not content with tracking my master, do these gentlemen suspect his good face and wish to put obstacles in his way? I am ashamed of them."

"What are you talking about?" said Fix.

"I say it is a piece of meanness; they might just as well pick Mr. Fogg's pocket."

"That is just the very thing we want to do."

"Then it is a conspiracy, is it?" exclaimed Passe-partout, who was getting excited by the brandy which he unconsciously had swallowed, "a regular conspiracy; and they call themselves gentlemen and friends!"

Fix began to feel very puzzled.

"Friends!" exclaimed Passe-partout, "members of the Reform Club, indeed! Do you know, Mr. Fix, that my master is an honest man, and when he has made a bet he wins it fairly?"

"But can you guess who I am?" said Fix, looking steadily at Passe-partout.

"An agent of the members of the club, whose business it is to hinder my master; and a dirty job it is, too; so although I have found you out long ago, I did not like to betray you to Mr. Fogg."

"Then he knows nothing about it," said Fix quickly.

"Nothing," replied Passe-partout, emptying his glass once more.

The detective passed his hand over his eyes and considered what he was to do. Passe-partout appeared sincere, and this rendered his plan all the more difficult; he evidently was not his master's accomplice. "He will, therefore, help me," said Fix to himself.

There was no time to lose. At any risk Fogg must be stopped at Hong Kong.

"Listen," said Fix, in a sharp tone; "I am not what you think me."

"Bah!" said Passe-partout.

"I am a detective, sent out by the police authorities in London."

"You a detective?"

"Yes, I can prove it. Here is my authority"; and drawing a paper from his pocketbook, he exhibited his instructions to the stupefied Passe-partout, who was unable to utter a word.

"This wager of Mr. Fogg's," continued Fix, "is merely to blindfold you and his colleagues at the Reform Club. He had a motive in securing your unconscious complicity."

"But why?" said Passe-partout.

"For this reason. On the 28th of last September, the sum of fifty-five thousand pounds was stolen from the Bank of England, by a person whose description is fortunately known. That description tallies exactly with Mr. Fogg's appearance."

"Absurd," exclaimed Passe-partout, striking the table with his fist; "my master is the most honest man in the world."

"What do you know about it?" replied Fix. "You only entered his service on the day he left on a mad excursion, without luggage, and carrying an immense sum in bank-notes; and do you dare to maintain that he is an honest man?"

"Yes, yes," repeated the other mechanically.

"Do you wish to be arrested as an accomplice?"

Passe-partout clutched his head with both hands; he was stupefied. He did not dare to look at the detective. Phileas Fogg a robber! This brave, generous man, the rescuer of Aouda, a thief? And yet circumstantial evidence was strong. Passe-partout did not wish to believe it. He could not believe in his master's guilt.

"Well, then, what do you want me to do?" he said, with an effort.

"Look here," said Fix: "I have tracked Mr. Fogg so far, but as yet I have not received a warrant, which I asked to be sent from London. You must help me to keep your master in Hong Kong."

"But I—"

"If so, I will share with you the reward of two thousand pounds promised by the bank."

"Never!" replied Passe-partout, who attempted to rise, but fell back utterly exhausted and stupefied.

"Mr. Fix," he stammered, "even if you have told the truth, supposing my master is the thief you are searching for – which I deny – I have been, I am still in his service; he is kind and generous to me, and I will never betray him for all the gold in the world."

"You refuse, then?"

"Absolutely."

"Well, then," said Fix, "forget all I have said. And now let us have a drink."

"Yes, let us have another glass."

Passe-partout felt that the liquor was overcoming him more and more. Fix having made up his mind that he must be separated from his master at any price, determined to finish the matter. On the table were some pipes of opium. Fix handed one of these to Passe-partout, who took a few puffs and fell back perfectly insensible.

"At last," muttered Fix, as Passe-partout collapsed. "Mr. Fogg will not hear of the change of time for the sailing of the *Carnatic*, and if so, he will have to go without this infernal Frenchman."

Then paying the score, he quitted the tavern.

CHAPTER XX
SHOWING HOW FIX AND FOGG COME FACE TO FACE

WHILE THESE EVENTS, which gravely compromised Mr. Fogg's future, were passing, that gentleman and Mrs. Aouda were walking through the town. Since she had accepted Mr. Fogg's escort to England, she wished to make some purchases for the voyage, for a lady could not travel with a hand-bag, as a gentleman might do. So she bought some necessary clothing, etc., and Mr. Fogg overcame all her excuses with his characteristic generosity.

"It is in my own interest," he invariably replied; "a part of my programme."

Having purchased what they required, they returned to dinner at the hotel. Mrs. Aouda subsequently retired to rest, leaving Mr. Fogg reading *The Times* and *Illustrated News*.

Had Mr. Fogg been a man likely to be astonished at anything, he would have been surprised at the absence of his servant at bedtime; so believing that the steamer did not start for Yokohama till the following morning, he did not trouble himself, but Passepartout did not appear when Mr. Fogg rang for him next morning, and then he learnt that his servant had not come in during the night. Without a word Mr. Fogg packed his bag, and sent to call Mrs. Aouda and for a palanquin. It was eight o'clock, and the *Carnatic* was to sail at high-water at half-past nine. Mr. Fogg and his companion got into the palanquin and reached the quay. Then, and not till then, they were informed that the *Carnatic* had left the previous evening.

Mr. Fogg, who had made up his mind to find the steamer and the servant both awaiting him, was obliged to go without either. He showed no anxiety, merely remarking to Mrs. Aouda, "An incident of travel, madam, nothing more."

At this moment, a man who had been watching them approached. It was Fix. He approached Mr. Fogg, and said:

"Were you not one of the passengers on board the *Rangoon* yesterday, as well as myself?"

"Yes, sir," replied Mr. Fogg coldly; "but I have not the honour—"

"Excuse me, but I expected to find your servant here."

"Do you know where he is?" asked the young lady quickly.

"What!" exclaimed Fix, in feigned surprise, "is he not with you?"

"No," replied Mrs. Aouda, "he has been absent since yesterday. Perhaps he has sailed in the *Carnatic*."

"Without you, madam?" said the detective. "You will excuse my question, but you counted on leaving in that steamer?"

"Yes, sir."

"So did I, madam; and I am terribly disappointed. The fact is, the *Carnatic* was ready for sea twelve hours sooner than was expected, and now we shall have to wait twelve days for another steamer."

Fix was delighted as he said this. In eight days the warrant would arrive. His chances were good. But his disgust may be guessed when he heard Fogg say, in his usual calm tone, "I suppose there are other ships besides the *Carnatic* in Hong Kong harbour"; and offering his arm to Mrs. Aouda, he turned away towards the docks.

Fix followed him in a dogged sort of manner. He appeared to be attached to Fogg by some invisible cord. But fortune had evidently abandoned Phileas Fogg. For three mortal hours he wandered about the docks, endeavouring to charter a vessel to take him to Yokohama; but all the ships were either loading or unloading, and could not go. The detective's spirits rose again.

But Mr. Fogg was not discouraged. He made up his mind to continue his search, even if he had to cross to Macao. At length he was accosted by a sailor.

"Is your honour looking for a boat?"

"Have you a boat ready to sail?" asked Mr. Fogg.

"I have. A pilot-boat, No. 43; the best in the harbour."

"Can she sail fast?"

"She can make eight or nine knots an hour, or more. Would you like to see her?"

"Yes."

"You will be pleased, I am sure. Is it for a trip that you require her?"

"Somewhat more than that; for a voyage."

"A voyage?"

"I want you to take me to Yokohama."

The sailor folded his arms and looked steadily at Mr. Fogg. "Is your honour serious?" he said.

"Yes. I have lost the *Carnatic*, and I must be at Yokohama on the 14th, at latest, to catch the steamer for San Francisco."

"I am very sorry," replied the pilot, "but it is impossible."

"I will give you a hundred pounds a day and a bonus of two hundred pounds, if you arrive in time."

"Are you in earnest?" asked the pilot.

"Very much so," replied Mr. Fogg.

The pilot took a turn up and down the wharf, he looked out to sea, and was evidently struggling between his wish to get the money and his fear of venturing so far. Fix, all this time, was on tenter-hooks.

Mr. Fogg turned to Mrs. Aouda, and asked her if she were afraid.

"Not with you, Mr. Fogg," replied the young lady.

Just then the pilot returned, twirling his hat in his hands.

"Well, pilot?" said Mr. Fogg.

"Well, your honour," replied the pilot; "I cannot risk my life, or my men, or even you in such a voyage, in so small a ship, at this time of year. Besides, we could not get to Yokohama in time. It is one thousand six hundred and fifty miles away."

"Only one thousand six hundred," said Mr. Fogg.

"Oh, it is all the same." Fix breathed again. "But," continued the pilot, "we might manage it in another way."

Fix scarcely dared to breathe.

"How do you mean?" asked Fogg.

"By going to Nagasaki, which is only eleven hundred miles, or to Shanghai, which is eight hundred. In the latter case we shall be able to keep close inshore, and have advantage of the current."

"But," replied Fogg, "I must take the American mail steamer at Yokohama, and not at Shanghai or Nagasaki."

"Well, why not?" replied the pilot. "The *San Francisco* does not start from Yokohama; it starts from Shanghai, and only calls at Yokohama and Nagasaki."

"Are you quite sure of that?"

"Certain."

"And when does she leave Shanghai?"

"On the 11th, at seven o'clock in the evening. So we have four days, which are ninety-six hours; and at the rate of eight knots an hour, if the wind hold, we shall be able to reach Shanghai in time."

"And when will you be able to start?"

"In an hour. I only want to buy some provisions and bend the sails."

"Well, it is a bargain. Are you the owner?"

"Yes; my name is John Bunsby, owner of the *Tankadere*."

"Would you like something on account?"

"If convenient to your honour."

"Here are two hundred pounds. Sir," continued Fogg, turning to Fix, "if you would like to take advantage of this opportunity—"

"Thank you, sir," replied Fix. "I was about to beg the favour of you."

"Well, then, we shall be ready in half an hour."

"But what shall we do about the servant?" said Mrs. Aouda, who was much distressed at Passe-partout's absence.

"I will do all I can for him," replied Fogg; and while they directed their steps towards the police-office, Fix went on board the pilot-boat. Phileas left the description of his servant with the police, and a sum of money to be spent in seeking him. The same formality was gone through at the French Consulate; and then procuring their luggage, which had been sent back to the hotel, they went down to the wharf.

Three o'clock struck; the pilot-boat No. 43 was ready to start. She was a pretty little schooner, about twenty tons, built for speed, like a racing-yacht. She was as bright and clean as possible, and Bunsby evidently took a pride in his little craft. Her masts raked rather. She carried foresail and the usual sails for a ship of her tonnage. She could evidently make good way, as indeed she had proved by winning several prizes.

The crew consisted of the owner and four other men, all well acquainted with the neighbouring seas, which they scoured in search of ships wanting pilots. John Bunsby was a man of about five-and-forty, vigorous and full of decision and energy, calculated to reassure the most nervous passengers.

Phileas Fogg and Mrs. Aouda went on board, where they found Fix already installed. The accommodation was not extensive, but everything was clean and neat.

"I am sorry I have nothing better to offer you," said Mr. Fogg to Fix. The latter bowed without replying, for he felt somewhat humiliated in accepting Mr. Fogg's kindness under the circumstances.

"At any rate," he thought, "if he is a rascal he is a very polite one."

At ten minutes past three the sails were hoisted, the English flag was run up to the peak; the passengers took a last look at the quays in the hope of descrying Passe-partout, but they were disappointed. Fix was somewhat afraid that some chance might bring the lad whom he had treated so badly in that direction, and then an explanation would surely have ensued of a nature by no means satisfactory to the detective. But the Frenchman did not turn up, and no doubt he was still under the influence of the opium.

So John Bunsby stood out to sea, and the *Tankadere*, with the wind on the quarter, went bounding briskly over the waves.

CHAPTER XXI
SHOWING HOW THE OWNER OF THE *TANKADERE* NEARLY LOST THE BONUS OF TWO HUNDRED POUNDS

THIS VOYAGE OF eight hundred miles was one of great risk at that season of the year in those seas, which are usually very rough, particularly during the equinoxes, and it was then the beginning of November.

It would have been very much to the advantage of the owner of the *Tankadere* to have gone on to Yokohama, as he was paid so much a day, but such a voyage would have been extremely rash. It was a risk to go to Shanghai; still, John Bunsby had confidence in his ship, which sailed like a bird, and perhaps he was right.

"There is no need for me to urge you to speed," said Fogg to Bunsby, when they had got out to sea.

"Your honour may depend upon me," replied Bunsby; "I will do all I can."

"Well, it is your business and not mine, pilot, and I trust you thoroughly."

Phileas Fogg, standing upright, with his legs stretched apart, was as steady as a sailor as he gazed over the foaming sea. Mrs. Aouda, seated aft, was somewhat nervous as she contemplated the ocean. The sails bellied out overhead like great wings, and the schooner ran before the wind at a great pace. Night fell. The moon was only in the first quarter, and her light would soon be quenched beneath the horizon. Clouds were rising in the east, and already banking up.

The pilot hung out the vessel's lights, an indispensable proceeding, for collisions were by no means unfrequent, and any such occurrence, at the speed they were now going, would shatter the gallant little craft to pieces.

Fix, seated up in the bows, held himself aloof, as he knew Fogg was not much of a talker; besides, he did not quite like to enter into conversation with this man whose good offices he had accepted. He thought of the future, for it now seemed certain that Fogg would not stop at Yokohama, but would immediately take the steamer for San Francisco, so as to reach America, where he would be safe. Fogg's plan seemed to the detective to be very simple.

Instead of embarking in England for the United States, like a common swindler, Fogg had made a tour three-parts round the globe, so as to gain the American continent more safely; and once there, he could enjoy himself comfortably with his spoil. But what could Fix do in the United States? Should he give up the man? No, certainly not; and until he had obtained an act of extradition, he would not lose sight of him. This was his duty, and he would carry it out to the bitter end. There was one thing, at any rate, to be thankful for, Passe-partout was not now with his master; and after Fix's confidence imparted to him, it was very important that the servant should not see his master again in a hurry.

Phileas Fogg was himself thinking about his servant, who had so curiously disappeared. But after consideration of the circumstances, it did not appear improbable that the young man had gone on board the *Carnatic* at the last moment. This was also Mrs. Aouda's opinion, for she deeply regretted the worthy fellow's absence, as she was so deeply indebted to him. They might, therefore, find him at Yokohama, and if he were on the *Carnatic*, it would be easy to ascertain the fact.

About ten o'clock the breeze began to freshen, and though it might have been prudent to take in a reef or two, the pilot, after taking an observation, let the sails stand, for the *Tankadere* carried her canvas well; but everything was prepared to furl the sails in case of necessity.

At midnight, Phileas Fogg and Mrs. Aouda went below. Fix

had already turned in, but the owner and his crew remained on deck all night.

By sunrise next morning the schooner had made a hundred miles. The log showed they were going about eight or nine knots an hour. They were still carrying on, and, if the wind held, the chances were in their favour. The vessel made her way along the coast all that day. The sea was not so rough, as the wind blew off-shore, which was a very fortunate circumstance for such a small vessel.

About noon the breeze fell a little, and shifted to the south-east. The owner spread his topsails, but furled them again, as the breeze showed signs of freshening once more.

Mr. Fogg and Mrs. Aouda did not suffer from sea-sickness, and ate with a good appetite, and Fix, invited to partake of the meal, was obliged to accept very unwillingly. He did not like to travel and eat at the expense of the man he was tracking; but yet he was obliged to eat, and so he ate.

After dinner he found an opportunity to speak to Mr. Fogg privately. "Sir," he said – this term scorched his lips, so to speak, and he had to control himself; his impulse was to arrest this "gentleman" – "sir," said he, "it is very good of you to give me a passage; but although I cannot spend money as freely as you do, I shall be happy to pay my expenses."

"You need not say anything about that," replied Mr. Fogg.

"But if I insist upon it?"

"No, sir," replied Fogg, in a tone which admitted of no discussion, "this is included in my general expenses."

Fix bowed, he felt half stifled; and going forward, he sat down and did not speak for the whole day.

Meantime they were making good progress. John Bunsby was in hopes of succeeding, and frequently said to Mr. Fogg that "they would be in time"; to which Fogg merely replied that "he counted upon it". The crew, also inspired by the hope of reward, worked hard. Not a sheet required bracing, not a sail that was not well hoisted, not one unnecessary lurch could be attributed to the steersman. They could not have worked the schooner better if they had been sailing a match in the Royal Yacht Club Regatta.

By the evening the log showed that they had run two hundred and twenty miles, and Mr. Fogg hoped that when he arrived at Yokohama he would not have to record any delay in his journal.

If so, the only check he had met with since he left London would not affect his journey.

Towards morning the *Tankadere* entered the Straits of Fo-kien, which separate Formosa from the Chinese coasts. The sea was very rough, and it was difficult to stand on deck. At daybreak the wind freshened still more, and there was every appearance of a storm. The mercury rose and fell at intervals. In the south-east the sea rose in a long swell, which betokened a tempest.

The pilot studied the aspect of the heavens for a long time, and at last said to Mr. Fogg:

"I suppose I may tell your honour what I think?"

"Of course," replied Fogg.

"Well, then, we are going to have a storm."

"From the north or south?" asked Mr. Fogg calmly.

"From the south. A typhoon is approaching."

"I am glad it is coming from the south, it will help us on."

"Oh, if you look on it in that light," said Bunsby, "I have no more to say."

The presentiments of Bunsby were fulfilled. During the summer the typhoon would have been probably dissipated in an electric cascade, but in the winter it would probably have its course. So the pilot took his precautions. He took in his sails and set merely the storm-jib, and waited.

The pilot begged his passengers to go below, but in such a narrow and confined space the imprisonment was far from agreeable, so none of them would quit the deck.

About eight o'clock the hurricane, with torrents of rain, burst upon them. With nothing but the small jib, the *Tankadere* was almost lifted out of the water by the tempest. She darted through the sea like a locomotive at full-speed.

All that day the vessel was hurried towards the north, borne on the top of the monstrous waves. Time after time she was almost engulfed, but the careful steering of the pilot saved her. The passengers were drenched with spray, but took it philosophically. Fix grumbled, no doubt; but the brave Aouda regarded her companion and admired his coolness, while she endeavoured to imitate it. As for Phileas Fogg, he took it as a matter of course.

Hitherto the *Tankadere* had been sailing northwards, but towards evening, as the pilot had feared, the wind veered round to the north-west. The schooner plunged terribly in the trough of the sea, and it was fortunate she was so solidly built. The tempest increased if possible at night, and John Bunsby began to feel anxious; he consulted his crew as to what they should do.

He then came to Mr. Fogg, and said, "I think we should make for one of the ports hereabouts."

"So do I," replied Fogg.

"Yes," said the pilot; "but which?"

"I only know of one," said Fogg quietly.

"And that is—?"

"Shanghai."

This reply took the pilot aback rather at first; but recognizing Mr. Fogg's firmness, he said: "Yes, your honour is right. Shanghai be it."

So they kept their course.

The night was fearful; it seemed a miracle that the little vessel did not founder. Twice she was caught in the trough of the sea, and would have gone down, but that everything was let fly. Mrs. Aouda was knocked about, and more than once Mr. Fogg rushed to her assistance, though she made no complaint.

At daybreak the storm was still raging, but suddenly the wind backed to the south-east. This was a change for the better, and the *Tankadere* again proceeded on her course, though the cross-sea gave her some tremendous blows, sufficient to have crushed a less solid craft. The coast was occasionally visible through the mist, but not a sail was in sight.

At noon the weather cleared a little, the gale had blown itself out, and the travellers were enabled to take some rest. The night was comparatively quiet, and the pilot was induced to set a little more sail, and at daybreak next morning John Bunsby was able to declare that they were less than a hundred miles from Shanghai.

A hundred miles, and only one day to accomplish the distance. On that evening they ought to be at Shanghai if they wished to catch the steamer for Yokohama; but for the storm, which had delayed them several hours, they would then have been within thirty miles of their destination.

The breeze continued to fall, and the sea went down. All canvas was spread, and at twelve o'clock the *Tankadere* was only forty-five miles from Shanghai. Six hours still remained, and all were afraid they could not do it. Everyone on board, except Phileas Fogg no doubt, felt the keenest anxiety. They must maintain a speed of nine knots an hour, and the wind was falling rapidly, and coming in puffs.

Nevertheless, the schooner was so light and carried such a spread of canvas, besides being aided by the shore currents, that at six o'clock Bunsby reckoned they were only ten miles from the Shanghai river. The town itself was situate about twelve miles higher up.

At seven o'clock they were still three miles from Shanghai. The pilot swore a formidable oath as he perceived the bonus of two hundred pounds slipping away from him. He looked at Mr. Fogg; Mr. Fogg was impassible, although his whole fortune was in the balance.

At this moment a long black funnel, from which a thick train of smoke was issuing, appeared. This was the American steamer leaving Shanghai at the proper time.

"Confound it!" cried Bunsby, as he kept the schooner away a point.

"Signal her," said Fogg quietly.

There was a small brass cannon on the forecastle, which was used during fogs.

This piece was charged to the muzzle, but just as the pilot was going to fire, Phileas said:

"Hoist your flag."

The ensign was run up half-mast. This was a signal of distress, and they hoped that the steamer would see it and heave-to to assist them.

"Fire!" exclaimed Mr. Fogg.

And the report of the little cannon immediately boomed over the sea.

CHAPTER XXII
SHOWING HOW PASSE-PARTOUT FINDS OUT THAT, EVEN AT THE ANTIPODES, IT IS PRUDENT TO HAVE MONEY IN HIS POCKET

THE *CARNATIC*, BOUND for Japan, left Hong Kong on the 7th of November. Two cabins were unoccupied – they had been engaged by Mr. Phileas Fogg. The following morning the sailors were astonished to perceive a dishevelled, half-stupefied figure emerge from the fore-cabin and sit down on deck.

This passenger was Passe-partout, and this is what had happened:

Soon after Fix had left the opium-tavern, two waiters had laid Passe-partout upon the couch reserved for smokers; three hours later Passe-partout, haunted by one idea, woke up and struggled against the stupefying influence of the drug. The thought of his unfulfilled duties assisted him to shake off his torpor. He left the den of drunkenness, and guiding himself by the walls, he staggered on, crying out, as in a dream: "The *Carnatic*, the *Carnatic*!"

The steamer was alongside the wharf, ready to start. Passe-partout had but a few paces to traverse; he rushed across the gangway, and fell senseless on the deck just as the paddles began to revolve. The sailors, accustomed to this sort of thing, took him down to the fore-cabin, and when he awoke he was fifty miles from Hong Kong.

This is how he found himself on board the *Carnatic*, inhaling the sea-air, which sobered him by degrees He began to collect his thoughts, which was no easy matter, but at length he was able to recall the occurrences of the day before – Fix's confidence and the opium-smoking, etc.

"The fact is," he thought, "I have been very tipsy. What will Mr. Fogg say? At any rate, I have not missed the steamer, and that is the principal thing"; then he thought of Fix. "As for him," he muttered, "I trust he has not dared to follow us on board this ship, as he said. A detective tracking my master, and accusing him of robbing the Bank of England! Bosh! he is no more a robber than I am an assassin."

Now, was he to tell all this to his master? Would it not be better to wait till they all reached London, and when the detective had followed them all round the world, to have a good laugh at him? This was a point to be considered. The first thing was to find Mr. Fogg and ask his pardon.

Passe-partout accordingly got up; the sea was rough, and the ship rolled considerably. It was with some difficulty he reached the quarter-deck, but could not see anyone at all like his master or Mrs. Aouda.

"All right," he thought, "the lady is not up yet, and Mr. Fogg is probably playing whist as usual."

Passe-partout accordingly went down to the saloon. Mr. Fogg was not there. All he could do now was to ask the purser for his master's cabin. That individual replied that he knew no passenger by the name of Fogg.

"Excuse me," said Passe-partout, "he is a tall, cool, quiet-looking gentleman, and is accompanied by a young lady."

"There is no young lady on board," said the purser. "However, here is the passenger-list, and you can see for yourself."

Passe-partout did so. His master's name was not entered.

Suddenly an idea occurred to him, and he said: "Am I on the *Carnatic*?"

"Yes," replied the purser.

"On the way to Yokohama?"

"Yes, decidedly."

Passe-partout for the moment was afraid he had got on the wrong ship, but if he was on the *Carnatic* it was evident his master was not.

Passe-partout fell back on a chair. He was thunder-struck. All at once the light broke in upon his mind; he remembered that the hour of the ship sailing had been altered, that he ought to have told his master, and he had not done so. It was therefore his fault that they had missed the vessel.

His fault no doubt, but still more the fault of that traitor who had endeavoured to keep his master at Hong Kong, and had made him (Passe-partout) tipsy. He saw it all now. His master was ruined, arrested, and imprisoned perhaps. Passe-partout was furious. Ah, if Fix ever came within his reach, what a settling of accounts there would be!

Passe-partout by degrees recovered his composure, and began to look things in the face. He was on his route to Japan, at any rate, but he had no money in his pocket, and this was not a pleasant reflection. He literally did not possess a penny. Fortunately his passage had been paid, so he had five or six days to make up his mind. He ate accordingly for the whole party, and as if there was nothing to be got to eat when he reached Japan.

The *Carnatic* entered the harbour of Yokohama on the morning tide of the 13th, and came alongside the quay, near the Custom House, amidst a crowd of ships of every nationality.

Passe-partout went on shore to this curious land without any enthusiasm; he had nothing to do but to wander aimlessly through the streets. He first found himself in a thoroughly European quarter of the town, with houses ornamented with verandahs and elegant peristyles. This portion of the town occupied all the space between the promontory of the Treaty and the river, and included docks and warehouses, with many streets and squares. Here, as at Hong Kong and Calcutta, were a crowd of Americans, English, Chinese, and Dutch merchants ready to buy or sell almost anything, and Passe-partout felt as strange amongst them as a Hottentot might have done.

He had one resource at any rate, he could apply to the French or English consuls; but he shrank from telling his adventures, which were so intimately connected with his master. So before doing so, he thought he would try every other chance for a livelihood.

After traversing the European quarter, he entered the Japanese district, and made up his mind to push on to Yeddo if necessary.

The native quarter of Yokohama is called Benter, after the sea-goddess worshipped on the neighbouring islands. Here he noticed beautiful groves of fir and cedar; sacred gates of peculiar construction; bridges, enclosed by bamboos and reeds; and temples, surrounded by immense and melancholy-looking cedars, wherein Buddhist priests and votaries of Confucius resided. There were long streets with crowds of infants, who looked as if they were cut out of Japanese screens, and who were playing with bandy-legged poodles, and with yellow cats without tails, of a very lazy and very affectionate disposition.

The streets were crowded with people passing and repassing: priests, policemen, custom-house officers, and soldiers – the Mikado's guard, in silken doublets and coats of mail, as well as other soldiers of all descriptions; for in Japan the army is as much regarded as it is despised in China. There were friars, pilgrims with long robes, and civilians with long black hair, large heads, long waists, thin legs, and short of stature; with complexions, some copper-colour, some pale, but never yellow like the Chinese, from whom the Japanese differ essentially. Amongst the carriages, the palanquins, the barrows with sails, bamboo litters, he noticed many very pretty women moving about with tiny steps, on tiny feet, and shod with canvas shoes, with straw sandals and wooden clogs. They appeared to have small eyes, flat chests, black teeth, according to fashion; but wearing gracefully the national robe called "kirimon", a sort of dressing-gown, crossed with a silk scarf and tied behind in a large knot, a mode which Parisian ladies have borrowed from the Japanese.

Passe-partout wandered about in the crowd for some hours, looking at the shops, at the glittering jewellers' establishments; the restaurants, which he could not enter; the tea-houses, where they drank "saki", a liquor made from the fermentation of rice; and comfortable-looking tobacco-shops, where they smoked, not opium, which is almost unknown in Japan, but a fine tobacco. Thence he went on into the fields amongst the rice-plantations; there were flowers of all sorts, giving forth their last perfumes – beautiful camellias, not on bushes, but on trees; and bamboo enclosures, with cherry, plum, and apple trees, which the natives cultivate rather for their blossom than their fruit. On almost every cedar-tree an eagle was perched, and on the willows were melancholy herons, standing on one leg; and crows, ducks, hawks, wild geese, and a quantity of cranes, which are looked upon as sacred by the Japanese, as conferring upon them long life and happiness.

As he wandered on, Passe-partout noted some violets amid the grass. "Good," he said, "here is my supper"; but he found they were scentless.

"No chance there," he thought.

Certainly, as a precaution, he had taken care to have a good meal before he left the *Carnatic*; but after walking a whole day, he felt somewhat hungry. He had already remarked that the butchers' shops displayed neither mutton, pork, nor kids; and as he knew that it was forbidden to kill oxen, which are reserved for farming, he concluded that meat was scarce in Japan. He was not mistaken, but he could have put up with wild boar even, partridges, quails, fish, or fowl, which the Japanese eat almost exclusively with rice. However, he kept his spirits up, and looked forward to a meal next day.

Night fell, and Passe-partout re-entered the native quarter, where he wandered through the streets in the midst of coloured lanterns, looking on at the conjurers, and at the astrologers, who had collected a crowd round their telescopes. Then he wandered back to the harbour, lighted up by the fishermen's torches.

At length the streets began to get empty, and to the crowd succeeded the patrols. These officers, in their splendid uniforms and followed by their attendants, looked like ambassadors; and every time Passe-partout met one of these parties, he said to himself:

"Good, good; another Japanese embassy going to Europe."

CHAPTER XXIII
IN WHICH PASSE-PARTOUT'S NOSE GETS
IMMEASURABLY LONG

NEXT MORNING, Passe-partout, very tired and very hungry, began to think that he ought to eat something, and the sooner the better. He still had his watch, which he could sell, but he would rather die of hunger than do that; so now or never, he must make use of his powerful, if not melodious, voice, with which nature had endowed him. He knew several French and English songs, and resolved to make the attempt. The Japanese were no doubt fond of music, since they were always beating cymbals, tom-toms, and drums, and they would no doubt appreciate European talent.

But perhaps it was somewhat early to start a concert, and the *dilettanti*, awakened inopportunely, would not, perhaps, pay him in current coin of the realm. So Passe-partout decided to wait; and meantime it occurred to him that he might as well change his clothes for some more in keeping with his present position, and afterwards he might be able to purchase something to eat.

He immediately set about to carry out the idea, and after a long search he discovered a dealer in old clothes, with whom he made an exchange, and left the shop dressed in a Japanese robe and dis-coloured turban; but he had some money in his pocket also.

"All right," he thought; "I must only fancy myself at a carnival."

Passe-partout's first care was to enter a quiet-looking tea-house, and then, with a portion of fowl and some rice, he break-fasted like a man who had not yet solved the problem as to where dinner was to come from.

"Now," he thought, after a hearty meal, "I must consider what I am about. All I can do now is to sell this dress for another still more Japanesey. I must think of some means of quitting this Country of the Sun as quickly as possible, and I shall not have a very pleasant recollection of it."

He accordingly went to look at the steamers about to sail to America, for he intended to offer himself as a cook or steward, in exchange for his passage and food. Once at San Francisco he would manage to get on. The important thing was to cross the ocean. He was not the man to think about a thing very long, so he went at once to the docks; but his project, which had appeared so simple in idea, was not so easy to execute. What need was there for a cook or steward on board an American mail-boat? And how could they trust him in his present costume? What reference or recommendation could he offer?

As he was turning these questions over in his mind his gaze fell upon a placard, which a circus clown was carrying through the streets. The notice was in English, and read as follows:

THE

HONOURABLE WILLIAM BATULCAR'S TROUPE

OF

JAPANESE ACROBATS

POSITIVELY THE LAST REPRESENTATIONS, PRIOR TO THEIR
DEPARTURE FOR AMERICA,

OF THE

LONG-NOSES-LONG-NOSES

Under the Special Patronage of the God Tingou

GREAT ATTRACTION!

"The United States of America!" exclaimed Passe-partout; "that suits me all round."

He followed the "sandwich-man", and was soon in the Japanese quarter once again. In about a quarter of an hour they stopped before a large hut, adorned with flags, upon which a troupe of jugglers were depicted, without any attempt at perspective.

This was the establishment of the Honourable Mr. Batulcar, a sort of Barnum, a director of a troupe of acrobats and jugglers, who were giving their last representations, prior to their departure to the United States. Passe-partout entered and asked for the proprietor. Mr. Batulcar appeared in person.

"What do you want?" he said to Passe-partout, whom he took for a native.

"Do you need a servant, sir?" asked Passe-partout.

"A servant!" echoed the Barnum, as he stroked his beard; "I have two, obedient and faithful, who have never left me, and serve me for nothing but nourishment; and here they are," he added, as he extended his brawny arms, on which the great veins stood out like whipcord.

"So I can be of no use to you, then?"

"Not the least."

"The devil! It would have been very convenient if I could have sailed with you."

"Ah, yes," said the Honourable Batulcar; "you are just about as much a Japanese as I am a baboon, I guess. What are you dressed up like that for?"

"One is obliged to dress as one can."

"That's a fact. You are a Frenchman, ain't you?"

"Yes; a Parisian."

"Then I suppose you know how to make grimaces?"

"Well," replied Passe-partout, somewhat vexed that his nationality should provoke such a question. "It is true that we Frenchmen do know how to make grimaces, but no better than Americans."

"That's so. Well, if I cannot take you as a servant I can engage you as a clown. You see, my lad, this is how it is: in France they exhibit foreign clowns, and in foreign countries French clowns."

"I see."

"You are pretty strong, I suppose?"

"More particularly when I get up after dinner."

"And you know how to sing?"

"Yes," replied Passe-partout, who at one time had sung in the street concerts.

"But can you sing standing on your head with a top spinning on the sole of your left foot, and a sword balanced on your right foot?"

"Something of that sort," replied Passe-partout, who recalled the acrobatic performances of his youth.

"Well, that is the whole business," replied the Honourable Mr. Batulcar.

And the engagement was ratified there and then.

At length Passe-partout had found something to do. He was engaged to make one of a celebrated Japanese troupe. This was not a high position, but in eight days he would be on his way to San Francisco.

The performance was advertised to commence at three o'clock, and although Passe-partout had not rehearsed the "business", he was obliged to form one of the human pyramid composed of the "Long-Noses of the God Tingou". This was the great attraction, and was to close the performance.

The house was crowded before three o'clock by people of all races, ages, and sexes. The musicians took up their positions, and performed vigorously on their noisy instruments.

The performance was very much the same as all acrobatic displays; but it must be stated that the Japanese are the cleverest acrobats in the world. One of them, with a fan and a few bits of paper, did the butterfly and flower trick; another traced in the air with the smoke of his pipe a compliment to the audience; another juggled with some lighted candles which he extinguished successively as they passed his mouth, and which he relit one after the other without for a moment ceasing his sleight-of-hand performances; another produced a series of spinning-tops which, in his hands, played all kinds of pranks as they whirled round – they ran along the stems of pipes, on the edges of swords, upon wires, and even on hairs stretched across the stage; they spun round crystal goblets, crossed bamboo ladders, ran into all the corners of the stage, and made strange music, combining various tones, as they revolved. The jugglers threw them up in the air, knocked them from one to the other like shuttlecocks, put them into their pockets and took them out again, and all the time they never ceased to spin.

But after all the principal attraction was the performance of the "Long-Noses", which has never been seen in Europe.

These "Long-Noses" were the select company under the immediate patronage of the god Tingou. Dressed in a costume of the Middle Ages, each individual wore a pair of wings; but they were specially distinguished by the inordinate length of their noses and the uses they made of them. These noses were simply bamboos from five to ten feet long, some straight, some curved, some ribbed, and some with warts painted on them. On these noses, which were firmly fixed on their natural ones, they performed their acrobatic feats. A dozen of these artists lay upon their backs, while their comrades, dressed to represent lightning-conductors, leaped from one to the other of their friends' noses, performing the most skilful somersaults.

The whole was to conclude with the "Pyramid", as had been announced, in which fifty "Long-Noses" were to represent the

"Car of Juggernaut". But instead of forming the pyramid on each other's shoulders, these artistes mounted on each other's noses. Now one of them, who used to act as the base of the car, had left the troupe, and as only strength and adroitness were necessary for the position, Passe-partout had been selected to fill it on this occasion.

That worthy fellow felt very melancholy when he had donned his costume, adorned with parti-coloured wings, and had fixed his six-foot nose to his face; but, at any rate, the nose would procure him something to eat, and he made up his mind to do what he had to do.

He went on the stage and joined his colleagues; they all lay down on their backs, and then another party placed themselves on the long noses of the first, another tier of performers climbed up on them, then a third and fourth; and upon the noses a human monument was raised almost to the flies.

Then the applause rose loud and long. The orchestra played a deafening tune, when suddenly the pyramid shook, one of the noses at the base fell out, and the whole pyramid collapsed like a house of cards!

It was all owing to Passe-partout. Clearing himself from the scramble, and leaping over the footlights, without the aid of his wings, he scaled the gallery, and fell at the feet of one of the spectators, crying out, as he did so, "Oh my master, my master!"

"You!"

"Yes, it is I."

"Well then, under those circumstances you had better go on board the steamer."

So Mr. Fogg, Aouda, who accompanied him, and Passe-partout hastened out of the theatre. At the door they met the Honourable Mr. Batulcar, who was furious, and demanded damages for the breaking of the "Pyramid". Mr. Fogg quickly appeased him by handing him a roll of notes.

At half-past six, the appointed hour for the sailing of the vessel, Mr. Fogg, Mrs. Aouda, and Passe-partout, who still wore his wings and long nose, stepped upon the deck of the American mail-steamer.

CHAPTER XXIV
IN WHICH THE PACIFIC OCEAN IS CROSSED

THE READER WILL easily guess what happened at Shanghai. The signals made by the *Tankadere* were perceived by the mail-steamer, and soon afterwards, Phileas Fogg having paid the price agreed upon, as well as a bonus of five hundred and fifty pounds, he and his party were soon on board the steamer.

They reached Yokohama on the 14th, and Phileas Fogg, leaving Fix to his own devices, went on board the *Carnatic*, where he heard, to Aouda's great delight, and probably to his own though he did not betray it, that a Frenchman named Passe-partout had arrived in her the day before.

Mr. Fogg, who was obliged to leave for San Francisco that very evening, immediately set about searching for his servant. To no purpose was it that he inquired at the Consulate or walked about the streets, and he gave up the search. Was it by chance or presentiment that he visited Mr. Batulcar's entertainment? He would not certainly have recognized his servant in his eccentric dress, but Passe-partout had spied his master out. He could not restrain a movement of the nose, and so the collapse had occurred.

All this Passe-partout learnt from Mrs. Aouda, who also told him how they had come from Hong Kong with a certain Mr. Fix.

Passe-partout did not even wink at the name of Fix, for he thought the moment had not yet come to tell his master what had passed; so in his recital of his own adventures, he merely said that he had been overtaken by opium.

Mr. Fogg listened coldly to his excuses, and then lent him money sufficient to obtain proper clothes. In about an hour he had got rid of his nose and wings, and was once more himself again.

The steamer in which they were crossing was called the *General Grant*, and belonged to the Pacific Mail Company. She was a paddle-steamer of two thousand five hundred tons, had three masts, and at twelve knots an hour would not take more than twenty-one days to cross the ocean; so Phileas Fogg was justified in thinking that he would reach San Francisco on the 2nd of December, New York on the 11th, and London on the 20th, so gaining several hours on the fatal 21st.

Nothing of any consequence occurred on the voyage. The Pacific fully bore out its name, and was as calm as Mr. Fogg himself. Mrs. Aouda felt more and more attached to this taciturn man by even stronger ties than gratitude. She was more deeply impressed than she was aware of, and almost unconsciously gave herself up to emotion, which, however, did not appear to have any effect upon Mr. Fogg. Besides, she took the greatest interest in his projects – anything that threatened to interfere with his plans disquieted her extremely. She frequently consulted with Passe-partout, and he, guessing how deeply she was interested, praised his master all day long. He calmed her apprehensions, insisted that the most difficult part of the journey had been accomplished, that they would be soon in civilized countries, and the railway to New York and the transatlantic steamer to Liverpool would bring them home within their time.

Nine days after leaving Yokohama, Mr. Fogg had traversed just exactly one half of the globe. On the 23rd of November this *General Grant* passed the 180th meridian, the antipodes of London. Of the eighty days he had had, he had, it is true, spent fifty-two, and only twenty-eight remained; but it must be remarked that if he had only gone halfway, according to the difference of meridians, he had really accomplished two-thirds of his journey. He had been obliged to make long detours; but had he followed the 50th parallel, which is that of London, the distance would only have been twelve thousand miles, whereas by the caprices of locomotion he had actually been obliged to travel twenty-six thousand miles, of which he had now finished seventeen thousand five hundred. But now it was all plain sailing, and Fix was not there to interfere with him.

It also happened on that day that Passe-partout made a great discovery. It may be remembered that he had insisted on keeping London time with his famous family watch, and despised all other timekeepers on the journey. Now on this day, although he had not touched it, his watch agreed exactly with the ship's chronometer. His triumph was complete, and he almost wished Fix had been there that he might crow over him.

"What a lot of falsehoods the fellow told me about the meridians, the sun, and the moon. Nice sort of time we should keep if we listened to such as he. I was quite sure that the sun would regulate itself by my watch one of these days."

Passe-partout did not know that if his watch had been divided into the twenty-four hours like Italian clocks, the hands would now show that it was nine o'clock in the evening instead of nine o'clock in the morning – that is to say, the one-and-twentieth hour after midnight, which is the difference between London time and that at the 180th meridian. But this Passe-partout would not have acknowledged even if he understood it, and, in any case, if the detective had been on board, Passe-partout would have argued with him on any subject.

Now, where was Fix at that moment?

Fix was actually on board the *General Grant*.

In fact, when he reached Yokohama, the detective immediately went to the English Consulate, where he found the warrant which had come by the *Carnatic*, on which steamer they thought he himself had arrived. His disappointment may be guessed, for the warrant was now useless, and an act of extradition would be difficult to cause Fogg to be arrested.

"Well," he thought, when his first anger had evaporated, "if the warrant is no use here it will be in England. The fellow is returning to his native land, thinking he has put the police off the scent. I will follow him; but I hope to goodness some of this money will be left. He must already have spent more than five thousand pounds; however, the bank can afford it."

So he made up his mind to proceed on the *General Grant*, and was actually on board when Mr. Fogg and Mrs. Aouda arrived. He was surprised to recognize Passe-partout in such a dress, but he quickly went downstairs to avoid explanation, and hoped, thanks to the number of passengers, that he would remain unperceived by his enemy. But that very day he came face to face with Passe-partout.

Passe-partout, without a word, caught him by the throat, and greatly to the delight of the bystanders, who immediately made bets on the result, he proved the superiority of the French system of boxing over the English.

Passe-partout was much refreshed by this exercise. Fix rose in a very dishevelled condition, and asked his adversary "whether he had quite finished?"

"For the present, yes."

"Then let me speak to you."

"But—"

"It is all in your master's interest."

Passe-partout seemed conquered by the detective's coolness, and followed Fix to the fore part of the ship.

"You have given me a licking," said the detective. "So far, so good. I expected it; but just now you must listen to me. Hitherto I have been playing against Mr. Fogg. I am now in his favour."

"Oh, then you believe him honest at last?"

"By no means. I think he is a thief. Be quiet, hear me out. So long as Mr. Fogg was on British territory, I did all I could to detain him till the warrant for his arrest arrived. It was I who put the Bombay priests on your track. I hocussed you at Hong Kong. I separated you from your master, and caused him to lose the Yokohama steamer."

Passe-partout clenched his fists as he listened.

"But now," continued Fix, "Mr. Fogg appears likely to return to England. All right, I will follow him. But in future I will do as much to keep his way clear, as I have done to prevent his progress. I have changed my game, and have done so for my own interest; your interest is the same as mine, for it will be only in England that you will ever find out whether your master is honest or not."

Passe-partout listened attentively, and felt that Fix meant what he said.

"Are we friends?" asked Fix.

"Friends, no; allies, yes; but only to a certain point, for at the least sign of treason, I will twist your neck."

"That's a bargain," said the detective calmly.

Eleven days afterwards, viz., on the 3rd of December, the *General Grant* entered the Golden Gate of San Francisco.

Mr. Fogg had neither gained nor lost a day.

CHAPTER XXV
A GLIMPSE OF SAN FRANCISCO — A POLITICAL MEETING

AT SEVEN O'CLOCK in the morning, Mr. Fogg and his companions landed in America, or rather upon the floating pier at which the steamers load and unload. There they mingled with ships and steamers of all nationalities, and steam ferry-boats with two or three decks which performed the service on the Sacramento and its affluents.

Passe-partout was so delighted to reach America, that he thought it necessary to execute one of his most active leaps. But when he landed upon the quay, he found the planks worm-eaten, and he went through them. His cry of alarm frightened all the birds which perched upon these floating quays.

Mr. Fogg's first care was to ascertain when the next train left for New York. It started at six o'clock, so they had a whole day before them. Then hiring a carriage, they drove to the International Hotel. From his position on the box of the vehicle, Passe-partout observed with great curiosity the wide streets, the rows of lofty houses, the churches and other places of worship built in the Anglo-Saxon gothic style, immense docks, palatial warehouses, innumerable cabs, omnibuses, and tramway-cars; while Americans, Europeans, Chinese, and Indians occupied the pathways. San Francisco surprised Passe-partout. It was no longer the habitation of bandits, incendiaries, and assassins, who gambled for gold-dust, a revolver in one hand and a knife in the other. This "good time" had passed. The city was now the hive of commerce. The tower of the city-hall overlooked the labyrinth of streets and avenues, which crossed each other at right angles, amongst which verdant squares extended; and the Chinese quarter looked like an importation from the Celestial Empire in a toy-puzzle. Sombreros, red shirts, and Indian head-dresses had given way to silk hats and black coats, and some of the principal streets were lined with splendid shops, offering the products of the whole world for sale.

When Passe-partout reached the International Hotel, he could scarcely recognize that he was not in England. The ground-floor of this immense building was occupied by a bar, at which free lunch of cold meat, oyster soup, biscuits and cheese, was always to be had; wine or beer had to be paid for. The restaurant was comfortable. Mr. Fogg and Mrs. Aouda sat down to a table, and were waited on by the blackest of negroes.

After breakfast, Phileas Fogg, accompanied by Mrs. Aouda, went to the English Consul to have his passport *viséd*. On the pavement he met his servant, who wanted to know whether he should not purchase some revolvers and rifles. Passe-partout had heard of Sioux and Pawnees, who are in the habit of stopping the trains. His master replied that the precaution was needless, but permitted him to do what he pleased in the matter, and pursued his way to the Consulate.

He had not gone very far when, of course by the merest chance, he met Fix. The detective appeared very much astonished. Was it possible that he and Mr. Fogg had crossed in the same steamer, and never met? Fix professed himself honoured at meeting the gentleman to whom he owed so much. Business called him to Europe, and he would be proud to travel in such agreeable company.

Mr. Fogg replied that the honour would be his, and thereupon Fix, who had made up his mind not to lose sight of the other, requested permission to accompany Mr. Fogg in his walks about the city, which was granted.

So the three travellers soon found themselves in Montgomery Street, and on the outskirts of a great crowd. People were everywhere looking on and shouting, going about carrying large printed bills; flags, and streamers were waving, and everyone was calling out "Hurrah for Camerfield!" or "Hurrah for Maudiboy!"

It was a political meeting, at least Fix thought so; and said to Mr. Fogg that it might perhaps be better not to mingle with the crowd for fear of accidents.

Mr. Fogg agreed, and added "that blows, even though inflicted in a political sense, were nevertheless blows".

Fix smiled, and then in order to be able to see without being hustled, the three travellers mounted a flight of steps at the upper end of the street. Opposite was a large platform towards which the crowd appeared to be moving.

Mr. Fogg could not form any opinion as to what the meeting was about. Perhaps it was the nomination of a governor of a State, or of a member of Congress, which was not unlikely. Just then the excitement of the crowd became greater, fists were raised as if to register a vote by a show of hands. The crowd swayed backwards and forwards, flags were displayed and immediately torn to pieces, hats were smashed, and the greater part of the crowd seemed to have grown suddenly shorter.

"It is evidently a political meeting," said Fix; "perhaps it is about the Alabama Claims, although they are settled by this time."

"Perhaps it is," replied Mr. Fogg.

"At any rate," continued Fix, "here are the candidates. The Honourable Mr. Camerfield and the Honourable Mr. Maudiboy have met."

Aouda, leaning upon Mr. Fogg's arm, was regarding the tumult with curiosity, and Fix was about to ask the reason of the disturbance when the uproar increased to a terrific extent. The crowd became more excited, blows were exchanged, boots and shoes were sent whirling through the air, and the spectators thought they could hear the crack of revolvers mingling with the cries of men. The combatants approached the steps on which the party had taken refuge. One of the candidates had evidently been repulsed, but whether Camerfield or Maudiboy had got the best of it, mere spectators could not tell.

"I think we had better retire," said Fix; "if there is any discussion about England, and we were recognized, we might receive some injury."

"An Englishman—" began Mr. Fogg.

But he never finished the sentence, for a tremendous uproar arose on the terrace just behind them, and there were loud shouts for Maudiboy, a party of whose adherents were taking their opponents in the flank.

Our travellers were now between two fires; it was too late to escape; the torrent of men armed with life-preservers and sticks could not be withstood. Phileas Fogg and Fix did all they could to protect their fair companions with the weapons nature had provided, but unsuccessfully. A great ruffian, with a red beard, who appeared to be the chief of the band, was about to strike Mr. Fogg, and would probably have done him serious injury if Fix had not stepped in and received the blow in his stead, thereby getting his hat completely smashed.

"You low Yankee!" exclaimed Mr. Fogg contemptuously.

"You English beast!" replied the other.

"We shall meet again."

"Whenever you please."

"What is your name?"

"Phileas Fogg; and yours?"

"Colonel Stamp Proctor."

And the tide of humanity swept past, overturning Fix, who, however, speedily regained his feet, and though much dishevelled was not seriously hurt. His overcoat was torn in two, and his trousers were more like those worn by the Indians; but fortunately Aouda had escaped, and Fix only showed any traces of the encounter.

"Thank you," said Mr. Fogg to the detective when they were out of the crowd.

"Don't mention it," replied Fix; "let us go on."

"Where to?"

"To a tailor's."

In fact this course had become necessary, for the clothes of both men were torn as badly as if they had taken an active part in the contest, but in an hour they were newly clad and safely back at the hotel again.

There they found Passe-partout waiting and armed with a dozen six-barrelled central-fire revolvers. When he perceived Fix with Mr. Fogg he frowned, but when Mrs. Aouda had told him all that had passed his brow cleared. Fix evidently was no longer an enemy; he was an ally, and was adhering to his agreement.

After dinner they took a carriage and drove to the railway-station. As Mr. Fogg was getting into the cab he said to Fix: "Have you seen that Colonel Proctor since?"

"No," replied Fix.

"I will make a point of coming back to America to find him out," replied Fogg coolly. "It would never do for an Englishman to allow himself to be treated as he treated us."

The detective smiled, but made no reply. It was evident, however, that Mr. Fogg was of that race of Britons who, though they do not permit duelling at home, fight in foreign countries when their honour is in any way attacked.

At a quarter to six the travellers reached the railway-station, and found the train ready. Mr. Fogg called a porter and asked him the reason of the excitement that afternoon.

"It was a meeting, sir," replied the porter.

"I thought there was some great commotion in the streets."

"It was merely an election meeting."

"For a commander-in-chief, no doubt?" suggested Mr. Fogg.

"Oh dear no," replied the man. "It was for a justice of the peace."

On this reply Phileas Fogg entered the train, which started almost immediately.

CHAPTER XXVI
SHOWING HOW MR. FOGG AND PARTY JOURNEYED IN THE PACIFIC EXPRESS

"FROM OCEAN TO OCEAN", as the Americans say, and this sentence is the usual expression to intimate the crossing of the continent by the Pacific Railway. That line is really divided into two, viz. the Central Pacific, between San Francisco and Ogden; and the Union Pacific, between Ogden and Omaha. There are five trunk-lines from Omaha to New York.

New York and San Francisco are thus united by a continuous iron road more than three thousand seven hundred and eighty-six miles in length; between the Pacific and Omaha the railroad traverses a country still inhabited by Indians and wild beasts, and a vast extent of territory which the Mormons began to colonize in 1845, when they were driven out from Illinois.

Formerly, under the most favourable circumstances, the journey from New York to San Francisco occupied six months, now it is accomplished in seven days.

It was in 1862 that, notwithstanding the opposition of Confederate members of Congress, who desired a more southerly route, the railroad track was planned between the forty-first and the forty-second parallels of latitude. President Lincoln himself fixed the termination of the new line at Omaha, in Nebraska. The work was immediately begun and continued with characteristic American energy, which is neither red-tapeish nor bureaucratic. The rapidity of the work did not affect its completeness; they laid a mile and a half of line across the prairie every day; an engine, carrying the rails to be used next day, ran on the line only just laid, and advanced as quickly as they were fixed.

The Pacific railroad has several branches in the States of Iowa, Kansas, Colorado, and Oregon. When it leaves Omaha the line runs along the left bank of the river Platte, as far as the mouth of the northern branch, follows the south branch, crosses the Laramine territory and the Wahsatch Mountains to Salt Lake City (the Mormon capital), plunges into the Tuilla Valley across the desert, Mounts Cedar and Humboldt, the Humboldt river and the Sierra Nevada, and then descends by Sacramento to the

Pacific; the gradient all the way, even over the Rocky Mountains, not exceeding a hundred and twelve feet to the mile.

Such was the line along which Phileas Fogg hoped to be carried to New York in seven days in time to reach the steamer to Liverpool on the 11th.

The car in which our travellers were seated was a sort of long omnibus, with four wheels at each end, without compartments; rows of seats were placed at each side, a passage running between them from end to end of this carriage, and practically of the train, for every carriage was closely connected with the next. There were drawing-room cars, smoking-cars, and restaurants. The only thing wanting was the theatre-car, but no doubt that will some day be supplied. Vendors of books and papers, eatables, drinkables, and tobacco, continually passed through the train.

The train started from Oakland Station at six p.m. It was already dark, and snow was threatening; the pace did not exceed twenty miles an hour, including stoppages. There was not much conversation amongst the passengers, and most of them soon went to sleep. Passe-partout was next to the detective, but did not address him, for after what had happened there could be no sympathy between them. Fix had not altered, but Passe-partout was extremely reserved, and on the least suspicion would have strangled his former friend.

In about an hour snow began to fall, but not sufficiently thick to hinder the progress of the train. Nothing could be seen from the windows but an immense white sheet, against which the steam of the engine looked grey.

At eight o'clock the steward entered and said that bed-time had come. The backs of the seats were thrown down, bedsteads were pulled out, and berths improvised in a few moments. By this ingenious system each passenger was provided with a bed, and protected by curtains from prying eyes. The sheets were clean, the pillows soft. There was nothing to do but to go to bed and sleep, which everybody did as if they were on board ship, while the train rushed on across the State of California.

The territory between San Francisco and Sacramento is not very hilly, and the railroad runs in a north-easterly direction along the American river which falls into the Bay of San Pablo. The hundred and twenty miles' distance between these cities was accomplished in six hours, and as it was midnight when they

passed through Sacramento, the travellers could see nothing of
the city.

Leaving Sacramento and passing Junction, Rochin, Auburn,
and Colfax, the railroad passes through the Sierra Nevada range,
and the train reached Cisco at seven o'clock. An hour afterwards
the sleeping-car was retransformed to an ordinary carriage, and
the passengers were enabled to look out upon the magnificent
scenery of this mountainous country. The track followed all the
caprices of the mountains, at times suspended over a precipice,
boldly rounding angles, penetrating narrow gorges which had
apparently no outlet. The engine, with fire gleaming from the
grate and black smoke issuing from its funnel, the warning-bell
ringing, the "cowcatcher" extending like a spur, mingled its
whistlings and snortings with the roar of torrents and waterfalls,
and twining its black smoke around the stems of the pine-trees.
There are few tunnels or bridges on this portion of the route, for
the line winds round the sides of the mountains and does not
penetrate them.

About nine o'clock the train entered the State of Nevada by
the Carson Valley, still proceeding in a north-easterly direction.
At mid-day the train quitted Reno, where it had stopped twenty
minutes for luncheon.

After lunch the passengers took their places in the car again,
and admired the scenery. Sometimes great troops of buffaloes
were massed like an immense moveable dam on the horizon.
These immense troops frequently oppose an impassable barrier
to the trains, for they cross the track in close array in thousands
and thousands, occupying several hours in their passage. On
these occasions the train is brought to a standstill and obliged to
wait till the track is clear.

In fact, an incident of this kind happened on this occasion.
About three o'clock in the afternoon a troop of ten or twelve
thousand beasts blocked the line. The engineer slackened speed
and tried to proceed slowly, but he could not pass the mass of
buffaloes.

The passengers could see the buffaloes defiling quietly across
the track, and now and then bellowing loudly. They were larger
than European bulls, the head and shoulders being covered with
a long mane, beneath which rises a hump; the legs and tails are
short. No one would ever think of attempting to turn them aside.

When once they have taken a certain direction, they cannot be forced to swerve from it. They compose a torrent of living flesh which no dam can withstand.

The passengers gazed on this curious spectacle, but the man most interested of all in the speedy progress of the train, Phileas Fogg, remained calmly in his place to wait till the buffaloes had passed by. Passe-partout was furious at the delay which the animals caused, and wished to discharge his armoury of revolvers at them.

"What a country this is!" he exclaimed. "Fancy a whole train being stopped by a herd of cattle, which do not hurry themselves in the least, as if they were not hindering us; I should like to know whether Mr. Fogg anticipated this delay. And here we have an engine-driver who is afraid to run his train against a few cows."

The engine-driver certainly did not attempt to do so, and he was quite right. No doubt he might have killed two or three of the first buffaloes he came in contact with; but the engine would soon have been thrown off the line, and progress would have been hopeless.

The best thing to do, then, was to wait patiently, and trust to make up time when the buffaloes had passed; but the procession of animals lasted for fully three hours, and it was night before the track was clear. The head of the column had ere this disappeared below the southern horizon.

It was eight o'clock when the train had traversed the defiles of the Humboldt range, and half-past nine when it entered Utah, the region of the great Salt Lake and the curious Mormon territory.

CHAPTER XXVII
SHOWING HOW PASSE-PARTOUT WENT THROUGH
A COURSE OF MORMON HISTORY, AT THE RATE OF
TWENTY MILES AN HOUR

DURING THE NIGHT of the 5—6th December, the train kept in a south-easterly direction for about fifty miles, and then went up in a north-east course towards Salt Lake.

About nine o'clock in the morning, Passe-partout went out upon the platform to get a breath of fresh air. The weather was cold and the sky was dull, but there was no snow falling then.

The sun in the mist looked like an enormous disc of gold, and Passe-partout was calculating what it would be worth in English money, when he was disturbed by the appearance of a very curious personage.

This individual, who had got into the train at Elko, was tall and of dark complexion, had a black moustache, wore black stockings, and black hat and clothes, except his necktie, which was white, and his gloves, which were dog-skin. He looked like a minister. He went the whole length of the train, and fastened a small notice-bill on the door of every car. Passe-partout read one of these "posters", and learnt that the Honourable Elder William Hitch, Mormon Missionary, would take advantage of the occasion to deliver a lecture upon Mormonism, in car No. 117, at eleven o'clock in the forenoon till twelve noon, and invited all those who wished to learn something about the "Latter-day Saints" to attend the lecture.

"Faith, I'll go," muttered Passe-partout, who knew nothing about Mormonism, except the plurality of wives.

The news spread rapidly amongst the passengers, and about thirty out of the hundred travellers were attracted to car No. 117. Passe-partout took a front seat. Neither his master nor Fix troubled themselves about the matter.

At the hour named the elder William Hitch got up, and in a somewhat irritable manner, as if he had been already contradicted, cried out:

"I tell you that Joe Smith is a martyr, and his brother Hiram is another, and the way the Government is persecuting Brigham Young will make him a martyr also. Now who dares say anything to the contrary?"

No one ventured to contradict him, and his vehemence certainly contrasted strangely with his calm features. But no doubt his anger was kindled by the indignities to which the Mormons had been actually exposed. The United States Government had certainly had a great deal of trouble to bring these fanatics to reason. It was now master of Utah, after having imprisoned Brigham Young on the charges of rebellion and polygamy. Since that time the followers of the prophet had redoubled their efforts, and, if not by deeds, by words resisted the authority of the United States Government. Elder W. Hitch, as we have seen, was endeavouring to gain converts in the railroad-cars.

Then he went on to recite passionately the history of Mormonism from patriarchal times. How in Israel a Mormon prophet of the tribe of Joseph published the annals of the new religion, and left them to his son Morom; and how, many centuries later, a translation of this wonderful book was made by Joseph Smith, junior, a Vermont farmer, who revealed himself as a prophet in 1823, when the angel appeared to him and gave him the sacred roll of the book.

About this time several of the audience left the car, but the lecturer continued to relate how Smith, junior, his father and brothers, and a few disciples founded the religion of the Latter-day Saints, which can count its converts not only in America, but in Scandinavia, England, and Germany. Also how a colony was established, in Ohio, where a temple was erected at a cost of two hundred thousand dollars, and a town built at Kirkland. How Smith became an opulent banker, and received a papyrus scroll written by Abraham and several celebrated Egyptians.

The narrative being very tiresome, the greater part of the audience decamped, but the lecturer nevertheless continued his tale respecting Joe Smith, his bankruptcy, his tarring and feathering, his reappearance at Independence, Missouri, as the head of a flourishing community of about three thousand disciples, his pursuit, and settlement in the Far West.

By this time Passe-partout and ten others were all that remained of the audience, who were informed that after much persecution Smith reappeared in Illinois and founded the beautiful city of Nauvoo, on the Mississippi, of which he became chief magistrate; how he became a candidate for the Presidency of the United States; how he was drawn into an ambuscade at Carthage, imprisoned, and assassinated by a band of masked murderers.

Passe-partout was now absolutely the only listener, and the lecturer looking him steadily in the face recalled to his memory the actions of the pious Brigham Young, and showed him how the colony of Mormon had flourished.

"And this is why the jealousy of Congress is roused against us. Shall we yield to force? Never! Driven from State to State we shall yet find an independent soil on which to rest and erect our tents. And you," he continued to Passe-partout, "and you, my brother, will not you pitch your tent beneath the shadow of our flag?"

"No," replied Passe-partout firmly, as he walked away, leaving the Mormon elder by himself.

While the lecturer had been holding forth the train had been progressing rapidly, and had reached the north-west extremity of Salt Lake. From that point the passengers could see this immense inland sea – the Dead Sea, as it is sometimes called, and into which an American Jordan flows. It is even now a splendid sheet of water, but time and the falling-in of the banks have in some degree reduced its ancient size.

Salt Lake is seventy miles long and thirty-five wide, and is more than three miles above the level of the sea. Though quite different from Lake Asphaltites, it contains salt in large quantities. The specific gravity of the water is one thousand one hundred and seventy; the same distilled is one thousand. No fish can live in it; and though brought down by the Jordan, Weber, and other rivers, soon perish; but it is not true that its density is so great that no men can swim in it.

The surrounding country is well cultivated, for the Mormons are great farmers, and various flowers, etc., would have been observed later. Just then the ground was sprinkled with snow.

The train got to Ogden at two o'clock, and did not start again until six; so Mr. Fogg and party had time to visit the City of the Saints by the branch-line to Ogden. They passed a couple of hours in that very American town, built, like all cities in the Union, with the "melancholy sadness of right angles", as Victor Hugo said. In America, where everything is supposed to be done on the square, though the people do not reach that level, cities, houses, and follies are all done "squarely".

At three o'clock our travellers were walking about the city. They remarked very few churches, but the public buildings were the house of the prophet, the court, the arsenal; houses of blue brick, with porches and verandahs surrounded by gardens, in which were palm-trees and acacias, etc. A stone wall ran round the city. In the principal street was the market-place and several hotels; amongst them Salt Lake House rose up.

There was no crowd in the streets, except near the temple. There was a superabundance of females, which was accounted for by the peculiar tenets of Mormons; but it is a mistake to suppose that all the Mormons are polygamists. They can do as they please; but it may be stated that the females are chiefly anxious to wed, as unmarried women are not admitted to the full privileges of membership. These poor creatures do not appear to be well off or happy. Some perhaps are rich and clothed in European style, but the majority were dressed *à la Indienne*.

Passe-partout beheld these women with some degree of awe, but above all he pitied the husbands of these wives. It seemed to him to be an awful thing to guide so many wives through all the mazes of life, and to conduct them to the Mormon paradise, with the prospect of meeting the glorious Joe Smith, who no doubt was there a shining light. He felt quite disgusted, and he fancied – perhaps he was mistaken – that some of the young ladies gazed at him alarmingly, and in a manner to compromise his liberty.

Fortunately his sojourn in the City of the Saints was not of long duration. At four o'clock the travellers took their places in the return train. The whistle sounded, but just as the train began to move a cry was heard, "Stop, stop!"

But the train did not stop. The gentleman who uttered these cries was a Mormon too late for the train. He ran till he was out of breath. Fortunately the railroad was quite open, there were no barriers nor gates to pass. He rushed along the line, jumped upon the footboard of the last carriage, and then threw himself panting into the nearest seat. Passe-partout, who had been watching him intently, learnt that he had run away after some domestic quarrel, and when the Mormon had recovered his breath Passe-partout plucked up courage to inquire how many wives the fugitive had left, as, judging from his anxiety to get away, he must have had twenty at least.

"One, sir," replied the Mormon, raising his arms to heaven. "One, sir; and, by thunder, that one was quite enough!"

CHAPTER XXVIII
IN WHICH PASSE-PARTOUT CANNOT MAKE ANYONE
LISTEN TO THE LANGUAGE OF REASON

THE TRAIN LEAVING Salt Lake and Ogden Station went on northwards as far as Weber River, about nine hundred miles from San Francisco; from this point it turned to the west across the Wahsatch range. It was in this part of the State that the American engineers had found the greatest difficulty. In this portion of the line also the Government subsidy had been raised to forty-eight thousand dollars a mile, instead of the sixteen thousand dollars a mile on the plains; but the engineers, so it is said, had stolen a march on nature, turned all the difficulties instead of cutting through them, and pierced only one tunnel of fourteen thousand feet in length.

At Salt Lake the line reached its greatest altitude – from that point it took a long curve towards Bitter-creek Valley, and then rose again to the watershed between the valley and the Pacific. Creeks were numerous hereabout, and Muddy Creek, Green Creek, and others were successively crossed on culverts. As they approached the end of their journey Passe-partout became more and more impatient, while Fix was very anxious to get on, for he feared delays and accidents and was more anxious to reach England than even Phileas Fogg.

The train stopped for a short time at Fort Bridges at ten o'clock, and twenty miles farther on entered Wyoming State, formerly Dakota. The next day, the 7th of December, they stopped at Green River. Sleet had fallen during the night, but not sufficient to interfere with the traffic. However, this bad weather annoyed Passe-partout very much, for any great fall of snow would have compromised the success of the journey.

"Any way, it is absurd of my master having undertaken such a journey in winter; he might just as well have waited for fine weather and had a better chance."

But while the honest fellow was worrying himself about the weather, Mrs. Aouda was disquieted for an entirely different reason, as amongst the passengers who had alighted at Green River she recognized Colonel Stamp Proctor, who had insulted Mr. Fogg at the San Francisco meeting. She drew back, as she did not wish to be recognized, but the circumstance affected her deeply.

In fact she had become attached to the man who, notwithstanding his coldness of manner, betrayed every day the interest he took in her. No doubt she herself was not aware of the depth of the sentiment with which he inspired her, which she believed to be gratitude, but was doubtless a deeper feeling. Her heart almost ceased to beat at the moment she recognized Mr. Fogg's enemy. Evidently it was mere chance which had led Colonel Proctor to this particular train, but he and Mr. Fogg must be kept apart at all hazards.

She took an opportunity, when Mr. Fogg was asleep, to tell them whom she had seen.

"That man Proctor on the train!" cried Fix. "Well, you may be quite easy, madam; before he sees Mr. Fogg he has to settle with me. It seems to me that in this matter I have been the most insulted of any."

"And I have a little business with him also, though he is a colonel," added Passe-partout.

"Mr. Fix," replied Mrs. Aouda, "Mr. Fogg would permit nobody to interfere with his quarrel. He has declared that he will come back to America to find out that man who insulted him. If then he sees Colonel Proctor, we cannot prevent a meeting which might have most deplorable results. They must not see each other."

"You are right, madam," replied Fix; "a meeting would spoil everything. Whether victor or not, Mr. Fogg would be delayed, and—"

"And," added Passe-partout, "that would just play into the hands of the Reform Club. In four days we shall be in New York. If during that time my master does not leave his car, the chances are he will not meet the American. At any rate, we must try to prevent a meeting."

The conversation ceased, for Mr. Fogg just then awoke and looked out of window at the snow. Shortly afterwards Passe-partout whispered to the detective, "Would you really fight for him?"

"I would do anything in the world to get him back to Europe alive," replied the detective in a determined tone.

Passe-partout shuddered, but his confidence in his master was unshaken.

And now the question was, how could they detain Mr. Fogg in the car and prevent him meeting the Colonel? It ought not to be a very difficult matter, for Phileas was naturally of a sedentary disposition. However, the detective found a way, for shortly afterwards he said to Mr. Fogg:

"The time passes very slowly."

"Yes," replied Fogg, "but it does pass."

"On board the steamer," continued the detective, "you used to like a game of whist."

"Yes," replied Fogg, "but here I have neither cards nor partners."

"Ah, we can easily purchase cards. As for partners, if madam can take a hand—"

"Certainly," replied the young lady. "I know whist, it is part of an English education."

"And," continued Fix, "I also have some little knowledge of the game, so we can play dummy."

"As you like," said Fogg, delighted to play his favourite game even in the train.

Passe-partout was immediately despatched to the steward, and he quickly returned with two packs of cards, some markers, and a board covered with cloth.

The game commenced, Mrs. Aouda played fairly well, and was complimented by Phileas. As for the detective, he was a first-rate player, and a worthy opponent of Mr. Fogg.

"Now," thought Passe-partout, "we have got him down and he won't move."

At eleven o'clock in the morning the train reached the watershed at Bridger Pass, at an elevation of seven thousand five hundred and twenty-four feet above the level of the sea. After traversing about two hundred miles more, the travellers found themselves in one of those extensive plains which proved so convenient to the laying of the railway.

At half-past twelve the travellers got a glimpse of Fort Halleck, and in a few hours afterwards they had crossed the Rocky Mountains. They were now in hopes that no accident would imperil the journey; the snow had ceased, and the air was frosty. Some large birds, startled by the locomotive, rose up, but no wild beasts appeared; the whole plain was a desert.

After a comfortable breakfast in his own car, Mr. Fogg and his companions resumed their whist. Just then a loud whistling was heard, and the train came to a stop. Passe-partout put his head out, but could see no cause for the stoppage. Mrs. Aouda and Fix were afraid that Mr. Fogg would get up and see what was the matter, but he merely told his servant to ascertain the reason of the delay.

Passe-partout jumped down. He found a number of passengers already on the ground, and amongst them Colonel Proctor.

The train had been stopped by signal. The engine-driver and guard were talking excitedly with the signalman, whom the station-master at Medicine Bow had sent down. The passengers joined in the discussion, and prominent amongst them was Colonel Proctor.

Passe-partout, as he joined the group, heard the signalman say: "You cannot pass. The bridge is unsafe, and will not bear the weight of the train."

The viaduct in question was a suspension-bridge over a rapid about a mile farther on. The signalman said that many of the supports were broken, and that it was impossible to cross; he did not exaggerate the danger, and it may be taken for granted that when an American is prudent there is good reason for not being rash.

Passe-partout did not dare to tell his master, but remained listening with clenched teeth, motionless as a statue.

"That is all very fine," said Colonel Proctor, "but I guess we ain't going to stop here to take root in the snow."

"We have telegraphed to Omaha for a train, Colonel," said the guard; "but it can't reach Medicine Bow in less than six hours."

"Six hours!" exclaimed Passe-partout.

"Yes," replied the guard; "but it will take us that time to reach Medicine Bow on foot."

"Why, it is only a mile from here," said one of the passengers.

"Only a mile, but on the other side of the river."

"And can't we cross in a boat?" asked the Colonel.

"Quite impossible; the creek has swollen with the rains; we shall have to go round ten miles to a ford."

The Colonel vented a choice collection of oaths, condemning the company, the guard, and creation generally; and Passe-partout, who was very angry, felt inclined to join him. Here was a material obstacle which all his master's money would not be able to remove.

The disappointment of the passengers was general, for, without reckoning the delay, they found themselves obliged to walk fifteen miles in the snow. The commotion would have attracted Phileas Fogg's attention had he not been entirely absorbed in his game.

Nevertheless, Passe-partout would have told him of it if the engineer, a true Yankee, named Foster, had not said:

"Perhaps there is a way we can get over after all, gentlemen."

"Over the bridge?" asked a passenger.

"Yes."

"With the train, do you mean?" asked the Colonel.

"With the train."

Passe-partout stopped and listened anxiously for the engineer's explanation.

"But the bridge is almost broken," said the guard.

"Never mind," replied Foster: "I think that by putting on full-steam we may have a chance of getting across."

"The devil!" muttered Passe-partout.

But a certain number of the passengers were attracted by the suggestion; Colonel Proctor was particularly pleased, and thought the plan quite feasible. He related various anecdotes concerning engineers, whom he had known, who crossed over rivers without any bridges at all by merely putting on full-steam, etc. The end of it was that many of the passengers agreed with the engineer.

"The chances are fifty to a hundred about our getting over," said one.

"Sixty!" said another.

"Eighty, ninety!" said a third.

Passe-partout was dumbfounded, and although he was very anxious to cross the river, he thought the proposed plan a little too American.

"Besides," he thought, "there is an easier way, which does not seem to have occurred to either of them"; so he said aloud to one of the passengers:

"The engineer's plan seems to me somewhat dangerous; but—"

"Eighty chances!" replied the person addressed, turning away.

"I know that," replied Passe-partout, as he spoke to another; "but an idea—"

"Ideas are no use," replied the American; "the engineer tells us we can cross."

"No doubt," replied Passe-partout; "but perhaps it would be more prudent—"

"What, prudent!" exclaimed Colonel Proctor, who was ready

to quarrel with anyone suggesting prudence. "Do you not understand that we are going across at full speed? Do you hear, at full speed?"

"I know, I know," said Passe-partout, whom no one would allow to finish his sentence; "but it would be, if not more prudent, since that word displeases you, at any rate more natural—"

"Who is this, what's this? Who is talking about natural?" cried the passengers on all sides.

Poor Passe-partout did not know which way to turn.

"Are you afraid?" asked Colonel Proctor.

"I afraid?" cried Passe-partout; "you think so, do you? I will show these people when a Frenchman can be as American as themselves."

"All aboard!" cried the guard.

"Yes, all get in," muttered Passe-partout; "but you cannot prevent my thinking that it would be much more natural for us to cross the bridge on foot and let the train follow."

But no one heard this wise reflection, and if so, probably no one would have acknowledged its justice.

The passengers took their places, as did Passe-partout, without saying what had happened. The whist-players were still deep in their game.

The engine-driver whistled and then backed his train for nearly a mile, then whistling again he started forward. The speed increased to a fearful extent, and rushing along at a pace of nearly a hundred miles an hour, seemed hardly to touch the rails at all.

They passed over like a flash of lightning. No one saw anything of the bridge; the train leaped, as it were, from bank to bank, and could not be stopped till it had passed the station for some miles.

Scarcely had the train crossed the bridge when the whole structure fell with a tremendous crash into the rapids beneath!

CHAPTER XXIX
IN WHICH CERTAIN INCIDENTS ARE TOLD WHICH
ARE NEVER MET WITH EXCEPT ON RAILROADS IN
THE UNITED STATES

THAT EVENING THE train proceeded without interruption; passed Fort Saunders, crossed Cheyenne Pass, and arrived at Evans' Pass. Here the railroad reached its greatest elevation, eight thousand and ninety-one feet above the sea. The track was now downhill all the way to the Atlantic, across naturally level plains. From here the Grand Trunk Line led to Denver, the capital of Colorado State, rich in gold and silver mines, and boasting more than fifty thousand inhabitants.

Three days and three nights had now been passed in accomplishing one thousand three hundred and eighty-two miles; four days and four nights more would suffice to reach New York, and Phileas Fogg had not lost time.

During the night they had passed Camp Walbach, and entered Nebraska at eleven, passing Julesburg on the south branch of the Platte river. It was here that General Dodge inaugurated the Union Pacific road on the 23rd of October, 1867. Here two powerful locomotives with nine carriages full of guests stopped, three cheers were given, the Sioux and Pawnee Indians had a sham fight, fireworks were let off, and the first number of a paper called *The Railway Pioneer* was printed in a press carried in the train.

Fort MacPherson was passed at eight in the morning; they had still three hundred and fifty-seven miles to go to Omaha. At nine o'clock the train stopped at North Platte, a town built between the two arms of the river.

The hundred-and-first meridian was now passed.

Mr. Fogg and his partner had resumed their whist; none of them, not even the dummy, complained of the length of the journey. Fix had at first won several guineas which he now seemed about to lose, but he was not a less passionate player than Fogg. Fortune distinctly favoured that gentleman, and showered trumps and honours upon him.

On one occasion he was on the point of playing a spade, when a voice behind him said, "I should play a diamond."

The players all looked up, and beheld Colonel Proctor. He and Fogg recognized each other at the same moment.

"Oh, you are that Britisher, are you?" exclaimed the Colonel. "So you are going to play a spade?"

"Yes, and I play it too," replied Fogg coldly, as he threw down the ten.

"Well, I choose to have diamonds," said Proctor insolently. He made a movement as if to seize the card just played, adding, "You know nothing about whist."

"Perhaps I do, as well as other people," said Fogg, rising.

"You have only got to try, you son of a John Bull," said the stout man.

Mrs. Aouda now turned very pale; she seized Fogg by the arm, and pulled him back. Passe-partout was quite ready to throw himself upon the American, who continued to regard his adversary with an insolent stare, but Fix rose and said, "You forget that this is my business, sir; I was not only insulted, but struck."

"Mr. Fix, excuse me," said Fogg; "this is entirely my business. By pretending that I did not know how to play, the Colonel has insulted me, and shall give me satisfaction."

"When and where you please," said the American; "name your weapons."

Aouda tried to keep Mr. Fogg back; the detective also tried to make the quarrel his own; Passe-partout wanted to throw the Colonel out of the window, but a sign from his master checked him. Mr. Fogg left the car, and the American followed him to the platform.

"Sir," said Fogg, "I am in a great hurry to return to Europe; any delay will be very prejudicial to my interest."

"What is all that to me?" said the Colonel.

"Sir," continued Fogg, very politely, "after our dispute at San Francisco, I had promised myself to return to America and find you out, when I had finished my business in England."

"Really!"

"Will you meet me six months hence?"

"Why don't you say six years?"

"I said six months," said Fogg, "and I shall not fail to be at the rendezvous."

"This is all humbug," cried Proctor, "it must be now or never."

"Very well," said Mr. Fogg; "are you going to New York?"

"No."

"To Chicago?"

"No."

"To Omaha?"

"It can't matter to you. Do you know Plum Creek?"

"No," replied Mr. Fogg.

"It is the next station. We shall stop there ten minutes; we shall have lots of time to exchange shots."

"All right," replied Mr. Fogg; "I will stop at Plum Creek."

"I guess you will stay there altogether," replied the American, with unparalleled insolence.

"Who knows?" replied Mr. Fogg, entering the car as coolly as ever, and commenced to reassure Mrs. Aouda, by telling her that braggarts need never be feared. He then asked Fix to be his second in the approaching duel, which Fix could not well refuse to be; and then Phileas Fog sat down quietly and resumed his whist, without betraying the least emotion.

At eleven o'clock the whistle of the engine announced their approach to Plum Creek. Mr. Fogg got up, and followed by Fix and Passe-partout, carrying a brace of revolvers, went out upon the platform. Mrs. Aouda remained in the car, as pale as death.

At that moment the door of the next car opened, and Colonel Proctor appeared, followed by his second, a Yankee of the same stamp as himself. They were about to descend when the guard ran up and said, "You cannot get out, gentlemen."

"Why not?" demanded the Colonel.

"We are twenty minutes late, and cannot stop."

"But I am going to fight a duel with this gentleman."

"I am very sorry," said the guard, "but we must be off at once; there is the bell ringing."

As he was speaking the train started.

"I am really extremely grieved, gentlemen," said the guard, "and under any other circumstances I should have been able to have obliged you. But though you cannot stop to fight, there is nothing to prevent your doing so as you go along."

"Perhaps that would not suit that gentleman," said the Colonel in a jeering tone.

"It will suit me quite well," replied Phileas Fogg.

"Well, we are actually in America, I see," thought Passe-partout; "and the guard is a gentleman of the highest standing."

The two adversaries, their seconds, and the guard passed down to the rear of the train. The last car had only about a dozen passengers in it, and the conductor asked them if they would mind moving, as the two gentlemen had a little affair of honour to settle.

The passengers were very glad to oblige the gentlemen, and they retired accordingly.

The car, about fifty feet long, was very suitable for the purpose. The combatants could advance towards one another between the seats, and fire at their leisure. Never had there been a duel more easy to arrange. Mr. Fogg and Colonel Proctor, each carrying a six-barrelled revolver, entered the car. Their seconds, having locked them in, withdrew to the platform. The duellists were to begin to fire at the first whistle of the engine, then, after a lapse of two minutes, what remained of the two gentlemen would be taken from the car.

Nothing could be easier. It was even so simple, that Fix and Passe-partout could hear their hearts beating as they listened.

Everyone was on the *qui vive* for the first whistle, when suddenly savage cries resounded, accompanied by shots, which certainly did not come from the duellists. On the contrary, the reports rose all along the train; cries of terror were heard inside the cars.

Colonel Proctor and Mr. Fogg, revolvers in hand, were hastily released, and rushed forward into the thick of the struggle, when they perceived that the train had been attacked by a band of Sioux. This was not the first time that this hardy tribe had attacked the train. According to custom, they leaped on the footboards as the train proceeded, as easy as a circus-rider would mount a horse at full gallop. The Sioux were armed with guns, to which the passengers replied with revolvers. The Indians had first mounted the engine, and stunned the engine-driver and firemen with blows on the head. A chief wished to stop the train, but not knowing how to do so had opened instead of closing the regulator, and the train was now proceeding at tremendous speed. Others of the tribe had entered the cars as actively as apes, and were now engaged in a hand-to-hand fight with the passengers. They pillaged the baggage-waggon, and were all the time fighting incessantly.

The travellers defended themselves courageously; they barricaded some of the cars which were besieged like forts, carried along at the rate of forty or fifty miles an hour. Mrs. Aouda had been most courageous. Revolver in hand, she defended herself heroically, firing through the broken windows whenever she caught sight of a savage. As many as twenty Sioux had fallen, and lay crushed by the wheels; and many passengers, grievously wounded, lay stretched upon the seats.

But it was necessary to put an end to the fight, which had lasted for ten minutes, and would result in a victory for the Indians if the train were not stopped. Fort Kearney Station, where there was a guard, was only a couple of miles farther on, and if that were passed, the Indians would be masters of the train till the next station was reached. The guard was fighting bravely by the side of Mr. Fogg, when he was shot down. As he fell he cried, "If the train is not stopped in less than five minutes, we are all lost!"

"It shall be stopped," said Fogg, who was about to rush out.

"Stay where you are, sir," said Passe-partout, "this is my business."

His master had not time to stop the brave fellow, who, unseen by the Indians, managed to creep along beneath the carriages, and then calling all his agility to his aid, with marvellous dexterity he managed to reach the fore part of the train without being seen. There, suspended by one hand between the baggage-waggon and the tender, with the other hand he unfastened the coupling-chains; but owing to the great tension, he was not able to loose the draw-bar, but it was fortunately jerked out as the train jolted. The locomotive, thus detached, sped along at a tremendous pace in front, while the train gradually slackened speed, and the brakes assisting it, it was pulled up within a hundred feet of Fort Kearney. The soldiers, attracted by the sound of firing, hastily turned out; but the Indians did not wait for them. They all disappeared before the train stopped.

But when the travellers came to count the passengers, they found that several were missing, and amongst the absentees was the brave Frenchman who had devoted himself to save them.

CHAPTER XXX
IN WHICH PHILEAS FOGG SIMPLY DOES HIS DUTY

THREE OF THE travellers, including Passe-partout, had disappeared, but it was impossible to say whether they had been killed or taken prisoners.

Several were wounded, but none mortally. Colonel Proctor was one of the most severely hurt; he had fought bravely, and was carried with the other wounded into the station, where he was attended to as well as the circumstances admitted of.

Mrs. Aouda was safe, and Phileas Fogg, who had been in the midst of the fight, had not received a scratch. Fix had a flesh-wound in the arm, but Passe-partout was missing, and Aouda could not help weeping. Meanwhile the travellers all got out of the train, the wheels of which were covered with blood and jagged pieces of flesh. Red tracks were visible on the whitened plain. The Indians were disappearing in the south along the Republican River.

Mr. Fogg was standing motionless with folded arms, and Aouda looked at him without speaking, but he understood her; he had to make up his mind. If his servant were a prisoner, ought he not to rescue him from the Indians?

"I will find him, living or dead," he said simply to Aouda.

"Oh Mr. Fogg!" exclaimed the young lady, seizing his hands, upon which her tears fell fast.

"Living," added Mr. Fogg, "if we lose no time."

By this resolution Phileas Fogg sacrificed everything, he pronounced his own ruin. A delay of even one day would lose the steamer at New York and his wager. But he thought it was his duty, and did not hesitate.

The commandant of Fort Kearney was present; his company were under arms to repel any further attack.

"Sir," said Mr. Fogg to him, "three passengers are missing."

"Dead?" asked the captain.

"Dead or prisoners," replied Fogg; "I must find out which. Is it your intention to pursue the Sioux?"

"That would be a very serious thing," replied the captain. "The Indians may retreat beyond the Arkansas, and I cannot leave the fort undefended."

"Sir," replied Fogg, "the lives of three men are in question."

"No doubt; but can I risk fifty to save three?"

"I do not know if you can, sir; but I know you ought."

"Sir," replied the captain, "no one here is fit to teach me my duty."

"Very well," said Fogg coldly, "I will go alone."

"You, sir!" exclaimed Fix, who now approached "Do you mean to go alone in pursuit of the Indians?"

"Do you wish me to leave that unfortunate man to perish to whom everyone here owes his life? I shall certainly go."

"No, sir, you shall not go alone," said the captain, who was moved in spite of himself. "You are a brave fellow. Now, then, thirty volunteers," he added, turning to the troops.

The whole company advanced at once. The captain had only to pick his men. Thirty were chosen, and a steady old non-commissioned officer put in command.

"Thanks, captain," said Mr. Fogg.

"You will let me go with you?" said Fix.

"You can do as you please, sir, but if you wish to do me a service you will remain with Mrs. Aouda. Should anything happen to me—"

The detective turned very pale. Should he separate from the man he had followed so persistently? Should he leave him to wander thus in the prairie? Fix gazed attentively at Mr. Fogg, and notwithstanding his suspicions and the struggle going on within him, his eyes fell before that frank look.

"I will remain," he said.

In a few moments Mr. Fogg, having shaken hands with the young lady and confided his precious bag to her care, departed with the soldiers. But before marching away he said to his escort, "My friends, I will divide a thousand pounds amongst you if we save the prisoners."

It was then a little past mid-day.

Mrs. Aouda retired to a waiting-room, and there she remained thinking of the generosity and courage of Phileas Fogg, who had sacrificed his fortune and was now risking his life for what he believed to be his duty. In her eyes Mr. Fogg was a hero.

But Fix's thoughts were very different; he could scarcely conceal his agitation; he walked up and down the station and soon recovered himself. Now that Fogg had gone, Fix perceived

how foolish he had been to let him go. He began to accuse himself in pretty round terms, as if he had been his own inspector.

"What a fool I have been," he thought. "The fellow has gone
and won't come back. How is it that I, actually with a warrant
for his arrest in my pocket, could have been so played upon?
Well, I am an ass!"

Thus reasoned the detective as he walked up and down the
platform. He did not know what to do. Sometimes he thought
he would tell Aouda everything, but he knew how she would
receive his confidence. He then thought of following Fogg over
the prairie, and he thought it not impossible he might find him,
as the footsteps of the escort would be imprinted in the snow.
But after a further fall they would soon be obliterated.

Fix became discouraged, and felt inclined to give up the whole
thing. He had now an opportunity to leave Kearney Station and
pursue his way homewards. In fact about two o'clock, in the
midst of a snowstorm, long whistles were heard from eastward;
a great shadow was slowly advancing; no train was expected from
that direction. The assistance telegraphed for could not possibly
arrive so soon, and the train to San Francisco was not due till the
next day. The mystery was soon explained.

It was the runaway locomotive that was approaching. After it
had left the train, it had run a long distance till the fire got low
and the steam went down. Then it stopped, still bearing the half-
conscious engine-driver and firemen. When they found themselves alone in the prairie they understood what had happened,
and they had no doubt they would find the train somewhere on
the track, helpless. The engine-driver did not hesitate. To go
on to Omaha would be only prudent, while to return would be
dangerous. He nevertheless built up the fire and ran back to Fort
Kearney, whistling through the mist as he went.

The travellers were all delighted to see the engine attached to
the train once more. They could now resume their journey, so
fatally interrupted.

When the engine was coupled on, Mrs. Aouda asked the guard
if he were really going to start?

"Right away, ma'am," he replied.

"But the prisoners, our unfortunate companions—"

"I cannot interrupt the service," he replied; "we are three
hours late already."

"And when will the next train arrive from San Francisco?"

"To-morrow evening."

"That will be too late. It must wait."

"That is impossible. If you wish to go on, please get in."

"I will not go," replied the lady.

Fix heard this conversation. A short time before, when there was no chance of his going on, he had decided to leave Kearney, and now that it was necessary for him to take his place, something seemed to detain him. The conflict in his mind waxed fiercer, he wished to fight it out.

Meantime the passengers, some of them wounded, including Colonel Proctor, took their places in the train, which started immediately and soon disappeared, the steam mingling with the falling snow.

Fix had remained behind.

Some hours passed away. The weather was wretched and very cold. Fix remained seated, apparently asleep, on a bench. Aouda, notwithstanding the tempest, continually came out of the room set apart for her, and walking to the extremity of the platform, attempted to penetrate the thick falling snow, as she listened intently for some sound of the return of the escort. But she saw and heard nothing, and would return chilled to the bone only to sally forth once more in vain.

Night fell, the troops had not returned; the commandant began to feel anxious, though he did not betray his anxiety. The snow fell less thickly now, but the cold was intense; absolute silence reigned around. All night Mrs. Aouda kept wandering about, filled with the most dismal forebodings – her imagination suggested a thousand dangers, and her anxiety was terrible.

Fix remained immovable, but he did not sleep either. A man approached him once and spoke to him, but a shake of the head was the only reply he received.

Thus passed the night. At sunrise it was possible to distinguish objects at the distance of two miles; but towards the south, in which direction the party had gone, there was no sign. It was then seven o'clock.

The captain, who was now seriously alarmed, did not know what to do. Should he send a second detachment after the first, and sacrifice more men on the slender chance of saving those who had already gone? But he did not hesitate long, and was on the point of ordering a reconnaissance to be made, when the sound of firing was heard. The soldiers rushed out of the fort and perceived the little troop returning in good order.

Mr. Fogg was marching at their head. Close to him were Passe-partout and the other two passengers, rescued from the hands of the Sioux. They had encountered the Indians ten miles from Kearney. Just before they arrived Passe-partout and his companions had turned upon their captors, three of whom the Frenchman had knocked down with his fists, when his master and the escort came to his assistance.

The party was welcomed most joyously.

Phileas Fog distributed the promised reward to the soldiers, while Passe-partout muttered, and not without reason, "I must confess that I cost my master pretty dearly."

Fix looked at Mr. Fogg without speaking, and it would have been difficult to analyse his thoughts at that moment. Mrs. Aouda, whose feelings were too deep for expression, took Mr. Fogg's hands in hers and pressed them without speaking.

Ever since his return Passe-partout had been looking for the train; he hoped to find it there ready to start for Omaha, and trusted that the lost time might be regained.

"But where is the train?" he exclaimed.

"Gone," replied Fix.

"When is the next train due here?" asked Mr. Fogg.

"Not until this evening."

"Ah!" replied the impassible gentleman simply.

CHAPTER XXXI
IN WHICH THE DETECTIVE FORWARDS MR. FOGG'S INTEREST CONSIDERABLY

PHILEAS FOGG WAS twenty hours behind time, and Passe-partout, the involuntary cause of the delay, was desperate; he had decidedly ruined his master.

The detective approached Mr. Fogg, and, looking at him attentively, said, "Seriously, sir, are you really in such a hurry?"

"Very seriously I am," replied Fogg.

"It is absolutely necessary, then, for you to be in New York on the 11th – before the departure of the English mail-steamer?"

"I have a very great interest in so doing."

"If, then, your voyage had not been interrupted, you would have reached New York on the morning of the 11th?"

"Yes, with twelve hours to spare."

"Well, you are now twenty hours late. Twelve from twenty leaves eight – you must regain those eight hours. Do you wish to try?"

"On foot?"

"No, on a sledge," replied Fix; "on a sledge with sails; a man has proposed it to me."

It was, in fact, the man who had spoken to Fix during the night, and whose offer he had refused.

Mr. Fogg did not immediately reply, but Fix pointed out the man, and Fogg went up and spoke to him. Shortly after they entered a hut built just beyond the fort. Here Mr. Fogg was shown a very curious vehicle – a sort of sledge, with room for five or six people. A high mast was firmly supported by wire rigging, and carried a large sail; it was also furnished with a rudder. In fact it was a sledge rigged like a cutter. During the winter, on the frozen plains, the trains cannot run, and these sledges make rapid passages from station to station, and when running before the wind they equal, if they do not exceed, the speed of the train.

The arrangement was soon made. The strong west wind was in their favour. The snow was hard, and Mr. Mudge, the owner, was confident of being able to reach Omaha in a few hours. Thence were plenty of trains to Chicago and New York. It was just possible to recover the lost time, and they did not hesitate to make the attempt.

Mr. Fogg did not wish to expose Aouda to the cold, and suggested that she should remain at the station with Passe-partout, who would escort her to England under more favourable circumstances; but she refused to leave Mr. Fogg, greatly to the delight of Passe-partout, who would not leave his master alone with Fix.

The detective's thoughts would be difficult to guess. Was his conviction shaken by Fogg's return, or did he still regard him as a scoundrel who hoped to be safe in England on his return? Perhaps Fix's opinion concerning Fogg had altered; but he would do his duty, nevertheless; and he would do his duty and hasten his return to England as much as possible.

At eight o'clock the sledge was ready. The passengers took

their places, the sails were hoisted, and the vehicle sped over the snow at forty miles an hour. The distance between Fort Kearney and Omaha, as the crow flies, is two hundred miles at most. If the wind held they could reach Omaha by one o'clock, if no accident happened.

What a journey it was! The travellers huddled close together, unable to speak in consequence of the intense cold. The sledge glided over the snow like a boat on a lake, and when the wind rose it was almost lifted off the ground. Mudge steered in a straight line, and counteracted the occasional lurches of the vessel. They hoisted all sail, and certainly could not be going less than forty miles an hour.

"If nothing carries away," said Mudge, "we shall get there in time."

Mr. Mudge had an interest in accomplishing the journey, for Mr. Fogg, as usual, had promised him a handsome reward.

The prairie was as flat as possible, and Mudge steered perfectly straight, taking the chord of the arc described by the railroad, which follows the right bank of the Platte River. Mudge was not afraid of being stopped by the stream, for it was frozen over. So the way was free from all obstacles, and there were but two things to fear – an accident or a change of wind. But the breeze blew steadily in the same direction, and even increased in force. The wire lashing hummed like the chords of a musical instrument, and the sledge sped along accompanied by a plaintive harmony of peculiar intensity.

"Those wires give us the fifth and the octave," said Mr. Fogg.

These were the only words he spoke throughout the passage. Mrs. Aouda was well wrapped up in furs. Passe-partout's face was as red as the setting sun, and, with his usual confidence, began to hope again. Instead of reaching New York in the morning they would get there in the evening, perhaps before the departure of the steamer for Liverpool. Passe-partout had a great desire to clasp Fix by the hand, for he did not forget that it was the detective who had procured the sledge, the only means of reaching Omaha in good time; but some presentiment induced him to remain quiet. However, Passe-partout would never forget Mr. Fogg's devotion in rescuing him from the Indians.

The sledge still flew along. The plain and the streams were covered with the mantle of snow. A great uninhabited island appeared to be enclosed between the Union and Pacific Railroad and the branch-line which unites Kearney with St. Joseph. Not a house was in sight. They occasionally passed some gaunt tree, and sometimes flocks of wild birds rose about them, or a band of starving wolves pursued the sledge. On these occasions Passe-partout, revolver in hand, was ready to fire on those which came too near. Had an accident happened, the wolves would have made short work of the travellers; but the sledge held on its course, and soon left the howling brutes behind.

At mid-day Mudge thought they were crossing the Platte River. He said nothing, but he was sure that Omaha was only twenty miles farther on. And in fact in less than an hour their skilful steersman left the helm and hauled down his sails, while the sledge ran on with its acquired impetus. At length it stopped, and Mudge, pointing to a cluster of snow-covered houses, said, "Here we are!"

They had arrived at the desired station, which was in constant communication with the Eastern States. Passe-partout and Fix jumped down and stretched their stiffened limbs. They then assisted Mr. Fogg and Mrs. Aouda to alight. The former paid Mudge handsomely. Passe-partout shook his hands warmly, and then the whole party rushed towards the railway-station.

A train was ready to start, and they had only just time to jump in; though they had seen nothing of Omaha, they did not regret it, as they were not travelling for pleasure.

The train rushed across the State of Iowa, past Conneil Bluffs, Des Morines, and Iowa city. During the night they crossed the Mississippi at Davenport and entered Illinois. Next day, the 10th, at four p.m., they reached Chicago, which had risen from its ashes, and, more proudly than ever, was seated on the borders of the beautiful Lake of Michigan.

They were still nine hundred miles from New York, but there were plenty of trains. Mr. Fogg passed at once from one train to another, which started at full-speed as if it knew he had no time to lose. It crossed Indiana, Ohio, Pennsylvania, and New Jersey like lightning, through towns with antique names containing streets and tramways, but as yet no houses. At length the Hudson Plain appeared, and at a quarter past eleven p.m., on the 11th, the train stopped in the station on the right bank of the river, before the very pier from which the Cunard, otherwise known

as the British and North American, Royal Mail Steam Packet
Company's steamers start.

The *China* had left for Liverpool three-quarters of an hour
previously.

CHAPTER XXXII
IN WHICH PHILEAS FOGG STRUGGLES AGAINST ILL-LUCK

THE *CHINA* SEEMED to have carried off Mr. Fogg's last hope, for
no other steamers of any other line would be of use. The *Pereire*,
of the French Transatlantic Company, did not leave till the 14th,
while the boats of the Hamburg American Company also went
to Havre, and not direct to Liverpool or London; and this extra
passage from Havre to Southampton would upset his calculations.

The Inman steamer *City of Paris* would not start till next day
– that would be too late. Nor would the White Star Line serve his
purpose; all of which Mr. Fogg learnt from "Bradshaw". Passe-
partout was completely upset; it was maddening to lose the
steamer by three-quarters of an hour, and it was his fault, too,
for putting obstacles in his master's way; and when he looked
back at the incidents of the journey, the sums expended on his
account, the enormous wager, and tremendous charges of the
now useless trip, he was overwhelmed. Mr. Fogg, however, did
not reproach him, but as he quitted the pier, said: "We will see
to-morrow what is best to be done. Come along."

The party crossed the river, and drove to the St. Nicholas
Hotel, in Broadway, where they engaged rooms; but Fogg was
the only one who slept. Next day was the 12th of December.
From that day, at seven in the morning, to the 21st, at a quarter
to nine in the evening, was a period of nine days, thirteen hours,
and forty-five minutes; so if Phileas Fogg had sailed in the *China*,
he would have reached London in time to win his wager.

Mr. Fogg left the hotel by himself, telling the others to wait
his return, but to be ready to leave at a moment's notice. He went
down to the Hudson River, to see if there were any vessels about
to start. Several were getting ready to go to sea, but the majority
of them were sailing ships, which of course did not suit Mr Fogg.
He appeared to have lost his last hope, when he perceived a small
screw-steamer moored off the battery; the funnel was pouring

forth black smoke, and every thing looked like a speedy departure. Mr. Fogg hailed a boat, and soon found himself on board
the *Henrietta*, which was an iron steamer. The captain was on
board, and approached Mr. Fogg to answer his inquiries. This
captain was a man about fifty, a regular sea-wolf.

"Are you the captain?" asked Mr. Fogg.

"I am."

"I am Phileas Fogg, of London."

"And I am Andrew Speedy, of Cardiff."

"You are about to sail, I suppose?"

"In an hour."

"Where are you bound?"

"For Bordeaux."

"And your cargo?"

"I am only in ballast."

"Have you any passengers?"

"I never take passengers; they are always in the way, and always
talking."

"Does your ship steam well?"

"Between eleven and twelve knots. The *Henrietta* is well
known."

"Would you like to take me and my three friends to Liverpool?"

"To Liverpool! Why not China at once?"

"I said Liverpool."

"No."

"No?"

"No, I tell you. I am bound for Bordeaux, and to Bordeaux
I shall go."

"Will money have any effect?"

"Not the least."

The captain spoke in a tone which did not admit of argument.

"But the owners of the *Henrietta*?" began Fogg.

"I am the owner. The vessel belongs to me."

"I will hire it from you."

"No."

"I will buy it, then."

"No."

Mr. Fogg did not betray the slightest disappointment, notwithstanding the gravity of the situation. Things were not at

New York as at Hong Kong, nor was the captain of the *Henrietta* like the pilot of the *Tankadere*. Hitherto money had smoothed all obstacles. Now it failed.

Nevertheless, some means of crossing the Atlantic must be found, and Phileas Fogg, apparently, had an idea, for he said to the captain:

"Will you take me to Bordeaux, then?"

"Not if you gave me two hundred dollars."

"I will give you two thousand dollars."

"What, for each passenger?"

"Yes."

"And there are four of you?"

"Yes."

This reply caused Captain Speedy to scratch his head. There were eight thousand dollars to be gained, by simply going his own route; and such a sum might well overcome his antipathy to passengers. Besides, passengers at two thousand dollars apiece become valuable merchandise.

"I start at nine o'clock," said Captain Speedy quietly; "and if you and your party are ready, why, there you are."

"We shall be on board at nine," replied Mr. Fogg, not less quietly.

It was then half-past eight. To land again, drive up to the hotel, and bring off his party to the *Henrietta*, did not take Mr. Fogg very long. He even offered a passage to the inseparable Fix. All this was done by Mr. Fogg as coolly as possible.

They were all on board by the time the *Henrietta* was ready to start.

When Passe-partout heard what the voyage was going to cost, he uttered a prolonged "Oh!" which descended through all the notes of the gamut.

As for Fix, he concluded at once that the Bank of England would not recover much of the money, for by the time they reached England, if Mr. Fogg did not throw away any more money, at least seven thousand pounds would have been spent.

CHAPTER XXXIII
IN WHICH PHILEAS FOGG RISES TO THE OCCASION

AN HOUR LATER the *Henrietta* passed the light-ship at the mouth of the Hudson, rounded Sandy Hook, and skirting Fire Island and Long Island, steamed rapidly eastward.

At noon next day Phileas Fogg mounted the bridge, to ascertain the ship's position, for Captain Speedy was safely locked up in his cabin, where he was using some very strong, but, under the circumstances, excusable language.

The fact was that Mr. Fogg wished to go to Liverpool, and the captain did not; and had made such good use of the time he had been on board, and of his money, that he had won the whole crew, who were not on the best terms with the captain, over to his side. And this is why Phileas Fogg was in command, why the captain was shut up in his cabin, and why the ship was heading for Liverpool. By the way Mr. Fogg managed the vessel, it was evident he had been a sailor.

How the adventure ended will be seen later on. Aouda was anxious, but said nothing. Fix had been completely upset from the first; but Passe-partout thought the manœuvre simply splendid. The captain had said that the *Henrietta* could make between eleven and twelve knots, and he had not exaggerated.

If, then – for there were still ifs – if the sea did not get too rough, nor the wind shift to the east, nor any accident happen to the machinery, it was possible for the *Henrietta* to cross the Atlantic in nine days. But it was not improbable that, when he reached Liverpool, Mr. Fogg would have to answer some awkward questions about the *Henrietta*, as well as about the bank business.

For the first few days everything went well, and the *Henrietta* steamed and sailed like a transatlantic liner.

Passe-partout was charmed. This last exploit of his master delighted him above everything; he was the life and soul of the crew, and his good spirits were infectious. He had forgotten the past vexation, and only looked forward to the future. He kept his eye warily upon Fix, but scarcely spoke, for the old intimacy no longer existed between them.

It must be confessed that Fix did not understand what was going on. The seizure of the *Henrietta*, the bribery of the crew, and Fogg's seamanlike qualities perfectly astounded him; he did not know what to think; for a gentleman who had begun by stealing fifty-five thousand pounds might end by stealing a vessel, and Fix not unnaturally came to the conclusion that the *Henrietta* would not reach Liverpool at all, but proceed to some port where Mr. Fogg, turned pirate, would be in safety. The detective was sorry he had gone into the business.

All this time Captain Speedy continued to grumble and swear in his cabin, and Passe-partout, who took him his meals, was obliged to be very circumspect. Mr. Fogg did not seem to care whether there was a captain on board or not.

On the 13th they passed the Banks of Newfoundland. This was a dangerous part of the coast, particularly in winter, when fogs and gales are frequent. On this occasion the barometer had been falling all the preceding day, and during the night the cold became more intense, and the wind chopped to the south-east.

This was unfortunate. Mr. Fogg furled his sails and put on full-steam; nevertheless the speed fell off, as the vessel pitched heavily. The wind rose, and the position of the *Henrietta* became precarious.

Passe-partout's face darkened as the sky, and for two days he was in mortal terror. But Mr. Fogg was a bold sailor, and kept the ship head to sea without even reducing the steam. The *Henrietta* rushed through the waves and deluged her decks. Sometimes the screw was clear out of the water, but still they kept on.

Although the wind did not increase to a tempest, it held to the south-east, so the sails were rendered useless, and a great aid to the screw was thus lost.

The 16th of December was the seventy-fifth day since Fogg's departure from London, and half the voyage across the Atlantic had been accomplished, and the worst was over. In the summer, success would have been assured, but in winter the weather had them at its mercy. Passe-partout said nothing, but consoled himself with the reflection that the steam would not fail them, and he hoped on.

One day the engineer came on deck and spoke anxiously to Mr. Fogg. This consultation made Passe-partout very uneasy; he would have given his ears to have heard what they were saying; he managed to catch a few words, and heard his master say, "Are you sure?"

"Quite certain," replied the engineer; "you must not forget that we have been piling up the fire ever since we left, and though we had sufficient coal to go under easy steam to Bordeaux, we had not enough to carry us to Liverpool at full pressure."

"I will think about it," said Mr. Fogg; and then Passe-partout understood it all.

The coal was failing!

"If my master can get over this," he thought, "he will be a clever fellow."

He was so agitated he could not help imparting his knowledge to Fix, who replied, "Then you really think we are going to Liverpool?"

"Of course we are."

"You idiot!" replied the detective, shrugging his shoulders, as he turned away.

Passe-partout would have revenged himself for this insult if he had not reflected that the unlucky Fix was very probably disappointed and humiliated at having followed a false scent all the way round the world.

But what would Phileas Fogg do now? No one could say; but he himself appeared as cool as ever, and to have decided, for he told the engineer, the same evening, to keep the full-steam on till the coal was exhausted.

So the *Henrietta* proceeded at full-steam until, on the 18th, the coals began to give out, as the engineer had foretold.

"Keep up the steam as much as possible," said Mr. Fogg.

About mid-day, Phileas Fogg, having taken the ship's reckoning, told Passe-partout to release Captain Speedy. The Frenchman would rather have unloosed a tiger, and said, as he went aft, "What an awful rage he will be in."

A few minutes later a bomb appeared on deck. This bomb was Captain Speedy, and looked ready to burst.

"Where are we?" was his first remark, as soon as his anger would allow him to speak. "Where are we?" he repeated, looking round.

"Seven hundred and seventy miles from Liverpool," replied Mr. Fogg calmly.

"Pirate!" roared Andrew Speedy.

"I requested your attendance, sir."

"You robber!"

"Sir," said Mr. Fogg, "I wish to ask you to sell me your vessel."

"Never, by all the devils!"

"Then I shall be obliged to burn her."

"Burn my ship?"

"Yes, at least the upper works, as we are in want of fuel."

"Burn my ship!" roared Captain Speedy; "why she is worth fifty thousand dollars!"

"Here are sixty thousand dollars," replied Fogg, as he offered him a roll of bank-notes.

This had a great effect upon Captain Speedy. In an instant he forgot his anger, his incarceration, and all his complaints. The ship was twenty years old, he would make his fortune. The bomb would not burst after all. Mr. Fogg had extinguished the fuse.

"I shall still keep the hulk, I suppose?"

"The hulk and the engine are yours. Is it a bargain?"

"Yes." And Speedy, seizing the proffered money, put it (speedily) into his pocket.

All this time Passe-partout was as pale as a ghost, while Fix looked as if he were going into a fit. Twenty thousand pounds expended, and the captain still possessed the hull and the machinery, the most valuable portion of the vessel! It was true that fifty-five thousand pounds had been stolen.

When Speedy had pocketed the money, Mr. Fogg said to him: "Don't be astonished at all this; you must know that if I do not reach London on the 21st of December, I shall lose twenty thousand pounds. Now you see I lost the steamer at New York – you refused to take me to Liverpool—"

"And I was right," replied the captain, "for I have made twenty thousand dollars by the refusal." Then he added, more seriously:

"Do you know one thing, Captain—"

"Fogg," said that worthy.

"Captain Fogg; you've got a spice of the Yankee in you!" And having paid him this compliment, as he fancied, he was going below, when Fogg said, "Now the vessel is mine!"

"Certainly; from truck to keelson – the wood I mean!"

"All right. Please have all the woodwork cut away and burnt."

It was absolutely necessary to burn the dry wood for fuel; and that day the poop, cabin fittings, bunks, and the spar-deck were consumed.

Next day, the 19th December, they burned the masts and spars. The crew worked with a will, and Passe–partout sawed away as lustily as any ten men. Next day the upper works disappeared, and the *Henrietta* was then only a hulk. But on that day they sighted the Fastnet Light and the Irish coast. By ten o'clock they passed Queenstown. Phileas Fogg had now only twenty-four hours left to reach Liverpool, even if he kept up full-speed; and the steam was likely to give out apparently.

"Sir," said Speedy, who was now almost as much interested as the rest, "I should really suggest your giving up the game. Everything is against you. We are only just passing Queenstown."

"Ah," exclaimed Fogg, "is that Queenstown where the lights are?"

"Yes."

"Cannot we enter the harbour?"

"Not before three o'clock; the tide will not serve."

"Let us wait then," said Fogg calmly, without betraying any emotion that, by a last effort, he was about to conquer his ill-luck.

Queenstown is the port at which the American mails are landed, which are then forwarded to Dublin by an express train, and from thence to Liverpool* by fast steamers, thus gaining twelve hours upon the fastest vessels.

Mr. Fogg calculated upon gaining this space of time, and so, instead of reaching Liverpool next evening, he would be there at noon, and be able to reach London by a quarter to nine p.m.

About one a.m. the *Henrietta* entered Queenstown, and Mr. Fogg, exchanging a clasp of the hand with Captain Speedy, left that personage upon the vessel, now a mere hulk.

All the party went ashore at once. Fix was much inclined to arrest Fogg on the spot, but refrained. Why? Did he think he was mistaken after all? At any rate he would not abandon Mr. Fogg. They all got into the train at half-past one a.m., and were in Dublin at daybreak, and immediately embarked on the mail-steamer which, disdaining to ride over the waves, cut through them.

At twenty minutes to twelve (noon) Mr. Fogg disembarked at Liverpool.* He was within six hours' run from London now.

*Holyhead. – *Trans.*

But at that moment Fix approached him, and putting his hand upon Mr. Fogg's shoulder, said:

"Are you really Phileas Fogg?"

"Yes," was the reply.

"Then I arrest you in the Queen's name!"

CHAPTER XXXIV
IN WHICH PASSE-PARTOUT USES STRONG LANGUAGE

PHILEAS FOGG WAS in prison. He had been shut up in the Custom House, pending his removal to London.

Passe-partout would have attacked Fix when he arrested his master, had not some policemen prevented him. Mrs. Aouda was quite upset by the occurrence, which was quite unintelligible to her. Passe-partout explained to her how it had come to pass, and the young lady, who was of course powerless, wept bitterly.

Fix had merely done his duty, whether Mr. Fogg was guilty or not guilty. The judge would decide that.

It then occurred to Passe-partout that this was all his fault. Why had he not communicated the facts to Mr. Fogg? He should have told him who Fix was and his errand. Thus forewarned he could have given proofs of his innocence, and at any rate the detective would not in that case have travelled at Mr. Fogg's expense, and arrested him the moment he landed. As he thought of all this Passe-partout was ready to shoot himself. Neither he nor Aouda left the Custom House, notwithstanding the cold weather. They were anxious to see Mr. Fogg once more.

As for that gentleman he was completely ruined, and at the very moment he had succeeded in his attempt. The arrest was fatal. He had just eight hours and forty-five minutes to reach the Reform Club, and six hours would have sufficed to get to London.

Could anyone have seen Mr. Fogg they would have found him seated calmly on a form in the Custom House, as cool as ever. Resigned is scarcely the word to apply to him, but to all appearance he was as unmoved as ever. If he was raging within he did not betray any symptoms of anger. Was it possible that he still hoped to succeed?

At any rate he had carefully placed his watch on the table before him, and was watching it intently. Not a word escaped him, but his eyes wore a curious fixed expression. Honest or not, he was caught and ruined.

Was he thinking of escape, did he think of looking for an outlet? It was not unlikely, for every now and then he got up and walked round the room. But the door and window were both firmly closed and barred. He sat down, and drawing his journal from his pocket, read:

"21st December, Saturday, Liverpool."

To this he added –

"Eightieth day, 11.40 a.m."

Then he waited. The clock of the Custom House struck one. Mr. Fogg perceived that his watch was two minutes fast.

Two o'clock came! Admitting that he could at that moment get into an express train, he might yet arrive in London and reach the Reform Club in time.

At 2.33 he heard a noise outside of opening doors. He could distinguish Passe-partout and Fix's voices. Mr. Fogg's eyes glittered. The door was flung open and Mrs. Aouda, Fix, and Passe-partout rushed in.

"Ah sir!" exclaimed Fix, hurrying up to the prisoner, "a thousand pardons – an unfortunate resemblance! The true thief is arrested. You are free, free!"

Phileas Fogg was free. He walked quietly up to the detective, looked him steadily in the face for a second, and with a movement of his arm knocked him down!

"Well hit!" exclaimed Passe-partout. "By jingo, that's a proper application of the art of self-defence!"

Fix lay flat on the ground, and did not say a word. He had only received his deserts. Mr. Fogg, Aouda, and Passe-partout immediately quitted the Custom House, jumped into a cab, and drove to the railway-station.

Mr. Fogg inquired when there would be a train for London. It was 2.40; the train had left five-and-thirty minutes before. Mr. Fogg ordered a "special".

There were plenty of engines capable of running at a high speed, but the train could not be got in readiness before three. At that hour Mr. Fogg having said a few words to the engine-driver respecting a certain "tip", was rushing up to London, accompanied by Mrs. Aouda and his faithful Passe-partout.

The distance was accomplished in five hours and a half, a very easy thing when the line is clear, but there were some unavoidable delays, and when the special arrived in London the clock pointed to ten minutes to nine.

Thus Phileas Fogg, having accomplished his journey round the world, had returned five minutes too late!

He had lost his wager.

CHAPTER XXXV
PASSE-PARTOUT OBEYS ORDERS QUICKLY

THE INHABITANTS OF Saville Row would have been astonished, next day, if they had been told that Mr. Fogg had returned, for the doors and windows of his house were still shut, and there was no change visible exteriorly.

When he left the railway-station, Mr. Fogg had told Passe-partout to purchase some provisions, and then, he quietly went home.

Mr. Fogg preserved his usual impassibility under the trying circumstances; he was ruined, and all through the fault of that blundering detective. After having achieved his long journey, overcome a thousand obstacles, braved a thousand dangers, and even found time to do some good on the way, to fail at the very moment that success was certain was indeed terrible. A very small portion remained to him of the large sum he had taken away with him; his whole fortune was comprised in the twenty thousand pounds deposited at Baring's, and that sum he owed to his colleagues at the club. After having paid all expenses, even had he won he would have been none the richer, and it is not likely he wished to be richer, for he was one of those men who bet for reputation; but this wager would ruin his altogether. However, he had fully made up his mind what to do.

A room had been set aside for Aouda, who felt Mr. Fogg's ruin very deeply. From certain words she had heard she understood he was meditating some serious measures. Knowing that Englishmen of an eccentric turn of mind sometimes commit suicide, Passe-partout kept watch on his master unobserved; but the first thing the lad did was to extinguish the gas in his room, which had been burning for eighty days. In the letter-box he had found the gas company's bill, and thought it was quite time to put a stop to such an expense.

The night passed. Mr. Fogg went to bed, but it is doubtful whether he slept. Aouda was quite unable to rest, and Passe-partout kept watch like a dog at his master's door.

Next day, Mr. Fogg told him, shortly, to attend to Mrs. Aouda's breakfast, while he would have a cup of tea and a chop. He excused himself from joining Aouda at meals on the plea of putting his affairs in order, and it was not till evening that he asked for an interview with the young lady.

Passe-partout having received his orders had only to obey them, but he found it impossible to leave his master's room. His heart was full, his conscience was troubled with remorse, for he could not help blaming himself for the disaster. If he had only warned his master about Fix, Mr. Fogg would not have brought the detective to Liverpool, and then—

Passe-partout could hold out no longer.

"Oh, Mr. Fogg!" he exclaimed, "do you not curse me? It is all my fault—"

"I blame no one," replied Phileas Fogg, in his usual calm tone. "Go!"

Passe-partout quitted the room and sought Mrs. Aouda, to whom he delivered his message.

"Madam," he added, "I am powerless. I have no influence over my master's mind; perhaps you may have."

"What influence can I have?" she replied. "Mr. Fogg will submit to no one. Has he really ever understood how grateful I am to him? Has he ever read my heart? He must not be left alone an instant. You say he is going to see me this evening?"

"Yes, madam. No doubt to make arrangements for your sojourn in England."

"Let us wait, then," replied the young lady, becoming suddenly thoughtful.

So, through all that Sunday, the house in Saville Row appeared uninhabited; and for the first time since he had lived in it, Phileas Fogg did not go to his club as Big Ben was striking half-past eleven.

And why should he go to the Reform Club? His friends did

not expect him. As he had not appeared in time to win the wager, it was not necessary for him to go to the bank and draw his twenty thousand pounds. His antagonists had his blank cheque; it only remained for them to fill it up and present it for payment.

As Mr. Fogg, then, had no object in going out, he stayed in his room and arranged his business matters. Passe-partout was continually running up and down stairs, and thought the day passed very slowy. He listened at his master's door, and did not think it wrong; he looked through the keyhole, for every instant he feared some catastrophe. Sometimes he thought of Fix, but without any animosity. Fix, like everyone else, had been mistaken, and had only done his duty in following Mr. Fogg, while he (Passe-partout)— The thought haunted him, and he thought himself the most wretched of men.

He was so unhappy that he could not bear to remain alone, so he knocked at Mrs. Aouda's sitting-room, and, permitted to enter, sat down in a corner, without speaking. She, too, was very pensive.

About half-past seven Mr. Fogg asked permission to go in; he took a chair and sat close by the fire-place, opposite to the young lady; he betrayed no emotion – the Fogg who had come back was the same as the Fogg who had gone away. There was the same calmness, the same impassibility.

For five minutes he did not speak, then he said; "Madam, can you forgive me for having brought you to England?"

"I, Mr. Fogg!" exclaimed Mrs. Aouda, trying to check the beating of her heart.

"Pray allow me to finish," continued Mr. Fogg. "When I asked you to come to this country I was rich, and had determined to place a portion of my fortune at your disposal. You would have been free and happy. Now I am ruined."

"I know it, Mr. Fogg," she replied; "and I, in my turn, have to ask your pardon for having followed you, and, who knows, retarded you, and thus contributed to your ruin."

"You could not have remained in India," replied Mr. Fogg, "and your safety was only assured by taking you quite away from those fanatics who wished to arrest you."

"So, Mr. Fogg," she replied, "not satisfied with having saved me from death, you wished to insure my comfort in a foreign country."

"I did," replied Fogg; "but fate was unpropitious. However, I wish to place at your disposal the little I have left."

"But," she exclaimed, "what will become of you, Mr. Fogg?"

"Of me, madam? I am in want of nothing."

"But," she continued, "how can you bear to look upon the fate in store for you?"

"As I always look at everything," replied Mr. Fogg; "in the best way I can."

"At any rate," said Aouda, "your friends will not permit you to want anything."

"I have no friends, madam."

"Your relations, then."

"I have no relations now."

"Oh then indeed I pity you, Mr. Fogg. Solitude is a terrible thing. Not a single person to whom you can confide your sorrow? Though they say that even grief, shared with another, is more easily supported."

"So they say, madam."

"Mr. Fogg," said Aouda, rising and extending her hand to him, "do you care to possess at the same time a relative and a friend? Will you take me for your wife?"

Mr. Fogg had risen also. There was an unusual gleam in his eyes, and his lips trembled. Aouda looked at him. In this regard of a noble woman, who had dared everything to save the man to whom she owed her life, her sincerity, firmness, and sweetness were all apparent. He was at first astonished, and then completely overcome. For a moment his eyes closed, as if to avoid her glance, and when he opened them again he said simply:

"I love you. By all I hold sacred, I love you dearly; and I am yours for ever."

"Ah!" exclaimed Mrs. Aouda, as she pressed her hand upon her bosom.

Passe-partout was immediately summoned. Mr. Fogg was still holding the lady's hand. Passe-partout understood it all, and his face became radiant.

Mr. Fogg asked him if it were too late to notify the Rev. Samuel Wilson, of Marylebone Church, about the wedding.

Passe-partout smiled, as he replied, "It is never too late." It was then five minutes past eight.

"Will the wedding take place to-morrow, Monday?" he said.

"Shall we say to-morrow?" asked Mr. Fogg, turning to Aouda.
"If you please," she replied, blushing.
Passe-partout hurried away as fast as he could go.

CHAPTER XXXVI
IN WHICH PHILEAS FOGG'S NAME IS ONCE AGAIN AT
A PREMIUM ON THE EXCHANGE

IT IS NOW time to say something of the change which English opinion underwent when the true bank robber, one James Strand, was arrested in Edinburgh on the 17th of December.

Three days before Fogg was a criminal, followed by the police; now he was a gentleman, who had only been taking an eccentric journey round the world. There was great discussion in the papers, and those who had laid wagers for or against Mr. Fogg rose once more as if by magic. The "Fogg Bonds" were once more negotiated, and Phileas Fogg's name was at a premium.

The members of the Reform Club passed those three days in great discomfort. Would Phileas Fogg, whom they had forgotten, return? Where was he on that 17th of December, which was the seventy-sixth day after his departure, and they had had no news of him? Had he given in, and renounced the struggle, or was he continuing the journey at a more reasonable rate, and would he appear on Saturday, the 21st of December, at a quarter to nine in the evening, as agreed upon?

We cannot depict the intense agitation which moved all classes of society during those three days. Telegrams were sent to America and Asia for news of Mr. Fogg, and people were sent, morning and night, to Saville Row; but there was no news. Even the police did not know what had become of Fix. But all these things did not prevent bets being made, even to a greater amount than formerly. Bonds were quoted no longer at a hundred per cent. discount, but went up to ten and five; and even old Lord Albemarle was betting at evens.

So that Saturday night a great crowd was assembled in Pall Mall and the Reform Club. Traffic was impeded; disputes, arguments, and bets were raging in every direction. The police had the greatest difficulty to keep back the crowd, and as the hour when Mr. Fogg was due approached, the excitement rose to fever-heat.

That evening that gentleman's five friends had assembled in the drawing-room of the club. There were the two bankers, John Sullivan and Samuel Fallentin; Andrew Stuart, the engineer; Gauthier Ralph, the director of the Bank of England; and Thomas Flanagan, the brewer; all awaiting Mr. Fogg's return with the greatest anxiety.

At twenty minutes past eight Stuart rose and said: "Gentlemen, in twenty-five minutes the time agreed upon will have expired."

"At what time was the last train due from Liverpool?" asked Flanagan.

"At 7.23," replied Ralph; "and the next does not arrive till past midnight."

"Well, then, gentlemen," replied Stuart, "if Mr. Fogg had arrived by the 7.23, he would have been here before now, so we may look upon the bet as won."

"Do not be in too great a hurry," replied Fallentin. "You know that our friend is very eccentric, and his punctuality is proverbial. I, for one, shall be astonished if he does not turn up at the last minute."

"For my part," said Stuart, who was very nervous, "if I should see him I could not believe it was he."

"In fact," replied Flanagan, "Mr. Fogg's project was insane. No matter how punctual he may he, he cannot prevent some delay; and a day or two would throw all his arrangements out of gear."

"And you will remark besides," said Sullivan, "that we have not received any news from him all the time he has been away, although there are telegraphs all along his route."

"He has lost, gentlemen," said Stuart, "a hundred times over. The only ship he could have come by and been in time was the *China*, and she arrived yesterday. Here is a list of the passengers, and Phileas Fogg's name is not included. On the most favourable computation our friend can scarcely have reached America. I do not expect him for the next twenty days, and my Lord Albemarle will lose his five thousand pounds."

"Then we have nothing to do," replied Ralph, "but to present his cheque at Baring's to-morrow."

The hands of the clock were then pointing to twenty minutes to nine.

"Five minutes more," said Stuart.

The five friends looked at each other. One could almost hear their hearts beating, for it must be confessed that even for such seasoned players the stakes were pretty high, but they did not wish their anxiety to be remarked, and on Fallentin's suggestion they sat down to whist.

"I would not give up my four thousand pounds," said Stuart as he sat down, "if anyone were to offer me three thousand nine hundred and ninety-nine."

The clock pointed to eighteen minutes to nine.

The players took up their cards, but kept looking at the clock. No matter how safe they felt, the minutes had never appeared so long.

"8.43," said Flanagan, as he cut the pack Ralph passed to him.

At that moment the silence was profound, but the cries of the crowd outside soon rose again. The clock beat out the seconds with mathematical regularity, and each of the players checked every tick of the pendulum.

"8.44," said Sullivan, in a voice which betrayed his nervousness.

One minute more and they would have won their bet. They laid down their cards and counted the seconds.

At the fortieth second no news; at the fiftieth still nothing. At the fifty-fifth second a loud roar was heard from the street mingled with cheers and oaths.

All the players rose simultaneously.

At the fifty-seventh second the door of the room was thrust open, and before the pendulum had marked the minute Phileas Fogg advanced into the room, followed to the door by an excited crowd who had forced their way in, and he said in his usual calm tone,

"Here I am, gentlemen."

CHAPTER XXXVII
SHOWING HOW PHILEAS FOGG GAINED ONLY HAPPINESS
BY HIS TOUR ROUND THE WORLD

YES, IT WAS Phileas Fogg in person.

Our readers will recollect that at five minutes after eight that evening – about twenty-five hours after our travellers' arrival in London – Passe-partout had been requested to arrange about a certain marriage with the Rev. Samuel Wilson. Passe-partout had gone on his mission rejoicing, but the clergyman was not at home. He naturally waited, but he was kept at least twenty minutes.

It was 8.35 when he left the clergyman's house, but what a state he was in! His hair was disordered, he ran home without his hat, overturning the passers-by as he went rushing along the pathway.

In three minutes he was back in Saville Row, and he rushed breathlessly into Mr. Fogg's room.

He was unable to speak.

"What is the matter?" asked Mr. Fogg.

"Oh, sir – the marriage – impossible."

"Impossible?"

"Impossible for to-morrow."

"Why so?"

"Because to-morrow is – Sunday."

"It is Monday," said Mr. Fogg.

"No, to-day is Saturday."

"Saturday? impossible."

"It is, it is!" exclaimed Passe-partout. "You have made a mistake of one day. We arrived twenty-four hours before our time, but we have only ten minutes left now."

As he spoke Passe-partout fairly dragged his master out of his chair.

Phileas Fogg, thus seized, had no choice. He rushed downstairs, jumped into a cab, promised the driver a hundred pounds, ran over two dogs, came into collision with five cabs, and reached the Reform Club at 8.45.

So Phileas Fogg had accomplished the journey round the world in eighty days, and had won his bet of twenty thousand pounds.

Now how was it that such a methodical man could have made a mistake of a day? How could he imagine that he had got back on Saturday the 21st when it was really Friday the 20th, seventy-nine days after his departure?

The reason is very simple.

Phileas Fogg had unconciously gained a day, simply because he journeyed always eastward, whereas, had he journeyed west-ward, he would have lost a day.

In fact, travelling towards the east, he had gone towards the south, and consequently the days got shorter as many times four minutes as he crossed degrees in that direction. There are three hundred and sixty degrees, and these multiplied by four minutes give exactly twenty-four hours; that is the day Fogg gained. In other words, while Phileas Fogg, going east, saw the sun pass the meridian eighty times, his friends in London only saw it seventy-nine times, and that is why on that day, which was Saturday, and not Sunday, as Mr. Fogg thought, they expected him at the Reform Club.

Passe-partout's wonderful watch, which had always kept London time, would have confirmed this had it only marked the days as well as the hours and minutes.

So Phileas Fogg had won his twenty thousand pounds, but as he had expended nearly nineteen thousand pounds, his gain was small. However, he had not bet for money. He actually divided the thousand pounds that remained between honest Passe-partout and the unfortunate Fix, against whom he bore no malice. But from Passe-partout's share he deducted, on principle, the cost of the gas which had been burning for one thousand nine hundred and twenty hours. That same evening Mr. Fogg, as tranquilly as ever, said to Aouda, "Is the prospect of our marriage still agreeable to you?"

"Mr. Fogg," she replied, "it is I who ought to have asked you that question. You were ruined then, but now you are rich."

"Excuse me, madam," he replied, "this fortune belongs to you. If you had not thought of the wedding, my servant would never have gone to see Mr. Wilson, and I should not have found out my mistake."

"Dear Mr. Fogg," said the young lady.

"My dearest Aouda," replied Phileas Fogg.

The marriage took place forty-eight hours afterwards, and

Passe-partout, beaming and resplendent, gave the bride away. Had he not saved her life, and was he not entitled to the honour?

On the wedding morning Passe-partout knocked at his master's door.

"What is the matter, Passe-partout?"

"Well, sir, I have just this moment found out that we might have gone round the world in seventy-eight days only."

"No doubt," replied Mr. Fogg, "if we had not crossed India; but if I had not crossed India we should not have rescued Mrs. Aouda, and she would never have been my wife."

And Mr. Fogg shut the door quietly.

So Phileas Fogg won his wager, and made the tour of the world in eighty days. To do this he had made use of every means of transport – steamers, railways, carriages, yacht, trading-ship, sledges, and elephants. That eccentric gentleman had displayed all through his most marvellous qualities of coolness and exactness; and after all what had he really gained? What had he brought back?

"Nothing," do you say? Well, perhaps so, if a charming woman is nothing, who, however extraordinary it may appear, made him the happiest of men.

And in truth, reader, would not you go round the world for less than that?

ABOUT THE TRANSLATOR

HENRY FRITH (1840–1910) was an Irish author, editor and translator. He translated several novels by Jules Verne shortly after they appeared in French, and is considered the best of Verne's contemporary translators.

ABOUT THE INTRODUCER

TIM FARRANT is Reader in Nineteenth-Century French Literature and a Fellow of Pembroke College in the University of Oxford. His books include *An Introduction to Nineteenth-Century French Literature* and *Balzac's Shorter Fictions*.

TITLES IN EVERYMAN'S LIBRARY

ALEXANDRE DUMAS
The Count of Monte Cristo
The Three Musketeers

UMBERTO ECO
The Name of the Rose

GEORGE ELIOT
Adam Bede
Daniel Deronda
Middlemarch
The Mill on the Floss
Silas Marner

JOHN EVELYN
The Diary of John Evelyn
(UK only)

J. G. FARRELL
The Siege of Krishnapur
and Troubles

WILLIAM FAULKNER
The Sound and the Fury
(UK only)

HENRY FIELDING
Joseph Andrews and Shamela
(UK only)
Tom Jones

F. SCOTT FITZGERALD
The Great Gatsby
This Side of Paradise
(UK only)

PENELOPE FITZGERALD
The Bookshop
The Gate of Angels
The Blue Flower (in 1 vol.)
Offshore
Human Voices
The Beginning of Spring
(in 1 vol.)

GUSTAVE FLAUBERT
Madame Bovary

FORD MADOX FORD
The Good Soldier
Parade's End

RICHARD FORD
The Bascombe Novels

E. M. FORSTER
Howards End
A Passage to India
A Room with a View,
Where Angels Fear to Tread
(in 1 vol., US only)

ANNE FRANK
The Diary of a Young Girl
(US only)

GEORGE MACDONALD
FRASER
Flashman
Flash for Freedom!
Flashman in the Great Game
(in 1 vol.)

ELIZABETH GASKELL
Mary Barton

EDWARD GIBBON
The Decline and Fall of the
Roman Empire
Vols 1 to 3: The Western Empire
Vols 4 to 6: The Eastern Empire

KAHLIL GIBRAN
The Collected Works

J. W. VON GOETHE
Selected Works

NIKOLAI GOGOL
The Collected Tales
Dead Souls

IVAN GONCHAROV
Oblomov

GÜNTER GRASS
The Tin Drum

GRAHAM GREENE
Brighton Rock
The Human Factor

DASHIELL HAMMETT
The Maltese Falcon
The Thin Man
Red Harvest
(in 1 vol.)
The Dain Curse,
The Glass Key,
and Selected Stories

THOMAS HARDY
Far From the Madding Crowd
Jude the Obscure
The Mayor of Casterbridge
The Return of the Native
Tess of the d'Urbervilles
The Woodlanders

JAROSLAV HAŠEK
The Good Soldier Švejk

NATHANIEL HAWTHORNE
The Scarlet Letter

JOSEPH HELLER
Catch-22

ERNEST HEMINGWAY
A Farewell to Arms
The Collected Stories
(UK only)

GEORGE HERBERT
The Complete English Works

HERODOTUS
The Histories

MICHAEL HERR
Dispatches (US only)

PATRICIA HIGHSMITH
The Talented Mr. Ripley
Ripley Under Ground
Ripley's Game
(in 1 vol.)

HINDU SCRIPTURES
(tr. R. C. Zaehner)

JAMES HOGG
Confessions of a Justified Sinner

HOMER
The Iliad
The Odyssey

VICTOR HUGO
The Hunchback of Notre-Dame
Les Misérables

ALDOUS HUXLEY
Brave New World

KAZUO ISHIGURO
The Remains of the Day

HENRY JAMES
The Awkward Age
The Bostonians
The Golden Bowl
The Portrait of a Lady
The Princess Casamassima
Washington Square
The Wings of the Dove
Collected Stories (in 2 vols)

SAMUEL JOHNSON
A Journey to the Western
Islands of Scotland

JAMES JOYCE
Dubliners
A Portrait of the Artist as
a Young Man
Ulysses

FRANZ KAFKA
Collected Stories
The Castle
The Trial

JOHN KEATS
The Poems

SØREN KIERKEGAARD
Fear and Trembling and
The Book on Adler

MAXINE HONG KINGSTON
The Woman Warrior and
China Men
(US only)

RUDYARD KIPLING
Collected Stories
Kim

THE KORAN
(tr. Marmaduke Pickthall)

GIUSEPPE TOMASI DI
LAMPEDUSA
The Leopard

WILLIAM LANGLAND
Piers Plowman
with (anon.) Sir Gawain and the
Green Knight, Pearl, Sir Orfeo
(UK only)

D. H. LAWRENCE
Collected Stories
The Rainbow
Sons and Lovers
Women in Love

MIKHAIL LERMONTOV
A Hero of Our Time

DORIS LESSING
Stories

PRIMO LEVI
If This is a Man and The Truce
(UK only)
The Periodic Table

THE MABINOGION

NICCOLÒ MACHIAVELLI
The Prince

ORHAN PAMUK
My Name is Red
Snow

BORIS PASTERNAK
Doctor Zhivago

SYLVIA PLATH
The Bell Jar (US only)

PLATO
The Republic
Symposium and Phaedrus

EDGAR ALLAN POE
The Complete Stories

MARCO POLO
The Travels of Marco Polo

MARCEL PROUST
In Search of Lost Time
(in 4 vols, UK only)

PHILIP PULLMAN
His Dark Materials

ALEXANDER PUSHKIN
The Collected Stories

FRANÇOIS RABELAIS
Gargantua and Pantagruel

JOSEPH ROTH
The Radetzky March

JEAN-JACQUES
ROUSSEAU
Confessions
The Social Contract and
the Discourses

SALMAN RUSHDIE
Midnight's Children

JOHN RUSKIN
Praeterita and Dilecta

PAUL SCOTT
The Raj Quartet (in 2 vols)

WALTER SCOTT
Rob Roy

WILLIAM SHAKESPEARE
Comedies Vols 1 and 2
Histories Vols 1 and 2
Romances
Sonnets and Narrative Poems
Tragedies Vols 1 and 2

MARY SHELLEY
Frankenstein

ADAM SMITH
The Wealth of Nations

ALEXANDER SOLZHENITSYN
One Day in the Life of
Ivan Denisovich

SOPHOCLES
The Theban Plays

MURIEL SPARK
The Prime of Miss Jean Brodie,
The Girls of Slender Means, The
Driver's Seat, The Only Problem
(in 1 vol.)

CHRISTINA STEAD
The Man Who Loved Children

JOHN STEINBECK
The Grapes of Wrath

STENDHAL
The Charterhouse of Parma
Scarlet and Black

LAURENCE STERNE
Tristram Shandy

ROBERT LOUIS STEVENSON
The Master of Ballantrae and
Weir of Hermiston
Dr Jekyll and Mr Hyde
and Other Stories

BRAM STOKER
Dracula

HARRIET BEECHER STOWE
Uncle Tom's Cabin

ITALO SVEVO
Zeno's Conscience

GRAHAM SWIFT
Waterland

JONATHAN SWIFT
Gulliver's Travels

TACITUS
Annals and Histories

JUNICHIRŌ TANIZAKI
The Makioka Sisters

W. M. THACKERAY
Vanity Fair

HENRY DAVID THOREAU
Walden

ALEXIS DE TOCQUEVILLE
Democracy in America